# The Golden Dog

## William Kirby

# AUTHOR'S PREFATORY NOTE.

TO THE PUBLIC:

In the year 1877 the first edition of "The Golden Dog" (Le Chien d'Or) was brought out in the United States, entirely without my knowledge or sanction. Owing to the inadequacy of the then existing copyright laws, I have been powerless to prevent its continued publication, which I understand to have been a successful and profitable undertaking for all concerned, except the author, the book having gone through many editions.

It was, consequently, a source of gratification to me when I was approached by Messrs. L. C. Page & Company, of Boston, with a request to revise "The Golden Dog," and re-publish it through them. The result is the present edition, which I have corrected and revised in the light of the latest developments in the history of Quebec, and which is the only edition offered to my readers with the sanction and approval of its author.

**William Kirby. Niagara, Canada, May, 1897.Contents**

# Chapter I: Men of the Old Regime

"'See Naples, and then die!' That was a proud saying, Count, which we used to hear as we cruised under lateen sails about the glorious bay that reflects from its waters the fires of Vesuvius. We believed the boast then, Count. But I say now, 'See Quebec, and live forever!' Eternity would be too short to weary me of this lovely scene--this bright Canadian morning is worthy of Eden, and the glorious landscape worthy of such a sun-rising."

Thus exclaimed a tall, fair Swedish gentleman, his blue eyes sparkling, and every feature glowing with enthusiasm, Herr Peter Kalm, to His Excellency Count de la Galissoniere, Governor of New France, as they stood together on a bastion of the ramparts of Quebec, in the year of grace 1748.

A group of French and Canadian officers, in the military uniforms of Louis XV., stood leaning on their swords, as they conversed gaily together on the broad gravelled walk at the foot of the rampart. They formed the suite in attendance upon the Governor, who was out by sunrise this morning to inspect the work done during the night by the citizens of Quebec and the habitans of the surrounding country, who had been hastily summoned to labor upon the defences of the city.

A few ecclesiastics, in black cassocks, dignitaries of the Church, mingled cheerfully in the conversation of the officers. They had accompanied the Governor, both to show their respect, and to encourage, by their presence and exhortations, the zeal of the colonists in the work of fortifying the capital.

War was then raging between old England and old France, and between New England and New France. The vast region of North America, stretching far into the interior and southwest from Canada to Louisiana, had for three years past been the scene of fierce hostilities between the rival nations, while the savage Indian tribes, ranged on the one side and on the other, steeped their moccasins in the blood of French and English colonists, who, in their turn, became as fierce, and carried on the war as relentlessly, as the savages themselves.

Louisbourg, the bulwark of New France, projecting its mailed arm boldly into the Atlantic, had been cut off by the English, who now overran Acadia, and began to threaten Quebec with invasion by sea and land. Busy rumors of approaching danger were rife in the colony, and the gallant Governor issued orders, which were enthusiastically obeyed, for the people to proceed to the walls and place the city in a state of defence, to bid defiance to the enemy.

Rolland Michel Barrin, Count de la Galissoniere, was remarkable no less for his philosophical attainments, that ranked him high among the savans of the French Academy, than for his political abilities and foresight as a statesman. He felt strongly the vital interests involved in the present war, and saw clearly what was the sole policy necessary for France to adopt in order to preserve her magnificent dominion in North America. His counsels were neither liked nor followed by the Court of Versailles, then sinking fast into the slough of corruption that marked the closing years of the reign of Louis XV.

Among the people who admired deeds more than words the Count was honored as a brave and skilful admiral, who had borne the flag of France triumphantly over the seas, and in the face of her most powerful enemies--the English and Dutch. His memorable repulse of Admiral Byng, eight years after the events here recorded,--which led to the death of that brave and unfortunate officer, who was shot by sentence of court martial to atone for that repulse,--was a glory to France, but to the Count brought after it a manly sorrow for the fate of his opponent, whose death he regarded as a cruel and unjust act, unworthy of the English nation, usually as generous and merciful as it is brave and considerate.

The Governor was already well-advanced in years. He had entered upon the winter of life, that sprinkles the head with snow that never melts, but he was still hale, ruddy, and active. Nature had, indeed, moulded him in an unpropitious hour for personal comeliness, but in compensation had seated a great heart and a graceful mind in a body low of stature, and marked by a slight deformity. His piercing eyes, luminous with intelligence and full of sympathy for everything noble and elevated, overpowered with their fascination the blemishes that a too curious scrutiny might discover upon his figure; while his mobile, handsome lips poured out the natural eloquence of clear thoughts and noble sentiments. The Count grew great while speaking: his listeners were carried away by the magic of his voice and the clearness of his intellect.

He was very happy this morning by the side of his old friend, Peter Kalm, who was paying him a most welcome visit in New France. They had been fellow-students, both at Upsal and at Paris, and loved each other with a cordiality that, like good wine, grew richer and more generous with age.

Herr Kalm, stretching out his arms as if to embrace the lovely landscape and clasp it to his bosom, exclaimed with fresh enthusiasm, "See Quebec, and live forever!"

"Dear Kalm," said the Governor, catching the fervor of his friend, as he rested his hand affectionately on his shoulder, "you are as true a lover of nature as when we sat together at the feet of Linnaeus, our glorious young master, and heard him open up for us the arcana of God's works; and we used to feel like him, too, when he thanked God for permitting him to look into his treasure-house and see the precious things of creation which he had made."

"Till men see Quebec," replied Kalm, "they will not fully realize the meaning of the term, 'God's footstool.' It is a land worth living for!"

"Not only a land to live for, but a land to die for, and happy the man who dies for it! Confess, Kalm,--thou who hast travelled in all lands,--think'st thou not it is indeed worthy of its proud title of New France?"

"It is indeed worthy," replied Kalm; "I see here a scion of the old oak of the Gauls, which, if let grow, will shelter the throne of France itself in an empire wider than Caesar wrested from Ambiotrix."

"Yes," replied the Count, kindling at the words of his friend, "it is old France transplanted, transfigured, and glorified,--where her language, religion, and laws shall be handed down to her posterity, the glory of North America as the mother-land is the glory of Europe!"

The enthusiastic Galissoniere stretched out his hands and implored a blessing upon the land entrusted to his keeping.

It was a glorious morning. The sun had just risen over the hilltops of Lauzon, throwing aside his drapery of gold, purple, and crimson. The soft haze of the summer morning was floating away into nothingness, leaving every object fresh with dew and magnified in the limpid purity of the air.

The broad St. Lawrence, far beneath their feet, was still partially veiled in a thin blue mist, pierced here and there by the tall mast of a King's ship or merchantman lying unseen at anchor; or, as the fog rolled slowly off, a swift canoe might be seen shooting out into a streak of sunshine, with the first news of the morning from the south shore.

Behind the Count and his companions rose the white glistening walls of the Hotel Dieu, and farther off the tall tower of the newly- restored Cathedral, the belfry of the Recollets, and the roofs of the ancient College of the Jesuits. An avenue of old oaks and maples shaded the walk, and in the branches of the trees a swarm of birds fluttered and sang, as if in rivalry with the gay French talk and laughter of the group of officers, who waited the return of the Governor from the bastion where he stood, showing the glories of Quebec to his friend.

The walls of the city ran along the edge of the cliff upwards as they approached the broad gallery and massive front of the Castle of St. Louis, and ascending the green slope of the broad glacis, culminated in the lofty citadel, where, streaming in the morning breeze, radiant in the sunshine, and alone in the blue sky, waved the white banner of France, the sight of which sent a thrill of joy and pride into the hearts of her faithful subjects in the New World.

The broad bay lay before them, round as a shield, and glittering like a mirror as the mist blew off its surface. Behind the sunny slopes of Orleans, which the river encircled in its arms like a giant lover his fair mistress, rose the bold, dark crests of the Laurentides, lifting their bare summits far away along the course of the ancient river, leaving imagination to wander over the wild scenery in their midst--the woods, glens, and unknown lakes and rivers that lay hid far from human ken, or known only to rude savages, wild as the beasts of chase they hunted in those strange regions.

Across the broad valley of the St. Charles, covered with green fields and ripening harvests, and dotted with quaint old homesteads, redolent with memories of Normandy and Brittany, rose a long mountain ridge covered with primeval woods, on the slope of which rose the glittering spire of Charlebourg, once a dangerous outpost of civilization. The pastoral Lairet was seen mingling its waters with the St. Charles in a little bay that preserves the name of Jacques Cartier, who with his hardy companions spent their first winter in Canada on this spot, the guests of the hospitable Donacana, lord of Quebec and of all the lands seen from its lofty cape.

Directly beneath the feet of the Governor, on a broad strip of land that lay between the beach and the precipice, stood the many-gabled Palace of the Intendant, the most magnificent structure in New France. Its long front of eight hundred feet overlooked the royal terraces and gardens, and beyond these the quays and magazines, where lay the ships of Bordeaux, St. Malo, and Havre, unloading the merchandise and luxuries of France in exchange for the more rude, but not less valuable, products of the Colony.

Between the Palace and the Basse Ville the waves at high tide washed over a shingly beach where there were already the beginnings of a street. A few rude inns displayed the sign of the fleur-de-lis or the imposing head of Louis XV. Round the doors of these inns in summer-time might always be found groups of loquacious Breton and Norman sailors in red caps and sashes, voyageurs and canoemen from the far West in half Indian costume, drinking Gascon wine and Norman cider, or the still more potent liquors filled with the fires of the Antilles. The Batture kindled into life on the arrival of the fleet from home, and in the evenings of summer, as the sun set behind the Cote a Bonhomme, the natural magnetism of companionship drew the lasses of Quebec down to the beach, where, amid old refrains of French ditties and the music of violins and tambours de Basque, they danced on the green with the jovial sailors who brought news from the old land beyond the Atlantic.

"Pardon me, gentlemen, for keeping you waiting," said the Governor, as he descended from the bastion and rejoined his suite. "I am so proud of our beautiful Quebec that I can scarcely stop showing off its charms to my friend Herr Kalm, who knows so well how to appreciate them. But," continued he, looking round admiringly on the bands of citizens and habitans who were at work strengthening every weak point in the fortifications, "my brave Canadians are busy as beavers on their dam. They are determined to keep the saucy English out of Quebec. They deserve to have the beaver for their crest, industrious fellows that they are! I am sorry I kept you waiting, however."

"We can never count the moments lost which your Excellency gives to the survey of our fair land," replied the Bishop, a grave, earnest- looking man. "Would that His Majesty himself could stand on these walls and see with his own eyes, as you do, this splendid patrimony of the crown of France. He would not dream of bartering it away in exchange for petty ends and corners of Germany and Flanders, as is rumored, my Lord."

"True words and good, my Lord Bishop," replied the Governor; "the retention of all Flanders now in the strong hands of the Marshal de Saxe would be a poor compensation for the surrender of a glorious land like this to the English."

Flying rumors of some such proposal on the part of France had reached the Colony, with wild reports arising out of the endless chaffering between the negotiators for peace, who had already assembled at Aix la Chapelle. "The fate of America will one day be decided here," continued the Governor; "I see it written upon this rock, 'Whoever rules Quebec will sway the destinies of the continent.' May our noble France be wise, and understand in time the signs of empire and of supremacy!"

The Bishop looked upwards with a sigh. "Our noble France has not yet read those tokens, or she misunderstands them. Oh, these faithful subjects of hers! Look at them, your Excellency." The Bishop pointed toward the crowd of citizens hard at work on the walls. "There is not a man of them but is ready to risk life and fortune for the honor and dominion of France, and yet they are treated by the Court with such neglect, and burdened with exactions that take from life the sweet reward of labor! They cannot do the impossible that France requires of them--fight her battles, till her fields, and see their bread taken from them by these new ordinances of the Intendant."

"Well, my Lord," replied the Governor, affecting a jocularity he did not feel, for he knew how true were the words of the Bishop, "we must all do our duty, nevertheless: if France requires impossibilities of us, we must perform them! That is the old spirit! If the skies fall upon our heads, we must, like true Gauls, hold them up on the points of our lances! What say you, Rigaud de Vaudreuil? Cannot one Canadian surround ten New Englanders?" The Governor alluded to an exploit of the gallant officer whom he turned to address.

"Probatum est, your Excellency! I once with six hundred Canadians surrounded all New England. Prayers were put up in all the churches of Boston for deliverance when we swept the Connecticut from end to end with a broom of fire."

"Brave Rigaud! France has too few like you!" remarked the Governor with a look of admiration.

Rigaud bowed, and shook his head modestly. "I trust she has ten thousand better;" but added, pointing at his fellow-officers who stood conversing at a short distance, "Marshal de Saxe has few the equals of these in his camp, my Lord Count!" And well was the compliment deserved: they were gallant men, intelligent in looks, polished in manners, and brave to a fault, and all full of that natural gaiety that sits so gracefully on a French soldier.

Most of them wore the laced coat and waistcoat, chapeau, boots, lace ruffles, sash, and rapier of the period--a martial costume befitting brave and handsome men. Their names were household words in every cottage in New France, and many of them as frequently spoken of in the English Colonies as in the streets of Quebec.

There stood the Chevalier de Beaujeu, a gentleman of Norman family, who was already famed upon the frontier, and who, seven years later, in the forests of the Monongahela, crowned a life of honor by a soldier's death on the bloody field won from the unfortunate Braddock, defeating an army ten times more numerous than his own.

Talking gayly with De Beaujeu were two gallant-looking young men of a Canadian family which, out of seven brothers, lost six slain in the service of their King--Jumonville de Villiers, who was afterwards, in defiance of a flag of truce, shot down by order of Colonel Washington, in the far-off forests of the Alleghenies, and his brother, Coulon de Villiers, who received the sword of Washington when he surrendered himself and garrison prisoners of war, at Fort Necessity, in 1754.

Coulon de Villiers imposed ignominious conditions of surrender upon Washington, but scorned to take other revenge for the death of his brother. He spared the life of Washington, who lived to become the leader and idol of his nation, which, but for the magnanimity of the noble Canadian, might have never struggled into independence.

There stood also the Sieur de Lery, the King's engineer, charged with the fortification of the Colony, a man of Vauban's genius in the art of defence. Had the schemes which he projected, and vainly urged upon the heedless Court of Versailles, been carried into effect, the conquest of New France would have been an impossibility.

Arm in arm with De Lery, in earnest conversation, walked the handsome Claude de Beauharnais,--brother of a former Governor of the Colony,--a graceful, gallant-looking soldier. De Beauharnais was the ancestor of a vigorous and beautiful race, among whose posterity was the fair Hortense de Beauharnais, who in her son, Napoleon III., seated an offshoot of Canada upon the imperial throne of France long after the abandonment of their ancient colony by the corrupt House of Bourbon.

Conspicuous among the distinguished officers by his tall, straight figure and quick movements, was the Chevalier La Corne St. Luc, supple as an Indian, and almost as dark, from exposure to the weather and incessant campaigning. He was fresh from the blood and desolation of Acadia, where France, indeed, lost her ancient colony, but St. Luc reaped a full sheaf of glory at Grand Pre, in the Bay of Minas, by the capture of an army of New Englanders. The rough old soldier was just now all smiles and gaiety, as he conversed with Monseigneur de Pontbriant, the venerable Bishop of Quebec, and Father de Berey, the Superior of the Recollets.

The Bishop, a wise ruler of his Church, was also a passionate lover of his country: the surrender of Quebec to the English broke his heart, and he died a few months after the announcement of the final cession of the Colony.

Father de Berey, a jovial monk, wearing the gray gown and sandals of the Recollets, was renowned throughout New France for his wit more than for his piety. He had once been a soldier, and he wore his gown, as he had worn his uniform, with the gallant bearing of a King's Guardsman. But the people loved him all the more for his jests, which never lacked the accompaniment of genuine charity. His sayings furnished all New France with daily food for mirth and laughter, without detracting an iota of the respect in which the Recollets were held throughout the colony.

Father Glapion, the Superior of the Jesuits, also accompanied the Bishop. His close, black soutane contrasted oddly with the gray, loose gown of the Recollet. He was a meditative, taciturn man,-- seeming rather to watch the others than to join in the lively conversation that went on around him. Anything but cordiality and brotherly love reigned between the Jesuits and the Order of St. Francis, but the Superiors were too wary to manifest towards each other the mutual jealousies of their subordinates.

The long line of fortifications presented a stirring appearance that morning. The watch-fires that had illuminated the scene during the night were dying out, the red embers paling under the rays of the rising sun. From a wide circle surrounding the city the people had come in--many were accompanied by their wives and daughters--to assist in making the bulwark of the Colony impregnable against the rumored attack of the English.

The people of New France, taught by a hundred years of almost constant warfare with the English and with the savage nations on their frontiers, saw as clearly as the Governor that the key of French dominion hung inside the walls of Quebec, and that for an enemy to grasp it was to lose all they valued as subjects of the Crown of France.

## Chapter II: The Walls of Quebec

Count de la Galissoniere, accompanied by his distinguished attendants, proceeded again on their round of inspection. They were everywhere saluted with heads uncovered, and welcomed by hearty greetings. The people of New France had lost none of the natural politeness and ease of their ancestors, and, as every gentleman of the Governor's suite was at once recognized, a conversation, friendly even to familiarity, ensued between them and the citizens and habitans, who worked as if they were building their very souls into the walls of the old city.

"Good morning, Sieur de St. Denis!" gaily exclaimed the Governor to a tall, courtly gentleman, who was super-intending the labor of a body of his censitaires from Beauport. "'Many hands make light work,' says the proverb. That splendid battery you are just finishing deserves to be called Beauport. What say you, my Lord Bishop?" turning to the smiling ecclesiastic. "Is it not worthy of baptism?"

"Yes, and blessing both; I give it my episcopal benediction," replied the Bishop, "and truly I think most of the earth of it is taken from the consecrated ground of the Hotel Dieu--it will stand fire!"

"Many thanks, my Lord!"--the Sieur de St. Denis bowed very low-- "where the Church bars the door Satan will never enter, nor the English either! Do you hear, men?" continued he, turning to his censitaires, "my Lord Bishop christens our battery Beauport, and says it will stand fire!"

"Vive le Roi!" was the response, an exclamation that came spontaneously to the lips of all Frenchmen on every emergency of danger or emotion of joy.

A sturdy habitan came forward, and doffing his red tuque or cap, addressed the Governor: "This is a good battery, my Lord Governor, but there ought to be one as good in our village. Permit us to build one and man it, and we promise your Excellency that no Englishman shall ever get into the back door of Quebec while we have lives to defend it." The old habitan had the eye of a soldier--he had been one. The Governor knew the value of the suggestion, and at once assented to it, adding, "No better defenders of the city could be found anywhere than the brave habitans of Beauport."

The compliment was never forgotten; and years afterwards, when Wolfe besieged the city, the batteries of Beauport repelled the assault of his bravest troops, and well-nigh broke the heart of the young hero over the threatened defeat of his great undertaking, as his brave Highlanders and grenadiers lay slain by hundreds upon the beach of Beauport.

The countenances of the hardy workers were suddenly covered with smiles of welcome recognition at the sight of the well-known Superior of the Recollets.

"Good morning!" cried out a score of voices; "good morning, Father de Berey! The good wives of Beauport send you a thousand compliments. They are dying to see the good Recollets down our way again. The Gray Brothers have forsaken our parish."

"Ah!" replied the Superior, in a tone of mock severity, while his eyes overran with mirthfulness, "you are a crowd of miserable sinners who will die without benefit of clergy--only you don't know it! Who was it boiled the Easter eggs hard as agates, which you gave to my poor brother Recollets for the use of our convent? Tell me that, pray! All the salts and senna in Quebec have not sufficed to restore the digestion of my poor monks since you played that trick upon them down in your misnamed village of Beauport!"

"Pardon, Reverend Father de Berey!" replied a smiling habitan, "it was not we, but the sacrilegious canaille of St. Anne who boiled the Easter eggs! If you don't believe us, send some of the good Gray Friars down to try our love. See if they do not find everything soft for them at Beauport, from our hearts to our feather beds, to say nothing of our eggs and bacon. Our good wives are fairly melting with longing for a sight of the gray gowns of St. Francis once more in our village."

"Oh! I dare be bound the canaille of St. Anne are lost dogs like yourselves--catuli catulorum."

The habitans thought this sounded like a doxology, and some crossed themselves, amid the dubious laughter of others, who suspected Father de Berey of a clerical jest.

"Oh!" continued he, "if fat Father Ambrose, the cook of the convent, only had you, one at a time, to turn the spit for him, in place of the poor dogs of Quebec, which he has to catch as best he can, and set to work in his kitchen! but, vagabonds that you are, you are rarely set to work now on the King's corvee--all work, little play, and no pay!"

The men took his raillery in excellent part, and one, their spokesman, bowing low to the Superior, said,--"Forgive us all the same, good Father. The hard eggs of Beauport will be soft as lard compared with the iron shells we are preparing for the English breakfast when they shall appear some fine morning before Quebec."

"Ah, well, in that case I must pardon the trick you played upon Brothers Mark and Alexis; and I give you my blessing, too, on condition you send some salt to our convent to cure our fish, and save your reputations, which are very stale just now among my good Recollets."

A general laugh followed this sally, and the Reverend Superior went off merrily, as he hastened to catch up with the Governor, who had moved on to another point in the line of fortifications.

Near the gate of St. John they found a couple of ladies, encouraging by their presence and kind words a numerous party of habitans,--one an elderly lady of noble bearing and still beautiful, the rich and powerful feudal Lady of the Lordship, or Seigniory, of Tilly; the other her orphan niece, in the bloom of youth, and of surpassing loveliness, the fair Amelie de Repentigny, who had loyally accompanied her aunt to the capital with all the men of the Seigniory of Tilly, to assist in the completion of its defences.

To features which looked as if chiselled out of the purest Parian marble, just flushed with the glow of morn, and cut in those perfect lines of proportion which nature only bestows on a few chosen favorites at intervals to show the possibilities of feminine beauty, Amelie de Repentigny added a figure which, in its perfect symmetry, looked smaller than it really was, for she was a tall girl: it filled the eye and held fast the fancy with the charms of a thousand graces as she moved or stood, suggestive of the beauty of a tame fawn, that in all its movements preserves somewhat of the coyness and easy grace of its free life.

Her hair was very dark and thick, matching her deep liquid eyes, that lay for the most part so quietly and restfully beneath their long shading lashes,--eyes gentle, frank, and modest, looking tenderly on all things innocent, fearlessly on all things harmful; eyes that nevertheless noted every change of your countenance, and read unerringly your meaning more from your looks than from your words. Nothing seemed to hide itself from that pure, searching glance when she chose to look at you.

In their depths you might read the tokens of a rare and noble character--a capability of loving which, once enkindled by a worthy object, might make all things that are possible to devoted womanhood possible to this woman, who would not count her life anything either for the man she loved or the cause she espoused. Amelie de Repentigny will not yield her heart without her judgment; but when she does, it will be a royal gift--never to be recalled, never to be repented of, to the end of her life. Happy the man upon whom she shall bestow her affection! It will be his forever. Unhappy all others who may love her! She may pity, but she will listen to no voice but the one which rules her heart, to her life's end!

Both ladies were in mourning, yet dressed with elegant simplicity, befitting their rank and position in society. The Chevalier Le Gardeur de Tilly had fallen two years ago, fighting gallantly for his King and country, leaving a childless widow to manage his vast domain and succeed him as sole guardian of their orphan niece, Amelie de Repentigny, and her brother Le Gardeur, left in infancy to the care of their noble relatives, who in every respect treated them as their own, and who indeed were the legal inheritors of the Lordship of Tilly.

Only a year ago, Amelie had left the ancient Convent of the Ursulines, perfected in all the graces and accomplishments taught in the famous cloister founded by Mere Marie de l'Incarnation for the education of the daughters of New France, generation after generation of whom were trained, according to her precepts, in graces of manner as well as in the learning of the age--the latter might be forgotten; the former, never. As they became the wives and mothers of succeeding times, they have left upon their descendants an impress of politeness and urbanity that distinguishes the people of Canada to this day.

Of all the crowd of fair, eager aspirants contending for honors on the day of examination in the great school, crowns had only been awarded to Amelie and to Angelique des Meloises-- two girls equal in beauty, grace, and accomplishments, but unlike in character and in destiny. The currents of their lives ran smoothly together at the beginning. How widely different was to be the ending of them!

The brother of Amelie, Le Gardeur de Repentigny, was her elder by a year--an officer in the King's service, handsome, brave, generous, devoted to his sister and aunt, but not free from some of the vices of the times prevalent among the young men of rank and fortune in the colony, who in dress, luxury, and immorality, strove to imitate the brilliant, dissolute Court of Louis XV.

Amelie passionately loved her brother, and endeavored--not without success, as is the way with women--to blind herself to his faults. She saw him seldom, however, and in her solitary musings in the far- off Manor House of Tilly, she invested him with all the perfections he did and did not possess; and turned a deaf, almost an angry ear, to tales whispered in his disparagement.

# Chapter III: A Chatelaine of New France

The Governor was surprised and delighted to encounter Lady de Tilly and her fair niece, both of whom were well known to and highly esteemed by him. He and the gentlemen of his suite saluted them with profound respect, not unmingled with chivalrous admiration for noble, high-spirited women.

"My honored Lady de Tilly and Mademoiselle de Repentigny," said the Governor, hat in hand, "welcome to Quebec. It does not surprise, but it does delight me beyond measure to meet you here at the head of your loyal censitaires. But it is not the first time that the ladies of the House of Tilly have turned out to defend the King's forts against his enemies."

This he said in allusion to the gallant defence of a fort on the wild Iroquois frontier by a former lady of her house.

"My Lord Count," replied the lady, with quiet dignity, "'tis no special merit of the house of Tilly to be true to its ancient fame-- it could not be otherwise. But your thanks are at this time more due to these loyal habitans, who have so promptly obeyed your proclamation. It is the King's corvee to restore the walls of Quebec, and no Canadian may withhold his hand from it without disgrace."

"The Chevalier La Corne St. Luc will think us two poor women a weak accession to the garrison," added she, turning to the Chevalier and cordially offering her hand to the brave old officer, who had been the comrade in arms of her husband and the dearest friend of her family.

"Good blood never fails, my Lady," returned the Chevalier, warmly grasping her hand. "You out of place here? No! no! you are at home on the ramparts of Quebec, quite as much as in your own drawing-room at Tilly. The walls of Quebec without a Tilly and a Repentigny would be a bad omen indeed, worse than a year without a spring or a summer without roses. But where is my dear goddaughter Amelie?"

As he spoke the old soldier embraced Amelie and kissed her cheek with fatherly effusion. She was a prodigious favorite. "Welcome, Amelie!" said he, "the sight of you is like flowers in June. What a glorious time you have had, growing taller and prettier every day all the time I have been sleeping by camp-fires in the forests of Acadia! But you girls are all alike; why, I hardly knew my own pretty Agathe when I came home. The saucy minx almost kissed my eyes out--to dry the tears of joy in them, she said!"

Amelie blushed deeply at the praises bestowed upon her, yet felt glad to know that her godfather retained all his old affection. "Where is Le Gardeur?" asked he, as she took his arm and walked a few paces apart from the throng.

Amelie colored deeply, and hesitated a moment. "I do not know, godfather! We have not seen Le Gardeur since our arrival." Then after a nervous silence she added, "I have been told that he is at Beaumanoir, hunting with His Excellency the Intendant."

La Corne, seeing her embarrassment, understood the reluctance of her avowal, and sympathized with it. An angry light flashed beneath his shaggy eyelashes, but he suppressed his thoughts. He could not help remarking, however, "With the Intendant at Beaumanoir! I could have wished Le Gardeur in better company! No good can come of his intimacy with Bigot; Amelie, you must wean him from it. He should have been in the city to receive you and the Lady de Tilly."

"So he doubtless would have been, had he known of our coming. We sent word, but he was away when our messenger reached the city."

Amelie felt half ashamed, for she was conscious that she was offering something unreal to extenuate the fault of her brother-- her hopes rather than her convictions.

"Well, well! goddaughter! we shall, at any rate, soon have the pleasure of seeing Le Gardeur. The Intendant himself has been summoned to attend a council of war today. Colonel Philibert left an hour ago for Beaumanoir."

Amelie gave a slight start at the name; she looked inquiringly, but did not yet ask the question that trembled on her lips.

"Thanks, godfather, for the good news of Le Gardeur's speedy return." Amelie talked on, her thoughts but little accompanying her words as she repeated to herself the name of Philibert. "Have you heard that the Intendant wishes to bestow an important and honorable post in the Palace upon Le Gardeur--my brother wrote to that effect?"

"An important and honorable post in the Palace?" The old soldier emphasized the word HONORABLE. "No, I had not heard of it,--never expect to hear of an honorable post in the company of Bigot, Cadet, Varin, De Pean, and the rest of the scoundrels of the Friponne! Pardon me, dear, I do not class Le Gardeur among them, far from it, dear deluded boy! My best hope is that Colonel Philibert will find him and bring him clean and clear out of their clutches."

The question that had trembled on her lips came out now. For her life she could not have retained it longer.

"Who is Colonel Philibert, godfather?" asked she, surprise, curiosity, and a still deeper interest marking her voice, in spite of all she could do to appear indifferent.

"Colonel Philibert?" repeated La Corne. "Why, do not you know? Who but our young Pierre Philibert; you have not forgotten him, surely, Amelie? At any rate he has not forgotten you: in many a long night by our watch-fires in the forest has Colonel Philibert passed the hours talking of Tilly and the dear friends he left there. Your brother at any rate will gratefully remember Philibert when he sees him."

Amelie blushed a little as she replied somewhat shyly, "Yes, godfather, I remember Pierre Philibert very well,--with gratitude I remember him,--but I never heard him called Colonel Philibert before."

"Oh, true! He has been so long absent. He left a simple ensign en second and returns a colonel, and has the stuff in him to make a field-marshal! He gained his rank where he won his glory--in Acadia. A noble fellow, Amelie! loving as a woman to his friends, but to his foes stern as the old Bourgeois, his father, who placed that tablet of the golden dog upon the front of his house to spite the Cardinal, they say,--the act of a bold man, let what will be the true interpretation of it."

"I hear every one speak well of the Bourgeois Philibert," remarked Amelie. "Aunt de Tilly is ever enthusiastic in his commendation. She says he is a true gentleman, although a trader."

"Why, he is noble by birth, if that be needed, and has got the King's license to trade in the Colony like some other gentlemen I wot of. He was Count Philibert in Normandy, although he is plain Bourgeois Philibert in Quebec; and a wise man he is too, for with his ships and his comptoirs and his ledgers he has traded himself into being the richest man in New France, while we, with our nobility and our swords, have fought ourselves poor, and receive nothing but contempt from the ungrateful courtiers of Versailles."

Their conversation was interrupted by a sudden rush of people, making room for the passage of the Regiment of Bearn, which composed part of the garrison of Quebec, on their march to their morning drill and guard-mounting,--bold, dashing Gascons in blue and white uniforms, tall caps, and long queues rollicking down their supple backs, seldom seen by an enemy.

Mounted officers, laced and ruffled, gaily rode in front. Subalterns with spontoons and sergeants with halberds dressed the long line of glistening bayonets. The drums and fifes made the streets ring again, while the men in full chorus, a gorge deployee, chanted the gay refrain of La Belle Canadienne in honor of the lasses of Quebec.

The Governor and his suite had already mounted their horses, and cantered off to the Esplanade to witness the review.

"Come and dine with us today," said the Lady de Tilly to La Corne St. Luc, as he too bade the ladies a courteous adieu, and got on horseback to ride after the Governor.

"Many thanks! but I fear it will be impossible, my Lady: the council of war meets at the Castle this afternoon. The hour may be deferred, however, should Colonel Philibert not chance to find the Intendant at Beaumanoir, and then I might come; but best not expect me."

A slight, conscious flush just touched the cheek of Amelie at the mention of Colonel Philibert.

"But come if possible, godfather," added she; "we hope to have Le Gardeur home this afternoon. He loves you so much, and I know you have countless things to say to him."

Amelie's trembling anxiety about her brother made her most desirous to bring the powerful influence of La Corne St. Luc to bear upon him.

Their kind old godfather was regarded with filial reverence by both. Amelie's father, dying on the battle-field, had, with his latest breath, commended the care of his children to the love and friendship of La Corne St. Luc.

"Well, Amelie, blessed are they who do not promise and still perform. I must try and meet my dear boy, so do not quite place me among the impossibles. Good-by, my Lady. Good-by, Amelie." The old soldier gaily kissed his hand and rode away.

Amelie was thoroughly surprised and agitated out of all composure by the news of the return of Pierre Philibert. She turned aside from the busy throng that surrounded her, leaving her aunt engaged in eager conversation with the Bishop and Father de Berey. She sat down in a quiet embrasure of the wall, and with one hand resting her drooping cheek, a train of reminiscences flew across her mind like a flight of pure doves suddenly startled out of a thicket.

She remembered vividly Pierre Philibert, the friend and fellow- student of her brother: he spent so many of his holidays at the old Manor-House of Tilly, when she, a still younger girl, shared their sports, wove chaplets of flowers for them, or on her shaggy pony rode with them on many a scamper through the wild woods of the Seigniory. Those summer and winter vacations of the old Seminary of Quebec used to be looked forward to by the young, lively girl as the brightest spots in the whole year, and she grew hardly to distinguish the affection she bore her brother from the regard in which she held Pierre Philibert.

A startling incident happened one day, that filled the inmates of the Manor House with terror, followed by a great joy, and which raised Pierre Philibert to the rank of an unparalleled hero in the imagination of the young girl.

Her brother was gambolling carelessly in a canoe, while she and Pierre sat on the bank watching him. The light craft suddenly upset. Le Gardeur struggled for a few moments, and sank under the blue waves that look so beautiful and are so cruel.

Amelie shrieked in the wildest terror and in helpless agony, while Philibert rushed without hesitation into the water, swam out to the spot, and dived with the agility of a beaver. He presently reappeared, bearing the inanimate body of her brother to the shore. Help was soon obtained, and, after long efforts to restore Le Gardeur to consciousness,--efforts which seemed to last an age to the despairing girl,--they at last succeeded, and Le Gardeur was restored to the arms of his family. Amelie, in a delirium of joy and gratitude, ran to Philibert, threw her arms round him, and kissed him again and again, pledging her eternal gratitude to the preserver of her brother, and vowing that she would pray for him to her life's end.

Soon after that memorable event in her young life, Pierre Philibert was sent to the great military schools in France to study the art of war with a view to entering the King's service, while Amelie was placed in the Convent of the Ursulines to be perfected in all the knowledge and accomplishments of a lady of highest rank in the Colony.

Despite the cold shade of a cloister, where the idea of a lover is forbidden to enter, the image of Pierre Philibert did intrude, and became inseparable from the recollection of her brother in the mind of Amelie. He mingled as the fairy prince in the day-dreams and bright imaginings of the young, poetic girl. She had vowed to pray for him to her life's end, and in pursuance of her vow added a golden bead to her chaplet to remind her of her duty in praying for the safety and happiness of Pierre Philibert.

But in the quiet life of the cloister, Amelie heard little of the storms of war upon the frontier and down in the far valleys of Acadia. She had not followed the career of Pierre from the military school to the camp and the battlefield, nor knew of his rapid promotion, as one of the ablest officers in the King's service, to a high command in his native Colony.

Her surprise, therefore, was extreme when she learned that the boy companion of her brother and herself was no other than the renowned Colonel Philibert, Aide-de-Camp of His Excellency the Governor- General.

There was no cause for shame in it; but her heart was suddenly illuminated by a flash of introspection. She became painfully conscious how much Pierre Philibert had occupied her thoughts for years, and now all at once she knew he was a man, and a great and noble one. She was thoroughly perplexed and half angry. She questioned herself sharply, as if running thorns into her flesh, to inquire whether she had failed in the least point of maidenly modesty and reserve in thinking so much of him; and the more she questioned herself, the more agitated she grew under her self- accusation: her temples throbbed violently; she hardly dared lift her eyes from the ground lest some one, even a stranger, she thought, might see her confusion and read its cause. "Sancta Maria," she murmured, pressing her bosom with both hands, "calm my soul with thy divine peace, for I know not what to do!"

So she sat alone in the embrasure, living a life of emotion in a few minutes; nor did she find any calm for her agitated spirits until the thought flashed upon her that she was distressing herself needlessly. It was most improbable that Colonel Philibert, after years of absence and active life in the world's great affairs, could retain any recollection of the schoolgirl of the Manor House of Tilly. She might meet him, nay, was certain to do so in the society in which both moved; but it would surely be as a stranger on his part, and she must make it so on her own.

With this empty piece of casuistry, Amelie, like others of her sex, placed a hand of steel, encased in a silken glove, upon her heart, and tyrannically suppressed its yearnings. She was a victim, with the outward show of conquest over her feelings. In the consciousness of Philibert's imagined indifference and utter forgetfulness, she could meet him now, she thought, with equanimity--nay, rather wished to do so, to make sure that she had not been guilty of weakness in regard to him. She looked up, but was glad to see her aunt still engaged in conversation with the Bishop on a topic which Amelie knew was dear to them both,--the care of the souls and bodies of the poor, in particular those for whom the Lady de Tilly felt herself responsible to God and the King.

While Amelie sat thinking over the strange chances of the morning, a sudden whirl of wheels drew her attention.

A gay caleche, drawn by two spirited horses en fleche, dashed through the gateway of St. John, and wheeling swiftly towards Amelie, suddenly halted. A young lady attired in the gayest fashion of the period, throwing the reins to the groom, sprang out of the caleche with the ease and elasticity of an antelope. She ran up the rampart to Amelie with a glad cry of recognition, repeating her name in a clear, musical voice, which Amelie at once knew belonged to no other than the gay, beautiful Angelique des Meloises. The newcomer embraced Amelie and kissed her, with warmest expressions of joy at meeting her thus unexpectedly in the city. She had learned that Lady de Tilly had returned to Quebec, she said, and she had, therefore, taken the earliest opportunity to find out her dear friend and school-fellow to tell her all the doings in the city.

"It is kind of you, Angelique," replied Amelie, returning her caress warmly, but without effusion. "We have simply come with our people to assist in the King's corvee; when that is done, we shall return to Tilly. I felt sure I should meet you, and thought I should know you again easily, which I hardly do. How you are changed--for the better, I should say, since you left off conventual cap and costume!" Amelie could not but look admiringly on the beauty of the radiant girl. "How handsome you have grown! but you were always that. We both took the crown of honor together, but you would alone take the crown of beauty, Angelique." Amelie stood off a pace or two, and looked at her friend from head to foot with honest admiration, "and would deserve to wear it too," added she.

"I like to hear you say that, Amelie; I should prefer the crown of beauty to all other crowns! You half smile at that, but I must tell the truth, if you do. But you were always a truth-teller, you know, in the convent, and I was not so! Let us cease flatteries."

Angelique felt highly flattered by the praise of Amelie, whom she had sometimes condescended to envy for her graceful figure and lovely, expressive features.

"Gentlemen often speak as you do, Amelie," continued she, "but, pshaw! they cannot judge as girls do, you know. But do you really think me beautiful? and how beautiful? Compare me to some one we know."

"I can only compare you to yourself, Angelique. You are more beautiful than any one I know," Amelie burst out in frank enthusiasm.

"But, really and truly, do you think me beautiful, not only in your eyes, but in the judgment of the world?"

Angelique brushed back her glorious hair and stared fixedly in the face of her friend, as if seeking confirmation of something in her own thoughts.

"What a strange question, Angelique! Why do you ask me in that way?"

"Because," replied she with bitterness, "I begin to doubt it. I have been praised for my good looks until I grow weary of the iteration; but I believed the lying flattery once,--as what woman would not, when it is repeated every day of her life?"

Amelie looked sufficiently puzzled. "What has come over you, Angelique? Why should you doubt your own charms? or really, have you found at last a case in which they fail you?"

Very unlikely, a man would say at first, second, or third sight of Angelique des Meloises. She was indeed a fair girl to look upon,-- tall, and fashioned in nature's most voluptuous mould, perfect in the symmetry of every part, with an ease and beauty of movement not suggestive of spiritual graces, like Amelie's, but of terrestrial witcheries, like those great women of old who drew down the very gods from Olympus, and who in all ages have incited men to the noblest deeds, or tempted them to the greatest crimes.

She was beautiful of that rare type of beauty which is only reproduced once or twice in a century to realize the dreams of a Titian or a Giorgione. Her complexion was clear and radiant, as of a descendant of the Sun God. Her bright hair, if its golden ripples were shaken out, would reach to her knees. Her face was worthy of immortality by the pencil of a Titian. Her dark eyes drew with a magnetism which attracted men, in spite of themselves, whithersoever she would lead them. They were never so dangerous as when, in apparent repose, they sheathed their fascination for a moment, and suddenly shot a backward glance, like a Parthian arrow, from under their long eyelashes, that left a wound to be sighed over for many a day.

The spoiled and petted child of the brave, careless Renaud d'Avesne des Meloises, of an ancient family in the Nivernois, Angelique grew up a motherless girl, clever above most of her companions, conscious of superior charms, always admired and flattered, and, since she left the Convent, worshipped as the idol of the gay gallants of the city, and the despair and envy of her own sex. She was a born sovereign of men, and she felt it. It was her divine right to be preferred. She trod the earth with dainty feet, and a step aspiring as that of the fair Louise de La Valliere when she danced in the royal ballet in the forest of Fontainebleau and stole a king's heart by the flashes of her pretty feet. Angelique had been indulged by her father in every caprice, and in the gay world inhaled the incense of adulation until she regarded it as her right, and resented passionately when it was withheld.

She was not by nature bad, although vain, selfish, and aspiring. Her footstool was the hearts of men, and upon it she set hard her beautiful feet, indifferent to the anguish caused by her capricious tyranny. She was cold and calculating under the warm passions of a voluptuous nature. Although many might believe they had won the favor, none felt sure they had gained the love of this fair, capricious girl.

# Chapter IV: Confidences

Angelique took the arm of Amelie in her old, familiar schoolgirl way, and led her to the sunny corner of a bastion where lay a dismounted cannon.

The girls sat down upon the old gun. Angelique held Amelie by both hands, as if hesitating how to express something she wished to say. Still, when Angelique did speak, it was plain to Amelie that she had other things on her mind than what her tongue gave loose to.

"Now we are quite alone, Amelie," said she, "we can talk as we used to do in our school-days. You have not been in the city during the whole summer, and have missed all its gaieties?"

"I was well content. How beautiful the country looks from here!" replied Amelie. "How much pleasanter to be in it, revelling among the flowers and under the trees! I like to touch the country as well as to look at it from a distance, as you do in Quebec."

"Well, I never care for the country if I can only get enough of the city. Quebec was never so gay as it has been this year. The Royal Roussillon, and the freshly arrived regiments of Bearn and Ponthieu, have turned the heads of all Quebec,--of the girls, that is. Gallants have been plenty as bilberries in August. And you may be sure I got my share, Amelie." Angelique laughed aloud at some secret reminiscences of her summer campaign.

"It is well that I did not come to the city, Angelique, to get my head turned like the rest; but now that I am here, suppose I should mercifully try to heal some of the hearts you have broken!"

"I hope you won't try. Those bright eyes of yours would heal too effectually the wounds made by mine, and that is not what I desire," replied Angelique, laughing.

"No! then your heart is more cruel than your eyes. But, tell me, who have been your victims this year, Angelique?"

"Well, to be frank, Amelie, I have tried my fascinations upon the King's officers very impartially, and with fair success. There have been three duels, two deaths, and one captain of the Royal Roussillon turned cordelier for my sake. Is that not a fair return for my labor?"

"You are shocking as ever, Angelique! I do not believe you feel proud of such triumphs," exclaimed Amelie.

"Proud, no! I am not proud of conquering men. That is easy! My triumphs are over the women! And the way to triumph over them is to subdue the men. You know my old rival at school, the haughty Francoise de Lantagnac: I owed her a grudge, and she has put on the black veil for life, instead of the white one and orange-blossoms for a day! I only meant to frighten her, however, when I stole her lover, but she took it to heart and went into the Convent. It was dangerous for her to challenge Angelique des Meloises to test the fidelity of her affianced, Julien de St. Croix."

Amelie rose up in honest indignation, her cheek burning like a coal of fire. "I know your wild talk of old, Angelique, but I will not believe you are so wicked as to make deadly sport of our holiest affections."

"Ah, if you knew men as I do, Amelie, you would think it no sin to punish them for their perjuries."

"No, I don't know men," replied Amelie, "but I think a noble man is, after God, the worthiest object of a woman's devotion. We were better dead than finding amusement in the pain of those who love us; pray what became of Julien de St. Croix after you broke up his intended marriage with poor Francoise?"

"Oh! I threw him to the fishes! What did I care for him? It was mainly to punish

Francoise's presumption that I showed my power and made him fight that desperate duel with Captain Le Franc."

"O Angelique, how could you be so unutterably wicked?"

"Wicked? It was not my fault, you know, that he was killed. He was my champion, and ought to have come off victor. I wore a black ribbon for him a full half-year, and had the credit of being devoted to his memory; I had my triumph in that if in nothing else."

"Your triumph! for shame, Angelique! I will not listen to you: you profane the very name of love by uttering such sentiments. The gift of so much beauty was for blessing, not for pain. St. Mary pray for you, Angelique: you need her prayers!" Amelie rose up suddenly.

"Nay, do not get angry and go off that way, Amelie," ejaculated Angelique. "I will do penance for my triumphs by relating my defeats, and my special failure of all, which I know you will rejoice to hear."

"I, Angelique? What have your triumphs or failures to do with me? No, I care not to hear." Angelique held her half forcibly by the scarf.

"But you will care when I tell you that I met an old and valued friend of yours last night at the Castle--the new Aide-de-Camp of the Governor, Colonel Philibert. I think I have heard you speak of Pierre Philibert in the Convent, Amelie?"

Amelie felt the net thrown over her by the skilful retiaria. She stood stock-still in mute surprise, with averted eye and deeply blushing cheek, fighting desperately with the confusion she feared to let Angelique detect. But that keen-sighted girl saw too clearly--she had caught her fast as a bird is caught by the fowler.

"Yes, I met with a double defeat last night," continued Angelique.

"Indeed! pray, from whom?" Amelie's curiosity, though not usually a troublesome quality, was by this time fairly roused.

Angelique saw her drift, and played with her anxiety for a few moments.

"My first rebuff was from that gentlemanly philosopher from Sweden, a great friend of the Governor, you know. But, alas, I might as well have tried to fascinate an iceberg! I do not believe that he knew, after a half-hour's conversation with me, whether I was man or woman. That was defeat number one."

"And what was number two?" Amelie was now thoroughly interested in Angelique's gossip.

"I left the dry, unappreciative philosopher, and devoted myself to charm the handsome Colonel Philibert. He was all wit and courtesy, but my failure was even more signal with him than with the cold Swede."

Amelie's eyes gave a sparkle of joy, which did not escape Angelique, but she pretended not to see it. "How was that? Tell me, pray, how you failed with Colonel Philibert?"

"My cause of failure would not be a lesson for you, Amelie. Listen! I got a speedy introduction to Colonel Philibert, who, I confess, is one of the handsomest men I ever saw. I was bent on attracting him."

"For shame, Angelique! How could you confess to aught so unwomanly!" There was a warmth in Amelie's tone that was less noticed by herself than by her companion.

"Well, it is my way of conquering the King's army. I shot my whole quiver of arrows at Colonel Philibert, but, to my chagrin, hit not a vital part! He parried every one, and returned them broken at my feet. His persistent questioning about yourself, as soon as he discovered we had been school companions at the Convent, quite foiled me. He was full of interest about you, and all that concerned you, but cared not a fig about me!"

"What could Colonel Philibert have to ask you about me?" Amelie unconsciously drew closer to her companion, and even clasped her arm by an involuntary movement which did not escape her friend.

"Why, he asked everything a gentleman could, with proper respect, ask about a lady."

"And what did you say?"

"Oh, not half enough to content him. I confess I felt piqued that he only looked on me as a sort of pythoness to solve enigmas about you. I had a grim satisfaction in leaving his curiosity irritated, but not satisfied. I praised your beauty, goodness, and cleverness up to the skies, however. I was not untrue to old friendship, Amelie!" Angelique kissed her friend on the cheek, who silently allowed what, in her indignation a few moments ago, she would have refused.

"But what said Colonel Philibert of himself? Never mind about me."

"Oh, impatient that you are! He said nothing of himself. He was absorbed in my stories concerning you. I told him as pretty a fable as La Fontaine related of the Avare qui avait perdu son tresor! I said you were a beautiful chatelaine besieged by an army of lovers, but the knight errant Fortunatus had alone won your favor, and would receive your hand! The brave Colonel! I could see he winced at this. His steel cuirass was not invulnerable. I drew blood, which is more than you would have dared to do, Amelie! But I discovered the truth hidden in his heart. He is in love with you, Amelie de Repentigny!"

"Mad girl! How could you? How dare you speak so of me? What must Colonel Philibert think?"

"Think? He thinks you must be the most perfect of your sex! Why, his mind was made up about you, Amelie, before he said a word to me. Indeed, he only just wanted to enjoy the supernal pleasure of hearing me sing the praises of Amelie De Repentigny to the tune composed by himself."

"Which you seem to have done, Angelique!"

"As musically as Mere St. Borgia when singing vespers in the Ursulines," was Angelique's flippant reply.

Amelie knew how useless it was to expostulate. She swallowed her mingled pleasure and vexation salt with tears she could not help. She changed the subject by a violent wrench, and asked Angelique when she had last seen Le Gardeur.

"At the Intendant's levee the other day. How like you he is, too, only less amiable!"

Angelique did not respond readily to her friend's question about her brother.

"Less amiable? that is not like my brother. Why do you think him less amiable than me?"

"Because he got angry with me at the ball given in honor of the arrival of the Intendant, and I have not been able to restore him to perfect good humor with me since."

"Oh, then Le Gardeur completes the trio of those who are proof against your fascinations?" Amelie was secretly glad to hear of the displeasure of Le Gardeur with Angelique."

"Not at all, I hope, Amelie. I don't place Le Gardeur in the same category with my other admirers. But he got offended because I seemed to neglect him a little to cultivate this gay new Intendant. Do you know him?"

"No; nor wish to! I have heard much said to his disadvantage. The Chevalier La Corne St. Luc has openly expressed his dislike of the Intendant for something that happened in Acadia."

"Oh, the Chevalier La Corne is always so decided in his likes and dislikes: one must either be very good or very bad to satisfy him!" replied Angelique with a scornful pout of her lips."

"Don't speak ill of my godfather, Angelique; better be profane on any other topic: you know my ideal of manly virtues is the Chevalier La Corne," replied Amelie.

"Well, I won't pull down your idol, then! I respect the brave old soldier, too; but could wish him with the army in Flanders!"

"Thousands of estimable people augur ill from the accession of the Intendant Bigot in New France, besides the Chevalier La Corne," Amelie said after a pause. She disliked censuring even the Intendant.

"Yes," replied Angelique, "the Honnetes Gens do, who think themselves bound to oppose the Intendant, because he uses the royal authority in a regal way, and makes every one, high and low, do their devoir to Church and State."

"While he does his devoir to none! But I am no politician, Angelique. But when so many good people call the Intendant a bad man, it behooves one to be circumspect in 'cultivating him,' as you call it."

"Well, he is rich enough to pay for all the broken pots: they say he amassed untold wealth in Acadia, Amelie!"

"And lost the province for the king!" retorted Amelie, with all the asperity her gentle but patriotic spirit was capable of. "Some say he sold the country."

"I don't care!" replied the reckless beauty, "he is like Joseph in Egypt, next to Pharaoh in authority. He can shoe his horses with gold! I wish he would shoe me with golden slippers--I would wear them, Amelie!"

Angelique stamped her dainty foot upon the ground, as if in fancy she already had them on.

"It is shocking if you mean it!" remarked Amelie pityingly, for she felt Angclique was speaking her genuine thoughts. "But is it true that the Intendant is really as dissolute as rumor says?"

"I don't care if it be true: he is noble, gallant, polite, rich, and all-powerful at Court. He is reported to be prime favorite of the Marquise de Pompadour. What more do I want?" replied Angelique warmly.

Amelie knew enough by report of the French Court to cause her to shrink instinctively, as from a repulsive insect, at the name of the mistress of Louis XV. She trembled at the thought of Angelique's infatuation, or perversity, in suffering herself to be attracted by the glitter of the vices of the Royal Intendant.

"Angelique!" exclaimed she, "I have heard things of the Intendant that would make me tremble for you, were you in earnest."

"But I am in earnest! I mean to win and wear the Intendant of New France, to show my superiority over the whole bevy of beauties competing for his hand. There is not a girl in Quebec but would run away with him tomorrow."

"Fie, Angelique! such a libel upon our sex! You know better. But you cannot love him?"

"Love him? No!" Angelique repeated the denial scornfully. "Love him! I never thought of love and him together! He is not handsome, like your brother Le Gardeur, who is my beau-ideal of a man I could love; nor has the intellect and nobility of Colonel Philibert, who is my model of a heroic man. I could love such men as them. But my ambition would not be content with less than a governor or royal intendant in New France. In old France I would not put up with less than the King himself!"

Angelique laughed at her own extravagance, but she believed in it all the same. Amelie, though shocked at her wildness, could not help smiling at her folly.

"Have you done raving?" said she; "I have no right to question your selection of a lover or doubt your power, Angelique. But are you sure there exists no insurmountable obstacle to oppose these high aspirations? It is whispered that the Intendant has a wife, whom he keeps in the seclusion of Beaumanoir. Is that true?"

The words burnt like fire. Angelique's eyes flashed out daggers. She clenched her delicate hands until her nails drew blood from her velvet palms. Her frame quivered with suppressed passion. She grasped her companion fiercely by the arm, exclaiming,--"You have hit the secret now, Amelie! It was to speak of that I sought you out this morning, for I know you are wise, discreet, and every way better than I. It is all true what I have said, and more too, Amelie. Listen! The Intendant has made love to me with pointed gallantry that could have no other meaning but that he honorably sought my hand. He has made me talked of and hated by my own sex, who envied his preference of me. I was living in the most gorgeous of fool's paradises, when a bird brought to my ear the astounding news that a woman, beautiful as Diana, had been found in the forest of Beaumanoir by some Hurons of Lorette, who were out hunting with the Intendant. She was accompanied by a few Indians of a strange tribe, the Abenaquais of Acadia. The woman was utterly exhausted by fatigue, and lay asleep on a couch of dry leaves under a tree, when the astonished Hurons led the Intendant to the spot where she lay.

"Don't interrupt me, Amelie; I see you are amazed, but let me go on!" She held the hands of her companion firmly in her lap as she proceeded:

"The Intendant was startled out of all composure at the apparition of the sleeping lady. He spoke eagerly to the Abenaquais in their own tongue, which was unintelligible to the Hurons. When he had listened to a few words of their explanation, he ran hastily to the lady, kissed her, called her by name, 'Caroline!' She woke up suddenly, and recognizing the Intendant, embraced him, crying 'Francois! 'Francois!' and fainted in his arms.

"The Chevalier was profoundly agitated, blessing and banning, in the same breath, the fortune that had led her to him. He gave her wine, restored her to consciousness, talked with her long, and sometimes angrily; but to no avail, for the woman, in accents of despair, exclaimed in French, which the Hurons understood, that the Intendant might kill and bury her there, but she would never, never return home any more."

Angelique scarcely took breath as she continued her eager recital.

"The Intendant, overpowered either by love of her or fear of her, ceased his remonstrances. He gave some pieces of gold to the Abenaquais, and dismissed them. The strange Indians kissed her on both hands as they would a queen, and with many adieus vanished into the forest. The lady, attended by Bigot, remained seated under the tree till nightfall, when he conducted her secretly to the Chateau, where she still remains in perfect seclusion in a secret chamber, they say, and has been seen by none save one or two of the Intendant's most intimate companions."

"Heavens! what a tale of romance! How learned you all this, Angelique?" exclaimed Amelie, who had listened with breathless attention to the narrative.

"Oh, partly from a hint from a Huron girl, and the rest from the Intendant's Secretary. Men cannot keep secrets that women are interested in knowing! I could make De Pean talk the Intendant's head off his shoulders, if I had him an hour in my confessional. But all my ingenuity could not extract from him what he did not know--who that mysterious lady is, her name and family."

"Could the Huron hunters give no guess?" asked Amelie, thoroughly interested in Angelique's story.

"No. They learned by signs, however, from the Abenaquais, that she was a lady of a noble family in Acadia which had mingled its patrician blood with that of the native chiefs and possessors of the soil. The Abenaquais were chary of their information, however: they would only say she was a great white lady, and as good as any saint in the calendar."

"I would give five years of my life to know who and what that woman is!" Angelique added, as she leaned over the parapet, gazing intently at the great forest that lay beyond Charlebourg, in which was concealed the Chateau of Beaumanoir."

"It is a strange mystery. But I would not seek to unravel it, Angelique," remarked Amelie, "I feel there is sin in it. Do not touch it: it will only bring mischief upon you if you do!"

"Mischief! So be it! But I will know the worst! The Intendant is deceiving me! Woe be to him and her if I am to be their intended victim! Will you not assist me, Amelie, to discover the truth of this secret?"

"I? how can I? I pity you, Angelique, but it were better to leave this Intendant to his own devices."

"You can very easily help me if you will. Le Gardeur must know this secret. He must have seen the woman--but he is angry with me, for-- for--slighting him--as he thinks--but he was wrong. I could not avow to him my jealousy in this matter. He told me just enough to madden me, and angrily refused to tell the rest when he saw me so infatuated--he called it--over other people's love affairs. Oh, Amelie, Le Gardeur will tell you all if you ask him!"

"And I repeat it to you, Angelique, I cannot question Le Gardeur on such a hateful topic. At any rate I need time to reflect, and will pray to be guided right."

"Oh, pray not at all! If you pray you will never aid me! I know you will say the end is wicked and the means dishonorable. But find out I will--and speedily! It will only be the price of another dance with the Chevalier de Pean, to discover all I want. What fools men are when they believe we love them for their sakes and not for our own!"

Amelie, pitying the wild humors, as she regarded them, of her old school companion, took her arm to walk to and fro in the bastion, but was not sorry to see her aunt and the Bishop and Father de Berey approaching.

"Quick," said she to Angelique, "smooth your hair, and compose your looks. Here comes my aunt and the Bishop--Father de Berey too!"

Angelique prepared at once to meet them, and with her wonderful power of adaptation transformed herself in a moment into a merry creature, all light and gaiety. She saluted the Lady de Tilly and the reverend Bishop in the frankest manner, and at once accepted an interchange of wit and laughter with Father de Berey.

"She could not remain long, however, in the Church's company," she said, "she had her morning calls to finish." She kissed the cheek of Amelie and the hand of the Lady de Tilly, and with a coquettish courtesy to the gentlemen, leaped nimbly into her caleche, whirled round her spirited horses like a practised charioteer, and drove with rapid pace down the crowded street of St. John, the observed of all observers, the admiration of the men and the envy of the women as she flashed by.

Amelie and the Lady de Tilly, having seen a plenteous meal distributed among their people, proceeded to their city home--their seigniorial residence, when they chose to live in the capital.

## Chapter V: The Itinerant Notary

Master Jean Le Nocher the sturdy ferryman's patience had been severely tried for a few days back, passing the troops of habitans over the St. Charles to the city of Quebec. Being on the King's corvee, they claimed the privilege of all persons in the royal service: they travelled toll-free, and paid Jean with a nod or a jest in place of the small coin which that worthy used to exact on ordinary occasions.

This morning had begun auspiciously for Jean's temper however. A King's officer, on a gray charger, had just crossed the ferry; and without claiming the exemption from toll which was the right of all wearing the King's uniform, the officer had paid Jean more than his fee in solid coin and rode on his way, after a few kind words to the ferryman and a polite salute to his wife Babet, who stood courtesying at the door of their cottage.

"A noble gentleman that, and a real one!" exclaimed Jean, to his buxom, pretty wife, "and as generous as a prince! See what he has given me." Jean flipped up a piece of silver admiringly, and then threw it into the apron of Babet, which she spread out to catch it.

Babet rubbed the silver piece caressingly between her fingers and upon her cheek. "It is easy to see that handsome officer is from the Castle," said Babet, "and not from the Palace--and so nice- looking he is too, with such a sparkle in his eye and a pleasant smile on his mouth. He is as good as he looks, or I am no judge of men."

"And you are an excellent judge of men, I know, Babet," he replied, "or you would never have taken me!" Jean chuckled richly over his own wit, which Babet nodded lively approval to. "Yes, I know a hawk from a handsaw," replied Babet, "and a woman who is as wise as that will never mistake a gentleman, Jean! I have not seen a handsomer officer than that in seven years!"

"He is a pretty fellow enough, I dare say, Babet; who can he be? He rides like a field-marshal too, and that gray horse has ginger in his heels!" remarked Jean, as the officer was riding at a rapid gallop up the long, white road of Charlebourg. "He is going to Beaumanoir, belike, to see the Royal Intendant, who has not returned yet from his hunting party."

"Whither they went three days ago, to enjoy themselves in the chase and drink themselves blind in the Chateau while everybody else is summoned to the city to work upon the walls!" replied Babet, scornfully. "I'll be bound that officer has gone to order the gay gallants of the Friponne back to the city to take their share of work with honest people."

"Ah! the Friponne! The Friponne!" ejaculated Jean. "The foul fiend fly away with the Friponne! My ferryboat is laden every day with the curses of the habitans returning from the Friponne, where they cheat worse than a Basque pedler, and without a grain of his politeness!"

The Friponne, as it was styled in popular parlance, was the immense magazine established by the Grand Company of Traders in New France. It claimed a monopoly in the purchase and sale of all imports and exports in the Colony. Its privileges were based upon royal ordinances and decrees of the Intendant, and its rights enforced in the most arbitrary manner--and to the prejudice of every other mercantile interest in the Colony. As a natural consequence it was cordially hated, and richly deserved the maledictions which generally accompanied the mention of the Friponne--the swindle--a rough and ready epithet which sufficiently indicated the feeling of the people whom it at once cheated and oppressed.

"They say, Jean," continued Babet, her mind running in a very practical and womanly way upon the price of commodities and good bargains, "they say, Jean, that the Bourgeois Philibert will not give in like the other merchants. He sets the Intendant at defiance, and continues to buy and sell in his own comptoir as he has always done, in spite of the Friponne."

"Yes, Babet! that is what they say. But I would rather he stood in his own shoes than I in them if he is to fight this Intendant--who is a Tartar, they say."

"Pshaw, Jean! you have less courage than a woman. All the women are on the side of the good Bourgeois: he is an honest merchant--sells cheap, and cheats nobody!" Babet looked down very complacently upon her new gown, which had been purchased at a great bargain at the magazine of the Bourgeois. She felt rather the more inclined to take this view of the question inasmuch as Jean had grumbled, just a little--he would not do more--at his wife's vanity in buying a gay dress of French fabric, like a city dame, while all the women of the parish were wearing homespun,--grogram, or linsey-woolsey,--whether at church or market.

Jean had not the heart to say another word to Babet about the French gown. In truth, he thought she looked very pretty in it, better than in grogram or in linsey-woolsey, although at double the cost. He only winked knowingly at Babet, and went on to speaking of the Bourgeois.

"They say the King has long hands, but this Intendant has claws longer than Satan. There will be trouble by and by at the Golden Dog--mark that, Babet! It was only the other day the Intendant was conversing with the Sieur Cadet as they crossed the ferry. They forgot me, or thought I did not hear them; but I had my ears open, as I always have. I heard something said, and I hope no harm, will come to the good Bourgeois, that is all!"

"I don't know where Christian folk would deal if anything happened him," said Babet, reflectively. "We always get civility and good pennyworths at the Golden Dog. Some of the lying cheats of the Friponne talked in my hearing one day about his being a Huguenot. But how can that be, Jean, when he gives the best weight and the longest measure of any merchant in Quebec? Religion is a just yard wand, that is my belief, Jean!"

Jean rubbed his head with a perplexed air. "I do not know whether he be a Huguenot, nor what a Huguenot is. The Cure one day said he was a Jansenist on all fours, which I suppose is the same thing, Babet--and it does not concern either you or me. But a merchant who is a gentleman and kind to poor folk, and gives just measure and honest weight, speaks truth and harms nobody, is Christian enough for me. A bishop could not trade more honestly; and the word of the Bourgeois is as reliable as a king's."

"The Cure may call the Bourgeois what he likes," replied Babet, "but there is not another Christian in the city if the good Bourgeois be not one; and next the Church there is not a house in Quebec better known or better liked by all the habitans, than the Golden Dog; and such bargains too, as one gets there!"

"Ay, Babet! a good bargain settles many a knotty point with a woman."

"And with a man too, if he is wise enough to let his wife do his marketing, as you do, Jean! But whom have we here?" Babet set her arms akimbo and gazed.

A number of hardy fellows came down towards the ferry to seek a passage.

"They are honest habitans of St. Anne," replied Jean. "I know them; they too are on the King's corvee, and travel free, every man of them! So I must cry Vive le Roi! and pass them over to the city. It is like a holiday when one works for nothing!"

Jean stepped nimbly into his boat, followed by the rough country fellows, who amused themselves by joking at Jean Le Nocher's increasing trade and the need of putting on an extra boat these stirring times. Jean put a good face upon it, laughed, and retorted their quips, and plying his oars, stoutly performed his part in the King's corvee by safely landing them on the other shore.

Meantime the officer who had lately crossed the ferry rode rapidly up the long, straight highway that led up on the side of the mountain to a cluster of white cottages and an old church, surmounted by a belfry whose sweet bells were ringing melodiously in the fresh air of the morning.

The sun was pouring a flood of golden light over the landscape. The still glittering dewdrops hung upon the trees, shrubs, and long points of grass by the wayside. All were dressed with jewels to greet the rising king of day.

The wide, open fields of meadow, and corn-fields, ripening for harvest, stretched far away, unbroken by hedge or fence. Slight ditches or banks of turf, covered with nests of violets, ferns, and wild flowers of every hue, separated contiguous fields. No other division seemed necessary in the mutual good neighborhood that prevailed among the colonists, whose fashion of agriculture had been brought, with many hardy virtues, from the old plains of Normandy.

White-walled, red-roofed cottages, or more substantial farmhouses, stood conspicuously in the green fields, or peered out of embowering orchards. Their casements were open to catch the balmy air, while in not a few the sound of clattering hoofs on the hard road drew fair faces to the window or door, to look inquisitively after the officer wearing the white plume in his military chapeau, as he dashed by on the gallant gray.

Those who caught sight of him saw a man worth seeing--tall, deep- chested, and erect. His Norman features, without being perfect, were handsome and manly. Steel-blue eyes, solidly set under a broad forehead, looked out searchingly yet kindly, while his well-formed chin and firm lips gave an air of resolution to his whole look that accorded perfectly with the brave, loyal character of Colonel Philibert. He wore the royal uniform. His auburn hair he wore tied with a black ribbon. His good taste discarded perukes and powder, although very much in fashion in those days.

It was long since he had travelled on the highway of Charlebourg, and he thoroughly enjoyed the beauty of the road he traversed. But behind him, as he knew, lay a magnificent spectacle, the sight of the great promontory of Quebec, crowned with its glorious fortifications and replete with the proudest memories of North America. More than once the young soldier turned his steed, and halted a moment or two to survey the scene with enthusiastic admiration. It was his native city, and the thought that it was threatened by the national enemy roused, like an insult offered to the mother that bore him. He rode onward, more than ever impatient of delay, and not till he passed a cluster of elm trees which reminded him of an adventure of his youth, did the sudden heat pass away, caused by the thought of the threatened invasion.

Under these trees he remembered that he and his school companion, Le Gardeur de Repentigny, had once taken refuge during a violent storm. The tree they stood under was shattered by a thunderbolt. They were both stunned for a few minutes, and knew they had had a narrow escape from death. Neither of them ever forgot it.

A train of thoughts never long absent from the mind of Philibert started up vividly at the sight of these trees. His memory flew back to Le Gardeur and the Manor House of Tilly, and the fair young girl who captivated his boyish fancy and filled his youth with dreams of glorious achievements to win her smiles and do her honor. Among a thousand pictures of her hung up in his mind and secretly worshipped he loved that which presented her likeness on that day when he saved her brother's life and she kissed him in a passion of joy and gratitude, vowing she would pray for him to the end of her life.

The imagination of Pierre Philibert had revelled in the romantic visions that haunt every boy destined to prominence, visions kindled by the eye of woman and the hope of love.

The world is ruled by such dreams, dreams of impassioned hearts, and improvisations of warm lips, not by cold words linked in chains of iron sequence,--by love, not by logic. The heart with its passions, not the understanding with its reasoning, sways, in the long run, the actions of mankind.

Pierre Philibert possessed that rich gift of nature, a creative imagination, in addition to the solid judgment of a man of sense, schooled by experience and used to the considerations and responsibilities of weighty affairs.

His love for Amelie de Repentigny had grown in secret. Its roots reached down to the very depths of his being. It mingled, consciously or unconsciously, with all his motives and plans of life, and yet his hopes were not sanguine. Years of absence, he remembered, work forgetfulness. New ties and associations might have wiped out the memory of him in the mind of a young girl fresh to society and its delights. He experienced a disappointment in not finding her in the city upon his return a few days ago, and the state of the Colony and the stress of military duty had so far prevented his renewing his acquaintance with the Manor House of Tilly.

The old-fashioned hostelry of the Couronne de France, with its high- pitched roof, pointed gables, and broad gallery, stood directly opposite the rustic church and tall belfry of Charlebourg, not as a rival, but as a sort of adjunct to the sacred edifice. The sign of the crown, bright with gilding, swung from the low, projecting arm of a maple-tree, thick with shade and rustling with the beautiful leaves of the emblem of Canada. A few rustic seats under the cool maple were usually occupied, toward the close of the day, or about the ringing of the Angelus, by a little gathering of parishioners from the village, talking over the news of the day, the progress of the war, the ordinances of the Intendant, or the exactions of the Friponne.

On Sundays, after Mass and Vespers, the habitans of all parts of the extended parish naturally met and talked over the affairs of the Fabrique--the value of tithes for the year, the abundance of Easter eggs, and the weight of the first salmon of the season, which was always presented to the Cure with the first-fruits of the field, to ensure the blessing of plenty for the rest of the year.

The Reverend Cure frequently mingled in these discussions. Seated in his accustomed armchair, under the shade of the maple in summer, and in winter by the warm fireside, he defended, ex cathedra, the rights of the Church, and good-humoredly decided all controversies. He found his parishioners more amenable to good advice over a mug of Norman cider and a pipe of native tobacco, under the sign of the Crown of France, than when he lectured them in his best and most learned style from the pulpit.

This morning, however, all was very quiet round the old inn. The birds were singing, and the bees humming in the pleasant sunshine. The house looked clean and tidy, and no one was to be seen except three persons bending over a table, with their heads close together, deeply absorbed in whatever business they were engaged in. Two of these persons were Dame Bedard, the sharp landlady of the Crown of France, and her no less sharp and pretty daughter, Zoe. The third person of the trio was an old, alert-looking little man, writing at the table as if for very life. He wore a tattered black robe, shortened at the knees to facilitate walking, a frizzled wig, looking as if it had been dressed with a currycomb, a pair of black breeches, well-patched with various colors; and gamaches of brown leather, such as the habitans wore, completed his odd attire, and formed the professional costume of Master Pothier dit Robin, the travelling notary, one of that not unuseful order of itinerants of the law which flourished under the old regime in New France.

Upon the table near him stood a black bottle, an empty trencher, and a thick scatter of crumbs, showing that the old notary had despatched a hearty breakfast before commencing his present work of the pen.

A hairy knapsack lay open upon the table near his elbow, disclosing some bundles of dirty papers tied up with red tape, a tattered volume or two of the "Coutume de Paris," and little more than the covers of an odd tome of Pothier, his great namesake and prime authority in the law. Some linen, dirty and ragged as his law papers, was crammed into his knapsack with them. But that was neither here nor there in the estimation of the habitans, so long as his law smelt strong in the nostrils of their opponents in litigation. They rather prided themselves upon the roughness of their travelling notary.

The reputation of Master Pothier dit Robin was, of course, very great among the habitans, as he travelled from parish to parish and from seigniory to seigniory, drawing bills and hypothecations, marriage contracts and last wills and testaments, for the peasantry, who had a genuine Norman predilection for law and chicanery, and a respect amounting to veneration for written documents, red tape, and sealing-wax. Master Pothier's acuteness in picking holes in the actes of a rival notary was only surpassed by the elaborate intricacy of his own, which he boasted, not without reason, would puzzle the Parliament of Paris, and confound the ingenuity of the sharpest advocates of Rouen. Master Pothier's actes were as full of embryo disputes as a fig is full of seeds, and usually kept all parties in hot water and litigation for the rest of their days. If he did happen now and then to settle a dispute between neighbors, he made ample amends for it by setting half the rest of the parish by the ears.

Master Pothier's nose, sharp and fiery as if dipped in red ink, almost touched the sheet of paper on the table before him, as he wrote down from the dictation of Dame Bedard the articles of a marriage contract between her pretty daughter, Zoe, and Antoine La Chance, the son of a comfortable but keen widow of Beauport.

Dame Bedard had shrewdly availed herself of the presence of Master Pothier, and in payment of a night's lodging at the Crown of France, to have him write out the contract of marriage in the absence of Dame La Chance, the mother of Antoine, who would, of course, object to the insertion of certain conditions in the contract which Dame Bedard was quite determined upon as the price of Zoe's hand and fortune.

"There! Dame Bedard!" cried Master Pothier, sticking the pen behind his ear, after a magnificent flourish at the last word," there is a marriage contract fit to espouse King Solomon to the Queen of Sheba! A dowry of a hundred livres tournoises, two cows, and a feather bed, bedstead, and chest of linen! A donation entre vifs!"

"A what? Master Pothier, now mind! are you sure that is the right word of the grimoire?" cried Dame Bedard, instinctively perceiving that here lay the very point of the contract. "You know I only give on condition, Master Pothier."

"Oh, yes! trust me, Dame Bedard. I have made it a donation entre vifs, revocable pour cause d'ingratitude, if your future son-in-law, Antoine la Chance, should fail in his duty to you and to Zoe."

"And he won't do his duty to Zoe, unless he does it to me, Master Pothier. But are you sure it is strong enough? Will it hold Dame La Chance by the foot, so that she cannot revoke her gifts although I may revoke mine?"

"Hold Dame La Chance by the foot? It will hold her as fast as a snapping-turtle does a frog. In proof of it, see what Ricard says, page 970; here is the book." Master Pothier opened his tattered volume, and held it up to the dame. She shook her head.

"Thanks, I have mislaid my glasses. Do you read, please!"

"Most cheerfully, good dame! A notary must have eyes for everybody-- eyes like a cat's, to see in the dark, and power to draw them in like a turtle, so that he may see nothing that he does not want to see."

"Oh, bless the eyes of the notary!" Dame Bedard grew impatient. "Tell me what the book says about gifts revocable--that is what concerns me and Zoe."

"Well, here it is, dame: 'Donations stipulated revocable at the pleasure of the donor are null. But this condition does not apply to donations by contract of marriage.' Bourdon also says--"

"A fig for Bourdon, and all such drones! I want my gift made revocable, and Dame La Chance's not! I know by long experience with my dear feu Bedard how necessary it is to hold the reins tight over the men. Antoine is a good boy, but he will be all the better for a careful mother-in-law's supervision."

Master Pothier rubbed the top of his wig with his forefinger.

"Are you sure, dame, that Antoine La Chance will wear the bridle easily?"

"Assuredly! I should like to see son-in-law of mine who would not! Besides, Antoine is in the humor just now to refuse nothing for sake of Zoe. Have you mentioned the children, Master Pothier? I do not intend to let Dame La Chance control the children any more than Zoe and Antoine."

"I have made you tutrice perpetuelle, as we say in the court, and here it is," said he, placing the tip of his finger on a certain line in the document.

Zoe looked down and blushed to her finger-ends. She presently rallied, and said with some spirit,--"Never mind them, Master Pothier! Don't put them in the contract! Let Antoine have something to say about them. He would take me without a dower, I know, and time enough to remind him about children when they come."

"Take you without dower! Zoe Bedard! you must be mad!" exclaimed the dame, in great heat. "No girl in New France can marry without a dower, if it be only a pot and a bedstead! You forget, too, that the dower is given, not so much for you, as to keep up the credit of the family. As well be married without a ring! Without a dower, indeed!"

"Or without a contract written by a notary, signed, sealed, and delivered!" chimed in Master Pothier.

"Yes, Master Pothier, and I have promised Zoe a three-days wedding, which will make her the envy of all the parish of Charlebourg. The seigneur has consented to give her away in place of her poor defunct father; and when he does that he is sure to stand godfather for all the children, with a present for every one of them! I shall invite you too, Master Pothier!"

Zoe affected not to hear her mother's remark, although she knew it all by heart, for it had been dinned into her ears twenty times a day for weeks, and sooth to say, she liked to hear it, and fully appreciated the honors to come from the patronage of the seigneur.

Master Pothier pricked up his ears till they fairly raised his wig, at the prospect of a three days wedding at the Crown of France. He began an elaborate reply, when a horse's tramp broke in upon them and Colonel Philibert wheeled up to the door of the hostelry.

Master Pothier, seeing an officer in the King's uniform, rose on the instant and saluted him with a profound bow, while Dame Bedard and Zoe, standing side by side, dropped their lowest courtesy to the handsome gentleman, as, with woman's glance, they saw in a moment he was.

Philibert returned their salute courteously, as he halted his horse in front of Dame Bedard. "Madame!" said he, "I thought I knew all roads about Charlebourg, but I have either forgotten or they have changed the road through the forest to Beaumanoir. It is surely altered from what it was."

"Your Honor is right," answered Dame Bedard, "the Intendant has opened a new road through the forest." Zoe took the opportunity, while the officer looked at her mother, to examine his features, dress, and equipments, from head to foot, and thought him the handsomest officer she had ever seen.

"I thought it must be so," replied Philibert; "you are the landlady of the Crown of France, I presume?" Dame Bedard carried it on her face as plainly marked as the royal emblem on the sign over her head.

"Yes, your Honor, I am Widow Bedard, at your service, and, I hope, keep as good a hostelry as your Honor will find in the Colony. Will your Honor alight and take a cup of wine, such as I keep for guests of quality?"

"Thanks, Madame Bedard, I am in haste: I must find the way to Beaumanoir. Can you not furnish me a guide, for I like not to lose time by missing my way?"

"A guide, sir! The men are all in the city on the King's corvee; Zoe could show you the way easily enough." Zoe twitched her mother's arm nervously, as a hint not to say too much. She felt flattered and fluttered too, at the thought of guiding the strange, handsome gentleman through the forest, and already the question shot through her fancy, "What might come of it? Such things have happened in stories!" Poor Zoe! she was for a few seconds unfaithful to the memory of Antoine La Chance. But Dame Bedard settled all surmises by turning to Master Pothier, who stood stiff and upright as became a limb of the law. "Here is Master Pothier, your Honor, who knows every highway and byway in ten seigniories. He will guide your Honor to Beaumanoir."

"As easy as take a fee or enter a process, your Honor," remarked Master Pothier, whose odd figure had several times drawn the criticizing eye of Colonel Philibert.

"A fee! ah! you belong to the law, then, my good friend? I have known many advocates--" but Philibert stopped; he was too good- natured to finish his sentence.

"You never saw one like me, your Honor was going to say? True, you never did. I am Master Pothier dit Robin, the poor travelling notary, at your Honor's service, ready to draw you a bond, frame an acte of convention matrimoniale, or write your last will and testament, with any notary in New France. I can, moreover, guide your Honor to Beaumanoir as easy as drink your health in a cup of Cognac."

Philibert could not but smile at the travelling notary, and thinking to himself, "too much Cognac at the end of that nose of yours, my friend!" which, indeed, looked fiery as Bardolph's, with hardly a spot for a fly to rest his foot upon without burning.

"But how will you go, friend?" asked Philibert, looking down at Master Pothier's gamaches; "you don't look like a fast walker."

"Oh, your Honor," interrupted Dame Bedard, impatiently, for Zoe had been twitching her hard to let her go. "Master Pothier can ride the old sorrel nag that stands in the stable eating his head off for want of hire. Of course your Honor will pay livery?"

"Why, certainly, Madame, and glad to do so! So Master Pothier make haste, get the sorrel nag, and let us be off."

"I will be back in the snap of a pen, or in the time Dame Bedard can draw that cup of Cognac, your Honor."

"Master Pothier is quite a personage, I see," remarked Philibert, as the old notary shuffled off to saddle the nag.

"Oh, quite, your Honor. He is the sharpest notary, they say, that travels the road. When he gets people into law they never can get out. He is so clever, everybody says! Why, he assures me that even the Intendant consults him sometimes as they sit eating and drinking half the night together in the buttery at the Chateau!"

"Really! I must be careful what I say," replied Philibert, laughing, "or I shall get into hot water! But here he comes."

As he spoke, Master Pothier came up, mounted on a raw-boned nag, lank as the remains of a twenty-years lawsuit. Zoe, at a hint from the Colonel, handed him a cup of Cognac, which he quaffed without breathing, smacking his lips emphatically after it. He called out to the landlady,--"Take care of my knapsack, dame! You had better burn the house than lose my papers! Adieu, Zoe! study over the marriage contract till I return, and I shall be sure of a good dinner from your pretty hands."

They set off at a round trot. Colonel Philibert, impatient to reach Beaumanoir, spurred on for a while, hardly noticing the absurd figure of his guide, whose legs stuck out like a pair of compasses beneath his tattered gown, his shaking head threatening dislodgment to hat and wig, while his elbows churned at every jolt, making play with the shuffling gait of his spavined and wall-eyed nag.

## Chapter VI: Beaumanoir

They rode on in silence. A little beyond the village of Charlebourg they suddenly turned into the forest of Beaumanoir, where a well- beaten track, practicable both for carriages and horses, gave indications that the resort of visitors to the Chateau was neither small nor seldom.

The sun's rays scarcely penetrated the sea of verdure overhead. The ground was thickly strewn with leaves, the memorials of past summers; and the dark green pines breathed out a resinous odor, fresh and invigorating to the passing rider.

Colonel Philibert, while his thoughts were for the most part fixed on the public dangers which led to this hasty visit of his to the Chateau of Beaumanoir, had still an eye for the beauty of the forest, and not a squirrel leaping, nor a bird fluttering among the branches, escaped his notice as he passed by. Still he rode on rapidly, and having got fairly into the road, soon outstripped his guide.

"A crooked road this to Beaumanoir," remarked he at length, drawing bridle to allow Master Pothier to rejoin him. "It is as mazy as the law. I am fortunate, I am sure, in having a sharp notary like you to conduct me through it."

"Conduct you! Your Honor is leading me! But the road to Beaumanoir is as intricate as the best case ever drawn up by an itinerant notary."

"You seldom ride, Master Pothier?" said Philibert, observing his guide jolting with an audible grunt at every step of his awkward nag.

"Ride, your Honor! N--no! Dame Bedard shall call me plaisant Robin if she ever tempts me again to mount her livery horse--'if fools only carried cruppers!' as Panurge says."

"Why, Master Pothier?" Philibert began to be amused at his odd guide.

"Why? Then I should be able to walk to-morrow--that is all! This nag will finish me. Hunc! hanc! hoc! He is fit to be Satan's tutor at the seminary! Hoc! hanc! hunc! I have not declined my pronouns since I left my accidence at the High School of Tours--not till to- day. Hunc! hanc! hoc! I shall be jolted to jelly! Hunc! hanc! hoc!"

Philibert laughed at the classical reminiscences of his guide; but, fearing that Pothier might fall off his horse, which he straddled like a hay-fork, he stopped to allow the worthy notary to recover his breath and temper.

"I hope the world appreciates your learning and talent, and that it uses you more gently than that horse of yours," remarked he.

"Oh, your Honor! it is kind of you to rein up by the way. I find no fault with the world if it find none with me. My philosophy is this, that the world is as men make it."

"As the old saying is,--

"'To lend, or to spend, or to give in,
'Tis a very good world that we live in;
But to borrow, or beg, or get a man's own,
'Tis the very worst world that ever was known.'

And you consider yourself in the latter category, Master Pothier?" Philibert spoke doubtingly, for a more self-complacent face than his companion's he never saw--every wrinkle trembled with mirth; eyes, cheeks, chin, and brows surrounded that jolly red nose of his like a group of gay boys round a bonfire.

"Oh, I am content, your Honor! We notaries are privileged to wear furred cloaks in the Palais de Justice, and black robes in the country when we can get them! Look here at my robe of dignity!" He held up the tattered tail of his gown with a ludicrous air. "The profession of notary is meat, drink, and lodging: every man's house is free to me--his bed and board I share, and there is neither wedding, christening, nor funeral, in ten parishes that can go on without me. Governors and intendants flourish and fall, but Jean Pothier dit Robin, the itinerant notary, lives merrily: men may do without bread, but they will not live without law--at least, in this noble, litigious New France of ours."

"Your profession seems quite indispensable, then!" remarked Philibert.

"Indispensable! I should think so! Without proper actes the world would soon come to an end, as did Adam's happiness in Eden, for want of a notary."

"A notary, Master Pothier?"

"Yes, your Honor. It is clear that Adam lost his first estate de usis et fructibus in the Garden of Eden, simply because there was no notary to draw up for him an indefeasable lease. Why, he had not even a bail a chaptal (a chattel mortgage) over the beasts he had himself named!"

"Ah!" replied Philibert, smiling, "I thought Adam lost his estate through a cunning notary who persuaded his wife to break the lease he held; and poor Adam lost possession because he could not find a second notary to defend his title."

"Hum! that might be; but judgment went by default, as I have read. It would be different now; there are notaries, in New France and Old, capable of beating Lucifer himself in a process for either soul, body, or estate! But, thank fortune, we are out of this thick forest now."

The travellers had reached the other verge of the forest of Beaumanoir. A broad plain dotted with clumps of fair trees lay spread out in a royal domain, overlooked by a steep, wooded mountain. A silvery brook crossed by a rustic bridge ran through the park. In the centre was a huge cluster of gardens and patriarchal trees, out of the midst of which rose the steep roof, chimneys, and gilded vanes, flashing in the sun, of the Chateau of Beaumanoir.

The Chateau was a long, heavy structure of stone, gabled and pointed in the style of the preceding century--strong enough for defence, and elegant enough for the abode of the Royal Intendant of New France. It had been built, some four-score years previously, by the Intendant Jean Talon, as a quiet retreat when tired with the importunities of friends or the persecution of enemies, or disgusted with the cold indifference of the Court to his statesmanlike plans for the colonization of New France.

A short distance from the Chateau rose a tower of rough masonry-- crenellated on top, and loopholed on the sides--which had been built as a place of defence and refuge during the Indian wars of the preceding century. Often had the prowling bands of Iroquois turned away baffled and dismayed at the sight of the little fortalice surmounted by a culverin or two, which used to give the alarm of invasion to the colonists on the slopes of Bourg Royal, and to the dwellers along the wild banks of the Montmorency.

The tower was now disused and partly dilapidated, but many wonderful tales existed among the neighboring habitans of a secret passage that communicated with the vaults of the Chateau; but no one had ever seen the passage--still less been bold enough to explore it had they found it, for it was guarded by a loup-garou that was the terror of children, old and young, as they crowded close together round the blazing fire on winter nights, and repeated old legends of Brittany and Normandy, altered to fit the wild scenes of the New World.

Colonel Philibert and Master Pothier rode up the broad avenue that led to the Chateau, and halted at the main gate--set in a lofty hedge of evergreens cut into fantastic shapes, after the fashion of the Luxembourg. Within the gate a vast and glowing garden was seen-- all squares, circles, and polygons. The beds were laden with flowers shedding delicious odors on the morning air as it floated by, while the ear was soothed by the hum of bees and the songs of birds revelling in the bright sunshine.

Above the hedge appeared the tops of heavily-laden fruit-trees brought from France and planted by Talon--cherries red as the lips of Breton maidens, plums of Gascony, Norman apples, with pears from the glorious valleys of the Rhone. The bending branches were just transmuting their green unripeness into scarlet, gold, and purple-- the imperial colors of Nature when crowned for the festival of autumn.

A lofty dove-cote, surmounted by a glittering vane, turning and flashing with every shift of the wind, stood near the Chateau. It was the home of a whole colony of snow-white pigeons, which fluttered in and out of it, wheeled in circles round the tall chimney-stacks, or strutted, cooing and bowing together, on the high roof of the Chateau, a picture of innocence and happiness.

But neither happiness nor innocence was suggested by the look of the Chateau itself, as it stood bathed in bright sunshine. Its great doors were close-shut in the face of all the beauty of the world without. Its mullioned windows, that should have stood wide open to let in the radiance and freshness of morning, were closely blinded, like eyes wickedly shut against God's light that beat upon them, vainly seeking entrance.

Outside all was still: the song of birds and the rustle of leaves alone met the ear. Neither man nor beast was stirring to challenge Colonel Philibert's approach, but long ere he reached the door of the Chateau, a din of voices within, a wild medley of shouts, song, and laughter, a clatter of wine-cups, and pealing notes of violins struck him with amazement and disgust. He distinguished drunken voices singing snatches of bacchanalian songs, while now and then stentorian mouths called for fresh brimmers, and new toasts were drunk with uproarious applause.

The Chateau seemed a very pandemonium of riot and revelry, that prolonged the night into the day, and defied the very order of nature by its audacious disregard of all decency of time, place, and circumstance.

"In God's name, what means all this, Master Pothier?" exclaimed Philibert, as they hastily dismounted and, tying their horses to a tree, entered the broad walk that led to the terrace.

"That concert going on, your Honor?"--Master Pothier shook his head to express disapproval, and smiled to express his inborn sympathy with feasting and good-fellowship--"that, your Honor, is the heel of the hunt, the hanging up of the antlers of the stag by the gay chasseurs who are visiting the Intendant!"

"A hunting party, you mean? To think that men could stand such brutishness, even to please the Intendant!"

"Stand! your Honor. I wager my gown that most of the chasseurs are lying under the table by this time, although by the noise they make it must be allowed there are some burly fellows upon their legs yet, who keep the wine flowing like the cow of Montmorency."

"'Tis horrible! 'tis damnable!" Philibert grew pale with passion and struck his thigh with his palm, as was his wont when very angry. "Rioting in drunkenness when the Colony demands the cool head, the strong arm, and the true heart of every man among us! Oh, my country! my dear country! what fate is thine to expect when men like these are thy rulers?"

"Your Honor must be a stranger in New France or you would not express such hasty, honest sentiments upon the Intendant's hospitality. It is not the fashion, except among plain-spoken habitans, who always talk downright Norman." Master Pothier looked approvingly at Colonel Philibert, who, listening with indignant ears, scarcely heeded his guide.

"That is a jolly song, your Honor," continued Pothier, waving one hand in cadence to a ditty in praise of wine, which a loud voice was heard singing in the Chateau, accompanied by a rousing chorus which startled the very pigeons on the roof and chimney-stacks. Colonel Philibert recognized the song as one he had heard in the Quartier Latin, during his student life in Paris--he fancied he recognized the voice also:

"'Pour des vins de prix
Vendons tous nos livres!
C'est pen d'etre gris,
Amis, soyons ivres!
        Bon.
La Faridondaine!
        Gai.
La Faridonde!'"

A roar of voices and a clash of glasses followed the refrain. Master Pothier's eyes winked and blinked in sympathy. The old notary stood on tiptoe, with outspread palms, as with ore rotundo he threw in a few notes of his own to fill up the chorus.

Philibert cast upon his guide a look of scorn, biting his lip angrily. "Go," said he, "knock at the door--it needs God's thunder to break in upon that infamous orgie. Say that Colonel Philibert brings orders from His Excellency the Governor to the Chevalier Intendant."

"And be served with a writ of ejectment! Pardon me! Be not angry, sir," pleaded Pothier supplicatingly, "I dare not knock at the door when they are at the devil's mass inside. The valets! I know them all! They would duck me in the brook, or drag me into the hall to make sport for the Philistines. And I am not much of a Samson, your Honor. I could not pull the Chatcau down upon their heads--I wish I could!"

Master Pothier's fears did not appear ill-grounded to Philibert as a fresh burst of drunken uproar assailed his ears. "Wait my return," said he, "I will knock on the door myself." He left his guide, ran up the broad stone steps, and knocked loudly upon the door again and again! He tried it at last, and to his surprise found it unlatched; he pushed it open, no servitor appearing to admit him. Colonel Philibert went boldly in. A blaze of light almost dazzled his eyes. The Chateau was lit up with lamps and candelabra in every part. The bright rays of the sun beat in vain for admittance upon the closed doors and blinded windows, but the splendor of midnight oil pervaded the interior of the stately mansion, making an artificial night that prolonged the wild orgies of the Intendant into the hours of day.

## Chapter VII: The Intendant Bigot

The Chateau of Beaumanoir had, since the advent of the Intendant Bigot, been the scene of many a festive revelry that matched, in bacchanalian frenzy, the wild orgies of the Regency and the present debaucheries of Croisy and the petits appartements of Versailles. Its splendor, its luxury, its riotous feasts lasting without intermission sometimes for days, were the themes of wonder and disgust to the unsophisticated people of New France, and of endless comparison between the extravagance of the Royal Intendant and the simple manners and inflexible morals of the Governor-General.

The great hall of the Chateau, the scene of the gorgeous feasts of the Intendant, was brilliantly illuminated with silver lamps, glowing like globes of sunlight as they hung from the lofty ceiling, upon which was painted a fresco of the apotheosis of Louis XIV., where the Grand Monarque was surrounded by a cloud of Condes, Orleanois, and Bourbons, of near and more remote consanguinity. At the head of the room hung a full-length portrait of Marquise de Pompadour, the mistress of Louis XV., and the friend and patroness of the Intendant Bigot; her bold, voluptuous beauty seemed well fitted to be the presiding genius of his house. The walls bore many other paintings of artistic and historic value. The King and Queen; the dark-eyed Montespan; the crafty Maintenon; and the pensive beauty of Louise de la Valliere, the only mistress of Louis XIV. who loved him for his own sake, and whose portrait, copied from this picture, may still be seen in the chapel of the Ursulines of Quebec, where the fair Louise is represented as St. Thais kneeling at prayer among the nuns.

The table in the great hall, a masterpiece of workmanship, was made of a dark Canadian wood then newly introduced, and stretched the length of the hall. A massive gold epergne of choicest Italian art, the gift of La Pompadour, stood on the centre of the table. It represented Bacchus enthroned on a tun of wine, presenting flowing cups to a dance of fauns and satyrs.

Silver cups of Venetian sculpture and goblets of Bohemian manufacture sparkled like stars upon the brilliant table, brimming over with the gold and ruby vintages of France and Spain; or lay overturned amid pools of wine that ran down upon the velvet carpet. Dishes of Parmesan cheese, caviare, and other provocatives to thirst stood upon the table, amid vases of flowers and baskets of the choicest fruits of the Antilles.

Round this magnificent table sat a score or more of revellers--in the garb of gentlemen, but all in disorder and soiled with wine; their countenances were inflamed, their eyes red and fiery, their tongues loose and loquacious. Here and there a vacant or overturned chair showed where a guest had fallen in the debauch and been carried off by the valets, who in gorgeous liveries waited on the table. A band of musicians sat up in a gallery at the end of the hall, and filled the pauses of the riotous feast with the ravishing strains of Lulli and Destouches.

At the head of the table, first in place as in rank, sat Francois Bigot, Intendant of New France. His low, well-set figure, dark hair, small, keen black eyes, and swarthy features full of fire and animation, bespoke his Gascon blood. His countenance was far from comely,--nay, when in repose, even ugly and repulsive,--but his eyes were magnets that drew men's looks towards him, for in them lay the force of a powerful will and a depth and subtlety of intellect that made men fear, if they could not love him. Yet when he chose--and it was his usual mood--to exercise his blandishments on men, he rarely failed to captivate them, while his pleasant wit, courtly ways, and natural gallantry towards women, exercised with the polished seductiveness he had learned in the Court of Louis XV., made Francois Bigot the most plausible and dangerous man in New France.

He was fond of wine and music, passionately addicted to gambling, and devoted to the pleasant vices that were rampant in the Court of France, finely educated, able in the conduct of affairs, and fertile in expedients to accomplish his ends. Francois Bigot might have saved New France, had he been honest as he was clever; but he was unprincipled and corrupt: no conscience checked his ambition or his love of pleasure. He ruined New France for the sake of himself and his patroness and the crowd of courtiers and frail beauties who surrounded the King, whose arts and influence kept him in his high office despite all the efforts of the Honnetes Gens, the good and true men of the Colony, to remove him.

He had already ruined and lost the ancient Colony of Acadia, through his defrauds and malversations as Chief Commissary of the Army, and instead of trial and punishment, had lately been exalted to the higher and still more important office of Royal Intendant of New France.

On the right of the Intendant sat his bosom friend, the Sieur Cadet, a large, sensual man, with twinkling gray eyes, thick nose, and full red lips. His broad face, flushed with wine, glowed like the harvest moon rising above the horizon. Cadet had, it was said, been a butcher in Quebec. He was now, for the misfortune of his country, Chief Commissary of the Army and a close confederate of the Intendant.

On the left of the Intendant sat his Secretary, De Pean, crafty and unscrupulous, a parasite, too, who flattered his master and ministered to his pleasures. De Pean was a military man, and not a bad soldier in the field; but he loved gain better than glory, and amassed an enormous fortune out of the impoverishment of his country.

Le Mercier, too, was there, Commandant of Artillery, a brave officer, but a bad man; Varin, a proud, arrogant libertine, Commissary of Montreal, who outdid Bigot in rapine and Cadet in coarseness; De Breard, Comptroller of the Marine, a worthy associate of Penisault, whose pinched features and cunning leer were in keeping with his important office of chief manager of the Friponne. Perrault, D'Estebe, Morin, and Vergor, all creatures of the Intendant, swelled the roll of infamy, as partners of the Grand Company of Associates trading in New France, as their charter named them--the "Grand Company of Thieves," as the people in their plain Norman called them who robbed them in the King's name and, under pretence of maintaining the war, passed the most arbitrary decrees, the only object of which was to enrich themselves and their higher patrons at the Court of Versailles.

The rest of the company seated round the table comprised a number of dissolute seigneurs and gallants of fashion about town--men of great wants and great extravagance, just the class so quaintly described by Charlevoix, a quarter of a century previous, as "gentlemen thoroughly versed in the most elegant and agreeable modes of spending money, but greatly at a loss how to obtain it."

Among the gay young seigneurs who had been drawn into the vortex of Bigot's splendid dissipation, was the brave, handsome Le Gardeur de Repentigny--a captain of the Royal Marine, a Colonial corps recently embodied at Quebec. In general form and feature Le Gardeur was a manly reflex of his beautiful sister Amelie, but his countenance was marred with traces of debauchery. His face was inflamed, and his dark eyes, so like his sister's, by nature tender and true, were now glittering with the adder tongues of the cursed wine-serpent.

Taking the cue from Bigot, Le Gardeur responded madly to the challenges to drink from all around him. Wine was now flooding every brain, and the table was one scene of riotous debauch.

"Fill up again, Le Gardeur!" exclaimed the Intendant, with a loud and still clear voice; "the lying clock says it is day--broad day, but neither cock crows nor day dawns in the Chateau of Beaumanoir, save at the will of its master and his merry guests! Fill up, companions all! The lamplight in the wine-cup is brighter than the clearest sun that ever shone!"

"Bravo Bigot! name your toast, and we will pledge it till the seven stars count fourteen!" replied Le Gardeur, looking hazily at the great clock in the hall. "I see four clocks in the room, and every one of them lies if it says it is day!"

"You are mending, Le Gardeur de Repentigny! You are worthy to belong to the Grand Company! But you shall have my toast. We have drank it twenty times already, but it will stand drinking twenty times more. It is the best prologue to wine ever devised by wit of man--a woman--"

"And the best epilogue too, Bigot!" interjected Varin, visibly drunk; "but let us have the toast, my cup is waiting."

"Well, fill up all, then; and we will drink the health, wealth, and love by stealth, of the jolliest dame in sunny France--The Marquise de Pompadour!"

"La Pompadour! La Pompadour!" Every tongue repeated the name, the goblets were drained to the bottoms, and a thunder of applause and clattering of glasses followed the toast of the mistress of Louis XV., who was the special protectress of the Grand Company,--a goodly share of whose profits in the monopoly of trade in New France was thrown into the lap of the powerful favorite.

"Come, Varin! your turn now!" cried Bigot, turning to the Commissary; "a toast for Ville Marie! Merry Montreal! where they eat like rats of Poitou, and drink till they ring the fire-bells, as the Bordelais did to welcome the collectors of the gabelle. The Montrealers have not rung the fire-bells yet against you, Varin, but they will by and by!"

Varin filled his cup with an unsteady hand until it ran over, and propping his body against the table as he stood up, replied, "A toast for Ville Marie! and our friends in need!--The blue caps of the Richelieu!" This was in allusion to a recent ordinance of the Intendant, authorizing him to seize all the corn in store at Montreal and in the surrounding country--under pretence of supplying the army, and really to secure the monopoly of it for the Grand Company.

The toast was drunk, amid rapturous applause. "Well said, Varin!" exclaimed Bigot; "that toast implied both business and pleasure: the business was to sweep out the granges of the farmers; the pleasure is to drink in honor of your success."

"My foragers sweep clean!" said Varin, resuming his seat, and looking under his hand to steady his gaze. "Better brooms were never made in Besancon. The country is swept as clean as a ball- room. Your Excellency and the Marquise might lead the dance over it, and not a straw lie in your way!"

"And did you manage it without a fight, Varin?" asked the Sieur d'Estebe, with a half sneer.

"Fight! Why fight? The habitans will never resist the King's name. We conjure the devil down with that. When we skin our eels we don't begin at the tail! If we did, the habitans would be like the eels of Melun--cry out before they were hurt. No! no! D'Estebe! We are more polite in Ville Marie. We tell them the King's troops need the corn. They doff their caps, and with tears in their eyes, say, 'Monsieur le Commissaire, the King can have all we possess, and ourselves too, if he will only save Canada from the Bostonnais.' This is better than stealing the honey and killing the bees that made it, D'Estebe!"

"But what became of the families of the habitans after this swoop of your foragers?" asked the Seigneur de Beauce, a country gentleman who retained a few honorable ideas floating on top of the wine he had swallowed.

"Oh! the families--that is, the women and children, for we took the men for the army. You see, De Beauce," replied Varin, with a mocking air, as he crossed his thumbs like a peasant of Languedoc when he wishes to inspire belief in his words, "the families have to do what the gentlemen of Beauce practise in times of scarcity-- breakfast by gaping! or they can eat wind, like the people of Poitou: it will make them spit clean!"

De Beauce was irritated at the mocking sign and the proverbial allusion to the gaping of the people of Beauce. He started up in wrath, and striking his fist on the table, "Monsieur Varin!" cried he, "do not cross your thumbs at me, or I will cut them off! Let me tell you the gentlemen of Beauce do not breakfast on gaping, but have plenty of corn to stuff even a Commissary of Montreal!"

The Sieur Le Mercier, at a sign from Bigot, interposed to stop the rising quarrel. "Don't mind Varin," said he, whispering to De Beauce; "he is drunk, and a row will anger the Intendant. Wait, and by and by you shall toast Varin as the chief baker of Pharoah, who got hanged because he stole the King's corn."

"As he deserves to be, for his insult to the gentlemen of Beauce," insinuated Bigot, leaning over to his angry guest, at the same time winking good-humoredly to Varin. "Come, now, De Beauce, friends all, amantium irae, you know--which is Latin for love--and I will sing you a stave in praise of this good wine, which is better than Bacchus ever drank." The Intendant rose up, and holding a brimming glass in his hand, chanted in full, musical voice a favorite ditty of the day, as a ready mode of restoring harmony among the company:

"'Amis! dans ma bouteille,
Voila le vin de France!
C'est le bon vin qui danse ici,
C'est le bon vin qui danse.
        Gai lon la!
        Vive la lirette!
        Des Filettes
        Il y en aura!'

Vivent les Filettes! The girls of Quebec--first in beauty, last in love, and nowhere in scorn of a gallant worthy of them!" continued Bigot. "What say you, De Pean? Are you not prepared to toast the belles of Quebec?"

"That I am, your Excellency!" De Pean was unsteady upon his feet, as he rose to respond to the Intendant's challenge. He pot- valiantly drew his sword, and laid it on the table. "I will call on the honorable company to drink this toast on their knees, and there is my sword to cut the legs off any gentleman who will not kneel down and drink a full cup to the bright eyes of the belle of Quebec-- The incomparable Angelique des Meloises!"

The toast suited their mood. Every one filled up his cup in honor of a beauty so universally admired.

"Kneel down, all," cried the Intendant, "or De Pean will hamstring us!" All knelt down with a clash--some of them unable to rise again. "We will drink to the Angelique charms of the fair Des Meloises. Come now, all together!--as the jolly Dutchmen of Albany say, 'Upp seys over!'"

Such of the company as were able resumed their seats amid great laughter and confusion, when the Sieur Deschenaux, a reckless young gallant, ablaze with wine and excitement, stood up, leaning against the table. His fingers dabbled in his wine-cup as he addressed them, but he did not notice it.

"We have drunk with all the honors," said he, "to the bright eyes of the belle of Quebec. I call on every gentleman now, to drink to the still brighter eyes of the belle of New France!"

"Who is she? Name! name!" shouted a dozen voices; "who is the belle of New France?"

"Who is she? Why, who can she be but the fair Angelique, whom we have just honored?" replied De Pean, hotly, jealous of any precedence in that quarter.

"Tut!" cried Deschenaux, "you compare glowworms with evening stars, when you pretend to match Angelique des Meloises with the lady I propose to honor! I call for full brimmers--cardinal's hats--in honor of the belle of New France--the fair Amelie de Repentigny!"

Le Gardeur de Repentigny was sitting leaning on his elbow, his face beaming with jollity, as he waited, with a full cup, for Deschenaux's toast. But no sooner did he hear the name of his sister from those lips than he sprang up as though a serpent had bit him. He hurled his goblet at the head of Deschenaux with a fierce imprecation, and drew his sword as he rushed towards him.

"A thousand lightnings strike you! How dare you pollute that holy name, Deschenaux? Retract that toast instantly, or you shall drink it in blood--retract, I say!"

The guests rose to their feet in terrible uproar. Le Gardeur struggled violently to break through a number of those who interposed between him and Deschenaux, who, roused to frenzy by the insult from Le Gardeur, had also drawn his sword, and stood ready to receive the assault of his antagonist.

The Intendant, whose courage and presence of mind never forsook him, pulled Deschenaux down upon his seat and held fast his sword arm, shouting in his ear,--

"Are you mad, Deschenaux? You knew she was his sister, and how he worships her! Retract the toast--it was inopportune! Besides, recollect we want to win over De Repentigny to the Grand Company!"

Deschenaux struggled for a minute, but the influence of the Intendant was all-powerful over him. He gave way. "Damn De Repentigny," said he, "I only meant to do honor to the pretty witch. Who would have expected him to take it up in that manner?"

"Any one who knows him; besides," continued the Intendant, "if you must toast his sister, wait till we get him body and soul made over to the Grand Company, and then he will care no more for his sister's fame than you do for yours."

"But the insult! He has drawn blood with the goblet," said Deschenaux, wiping his forehead with his fingers; "I cannot pardon that!"

"Tut, tut; fight him another day. But you shall not fight here! Cadet and Le Mercier have pinned the young Bayard, I see; so you have a chance to do the honorable; Deschenaux; go to him, retract the toast, and say you had forgotten the fair lady was his sister."

Deschenaux swallowed his wrath, rose up, and sheathed his sword. Taking the Intendant by the arm, he went up to Le Gardeur, who was still trying to advance. Deschenaux held up his hand deprecatingly. "Le Gardeur," said he, with an air of apparent contrition, "I was wrong to offer that toast. I had forgotten the fair lady was your sister. I retract the toast, since it is disagreeable to you, although all would have been proud to drink it."

Le Gardeur was as hard to appease as he was easy to excite to anger. He still held his drawn sword in his hand.

"Come!" cried Bigot, "you are as hard to please as Villiers Vendome, whom the King himself could not satisfy. Deschenaux says he is sorry. A gentleman cannot say more; so shake hands and be friends, De Repentigny."

Impervious to threats, and often to reason, Le Gardeur could not resist an appeal to his generosity.

He sheathed his sword, and held out his hand with frank forgiveness. "Your apology is ample, Sieur Deschenaux. I am satisfied you meant no affront to my sister! It is my weak point, messieurs," continued he, looking firmly at the company, ready to break out had he detected the shadow of a sneer upon any one's countenance. "I honor her as I do the queen of heaven. Neither of their names ought to be spoken here."

"Well said! Le Gardeur," exclaimed the Intendant. "That's right, shake hands, and be friends again. Blessed are quarrels that lead to reconciliation and the washing out of feuds in wine. Take your seats, gentlemen."

There was a general scramble back to the table. Bigot stood up in renewed force.

"Valets!" cried he, "bring in now the largest cups! We will drink a toast five fathoms deep, in water of life strong enough to melt Cleopatra's pearls, and to a jollier dame than Egypt's queen. But first we will make Le Gardeur de Repentigny free of the guild of noble partners of the company of adventurers trading in New France."

The valets flew in and out. In a few moments the table was replenished with huge drinking-cups, silver flagons, and all the heavy impedimenta of the army of Bacchus.

"You are willing to become one of us, and enter the jolly guild of the Grand Company?" exclaimed the Intendant, taking Le Gardeur by the hand.

"Yes, I am a stranger, and you may take me in. I claim admission," replied Le Gardeur with drunken gravity, "and by St. Pigot! I will be true to the guild!"

Bigot kissed him on both cheeks. "By the boot of St. Benoit! you speak like the King of Yvetot. Le Gardeur de Repentigny, you are fit to wear fur in the Court of Burgundy."

"You can measure my foot, Bigot," replied Le Gardeur, "and satisfy the company that I am able to wear the boot of St. Benoit."

"By jolly St. Chinon! and you shall wear it, Le Gardeur," exclaimed Bigot, handing him a quart flagon of wine, which Le Gardeur drank without drawing breath. "That boot fits," shouted the Intendant exultingly; "now for the chant! I will lead. Stop the breath of any one who will not join in the chorus."

The Intendant in great voice led off a macaronic verse of Moliere, that had often made merry the orgies of Versailles:

"'Bene, bene, bene, respondere!
Dignus, dignus es, entrare
In nostro laeto corpore!'"

A tintamarre of voices and a jingle of glasses accompanied the violins and tambours de Basque as the company stood up and sang the song, winding up with a grand burst at the chorus:

"'Vivat! vivat! vivat! cent fois vivat!
Novus socius qui tam bene parlat!
Mille mille annis et manget et bibat,
Fripet et friponnat!'"

Hands were shaken all round, congratulations, embracings, and filthy kisses showered upon Le Gardeur to honor his admission as a partner of the Grand Company.

"And now," continued Bigot, "we will drink a draught long as the bell rope of Notre Dame. Fill up brimmers of the quintessence of the grape, and drain them dry in honor of the Friponne!"

The name was electric. It was, in the country, a word of opprobrium, but at Beaumanoir it was laughed at with true Gallic nonchalance. Indeed, to show their scorn of public opinion, the Grand Company had lately launched a new ship upon the Great Lakes to carry on the fur trade, and had appropriately and mockingly named her, "La Friponne."

The toast of La Friponne was drunk with applause, followed by a wild bacchanalian song.

The Sieur Morin had been a merchant in Bordeaux whose bond was held in as little value as his word. He had lately removed to New France, transferred the bulk of his merchandise to the Friponne, and become an active agent of the Grand Company.

"La Friponne!" cried he; "I have drunk success to her with all my heart and throat; but I say she will never wear a night-cap and sleep quietly in our arms until we muzzle the Golden Dog that barks by night and by day in the Rue Buade."

"That is true, Morin!", interrupted Varin. "The Grand Company will never know peace until we send the Bourgeois, his master, back to the Bastille. The Golden Dog is--"

"Damn the Golden Dog!" exclaimed Bigot, passionately. "Why do you utter his name, Varin, to sour our wine? I hope one day to pull down the Dog, as well as the whole kennel of the insolent Bourgeois." Then, as was his wont, concealing his feelings under a mocking gibe, "Varin," said he, "they say that it is your marrow bone the Golden Dog is gnawing--ha! ha! ha!"

"More people believe it is your Excellency's!" Varin knew he was right, but aware of Bigot's touchiness on that point, added, as is the wont of panders to great men, "It is either yours or the Cardinal's."

"Let it be the Cardinal's, then! He is still in purgatory, and there will wait the arrival of the Bourgeois, to balance accounts with him."

Bigot hated the Bourgeois Philibert as one hates the man he has injured. Bigot had been instrumental in his banishment years ago from France, when the bold Norman count defended the persecuted Jansenists in the Parliament of Rouen. The Intendant hated him now for his wealth and prosperity in New France. But his wrath turned to fury when he saw the tablet of the Golden Dog, with its taunting inscription, glaring upon the front of the magazine in the Rue Buade. Bigot felt the full meaning and significance of the words that burned into his soul, and for which he hoped one day to be revenged.

"Confusion to the whole litter of the Golden Dog, and that is the party of the Honnetes Gens!" cried he. "But for that canting savant who plays the Governor here, I would pull down the sign and hang its master up in its stead to-morrow!"

The company now grew still more hilarious and noisy in their cups. Few paid attention to what the Intendant was saying. But De Repentigny heard him utter the words, "Oh, for men who dare do men's deeds!" He caught the eye of De Repentigny, and added, "But we are all cowards in the Grand Company, and are afraid of the Bourgeois."

The wine was bubbling in the brain of Le Gardeur. He scarcely knew what the Intendant said, but he caught the last words.

"Whom do you call cowards, Chevalier? I have joined the Grand Company. If the rest are cowards, I am not: I stand ready to pluck the peruke off the head of any man in New France, and carry it on my sword to the Place d' Armes, where I will challenge all the world to come and take it!"

"Pish! that is nothing! give me man's work. I want to see the partner in the Grand Company who dare pull down the Golden Dog."

"I dare! and I dare!" exclaimed a dozen voices at once in response to the appeal of the Intendant, who craftily meant his challenge to ensnare only Le Gardeur.

"And I dare; and I will, too, if you wish it, Chevalier!" shouted Le Gardeur, mad with wine, and quite oblivious of the thousand claims of the father of his friend, Pierre Philibert, upon him.

"I take you at your word, Le Gardeur! and bind your honor to it in the presence of all these gentlemen," said Bigot with a look of intense satisfaction.

"When shall it be done--to-day?" Le Gardeur seemed ready to pluck the moon from the sky in his present state of ecstasy.

"Why, no, not to-day; not before the pear is ripe will we pluck it! Your word of honor will keep till then?"

Bigot was in great glee over the success of his stratagem to entrap De Repentigny.

"It will keep a thousand years!" replied Le Gardeur, amid a fresh outburst of merriment round the board which culminated in a shameless song, fit only for a revel of satyrs.

The Sieur Cadet lolled lazily in his chair, his eyes blinking with a sleepy leer. "We are getting stupidly drunk. Bigot," said he; "we want something new to rouse us all to fresh life. Will you let me offer a toast?"

"Go on, Cadet! offer what toast you please. There is nothing in heaven, hell, or upon earth that I won't drink to for your sake."

"I want you to drink it on your knees, Bigot! pledge me that, and fill your biggest cup."

"We will drink it on all fours if you like! come, out with your toast, Cadet; you are as long over it as Father Glapion's sermon in Lent! and it will be as interesting, I dare say!"

"Well, Chevalier, the Grand Company, after toasting all the beauties of Quebec, desire to drink the health of the fair mistress of Beaumanoir, and in her presence too!" said Cadet with owlish gravity.

Bigot started; drunk and reckless as he was, he did not like his secret to be divulged. He was angry with Cadet for referring to it in the presence of so many who knew not that a strange lady was residing at Beaumanoir. He was too thoroughly a libertine of the period to feel any moral compunction for any excess he committed. He was habitually more ready to glory over his conquests, than to deny or extenuate them. But in this case he had, to the surprise of Cadet, been very reticent, and shy of speaking of this lady even to him.

"They say she is a miracle of beauty, Bigot!" continued Cadet, "and that you are so jealous of the charms of your belle Gabrielle that you are afraid to show her to your best friends."

"My belle Gabrielle is at liberty to go where she pleases, Cadet!" Bigot saw the absurdity of anger, but he felt it, nevertheless. "She chooses not to leave her bower, to look even on you, Cadet! I warrant you she has not slept all night, listening to your infernal din."

"Then, I hope you will allow us to go and beg pardon on our knees for disturbing her rest. What say the good company?"

"Agreed, agreed!" was the general response, and all pressed the Intendant vociferously to allow them to see the fair mistress of Beaumanoir.

Varin, however, proposed that she should be brought into the hall. "Send her to us, O King," cried he; "we are nobles of Persia, and this is Shushan the palace, where we carouse according to the law of the Medes, seven days at a stretch. Let the King bring in Queen Vashti, to show her beauty to the princes and nobles of his court!"

Bigot, too full of wine to weigh scruples, yielded to the wish of his boon companions. He rose from his chair, which in his absence was taken by Cadet. "Mind!" said he, "if I bring her in, you shall show her every respect."

"We will kiss the dust of her feet," answered Cadet, "and consider you the greatest king of a feast in New France or Old."

Bigot, without further parley, passed out of the hall, traversed a long corridor and entered an anteroom, where he found Dame Tremblay, the old housekeeper, dozing on her chair. He roused her up, and bade her go to the inner chamber to summon her mistress.

The housekeeper rose in a moment at the voice of the Intendant. She was a comely dame, with a ruddy cheek, and an eye in her head that looked inquisitively at her master as she arranged her cap and threw back her rather gay ribbons.

"I want your mistress up in the great hall! Go summon her at once," repeated the Intendant.

The housekeeper courtesied, but pressed her lips together as if to prevent them from speaking in remonstrance. She went at once on her ungracious errand.

## Chapter VIII: Caroline de St. Castin

Dame Tremblay entered the suite of apartments and returned in a few moments, saying that her lady was not there, but had gone down to the secret chamber, to be, she supposed, more out of hearing of the noise, which had disturbed her so much.

"I will go find her then," replied the Intendant; "you may return to your own room, dame."

He walked across the drawing-room to one of the gorgeous panels that decorated the wall, and touched a hidden spring. A door flew open, disclosing a stair heavily carpeted that led down to the huge vaulted foundations of the Chateau.

He descended the stair with hasty though unsteady steps. It led to a spacious room, lighted with a gorgeous lamp that hung pendant in silver chains from the frescoed ceiling. The walls were richly tapestried with products of the looms of the Gobelins, representing the plains of Italy filled with sunshine, where groves, temples, and colonnades were pictured in endless vistas of beauty. The furniture of the chamber was of regal magnificence. Nothing that luxury could desire, or art furnish, had been spared in its adornment. On a sofa lay a guitar, and beside it a scarf and a dainty glove fit for the hand of the fairy queen.

The Intendant looked eagerly round, as he entered this bright chamber of his fancy, but saw not its expected occupant. A recess in the deep wall at the farthest side of the room contained an oratory with an altar and a crucifix upon it. The recess was partly in the shade. But the eyes of the Intendant discerned clearly enough the kneeling, or rather the prostrate, figure of Caroline de St. Castin. Her hands were clasped beneath her head, which was bowed to the ground. Her long, black hair lay dishevelled over her back, as she lay in her white robe like the Angel of Sorrow, weeping and crying from the depths of her broken heart, "Lamb of God, that taketh away the sins of the world, have mercy upon me!" She was so absorbed in her grief that she did not notice the entrance of the Intendant.

Bigot stood still for a moment, stricken with awe at the spectacle of this lovely woman weeping by herself in the secret chamber. A look of something like pity stole into his eyes; he called her by name, ran to her, assisted her to rise, which she did, slowly turning towards him that weeping, Madonna-like face which haunts the ruins of Beaumanoir to this day.

She was of medium stature, slender and lissome, looking taller than she really was. Her features were chiselled with exquisite delicacy; her hair of a raven blackness, and eyes of that dark lustre which reappears for generations in the descendants of Europeans who have mingled their blood with that of the aborigines of the forest. The Indian eye is preserved as an heirloom, long after all memory of the red stain has vanished from the traditions of the family. Her complexion was pale, naturally of a rich olive, but now, through sorrow, of a wan and bloodless hue--still very beautiful, and more appealing than the rosiest complexion.

Caroline de St. Castin was an Acadienne of ancient and noble family, whose head and founder, the Baron de St. Castin, had married the beautiful daughter of the high chief of the Abenaquais.

Her father's house, one of the most considerable in the Colony, had been the resort of the royal officers, civil and military, serving in Acadia. Caroline, the only daughter of the noble house, had been reared in all the refinements and luxuries of the period, as became her rank and position both in France and her native Province.

In an evil hour for her happiness this beautiful and accomplished girl met the Chevalier Bigot, who as Chief Commissary of the Army, was one of the foremost of the royal officers in

Acadia.

His ready wit and graceful manners pleased and flattered the susceptible girl, not used to the seductions of the polished courtesies of the mother-land of France. She was of a joyous temper--gay, frank, and confiding. Her father, immersed in public affairs, left her much to herself, nor, had he known it, would he have disapproved of the gallant courtesies of the Chevalier Bigot. For the Baron had the soul of honor, and dreamt every gentleman as well as himself possessed it.

Bigot, to do him justice, felt as sincere a regard for this beautiful, amiable girl as his nature was capable of entertaining. In rank and fortune she was more than his equal, and left to himself, he would willingly have married her. Before he learned that his project of a marriage in the Colony was scouted at Court he had already offered his love to Caroline de St. Castin, and won easily the gentle heart that was but too well disposed to receive his homage.

Her trust went with her love. Earth was never so green, nor air so sweet, nor skies so bright and azure, as those of Caroline's wooing, on the shores of the beautiful Bay of Minas. She loved this man with a passion that filled with ecstasy her whole being. She trusted his promises as she would have trusted God's. She loved him better than she loved herself--better than she loved God, or God's law; and counted as a gain every loss she suffered for his sake, and for the affection she bore him.

After some months spent in her charming society, a change came over Bigot. He received formidable missives from his great patroness at Versailles, the Marquise de Pompadour, who had other matrimonial designs for him. Bigot was too slavish a courtier to resent her interference, nor was he honest enough to explain his position to his betrothed. He deferred his marriage. The exigencies of the war called him away. He had triumphed over a fond, confiding woman; but he had been trained among the dissolute spirits of the Regency too thoroughly to feel more than a passing regret for a woman whom, probably, he loved better than any other of the victims of his licentious life.

When he finally left Acadia a conquered province in the hands of the English, he also left behind him the one true, loving heart that believed in his honor and still prayed for his happiness.

The days of Caroline's disillusion soon came; she could not conceal from herself that she had been basely deceived and abandoned by the man she loved so ardently. She learned that Bigot had been elevated to the high office of Intendant of New France, but felt herself as utterly forgotten by him as the rose that had bloomed and withered in her garden two summers ago.

Her father had been summoned to France on the loss of the Colony; and fearing to face him on his return, Caroline suddenly left her home and sought refuge in the forest among her far-off kindred, the red Abenaquais.

The Indians welcomed her with joy and unbounded respect, recognizing her right to their devotion and obedience. They put upon her feet the moccasins of their tribe, and sent her, with a trusty escort, through the wilderness to Quebec, where she hoped to find the Intendant, not to reproach him for his perfidy,--her gentle heart was too much subdued for that,--but to claim his protection, and if refused, to die at his door.

It was under such circumstances that the beautiful, highborn Caroline de St. Castin became an inmate of Beaumanoir. She had passed the night of this wild debauch in a vigil of prayers, tears, and lamentations over her sad lot and over the degradation of Bigot by the life which she now knew he led. Sometimes her maddened fancy was ready to accuse Providence itself of cruelty and injustice; sometimes, magnifying her own sin, she was ready to think all earthly punishment upon herself as too light, and invoked death and judgment as alone adequate to her fault. All night she had knelt before the altar, asking for mercy and forgiveness,-- sometimes starting to her feet in terror, as a fresh burst of revelry came rushing from the great hall above, and shook the door of her secret chamber. But no one came to her help, no one looked in upon her desolation. She deemed herself utterly forgotten and forsaken of God and man.

Occasionally she fancied she could distinguish the voice of the Intendant amid the drunken uproar, and she shuddered at the infatuation which bound her very soul to this man; and yet when she questioned her heart, she knew that, base as he was, all she had done and suffered for him she would infallibly do again. Were her life to live over, she would repeat the fault of loving this false, ungrateful man. The promise of marriage had been equivalent to marriage in her trust of him, and nothing but death could now divorce her from him.

Hour after hour passed by, each seeming an age of suffering. Her feelings were worked up to frenzy: she fancied she heard her father's angry voice calling her by name, or she heard accusing angels jeering at her fall. She sank prostrate at last, in the abandonment of despair, calling upon God to put an end to her miserable life.

Bigot raised her from the floor, with words of pity and sympathy. She turned on him a look of gratitude which, had he been of stone, he must have felt. But Bigot's words meant less than she fancied. He was still too intoxicated to reflect, or to feel shame of his present errand.

"Caroline!" said he, "what do you here? This is the time to make merry--not to pray! The honorable company in the great hall desire to pay their respects to the lady of Beaumanoir--come with me!"

He drew her hand through his arm with a courtly grace that seldom forsook him, even in his worst moments. Caroline looked at him in a dazed manner, not comprehending his request. "Go with you, Francois? You know I will, but where?"

"To the great hall," repeated he; "my worthy guests desire to see you, and to pay their respects to the fair lady of Beaumanoir."

It flashed upon her mind what he wanted. Her womanly pride was outraged as it had never been before; she withdrew her hand from his arm with shame and terror stamped on every feature.

"Go up there! Go to show myself to your guests!" exclaimed she, with choking accents, as she stepped back a pace from him. "Oh, Francois Bigot, spare me that shame and humiliation! I am, I know, contemptible beyond human respect, but still--God help me!--I am not so vile as to be made a spectacle of infamy to those drunken men whom I hear clamoring for me, even now."

"Pshaw! You think too much of the proprieties, Caroline!" Bigot felt sensibly perplexed at the attitude she assumed. "Why! The fairest dames of Paris, dressed as Hebes and Ganymedes, thought it a fine jest to wait on the Regent Duke of Orleans and the Cardinal du Bois in the gay days of the King's bachelorhood, and they do the same now when the King gets up one of his great feasts at Choisy; so come, sweetheart--come!" He drew her towards the door.

"Spare me, Francois!" Caroline knelt at his feet, clasping his hand, and bathing it in tears- -"Spare me!" cried she. "Oh, would to God I had died ere you came to command me to do what I cannot and will not do, Francois!" added she, clasping hard the hand of the Intendant, which she fancied relaxed somewhat of its iron hardness.

"I did not come to command you, Caroline, but to bear the request of my guests. No, I do not even ask you on my account to go up to the great hall: it is to please my guests only." Her tears and heartrending appeal began to sober him. Bigot had not counted on such a scene as this.

"Oh, thanks, Francois, for that word! You did not come to command my obedience in such a shameful thing: you had some small regard left for the unfortunate Caroline. Say you will not command me to go up there," added she, looking at him with eyes of pitiful pleading, such as no Italian art ever portrayed on the face of the sorrowing Madonna.

"No," he replied, impatiently. "It was not I proposed it: it was Cadet. He is always a fool when the wine overflows, as I am too, or I would not have hearkened to him! Still, Caroline, I have promised, and my guests will jeer me finely if I return without you." He thought she hesitated a moment in her resolve at this suggestion. "Come, for my sake, Caroline! Do up that disordered hair; I shall be proud of you, my Caroline; there is not a lady in New France can match you when you look yourself, my pretty Caroline!"

"Francois," said she, with a sad smile, "it is long since you flattered me thus! But I will arrange my hair for you alone," added she, blushing, as with deft fingers she twisted her raven locks into a coronal about her head. "I would once have gone with you to the end of the world to hear you say you were proud of me. Alas! you can never be proud of me any more, as in the old happy days at Grand Pre. Those few brief days of love and joy can never return--never, never!"

Bigot stood silent, not knowing what to say or do. The change from the bacchanalian riot in the great hall to the solemn pathos and woe of the secret chamber sobered him rapidly. Even his obduracy gave way at last. "Caroline," said he, taking both her hands in his, "I will not urge you longer. I am called bad, and you think me so; but I am not brutal. It was a promise made over the wine. Varin, the drunken beast, called you Queen Vashti, and challenged me to show your beauty to them; and I swore not one of their toasted beauties could match my fair Acadienne."

"Did the Sieur Varin call me Queen Vashti? Alas! he was a truer prophet than he knew," replied she, with ineffable sadness. "Queen Vashti refused to obey even her king, when commanded to unveil her face to the drunken nobles. She was deposed, and another raised to her place. Such may be my fate, Francois."

"Then you will not go, Caroline?"

"No; kill me if you like, and bear my dead body into the hall, but living, I can never show my face again before men--hardly before you, Francois," added she, blushing, as she hid her tearful eyes on his shoulder.

"Well then, Caroline," replied, he, really admiring her spirit and resolution, "they shall finish their carouse without seeing you. The wine has flowed to-night in rivers, but they shall swim in it without you."

"And tears have flowed down here," said she, sadly,--"oh, so bitter! May you never taste their bitterness, Francois!"

Bigot paced the chamber with steadier steps than he had entered it. The fumes were clearing from his brain; the song that had caught the ear of Colonel Philibert as he approached the Chateau was resounding at this moment. As it ceased Bigot heard the loud impatient knocking of Philibert at the outer door.

"Darling!" said he, "lie down now, and compose yourself. Francois Bigot is not unmindful of your sacrifices for his sake. I must return to my guests, who are clamoring for me, or rather for you, Caroline!"

He kissed her cheek and turned to leave her, but she clung to his hand as if wanting to say something more ere he went. She trembled visibly as her low plaintive tones struck his ear.

"Francois! if you would forsake the companionship of those men and purify your table of such excess, God's blessing would yet descend upon you, and the people's love follow you! It is in your power to be as good as you are great! I have many days wished to say this to you, but alas, I feared you too much. I do not fear you to-day, Francois, after your kind words to me."

Bigot was not impenetrable to that low voice so full of pathos and love. But he was at a loss what to reply: strange influences were flowing round him, carrying him out of himself. He kissed the gentle head that reclined on his bosom. "Caroline," said he, "your advice is wise and good as yourself. I will think of it for your sake, if not for my own. Adieu, darling! Go, and take rest: these cruel vigils are killing you, and I want you to live in hope of brighter days."

"I will," replied she, looking up with ineffable tenderness. "I am sure I shall rest after your kind words, Francois. No dew of Heaven was ever more refreshing than the balm they bring to my weary soul. Thanks, O my Francois, for them!" She kissed his lips, and Bigot left the secret chamber a sadder and for the moment a better man than he had ever been before.

Caroline, overcome by her emotions, threw herself on a couch, invoking blessings upon the head of the man by whom she had been so cruelly betrayed. But such is woman's heart--full of mercy, compassion, and pardon for every wrong, when love pleads for forgiveness.

"Ha! ha!" said Cadet, as the Intendant re-entered the great hall, which was filled with bacchanalian frenzy. "Ha! ha! His Excellency has proposed and been rejected! The fair lady has a will of her own and won't obey! Why, the Intendant looks as if he had come from Quintin Corentin, where nobody gets anything he wants!"

"Silence, Cadet! don't be a fool!" replied Bigot, impatiently, although in the Intendant's usual mood nothing too gross or too bad could be said in his presence but he could cap it with something worse.

"Fool, Bigot! It is you who have been the fool of a woman!" Cadet was privileged to say anything, and he never stinted his speech. "Confess, your Excellency! she is splay-footed as St. Pedauque of Dijon! She dare not trip over our carpet for fear of showing her big feet!"

Cadet's coarse remark excited the mirth of the Intendant. The influences of the great hall were more powerful than those of the secret chamber. He replied curtly, however,--"I have excused the lady from coming, Cadet. She is ill, or she does not please to come, or she has a private fancy of her own to nurse--any reason is enough to excuse a lady, or for a gentleman to cease pressing her."

"Dear me!" muttered Cadet, "the wind blows fresh from a new quarter! It is easterly, and betokens a storm!" and with drunken gravity he commenced singing a hunting refrain of Louis XIV.:

"'Sitot qu'il voit sa Chienne
Il quitte tout pour elle.'"

Bigot burst out into immoderate laughter. "Cadet," said he, "you are, when drunk, the greatest ruffian in Christendom, and the biggest knave when sober. Let the lady sleep in peace, while we drink ourselves blind in her honor. Bring in brandy, valets, and we will not look for day until midnight booms on the old clock of the Chateau."

The loud knocking of Philibert in the great hall reverberated again and again through the house. Bigot bade the valets go see who disturbed the Chateau in that bold style.

"Let no one in!" added he "'tis against the rule to open the doors when the Grand Company are met for business! Take whips, valets, and scourge the insolent beggars away. Some miserable habitans, I warrant, whining for the loss of their eggs and bacon taken by the King's purveyors!"

A servant returned with a card on a silver salver. "An officer in uniform waits to see your Excellency: he brings orders from the Governor," said he to the Intendant.

Bigot looked at the card with knitted brows; fire sparkled in his eyes as he read the name.

"Colonel Philibert!" exclaimed he, "Aide-de-Camp of the Governor! What the fiend brings HIM at such a time? Do you hear?" continued he, turning to Varin. "It is your friend from Louisbourg, who was going to put you in irons, and send you to France for trial when the mutinous garrison threatened to surrender the place if we did not pay them."

Varin was not so intoxicated but the name of Philibert roused his anger. He set his cup down with a bang upon the table. "I will not taste a drop more till he is gone," said he; "curse Galissoniere's crooked neck--could he not have selected a more welcome messenger to send to Beaumanoir? But I have got his name in my list of debtors, and he shall pay up one day for his insolence at Louisbourg."

"Tut, tut, shut up your books! you are too mercantile for gentlemen," replied Bigot. "The question is, shall we allow Colonel Philibert to bring his orders into the hall? Par Dieu! we are scarcely presentable!"

But whether presentable or no, the words were scarcely spoken, when, impatient at the delay, Philibert took advantage of the open door and entered the great hall. He stood in utter amazement for a moment at the scene of drunken riot which he beheld. The inflamed faces, the confusion of tongues, the disorder, filth, and stench of the prolonged debauch sickened him, while the sight of so many men of rank and high office revelling at such an hour raised a feeling of indignation which he had difficulty in keeping down while he delivered his message to the Intendant.

Bigot, however, was too shrewd to be wanting in politeness. "Welcome, Colonel Philibert," said he; "you are an unexpected guest, but a welcome one! Come and taste the hospitality of Beaumanoir before you deliver your message. Bustle, valets, bring fresh cups and the fullest carafes for Colonel Philibert."

"Thanks for your politeness, Chevalier! Your Excellency will please excuse me if I deliver my message at once. My time is not my own to-day, so I will not sit down. His Excellency the Governor desires your presence and that of the Royal Commissaries at the council of war this afternoon. Despatches have just arrived by the Fleur-de- Lis from home, and the council must assemble at once."

A red flush rested upon the brow of Philibert as in his mind he measured the important business of the council with the fitness of the men whom he summoned to attend it. He declined the offer of wine, and stepped backward from the table, with a bow to the Intendant and the company, and was about to depart, when a loud voice on the further side of the table cried out,--

"It is he, by all that is sacred! Pierre Philibert! wait!" Le Gardeur de Repentigny rushed like a storm through the hall, upsetting chairs and guests in his advance. He ran towards Colonel Philibert, who, not recognizing the flushed face and disordered figure that greeted him, shrank back from his embrace.

"My God! do you not know me, Pierre?" exclaimed Le Gardeur, wounded to the quick by the astonished look of his friend. "I am Le Gardeur de Repentigny! O dear friend, look and recognize me!"

Philibert stood transfixed with surprise and pain, as if an arrow had stricken his eyes. "You! you Le Gardeur de Repentigny? It is impossible! Le Gardeur never looked like you--much less, was ever found among people like these!" The last words were rashly spoken, but fortunately not heard amid the hubbub in the hall, or Philibert's life might have paid the penalty from the excited guests.

"And yet it is true; Pierre, look at me again. I am no other than he whom you drew out of the St. Lawrence, the only brother of Amelie!"

Philibert looked hard in the eyes of Le Gardeur, and doubted no longer. He pressed his old friend to his heart, saying, in a voice full of pathos,--

"O Le Gardeur! I recognize you now, but under what change of look and place! Often have I forecast our meeting again, but it was in your pure, virtuous home of Tilly, not in this place. What do you here, Le Gardeur?"

"Forgive me, Pierre, for the shame of meeting me here." Le Gardeur stood up like a new man in the glance of his friend; the shock seemed to have sobered him at once. "'What do I do here?' say you, O dear friend!" said he, glancing round the hall, "it is easier seen than told what I do here. But by all the saints, I have finished here for to-day! You return to the city at once, Pierre?"

"At once, Le Gardeur. The Governor awaits my return."

"Then I will return with you. My dear aunt and sister are in the city. News of their arrival reached me here; my duty was to return at once, but the Intendant's wine-cups were too potent for me--curse them, for they have disgraced me in your eyes, Pierre, as well as my own!"

Philibert started at the information that Amelie was in the city. "Amelie in the city?" repeated he, with glad surprise, "I did not expect to be able to salute her and the noble Lady de Tilly so soon." His heart bounded in secret at the prospect of again seeing this fair girl, who had filled his thoughts for so many years and been the secret spring of so much that was noble and manly in his character.

"Come, Le Gardeur, let us take leave of the Intendant, and return at once to the city, but not in that plight!" added he, smiling, as Le Gardeur, oblivious of all but the pleasure of accompanying him, grasped his arm to leave the great hall. "Not in that garb, Le Gardeur! Bathe, purify, and clean yourself; I will wait outside in the fresh air. The odor of this room stifles me!"

"You are not going to leave us, Le Gardeur!" Varin called, across the table, "and break up good company? Wait till we finish a few more rounds, and we will all go together."

"I have finished all the rounds for to-day, Varin, may be forever! Colonel Philibert is my dearest friend in life; I must leave even you to go with him, so pray excuse me."

"You are excused, Le Gardeur." Bigot spoke very courteously to him, much as he disliked the idea of his companionship with Philibert. "We must all return by the time the Cathedral bells chime noon. Take one parting cup before you go, Le Gardeur, and prevail on Colonel Philibert to do the same, or he will not praise our hospitality, I fear."

"Not one drop more this day, were it from Jove's own poculum!" Le Gardeur repelled the temptation more readily as he felt a twitch on his sleeve from the hand of Philibert.

"Well, as you will, Le Gardeur; we have all had enough and over, I dare say. Ha! ha! Colonel Philibert rather puts us to the blush, or would were not our cheeks so well-painted in the hues of rosy Bacchus."

Philibert, with official courtesy, bade adieu to the Intendant and the company. A couple of valets waited upon Le Gardeur, whom they assisted to bathe and dress. In a short time he left the Chateau almost sobered, and wholly metamorphosed into a handsome, fresh chevalier. A perverse redness about the eyes alone remained, to tell the tale of the last night's debauch.

Master Pothier sat on a horse-block at the door with all the gravity of a judge, while he waited for the return of Colonel Philibert and listened to the lively noise in the Chateau, the music, song, and jingle of glass forming a sweet concert in the ears of the jolly old notary.

"I shall not need you to guide me back, Master Pothier," said Philibert, as he put some silver pieces in his hollow palm; "take your fee. The cause is gained, is it not, Le Gardeur?" He glanced triumphantly at his friend.

"Good-by, Master Pothier," said he, as he rode off with Le Gardeur. The old notary could not keep up with them, but came jolting on behind, well pleased to have leisure to count and jingle his coins. Master Pothier was in that state of joyful anticipation when hope outruns realization. He already saw himself seated in the old armchair in the snug parlor of Dame Bedard's inn, his back to the fire, his belly to the table, a smoking dish of roast in the middle, an ample trencher before him with a bottle of Cognac on one flank and a jug of Norman cider on the other, an old crony or two to eat and drink with him, and the light foot and deft hand of pretty Zoe Bedard to wait upon them.

This picture of perfect bliss floated before the winking eyes of Master Pothier, and his mouth watered in anticipation of his Eden, not of flowers and trees, but of tables, cups, and platters, with plenty to fill them, and to empty them as well.

"A worthy gentleman and a brave officer, I warrant!" said Pothier, as he jogged along. "He is generous as a prince, and considerate as a bishop, fit for a judge, nay, for a chief justice! What would you do for him, Master Pothier?" the old notary asked himself. "I answer the interrogatory of the Court: I would draw up his marriage contract, write his last will and testament with the greatest of pleasure and without a fee!--and no notary in New France could do more for him!" Pothier's imagination fell into a vision over a consideration of his favorite text-- that of the great sheet, wherein was all manner of flesh and fowl good for food, but the tongue of the old notary would trip at the name of Peter, and perversely say, "Rise, Pothier; kill, and eat."

## Chapter IX: Pierre Philibert

Colonel Philibert and Le Gardeur rode rapidly through the forest of Beaumanoir, pulling up occasionally in an eager and sympathetic exchange of questions and replies, as they recounted the events of their lives since their separation, or recalled their school-days and glorious holidays and rambles in the woods of Tilly--with frequent mention of their gentle, fair companion, Amelie de Repentigny, whose name on the lips of her brother sounded sweeter than the chime of the bells of Charlebourg to the ear of Pierre Philibert.

The bravest man in New France felt a tremor in his breast as he asked Le Gardeur a seemingly careless question--seemingly, for, in truth, it was vital in the last degree to his happiness, and he knew it. He expressed a fear that Amelie would have wholly forgotten him after so long an absence from New France.

His heart almost ceased beating as he waited the reply of Le Gardeur, which came impetuously: "Forgotten you, Pierre Philibert? She would forget me as soon! But for you she would have had no brother to-day, and in her prayers she ever remembers both of us-- you by right of a sister's gratitude, me because I am unworthy of her saintly prayers and need them all the more! O Pierre Philibert, you do not know Amelie if you think she is one ever to forget a friend like you!"

The heart of Philibert gave a great leap for joy. Too happy for speech, he rode on a while in silence.

"Amelie will have changed much in appearance?" he asked, at last. A thousand questions were crowding upon his lips.

"Changed? Oh, yes!" replied Le Gardeur, gaily. "I scarcely recognize my little bright-eyed sister in the tall, perfect young lady that has taken her place. But the loving heart, the pure mind, the gentle ways, and winning smiles are the same as ever. She is somewhat more still and thoughtful, perhaps--more strict in the observances of religion. You will remember, I used to call her in jest our St. Amelie: I might call her that in earnest now, Pierre, and she would be worthy of the name!"

"God bless you, Le Gardeur!" burst out Colonel Philibert,--his voice could not repress the emotion he felt,--"and God bless Amelie! Think you she would care to see me to-day, Le Gardeur?" Philibert's thoughts flew far and fast, and his desire to know more of Amelie was a rack of suspense to him. She might, indeed, recollect the youth Pierre Philibert, thought he, as she did a sunbeam that gladdened long-past summers; but how could he expect her to regard him--the full-grown man--as the same? Nay, was he not nursing a fatal fancy in his breast that would sting him to death? for among the gay and gallant throng about the capital was it not more than possible that so lovely and amiable a woman had already been wooed, and given the priceless treasure of her love to another? It was, therefore, with no common feeling that Philibert said, "Think you she will care to see me to-day, Le Gardeur?"

"Care to see you, Pierre Philibert? What a question! She and Aunt de Tilly take every occasion to remind me of you, by way of example, to shame me of my faults--and they succeed, too! I could cut off my right hand this moment, Pierre, that it should never lift wine again to my lips--and to have been seen by you in such company! What must you think of me?"

"I think your regret could not surpass mine; but tell me how you have been drawn into these rapids and taken the wrong turn, Le Gardeur?"

Le Gardeur winced as he replied,--"Oh, I do not know. I found myself there before I thought. It was the wit, wine, and enchantments of Bigot, I suppose,--and the greatest temptation of all, a woman's smiles,--that led me to take the wrong turn, as you call it. There, you have my confession!--and I would put my sword through any man but you, Pierre, who dared ask me to give such an account of myself. I am ashamed of it all, Pierre Philibert!"

"Thanks, Le Gardeur, for your confidence. I hope you will outride this storm!" He held out his hand, nervous and sinewy as that of Mars. Le Gardeur seized it, and pressed it hard in his. "Don't you think it is still able to rescue a friend from peril?" added Philibert smiling.

Le Gardeur caught his meaning, and gave him a look of unutterable gratitude. "Besides this hand of mine, are there not the gentler hands of Amelie to intercede for you with your better self?" said Philibert.

"My dear sister!" interjected Le Gardeur. "I am a coward when I think of her, and I shame to come into her pure presence."

"Take courage, Le Gardeur! There is hope where there is shame of our faults. Be equally frank with your sister as with me, and she will win you, in spite of yourself, from the enchantments of Bigot, Cadet, and the still more potent smiles you speak of that led you to take the wrong turn in life."

"I doubt it is too late, Pierre! although I know that, were every other friend in the world to forsake me, Amelie would not! She would not even reproach me, except by excess of affection."

Philibert looked on his friend admiringly, at this panegyric of the woman he loved. Le Gardeur was in feature so like his sister that Philibert at the moment caught the very face of Amelie, as it were, looking at him through the face of her brother. "You will not resist her pleadings, Le Gardeur,"--Philibert thought it an impossible thing. "No guardian angel ever clung to the skirts of a sinner as Amelie will cling to you," said he; "therefore I have every hope of my dear friend Le Gardeur Repentigny."

The two riders emerged from the forest, and drew up for a minute in front of the hostelry of the Crown of France, to water their horses at the long trough before the door and inform Dame Bedard, who ran out to greet them, that Master Pothier was following with his ambling nag at a gentle pace, as befitted the gravity of his profession.

"Oh! Master Pothier never fails to find his way to the Crown of France; but won't your Honors take a cup of wine? The day is hot and the road dusty. 'A dry rider makes a wet nag,'" added the Dame, with a smile, as she repeated an old saying, brought over with the rest of the butin in the ships of Cartier and Champlain.

The gentlemen bowed their thanks, and as Philibert looked up, he saw pretty Zoe Bedard poring over a sheet of paper bearing a red seal, and spelling out the crabbed law text of Master Pothier. Zoe, like other girls of her class, had received a tincture of learning in the day schools of the nuns; but, although the paper was her marriage contract, it puzzled her greatly to pick out the few chips of plain sense that floated in the sea of legal verbiage it contained. Zoe, with a perfect comprehension of the claims of meum and tuum, was at no loss, however, in arriving at a satisfactory solution of the true merits of her matrimonial contract with honest Antoine La Chance.

She caught the eye of Philibert, and blushed to the very chin as she huddled away the paper and returned the salute of the two handsome gentlemen, who, having refreshed their horses, rode off at a rapid trot down the great highway that led to the city.

Babet Le Nocher, in a new gown, short enough to reveal a pair of shapely ankles in clocked stockings and well-clad feet that would have been the envy of many a duchess, sat on the thwart of the boat knitting. Her black hair was in the fashion recorded by the grave Peter Kalm, who, in his account of New France, says, "The peasant women all wear their hair in ringlets, and nice they look!"

"As I live!" exclaimed she to Jean, who was enjoying a pipe of native tobacco, "here comes that handsome officer back again, and in as great a hurry to return as he was to go up the highway!"

"Ay, ay, Babet! It is plain to see he is either on the King's errand or his own. A fair lady awaits his return in the city, or one has just dismissed him where he has been! Nothing like a woman to put quicksilver in a man's shoes--eh! Babet?"

"Or foolish thoughts into their hearts, Jean!" replied she, laughing.

"And nothing more natural, Babet, if women's hearts are wise enough in their folly to like our foolish thoughts of them. But there are two! Who is that riding with the gentleman? Your eyes are better than mine, Babet!"

"Of course, Jean! that is what I always tell you, but you won't believe me--trust my eyes, and doubt your own! The other gentleman," said she, looking fixedly, while her knitting lay still in her lap, "the other is the young Chevalier de Repentigny. What brings him back before the rest of the hunting party, I wonder?"

"That officer must have been to Beaumanoir, and is bringing the young seigneur back to town," remarked Jean, puffing out a long thread of smoke from his lips.

"Well, it must be something better than smoke, Jean!"--Babet coughed: she never liked the pipe--"The young chevalier is always one of the last to give up when they have one of their three days drinking bouts up at the Chateau. He is going to the bad, I fear-- more's the pity! such a nice, handsome fellow, too!"

"All lies and calumny!" replied Jean, in a heat. "Le Gardeur de Repentigny is the son of my dear old seigneur. He may get drunk, but it will be like a gentleman if he does, and not like a carter, Babet, or like a--"

"Boatman! Jean; but I don't include you--you have never been the worse for drinking water since I took care of your liquor, Jean!"

"Ay, you are intoxication enough of yourself for me, Babet! Two bright eyes like yours, a pipe and bitters, with grace before meat, would save any Christian man in this world." Jean stood up, politely doffing his red tuque to the gentlemen. Le Gardeur stooped from his horse to grasp his hand, for Jean had been an old servitor at Tilly, and the young seigneur was too noble-minded and polite to omit a kindly notice of even the humblest of his acquaintance.

"Had a busy day, Jean, with the old ferry?" asked Le Gardeur, cheerily.

"No, your Honor, but yesterday I think half the country-side crossed over to the city on the King's corvee. The men went to work, and the women followed to look after them, ha! ha!" Jean winked provokingly at Babet, who took him up sharply.

"And why should not the women go after the men? I trow men are not so plentiful in New France as they used to be before this weary war began. It well behooves the women to take good care of all that are left."

"That is true as the Sunday sermon," remarked Jean. "Why, it was only the other day I heard that great foreign gentleman, who is the guest of His Excellency the Governor, say, sitting in this very boat, that 'there are at this time four women to every man in New France!' If that is true, Babet,--and you know he said it, for you were angry enough,--a man is a prize indeed, in New France, and women are plenty as eggs at Easter!"

"The foreign gentleman had much assurance to say it, even if it were true: he were much better employed picking up weeds and putting them in his book!" exclaimed Babet, hotly.

"Come! come!" cried Le Gardeur, interrupting this debate on the population; "Providence knows the worth of Canadian women, and cannot give us too many of them. We are in a hurry to get to the city, Jean, so let us embark. My aunt and Amelie are in the old home in the city; they will be glad to see you and Babet," added he, kindly, as he got into the boat.

Babet dropped her neatest courtesy, and Jean, all alive to his duty, pushed off his boat, bearing the two gentlemen and their horses across the broad St. Charles to the King's Quay, where they remounted, and riding past the huge palace of the Intendant, dashed up the steep Cote au Chien and through the city gate, disappearing from the eyes of Babet, who looked very admiringly after them. Her thoughts were especially commendatory of the handsome officer in full uniform who had been so polite and generous in the morning.

"I was afraid, Jean, you were going to blurt out about Mademoiselle des Meloises," remarked Babet to Jean on his return; "men are so indiscreet always!"

"Leaky boats! leaky boats! Babet! no rowing them with a woman aboard! sure to run on the bank. But what about Mademoiselle des Meloises?" Honest Jean had passed her over the ferry an hour ago, and been sorely tempted to inform Le Gardeur of the interesting fact.

"What about Mademoiselle des Meloises?" Babet spoke rather sharply. "Why, all Quebec knows that the Seigneur de Repentigny is mad in love with her."

"And why should he not be mad in love with her if he likes?" replied Jean; "she is a morsel fit for a king, and if Le Gardeur should lose both his heart and his wits on her account, it is only what half the gallants of Quebec have done."

"Oh, Jean, Jean! it is plain to see you have an eye in your head as well as a soft place!" ejaculated Babet, recommencing her knitting with fresh vigor, and working off the electricity that was stirring in her.

"I had two eyes in my head when I chose you, Babet, and the soft place was in my heart!" replied Jean, heartily. The compliment was taken with a smile, as it deserved to be. "Look you, Babet, I would not give this pinch of snuff," said Jean, raising his thumb and two fingers holding a good dose of the pungent dust,--"I would not give this pinch of snuff for any young fellow who could be indifferent to the charms of such a pretty lass as Angelique des Meloises!"

"Well, I am glad you did not tell the Seigneur de Repentigny that she had crossed the ferry and gone--not to look for him, I'll be bound! I will tell you something by and by, Jean, if you will come in and eat your dinner; I have something you like."

"What is it, Babet?" Jean was, after all, more curious about his dinner than about the fair lady.

"Oh, something you like--that is a wife's secret: keep the stomach of a man warm, and his heart will never grow cold. What say you to fried eels?"

"Bravo!" cried the gay old boatman, as he sang,

"'Ah! ah! ah! frit a l'huile,
Frit au beurre et a l'ognon!'"

and the jolly couple danced into their little cottage--no king and queen in Christendom half so happy as they.

# Chapter X: Amelie de Repentigny

The town house of the Lady de Tilly stood on the upper part of the Place d'Armes, a broad, roughly-paved square. The Chateau of St. Louis, with its massive buildings and high, peaked roofs, filled one side of the square. On the other side, embowered in ancient trees that had escaped the axe of Champlain's hardy followers, stood the old-fashioned Monastery of the Recollets, with its high belfry and broad shady porch, where the monks in gray gowns and sandals sat in summer, reading their breviaries or exchanging salutations with the passers-by, who always had a kind greeting for the brothers of St. Francis.

The mansion of the Lady de Tilly was of stone, spacious and ornate, as became the rank and wealth of the Seigneurs de Tilly. It overlooked the Place d'Armes and the noble gardens of the Chateau of St. Louis, with a magnificent sweep of the St. Lawrence, flowing majestically under the fortress-crowned cape and the high, wooded hills of Lauzon, the farther side of the river closing the view.

In the recess of an ornate mullioned window, half concealed by the rich, heavy curtains of a noble room, Amelie de Repentigny sat alone--very quiet in look and demeanor, but no little agitated in mind, as might be noticed in the nervous contact of her hands, which lay in her lap clasping each other very hard, as if trying to steady her thoughts.

Her aunt was receiving some lady visitors in the great drawing-room. The hum of loud feminine voices reached the ear of Amelie, but she paid no attention, so absorbed was she in the new and strange thoughts that had stirred in her mind since morning, when she had learned from the Chevalier La Corne of the return to New France of Pierre Philibert. The news had surprised her to a degree she could not account for. Her first thought was, how fortunate for her brother that Pierre had returned; her second, how agreeable to herself. Why? She could not think why: she wilfully drew an inference away from the truth that lay in her heart--it was wholly for the sake of her brother she rejoiced in the return of his friend and preserver. Her heart beat a little faster than usual--that was the result of her long walk and disappointment at not meeting Le Gardeur on her arrival yesterday. But she feared to explore her thoughts: a rigid self-examination might discover what she instinctively felt was deeply concealed there.

A subtile, indefinable prevision had suggested to her that Colonel Philibert would not have failed to meet Le Gardeur at Beaumanoir, and that he would undoubtedly accompany her brother on his return and call to pay his respects to the Lady de Tilly and--to herself. She felt her cheek glow at the thought, yet she was half vexed at her own foolish fancy, as she called it. She tried to call upon her pride, but that came very laggardly to the relief of her discomposure.

Her interview, too, with Angelique des Meloises had caused her no little disquiet. The bold avowals of Angelique with reference to the Intendant had shocked Amelie. She knew that her brother had given more of his thoughts to this beautiful, reckless girl than was good for his peace, should her ambition ever run counter to his love.

The fond sister sighed deeply when she reflected that the woman who had power to make prize of Le Gardeur's love was not worthy of him.

It is no rare thing for loving sisters who have to resign their brothers to others' keeping to think so. But Amelie knew that Angelique des Meloises was incapable of that true love which only finds its own in the happiness of another. She was vain, selfish, ambitious, and--what Amelie did not yet know--possessed of neither scruple nor delicacy in attaining her objects.

It had chimed the hour of noon upon the old clock of the Recollets, and Amelie still sat looking wistfully over the great square of the Place d'Armes, and curiously scanning every horseman that rode across it. A throng of people moved about the square, or passed in and out of the great arched gateway of the Castle of St. Louis. A bright shield, bearing the crown and fleur-de-lis, surmounted the gate, and under it walked, with military pace, a couple of sentries, their muskets and bayonets flashing out in the sun every time they wheeled to return on their beat. Occasionally there was a ruffle of drums: the whole guard turned out and presented arms, as some officer of high rank, or ecclesiastical dignitary, passed through to pay his respects to the Governor, or transact business at the vice- regal court. Gentlemen on foot, with chapeaux and swords, carrying a cloak on their shoulders; ladies in visiting dress; habitans and their wives in unchanging costume; soldiers in uniform, and black- gowned clergy, mingled in a moving picture of city life, which, had not Amelie's thoughts been so preoccupied to-day, would have afforded her great delight to look out upon.

The Lady de Tilly had rather wearied of the visit of the two ladies of the city, Madame de Grandmaison and Madame Couillard, who had bored her with all the current gossip of the day. They were rich and fashionable, perfect in etiquette, costume, and most particular in their society; but the rank and position of the noble Lady de Tilly made her friendship most desirable, as it conferred in the eyes of the world a patent of gentility which held good against every pretension to overtop it.

The stream of city talk from the lips of the two ladies had the merit of being perfect of its kind--softly insinuating and sweetly censorious, superlative in eulogy and infallible in opinion. The good visitors most conscientiously discharged what they deemed a great moral and social duty by enlightening the Lady de Tilly on all the recent lapses and secrets of the capital. They slid over slippery topics like skaters on thin ice, filling their listener with anxiety lest they should break through. But Madame de Grandmaison and her companion were too well exercised in the gymnastics of gossip to overbalance themselves. Half Quebec was run over and run down in the course of an hour.

Lady de Tilly listened with growing impatience to their frivolities, but she knew society too well to quarrel with its follies when it was of no service to do so: she contented herself with hoping it was not so bad. The Pope was not Catholic enough to suit some people, but, for her part, she had generally found people better than they were called.

A rather loud but well-bred exclamation of Madame de Grandmaison roused Amelie from her day-dream.

"Not going to the Intendant's ball at the Palace, my Lady de Tilly! neither you nor Mademoiselle de Repentigny, whom we are so sorry not to have seen to-day? Why, it is to be the most magnificent affair ever got up in New France. All Quebec has rung with nothing else for a fortnight, and every milliner and modiste in the city has gone almost insane over the superlative costumes to be worn there."

"And it is to be the most select in its character," chimed in Madame Couillard; "all gentry and noblesse, not one of the bourgeois to be invited. That class, especially the female portion of them, give themselves such airs nowadays! As if their money made them company for people of quality! They must be kept down, I say, or--"

"And the Royal Intendant quite agrees with the general sentiment of the higher circles," responded Madame de Grandmaison. "He is for keeping down--"

"Noblesse! Noblesse!" The Lady de Tilly spoke with visible impatience. "Who is this Royal Intendant who dares cast a slight upon the worthy, honest bourgeoisie of this city? Is he noble himself? Not that I would think worse of him were he not, but I have heard it disputed. He is the last one who should venture to scorn the bourgeoisie."

Madame de Grandmaison fanned herself in a very stately manner. "Oh, my Lady, you surely forget! The Chevalier Bigot is a distant relative of the Count de Marville, and the Chevalier de Grandmaison is a constant visitor at the Intendant's! But he would not have sat at his table an hour had he not known that he was connected with the nobility. The Count de Marville--"

"The Count de Marville!" interrupted the Lady de Tilly, whose politeness almost gave way. "Truly, a man is known by the company he keeps. No credit to any one to be connected with the Count de Marville."

Madame de Grandmaison felt rather subdued. She perceived that the Lady de Tilly was not favorably impressed towards the Intendant. But she tried again: "And then, my Lady, the Intendant is so powerful at Court. He was a particular friend of Madame d'Etioles before she was known at Court, and they say he managed her introduction to the King at the famous masked ball at the Hotel de Ville, when His Majesty threw his handkerchief at her, and she became first dame du palais and the Marquise de Pompadour. She has ever remained his firm friend, and in spite of all his enemies could do to prevent it His Majesty made him Intendant of New France."

"In spite of all the King's friends could do, you mean," replied the Lady de Tilly, in a tone the sound of which caught the ear of Amelie, and she knew her aunt was losing patience with her visitors. Lady de Tilly heard the name of the royal mistress with intense disgust, but her innate loyalty prevented her speaking disparagingly of the King. "We will not discuss the Court," said she, "nor the friendships of this Intendant. I can only pray his future may make amends for his past. I trust New France may not have as much reason as poor lost Acadia to lament the day of his coming to the Colonies."

The two lady visitors were not obtuse. They saw they had roused the susceptibilities-- prejudices, they called them--of the Lady de Tilly. They rose, and smothering their disappointment under well- bred phrases, took most polite leave of the dignified old lady, who was heartily glad to be rid of them.

"The disagreeable old thing--to talk so of the Intendant!" exclaimed Madame Couillard, spitefully, "when her own nephew, and heir in the Seigniory of Tilly, is the Intendant's firmest friend and closest companion."

"Yes, she forgot about her own house; people always forget to look at home when they pass judgment upon their neighbors," replied Madame de Grandmaison. "But I am mistaken if she will be able to impress Le Gardeur de Repentigny with her uncharitable and unfashionable opinions of the Intendant. I hope the ball will be the greatest social success ever seen in the city, just to vex her and her niece, who is as proud and particular as she is herself."

Amelie de Repentigny had dressed herself to-day in a robe of soft muslin of Deccan, the gift of a relative in Pondicherry. It enveloped her exquisite form, without concealing the grace and lissomeness of her movements. A broad blue ribbon round her waist, and in her dark hair a blue flower, were all her adornments, except a chain and cross of gold, which lay upon her bosom, the rich gift of her brother, and often kissed with a silent prayer for his welfare and happiness. More than once, under the influence of some indefinable impulse, she rose and went to the mirror, comparing her features now with a portrait of herself taken as a young girl in the garb of a shepherdess of Provence. Her father used to like that picture of her, and to please him she often wore her hair in the fashion of Provence. She did so to-day. Why? The subtle thought in many Protean shapes played before her fancy, but she would not try to catch it--no! rather shyly avoided its examination.

She was quite restless, and sat down again in the deep recess of the window, watching the

Place d'Armes for the appearance of her brother.

She gave a sudden start at last, as a couple of officers galloped in to the square and rode towards the great gate of the Chateau; one of them she instantly recognized as her brother, the other, a tall martial figure in full uniform, upon a fiery gray, she did not recognize, but she knew in her heart it could be no other than Colonel Philibert.

Amelie felt a thrill, almost painful in its pleasure, agitating her bosom, as she sat watching the gateway they had entered. It was even a momentary relief to her that they had turned in there instead of riding directly to the house. It gave her time to collect her thoughts and summon all her fortitude for the coming interview. Her fingers wandered down to the rosary in the folds of her dress, and the golden bead, which had so often prompted her prayer for the happiness of Pierre Philibert, seemed to burn to the touch. Her cheek crimsoned, for a strange thought suddenly intruded--the boy Pierre Philibert, whose image and memory she had so long and innocently cherished, was now a man, a soldier, a councillor, trained in courts and camps! How unmaidenly she had acted, forgetting all this in her childish prayers until this moment! "I mean no harm," was all the defence she could think of. Nor had she time to think more of herself, for, after remaining ten minutes in the Chateau, just long enough to see the Governor and deliver the answer of the Intendant to his message, the gray charger emerged from the gate. His rider was accompanied by her brother and the well-known figure of her godfather, La Corne St. Luc, who rode up the hill and in a minute or two dismounted at the door of the mansion of the Lady de Tilly.

The fabled lynx, whose eye penetrates the very earth to discover hidden treasure, did not cast a keener and more inquisitive glance than that which Amelie, shrouded behind the thick curtains, directed from the window at the tall, manly figure and handsome countenance of him whom she knew to be Pierre Philibert. Let it not detract from her that she gave way to an irresistible impulse of womanly curiosity. The Queen of France would, under the same temptation, have done the same thing, and perhaps without feeling half the modest shame of it that Amelie did. A glance sufficed--but a glance that impressed upon her mind forever the ineffaceable and perfect image of Pierre Philibert the man, who came in place of Pierre Philibert the boy friend of Le Gardeur and of herself.

## Chapter XI: The Soldier's Welcome

The voices of the gentlemen mingled with her aunt's in eager greetings. She well knew which must be the voice of Colonel Philibert--the rest were all so familiar to her ear. Suddenly footsteps ran up the grand stair, clearing three at a time. She waited, trembling with anticipation. Le Gardeur rushed into the room with outstretched arms, embraced her, and kissed her in a transport of brotherly affection.

"Oh, Le Gardeur!" cried she, returning his kiss with fond affection, and looking in his face with tenderness and joy. "O my brother, how I have prayed and longed for your coming. Thank God! you are here at last. You are well, brother, are you not?" said she, looking up with a glance that seemed to betray some anxiety.

"Never better, Amelie," replied he, in a gayer tone than was quite natural to him, and shyly averting his eyes from her tender scrutiny. "Never better. Why, if I had been in my grave, I should have risen up to welcome a friend whom I have met to-day after years of separation. Oh, Amelie, I have such news for you!"

"News for me, Le Gardeur! What can it be?" A blush stole over her countenance, and her bosom heaved, for she was very conscious of the nature of the news her brother was about to impart.

"Guess! you unsuspecting queen of shepherdesses," cried he, archly twisting a lock of her hair that hung over her shoulder. "Guess, you pretty gipsy, you!"

"Guess? How can I guess, Le Gardeur? Can there be any news left in the city of Quebec after an hour's visit from Madame de Grandmaison and Madame Couillard? I did not go down, but I know they inquired much after you, by the way!" Amelie, with a little touch of feminine perversity, shyly put off the grand burst of Le Gardeur's intelligence, knowing it was sure to come.

"Pshaw! who cares for those old scandal-mongers! But you can never guess my news, Amelie, so I may as well tell you." Le Gardeur fairly swelled with the announcement he was about to make.

"Have mercy then, brother, and tell me at once, for you do now set my curiosity on tiptoe." She was a true woman, and would not for anything have admitted her knowledge of the presence of Colonel Philibert in the house.

"Amelie," said he, taking her by both hands, as if to prevent her escape, "I was at Beaumanoir--you know the Intendant gave a grand hunting party," added he, noticing the quick glance she gave him; "and who do you think came to the Chateau and recognized me, or rather I recognized him? A stranger--and not such a stranger, either Amelie."

"Nay; go on, brother! Who could this mysterious stranger and no stranger have been?"

"Pierre Philibert, Amelie! Pierre--our Pierre, you know! You recollect him, sister!"

"Recollect Pierre Philibert? Why, how could I ever forget him while you are living? since to him we are all indebted for your life, brother!"

"I know that; are you not glad, as I am, at his return?" asked Le Gardeur, with a penetrating look.

She threw her arms round him involuntarily, for she was much agitated. "Glad, brother? Yes, I am glad because you are glad."

"No more than that, Amelie? That is a small thing to be glad for."

"Oh, brother! I am glad for gladness's sake! We can never overpay the debt of gratitude we owe Pierre Philibert."

"O my sweet sister," replied he, kissing her, "I knew my news would please you. Come, we will go down and see him at once, for Pierre is in the house."

"But, Le Gardeur!" She blushed and hesitated. "Pierre Philibert I knew--I could speak to him; but I shall hardly dare recognize him in the stately soldier of to-day. Voila la difference!" added she, repeating the refrain of a song very popular both in New France and in Old at that period.

Le Gardeur did not comprehend her hesitation and tone. Said he,-- "Pierre is wonderfully changed since he and I wore the green sash of the seminary. He is taller than I, wiser and better,-- he was always that,--but in heart the same generous, noble Pierre Philibert he was when a boy. Voila la ressemblance!" added he, pulling her hair archly as he repeated the antistrophe of the same ditty.

Amelie gave her brother a fond look, but she did not reply, except by a tight pressure of the hand. The voices of the Chevalier La Corne and the Lady de Tilly and Colonel Philibert were again heard in animated conversation. "Come, brother, we will go now," said she; and quick in executing any resolution she had formed, she took the arm of her brother, swept with him down the broad stair, and entered the drawing-room.

Philibert rose to his feet in admiration of the vision of loveliness that suddenly beamed upon his eyes. It was the incarnation of all the shapes of grace and beauty that had passed through his fervid fancy during so many years of absence from his native land. Something there was of the features of the young girl who had ridden with flying locks, like a sprite, through the woods of Tilly. But comparing his recollection of that slight girl with the tall, lithe, perfect womanhood of the half-blushing girl before him, he hesitated, although intuitively aware that it could be no other than the idol of his heart, Amelie de Repentigny.

Le Gardeur solved the doubt in a moment by exclaiming, in a tone of exultation, "Pierre Philibert, I bring an old young friend to greet you--my sister!"

Philibert advanced, and Amelie raised her dark eyes with a momentary glance that drew into her heart the memory of his face forever. She held out her hand frankly and courteously. Philibert bent over it as reverently as he would over the hand of the Madonna.

The greeting of the Lady de Tilly and La Corne St. Luc had been cordial, nay, affectionate in its kindness. The good lady kissed Pierre as a mother might have done a long-absent son.

"Colonel Philibert," said Amelie, straining her nerves to the tension of steel to preserve her composure, "Colonel Philibert is most welcome; he has never been forgotten in this house." She glanced at her aunt, who smiled approvingly at Amelie's remark.

"Thanks, Mademoiselle de Repentigny; I am indeed happy to be remembered here; it fulfils one of my most cherished hopes in returning to my native land."

"Ay, ay, Pierre," interrupted La Corne St. Luc, who looked on this little scene very admiringly, "good blood never lies. Look at Colonel Philibert there, with the King's epaulets on his shoulders. I have a sharp eye, as you know, Amelie, when I look after my pretty goddaughter, but I should not have recognized our lively Pierre in him, had Le Gardeur not introduced him to me, and I think you would not have known him either."

"Thanks for your looking after me, godfather," replied Amelie, merrily, very grateful in her heart for his appreciation of Pierre, "but I think neither aunt nor I should have failed to recognize him."

"Right, my Amelie!" said the Lady de Tilly. "We should not, and we shall not be afraid, Pierre,--I must call you Pierre or nothing,-- we shall not be afraid, although you do lay in a new stock of acquaintances in the capital, that old friends will be put aside as unfashionable remnants."

"My whole stock of friendship consists of those remnants, my Lady,-- memories of dear friends I love and honor. They will never be unfashionable with me: I should be bankrupt indeed, were I to part with one of them."

"Then they are of a truer fabric than Penelope's web, for she, I read, pulled in pieces at night what she had woven through the day," replied Lady de Tilly. "Give me the friendship that won't unravel."

"But not a thread of my recollections has ever unravelled, or ever will," replied Pierre, looking at Amelie as she clasped the arm of her aunt, feeling stronger, as is woman's way, by the contact with another.

"Zounds! What is all this merchant's talk about webs and threads and thrums?" exclaimed La Corne. "There is no memory so good as a soldier's, Amelie, and for good reason: a soldier on our wild frontiers is compelled to be faithful to old friends and old flannels; he cannot help himself to new ones if he would. I was five years and never saw a woman's face except red ones--some of them were very comely, by the way," added the old warrior with a smile.

"The gallantry of the Chevalier La Corne is incontestable," remarked Pierre, "for once, when we captured a convoy of soldiers' wives from New England, he escorted them, with drums beating, to Grand Pre, and sent a cask of Gascon wine for them to celebrate their reunion with their husbands."

"Frowzy huzzies! not worth the keeping, or I would not have sent them; fit only for the bobtailed militia of New England!" exclaimed La Corne.

"Not so thought the New Englanders, who had a three days feast when they remarried their wives--and handsome they were, too," said Philibert; "the healths they drank to the Chevalier were enough to make him immortal."

La Corne always brushed aside compliments to himself: "Tut, my Lady! it was more Pierre's good-nature than mine--he out of kindness let the women rejoin their husbands; on my part it was policy and stratagem, of war. Hear the sequel! The wives spoiled the husbands, as I guessed they would do, taught them to be too late at reveille, too early at tattoo. They neglected guards and pickets, and when the long nights of winter set in, the men hugged their wives by the firesides instead of their muskets by their watch- fires. Then came destruction upon them! In a blinding storm, amid snow-drifts and darkness, Coulon de Villiers, with his troops on snow-shoes, marched into the New England camp, and made widows of the most of the poor wives, who fell into our hands the second time. Poor creatures! I saw that day how hard it was to be a soldier's wife." La Corne's shaggy eyelash twinkled with moisture. "But it was the fortune of war!--the fortune of war, and a cruel fortune it is at the best!"

The Lady de Tilly pressed her hand to her bosom to suppress the rising emotion. "Alas, Chevalier! poor widows! I feel all they suffered. War is indeed a cruel fortune, as I too have had reason to learn."

"And what became of the poor women, godfather?" Amelie's eyes were suffused with tears: it was in her heart, if ever in any mortal's, to love her enemies.

"Oh, we cared for them the best we could. The Baron de St. Castin sheltered them in his chateau for the winter, and his daughter devoted herself to them with the zeal and tenderness of a saint from Heaven--a noble, lovely girl, Amelie!" added La Corne, impressively; "the fairest flower in all Acadia, and most unfortunate, poor girl! God's blessing rest upon her, wherever she may be!" La Corne St. Luc spoke with a depth of emotion he rarely manifested.

"How was she unfortunate, godfather?" Philibert watched the cheek flush and the eyelid quiver of the fair girl as she spoke, carried away by her sympathy. His heart went with his looks.

"Alas!" replied La Corne, "I would fain not answer, lest I distrust the moral government of the universe. But we are blind creatures, and God's ways are not fashioned in our ways. Let no one boast that he stands, lest he fall! We need the help of the host of Heaven to keep us upright and maintain our integrity. I can scarcely think of that noble girl without tears. Oh, the pity of it! The pity of it!"

Lady de Tilly looked at him wonderingly. "I knew the Baron de St. Castin," said she. "When he came to perform homage at the Castle of St. Louis, for the grant of some lands in Acadia, he was accompanied by his only daughter, a child perfect in goodness, grace, and loveliness. She was just the age of Amelie. The ladies of the city were in raptures over the pretty Mayflower, as they called her. What, in heaven's name, has happened to that dear child, Chevalier La Corne?"

La Corne St. Luc, half angry with himself for having broached the painful topic, and not used to pick his words, replied bluntly,-- "Happened, my Lady! what is it happens worst to a woman? She loved a man unworthy of her love--a villain in spite of high rank and King's favor, who deceived this fond, confiding girl, and abandoned her to shame! Faugh! It is the way of the Court, they say; and the King has not withdrawn his favor, but heaped new honors upon him!" La Corne put a severe curb upon his utterance and turned impatiently away, lest he might curse the King as well as the favorite.

"But what became of the poor deceived girl?" asked the Lady de Tilly, after hastily clearing her eyes with her handkerchief.

"Oh, the old, old story followed. She ran away from home in an agony of shame and fear, to avoid the return of her father from France. She went among the Indians of the St. Croix, they say, and has not been heard of since. Poor, dear girl! her very trust in virtue was the cause of her fall!"

Amelie turned alternately pale and red at the recital of her godfather. She riveted her eyes upon the ground as she pressed close to her aunt, clasping her arm, as if seeking strength and support.

Lady de Tilly was greatly shocked at the sad recital. She inquired the name of the man of rank who had acted so treacherously to the hapless girl.

"I will not utter the name to-day, my Lady! It has been revealed to me as a great secret. It is a name too high for the stroke of the law, if there be any law left us but the will of a King's mistress! God, however, has left us the law of a gentleman's sword to avenge its master's wrong. The Baron de St. Castin will soon return to vindicate his own honor, and whether or no, I vow to heaven, my Lady, that the traitor who has wronged that sweet girl will one day have to try whether his sword be sharper than that of La Corne St. Luc! But pshaw! I am talking bravado like an Indian at the war post. The story of those luckless New England wives has carried us beyond all bounds."

Lady de Tilly looked admiringly, without a sign of reproof, at the old soldier, sympathizing with his honest indignation at so foul a wrong to her sex. "Were that dear child mine, woman as I am, I would do the same thing!" said she, with a burst of feeling. She felt Amelie press her arm as if she too shared the spirit of her bolder aunt.

"But here comes Felix Baudoin to summon us to dinner!" exclaimed Lady de Tilly, as an old, white-headed servitor in livery appeared at the door with a low bow, announcing that dinner was served.

Le Gardeur and La Corne St. Luc greeted the old servitor with the utmost kindness, inquired after his health, and begged a pinch from his well-worn snuff-box. Such familiarities were not rare in that day between the gentlemen of New France and their old servants, who usually passed their lifetime in one household. Felix was the majordomo of the Manor House of Tilly, trusty, punctilious, and polite, and honored by his mistress more as an humble friend than as a servant of her house.

"Dinner is served, my Lady!" repeated Felix, with a bow. "But my Lady must excuse! The kitchen has been full of habitans all day. The Trifourchettes, the Doubledents, and all the best eaters in Tilly have been here. After obeying my Lady's commands to give them all they could eat we have had difficulty in saving anything for my Lady's own table."

"No matter, Felix, we shall say grace all the same. I could content myself with bread and water, to give fish and flesh to my censitaires, who are working so willingly on the King's corvee! But that must be my apology to you, Pierre Philibert and the Chevalier La Corne, for a poorer dinner than I could wish."

"Oh, I feel no misgivings, my Lady!" remarked La Corne St. Luc, laughing. "Felix Baudoin is too faithful a servitor to starve his mistress for the sake of the Trifourchettes, the Doubledents, and all the best eaters in the Seigniory! No! no! I will be bound your Ladyship will find Felix has tolled and tithed from them enough to secure a dinner for us all--come, Amelie, with me."

Lady de Tilly took the arm of Colonel Philibert, followed by Le Gardeur, La Corne, and Amelie, and, marshalled by the majordomo, proceeded to the dining-room--a large room, wainscotted with black walnut, a fine wood lately introduced. The ceiling was coved, and surrounded by a rich frieze of carving. A large table, suggestive of hospitality, was covered with drapery of the snowiest linen, the product of the spinning-wheels and busy looms of the women of the Seigniory of Tilly. Vases of china, filled with freshly-gathered flowers, shed sweet perfumes, while they delighted the eye with their beauty, etherializing the elements of bread and meat by suggestions of the poetry and ideals of life. A grand old buffet, a prodigy of cabinet-maker's art, displayed a mass of family plate, and a silver shield embossed with the arms of Tilly, a gift of Henry of Navarre to their ancient and loyal house, hung upon the wall over the buffet.

In spite of the Trifourchettes and the Doubledents, Felix Baudoin had managed to set an excellent dinner upon the table of his lady, who looked archly at the Chevalier La Corne, as if assenting to his remark on her old servitor.

The lady remained standing at the head of her table until they all sat down, when, clasping her hands, she recited with feeling and clearness the old Latin grace, "Benedic, Domine, nos et haec tua dona," sanctifying her table by the invocation of the blessing of God upon it and upon all who sat round it.

A soup, rich and savory, was the prelude at all dinners in New France. A salmon speared in the shallows of the Chaudiere, and a dish of blood-speckled trout from the mountain streams of St. Joachim, smoked upon the board. Little oval loaves of wheaten bread were piled up in baskets of silver filigree. For in those days the fields of New France produced crops of the finest wheat--a gift which Providence has since withheld. "The wheat went away with the Bourbon lilies, and never grew afterwards," said the old habitans. The meat in the larder had all really been given to the hungry censitaires in the kitchen, except a capon from the basse cour of Tilly and a standing pie, the contents of which came from the manorial dovecote. A reef of raspberries, red as corals, gathered on the tangled slopes of Cote a Bonhomme, formed the dessert, with blue whortleberries from Cape Tourment, plums sweet as honey drops, and small, gray-coated apples from Beaupre, delicious as those that comforted the Rose of Sharon. A few carafes of choice wine from the old manorial cellar, completed the entertainment.

The meal was not a protracted one, but to Pierre Philibert the most blissful hour of his life. He sat by the side of Amelie, enjoying every moment as if it were a pearl dropped into his bosom by word, look, or gesture of the radiant girl who sat beside him.

He found Amelie, although somewhat timid at first to converse, a willing, nay, an eager listener. She was attracted by the magnetism of a noble, sympathetic nature, and by degrees ventured to cast a glance at the handsome, manly countenance where feature after feature revealed itself, like a landscape at dawn of day, and in Colonel Philibert she recognized the very looks, speech, and manner of Pierre Philibert of old.

Her questioning eyes hardly needed the interpretation of her tongue to draw him out to impart the story of his life during his long absence from New France, and it was with secret delight she found in him a powerful, cultivated intellect and nobility of sentiment such as she rightly supposed belonged only to a great man, while his visible pleasure at meeting her again filled her with a secret joy that, unnoticed by herself, suffused her whole countenance with radiance, and incited her to converse with him more freely than she had thought it possible when she sat down at table.

"It is long since we all sat together, Mademoiselle, at the table of your noble aunt," remarked Philibert. "It fulfills an often and often repeated day-dream of mine, that I should one day find you just the same."

"And do you find me just the same?" answered she, archly. "You take down the pride of ladyhood immensely, Colonel! I had imagined I was something quite other than the wild child of Tilly!"

"I hardly like to consider you as in the pride of ladyhood, Mademoiselle, for fear I should lose the wild child of Tilly, whom I should be so glad to find again."

"And whom you do find just the same in heart, mind, and regard too!" thought she to herself, but her words were,--"My school mistresses would be ashamed of their work, Colonel, if they had not improved on the very rude material my aunt sent them up from Tilly to manufacture into a fine lady! I was the crowned queen of the year when I left the Ursulines, so beware of considering me 'the child of Tilly' any longer."

Her silvery laugh caught his heart, for in that he recognized vividly the gay young girl whose image he was every instant developing out of the tall, lovely woman beside him.

La Corne St. Luc and the Lady de Tilly found a thousand delights in mutual reminiscences of the past. Le Gardeur, somewhat heavy, joined in conversation with Philibert and his sister. Amelie guessed, and Philibert knew, the secret of Le Gardeur's dulness; both strove to enliven and arouse him. His aunt guessed too, that he had passed the night as the guests of the Intendant always passed it, and knowing his temper and the regard he had for her good opinion, she brought the subject of the Intendant into conversation, in order, casually as it were, to impress Le Gardeur with her opinion of him. "Pierre Philibert too," thought she, "shall be put upon his guard against the crafty Bigot."

"Pierre," said she, "you are happy in a father who is a brave, honorable man, of whom any son in the world might be proud. The country holds by him immensely, and he deserves their regard. Watch over him now you are at home, Pierre. He has some relentless and powerful enemies, who would injure him if they could."

"That has he," remarked La Corne St. Luc; "I have spoken to the Sieur Philibert and cautioned him, but he is not impressible on the subject of his own safety. The Intendant spoke savagely of him in public the other day."

"Did he, Chevalier?" replied Philibert, his eyes flashing with another fire than that which had filled them looking at Amelie. "He shall account to me for his words, were he Regent instead of Intendant!"

La Corne St. Luc looked half approvingly at Philibert.

"Don't quarrel with him yet, Pierre! You cannot make a quarrel of what he has said."

Lady de Tilly listened uneasily, and said,--

"Don't quarrel with him at all, Pierre Philibert! Judge him and avoid him, as a Christian man should do. God will deal with Bigot as he deserves: the crafty man will be caught in his own devices some day."

"Oh, Bigot is a gentleman, aunt, too polite to insult any one," remarked Le Gardeur, impatient to defend one whom he regarded as a friend. "He is the prince of good fellows, and not crafty, I think, but all surface and sunshine."

"You never explored the depths of him, Le Gardeur," remarked La Corne. "I grant he is a gay, jesting, drinking, and gambling fellow in company; but, trust me, he is deep and dark as the Devil's cave that I have seen in the Ottawa country. It goes story under story, deeper and deeper, until the imagination loses itself in contemplating the bottomless pit of it--that is Bigot, Le Gardeur."

"My censitaires report to me," remarked the Lady de Tilly, "that his commissaries are seizing the very seed-corn of the country. Heaven knows what will become of my poor people next year if the war continue!"

"What will become of the Province in the hands of Francois Bigot?" replied La Corne St. Luc. "They say, Philibert, that a certain great lady at Court, who is his partner or patroness, or both, has obtained a grant of your father's sequestered estate in Normandy, for her relative, the Count de Marville. Had you heard of that, Philibert? It is the latest news from France."

"Oh, yes, Chevalier! Ill news like that never misses the mark it is aimed at. The news soon reached my father!"

"And how does your father take it?"

"My father is a true philosopher; he takes it as Socrates might have taken it; he laughs at the Count de Marville, who will, he says, want to sell the estate before the year is out, to pay his debts of honor--the only debts he ever does pay."

"If Bigot had anything to do with such an outrage," exclaimed Le Gardeur warmly, "I would renounce him on the spot. I have heard Bigot speak of this gift to De Marville, whom he hates. He says it was all La Pompadour's doing from first to last, and I believe it."

"Well," remarked La Corne, "Bigot has plenty of sins of his own to answer for to the Sieur Philibert, on the day of account, without reckoning this among them."

The loud report of a cannon shook the windows of the room, and died away in long-repeated echoes among the distant hills.

"That is the signal for the Council of War, my Lady," said La Corne. "A soldier's luck! just as we were going to have music and heaven, we are summoned to field, camp, or council."

The gentlemen rose and accompanied the ladies to the drawing-room, and prepared to depart. Colonel Philibert took a courteous leave of the ladies of Tilly, looking in the eyes of Amelie for something which, had she not turned them quickly upon a vase of flowers, he might have found there. She plucked a few sprays from the bouquet, and handed them to him as a token of pleasure at meeting him again in his own land.

"Recollect, Pierre Philibert!" said the Lady de Tilly, holding him cordially by the hand, "the Manor House of Tilly is your second home, where you are ever welcome."

Philibert was deeply touched by the genuine and stately courtesy of the lady. He kissed her hand with grateful reverence, and bowing to both the ladies, accompanied La Corne St. Luc and Le Gardeur to the castle of St. Louis.

Amelie sat in the recess of the window, resting her cheek upon her tremulous hand as she watched the gentlemen proceed on their way to the castle. Her mind was overflowing with thoughts and fancies, new, enigmatical, yet delightful. Her nervous manner did not escape the loving eye of her aunt; but she spoke not--she was silent under the burden of a secret joy that found not vent in words.

Suddenly Amelie rose from the window, and seated herself, in her impulsive way, at the organ. Her fingers touched the keys timidly at first as she began a trembling prelude of her own fantasy. In music her pent-up feelings found congenial expression. The fire kindled, and she presently burst out with the voice of a seraph in that glorious psalm, the 116th:

"'Toto pectore diligam
Unice et Dominum colam,
Qui lenis mihi supplici
Non duram appulit aurem.

Aurem qui mihi supplici,
Non duram dedit; hunc ego
Donec pectora spiritus
Pulset semper, amabo.'"

The Lady de Tilly, half guessing the truth, would not wound the susceptibilities of her niece by appearing to do so; so rose quietly from her seat and placed her arms gently round Amelie when she finished the psalm. She pressed her to her bosom, kissed her fondly, and without a word, left her to find in music relief from her high-wrought feelings. Her voice rose in sweeter and loftier harmonies to the pealing of the organ as she sang to the end the joyful yet solemn psalm, in a version made for Queen Mary of France and Scotland when life was good, hope all brightness, and dark days as if they would never come.

## Chapter XII: The Castle of St. Louis

The Count de la Galissoniere, with a number of officers of rank in full uniform, was slowly pacing up and down the long gallery that fronted the Castle of St. Louis, waiting for the Council of War to open; for although the hour had struck, the Intendant, and many other high officials of the Colony, had not yet arrived from Beaumanoir.

The Castle of St. Louis, a massive structure of stone, with square flanking towers, rose loftily from the brink of the precipice, overlooking the narrow, tortuous streets of the lower town. The steeple of the old Church of Notre Dame des Victoires, with its gilded vane, lay far beneath the feet of the observer as he leaned over the balustrade of iron that guarded the gallery of the Chateau.

A hum of voices and dense sounds rose up from the market of Notre Dame and from the quay where ships and bateaux were moored. The cries of sailors, carters, and habitans in thick medley floated up the steep cliffs, pleasant sounds to the ear of the worthy Governor, who liked the honest noises of industry and labor better than all the music of the Academy.

A few merchantmen which had run the blockade of the English cruisers lay at anchor in the stream, where the broad river swept majestically round the lofty cape. In the midst of them a newly- arrived King's ship, the Fleur-de-Lis, decorated with streamers, floated proudly, like a swan among a flock of teal.

Le Gardeur, as an officer of the garrison, went to report himself to the military commandant, while La Corne St. Luc and Colonel Philibert proceeded to the gallery, where a crowd of officers were now assembled, waiting for the Council.

The Governor at once called Philibert aside, and took his arm. "Philibert," said he, "I trust you had no difficulty in finding the Intendant?"

"No difficulty whatever, your Excellency. I discovered the Intendant and his friends by ear long before I got sight of them." An equivocal smile accompanied Philibert's words, which the Governor rightly interpreted.

"Ah! I understand, Philibert; they were carousing at that hour of daylight? Were they all--? Faugh! I shame to speak the word. Was the Intendant in a condition to comprehend my summons?" The Governor looked sad, rather than surprised or angry, for he had expected no less than Philibert had reported to him.

"I found him less intoxicated, I think, than many of his guests. He received your message with more politeness than I expected, and promised to be here punctually at the hour for opening the Council."

"Oh, Bigot never lacks politeness, drunk or sober: that strong intellect of his seems to defy the power of wine, as his heart is proof against moral feeling. You did not prolong your stay in Beaumanoir, I fancy?" remarked the Governor, dinting the point of his cane into the floor.

"I hastened out of it as I would out of hell itself! After making prize of my friend De Repentigny and bringing him off with me, as I mentioned to you, I got quickly out of the Chateau."

"You did rightly, Philibert: the Intendant is ruining half the young men of birth in the Colony."

"He shall not ruin Le Gardeur if I can save him," said Philibert, resolutely. "May I count upon your Excellency's cooperation?" added he.

"Assuredly, Philibert! Command me in anything you can devise to rescue that noble young fellow from the fatal companionship of Bigot. But I know not how long I shall be permitted to remain in New France: powerful intrigues are at work for my removal!" added the Governor. "I care not for the removal, so that it be not accompanied with insult."

"Ah! you have received news to-day by the frigate?" said Philibert, looking down at the King's ship at anchor in the stream.

"News? Yes; and such news, Philibert!" replied the Governor in at one of despondency. "It needs the wisdom of Solon to legislate for this land, and a Hercules to cleanse its Augean stables of official corruption. But my influence at Court is nil--you know that, Philibert!"

"But while you are Governor your advice ought to prevail with the King," replied Philibert.

"My advice prevail! Listen, Philibert: my letters to the King and the Minister of Marine and Colonies have been answered by whom, think you?"

"Nay, I cannot conceive who, out of the legal channel, would dare to reply to them."

"No! no man could guess that my official despatches have been answered by the Marquise de Pompadour! She replies to my despatches to my sovereign!"

"La Pompadour!" exclaimed Philibert in a burst of indignation. "She, the King's mistress, reply to your despatches! Has France come to be governed by courtesans, like imperial Rome?"

"Yes! and you know the meaning of that insult, Philibert! They desire to force me to resign, and I shall resign as soon as I see my friends safe. I will serve the King in his fleet, but never more in a colony. This poor land is doomed to fall into the hands of its enemies unless we get a speedy peace. France will help us no more!"

"Don't say that, your Excellency! France will surely never be untrue to her children in the New World! But our resources are not yet all exhausted: we are not driven to the wall yet, your Excellency!"

"Almost, I assure you, Philibert! But we shall understand that better after the Council."

"What say the despatches touching the negotiations going on for peace?" asked Philibert, who knew how true were the Governor's vaticinations.

"They speak favorably of peace, and I think, correctly, Philibert; and you know the King's armies and the King's mistresses cannot all be maintained at the same time--women or war, one or other must give way, and one need not doubt which it will be, when the women rule Court and camp in France at the same time!"

"To think that a woman picked out of the gutters of Paris should rule France and answer your despatches!" said Philibert, angrily; "it is enough to drive honorable Frenchmen mad. But what says the Marquise de Pompadour?"

"She is especially severe upon my opposing the fiscal measures and commercial policy, as she calls it, of her friend the Intendant! She approves of his grant of a monopoly of trade to the Grand Company, and disputes my right, as Governor, to interfere with the Intendant in the finances of the Colony."

Philibert felt deeply this wound to the honor and dignity of his chief. He pressed his hand in warmest sympathy.

The Governor understood his feelings. "You are a true friend, Philibert," said he; "ten men like you might still save this Colony! But it is past the hour for the Council, and still Bigot delays! He must have forgotten my summons."

"I think not; but he might have to wait until Cadet, Varin, Deschenaux, and the rest of them were in a condition fit to travel," answered Philibert with an air of disgust.

"O Philibert! the shame of it! the shame of it! for such thieves to have the right to sit among loyal, honorable men," exclaimed, or rather groaned, the Governor. "They have the real power in New France, and we the empty title and the killing responsibility! Dine with me to-night after the Council, Philibert: I have much to say to you."

"Not to-night, your Excellency! My father has killed the fatted calf for his returned prodigal, and I must dine with him to-night," answered Philibert.

"Right! Be it to-morrow then! Come on Wednesday," replied the Governor. "Your father is a gentleman who carries the principles of true nobility into the walks of trade; you are happy in such a father, Philibert, as he is fortunate in such a son." The Governor bowed to his friend, and rejoined the groups of officers upon the terrace.

A flash, and a column of smoke, white and sudden, rose from the great battery that flanked the Chateau. It was the second signal for the Council to commence. The Count de la Galissoniere, taking the arm of La Corne St. Luc, entered the Castle, and followed by the crowd of officers, proceeded to the great Hall of Council and Audience. The Governor, followed by his secretaries, walked forward to the vice-regal chair, which stood on a dais at the head of a long table covered with crimson drapery. On each side of the table the members of the Council took the places assigned to them in the order of their rank and precedence, but a long array of chairs remained unoccupied. These seats, belonging to the Royal Intendant and the other high officers of the Colony who had not yet arrived to take their places in the Council, stood empty.

The great hall of the Castle of St. Louis was palatial in its dimensions and adornments. Its lofty coved ceiling rested on a cornice of rich frieze of carved work, supported on polished pilasters of oak. The panels of wainscoting upon the walls were surrounded by delicate arabesques, and hung with paintings of historic interest--portraits of the kings, governors, intendants, and ministers of state who had been instrumental in the colonization of New France.

Over the Governor's seat hung a gorgeous escutcheon of the royal arms, draped with a cluster of white flags sprinkled with golden lilies, the emblems of French sovereignty in the Colony.

Among the portraits on the walls, besides those of the late and present King,--which hung on each side of the throne,--might be seen the features of Richelieu, who first organized the rude settlements on the St. Lawrence into a body politic--a reflex of feudal France; and of Colbert, who made available its natural wealth and resources by peopling it with the best scions of the motherland, the noblesse and peasantry of Normandy, Brittany, and Aquitaine. There too might be seen the keen, bold features of Cartier, the first discoverer, and of Champlain, the first explorer of the new land and the founder of Quebec. The gallant, restless Louis Buade de Frontenac was pictured there side by side with his fair countess, called by reason of her surpassing loveliness "the divine;" Vaudreuil too, who spent a long life of devotion to his country, and Beauharnais, who nourished its young strength until it was able to resist not only the powerful confederacy of the Five Nations but the still more powerful league of New England and the other English Colonies. There, also, were seen the sharp, intellectual face of Laval, its first bishop, who organized the Church and education in the Colony; and of Talon, wisest of intendants, who devoted himself to the improvement of agriculture, the increase of trade, and the well- being of all the King's subjects in New France. And one more striking portrait was there, worthy to rank among the statesmen and rulers of New France,--the pale, calm, intellectual features of Mere Marie de l'Incarnation, the first superior of the Ursulines of Quebec, who, in obedience to heavenly visions, as she believed, left France to found schools for the children of the new colonists, and who taught her own womanly graces to her own sex, who were destined to become the future mothers of New France.

In marked contrast with the military uniforms of the officers surrounding the council-table were the black robes and tonsured heads of two or three ecclesiastics, who had been called in by the Governor to aid the council with their knowledge and advice. There were the Abbe Metavet, of the Algonquins of the North; Pere Oubal, the Jesuit missionary of the Abenaquais of the East, and his confrere, La Richardie, from the wild tribes of the Far West; but conspicuous among the able and influential missionaries who were the real rulers of the Indian nations allied with France was the famous Sulpicien, Abbe Piquet, "the King's missionary," as he was styled in royal ordinances, and the apostle to the Iroquois, whom he was laboring to convert and bring over to the side of France in the great dispute raised between France and England for supremacy in North America.

Upon the wall behind the vice-regal chair hung a great map, drawn by the bold hand of Abbe Piquet, representing the claims as well as actual possessions of France in America. A broad, red line, beginning in Acadia, traversed the map westerly, taking in Lake Ontario and running southerly along the crests and ridges of the Appalachian Mountains. It was traced with a firm hand down to far- off Louisiana, claiming for France the great valleys of the Ohio, the Mississippi, and the vast territories watered by the Missouri and the Colorado--thus hemming the English in between the walls of the Appalachian range on the west and the seacoast on the east.

The Abbe Piquet had lately, in a canoe, descended the Belle Riviere, as the voyageurs called the noble Ohio. From its source to its junction with the solitary Mississippi the Abbe had planted upon its conspicuous bluffs the ensigns of France, with tablets of lead bearing the fleur- de-lis and the proud inscription, "Manibus date lilia plenis,"--lilies destined, after a fierce struggle for empire, to be trampled into the earth by the feet of the victorious English.

The Abbe, deeply impressed with the dangers that impended over the Colony, labored zealously to unite the Indian nations in a general alliance with France. He had already brought the powerful Algonquins and Nipissings into his scheme, and planted them at Two Mountains as a bulwark to protect the city of Ville Marie. He had created a great schism in the powerful confederacy of the Five Nations by adroitly fanning into a flame their jealousy of English encroachments upon their ancient territory on Lake Ontario; and bands of Iroquois had, not long since, held conference with the Governor of New France, denouncing the English for disregarding their exclusive right to their own country. "The lands we possess," said they at a great council in Ville Marie, "the lands we possess were given to us by the Master of Life, and we acknowledge to hold of no other!"

The Abbe had now strong hopes of perfecting a scheme which he afterwards accomplished. A powerful body of the Iroquois left their villages and castles on the Mohawk and Genesee rivers, and under the guidance of the Abbe settled round the new Fort of La Presentation on the St. Lawrence, and thus barred that way, for the future, against the destructive inroads of their countrymen who remained faithful to the English alliance.

Pending the arrival of the Royal Intendant the members of the Council indulged freely in conversation bearing more or less upon the important matters to be discussed,--the state of the country, the movements of the enemy, and not seldom intermingled remarks of dissatisfaction and impatience at the absence of the Intendant.

The revel at Beaumanoir was well known to them; and eyes flashed and lips curled in open scorn at the well-understood reason of the Intendant's delay.

"My private letters by the Fleur-de-Lis," remarked Beauharnais, "relate, among other Court gossip, that orders will be sent out to stop the defensive works at Quebec, and pull down what is built! They think the cost of walls round our city can be better bestowed on political favorites and certain high personages at Court." Beauharnais turned towards the Governor. "Has your Excellency heard aught of this?" asked he.

"Yes! It is true enough, Beauharnais! I also have received communications to that effect!" replied the Governor, with an effort at calmness which ill-concealed the shame and disgust that filled his soul.

There was an indignant stir among the officers, and many lips seemed trembling with speech. The impetuous Rigaud de Vaudreuil broke the fierce silence. He struck his fist heavily on the table.

"Ordered us to stop the building of the walls of Quebec, and to pull down what we have done by virtue of the King's corvee!--did I hear your Excellency right?" repeated he in a tone of utmost incredulity. "The King is surely mad to think of such a thing!"

"Yes, Rigaud! it is as I tell you; but we must respect the royal command, and treat His Majesty's name as becomes loyal servants."

"Ventre saint bleu!--heard ever Canadian or Frenchman such moonshine madness! I repeat it, your Excellency--dismantle Quebec? How in God's name are the King's dominions and the King's subjects to be defended?" Rigaud got warmer. He was fearless, and would, as every one knew, have out his say had the King been present in person. "Be assured, your Excellency, it is not the King who orders that affront to his faithful colony; it is the King's ministers--the King's mistresses--the snuff-box-tapping courtiers at Versailles, who can spend the public money in more elegant ways than in raising up walls round our brave old city! Ancient honor and chivalry of France! what has become of you?"

Rigaud sat down angrily; the emotion he displayed was too much in accord with the feelings of the gallant officers present to excite other than marks of approbation, except among a few personal friends of the Intendant, who took their cue from the avowed wishes of the Court.

"What reason does His Majesty give," asked La Corne St. Luc, "for this singular communication?"

"The only reason given is found in the concluding paragraph of the despatch. I will allow the Secretary to read so much of it, and no more, before the Intendant arrives." The Governor looked up at the great clock in the hall with a grim glance of impatience, as if mentally calling down anything but a blessing upon the head of the loitering Intendant.

"The Count de le Galissoniere ought to know," said the despatch sneeringly, "that works like those of Quebec are not to be undertaken by the governors of colonies, except under express orders from the King; and therefore it is His Majesty's desire that upon the reception of this despatch your Excellency will discontinue the works that have been begun upon Quebec. Extensive fortifications require strong garrisons for their defence, and the King's treasury is already exhausted by the extraordinary expenses of the war in Europe. It cannot at the same time carry on the war in Europe and meet the heavy drafts made upon it from North America."

The Secretary folded the despatch, and sat down without altering a line of his impassive face. Not so the majority of the officers round the table: they were excited, and ready to spring up in their indignation. The King's name restrained them all but Rigaud de Vaudreuil, who impetuously burst out with an oath, exclaiming,-- "They may as well sell New France at once to the enemy, if we are not to defend Quebec! The treasury wants money for the war in Europe forsooth! No doubt it wants money for the war when so much is lavished upon the pimps, panders, and harlots of the Court!"

The Governor rose suddenly, striking the table with his scabbard to stop Rigaud in his rash and dangerous speech.

"Not a word more of comment, Chevalier Rigaud!" said he, with a sharp imperative tone that cut short debate; "not another word! His Majesty's name and those of his ministers must be spoken here respectfully, or not at all! Sit down, Chevalier de Vaudreuil; you are inconsiderate."

"I obey your Excellency--I am, I dare say, inconsiderate! but I am right!" Rigaud's passion was subsiding, but not spent. He obeyed the order, however. He had had his say, and flung himself heavily upon his chair.

"The King's despatch demands respectful and loyal consideration, remarked De Lery, a solid, grave officer of engineers, "and I doubt not that upon a proper remonstrance from this council His Majesty will graciously reconsider his order. The fall of Louisbourg is ominous of the fall of Quebec. It is imperative to fortify the city in time to meet the threatened invasion. The loss of Quebec would be the loss of the Colony; and the loss of the Colony, the disgrace of France and the ruin of our country."

"I cordially agree with the Chevalier de Lery," said La Corne St. Luc; "he has spoken more sense than would be found in a shipload of such despatches as that just read! Nay, your Excellency," continued the old officer, smiling, "I shall not affront my sovereign by believing that so ill-timed a missive came from him! Depend upon it, His Majesty has neither seen nor sanctioned it. It is the work of the minister and his mistresses, not the King's."

"La Corne! La Corne!" The Governor raised his finger with a warning look. "We will not discuss the point further until we are favored with the presence and opinion of the Intendant; he will surely be here shortly!" At this moment a distant noise of shouting was heard in some part of the city.

An officer of the day entered the hall in great haste, and whispered something in the Governor's ear.

"A riot in the streets!" exclaimed the Governor. "The mob attacking the Intendant! You do not say so! Captain Duval, turn out the whole guard at once, and let Colonel St. Remy take the command and clear the way for the Intendant, and also clear the streets of all disturbers."

A number of officers sprang to their feet. "Keep seated, gentlemen! We must not break up the Council," said the Governor. "We are sure to have the Intendant here in a few minutes and to learn the cause of this uproar. It is some trifling affair of noisy habitans, I have no doubt."

Another loud shout, or rather yell, made itself distinctly heard in the council-chamber. "It is the people cheering the Intendant on his way through the city!" remarked La Corne St. Luc, ironically. "Zounds! what a vacarme they make! See what it is to be popular with the citizens of Quebec!"

There was a smile all round the table at La Corne's sarcasm. It offended a few friends of the Intendant, however.

"The Chevalier La Corne speaks boldly in the absence of the Intendant," said Colonel Leboeuf. "A gentleman would give a louis d'or any day to buy a whip to lash the rabble sooner than a sou to win their applause! I would not give a red herring for the good opinion of all Quebec!"

"They say in France, Colonel," replied La Corne de St. Luc, scornfully, "that 'King's chaff is better than other people's corn, and that fish in the market is cheaper than fish in the sea!' I believe it, and can prove it to any gentleman who maintains the contrary!"

There was a laugh at La Corne's allusion to the Marquise de Pompadour, whose original name of Jeanne Poisson, gave rise to infinite jests and sarcasms among the people of low and high degree.

Colonel Leboeuf, choleric as he was, refrained from pressing the quarrel with La Corne St. Luc. He sat sulkily smothering his wrath-- longing to leave the hall and go to the relief of the

Intcndant, but kept against his will by the command of the Governor.

The drums of the main guard beat the assembly. The clash of arms and the tramp of many feet resounded from the court-yard of the Chateau. The members of the Council looked out of the windows as the troops formed in column, and headed by Colonel St. Remy, defiled out of the Castle gate, the thunder of their drums drowning every other sound and making the windows shake as they marched through the narrow streets to the scene of disturbance.

# Chapter XIII: The Chien d'Or

On the Rue Buade, a street commemorative of the gallant Fontenac, stood the large, imposing edifice newly built by the Bourgeois Philibert, as the people of the Colony fondly called Nicholas Jaquin Philibert, the great and wealthy merchant of Quebec and their champion against the odious monopolies of the Grand Company favored by the Intendant.

The edifice was of stone, spacious and lofty, but in style solid, plain, and severe. It was a wonder of architecture in New France and the talk and admiration of the Colony from Tadousac to Ville Marie. It comprised the city residence of the Bourgeois, as well as suites of offices and ware-rooms connected with his immense business.

The house was bare of architectural adornments; but on its facade, blazing in the sun, was the gilded sculpture that so much piqued the curiosity of both citizens and strangers and was the talk of every seigniory in the land. The tablet of the Chien D'or,--the Golden Dog,--with its enigmatical inscription, looked down defiantly upon the busy street beneath, where it is still to be seen, perplexing the beholder to guess its meaning and exciting our deepest sympathies over the tragedy of which it remains the sole sad memorial.

Above and beneath the figure of a couchant dog gnawing the thigh bone of a man is graven the weird inscription, cut deeply in the stone, as if for all future generations to read and ponder over its meaning:

"Je suis un chien qui ronge l'os,
En le rongeant je prends mon repos.
Un temps viendra qui n'est pas venu
Que je mordrai qui m'aura mordu."
1736.

Or in English:

"I am a dog that gnaws his bone,
I couch and gnaw it all alone--
A time will come, which is not yet,
When I'll bite him by whom I'm bit."

The magazines of the Bourgeois Philibert presented not only an epitome but a substantial portion of the commerce of New France. Bales of furs, which had been brought down in fleets of canoes from the wild, almost unknown regions of the Northwest, lay piled up to the beams--skins of the smooth beaver, the delicate otter, black and silver fox, so rich to the eye and silky to the touch that the proudest beauties longed for their possession; sealskins to trim the gowns of portly burgomasters, and ermine to adorn the robes of nobles and kings. The spoils of the wolf, bear, and buffalo, worked to the softness of cloth by the hands of Indian women, were stored for winter wear and to fill the sledges with warmth and comfort when the northwest wind freezes the snow to fine dust and the aurora borealis moves in stately possession, like an army of spear-men, across the northern sky. The harvests of the colonists, the corn, the wool, the flax; the timber, enough to build whole navies, and mighty pines fit to mast the tallest admiral, were stored upon the wharves and in the warehouses of the Bourgeois upon the banks of the St. Lawrence, with iron from the royal forges of the Three Rivers and heaps of ginseng from the forests, a product worth its weight in gold and eagerly exchanged by the Chinese for their teas, silks, and sycee silver.

The stately mansion of Belmont, overlooking the picturesque valley of the St. Charles, was the residence proper of the Bourgeois Philibert, but the shadow that in time falls over every hearth had fallen upon his when the last of his children, his beloved son Pierre, left home to pursue his military studies in France. During Pierre's absence the home at Belmont, although kept up with the same strict attention which the Bourgeois paid to everything under his rule, was not occupied by him. He preferred his city mansion, as more convenient for his affairs, and resided therein. His partner of many years of happy wedded life had been long dead; she left no void in his heart that another could fill, but he kept up a large household for friendship's sake, and was lavish in his hospitality. In secret he was a grave, solitary man, caring for the present only for the sake of the thousands dependent on him--living much with the memory of the dear dead, and much with the hope of the future in his son Pierre.

The Bourgeois was a man worth looking at and, at a glance, one to trust to, whether you sought the strong hand to help, the wise head to counsel, or the feeling heart to sympathize with you. He was tall and strongly knit, with features of a high patrician cast, a noble head, covered thick with grizzly hair--one of those heads so tenacious of life that they never grow bald, but carry to the grave the snows of a hundred years. His quick gray eyes caught your meaning ere it was half spoken. A nose and chin, moulded with beauty and precision, accentuated his handsome face. His lips were grave even in their smile, for gaiety was rarely a guest in the heart of the Bourgeois--a man keenly susceptible to kindness, but strong in resentments and not to be placated without the fullest atonement.

The Bourgeois sat by the table in his spacious, well-furnished drawing-room, which overlooked the Rue Buade and gave him a glimpse of the tall, new Cathedral and the trees and gardens of the Seminary. He was engaged in reading letters and papers just arrived from France by the frigate, rapidly extracting their contents and pencilling on their margins memos, for further reference to his clerks.

The only other occupant of the room was a very elderly lady, in a black gown of rigid Huguenot fashion. A close white cap, tied under her chin, set off to the worst advantage her sharp, yet kindly, features. Not an end of ribbon or edge of lace could be seen to point to one hair-breadth of indulgence in the vanities of the world by this strict old Puritan, who, under this unpromising exterior, possessed the kindliest heart in Christendom. Her dress, if of rigid severity, was of saintly purity, and almost pained the eye with its precision and neatness. So fond are we of some freedom from over-much care as from over-much righteousness, that a stray tress, a loose ribbon, a little rent even, will relieve the eye and hold it with a subtle charm. Under the snow white hair of Dame Rochelle--for she it was, the worthy old housekeeper and ancient governess of the House of Philibert--you saw a kind, intelligent face. Her dark eyes betrayed her Southern origin, confirmed by her speech, which, although refined by culture, still retained the soft intonation and melody of her native Languedoc.

Dame Rochelle, the daughter of an ardent Calvinist minister, was born in the fatal year of the revocation of the Edict of Nantes, when Louis XIV. undid the glorious work of Henri IV., and covered France with persecution and civil war, filling foreign countries with the elect of her population, her industry, and her wealth, exiled in the name of religion.

Dame Rochelle's childhood had passed in the trying scenes of the great persecution, and in the succeeding civil wars of the Cevennes she lost all that was nearest and dearest to her--her father, her brothers, her kindred nearly all, and lastly, a gallant gentleman of Dauphiny to whom she was betrothed. She knelt beside him at his place of execution--or martyrdom, for he died for his faith--and holding his hands in hers, pledged her eternal fidelity to his memory, and faithfully kept it all her life.

The Count de Philibert, elder brother of the Bourgeois, was an officer of the King; he witnessed this sad scene, took pity upon the hapless girl, and gave her a home and protection with his family in the Chateau of Philibert, where she spent the rest of her life until the Bourgeois succeeded to his childless brother. In the ruin of his house she would not consent to leave them, but followed their fortunes to New France. She had been the faithful friend and companion of the wife of the Bourgeois and the educator of his children, and was now, in her old age, the trusted friend and manager of his household. Her days were divided between the exercises of religion and the practical duties of life. The light that illumined her, though flowing through the narrow window of a narrow creed, was still light of divine origin. It satisfied her faith, and filled her with resignation, hope, and comfort.

Her three studies were the Bible, the hymns of Marot, and the sermons of the famous Jurieu. She had listened to the prophecies of Grande Marie, and had even herself been breathed upon on the top of Mount Peira by the Huguenot prophet, De Serre.

Good Dame Rochelle was not without a feeling that at times the spiritual gift she had received when a girl made itself manifest by intuitions of the future, which were, after all, perhaps only emanations of her natural good sense and clear intellect--the foresight of a pure mind.

The wasting persecutions of the Calvinists in the mountains of the Cevennes drove men and women wild with desperate fanaticism. De Serre had an immense following. He assumed to impart the Holy Spirit and the gift of tongues by breathing upon the believers. The refugees carried his doctrines to England, and handed down their singular ideas to modern times; and a sect may still be found which believes in the gift of tongues and practises the power of prophesying, as taught originally in the Cevennes.

The good dame was not reading this morning, although the volume before her lay open. Her glasses lay upon the page, and she sat musing by the open window, seldom looking out, however, for her thoughts were chiefly inward. The return of Pierre Philibert, her foster child, had filled her with joy and thankfulness, and she was pondering in her mind the details of a festival which the Bourgeois intended to give in honor of the return of his only son.

The Bourgeois had finished the reading of his packet of letters, and sat musing in silence. He too was intently thinking of his son. His face was filled with the satisfaction of old Simeon when he cried, out of the fulness of his heart, "Domine! nunc dimittis!"

"Dame Rochelle," said he. She turned promptly to the voice of her master, as she ever insisted on calling him. "Were I superstitious, I should fear that my great joy at Pierre's return might be the prelude to some great sorrow."

"God's blessing on Pierre!" said she, "he can only bring joy to this house. Thank the Lord for what He gives and what He takes! He took Pierre, a stripling from his home, and returns him a great man, fit to ride at the King's right hand and to be over his host like Benaiah, the son of Jehoiada, over the host of Solomon."

"Grand merci for the comparison, dame!" said the Bourgeois, smiling, as he leaned back in his chair. "But Pierre is a Frenchman, and would prefer commanding a brigade in the army of the Marshal de Saxe to being over the host of King Solomom. But," continued he, gravely, "I am strangely happy to-day, Deborah,"--he was wont to call her Deborah when very earnest,--"and I will not anticipate any mischief to mar my happiness. Pshaw! It is only the reaction of over-excited feelings. I am weak in the strength of my joy."

"The still, small voice speaks to us in that way, master, to remind us to place our trust in Heaven, not on earth, where all is transitory and uncertain; for if a man live many years, and rejoice in them all, let him remember the days of darkness, for they are many! We are no strangers to the vanity and shadows of human life, master! Pierre's return is like sunshine breaking through the clouds. God is pleased if we bask in the sunshine when he sends it."

"Right, dame! and so we will! The old walls of Belmont shall ring with rejoicing over the return of their heir and future owner."

The dame looked up delightedly at the remark of the Bourgeois. She knew he had destined Belmont as a residence for Pierre; but the thought suggested in her mind was, perhaps, the same which the Bourgeois had mused upon when he gave expression to a certain anxiety.

"Master," said she, "does Pierre know that the Chevalier Bigot was concerned in the false accusations against you, and that it was he, prompted by the Cardinal and the Princess de Carignan, who enforced the unjust decree of the Court?"

"I think not, Deborah. I never told Pierre that Bigot was ever more than the avocat du Roi in my persecution. It is what troubles me amidst my joy. If Pierre knew that the Intendant had been my false accuser on the part of the Cardinal, his sword would not rest a day in its scabbard without calling Bigot to a bloody account. Indeed, it is all I myself can do to refrain. When I met him for the first time here, in the Palace gate, I knew him again and looked him full in the eyes, and he knew me. He is a bold hound, and glared back at me without shrinking. Had he smiled I should have struck him; but we passed in silence, with a salute as mortal as enemies ever gave each other. It is well, perhaps, I wore not my sword that day, for I felt my passion rising--a thing I abhor. Pierre's young blood would not remain still if he knew the Intendant as I know him. But I dare not tell him! There would be bloodshed at once, Deborah!"

"I fear so, master! I trembled at Bigot in the old land! I tremble at him here, where he is more powerful than before. I saw him passing one day. He stopped to read the inscription of the Golden Dog. His face was the face of a fiend, as he rode hastily away. He knew well how to interpret it."

"Ha! you did not tell me that before, Deborah!" The Bourgeois rose, excitedly. "Bigot read it all, did he? I hope every letter of it was branded on his soul as with red-hot iron!"

"Dear master, that is an unchristian saying, and nothing good can come of it. 'Vengeance is mine, saith the Lord!' Our worst enemies are best left in His hands."

The dame was proceeding in a still more moralizing strain, when a noise arose in the street from a crowd of persons, habitans for the most part, congregated round the house. The noise increased to such a degree that they stopped their conversation, and both the dame and the Bourgeois looked out of the window at the increasing multitude that had gathered in the street.

The crowd had come to the Rue Buade to see the famous tablet of the Golden Dog, which was talked of in every seigniory in New France; still more, perhaps, to see the Bourgeois Philibert himself--the great merchant who contended for the rights of the habitans, and who would not yield an inch to the Friponne.

The Bourgeois looked down at the ever-increasing throng,--country people for the most part, with their wives, with not a few citizens, whom he could easily distinguish by their dress and manner. The Bourgeois stood rather withdrawn from the front, so as not to be recognized, for he hated intensely anything like a demonstration, still less an ovation. He could hear many loud voices, however, in the crowd, and caught up the chief topics they discussed with each other.

His eyes rested several times on a wiry, jerking little fellow, whom he recognized as Jean La Marche, the fiddler, a censitaire of the manor of Tilly. He was a well-known character, and had drawn a large circle of the crowd around himself.

"I want to see the Bourgeois Philibert!" exclaimed Jean La Marche. "He is the bravest merchant in New France--the people's friend. Bless the Golden Dog, and curse the Friponne!"

"Hurrah for the Golden Dog, and curse the Friponne!" exclaimed a score of voices; "won't you sing, Jean?"

"Not now; I have a new ballad ready on the Golden Dog, which I shall sing to-night--that is, if you will care to listen to me." Jean said this with a very demure air of mock modesty, knowing well that the reception of a new ballad from him would equal the furor for a new aria from the prima donna of the opera at Paris.

"We will all come to hear it, Jean!" cried they: "but take care of your fiddle or you will get it crushed in the crowd."

"As if I did not know how to take care of my darling baby!" said Jean, holding his violin high above his head. "It is my only child; it will laugh or cry, and love and scold as I bid it, and make everybody else do the same when I touch its heart-strings." Jean had brought his violin under his arm, in place of a spade, to help build up the walls of the city. He had never heard of Amphion, with his lyre, building up the walls of Thebes; but Jean knew that in his violin lay a power of work by other hands, if he played while they labored. "It lightened toil, and made work go merrily as the bells of Tilly at a wedding," said he.

There was immense talk, with plenty of laughter and no thought of mischief, among the crowd. The habitans of en haut and the habitans of en bas commingled, as they rarely did, in a friendly way. Nor was anything to provoke a quarrel said even to the Acadians, whose rude patois was a source of merry jest to the better-speaking Canadians.

The Acadians had flocked in great numbers into Quebec on the seizure of their Province by the English, sturdy, robust, quarrelsome fellows, who went about challenging people in their reckless way,-- Etions pas mon maitre, monsieur?--but all were civil to-day, and tuques were pulled off and bows exchanged in a style of easy politeness that would not have shamed the streets of Paris.

The crowd kept increasing in the Rue Buade. The two sturdy beggars who vigorously kept their places on the stone steps of the barrier, or gateway, of the Basse Ville reaped an unusual harvest of the smallest coin--Max Grimau, an old, disabled soldier, in ragged uniform, which he had worn at the defence of Prague under the Marshal de Belleisle, and blind Bartemy, a mendicant born--the former, loud-tongued and importunate, the latter, silent and only holding out a shaking hand for charity. No Finance Minister or Royal Intendant studied more earnestly the problem how to tax the kingdom than Max and Blind Bartemy how to toll the passers-by, and with less success, perhaps.

To-day was a red-letter day for the sturdy beggars, for the news flew fast that an ovation of some popular kind was to be given to the Bourgeois Philibert. The habitans came trooping up the rough mountain-road that leads from the Basse Ville to the Upper Town; and up the long stairs lined with the stalls of Basque pedlars-- cheating, loquacious varlets--which formed a by-way from the lower regions of the Rue de Champlain--a break-neck thoroughfare little liked by the old and asthmatical, but nothing to the sturdy "climbers," as the habitans called the lads of Quebec, or the light- footed lasses who displayed their trim ankles as they flew up the breezy steps to church or market.

Max Grimau and Blind Bartemy had ceased counting their coins. The passers-by came up in still increasing numbers, until the street, from the barrier of the Basse Ville to the Cathedral, was filled with a noisy, good-humored crowd, without an object except to stare at the Golden Dog and a desire to catch a glimpse of the Bourgeois Philibert.

The crowd had become very dense, when a troop of gentlemen rode at full speed into the

Rue Buade, and after trying recklessly to force their way through, came to a sudden halt in the midst of the surging mass.

The Intendant, Cadet, and Varin had ridden from Beaumanoir, followed by a train of still flushed guests, who, after a hasty purification, had returned with their host to the city--a noisy troop, loquacious, laughing, shouting, as is the wont of men reckless at all times, and still more defiant when under the influence of wine.

"What is the meaning of this rabble, Cadet?" asked Bigot; "they seem to be no friends of yours. That fellow is wishing you in a hot place!" added Bigot, laughing, as he pointed out a habitan who was shouting "A bas Cadet!"

"Nor friends of yours, either," replied Cadet. "They have not recognized you yet, Bigot. When they do, they will wish you in the hottest place of all!"

The Intendant was not known personally to the habitans as were Cadet, Varin, and the rest. Loud shouts and execrations were freely vented against these as soon as they were recognized.

"Has this rabble waylaid us to insult us?" asked Bigot. "But it can hardly be that they knew of our return to the city to-day." The Intendant began to jerk his horse round impatiently, but without avail.

"Oh, no, your Excellency! it is the rabble which the Governor has summoned to the King's corvee. They are paying their respects to the Golden Dog, which is the idol the mob worships just now. They did not expect us to interrupt their devotions, I fancy."

"The vile moutons! their fleece is not worth the shearing!" exclaimed Bigot angrily, at the mention of the Golden Dog, which, as he glanced upwards, seemed to glare defiantly upon him.

"Clear the way, villains!" cried Bigot loudly, while darting his horse into the crowd. "Plunge that Flanders cart-horse of yours into them, Cadet, and do not spare their toes!"

Cadet's rough disposition chimed well with the Intendant's wish. "Come on, Varin, and the rest of you," cried he, "give spur, and fight your way through the rabble."

The whole troop plunged madly at the crowd, striking right and left with their heavy hunting-whips. A violent scuffle ensued; many habitans were ridden down, and some of the horsemen dismounted. The Intendant's Gascon blood got furious: he struck heavily, right and left, and many a bleeding tuque marked his track in the crowd.

The habitans recognized him at last, and a tremendous yell burst out. "Long live the Golden Dog! Down with the Friponne!" while the more bold ventured on the cry, "Down with the Intendant and the thieves of the Grand Company!"

Fortunately for the troop of horsemen the habitans were utterly unarmed; but stones began to be thrown, and efforts were made by them, not always unsuccessfully, to pull the riders off of their horses. Poor Jean La Marche's darling child, his favorite violin, was crushed at the first charge. Jean rushed at the Intendant's bridle, and received a blow which levelled him.

The Intendant and all the troop now drew their swords. A bloody catastrophe seemed impending, when the Bourgeois Philibert, seeing the state of affairs, despatched a messenger with tidings to the Castle of St. Louis, and rushed himself into the street amidst the surging crowd, imploring, threatening, and compelling them to give way.

He was soon recognized and cheered by the people; but even his influence might have failed to calm the fiery passions excited by the Intendant's violence, had not the drums of the approaching soldiery suddenly resounded above the noise of the riot. In a few minutes long files of glittering bayonets were seen streaming down the Rue du Fort. Colonel St. Remi rode at their head, forming his troops in position to charge the crowd. The colonel saw at once the state of affairs, and being a man of judgment, commanded peace before resorting to force. He was at once obeyed. The people stood still and in silence. They fell back quietly before the troops. They had no purpose to resist the authorities--indeed, had no purpose whatever. A way was made by the soldiers, and the Intendant and his friends were extricated from their danger.

They rode at once out of the mob amid a volley of execrations, which were replied to by angry oaths and threats of the cavaliers as they galloped across the Place d'Armes and rode pell-mell into the gateway of the Chateau of St. Louis.

The crowd, relieved of their presence, grew calm; and some of the more timid of them got apprehensive of the consequences of this outrage upon the Royal Intendant. They dispersed quietly, singly or in groups, each one hoping that he might not be called upon to account for the day's proceedings.

The Intendant and his cortege of friends rode furiously into the courtyard of the Chateau of St. Louis, dishevelled, bespattered, and some of them hatless. They dismounted, and foaming with rage, rushed through the lobbies, and with heavy trampling of feet, clattering of scabbards, and a bedlam of angry tongues, burst into the Council Chamber.

The Intendant's eyes shot fire. His Gascon blood was at fever heat, flushing his swarthy cheek like the purple hue of a hurricane. He rushed at once to the council-table, and seeing the Governor, saluted him, but spoke in tones forcibly kept under by a violent effort.

"Your Excellency and gentlemen of the Council will excuse our delay," shouted Bigot, "when I inform you that I, the Royal Intendant of New France, have been insulted, pelted, and my very life threatened by a seditious mob congregated in the streets of Quebec."

"I grieve much, and sympathize with your Excellency's indignation," replied the Governor warmly; "I rejoice you have escaped unhurt. I despatched the troops to your assistance, but have not yet learned the cause of the riot."

"The cause of the riot was the popular hatred of myself for enforcing the royal ordinances, and the seditious example set the rabble by the notorious merchant, Philibert, who is at the bottom of all mischief in New France."

The Governor looked fixedly at the Intendant, as he replied quietly,--"The Sieur Philibert, although a merchant, is a gentleman of birth and loyal principles, and would be the last man alive, I think, to excite a riot. Did you see the Bourgeois, Chevalier?"

"The crowd filled the street near his magazines, cheering for the Bourgeois and the Golden Dog. We rode up and endeavored to force our way through. But I did not see the Bourgeois himself until the disturbance had attained its full proportions."

"And then, your Excellency? Surely the Bourgeois was not encouraging the mob, or participating in the riot?"

"No! I do not charge him with participating in the riot, although the mob were all his friends and partisans. Moreover," said Bigot, frankly, for he felt he owed his safety to the interference of the Bourgeois, "it would be unfair not to acknowledge that he did what he could to protect us from the rabble. I charge Philibert with sowing the sedition that caused the riot, not with rioting himself."

"But I accuse him of both, and of all the mob has done!" thundered Varin, enraged to hear the Intendant speak with moderation and justice. "The house of the Golden Dog is a den of traitors; it ought to be pulled down, and its stones built into a monument of infamy over its owner, hung like a dog in the market-place."

"Silence, Varin!" exclaimed the Governor sternly. "I will not hear the Sieur Philibert spoken of in these injurious terms. The Intendant does not charge him with this disturbance;

neither shall you."

"Par Dieu! you shall not, Varin!" burst in La Corne St. Luc, roused to unusual wrath by the opprobrium heaped upon his friend the Bourgeois; "and you shall answer to me for that you have said!"

"La Corne! La Corne!" The Governor saw a challenge impending, and interposed with vehemence. "This is a Council of War, and not a place for recriminations. Sit down, dear old friend, and aid me to get on with the business of the King and his Colony, which we are here met to consider."

The appeal went to the heart of La Corne. He sat down. "You have spoken generously, Chevalier Bigot, respecting the Bourgeois Philibert," continued the Governor. "I am pleased that you have done so. My Aide-de-Camp, Colonel Philibert, who is just entering the Council, will be glad to hear that your Excellency does justice to his father in this matter."

"The blessing of St. Bennet's boots upon such justice," muttered Cadet to himself. "I was a fool not to run my sword through Philibert when I had the chance."

The Governor repeated to Colonel Philibert what had been said by Bigot.

Colonel Philibert bowed to the Intendant. "I am under obligation to the Chevalier Bigot," said he, "but it astonishes me much that any one should dare implicate my father in such a disturbance. Certainly the Intendant does him but justice."

This remark was not pleasing to Bigot, who hated Colonel Philibert equally with his father. "I merely said he had not participated in the riot, Colonel Philibert, which was true. I did not excuse your father for being at the head of the party among whom these outrages arise. I simply spoke truth, Colonel Philibert. I do not eke out by the inch my opinion of any man. I care not for the Bourgeois Philibert more than for the meanest blue cap in his following."

This was an ungracious speech. Bigot meant it to be such. He repented almost of the witness he had borne to the Bourgeois's endeavors to quell the mob. But he was too profoundly indifferent to men's opinions respecting himself to care to lie.

Colonel Philibert resented the Intendant's sneer at his father. He faced Bigot, saying to him,--"The Chevalier Bigot has done but simple justice to my father with reference to his conduct in regard to the riot. But let the Intendant recollect that, although a merchant, my father is above all things a Norman gentleman, who never swerved a hair-breadth from the path of honor--a gentleman whose ancient nobility would dignify even the Royal Intendant." Bigot looked daggers at this thrust at his own comparatively humble origin. "And this I have further to say," continued Philibert, looking straight in the eyes of Bigot, Varin, and Cadet, "whoever impugns my father's honor impugns mine; and no man, high or low, shall do that and escape chastisement!"

The greater part of the officers seated round the council-board listened with marks of approval to Philibert's vindication of his father. But no one challenged his words, although dark, ominous looks glanced from one to another among the friends of the Intendant. Bigot smothered his anger for the present, however; and to prevent further reply from his followers he rose, and bowing to the Governor, begged His Excellency to open the Council.

"We have delayed the business of the King too long with these personal recriminations," said he. "I shall leave this riot to be dealt with by the King's courts, who will sharply punish both instigators and actors in this outrage upon the royal authority."

These words seemed to end the dispute for the present.

# Chapter XIV: The Council of War

The Council now opened in due form. The Secretary read the royal despatches, which were listened to with attention and respect, although with looks of dissent in the countenances of many of the officers.

The Governor rose, and in a quiet, almost a solemn strain, addressed the Council: "Gentlemen," said he, "from the tenor of the royal despatches just read by the Secretary, it is clear that our beloved New France is in great danger. The King, overwhelmed by the powers in alliance against him, can no longer reinforce our army here. The English fleet is supreme--for the moment only, I hope!" added the Governor, as if with a prevision of his own future triumphs on the ocean. "English troops are pouring into New York and Boston, to combine with the militia of New England and the Middle Colonies in a grand attack upon New France. They have commenced the erection of a great fort at Chouagen on Lake Ontario, to dispute supremacy with our stronghold at Niagara, and the gates of Carillon may ere long have to prove their strength in keeping the enemy out of the Valley of the Richelieu. I fear not for Carillon, gentlemen, in ward of the gallant Count de Lusignan, whom I am glad to see at our Council. I think Carillon is safe.

The Count de Lusignan, a gray-headed officer of soldierly bearing, bowed low to this compliment from the Governor. "I ask the Count de Lusignan," continued the Governor, "what he thinks would result from our withdrawing the garrison from Carillon, as is suggested in the despatches?"

"The Five Nations would be on the Richelieu in a week, and the English in Montreal a month after such a piece of folly on our part!" exclaimed the Count de Lusignan.

"You cannot counsel the abandonment of Carillon then, Count?" A smile played over the face of the Governor, as if he too felt the absurdity of his question.

"Not till Quebec itself fall into the enemy's hands. When that happens, His Majesty will need another adviser in the place of the old Count de Lusignan."

"Well spoken, Count! In your hands Carillon is safe, and will one day, should the enemy assail it, be covered with wreaths of victory, and its flag be the glory of New France."

"So be it, Governor. Give me but the Royal Roussillon and I pledge you neither English, Dutch, nor Iroquois shall ever cross the waters of St. Sacrament."

"You speak like your ancestor the crusader, Count. But I cannot spare the Royal Roussillon. Think you you can hold Carillon with your present garrison?"

"Against all the force of New England. But I cannot promise the same against the English regulars now landing at New York."

"They are the same whom the King defeated at Fontenoy, are they not?" interrupted the Intendant, who, courtier as he was, disliked the tenor of the royal despatches as much as any officer present,-- all the more as he knew La Pompadour was advising peace out of a woman's considerations rather than upholding the glory of France.

"Among them are many troops who fought us at Fontenoy. I learned the fact from an English prisoner whom our Indians brought in from Fort Lydius," replied the Count de Lusignan.

"Well, the more of them the merrier," laughed La Corne St. Luc. "The bigger the prize, the richer they who take it. The treasure- chests of the English will make up for the beggarly packs of the New Englanders. Dried stock fish, and eel-skin garters to drive away the rheumatism, were the usual prizes we got from them down in Acadia!"

"The English of Fontenoy are not such despicable foes," remarked the Chevalier de Lery; "they sufficed to take Louisbourg, and if we discontinue our walls, will suffice to take Quebec."

"Louisbourg was not taken by THEM, but fell through the mutiny of the base Swiss!" replied Bigot, touched sharply by any allusion to that fortress where he had figured so discreditably. "The vile hirelings demanded money of their commander when they should have drawn the blood of the enemy!" added he, angrily.

"Satan is bold, but he would blush in the presence of Bigot," remarked La Corne St. Luc to an Acadian officer seated next him. "Bigot kept the King's treasure, and defrauded the soldiers of their pay: hence the mutiny and the fall of Louisbourg."

"It is what the whole army knows," replied the officer. "But hark! the Abbe Piquet is going to speak. It is a new thing to see clergy in a Council of War!"

"No one has a better right to speak here than the Abbe Piquet," replied La Corne. "No one has sent more Indian allies into the field to fight for New France than the patriotic Abbe."

Other officers did not share the generous sentiments of La Corne St. Luc. They thought it derogatory to pure military men to listen to a priest on the affairs of the war.

"The Marshal de Belleisle would not permit even Cardinal de Fleury to put his red stockings beneath his council-table," remarked a strict martinet of La Serre; "and here we have a whole flock of black gowns darkening our regimentals! What would Voltaire say?"

"He would say that when priests turn soldiers it is time for soldiers to turn tinkers and mend holes in pots, instead of making holes in our enemies," replied his companion, a fashionable freethinker of the day.

"Well, I am ready to turn pedlar any day! The King's army will go to the dogs fast enough since the Governor commissions Recollets and Jesuits to act as royal officers," was the petulant remark of another officer of La Serre.

A strong prejudice existed in the army against the Abbe Piquet for his opposition to the presence of French troops in his Indian missionary villages. They demoralized his neophytes, and many of the officers shared in the lucrative traffic of fire-water to the Indians. The Abbe was zealous in stopping those abuses, and the officers complained bitterly of his over-protection of the Indians.

The famous "King's Missionary," as he was called, stood up with an air of dignity and authority that seemed to assert his right to be present in the Council of War, for the scornful looks of many of the officers had not escaped his quick glance.

The keen black eyes, thin resolute lips, and high swarthy forehead of the Abbe would have well become the plumed hat of a marshal of France. His loose black robe, looped up for freedom, reminded one of a grave senator of Venice whose eye never quailed at any policy, however severe, if required for the safety of the State.

The Abbe held in his hand a large roll of wampum, the tokens of treaties made by him with the Indian nations of the West, pledging their alliance and aid to the great Onontio, as they called the Governor of New France.

"My Lord Governor!" said the Abbe, placing his great roll on the table, "I thank you for admitting the missionaries to the Council. We appear less as churchmen on this occasion than as the King's ambassadors, although I trust that all we have done will redound to God's glory and the spread of religion among the heathen. These belts of wampum are tokens of the treaties we have made with the numerous and warlike tribes of the great West. I bear to the Governor pledges of alliance from the Miamis and Shawnees of the great valley of the Belle Riviere, which they call the Ohio. I am commissioned to tell Onontio that they are at peace with the King and at war with his enemies from this time forth forever. I have set up the arms of France on the banks of the Belle Riviere, and claimed all its lands and waters as the just appanage of our sovereign, from the Alleghanies to the plantations of Louisiana. The Sacs and Foxes, of the Mississippi; the Pottawatomies, Winnebagoes, and Chippewas of a hundred bands who fish in the great rivers and lakes of the West; the warlike Ottawas, who have carried the Algonquin tongue to the banks of Lake Erie,--in short, all enemies of the Iroquois have pledged themselves to take the field whenever the Governor shall require the axe to be dug up and lifted against the English and the Five Nations. Next summer the chiefs of all these tribes will come to Quebec, and ratify in a solemn General Council the wampums they now send by me and the other missionaries, my brothers in the Lord!"

The Abbe, with the slow, formal manner of one long accustomed to the speech and usages of the Indians, unrolled the belts of wampum, many fathoms in length, fastened end to end to indicate the length of the alliance of the various tribes with France. The Abbe interpreted their meaning, and with his finger pointed out the totems or signs manual--usually a bird, beast, or fish--of the chiefs who had signed the roll.

The Council looked at the wampums with intense interest, well knowing the important part these Indians were capable of assuming in the war with England.

"These are great and welcome pledges you bring us, Abbe," said the Governor; "they are proofs at once of your ability and of your zealous labors for the King. A great public duty has been ably discharged by you and your fellow-missionaries, whose loyalty and devotion to France it shall be my pleasure to lay before His Majesty. The Star of Hope glitters in the western horizon, to encourage us under the clouds of the eastern. Even the loss of Acadia, should it be final, will be compensated by the acquisition of the boundless fertile territories of the Belle Riviere and of the Illinois. The Abbe Piquet and his fellow-missionaries have won the hearts of the native tribes of the West. There is hope now, at last, of uniting New France with Louisiana in one unbroken chain of French territory.

"It has been my ambition, since His Majesty honored me with the Government of New France, to acquire possession of those vast territories covered with forests old as time, and in soil rich and fertile as Provence and Normandy.

"I have served the King all my life," continued the Governor, "and served him with honor and even distinction,--permit me to say this much of myself."

He spoke in a frank, manly way, for vanity prompted no part of his speech. "Many great services have I rendered my country, but I feel that the greatest service I could yet do Old France or New would be the planting of ten thousand sturdy peasants and artisans of France in the valley of the far West, to make its forests vocal with the speech of our native land.

"This present war may end suddenly,--I think it will: the late victory at Lawfelt has stricken the allies under the Duke of Cumberland a blow hard as Fontenoy. Rumors of renewed negotiations for peace are flying thick through Europe. God speed the peacemakers, and bless them, I say! With peace comes opportunity. Then, if ever, if France be true to herself and to her heritage in the New World, she will people the valley of the Ohio and secure forever her supremacy in America!

"But our forts far and near must be preserved in the meantime. We must not withdraw from one foot of French territory. Quebec must be walled, and made safe against all attack by land or water. I therefore will join the Council in a respectful remonstrance to the Count de Maurepas, against the inopportune despatches just received from His Majesty. I trust the Royal Intendant will favor the Council now with his opinion on this important matter, and I shall be happy to have the cooperation of His Excellency in measures of such vital consequence to the Colony and to France."

The Governor sat down, after courteously motioning the Intendant to rise and address the Council.

The Intendant hated the mention of peace. His interests, and the interests of his associates of the Grand Company, were all involved in the prolongation of the war.

War enabled the Grand Company to monopolize the trade and military expenditure of New France. The enormous fortunes its members made, and spent with such reckless prodigality, would by peace be dried up in their source; the yoke would be thrown off the people's neck, trade would again free.

Bigot was far-sighted enough to see that clamors would be raised and listened to in the leisure of peace. Prosecutions for illegal exactions might follow, and all the support of his friends at Court might not be able to save him and his associates from ruin--perhaps punishment.

The parliaments of Paris, Rouen, and Brittany still retained a shadow of independence. It was only a shadow, but the fury of Jansenism supplied the lack of political courage, and men opposed the Court and its policy under pretence of defending the rights of the Gallican Church and the old religion of the nation.

Bigot knew he was safe so long as the Marquise de Pompadour governed the King and the kingdom. But Louis XV. was capricious and unfaithful in his fancies; he had changed his mistresses, and his policy with them, many times, and might change once more, to the ruin of Bigot and all the dependents of La Pompadour.

Bigot's letters by the Fleur-de-Lis were calculated to alarm him. A rival was springing up at Court to challenge La Pompadour's supremacy: the fair and fragile Lange Vaubernier had already attracted the King's eye, and the courtiers versed in his ways read the incipient signs of a future favorite.

Little did the laughing Vaubernier forsee the day when, as Madame du Barry, she would reign as Dame du Palais, after the death of La Pompadour. Still less could she imagine that in her old age, in the next reign, she would be dragged to the guillotine, filling the streets of Paris with her shrieks, heard above the howlings of the mob of the Revolution: "Give me life! life! for my repentance! Life! to devote it to the Republic! Life! for the surrender of all my wealth to the nation!" And death, not life, was given in answer to her passionate pleadings.

These dark days were yet in the womb of the future, however. The giddy Vaubernier was at this time gaily catching at the heart of the King, but her procedure filled the mind of Bigot with anxiety: the fall of La Pompadour would entail swift ruin upon himself and associates. He knew it was the intrigues of this girl which had caused La Pompadour suddenly to declare for peace in order to watch the King more surely in his palace. Therefore the word peace and the name of Vaubernier were equally odious to Bigot, and he was perplexed in no small degree how to act.

Moreover, be it confessed that, although a bad man and a corrupt statesman, Bigot was a Frenchman, proud of the national success and glory. While robbing her treasures with one hand, he was ready with his sword in the other to risk life and all in her defence. Bigot was bitterly opposed to English supremacy in North America. The loss of Louisbourg, though much his fault, stung him to the quick, as a triumph of the national enemy; and in those final days of New France, after the fall of Montcalm, Bigot was the last man to yield, and when all others counselled retreat, he would not consent to the surrender of Quebec to the English.

To-day, in the Council of War, Bigot stood up to respond to the appeal of the Governor. He glanced his eye coolly, yet respectfully, over the Council. His raised hand sparkled with gems, the gifts of courtiers and favorites of the King. "Gentlemen of the Council of War!," said he, "I approve with all my heart of the words of His Excellency the Governor, with reference to our fortifications and the maintenance of our frontiers. It is our duty to remonstrate, as councillors of the King in the Colony, against the tenor of the despatches of the Count de Maurepas. The city of Quebec, properly fortified, will be equivalent to an army of men in the field, and the security and defence of the whole Colony depends upon its walls. There can be but one intelligent opinion in the Council on that point, and that opinion should be laid before His Majesty before this despatch be acted on.

"The pressure of the war is great upon us just now. The loss of the fleet of the Marquis de la Jonquiere has greatly interrupted our communications with France, and Canada is left much to its own resources. But Frenchmen! the greater the peril the greater the glory of our defence! And I feel a lively confidence,"--Bigot glanced proudly round the table at the brave, animated faces that turned towards him,--"I feel a lively confidence that in the skill, devotion, and gallantry of the officers I see around this council- table, we shall be able to repel all our enemies, and bear the royal flag to fresh triumphs in North America."

This timely flattery was not lost upon the susceptible minds of the officers present, who testified their approval by vigorous tapping on the table, and cries of "Well said, Chevalier Intendant!"

"I thank, heartily, the venerable Abbe Piquet," continued he, "for his glorious success in converting the warlike savages of the West from foes to fast friends of the King; and as Royal Intendant I pledge the Abbe all my help in the establishment of his proposed fort and mission at La Presentation, for the purpose of dividing the power of the Iroquois."

"That is right well said, if the Devil said it!" remarked La Corne St. Luc, to the Acadian sitting next him. "There is bell-metal in Bigot, and he rings well if properly struck. Pity so clever a fellow should be a knave!"

"Fine words butter no parsnips, Chevalier La Corne," replied the Acadian, whom no eloquence could soften. "Bigot sold Louisbourg!" This was a common but erroneous opinion in Acadia.

"Bigot butters his own parsnips well, Colonel," replied La Corne St. Luc; "but I did not think he would have gone against the despatches! It is the first time he ever opposed Versailles! There must be something in the wind! A screw loose somewhere, or another woman in the case! But hark, he is going on again!"

The Intendant, after examining some papers, entered into a detail of the resources of the Colony, the number of men capable of bearing arms, the munitions and material of war in the magazines, and the relative strength of each district of the Province. He manipulated his figures with the dexterity of an Indian juggler throwing balls; and at the end brought out a totality of force in the Colony capable unaided of prolonging the war for two years, against all the powers of the English.

At the conclusion of this speech Bigot took his seat. He had made a favorable impression upon the Council, and even his most strenuous opponents admitted that on the whole the Intendant had spoken like an able administrator and a true Frenchman.

Cadet and Varin supported their chief warmly. Bad as they were, both in private life and public conduct, they lacked neither shrewdness nor courage. They plundered their country--but were ready to fight for it against the national enemy.

Other officers followed in succession,--men whose names were already familiar, or destined to become glorious in New France,--La Corne, St. Luc, Celeron de Bienville, Colonel Philibert, the Chevalier de Beaujeu, the De Villiers, Le Gardeur de St. Pierre, and De Lery. One and all supported that view of the despatches taken by the Governor and the Intendant. All agreed upon the necessity of completing the walls of Quebec and of making a determined stand at every point of the frontier against the threatened invasion. In case of the sudden patching up of a peace by the negotiators at Aix La Chapelle--as really happened--on the terms of uti possidetis, it was of vital importance that New France hold fast to every shred of her territory, both East and West.

Long and earnest were the deliberations of the Council of War. The reports of the commanding officers from all points of the frontier were carefully studied. Plans of present defence and future conquest were discussed with reference to the strength and weakness of the Colony, and an accurate knowledge of the forces and designs of the English obtained from the disaffected remnant of Cromwellian republicans in New England, whose hatred to the Crown ever outweighed their loyalty, and who kept up a traitorous correspondence, for purposes of their own, with the governors of New France.

The lamps were lit and burned far into the night when the Council broke up. The most part of the officers partook of a cheerful refreshment with the Governor before they retired to their several quarters. Only Bigot and his friends declined to sup with the Governor: they took a polite leave, and rode away from the Chateau to the Palace of the Intendant, where a more gorgeous repast and more congenial company awaited them.

The wine flowed freely at the Intendant's table, and as the irritating events of the day were recalled to memory, the pent-up wrath of the Intendant broke forth. "Damn the Golden Dog and his master both!" exclaimed he. "Philibert shall pay with his life for the outrage of to-day, or I will lose mine! The dirt is not off my coat yet, Cadet!" said he, as he pointed to a spatter of mud upon his breast. "A pretty medal that for the Intendant to wear in a Council of War!"

"Council of War!" replied Cadet, setting his goblet down with a bang upon the polished table, after draining it to the bottom. "I would like to go through that mob again! and I would pull an oar in the galleys of Marseilles rather than be questioned with that air of authority by a botanizing quack like La Galissoniere! Such villainous questions as he asked me about the state of the royal magazines! La Galissoniere had more the air of a judge cross- examining a culprit than of a Governor asking information of a king's officer!"

"True, Cadet!" replied Varin, who was always a flatterer, and who at last saved his ill-gotten wealth by the surrender of his wife as a love-gift to the Duc de Choiseul. "We all have our own injuries to bear. The Intendant was just showing us the spot of dirt cast upon him by the mob; and I ask what satisfaction he has asked in the Council for the insult."

"Ask satisfaction!" replied Cadet with a laugh. "Let him take it! Satisfaction! We will all help him! But I say that the hair of the dog that bit him will alone cure the bite! What I laughed at the most was this morning at Beaumanoir, to see how coolly that whelp of the Golden Dog, young Philibert, walked off with De Repentigny from the very midst of all the Grand Company!"

"We shall lose our young neophyte, I doubt, Cadet! I was a fool to let him go with Philibert!" remarked Bigot.

"Oh, I am not afraid of losing him, we hold him by a strong triple cord, spun by the Devil. No fear of losing him!" answered Cadet, grinning good-humoredly.

"What do you mean, Cadet?" The Intendant took up his cup and drank very nonchalantly, as if he thought little of Cadet's view of the matter. "What triple cord binds De Repentigny to us?"

"His love of wine, his love of gaming, and his love of women--or rather his love of a woman, which is the strongest strand in the string for a young fool like him who is always chasing virtue and hugging vice!"

"Oh! a woman has got him! eh, Cadet? Pray who is she? When once a woman catches a fellow by the gills, he is a dead mackerel: his fate is fixed for good or bad in this world. But who is she, Cadet?--she must be a clever one," said Bigot, sententiously.

"So she is! and she is too clever for young De Repentigny: she has got her pretty fingers in his gills, and can carry her fish to whatever market she chooses!"

"Cadet! Cadet! out with it!" repeated a dozen voices. "Yes, out with it!" repeated Bigot. "We are all companions under the rose, and there are no secrets here about wine or women!"

"Well, I would not give a filbert for all the women born since mother Eve!" said Cadet, flinging a nut-shell at the ceiling. "But this is a rare one, I must confess. Now stop! Don't cry out again 'Cadet! out with it!' and I will tell you! What think you of the fair, jolly Mademoiselle des Meloises?"

"Angelique? Is De Repentigny in love with her?" Bigot looked quite interested now.

"In love with her? He would go on all fours after her, if she wanted him! He does almost, as it is."

Bigot placed a finger on his brow and pondered for a moment. "You say well, Cadet; if De Repentigny has fallen in love with that girl, he is ours forever! Angelique des Meloises never lets go her ox until she offers him up as a burnt offering! The Honnetes Gens will lose one of the best trout in their stream if Angelique has the tickling of him!"

Bigot did not seem to be quite pleased with Cadet's information. He rose from his seat somewhat flushed and excited by this talk respecting Angelique des Meloises. He walked up and down the room a few turns, recovered his composure, and sat down again.

"Come, gentlemen," said he; "too much care will kill a cat! Let us change our talk to a merrier tune; fill up, and we will drink to the loves of De Repentigny and the fair Angelique! I am much mistaken if we do not find in her the dea ex machina to help us out of our trouble with the Honnetes Gens!"

The glasses were filled and emptied. Cards and dice were then called for. The company drew their chairs into a closer circle round the table; deep play, and deeper drinking, set in. The Palais resounded with revelry until the morning sun looked into the great window, blushing red at the scene of drunken riot that had become habitual in the Palace of the Intendant.

# Chapter XV: The Charming Josephine

The few words of sympathy dropped by Bigot in the secret chamber had fallen like manna on the famine of Caroline's starving affections as she remained on the sofa, where she had half fallen, pressing her bosom with her hands as if a new-born thought lay there. "I am sure he meant it!" repeated she to herself. "I feel that his words were true, and for the moment his look and tone were those of my happy maiden days in Acadia! I was too proud then of my fancied power, and thought Bigot's love deserved the surrender of my very conscience to his keeping. I forgot God in my love for him; and, alas for me! that now is part of my punishment! I feel not the sin of loving him! My penitence is not sincere when I can still rejoice in his smile! Woe is me! Bigot! Bigot! unworthy as thou art, I cannot forsake thee! I would willingly die at thy feet, only spurn me not away, nor give to another the love that belongs to me, and for which I have paid the price of my immortal soul!"

She relapsed into a train of bitter reflections as her thoughts reverted to herself. Silence had been gradually creeping through the house. The noisy debauch was at an end. There were trampings, voices, and footfalls for a while longer, and then they died away. Everything was still and silent as the grave. She knew the feast was over and the guests departed; but not whether Bigot had accompanied them.

She sprang up as a low knock came to her door, thinking it was he, come to bid her adieu. It was with a feeling of disappointment she heard the voice of Dame Tremblay saying, "My Lady, may I enter?"

Caroline ran her fingers through her disordered hair, pressed her handkerchief into her eyes, and hastily tried to obliterate every trace of her recent agony. She bade her enter.

Dame Tremblay, shrewd as became the whilom Charming Josephine of Lake Beauport, had a kind heart, nevertheless, under her old- fashioned bodice. She sincerely pitied this young creature who was passing her days in prayer and her nights in weeping, although she might rather blame her in secret for not appreciating better the honor of a residence at Beaumanoir and the friendship of the Intendant.

"I do not think she is prettier than I, when I was the Charming Josephine!" thought the old dame. "I did not despise Beaumanoir in those days, and why should she now? But she will be neither maid nor mistress here long, I am thinking!" The dame saluted the young lady with great deference, and quietly asked if she needed her service.

"Oh! it is you, good dame!"--Caroline answered her own thoughts, rather than the question,--"tell me what makes this unusual silence in the Chateau?"

"The Intendant and all the guests have gone to the city, my Lady: a great officer of the Governor's came to summon them. To be sure, not many of them were fit to go, but after a deal of bathing and dressing the gentlemen got off. Such a clatter of horsemen as they rode out, I never heard before, my Lady; you must have heard them even here!"

"Yes, dame!" replied Caroline, "I heard it; and the Intendant, has he accompanied them?"

"Yes, my Lady; the freshest and foremost cavalier of them all. Wine and late hours never hurt the Intendant. It is for that I praise him, for he is a gallant gentleman, who knows what politeness is to women."

Caroline shrank a little at the thought expressed by the dame. "What causes you to say that?" asked she.

"I will tell, my Lady! 'Dame Tremblay!' said he, just before he left the Chateau. 'Dame Tremblay'--he always calls me that when he is formal, but sometimes when he is merry, he calls me 'Charming Josephine,' in remembrance of my young days, concerning which he has heard flattering stories, I dare say--"

"In heaven's name! go on, dame!" Caroline, depressed as she was, felt the dame's garrulity like a pinch on her impatience. "What said the Intendant to you, on leaving the Chateau?"

"Oh, he spoke to me of you quite feelingly--that is, bade me take the utmost care of the poor lady in the secret chamber. I was to give you everything you wished, and keep off all visitors, if such were your own desire."

A train of powder does not catch fire from a spark more quickly than Caroline's imagination from these few words of the old housekeeper. "Did he say that, good dame? God bless you, and bless him for those words!" Her eyes filled with tears at the thought of his tenderness, which, although half fictitious, she wholly believed.

"Yes, dame," continued she. "It is my most earnest desire to be secluded from all visitors. I wish to see no one but yourself. Have you many visitors--ladies, I mean--at the Chateau?"

"Oh, yes! the ladies of the city are not likely to forget the invitations to the balls and dinners of the bachelor Intendant of New France. It is the most fashionable thing in the city, and every lady is wild to attend them. There is one, the handsomest and gayest of them all, who, they say, would not object even to become the bride of the Intendant."

It was a careless shaft of the old dame's, but it went to the heart of Caroline. "Who is she, good dame?--pray tell me!"

"Oh, my Lady, I should fear her anger, if she knew what I say! She is the most terrible coquette in the city--worshipped by the men, and hated, of course, by the women, who all imitate her in dress and style as much as they possibly can, because they see it takes! But every woman fears for either husband or lover when Angelique des Meloises is her rival."

"Is that her name? I never heard it before, dame!" remarked Caroline, with a shudder. She felt instinctively that the name was one of direful omen to herself.

"Pray God you may never have reason to hear it again," replied Dame Tremblay. "She it was who went to the mansion of Sieur Tourangeau and with her riding-whip lashed the mark of a red cross upon the forehead of his daughter, Cecile, scarring her forever, because she had presumed to smile kindly upon a young officer, a handsome fellow, Le Gardeur de Repentigny-- whom any woman might be pardoned for admiring!" added the old dame, with a natural touch of the candor of her youth. "If Angelique takes a fancy to the Intendant, it will be dangerous for any other woman to stand in her way!"

Caroline gave a frightened look at the dame's description of a possible rival in the Intendant's love. "You know more of her, dame! Tell me all! Tell me the worst I have to learn!" pleaded the poor girl.

"The worst, my Lady! I fear no one can tell the worst of Angelique des Meloises,--at least, would not dare to, although I know nothing bad of her, except that she would like to have all the men to herself, and so spite all the women!"

"But she must regard that young officer with more than common affection, to have acted so savagely to Mademoiselle Tourangeau?" Caroline, with a woman's quickness, had caught at that gleam of hope through the darkness.

"Oh, yes, my Lady! All Quebec knows that Angelique loves the Seigneur de Repentigny, for nothing is a secret in Quebec if more than one person knows it, as I myself well recollect; for when I was the Charming Josephine, my very whispers were all over the city by the next dinner hour, and repeated at every table, as gentlemen cracked their almonds and drank their wine in toasts to the Charming Josephine."

"Pshaw! dame! Tell me about the Seigneur de Repentigny! Does Angelique des Meloises love him, think you?" Caroline's eyes were fixed like stars upon the dame, awaiting her reply.

"It takes women to read women, they say," replied the dame, "and every lady in Quebec would swear that Angelique loves the Seigneur de Repentigny; but I know that, if she can, she will marry the Intendant, whom she has fairly bewitched with her wit and beauty, and you know a clever woman can marry any man she pleases, if she only goes the right way about it: men are such fools!"

Caroline grew faint. Cold drops gathered on her brow. A veil of mist floated before her eyes. "Water! good dame water!" she articulated, after several efforts.

Dame Tremblay ran, and got her a drink of water and such restoratives as were at hand. The dame was profuse in words of sympathy: she had gone through life with a light, lively spirit, as became the Charming Josephine, but never lost the kindly heart that was natural to her.

Caroline rallied from her faintness. "Have you seen what you tell me, dame, or is it but the idle gossip of the city, no truth in it? Oh, say it is the idle gossip of the city! Francois Bigot is not going to marry this lady? He is not so faithless"--to me, she was about to add, but did not.

"So faithless to her, she means, poor soul!" soliliquized the dame. "It is but little you know my gay master if you think he values a promise made to any woman, except to deceive her! I have seen too many birds of that feather not to know a hawk, from beak to claw. When I was the Charming Josephine I took the measure of men's professions, and never was deceived but once. Men's promises are big as clouds, and as empty and as unstable!"

"My good dame, I am sure you have a kind heart," said Caroline, in reply to a sympathizing pressure of the hand. "But you do not know, you cannot imagine what injustice you do the Intendant"--Caroline hesitated and blushed--"by mentioning the report of his marriage with that lady. Men speak untruly of him--"

"My dear Lady, it is what the women say that frightens one! The men are angry, and won't believe it; but the women are jealous, and will believe it even if there be nothing in it! As a faithful servant I ought to have no eyes to watch my master, but I have not failed to observe that the Chevalier Bigot is caught man-fashion, if not husband-fashion, in the snares of the artful Angelique. But may I speak my real opinion to you, my Lady?"

Caroline was eagerly watching the lips of the garrulous dame. She started, brushed back with a stroke of her hand the thick hair that had fallen over her ear,--"Oh, speak all your thoughts, good dame! If your next words were to kill me, speak them!"

"My next words will not harm you, my Lady," said she, with a meaning smile, "if you will accept the opinion of an old woman, who learned the ways of men when she was the Charming Josephinè! You must not conclude that because the Chevalier Intendant admires, or even loves Angelique des Meloises, he is going to marry her. That is not the fashion of these times. Men love beauty, and marry money; love is more plenty than matrimony, both at Paris and at Quebec, at Versailles as well as at Beaumanoir or even at Lake Beauport, as I learned to my cost when I was the Charming Josephine!"

Caroline blushed crimson at the remark of Dame Tremblay. Her voice quivered with emotion. "It is sin to cheapen love like that, dame! And yet I know we have sometimes to bury our love in our heart, with no hope of resurrection."

"Sometimes? Almost always, my Lady! When I was the Charming Josephine--nay, listen, Lady: my story is instructive." Caroline composed herself to hear the dame's recital. "When I was the Charming Josephine of Lake Beauport I began by believing that men were angels sent for the salvation of us women. I thought that love was a better passport than money to lead to matrimony; but I was a fool for my fancy! I had a good score of lovers any day. The gallants praised my beauty, and it was the envy of the city; they flattered me for my wit,--nay, even fought duels for my favor, and called me the Charming Josephine, but not one offered to marry me! At twenty I ran away for love, and was forsaken. At thirty I married for money, and was rid of all my illusions. At forty I came as housekeeper to Beaumanoir, and have lived here comfortably ever since I know what royal intendants are! Old Hocquart wore night- caps in the daytime, took snuff every minute, and jilted a lady in France because she had not the dower of a duchess to match his hoards of wealth! The Chevalier Bigot's black eye and jolly laugh draw after him all the girls of the city, but not one will catch him! Angelique des Meloises is first in his favor, but I see it is as clear as print in the eye of the Intendant that he will never marry her-- and you will prevent him, my Lady!"

"I? I prevent him!" exclaimed Caroline in amazement. "Alas! good dame, you little know how lighter than thistledown floating on the wind is my influence with the Intendant."

"You do yourself injustice, my Lady. Listen! I never saw a more pitying glance fall from the eye of man than the Intendant cast upon you one day when he saw you kneeling in your oratory unconscious of his presence. His lips quivered, and a tear gathered under his thick eyelashes as he silently withdrew. I heard him mutter a blessing upon you, and curses upon La Pompadour for coming between him and his heart's desire. I was a faithful servant and kept my counsel. I could see, however, that the Intendant thought more of the lovely lady of Beaumanoir than of all the ambitious demoiselles of Quebec."

Caroline sprang up, and casting off the deep reserve she had maintained, threw her arms round the neck of Dame Tremblay, and half choked with emotion, exclaimed,--

"Is that true? good, dear friend of friends! Did the Chevalier Bigot bless me, and curse La Pompadour for coming between him and his heart's desire! His heart's desire! but you do not know--you cannot guess what that means, dame?"

"As if I did not know a man's heart's desire! but I am a woman, and can guess! I was not the Charming Josephine for nothing, good Lady!" replied the dame, smiling, as the enraptured girl laid her fair, smooth cheek upon that of the old housekeeper.

"And did he look so pityingly as you describe, and bless me as I was praying, unwitting of his presence?" repeated she, with a look that searched the dame through and through.

"He did, my Lady; he looked, just then, as a man looks upon a woman whom he really loves. I know how men look when they really love us and when they only pretend to? No deceiving me!" added she. "When I was the Charming Josephine--"

"Ave Maria!" said Caroline, crossing herself with deep devotion, not heeding the dame's reminiscences of Lake Beauport. "Heaven has heard my prayers! I can die happy!"

"Heaven forbid you should die at all, my Lady! You die? The Intendant loves you. I see it in his face that he will never marry Angelique des Meloises. He may indeed marry a great marchioness with her lap full of gold and chateaux--that is, if the King commands him: that is how the grand gentlemen of the Court marry. They wed rank, and love beauty--the heart to one, the hand to another. It would be my way too, were I a man and women so simple as we all are. If a girl cannot marry for love, she will marry for money; and if not for money, she can always marry for spite--I did, when I was the Charming Josephine!"

"It is a shocking and sinful way, to marry without love!" said Caroline, warmly.

"It is better than no way at all!" replied the dame, regretting her remark when she saw her lady's face flush like crimson. The dame's opinions were rather the worse for wear in her long journey through life, and would not be adopted by a jury of prudes. "When I was the Charming Josephine," continued she, "I had the love of half the gallants of Quebec, but not one offered his hand. What was I to do? 'Crook a finger, or love and linger,' as they say in Alencon, where I was born?"

"Fie, dame! Don't say such things!" said Caroline, with a shamed, reproving look. "I would think better of the Intendant." Her gratitude led her to imagine excuses for him. The few words reported to her by Dame Tremblay she repeated with silently moving lips and tender reiteration. They lingered in her ear like the fugue of a strain of music, sung by a choir of angelic spirits. "Those were his very words, dame?" added she again, repeating them-- not for inquiry, but for secret joy.

"His very words, my Lady! But why should the Royal Intendant not have his heart's desire as well as that great lady in France? If any one had forbidden my marrying the poor Sieur Tremblay, for whom I did not care two pins, I would have had him for spite--yes, if I had had to marry him as the crows do, on a tree-top!"

"But no one bade you or forbade you, dame! You were happy that no one came between you and your heart's desire!" replied Caroline.

Dame Tremblay laughed out merrily at the idea. "Poor Giles Tremblay my heart's desire! Listen, Lady, I could no more get that than you could. When I was the Charming Josephine there was but one, out of all my admirers, whom I really cared for, and he, poor fellow, had a wife already! So what was I to do? I threw my line at last in utter despair, and out of the troubled sea I drew the Sieur Tremblay, whom I married, and soon put cosily underground with a heavy tombstone on top of him to keep him down, with this inscription, which you may see for yourself, my Lady, if you will, in the churchyard where he lies:

"'Ci git mon Giles,
Ah! qu'il est bien,
Pour son repos,
Et pour le mien!'

"Men are like my Angora tabby: stroke them smoothly and they will purr and rub noses with you; but stroke them the wrong way and whirr! they scratch your hands and out of the window they fly! When I was the Charming--"

"Oh, good dame, thanks! thanks! for the comfort you have given me!" interrupted Caroline, not caring for a fresh reminiscence of the Charming Josephine. "Leave me, I pray. My mind is in a sad tumult. I would fain rest. I have much to fear, but something also to hope for now," she said, leaning back in her chair in deep and quiet thought.

"The Chateau is very still now, my Lady," replied the dame, "the servants are all worn out with long attendance and fast asleep. Let my Lady go to her own apartments, which are bright and airy. It will be better for her than this dull chamber."

"True, dame!" Caroline rose at the suggestion. "I like not this secret chamber. It suited my sad mood, but now I seem to long for air and sunshine. I will go with you to my own room."

They ascended the winding stair, and Caroline seated herself by the window of her own chamber, overlooking the park and gardens of the Chateau. The huge, sloping forest upon the mountain side, formed, in the distance, with the blue sky above it, a landscape of beauty, upon which her eyes lingered with a sense of freshness and delight.

Dame Tremblay left her to her musings, to go, she said, to rouse up the lazy maids and menservants, to straighten up the confusion of everything in the Chateau after the late long feast.

On the great stair she encountered M. Froumois, the Intendant's valet, a favorite gossip of the dame's, who used to invite him into her snug parlor, where she regaled him with tea and cake, or, if late in the evening, with wine and nipperkins of Cognac, while he poured into her ear stories of the gay life of Paris and the bonnes fortunes of himself and master--for the valet in plush would have disdained being less successful among the maids in the servants' hall than his master in velvet in the boudoirs of their mistresses.

M. Froumois accepted the dame's invitation, and the two were presently engaged in a melee of gossip over the sayings and doings of fashionable society in Quebec.

The dame, holding between her thumb and finger a little china cup of tea well laced, she called it, with Cognac, remarked,--"They fairly run the Intendant down, Froumois: there is not a girl in the city but laces her boots to distraction since it came out that the Intendant admires a neat, trim ankle. I had a trim ankle myself when I was the Charming Josephine, M. Froumois!"

"And you have yet, dame,--if I am a judge," replied Froumois, glancing down with an air of gallantry.

"And you are accounted a judge--and ought to be a good one, Froumois! A gentleman can't live at court as you have done, and learn nothing of the points of a fine woman!" The good dame liked a compliment as well as ever she had done at Lake Beauport in her hey- day of youth and beauty.

"Why, no, dame," replied he; "one can't live at Court and learn nothing! We study the points of fine women as we do fine statuary in the gallery of the Louvre, only the living beauties will compel us to see their best points if they have them!" M. Froumois looked very critical as he took a pinch from the dame's box, which she held out to him. Her hand and wrist were yet unexceptionable, as he could not help remarking.

"But what think you, really, of our Quebec beauties? Are they not a good imitation of Versailles?" asked the dame.

"A good imitation! They are the real porcelain! For beauty and affability Versailles cannot exceed them. So says the Intendant, and so say I!," replied the gay valet. "Why, look you, Dame Tremblay!" continued he, extending his well-ringed fingers, "they do give gentlemen no end of hopes here! We have only to stretch out our ten digits and a ladybird will light on every one of them! It was so at Versailles--it is just so here. The ladies in Quebec do know how to appreciate a real gentleman!"

"Yes, that is what makes the ladies of Ville Marie so jealous and angry," replied the dame; "the King's officers and all the great catches land at Quebec first, when they come out from France, and we take toll of them! We don't let a gentleman of them get up to Ville Marie without a Quebec engagement tacked to his back, so that all Ville Marie can read it, and die of pure spite! I say we, Froumois; but you understand I speak of myself only as the Charming Josephine of Lake Beauport. I must content myself now with telling over my past glories."

"Well dame, I don't know but you are glorious yet! But tell me, what has got over my master to-day? Was the unknown lady unkind? Something has angered him, I am sure!"

"I cannot tell you, Froumois: women's moods are not to be explained, even by themselves." The dame had been sensibly touched by Caroline's confidence in her, and she was too loyal to her sex to repeat even to Froumois her recent conversation with Caroline.

They found plenty of other topics, however, and over the tea and Cognac the dame and valet passed an hour of delightful gossip.

Caroline, left to the solitude of her chamber, sat silently with her hands clasped in her lap. Her thoughts pressed inward upon her. She looked out without seeing the fair landscape before her eyes.

Tears and sorrow she had welcomed in a spirit of bitter penitence for her fault in loving one who no longer regarded her. "I do not deserve any man's regard," murmured she, as she laid her soul on the rack of self-accusation, and wrung its tenderest fibres with the pitiless rigor of a secret inquisitor. She utterly condemned herself while still trying to find some excuse for her unworthy lover. At times a cold half-persuasion, fluttering like a bird in the snow, came over her that Bigot could not be utterly base. He could not thus forsake one who had lost all--name, fame, home, and kindred--for his sake! She clung to the few pitying words spoken by him as a shipwrecked sailor to the plank which chance has thrown in his way. It might float her for a few hours, and she was grateful.

Immersed in these reflections, Caroline sat gazing at the clouds, now transformed into royal robes of crimson and gold--the gorgeous train of the sun filled the western horizon. She raised her pale hands to her head, lifting the mass of dark hair from her temples. The fevered blood, madly coursing, pulsed in her ear like the stroke of a bell.

She remembered a sunset like this on the shores of the Bay of Minas, where the thrush and oriole twittered their even-song before seeking their nests, where the foliage of the trees was all ablaze with golden fire, and a shimmering path of sunlight lay upon the still waters like a glorious bridge leading from themselves to the bright beyond.

On that well-remembered night her heart had yielded to Bigot's pleadings. She had leaned her head upon his bosom, and received the kiss and gave the pledge that bound her to him forever.

The sun kept sinking--the forests on the mountain tops burst into a bonfire of glory. Shadows went creeping up the hill-sides until the highest crest alone flamed out as a beacon of hope to her troubled soul.

Suddenly, like a voice from the spirit world, the faint chime of the bells of Charlebourg floated on the evening breeze: it was the Angelus, calling men to prayer and rest from their daily labor. Sweetly the soft reverberation floated through the forests, up the hill-sides, by plain and river, entering the open lattices of Chateau and cottage, summoning rich and poor alike to their duty of prayer and praise. It reminded men of the redemption of the world by the divine miracle of the incarnation announced by Gabriel, the angel of God, to the ear of Mary blessed among women.

The soft bells rang on. Men blessed them, and ceased from their toils in field and forest. Mothers knelt by the cradle, and uttered the sacred words with emotions such as only mothers feel. Children knelt by their mothers, and learned the story of God's pity in appearing upon earth as a little child, to save mankind from their sins. The dark Huron setting his snares in the forest and the fishers on the shady stream stood still. The voyageur sweeping his canoe over the broad river suspended his oar as the solemn sound reached him, and he repeated the angel's words and went on his way with renewed strength.

The sweet bells came like a voice of pity and consolation to the ear of Caroline. She knelt down, and clasping her hands, repeated the prayer of millions,--

"'Ave Maria! gratia plena.'"

She continued kneeling, offering up prayer after prayer for God's forgiveness, both for herself and for him who had brought her to this pass of sin and misery. "'Mea culpa! Mea maxima culpa!'" repeated she, bowing herself to the ground. "I am the chief of sinners; who shall deliver me from this body of sin and affliction?"

The sweet bells kept ringing. They woke reminiscences of voices of by-gone days. She heard her father's tones, not in anger as he would speak now, but kind and loving as in her days of innocence. She heard her mother, long dead--oh, how happily dead! for she could not die of sorrow now over her dear child's fall. She heard the voices of the fair companions of her youth, who would think shame of her now; and amidst them all, the tones of the persuasive tongue that wooed her maiden love. How changed it all seemed! and yet, as the repetition of two or three notes of a bar of music brings to recollection the whole melody to which it belongs, the few kind words of Bigot, spoken that morning, swept all before them in a drift of hope. Like a star struggling in the mist the faint voice of an angel was heard afar off in the darkness.

The ringing of the Angelus went on. Her heart was utterly melted. Her eyes, long parched, as a spent fountain in the burning desert, were suddenly filled with tears. She felt no longer the agony of the eyes that cannot weep. The blessed tears flowed quietly as the waters of Shiloh, bringing relief to her poor soul, famishing for one true word of affection. Long after the sweet bells ceased their chime Caroline kept on praying for him, and long after the shades of night had fallen over the Chateau of Beaumanoir.

# Chapter XVI: Angelique des Meloises

"Come and see me to-night, Le Gardeur." Angelique des Meloises drew the bridle sharply as she halted her spirited horse in front of the officer of the guard at the St. Louis Gate. "Come and see me to- night: I shall be at home to no one but you. Will you come?"

Had Le Gardeur de Repentigny been ever so laggard and indifferent a lover the touch of that pretty hand, and the glance from the dark eye that shot fire down into his very heart, would have decided him to obey this seductive invitation.

He held her hand as he looked up with a face radiant with joy. "I will surely come, Angelique; but tell me--"

She interrupted him laughingly: "No; I will tell you nothing till you come! So good-by till then."

He would fain have prolonged the interview; but she capriciously shook the reins, and with a silvery laugh rode through the gateway and into the city. In a few minutes she dismounted at her own home, and giving her horse in charge of a groom, ran lightly up the broad steps into the house.

The family mansion of the Des Meloises was a tall and rather pretentious edifice overlooking the fashionable Rue St. Louis.

The house was, by a little artifice on the part of Angelique, empty of visitors this evening. Even her brother, the Chevalier des Meloises, with whom she lived, a man of high life and extreme fashion, was to-night enjoying the more congenial society of the officers of the Regiment de Bearn. At this moment, amid the clash of glasses and the bubbling of wine, the excited and voluble Gascons were discussing in one breath the war, the council, the court, the ladies, and whatever gay topic was tossed from end to end of the crowded mess-table.

"Mademoiselle's hair has got loose and looks like a Huron's," said her maid Lizette, as her nimble fingers rearranged the rich dark- golden locks of Angelique, which reached to the floor as she sat upon her fauteuil.

"No matter, Lizette; do it up a la Pompadour, and make haste. My brain is in as great confusion as my hair. I need repose for an hour. Remember, Lizette, I am at home to no one to-night except the Chevalier de Repentigny."

"The Chevalier called this afternoon, Mademoiselle, and was sorry he did not find you at home," replied Lizette, who saw the eyelashes of her mistress quiver and droop, while a flush deepened for an instant the roseate hue of her cheek.

"I was in the country, that accounts for it! There, my hair will do!" said Angelique, giving a glance in the great Venetian mirror before her. Her freshly donned robe of blue silk, edged with a foam of snowy laces and furbelows, set off her tall figure. Her arms, bare to the elbows, would have excited Juno's jealousy or Homer's verse to gather efforts in praise of them. Her dainty feet, shapely, aspiring, and full of character as her face, were carelessly thrust forward, and upon one of them lay a flossy spaniel, a privileged pet of his fair mistress.

The boudoir of Angelique was a nest of luxury and elegance. Its furnishings and adornings were of the newest Parisian style. A carpet woven in the pattern of a bed of flowers covered the floor. Vases of Sevres and Porcelein, filled with roses and jonquils, stood on marble tables. Grand Venetian mirrors reflected the fair form of their mistress from every point of view--who contemplated herself before and behind with a feeling of perfect satisfaction and sense of triumph over every rival.

A harpsichord occupied one corner of the room, and an elaborate bookcase, well-filled with splendidly bound volumes, another.

Angelique had small taste for reading, yet had made some acquaintance with the literature of the day. Her natural quick parts and good taste enabled her to shine, even in literary conversation. Her bright eyes looked volumes. Her silvery laugh was wiser than the wisdom of a precieuse. Her witty repartees covered acres of deficiencies with so much grace and tact that men were tempted to praise her knowledge no less than her beauty.

She had a keen eye for artistic effects. She loved painting, although her taste was sensuous and voluptuous--character is shown in the choice of pictures as much as in that of books or of companions.

There was a painting of Vanloo--a lot of full-blooded horses in a field of clover; they had broken fence, and were luxuriating in the rich, forbidden pasture. The triumph of Cleopatra over Antony, by Le Brun, was a great favorite with Angelique, because of a fancied, if not a real, resemblance between her own features and those of the famous Queen of Egypt. Portraits of favorite friends, one of them Le Gardeur de Repentigny, and a still more recent acquisition, that of the Intendant Bigot, adorned the walls, and among them was one distinguished for its contrast to all the rest--the likeness, in the garb of an Ursuline, of her beautiful Aunt Marie des Meloises, who, in a fit of caprice some years before, had suddenly forsaken the world of fashion, and retired to a convent.

The proud beauty threw back her thick golden tresses as she scanned her fair face and magnificent figure in the tall Venetian mirror. She drank the intoxicating cup of self-flattery to the bottom as she compared herself, feature by feature, with every beautiful woman she knew in New France. The longer she looked the more she felt the superiority of her own charms over them all. Even the portrait of her aunt, so like her in feature, so different in expression, was glanced at with something like triumph spiced with content.

"She was handsome as I!" cried Angelique. "She was fit to be a queen, and made herself a nun--and all for the sake of a man! I am fit to be a queen too, and the man who raises me nighest to a queen's estate gets my hand! My heart?" she paused a few moments. "Pshaw!" A slight quiver passed over her lips. "My heart must do penance for the fault of my hand!"

Petrified by vanity and saturated with ambition, Angelique retained under the hard crust of selfishness a solitary spark of womanly feeling. The handsome face and figure of Le Gardeur de Repentigny was her beau-ideal of manly perfection. His admiration flattered her pride. His love, for she knew infallibly, with a woman's instinct, that he loved her, touched her into a tenderness such as she felt for no man besides. It was the nearest approach to love her nature was capable of, and she used to listen to him with more than complacency, while she let her hand linger in his warm clasp while the electric fire passed from one to another and she looked into his eyes, and spoke to him in those sweet undertones that win man's hearts to woman's purposes.

She believed she loved Le Gardeur; but there was no depth in the soil where a devoted passion could take firm root. Still she was a woman keenly alive to admiration, jealous and exacting of her suitors, never willingly letting one loose from her bonds, and with warm passions and a cold heart was eager for the semblance of love, although never feeling its divine reality.

The idea of a union with Le Gardeur some day, when she should tire of the whirl of fashion, had been a pleasant fancy of Angelique. She had no fear of losing her power over him: she held him by the very heart-strings, and she knew it. She might procrastinate, play false and loose, drive him to the very verge of madness by her coquetries, but she knew she could draw him back, like a bird held by a silken string. She could excite, if she could not feel, the fire of a passionate love. In her heart she regarded men as beings created for her service, amazement, and sport,--to worship her beauty and adorn it with gifts. She took everything as her due, giving nothing in return. Her love was an empty shell that never held a kernel of real womanly care for any man.

Amid the sunshine of her fancied love for Le Gardeur had come a day of eclipse for him, of fresh glory for her. The arrival of the new Intendant, Bigot, changed the current of Angelique's ambition. His high rank, his fabulous wealth, his connections with the court, and his unmarried state, fanned into a flame the secret aspirations of the proud, ambitious girl. His wit and gallantry captivated her fancy, and her vanity was full fed by being singled out as the special object of the Intendant's admiration.

She already indulged in dreams which regarded the Intendant himself as but a stepping-stone to further greatness. Her vivid fancy, conjured up scenes of royal splendor, where, introduced by the courtly Bigot, princes and nobles would follow in her train and the smiles of majesty itself would distinguish her in the royal halls of Versailles.

Angelique felt she had power to accomplish all this could she but open the way. The name of Bigot she regarded as the open sesame to all greatness. "If women rule France by a right more divine than that of kings, no woman has a better right than I!" said she, gazing into the mirror before her. "The kingdom should be mine, and death to all other pretenders! And what is needed after all?" thought she, as she brushed her golden hair from her temples with a hand firm as it was beautiful. "It is but to pull down the heart of a man! I have done that many a time for my pleasure; I will now do it for my profit, and for supremacy over my jealous and envious sex!"

Angelique was not one to quail when she entered the battle in pursuit of any object of ambition or fancy. "I never saw the man yet," said she, "whom I could not bring to my feet if I willed it! The Chevalier Bigot would be no exception--that is, he would be no exception"--the voice of Angelique fell into a low, hard monotone as she finished the sentence--"were he free from the influence of that mysterious woman at Beaumanoir, who, they say, claims the title of wife by a token which even Bigot may not disregard! Her pleading eyes may draw his compassion where they ought to excite his scorn. But men are fools to woman's faults, and are often held by the very thing women never forgive. While she crouches there like a lioness in my path the chances are I shall never be chatelaine of Beaumanoir--never, until she is gone!"

Angelique fell into a deep fit of musing, and murmured to herself, "I shall never reach Bigot unless she be removed--but how to remove her?"

Ay, that was the riddle of the Sphinx! Angelique's life, as she had projected it, depended upon the answer to that question.

She trembled with a new feeling; a shiver ran through her veins as if the cold breath of a spirit of evil had passed over her. A miner, boring down into the earth, strikes a hidden stone that brings him to a dead stand. So Angelique struck a hard, dark thought far down in the depths of her secret soul. She drew it to the light, and gazed on it shocked and frightened.

"I did not mean that!" cried the startled girl, crossing herself. "Mere de Dieu! I did not conceive a wicked thought like that! I will not! I cannot contemplate that!" She shut her eyes, pressing both hands over them as if resolved not to look at the evil thought that, like a spirit of darkness, came when evoked, and would not depart when bidden. She sprang up trembling in every limb, and supporting herself against a table, seized a gilded carafe and poured out a full goblet of wine, which she drank. It revived her fainting spirit. She drank another, and stood up herself again, laughing at her own weakness.

She ran to the window, and looked out into the night. The bright stars shone overhead; the lights in the street reassured her. The people passing by and the sound of voices brought back her familiar mood. She thought no more of the temptation from which she had not prayed to be delivered, just as the daring skater forgets the depths that underlie the thin ice over which he skims, careless as a bird in the sunshine.

An hour more was struck by the loud clock of the Recollets. The drums and bugles of the garrison sounded the signal for the closing of the gates of the city and the setting of the watch for the night. Presently the heavy tramp of the patrol was heard in the street. Sober bourgeois walked briskly home, while belated soldiers ran hastily to get into their quarters ere the drums ceased beating the tattoo.

The sharp gallop of a horse clattered on the stony pavement, and stopped suddenly at the door. A light step and the clink of a scabbard rang on the steps. A familiar rap followed. Angelique, with the infallible intuition of a woman who recognizes the knock and foostep of her lover from ten thousand others, sprang up and met Le Gardeur de Repentigny as he entered the boudoir. She received him with warmth, even fondness, for she was proud of Le Gardeur and loved him in her secret heart beyond all the rest of her admirers.

"Welcome, Le Gardeur!" exclaimed she, giving both hands in his: "I knew you would come; you are welcome as the returned prodigal!"

"Dear Angelique!" repeated he, after kissing her hands with fervor, "the prodigal was sure to return, he could not live longer on the dry husks of mere recollections."

"So he rose, and came to the house that is full and overflowing with welcome for him! It is good of you to come, Le Gardeur! why have you stayed so long away?" Angelique in the joy of his presence forgot for the moment her meditated infidelity.

A swift stroke of her hand swept aside her flowing skirts to clear a place for him upon the sofa, where he sat down beside her.

"This is kind of you, Angelique," said he, "I did not expect so much condescension after my petulance at the Governor's ball; I was wicked that night--forgive me."

"The fault was more mine, I doubt, Le Gardeur." Angelique recollected how she had tormented him on that occasion by capricious slights, while bounteous of her smiles to others. "I was angry with you because of your too great devotion to Cecile Tourangeau."

This was not true, but Angelique had no scruple to lie to a lover. She knew well that it was only from his vexation at her conduct that Le Gardeur had pretended to renew some long intermitted coquetries with the fair Cecile. "But why were you wicked at all that night?" inquired she, with a look of sudden interest, as she caught a red cast in his eye, that spoke of much dissipation. "You have been ill, Le Gardeur!" But she knew he had been drinking deep and long, to drown vexation, perhaps, over her conduct.

"I have not been ill," replied he; "shall I tell you the truth, Angelique?"

"Always, and all of it! The whole truth and nothing but the truth!" Her hand rested fondly on his; no word of equivocation was possible under that mode of putting her lover to the question. "Tell me why you were wicked that night!"

"Because I loved you to madness, Angelique; and I saw myself thrust from the first place in your heart, and a new idol set up in my stead. That is the truth?"

"That is not the truth!" exclaimed she vehemently; and never will be the truth if I know myself and you. But you don't know women, Le Gardeur," added she, with a smile; "you don't know me, the one woman you ought to know better than that!"

It is easy to recover affection that is not lost. Angelique knew her power, and was not indisposed to excess in the exercise of it. "Will you do something for me, Le Gardeur?" asked she, tapping his fingers coquettishly with her fan.

"Will I not? Is there anything in earth, heaven, or hell, Angelique, I would not do for you if I only could win what I covet more than life?"

"What is that?" Angelique knew full well what he coveted more than life; her own heart began to beat responsively to the passion she had kindled in his. She nestled up closer to his side. "What is that, Le Gardeur?"

"Your love, Angelique! I have no other hope in life if I miss that! Give me your love and I will serve you with such loyalty as never man served woman with since Adam and Eve were created."

It was a rash saying, but Le Gardeur believed it, and Angelique too. Still she kept her aim before her. "If I give you my love," said she, pressing her hand through his thick locks, sending from her fingers a thousand electric fires, "will you really be my knight, my preux chevalier, to wear my colors and fight my battles with all the world?"

"I will, by all that is sacred in man or woman! Your will shall be my law, Angelique; your pleasure, my conscience; you shall be to me all reason and motive for my acts if you will but love me!"

"I do love you, Le Gardeur!" replied she, impetuously. She felt the vital soul of this man breathing on her cheek. She knew he spoke true, but she was incapable of measuring the height and immensity of such a passion. She accepted his love, but she could no more contain the fulness of his overflowing affection than the pitcher that is held to the fountain can contain the stream that gushes forth perpetually.

Angelique was ALMOST carried away from her purpose, however. Had her heart asserted its rightful supremacy--that is, had nature fashioned it larger and warmer--she had there and then thrown herself into his arms and blessed him by the consent he sought. She felt assured that here was the one man God had made for her, and she was cruelly sacrificing him to a false idol of ambition and vanity. The word he pleaded for hovered on her tongue, ready like a bird to leap down into his bosom; but she resolutely beat it back into its iron cage.

The struggle was the old one--old as the race of man. In the losing battle between the false and true, love rarely comes out of that conflict unshorn of life or limb. Untrue to him, she was true to her selfish self. The thought of the Intendant and the glories of life opening to her closed her heart, not to the pleadings of Le Gardeur,--them she loved,--but to the granting of his prayer.

The die was cast, but she still clasped hard his hand in hers, as if she could not let him go. "And will you do all you say, Le Gardeur-- make my will your law, my pleasure your conscience, and let me be to you all reason and motive? Such devotion terrifies me, Le Gardeur?"

"Try me! Ask of me the hardest thing, nay, the wickedest, that imagination can conceive or hands do--and I would perform it for your sake." Le Gardeur was getting beside himself. The magic power of those dark, flashing eyes of hers was melting all the fine gold of his nature to folly.

"Fie!" replied she, "I do not ask you to drink the sea: a small thing would content me. My love is not so exacting as that, Le Gardeur."

"Does your brother need my aid?" asked he. "If he does, he shall have it to half my fortune for your sake!" Le Gardeur was well aware that the prodigal brother of Angelique was in a strait for money, as was usual with him. He had lately importuned Le Gardeur, and obtained a large sum from him.

She looked up with well-affected indignation. "How can you think such a thing, Le

Gardeur? my brother was not in my thought. It was the Intendant I wished to ask you about,--you know him better than I."

This was not true. Angelique had studied the Intendant in mind, person, and estate, weighing him scruple by scruple to the last attainable atom of information. Not that she had sounded the depths of Bigot's soul--there were regions of darkness in his character which no eye but God's ever penetrated. Angelique felt that with all her acuteness she did not comprehend the Intendant.

"You ask what I think of the Intendant?" asked he, surprised somewhat at the question.

"Yes--an odd question, is it not, Le Gardeur?" and she smiled away any surprise he experienced.

"Truly, I think him the most jovial gentleman that ever was in New France," was the reply; "frank and open-handed to his friends, laughing and dangerous to his foes. His wit is like his wine, Angelique: one never tires of either, and no lavishness exhausts it. In a word, I, like the Intendant, I like his wit ,his wine, his friends,--some of them, that is!--but above all, I like you, Angelique, and will be more his friend than ever for your sake, since I have learned his generosity towards the Chevalier des Meloises."

The Intendant had recently bestowed a number of valuable shares in the Grand Company upon the brother of Angelique, making the fortune of that extravagant young nobleman.

"I am glad you will be his friend, if only for my sake," added she, coquettishly. "But some great friends of yours like him not. Your sweet sister Amelie shrank like a sensitive plant at the mention of his name, and the Lady de Tilly put on her gravest look to-day when I spoke of the Chevalier Bigot."

Le Gardeur gave Angelique an equivocal look at mention of his sister. "My sister Amelie is an angel in the flesh," said he. "A man need be little less than divine to meet her full approval; and my good aunt has heard something of the genial life of the Intendant. One may excuse a reproving shake of her noble head."

"Colonel Philibert too! he shares in the sentiments of your aunt and sister, to say nothing of the standing hostility of his father, the Bourgeois," continued Angelique, provoked at Le Gardeur's want of adhesion.

"Pierre Philibert! He may not like the Intendant: he has reason for not doing so; but I stake my life upon his honor--he will never be unjust towards the Intendant or any man." Le Gardeur could not be drawn into a censure of his friend.

Angelique shielded adroitly the stiletto of innuendo she had drawn. "You say right," said she, craftily; "Pierre Philibert is a gentleman worthy of your regard. I confess I have seen no handsomer man in New France. I have been dreaming of one like him all my life! What a pity I saw you first, Le Gardeur!" added she, pulling him by the hair.

"I doubt you would throw me to the fishes were Pierre my rival, Angelique," replied he, merrily; "but I am in no danger: Pierre's affections are, I fancy, forestalled in a quarter where I need not be jealous of his success."

"I shall at any rate not be jealous of your sister, Le Gardeur," said Angelique, raising her face to his, suffused with a blush; "if I do not give you the love you ask for it is because you have it already; but ask no more at present from me--this, at least, is yours," said she, kissing him twice, without prudery or hesitation.

That kiss from those adored lips sealed his fate. It was the first-- better it had been the last, better he had never been born than have drank the poison of her lips.

"Now answer me my questions, Le Gardeur," added she, after a pause of soft blandishments.

Le Gardeur felt her fingers playing with his hair, as, like Delilah, she cut off the seven locks of his strength.

"There is a lady at Beaumanoir; tell me who and what she is, Le Gardeur," said she.

He would not have hesitated to betray the gate of Heaven at her prayer; but, as it happened, Le Gardeur could not give her the special information she wanted as to the particular relation in which that lady stood to the Intendant. Angelique with wonderful coolness talked away, and laughed at the idea of the Intendant's gallantry. But she could get no confirmation of her suspicions from Le Gardeur. Her inquiry was for the present a failure, but she made Le Gardeur promise to learn what he could and tell her the result of his inquiries.

They sat long conversing together, until the bell of the Recollets sounded the hour of midnight. Angelique looked in the face of Le Gardeur with a meaning smile, as she counted each stroke with her dainty finger on his cheek. When finished, she sprang up and looked out of the lattice at the summer night.

The stars were twinkling like living things. Charles's Wain lay inverted in the northern horizon; Bootes had driven his sparkling herd down the slope of the western sky. A few thick tresses of her golden hair hung negligently over her bosom and shoulders. She placed her arm in Le Gardeur's, hanging heavily upon him as she directed his eyes to the starry heavens. The selfish schemes she carried in her bosom dropped for a moment to the ground. Her feet seemed to trample them into the dust, while she half resolved to be to this man all that he believed her to be, a true and devoted woman.

"Read my destiny, Le Gardeur," said she, earnestly. "You are a Seminarist. They say the wise fathers of the Seminary study deeply the science of the stars, and the students all become adepts in it."

"Would that my starry heaven were more propitious, Angelique," replied he, gaily kissing her eyes. "I care not for other skies than these! My fate and fortune are here."

Her bosom heaved with mingled passions. The word of hope and the word of denial struggled on her lips for mastery. Her blood throbbed quicker than the beat of the golden pendule on the marble table; but, like a bird, the good impulse again escaped her grasp.

"Look, Le Gardeur," said she. Her delicate finger pointed at Perseus, who was ascending the eastern heavens: "there is my star. Mere Malheur,--you know her,--she once said to me that that was my natal star, which would rule my life."

Like all whose passions pilot them, Angelique believed in destiny.

Le Gardeur had sipped a few drops of the cup of astrology from the venerable Professor Vallier. Angelique's finger pointed to the star Algol--that strange, mutable star that changes from bright to dark with the hours, and which some believe changes men's hearts to stone.

"Mere Malheur lied!" exclaimed he, placing his arm round her, as if to protect her from the baleful influence. "That cursed star never presided over your birth, Angelique! That is the demon star Algol."

Angelique shuddered, and pressed still closer to him, as if in fear.

"Mere Malheur would not tell me the meaning of that star, but bade me, if a saint, to watch and wait; if a sinner, to watch and pray. What means Algol, Le Gardeur?" she half faltered.

"Nothing for you, love. A fig for all the stars in the sky! Your bright eyes outshine them all in radiance, and overpower them in influence. All the music of the spheres is to me discord compared with the voice of Angelique des Meloises, whom alone I love!"

As he spoke a strain of heavenly harmony arose from the chapel of the Convent of the Ursulines, where they were celebrating midnight service for the safety of New France. Amid the sweet voices that floated up on the notes of the pealing organ was clearly distinguished that of Mere St. Borgia, the aunt of Angelique, who led the choir of nuns. In trills and cadences of divine melody the voice of Mere St. Borgia rose higher and higher, like a spirit mounting the skies. The words were indistinct, but Angelique knew them by heart. She had visited her aunt in the Convent, and had learned the new hymn composed by her for the solemn occasion.

As they listened with quiet awe to the supplicating strain, Angelique repeated to Le Gardeur the words of the hymn as it was sung by the choir of nuns:

"'Soutenez, grande Reine,
Notre pauvre pays!
Il est votre domaine,
Faites fleurir nos lis!
L'Anglais sur nos frontieres
Porte ses etendards;
Exauces nos prieres,
Protegez nos remparts!'"

The hymn ceased. Both stood mute until the watchman cried the hour in the silent street.

"God bless their holy prayers, and good-night and God bless you, Angelique!" said Le Gardeur, kissing her. He departed suddenly, leaving a gift in the hand of Lizette, who courtesied low to him with a smile of pleasure as he passed out, while Angelique leaned out of the window listening to his horse's hoofs until the last tap of them died away on the stony pavement.

She threw herself upon her couch and wept silently. The soft music had touched her feelings. Le Gardeur's love was like a load of gold, crushing her with its weight. She could neither carry it onward nor throw it off. She fell at length into a slumber filled with troubled dreams. She was in a sandy wilderness, carrying a pitcher of clear, cold water, and though dying of thirst she would not drink, but perversely poured it upon the ground. She was falling down into unfathomable abysses and pushed aside the only hand stretched out to save her. She was drowning in deep water and she saw Le Gardeur buffeting the waves to rescue her but she wrenched herself out of his grasp. She would not be saved, and was lost! Her couch was surrounded with indefinite shapes of embryo evil.

She fell asleep at last. When she awoke the sun was pouring in her windows. A fresh breeze shook the trees. The birds sang gaily in the garden. The street was alive and stirring with people.

It was broad day. Angelique des Meloises was herself again. Her day-dream of ambition resumed its power. Her night-dream of love was over. Her fears vanished, her hopes were all alive, and she began to prepare for a possible morning call from the Chevalier Bigot.

## Chapter XVII: Splendide Mendax

Amid the ruins of the once magnificent palace of the Intendant, massive fragments of which still remain to attest its former greatness, there may still be traced the outline of the room where Bigot walked restlessly up and down the morning after the Council of War. The disturbing letters he had received from France on both public and private affairs irritated him, while it set his fertile brain at work to devise means at once to satisfy the Marquise de Pompadour and to have his own way still.

The walls of his cabinet--now bare, shattered, and roofless with the blasts of six score winters--were hung with portraits of ladies and statesmen of the day; conspicuous among which was a fine picture from the pencil of Vanloo of the handsome, voluptuous Marquise de Pompadour.

With a world of faults, that celebrated dame, who ruled France in the name of Louis XV., made some amends by her persistent good nature and her love for art. The painter, the architect, the sculptor, and above all, the men of literature in France, were objects of her sincere admiration, and her patronage of them was generous to profusion. The picture of her in the cabinet of the Intendant had been a work of gratitude by the great artist who painted it, and was presented by her to Bigot as a mark of her friendship and demi-royal favor. The cabinet itself was furnished in a style of regal magnificence, which the Intendant carried into all details of his living.

The Chevalier de Pean, the Secretary and confidential friend of the Intendant, was writing at a table. He looked up now and then with a curious glance as the figure of his chief moved to and fro with quick turns across the room. But neither of them spoke.

Bigot would have been quite content with enriching himself and his friends, and turning out of doors the crowd of courtly sycophants who clamored for the plunder of the Colony. He had sense to see that the course of policy in which he was embarked might eventually ruin New France,--nay, having its origin in the Court, might undermine the whole fabric of the monarchy. He consoled himself, however, with the reflection that it could not be helped. He formed but one link in the great chain of corruption, and one link could not stand alone: it could only move by following those which went before and dragging after it those that came behind. Without debating a useless point of morals, Bigot quietly resigned himself to the service of his masters, or rather mistresses, after he had first served himself.

If the enormous plunder made out of the administration of the war by the great monopoly he had established were suddenly to cease, Bigot felt that his genius would be put to a severe test. But he had no misgivings, because he had no scruples. He was not the man to go under in any storm. He would light upon his feet, as he expressed it, if the world turned upside down.

Bigot suddenly stopped in his walk. His mind had been dwelling upon the great affairs of his Intendancy and the mad policy of the Court of Versailles. A new thought struck him. He turned and looked fixedly at his Secretary.

"De Pean!" said he. "We have not a sure hold of the Chevalier de Repentigny! That young fellow plays fast and loose with us. One who dines with me at the palace and sups with the Philiberts at the Chien d'Or cannot be a safe partner in the Grand Company!"

"I have small confidence in him, either," replied De Pean. "Le Gardeur has too many loose ends of respectability hanging about him to make him a sure hold for our game."

"Just so! Cadet, Varin, and the rest of you, have only half haltered the young colt. His training so far is no credit to you! The way that cool bully, Colonel Philibert, walked off with him out of Beaumanoir, was a sublime specimen of impudence. Ha! Ha! The recollection of it has salted my meat ever since! It was admirably performed! although, egad, I should have liked to run my sword through Philibert's ribs! and not one of you all was man enough to do it for me!"

"But your Excellency gave no hint, you seemed full of politeness towards Philibert," replied De Pean, with a tone that implied he would have done it had Bigot given the hint.

"Zounds! as if I do not know it! But it was provoking to be flouted, so politely too, by that whelp of the Golden Dog! The influence of that Philibert is immense over young De Repentigny. They say he once pulled him out of the water, and is, moreover, a suitor of the sister, a charming girl, De Pean! with no end of money, lands, and family power. She ought to be secured as well as her brother in the interests of the Grand Company. A good marriage with one of our party would secure her, and none of you dare propose, by God!"

"It is useless to think of proposing to her," replied De Pean. "I know the proud minx. She is one of the angelic ones who regard marriage as a thing of Heaven's arrangement. She believes God never makes but one man for one woman, and it is her duty to marry him or nobody. It is whispered among the knowing girls who went to school with her at the Convent,--and the Convent girls do know everything, and something more,--that she always cherished a secret affection for this Philibert, and that she will marry him some day."

"Marry Satan! Such a girl as that to marry a cursed Philibert!" Bigot was really irritated at the information. "I think," said he, "women are ever ready to sail in the ships of Tarshish, so long as the cargo is gold, silver, ivory, apes, and peacocks! It speaks ill for the boasted gallantry of the Grand Company if not one of them can win this girl. If we could gain her over we should have no difficulty with the brother, and the point is to secure him."

"There is but one way I can see, your Excellency." De Pean did not appear to make his suggestion very cheerfully, but he was anxious to please the Intendant.

"How is that?" the Intendant asked sharply. He had not the deepest sense of De Pean's wisdom.

"We must call in woman to fight woman in the interests of the Company," replied the Secretary.

"A good scheme if one could be got to fight and win! But do you know any woman who can lay her fingers on Le Gardeur de Repentigny and pull him out from among the Honnetes Gens?"

"I do, your Excellency. I know the very one can do it," replied De Pean confidently.

"You do! Why do you hesitate then? Have you any arriere pensee that keeps you from telling her name at once?" asked the Intendant impatiently.

"It is Mademoiselle des Meloises. She can do it, and no other woman in New France need try!" replied De Pean.

"Why, she is a clipper, certainly! Bright eyes like hers rule the world of fools--and of wise men, too," added Bigot in a parenthesis. "However, all the world is caught by that bird-lime. I confess I never made a fool of myself but a woman was at the bottom of it. But for one who has tripped me up, I have taken sweet revenge on a thousand. If Le Gardeur be entangled in Nerea's hair, he is safe in our toils. Do you think Angelique is at home, De Pean?"

The Intendant looked up at the clock. It was the usual hour for morning calls in Quebec.

"Doubtless she is at home at this hour, your Excellency," replied De Pean. "But she likes her bed, as other pretty women do, and is practising for the petite levee, like a duchess. I don't suppose she is up!"

"I don't know that," replied Bigot. "A greater runagate in petticoats there is not in the wholc city! I never pass through the streets but I see her."

"Ay, that is because she intends to meet your Excellency!" Bigot looked sharply at De Pean. A new thought flashed in his eyes.

"What! think you she makes a point of it, De Pean?"

"I think she would not go out of the way of your Excellency." De Pean shuffled among his papers, but his slight agitation was noticed by the Intendant.

"Hum! is that your thought, De Pean? Looks she in this quarter?" Bigot meditated with his hand on his chin for a moment or two. "You think she is doubtless at home this morning?" added he.

"It was late when De Repentigny left her last night, and she would have long and pleasant dreams after that visit, I warrant," replied the Secretary.

"How do you know? By St. Picot! You watch her closely, De Pean!"

"I do, your Excellency: I have reason," was the reply.

De Pean did not say what his reason for watching Angelique was; neither did Bigot ask. The Intendant cared not to pry into the personal matters of his friends. He had himself too much to conceal not to respect the secrets of his associates.

"Well, De Pean! I will wait on Mademoiselle des Meloises this morning. I will act on your suggestion, and trust I shall not find her unreasonable."

"I hope your Excellency will not find her unreasonable, but I know you will, for if ever the devil of contradiction was in a woman he is in Angelique des Meloises!" replied De Pean savagely, as if he spoke from some experience of his own.

"Well, I will try to cast out that devil by the power of a still stronger one. Ring for my horse, De Pean!"

The Secretary obeyed and ordered the horse. "Mind, De Pean!" continued the Intendant. "The Board of the Grand Company meet at three for business! actual business! not a drop of wine upon the table, and all sober! not even Cadet shall come in if he shows one streak of the grape on his broad face. There is a storm of peace coming over us, and it is necessary to shorten sail, take soundings, and see where we are, or we may strike on a rock."

The Intendant left the palace attended by a couple of equerries. He rode through the palace gate and into the city. Habitans and citizens bowed to him out of habitual respect for their superiors. Bigot returned their salutations with official brevity, but his dark face broke into sunshine as he passèd ladies and citizens whom he knew as partners of the Grand Company or partizans of his own faction.

As he rode rapidly through the streets many an ill wish followed him, until he dismounted before the mansion of the Des Meloises.

"As I live, it is the Royal Intendant himself," screamed Lizette, as she ran, out of breath, to inform her mistress, who was sitting alone in the summer-house in the garden behind the mansion, a pretty spot tastefully laid out with flower beds and statuary. A thick hedge of privet, cut into fantastic shapes by some disciple of the school of Lenotre, screened it from the slopes that ran up towards the green glacis of Cape Diamond.

Angelique looked beautiful as Hebe the golden-haired, as she sat in the arbor this morning. Her light morning dress of softest texture fell in graceful folds about her exquisite form. She held a Book of Hours in her hand, but she had not once opened it since she sat down. Her dark eyes looked not soft, nor kindly, but bright, defiant, wanton, and even wicked in their expression, like the eyes of an Arab steed, whipped, spurred, and brought to a desperate leap-- it may clear the wall before it, or may dash itself dead against the stones. Such was the temper of

Angelique this morning.

Hard thoughts and many respecting the Lady of Beaumanoir, fond almost savage regret at her meditated rejection of De Repentigny, glittering images of the royal Intendant and of the splendors of Versailles, passed in rapid succession through her brain, forming a phantasmagoria in which she colored everything according to her own fancy. The words of her maid roused her in an instant.

"Admit the Intendant and show him into the garden, Lizette. Now!" said she, "I shall end my doubts about that lady! I will test the Intendant's sincerity,--cold, calculating woman-slayer that he is! It shames me to contrast his half-heartedness with the perfect adoration of my handsome Le Gardeur de Repentigny!"

The Intendant entered the garden. Angelique, with that complete self-control which distinguishes a woman of half a heart or no heart at all, changed her whole demeanor in a moment from gravity to gayety. Her eyes flashed out pleasure, and her dimples went and came, as she welcomed the Intendant to her arbor.

"A friend is never so welcome as when he comes of his own accord!" said she, presenting her hand to the Intendant, who took it with empressement. She made room for him on the seat beside her, dashing her skirts aside somewhat ostentatiously.

Bigot looked at her admiringly. He thought he had never seen, in painting, statuary, or living form, a more beautiful and fascinating woman.

Angelique accepted his admiration as her due, feeling no thanks, but looking many.

"The Chevalier Bigot does not lose his politeness, however long he absents himself!" said she, with a glance like a Parthian arrow well aimed to strike home.

"I have been hunting at Beaumanoir," replied he extenuatingly; "that must explain, not excuse, my apparent neglect." Bigot felt that he had really been a loser by his absence.

"Hunting! indeed!" Angelique affected a touch of surprise, as if she had not known every tittle of gossip about the gay party and all their doings at the Chateau. "They say game is growing scarce near the city, Chevalier," continued she nonchalantly, "and that a hunting party at Beaumanoir is but a pretty metonomy for a party of pleasure is that true?"

"Quite true, mademoiselle," replied he, laughing. "The two things are perfectly compatible,--like a brace of lovers, all the better for being made one."

"Very gallantly said!" retorted she, with a ripple of dangerous laughter. "I will carry the comparison no farther. Still, I wager, Chevalier, that the game is not worth the hunt."

"The play is always worth the candle, in my fancy," said he, with a glance of meaning; "but there is really good game yet in Beaumanoir, as you will confess, Mademoiselle, if you will honor our party some day with your presence."

"Come now, Chevalier," replied she, fixing him mischievously with her eyes, "tell me, what game do you find in the forest of Beaumanoir?"

"Oh! rabbits, hares, and deer, with now and then a rough bear to try the mettle of our chasseurs."

"What! no foxes to cheat foolish crows? no wolves to devour pretty Red Riding Hoods straying in the forest? Come, Chevalier, there is better game than all that," said she.

"Oh, yes!" he half surmised she was rallying him now--"plenty, but we don't wind horns after them."

"They say," continued she, "there is much fairer game than bird or beast in the forest of Beaumanoir, Chevalier." She went on recklessly, "Stray lambs are picked up by intendants sometimes, and carried tenderly to the Chateau! The Intendant comprehends a gentleman's devoirs to our sex, I am sure."

Bigot understood her now, and gave an angry start. Angelique did not shrink from the temper she had evoked.

"Heavens! how you look, Chevalier!" said she, in a tone of half banter. "One would think I had accused you of murder instead of saving a fair lady's life in the forest; although woman-killing is no murder I believe, by the laws of gallantry, as read by gentlemen-- of fashion."

Bigot rose up with a hasty gesture of impatience and sat down again. After all, he thought, what could this girl know about Caroline de St. Castin? He answered her with an appearance of frankness, deeming that to be the best policy.

"Yes, Mademoiselle, I one day found a poor suffering woman in the forest. I took her to the Chateau, where she now is. Many ladies beside her have been to Beaumanoir. Many more will yet come and go, until I end my bachelordom and place one there in perpetuity as 'mistress of my heart and home,' as the song says."

Angelique could coquette in half-meanings with any lady of honor at Court. "Well, Chevalier, it will be your fault not to find one fit to place there. They walk every street of the city. But they say this lost and found lady is a stranger?"

"To me she is--not to you, perhaps, Mademoiselle!"

The fine ear of Angelique detected the strain of hypocrisy in his speech. It touched a sensitive nerve. She spoke boldly now.

"Some say she is your wife, Chevalier Bigot!" Angelique gave vent to a feeling long pent-up. She who trifled with men's hearts every day was indignant at the least symptom of repayment in kind. "They say she is your wife or, if not your wife, she ought to be, Chevalier,-- and will be, perhaps, one of these fine days, when you have wearied of the distressed damsels of the city."

It had been better for Bigot, better for Angelique, that these two could have frankly understood each other. Bigot, in his sudden admiration of the beauty of this girl, forgot that his object in coming to see her had really been to promote a marriage, in the interests of the Grand Company, between her and Le Gardeur. Her witcheries had been too potent for the man of pleasure. He was himself caught in the net he spread for another. The adroit bird- catching of Angelique was too much for him in the beginning: Bigot's tact and consummate heartlessness with women, might be too much for her in the end. At the present moment he was fairly dazzled with her beauty, spirit, and seductiveness.

"I am a simple quail," thought he, "to be caught by her piping. Par Dieu! I am going to make a fool of myself if I do not take care! Such a woman as this I have not found between Paris and Naples. The man who gets her, and knows how to use her, might be Prime Minister of France. And to fancy it--I came here to pick this sweet chestnut out of the fire for Le Gardeur de Repentigny! Francois Bigot! as a man of gallantry and fashion I am ashamed of you!"

These were his thoughts, but in words he replied, "The lady of Beaumanoir is not my wife, perhaps never will be." Angelique's eager question fell on very unproductive ground.

Angelique repeated the word superciliously. "'Perhaps!' 'Perhaps' in the mouth of a woman is consent half won; in the mouth of a man I know it has a laxer meaning. Love has nothing to say to 'perhaps': it is will or shall, and takes no 'perhaps' though a thousand times repeated!

"And you intend to marry this treasure trove of the forest-- perhaps?" continued Angelique, tapping the ground with a daintier foot than the Intendant had ever seen before.

"It depends much on you, Mademoiselle des Meloises," said he. "Had you been my treasure-trove, there had been no 'perhaps' about it." Bigot spoke bluntly, and to Angelique it sounded like sincerity. Her dreams were accomplished. She trembled with the intensity of her gratification, and felt no repugnance at his familiar address.

The Intendant held out his hand as he uttered the dulcet flattery, and she placed her hand in his, but it was cold and passionless. Her heart did not send the blood leaping into her finger-ends as when they were held in the loving grasp of Le Gardeur.

"Angelique!" said he. It was the first time the Intendant had called her by her name. She started. It was the unlocking of his heart she thought, and she looked at him with a smile which she had practised with infallible effect upon many a foolish admirer.

"Angelique, I have seen no woman like you, in New France or in Old; you are fit to adorn a Court, and I predict you will--if--if--"

"If what, Chevalier?" Her eyes fairly blazed with vanity and pleasure. "Cannot one adorn Courts, at least French Courts, without if's?"

"You can, if you choose to do so," replied he, looking at her admiringly; for her whole countenance flashed intense pleasure at his remark.

"If I choose to do so? I do choose to do so! But who is to show me the way to the Court, Chevalier? It is a long and weary distance from New France."

"I will show you the way, if you will permit me, Angelique: Versailles is the only fitting theatre for the display of beauty and spirit like yours."

Angelique thoroughly believed this, and for a few moments was dazzled and overpowered by the thought of the golden doors of her ambition opened by the hand of the Intendant. A train of images, full-winged and as gorgeous as birds of paradise, flashed across her vision. La Pompadour was getting old, men said, and the King was already casting his eyes round the circle of more youthful beauties in his Court for a successor. "And what woman in the world," thought she, "could vie with Angelique des Meloises if she chose to enter the arena to supplant La Pompadour? Nay, more! If the prize of the King were her lot, she would outdo La Maintenon herself, and end by sitting on the throne."

Angelique was not, however, a milkmaid to say yes before she was asked. She knew her value, and had a natural distrust of the Intendant's gallant speeches. Moreover, the shadow of the lady of Beaumanoir would not wholly disappear. "Why do you say such flattering things to me, Chevalier?" asked she. "One takes them for earnest coming from the Royal Intendant. You should leave trifling to the idle young men of the city, who have no business to employ them but gallanting us women."

"Trifling! By St. Jeanne de Choisy, I was never more in earnest, Mademoiselle!" exclaimed Bigot. "I offer you the entire devotion of my heart." St. Jeanne de Choisy was the sobriquet in the petits appartements for La Pompadour. Angelique knew it very well, although Bigot thought she did not.

"Fair words are like flowers, Chevalier," replied she, "sweet to smell and pretty to look at; but love feeds on ripe fruit. Will you prove your devotion to me if I put it to the test?"

"Most willingly, Angelique!" Bigot thought she contemplated some idle freak that might try his gallantry, perhaps his purse. But she was in earnest, if he was not.

"I ask, then, the Chevalier Bigot that before he speaks to me again of love or devotion, he shall remove that lady, whoever she may be, from Beaumanoir!" Angelique sat erect, and looked at him with a long, fixed look, as she said this.

"Remove that lady from Beaumanoir!" exclaimed he in complete surprise; "surely that poor shadow does not prevent your accepting my devotion, Angelique?"

"Yes, but it does, Chevalier! I like bold men. Most women do, but I did not think that even the Intendant of New France was bold enough to make love to Angelique des Meloises while he kept a wife or mistress in stately seclusion at Beaumanoir!"

Bigot cursed the shrewishness and innate jealousy of the sex, which would not content itself with just so much of a man's favor as he chose to bestow, but must ever want to rule single and alone. "Every woman is a despot," thought he, "and has no mercy upon pretenders to her throne."

"That lady," replied he, "is neither wife nor mistress, Mademoiselle: she sought the shelter of my roof with a claim upon the hospitality of Beaumanoir.

"No doubt"--Angelique's nostril quivered with a fine disdain--"the hospitality of Beaumanoir is as broad and comprehensive as its master's admiration for our sex!" said she.

Bigot was not angry. He gave a loud laugh. "You women are merciless upon each other, Mademoiselle!" said he.

"Men are more merciless to women when they beguile us with insincere professions," replied she, rising up in well-affected indignation.

"Not so, Mademoiselle!" Bigot began to feel annoyed. "That lady is nothing to me," said he, without rising as she had done. He kept his seat.

"But she has been! you have loved her at some time or other! and she is now living on the scraps and leavings of former affection. I am never deceived, Chevalier!" continued she, glancing down at him, a wild light playing under her long eyelashes like the illumined under-edge of a thundercloud.

"But how in St. Picot's name did you arrive at all this knowledge, Mademoiselle?" Bigot began to see that there was nothing for it but to comply with every caprice of this incomprehensible girl if he would carry his point.

"Oh, nothing is easier than for a woman to divine the truth in such matters, Chevalier," said she. "It is a sixth sense given to our sex to protect our weakness: no man can make love to two women but each of them knows instinctively to her finger-tips that he is doing it."

"Surely woman is a beautiful book written in golden letters, but in a tongue as hard to understand as hieroglyphics of Egypt." Bigot was quite puzzled how to proceed with this incomprehensible girl.

"Thanks for the comparison, Chevalier," replied she, with a laugh. "It would not do for men to scrutinize us too closely, yet one woman reads another easily as a horn-book of Troyes, which they say is so easy that the children read it without learning."

To boldly set at defiance a man who had boasted a long career of success was the way to rouse his pride, and determine him to overcome her resistance. Angelique was not mistaken. Bigot saw her resolution, and, although it was with a mental reservation to deceive her, he promised to banish Caroline from his chateau.

"It was always my good fortune to be conquered in every passage of arms with your sex, Angelique," said he, at once radiant and submissive. "Sit down by me in token of amity."

She complied without hesitation, and sat down by him, gave him her hand again, and replied with an arch smile, while a thousand inimitable coquetries played about her eyes and lips, "You speak now like an amant magnifique, Chevalier!

"'Quelque fort qu'on s'en defende,
Il y faut venir un jour!'"

"It is a bargain henceforth and forever, Angelique!" said he; "but I am a harder man than you imagine: I give nothing for nothing, and all for everything. Will you consent to aid me and the Grand Company in a matter of importance?"

"Will I not? What a question, Chevalier! Most willingly I will aid you in anything proper for a lady to do!" added she, with a touch of irony.

"I wish you to do it, right or wrong, proper or improper, although there is no impropriety in it. Improper becomes proper if you do it, Mademoiselle!"

"Well, what is it, Chevalier,--this fearful test to prove my loyalty to the Grand Company, and which makes you such a matchless flatterer?"

"Just this, Angelique!" replied he. "You have much influence with the Seigneur de Repentigny?"

Angelique colored up to the eyes. "With Le Gardeur! What of him? I can take no part against the Seigneur de Repentigny;" said she, hastily.

"Against him? For him! We fear much that he is about to fall into the hands of the Honnetes Gens: you can prevent it if you will, Angelique?"

"I have an honest regard for the Seigneur de Repentigny!" said she, more in answer to her own feelings than to the Intendant's remark-- her cheek flushed, her fingers twitched nervously at her fan, which she broke in her agitation and threw the pieces vehemently upon the ground. "I have done harm enough to Le Gardeur I fear," continued she. "I had better not interfere with him any more! Who knows what might result?" She looked up almost warningly at the Intendant.

"I am glad to find you so sincere a friend to Le Gardeur," remarked Bigot, craftily. "You will be glad to learn that our intention is to elevate him to a high and lucrative office in the administration of the Company, unless the Honnetes Gens are before us in gaining full possession of him."

"They shall not be before us if I can prevent it, Chevalier," replied she, warmly. She was indeed grateful for the implied compliment to Le Gardeur. "No one will be better pleased at his good fortune than myself."

"I thought so. It was partly my business to tell you of our intentions towards Le Gardeur."

"Indeed!" replied she, in a tone of pique. "I flattered myself your visit was all on my own account, Chevalier."

"So it was." Bigot felt himself on rather soft ground. "Your brother, the Chevalier des Meloises, has doubtless consulted you upon the plan of life he has sketched out for both of you?"

"My good brother sketches so many plans of life that I really am not certain I know the one you refer to." She guessed what was coming, and held her breath hard until she heard the reply.

"Well, you of course know that his plan of life depends mainly upon an alliance between yourself and the Chevalier de Repentigny."

She gave vent to her anger and disappointment. She rose up suddenly, and, grasping the Intendant's arm fiercely, turned him half round in her vehemence. "Chevalier Bigot! did you come here to propose for me on behalf of Le Gardeur de Repentigny?"

"Pardon me, Mademoiselle; it is no proposal of mine,--on behalf of Le Gardeur. I sanctioned his promotion. Your brother, and the Grand Company generally, would prefer the alliance. I don't!" He said this with a tone of meaning which Angelique was acute enough to see implied Bigot's unwillingness to her marrying any man--but himself, was the addendum she at once placed to his credit. "I regret I mentioned it," continued he, blandly, "if it be contrary to your wishes."

"It is contrary to my wishes," replied she, relaxing her clutch of his arm. "Le Gardeur de Repentigny can speak for himself. I will not allow even my brother to suggest it; still less will I discuss such a subject with the Chevalier Bigot."

"I hope you will pardon me, Mademoiselle--I will not call you Angelique until you are pleased with me again. To be sure, I should never have forgiven you had you conformed to your brother's wishes. It was what I feared might happen, and I--I wished to try you; that was all!"

"It is dangerous trying me, Chevalier," replied she, resuming her seat with some heat. "Don't try me again, or I shall take Le Gardeur out of pure SPITE," she said. Pure love was in her mind, but the other word came from her lips. "I will do all I can to rescue him from the Honnetes Gens, but not by marrying him, Chevalier,--at present."

They seemed to understand each other fully. "It is over with now," said Bigot. "I swear to you, Angelique, I did not mean to offend you,--you cut deep."

"Pshaw!" retorted she, smiling. "Wounds by a lady are easily cured: they seldom leave a mark behind, a month after."

"I don't know that. The slight repulse of a lady's finger--a touch that would not crush a gnat--will sometimes kill a strong man like a sword-stroke. I have known such things to happen," said Bigot.

"Well, happily, my touch has not hurt you, Chevalier. But, having vindicated myself, I feel I owe you reparation. You speak of rescuing Le Gardeur from the Honnetes Gens. In what way can I aid you?"

"In many ways and all ways. Withdraw him from them. The great festival at the Philiberts--when is it to be?"

"To-morrow! See, they have honored me with a special invitation." She drew a note from her pocket. "This is very polite of Colonel Philibert, is it not?" said she.

Bigot glanced superciliously at the note. "Do you mean to go, Angelique?" asked he.

"No; although, had I no feelings but my own to consult, I would certainly go."

"Whose feelings do you consult, Angelique," asked the Intendant, "if not your own?"

"Oh, don't be flattered,--the Grand Company's! I am loyal to the association without respect to persons."

"So much the better," said he. "By the way, it would not be amiss to keep Le Gardeur away from the festival. These Philiberts and the heads of the Honnetes Gens have great sway over him."

"Naturally; they are all his own kith and kin. But I will draw him away, if you desire it. I cannot prevent his going, but I can find means to prevent his staying!" added she, with a smile of confidence in her power.

"That will do, Angelique,--anything to make a breach between them!"

While there were abysses in Bigot's mind which Angelique could not fathom, as little did Bigot suspect that, when Angelique seemed to flatter him by yielding to his suggestions, she was following out a course she had already decided upon in her own mind from the moment she had learned that Cecile Tourangeau was to be at the festival of Belmont, with unlimited opportunities of explanation with Le Gardeur as to her treatment by Angelique.

The Intendant, after some pleasant badinage, rose and took his departure, leaving Angelique agitated, puzzled, and dissatisfied, on the whole, with his visit. She reclined on the seat, resting her head on her hand for a long time,--in appearance the idlest, in reality the busiest, brain of any girl in the city of Quebec. She felt she had much to do,--a great sacrifice to make,--but firmly resolved, at whatever cost, to go through with it; for, after all, the sacrifice was for herself, and not for others.

## Chapter XVIII: The Merovingian Princess

The interior of the Cathedral of St. Marie seemed like another world, in comparison with the noisy, bustling Market Place in front of it.

The garish sunshine poured hot and oppressive in the square outside, but was shorn of its strength as it passed through the painted windows of the Cathedral, filling the vast interior with a cool, dim, religious light, broken by tall shafts of columns, which swelled out into ornate capitals, supporting a lofty ceiling, on which was painted the open heavens with saints and angels adoring the Lord.

A lofty arch of cunning work overlaid with gold, the masterpiece of Le Vasseur, spanned the chancel, like the rainbow round the throne. Lights were burning on the altar, incense went up in spirals to the roof; and through the wavering cloud the saints and angels seemed to look down with living faces upon the crowd of worshippers who knelt upon the broad floor of the church.

It was the hour of Vespers. The voice of the priest was answered by the deep peal of the organ and the chanting of the choir. The vast edifice was filled with harmony, in the pauses of which the ear seemed to catch the sound of the river of life as it flows out of the throne of God and the Lamb.

The demeanor of the crowd of worshippers was quiet and reverential. A few gay groups, however, whose occupation was mainly to see and be seen, exchanged the idle gossip of the day with such of their friends as they met there. The fee of a prayer or two did not seem excessive for the pleasure, and it was soon paid.

The perron outside was a favorite resort of the gallants of fashion at the hour of Vespers, whose practice it was to salute the ladies of their acquaintance at the door by sprinkling their dainty fingers with holy water. Religion combined with gallantry is a form of devotion not quite obsolete at the present day, and at the same place.

The church door was the recognized spot for meeting, gossip, business, love-making, and announcements; old friends stopped to talk over the news, merchants their commercial prospects. It was at once the Bourse and the Royal Exchange of Quebec: there were promulgated, by the brazen lungs of the city crier, royal proclamations of the Governor, edicts of the Intendant, orders of the Court of Justice, vendues public and private,--in short, the life and stir of the city of Quebec seemed to flow about the door of St. Marie as the blood through the heart of a healthy man.

A few old trees, relics of the primeval forest, had been left for shade and ornament in the great Market Place. A little rivulet of clear water ran sparkling down the slope of the square, where every day the shadow of the cross of the tall steeple lay over it like a benediction.

A couple of young men, fashionably dressed, loitered this afternoon near the great door of the Convent in the narrow Street that runs into the great square of the market. They walked about with short, impatient turns, occasionally glancing at the clock of the Recollets, visible through the tall elms that bounded the garden of the Gray Friars. Presently the door of the Convent opened. Half a dozen gaily-attired young ladies, internes or pupils of the Convent, sallied out. They had exchanged their conventual dress for their usual outside attire, and got leave to go out into the world on some errand, real or pretended, for one hour and no more.

They tripped lightly down the broad steps, and were instantly joined by the young men who had been waiting for them. After a hasty, merry hand-shaking, the whole party proceeded in great glee towards the Market Place, where the shops of the mercers and confectioners offered the attractions they sought. They went on purchasing bonbons and ribbons from one shop to another until thcy reached the Cathedral, when a common impulse seized them to see who was there. They flew up the steps and disappeared in the church.

In the midst of their devotions, as they knelt upon the floor, the sharp eyes of the young ladies were caught by gesticulations of the well-gloved hand of the Chevalier des Meloises, as he saluted them across the aisle.

The hurried recitation of an Ave or two had quite satisfied the devotion of the Chevalier, and he looked round the church with an air of condescension, criticizing the music and peering into the faces of such of the ladies as looked up, and many did so, to return his scrutiny.

The young ladies encountered him in the aisle as they left the church before the service was finished. It had long since been finished for him, and was finished for the young ladies also when they had satisfied their curiosity to see who was there and who with whom.

"We cannot pray for you any longer, Chevalier des Meloises!" said one of the gayest of the group; "the Lady Superior has economically granted us but one hour in the city to make our purchases and attend Vespers. Out of that hour we can only steal forty minutes for a promenade through the city, so good-by, if you prefer the church to our company, or come with us and you shall escort two of us. You see we have only a couple of gentlemen to six ladies."

"I much prefer your company, Mademoiselle de Brouague!" replied he gallantly, forgetting the important meeting of the managers of the Grand Company at the Palace. The business, however, was being cleverly transacted without his help.

Louise de Brouague had no great esteem for the Chevalier des Meloises, but, as she remarked to a companion, he made rather a neat walking-stick, if a young lady could procure no better to promenade with.

"We come out in full force to-day, Chevalier," said she, with a merry glance round the group of lively girls. "A glorious sample of the famous class of the Louises, are we not?"

"Glorious! superb! incomparable!" the Chevalier replied, as he inspected them archly through his glass. "But how did you manage to get out? One Louise at a time is enough to storm the city, but six of them at once--the Lady Superior is full of mercy to-day."

"Oh! is she? Listen: we should not have got permission to come out to-day had we not first laid siege to the soft heart of Mere des Seraphins. She it was who interceded for us, and lo! here we are, ready for any adventure that may befall errant demoiselles in the streets of Quebec!"

Well might the fair Louise de Brouague boast of the famous class of "the Louises," all composed of young ladies of that name, distinguished for beauty, rank, and fashion in the world of New France.

Prominent among them at that period was the beautiful, gay Louise de Brouague. In the full maturity of her charms, as the wife of the Chevalier de Lery she accompanied her husband to England after the cession of Canada, and went to Court to pay homage to their new sovereign, George III., when the young king, struck with her grace and beauty, gallantly exclaimed,--

"If the ladies of Canada are as handsome as you, I have indeed made a conquest!"

To escort young ladies, internes of the Convent, when granted permission to go out into the city, was a favorite pastime, truly a labor of love, of the young gallants of that day,--an occupation, if very idle, at least very agreeable to those participating in these stolen promenades, and which have not, perhaps, been altogether discontinued in Quebec even to the present day.

The pious nuns were of course entirely ignorant of the contrivances of their fair pupils to amuse themselves in the city. At any rate they good-naturedly overlooked things they could not quite prevent. They had human hearts still under their snowy wimples, and perhaps did not wholly lack womanly sympathy with the dear girls in their charge.

"Why are you not at Belmont to-day, Chevalier des Meloises?" boldly asked Louise Roy, a fearless little questioner in a gay summer robe. She was pretty, and sprightly as Titania. Her long chestnut hair was the marvel and boast of the Convent and, what she prized more, the admiration of the city. It covered her like a veil down to her knees when she chose to let it down in a flood of splendor. Her deep gray eyes contained wells of womanly wisdom. Her skin, fair as a lily of Artois, had borrowed from the sun five or six faint freckles, just to prove the purity of her blood and distract the eye with a variety of charms. The Merovingian Princess, the long-haired daughter of kings, as she was fondly styled by the nuns, queened it wherever she went by right divine of youth, wit, and beauty.

"I should not have had the felicity of meeting you, Mademoiselle Roy, had I gone to Belmont," replied the Chevalier, not liking the question at all. "I preferred not to go."

"You are always so polite and complimentary," replied she, a trace of pout visible on her pretty lips. "I do not see how any one could stay away who was at liberty to go to Belmont! And the whole city has gone, I am sure! for I see nobody in the street!" She held an eye-glass coquettishly to her eye. "Nobody at all!" repeated she. Her companions accused her afterwards of glancing equivocally at the Chevalier as she made this remark; and she answered with a merry laugh that might imply either assent or denial.

"Had you heard in the Convent of the festival at Belmont, Mademoiselle Roy?" asked he, twirling his cane rather majestically.

"We have heard of nothing else and talked of nothing else for a whole week!" replied she. "Our mistresses have been in a state of distraction trying to stop our incessant whispering in the school instead of minding our lessons like good girls trying to earn good conduct marks! The feast, the ball, the dresses, the company, beat learning out of our heads and hearts! Only fancy, Chevalier," she went on in her voluble manner; "Louise de Beaujeu here was asked to give the Latin name for Heaven, and she at once translated it Belmont!"

"Tell no school tales, Mademoiselle Roy!" retorted Louise de Beaujeu, her black eyes flashing with merriment. "It was a good translation! But who was it stumbled in the Greek class when asked for the proper name of the anax andron, the king of men in the Iliad?" Louise Roy looked archly and said defiantly, "Go on!" "Would you believe it, Chevalier, she replied 'Pierre Philibert!' Mere Christine fairly gasped, but Louise had to kiss the floor as a penance for pronouncing a gentleman's name with such unction."

"And if I did I paid my penance heartily and loudly, as you may recollect, Louise de Beaujeu, although I confess I would have preferred kissing Pierre Philibert himself if I had had my choice!"

"Always her way! won't give in! never! Louise Roy stands by her translation in spite of all the Greek Lexicons in the Convent!" exclaimed Louise de Brouague.

"And so I do, and will; and Pierre Philibert is the king of men, in New France or Old! Ask Amelie de Repentigny!" added she, in a half whisper to her companion.

"Oh, she will swear to it any day!" was the saucy reply of Louise de Brouague. "But without whispering it, Chevalier des Meloises," continued she, "the classes in the Convent have all gone wild in his favor since they learned he was in love with one of our late companions in school. He is the Prince Camaralzaman of our fairy tales."

"Who is that?" The Chevalier spoke tartly, rather. He was excessively annoyed at all this enthusiasm in behalf of Pierre Philibert.

"Nay, I will tell no more fairy tales out of school, but I assure you, if our wishes had wings the whole class of Louises would fly away to Belmont to-day like a flock of ring-doves."

Louise de Brouague noticed the pique of the Chevalier at the mention of Philibert, but in that spirit of petty torment with which her sex avenges small slights she continued to irritate the vanity of the Chevalier, whom in her heart she despised.

His politeness nearly gave way. He was thoroughly disgusted with all this lavish praise of Philibert. He suddenly recollected that he had an appointment at the Palace which would prevent him, he said, enjoying the full hour of absence granted to the Greek class of the Ursulines.

"Mademoiselle Angelique has of course gone to Belmont, if pressing engagements prevent YOU, Chevalier," said Louise Roy. "How provoking it must be to have business to look after when one wants to enjoy life!" The Chevalier half spun round on his heel under the quizzing of Louise's eye-glass.

"No, Angelique has not gone to Belmont," replied he, quite piqued. "She very properly declined to mingle with the Messieurs and Mesdames Jourdains who consort with the Bourgeois Philibert! She was preparing for a ride, and the city really seems all the gayer by the absence of so many commonplace people as have gone out to Belmont."

Louise de Brouague's eyes gave a few flashes of indignation. "Fie, Chevalier! that was naughtily said of you about the good Bourgeois and his friends," exclaimed she, impetuously. "Why, the Governor, the Lady de Tilly and her niece, the Chevalier La Corne St. Luc, Hortense and Claude de Beauharnais, and I know not how many more of the very elite of society have gone to do honor to Colonel Philibert! And as for the girls in the Convent, who you will allow are the most important and most select portion of the community, there is not one of us but would willingly jump out of the window, and do penance on dry bread and salt fish for a month, just for one hour's pleasure at the ball this evening, would we not, Louises?"

Not a Louise present but assented with an emphasis that brought sympathetic smiles upon the faces of the two young chevaliers who had watched all this pretty play.

The Chevalier des Meloises bowed very low. "I regret so much, ladies, to have to leave you! but affairs of State, you know-- affairs of State! The Intendant will not proceed without a full board: I must attend the meeting to-day at the Palace."

"Oh, assuredly, Chevalier," replied Louise Roy. "What would become of the Nation, what would become of the world, nay, what would become of the internes of the Ursulines, if statesmen and warriors and philosophers like you and the Sieurs Drouillon and La Force here (this in a parenthesis, not to scratch the Chevalier too deep), did not take wise counsel for our safety and happiness, and also for the welfare of the nation?"

The Chevalier des Meloises took his departure under this shower of arrows.

The young La Force was as yet only an idle dangler about the city; but in the course of time became a man of wit and energy worthy of his name. He replied gaily,--

"Thanks, Mademoiselle Roy! It is just for sake of the fair internes of the Convent that Drouillon and I have taken up the vocation of statesmen, warriors, philosophers, and friends. We are quite ready to guide your innocent footsteps through the streets of this perilous city, if you are ready to go."

"We had better hasten too!" ejaculated Louise Roy, looking archly through her eye-glass. "I can see Bonhomme Michel peeping round the corner of the Cote de Lery! He is looking after us stray lambs of the flock, Sieur Drouillon!"

Bonhomme Michel was the old watchman and factotum of the monastery. He had a general commission to keep a sharp eye upon the young ladies who were allowed to go out into the city. A pair of horn spectacles usually helped his vision,--sometimes marred it, however, when the knowing gallants slipped a crown into his hand to put in the place of his magnifiers!

Bonhomme Michel placed all his propitiation money--he liked a pious word--in his old leathern sack, which contained the redemption of many a gadding promenade through the streets of Quebec. Whether he reported what he saw this time is not recorded in the Vieux Recit, the old annals of the Convent. But as Louise Roy called him her dear old Cupid, and knew so well how to bandage his eyes, it is probable the good nuns were not informed of the pleasant meeting of the class Louises and the gentlemen who escorted them round the city on the present occasion.

# Chapter XIX: Put Money in Thy Purse

The Chevalier des Meloises, quite out of humor with the merry Louises, picked his way with quick, dainty steps down the Rue du Palais. The gay Louises, before returning to the Convent, resolved to make a hasty promenade to the walls to see the people at work upon them. They received with great contentment the military salutes of the officers of their acquaintance, which they acknowledged with the courtesy of well-trained internes, slightly exaggerated by provoking smiles and mischievous glances which had formed no part of the lessons in politeness taught them by the nuns.

In justice be it said, however, the girls were actuated by a nobler feeling than the mere spirit of amusement--a sentiment of loyalty to France, a warm enthusiasm for their country, drew them to the walls: they wanted to see the defenders of Quebec, to show their sympathy and smile approval upon them.

"Would to heaven I were a man," exclaimed Louise de Brouague, "that I might wield a sword, a spade, anything of use, to serve my country! I shame to do nothing but talk, pray, and suffer for it, while every one else is working or fighting."

Poor girl! she did not foresee a day when the women of New France would undergo trials compared with which the sword stroke that kills the strong man is as the touch of mercy,--when the batteries of Wolfe would for sixty-five days shower shot and shell upon Quebec, and the South shore for a hundred miles together be blazing with the fires of devastation. Such things were mercifully withheld from their foresight, and the light-hearted girls went the round of the works as gaily as they would have tripped in a ballroom.

The Chevalier des Meloises, passing through the Porte du Palais, was hailed by two or three young officers of the Regiment of Bearn, who invited him into the Guard House to take a glass of wine before descending the steep hill. The Chevalier stopped willingly, and entered the well-furnished quarters of the officers of the guard, where a cool flask of Burgundy presently restored him to good humor with himself, and consequently with the world.

"What is up to-day at the Palace?" asked Captain Monredin, a vivacious Navarrois. "All the Gros Bonnets of the Grand Company have gone down this afternoon! I suppose you are going too, Des Meloises?"

"Yes! They have sent for me, you see, on affairs of State--what Penisault calls 'business.' Not a drop of wine on the board! Nothing but books and papers, bills and shipments, money paid, money received! Doit et avoir and all the cursed lingo of the Friponne! I damn the Friponne, but bless her money! It pays, Monredin! It pays better than fur-trading at a lonely outpost in the northwest." The Chevalier jingled a handful of coin in his pocket. The sound was a sedative to his disgust at the idea of trade, and quite reconciled him to the Friponne.

"You are a lucky dog nevertheless, to be able to make it jingle!" said Monredin, "not one of us Bearnois can play an accompaniment to your air of money in both pockets. Here is our famous Regiment of Bearn, second to none in the King's service, a whole year in arrears without pay! Gad! I wish I could go into 'business,' as you call it, and woo that jolly dame, La Friponne!"

"For six months we have lived on trust. Those leeches of Jews, who call themselves Christians, down in the Sault au Matelot, won't cash the best orders in the regiment for less than forty per cent. discount!"

"That is true!" broke in another officer, whose rather rubicund face told of credit somewhere, and the product of credit,--good wine and good dinners generally. "That is true, Monredin! The old curmudgeon of a broker at the corner of the Cul de Sac had the impudence to ask me fifty per cent. discount upon my drafts on Bourdeaux! I agree with Des Meloises there: business may be a good thing for those who handle it, but devil touch their dirty fingers for me!"

"Don't condemn all of them, Emeric," said Captain Poulariez, a quiet, resolute-looking officer. "There is one merchant in the city who carries the principles of a gentleman into the usages of commerce. The Bourgeois Philibert gives cent. per cent. for good orders of the King's officers, just to show his sympathy with the army and his love for France."

"Well, I wish he were paymaster of the forces, that is all, and then I could go to him if I wanted to," replied Monredin.

"Why do you not go to him?" asked Poulariez.

"Why, for the same reason, I suppose, so many others of us do not," replied Monredin. "Colonel Dalquier endorses my orders, and he hates the Bourgeois cordially, as a hot friend of the Intendant ought to do. So you see I have to submit to be plucked of my best pen-feathers by that old fesse-mathieu Penisault at the Friponne!"

"How many of yours have gone out to the great spread at Belmont?" asked Des Meloises, quite weary of commercial topics.

"Par Dieu!" replied Monredin, "except the colonel and adjutant, who stayed away on principle, I think every officer in the regiment, present company excepted--who being on duty could not go, much to their chagrin. Such a glorious crush of handsome girls has not been seen, they say, since our regiment came to Quebec."

"And not likely to have been seen before your distinguished arrival-- eh, Monredin?" ejaculated Des Meloises, holding his glass to be refilled. "That is delicious Burgundy," added he, "I did not think any one beside the Intendant had wine like that."

"That is some of La Martiniere's cargo," replied Poulariex. "It was kind of him, was it not, to remember us poor Bearnois here on the wrong side of the Atlantic?"

"And how earnestly we were praying for that same Burgundy," ejaculated Monredin, "when it came, as if dropped upon us by Providence! Health and wealth to Captain La Martiniere and the good frigate Fleur-de-Lis!"

Another round followed.

"They talk about those Jansenist convulsionnaires at the tomb of Mastcr Paris, which are setting all France by the ears," exclaimed Monredin, "but I say there is nothing so contagious as the drinking of a glass of wine like that."

"And the glass gives us convulsions too, Monredin, if we try it too often, and no miracle about it either," remarked Poulariez.

Monredin looked up, red and puffy, as if needing a bridle to check his fast gait.

"But they say we are to have peace soon. Is that true, Des Meloises?" asked Poulariez. "You ought to know what is under the cards before they are played."

"No, I don't know; and I hope the report is not true. Who wants peace yet? It would ruin the King's friends in the Colony." Des Meloises looked as statesmanlike as he could when delivering this dictum.

"Ruin the King's friends! Who are they, Des Meloises?" asked Poulariez, with a look of well-assumed surprise.

"Why, the associates of the Grand Company, to be sure! What other friends has the King got in New France?"

"Really! I thought he had the Regiment of Bearn for a number of them--to say nothing of the honest people of the Colony," replied Poulariez, impatiently.

"The Honnetes Gens, you mean!" exclaimed Des Meloises. "Well, Poulariez, all I have to say is that if this Colony is to be kept up for the sake of a lot of shopkeepers, wood-choppers, cobblers, and farmers, the sooner the King hands it over to the devil or the English the better!"

Poulariex looked indignant enough; but from the others a loud laugh followed this sally.

The Chevalier des Meloises pulled out his watch. "I must be gone to the Palace," said he. "I dare say Cadet, Varin, and Penisault will have balanced the ledgers by this time, and the Intendant, who is the devil for business on such occasions, will have settled the dividends for the quarter--the only part of the business I care about."

"But don't you help them with the work a little?" asked Poulariez.

"Not I; I leave business to them that have a vocation for it. Besides, I think Cadet, Vargin, and Penisault like to keep the inner ring of the company to themselves." He turned to Emeric: "I hope there will be a good dividend to-night, Emeric," said he. "I owe you some revenge at piquet, do I not?"

"You capoted me last night at the Taverne de Menut, and I had three aces and three kings."

"But I had a quatorze, and took the fishes," replied Des Meloises.

"Well, Chevalier, I shall win them back to-night. I hope the dividend will be good: in that way I too may share in the 'business' of the Grand Company."

"Good-by, Chevalier; remember me to St. Blague!" (This was a familiar sobriquet of Bigot.) "Tis the best name going. If I had an heir for the old chateau on the Adour, I would christen him Bigot for luck."

The Chevalier des Meloises left the officers and proceeded down the steep road that led to the Palace. The gardens were quiet to-day-- a few loungers might be seen in the magnificent alleys, pleached walks, and terraces; beyond these gardens, however, stretched the King's wharves and the magazines of the Friponne. These fairly swarmed with men loading and unloading ships and bateaux, and piling and unpiling goods.

The Chevalier glanced with disdain at the magazines, and flourishing his cane, mounted leisurely the broad steps of the Palace, and was at once admitted to the council-room.

"Better late than never, Chevalier des Meloises!" exclaimed Bigot, carelessly glancing at him as he took a seat at the board, where sat Cadet, Varin, Penisault, and the leading spirits of the Grand Company. "You are in double luck to-day. The business is over, and Dame Friponne has laid a golden egg worth a Jew's tooth for each partner of the Company."

The Chevalier did not notice, or did not care for, the slight touch of sarcasm in the Intendant's tone. "Thanks, Bigot!" drawled he. "My eggs shall be hatched to-night down at Menut's. I expect to have little more left than the shell of it to-morrow."

"Well, never mind! We have considered all that, Chevalier. What one loses another gets. It is all in the family. Look here," continued he, laying his finger upon a page of the ledger that lay open before him, "Mademoiselle Angelique des Meloises is now a shareholder in the Grand Company. The list of high, fair, and noble ladies of the Court who are members of the Company will be honored by the addition of the name of your charming sister."

The Chevalier's eyes sparkled with delight as he read Angelique's name on the book. A handsome sum of five digits stood to her credit. He bowed his thanks with many warm expressions of his sense of the honor done his sister by "placing her name on the roll of the ladies of the Court who honor the Company by accepting a share of its dividends."

"I hope Mademoiselle des Meloises will not refuse this small mark of our respect," observed Bigot, feeling well assured she would not deem it a small one.

"Little fear of that!" muttered Cadet, whose bad opinion of the sex was incorrigible. "The game fowls of Versailles scratch jewels out of every dung-hill, and Angelique des Meloises has longer claws than any of them!"

Cadet's ill-natured remark was either unheard or unheeded; besides, he was privileged to say anything. Des Meloises bowed with an air of perfect complaisance to the Intendant as he answered,--"I guarantee the perfect satisfaction of Angelique with this marked compliment of the Grand Company. She will, I am sure, appreciate the kindness of the Intendant as it deserves."

Cadet and Varin exchanged smiles, not unnoticed by Bigot, who smiled too. "Yes, Chevalier," said he, "the Company gives this token of its admiration for the fairest lady in New France. We have bestowed premiums upon fine flax and fat cattle: why not upon beauty, grace, and wit embodied in handsome women?"

"Angelique will be highly flattered, Chevalier," replied he, "at the distinction. She must thank you herself, as I am sure she will."

"I am happy to try to deserve her thanks," replied Bigot; and, not caring to talk further on the subject,--"what news in the city this afternoon, Chevalier?" asked he; "how does that affair at Belmont go off?"

"Don't know. Half the city has gone, I think. At the Church door, however, the talk among the merchants is that peace is going to be made soon. Is it so very threatening, Bigot?"

"If the King wills it, it is." Bigot spoke carelessly.

"But your own opinion, Chevalier Bigot; what think you of it?"

"Amen! amen! Quod fiat fiatur! Seigny John, the fool of Paris, could enlighten you as well as I could as to what the women at Versailles may decide to do," replied Bigot in a tone of impatience.

"I fear peace will be made. What will you do in that case, Bigot?" asked Des Meloises, not noticing Bigot's aversion to the topic.

"If the King makes it, invitus amabo! as the man said who married the shrew." Bigot laughed mockingly. "We must make the best of it, Des Meloises! and let me tell you privately, I mean to make a good thing of it for ourselves whichever way it turns."

"But what will become of the Company should the war expenditure stop?" The Chevalier was thinking of his dividend of five figures.

"Oh! you should have been here sooner, Des Meloises: you would have heard our grand settlement of the question in every contingency of peace or war."

"Be sure of one thing," continued Bigot, "the Grand Company will not, like the eels of Melun, cry out before they are skinned. What says the proverb, 'Mieux vaut engin que force' (craft beats strength)? The Grand Company must prosper as the first condition of life in New France. Perhaps a year or two of repose may not be amiss, to revictual and reinforce the Colony; and by that time we shall be ready to pick the lock of Bellona's temple again and cry Vive la guerre! Vive la Grande Compagnie! more merrily than ever!"

Bigot's far-reaching intellect forecast the course of events, which remained so much subject to his own direction after the peace of Aix la Chapelle--a peace which in America was never a peace at all, but only an armed and troubled truce between the clashing interests and rival ambitions of the French and English in the New World.

The meeting of the Board of Managers of the Grand Company broke up, and--a circumstance that rarely happened--without the customary debauch. Bigot, preoccupied with his own projects, which reached far beyond the mere interests of the Company, retired to his couch. Cadet, Varin, and Penisault, forming an interior circle of the Friponne, had certain matters to shape for the Company's eye. The rings of corruption in the Grand Company descended, narrower and more black and precipitous, down to the bottom where Bigot sat, the Demiurgos of all.

The Chevalier des Meloises was rather proud of his sister's beauty and cleverness, and in truth a little afraid of her. They lived together harmoniously enough, so long as each allowed the other his or her own way. Both took it, and followed their own pleasures, and were not usually disagreeable to one another, except when Angelique commented on what she called his penuriousness, and he upon her extravagance, in the financial administration of the family of the Des Meloises.

The Chevalier was highly delighted to-day to be able to inform Angelique of her good fortune in becoming a partner of the Friponne and that too by grace of his Excellency the Intendant. The information filled Angelique with delight, not only because it made her independent of her brother's mismanagement of money, but it opened a door to her wildest hopes. In that gift her ambition found a potent ally to enable her to resist the appeal to her heart which she knew would be made to-night by Le Gardeur de Repentigny.

The Chevalier des Meloises had no idea of his sister's own aims. He had long nourished a foolish fancy that, if he had not obtained the hand of the wealthy and beautiful heiress of Repentigny, it was because he had not proposed. Something to-day had suggested the thought that unless he did propose soon his chances would be nil, and another might secure the prize which he had in his vain fancy set down as his own.

He hinted to Angelique to-day that he had almost resolved to marry, and that his projected alliance with the noble and wealthy house of Tilly could be easily accomplished if Angelique would only do her share, as a sister ought, in securing her brother's fortune and happiness.

"How?" asked she, looking up savagely, for she knew well at what her brother was driving.

"By your accepting Le Gardeur without more delay! All the city knows he is mad in love, and would marry you any day you choose if you wore only the hair on your head. He would ask no better fortune!"

"It is useless to advise me, Renaud!" said she, "and whether I take Le Gardeur or no it would not help your chance with Amelie! I am sorry for it, for Amelie is a prize, Renaud! but not for you at any price. Let me tell you, that desirable young lady will become the bride of Pierre Philibert, and the bride of no other man living."

"You give one cold encouragement, sister! But I am sure, if you would only marry Le Gardeur, you could easily, with your tact and cleverness, induce Amelie to let me share the Tilly fortune. There are chests full of gold in the old Manor House, and a crow could hardly fly in a day over their broad lands!"

"Perfectly useless, brother! Amelie is not like most girls. She would refuse the hand of a king for the sake of the man she loves, and she loves Pierre Philibert to his finger-ends. She has married him in her heart a thousand times. I hate paragons of women, and would scorn to be one, but I tell you, brother, Amelie is a paragon of a girl, without knowing it!"

"Hum, I never tried my hand on a paragon: I should like to do so," replied he, with a smile of decided confidence in his powers. "I fancy they are just like other women when you can catch them with their armor off."

"Yes, but women like Amelie never lay off their armor! They seem born in it, like Minerva. But your vanity will not let you believe me, Renaud! So go try her, and tell me your luck! She won't scratch you, nor scold. Amelie is a lady, and will talk to you like a queen. But she will give you a polite reply to your proposal that will improve your opinions of our sex."

"You are mocking me, Angelique, as you always do! One never knows when you are in jest or when in earnest. Even when you get angry, it is often unreal and for a purpose! I want you to be serious for once. The fortune of the Tillys and De Repentignys is the best in New France, and we can make it ours if you will help me."

"I am serious enough in wishing you those chests full of gold, and those broad lands that a crow cannot fly over in a day; but I must forego my share of them, and so must you yours, brother!" Angelique leaned back in her chair, desiring to stop further discussion of a topic she did not like to hear.

"Why must you forego your share of the De Repentigny fortune, Angelique? You could call it your own any day you chose by giving your little finger to Le Gardeur! you do really puzzle me."

The Chevalier did look perplexed at his inscrutable sister, who only smiled over the table at him, as she nonchalantly cracked nuts and sipped her wine by drops.

"Of course I puzzle you, Renaud!" said she at last. "I am a puzzle to myself sometimes. But you see there are so many men in the world,--poor ones are so plenty, rich ones so scarce, and sensible ones hardly to be found at all,--that a woman may be excused for selling herself to the highest bidder. Love is a commodity only spoken of in romances or in the patois of milkmaids now-a-days!"

"Zounds, Angelique! you would try the patience of all the saints in the calendar! I shall pity the fellow you take in! Here is the fairest fortune in the Colony about to fall into the hands of Pierre Philibert--whom Satan confound for his assurance! A fortune which I always regarded as my own!"

"It shows the folly and vanity of your sex! You never spoke a word to Amelie de Repentigny in the way of wooing in your life! Girls like her don't drop into men's arms just for the asking."

"Pshaw! as if she would refuse me if you only acted a sister's part! But you are impenetrable as a rock, and the whole of your fickle sex could not match your vanity and caprice, Angelique."

She rose quickly with a provoked air.

"You are getting so complimentary to my poor sex, Renaud," said she, "that I must really leave you to yourself, and I could scarcely leave you in worse company."

"You are so bitter and sarcastic upon one!" replied he, tartly; "my only desire was to secure a good fortune for you, and another for myself. I don't see, for my part, what women are made for, except to mar everything a man wants to do for himself and for them!"

"Certainly everything should be done for us, brother; but I have no defence to make for my sex, none! I dare say we women deserve all that men think of us, but then it is impolite to tell us so to our faces. Now, as I advised you, Renaud, I would counsel you to study gardening, and you may one day arrive at as great distinction as the Marquis de Vandriere--you may cultivate chou chou if you cannot raise a bride like Amelie de Repentigny."

Angelique knew her brother's genius was not penetrating, or she would scarcely have ventured this broad allusion to the brother of La Pompadour, who, by virtue of his relationship to the Court favorite, had recently been created Director of the Royal Gardens. What fancy was working in the brain of Angelique when she alluded to him may be only surmised.

The Chevalier was indignant, however, at an implied comparison between himself and the plebeian Marquis de Vandriere. He replied, with some heat,--

"The Marquis de Vandriere! How dare you mention him and me together! There's not an officer's mess in the army that receives the son of the fishmonger! Why do you mention him, Angelique? You are a perfect riddle!"

"I only thought something might happen, brother, if I should ever go to Paris! I was acting a charade in my fancy, and that was the solution of it!"

"What was? You would drive the whole Sorbonne mad with your charades and fancies! But I must leave you."

"Good-by, brother,--if you will go. Think of it!--if you want to rise in the world you may yet become a royal gardener like the Marquis de Vandriere!" Her silvery laugh rang out good-humoredly as he descended the stairs and passed out of the house.

She sat down in her fauteuil. "Pity Renaud is such a fool!" said she; "yet I am not sure but he is wiser in his folly than I with all my tact and cleverness, which I suspect are going to make a greater fool of me than ever he is!"

She leaned back in her chair in a deep thinking mood. "It is growing dark," murmured she. "Le Gardeur will assuredly be here soon, in spite of all the attractions of Belmont. How to deal with him when he comes is more than I know: he will renew his suit, I am sure."

For a moment the heart of Angelique softened in her bosom. "Accept him I must not!" said she; "affront him I will not! cease to love him is out of my power as much as is my ability to love the Intendant, whom I cordially detest, and shall marry all the same!" She pressed her hands over her eyes, and sat silent for a few minutes. "But I am not sure of it! That woman remains still at Beaumanoir! Will my scheming to remove her be all in vain or no?" Angelique recollected with a shudder a thought that had leaped in her bosom, like a young Satan, engendered of evil desires. "I dare hardly look in the honest eyes of Le Gardeur after nursing such a monstrous fancy as that," said she; "but my fate is fixed all the same. Le Gardeur will vainly try to undo this knot in my life, but he must leave me to my own devices." To what devices she left him was a thought that sprang not up in her purely selfish nature.

In her perplexity Angelique tied knot upon knot hard as pebbles in her handkerchief. Those knots of her destiny, as she regarded them, she left untied, and they remain untied to this day--a memento of her character and of those knots in her life which posterity has puzzled itself over to no purpose to explain.

# Chapter XX: Belmont

A short drive from the gate of St. John stood the old mansion of Belmont, the country-seat of the Bourgeois Philibert--a stately park, the remains of the primeval forest of oak, maple, and pine; trees of gigantic growth and ample shade surrounded the high-roofed, many-gabled house that stood on the heights of St. Foye overlooking the broad valley of the St. Charles. The bright river wound like a silver serpent through the flat meadows in the bottom of the valley, while the opposite slopes of alternate field and forest stretched away to the distant range of the Laurentian hills, whose pale blue summits mingled with the blue sky at midday or, wrapped in mist at morn and eve, were hardly distinguishable from the clouds behind them.

The gardens and lawns of Belmont were stirring with gay company to-day in honor of the fete of Pierre Philibert upon his return home from the campaign in Acadia. Troops of ladies in costumes and toilettes of the latest Parisian fashion gladdened the eye with pictures of grace and beauty which Paris itself could not have surpassed. Gentlemen in full dress, in an age when dress was an essential part of a gentleman's distinction, accompanied the ladies with the gallantry, vivacity, and politeness belonging to France, and to France alone.

Communication with the mother country was precarious and uncertain by reason of the war and the blockade of the Gulf by the English cruisers. Hence the good fortune and daring of the gallant Captain Martiniere in running his frigate, the Fleur-de-Lis, through the fleet of the enemy, enabling him among other things to replenish the wardrobes of the ladies of Quebec with latest Parisian fashions, made him immensely popular on this gala day. The kindness and affability of the ladies extended without diminution of graciousness to the little midshipmen even, whom the Captain conditioned to take with him wherever he and his officers were invited. Captain Martiniere was happy to see the lads enjoy a few cakes on shore after the hard biscuit they had so long nibbled on shipboard. As for himself, there was no end to the gracious smiles and thanks he received from the fair ladies at Belmont.

At the great door of the Manor House, welcoming his guests as they arrived, stood the Bourgeois Philibert, dressed as a gentleman of the period, in attire rich but not ostentatious. His suit of dark velvet harmonized well with his noble manner and bearing. But no one for a moment could overlook the man in contemplating his dress. The keen, discriminating eye of woman, overlooking neither dress nor man, found both worthy of warmest commendation, and many remarks passed between the ladies on that day that a handsomer man and more ripe and perfect gentleman than the Bourgeois Philibert had never been seen in New France.

His grizzled hair grew thickly all over his head, the sign of a tenacious constitution. It was powdered and tied behind with a broad ribbon, for he hated perukes. His strong, shapely figure was handsomely conspicuous as he stood, chapeau in hand, greeting his guests as they approached. His eyes beamed with pleasure and hospitality, and his usually grave, thoughtful lips were wreathed in smiles, the sweeter because not habitually seen upon them.

The Bourgeois had this in common with all complete and earnest characters, that the people believed in him because they saw that he believed in himself. His friends loved and trusted him to the uttermost, his enemies hated and feared him in equal measure; but no one, great or small, could ignore him and not feel his presence as a solid piece of manhood.

It is not intellect, nor activity, nor wealth, that obtains most power over men; but force of character, self-control, a quiet, compressed will and patient resolve; these qualities make one man the natural ruler over others by a title they never dispute.

The party of the Honnetes Gens, the "honest folks" as they were derisively called by their opponents, regarded the Bourgeois Philibert as their natural leader. His force of character made men willingly stand in his shadow. His clear intellect, never at fault, had extended his power and influence by means of his vast mercantile operations over half the continent. His position as the foremost merchant of New France brought him in the front of the people's battle with the Grand Company, and in opposition to the financial policy of the Intendant and the mercantile assumption of the Friponne.

But the personal hostility between the Intendant and the Bourgeois had its root and origin in France, before either of them crossed the ocean to the hither shore of the Atlantic. The Bourgeois had been made very sensible of a fact vitally affecting him, that the decrees of the Intendant, ostensibly for the regulation of trade in New France, had been sharply pointed against himself. "They draw blood!" Bigot had boasted to his familiars as he rubbed his hands together with intense satisfaction one day, when he learned that Philibert's large trading-post in Mackinaw had been closed in consequence of the Indians having been commanded by royal authority, exercised by the Intendant, to trade only at the comptoirs of the Grand Company. "They draw blood!" repeated he, "and will draw the life yet out of the Golden Dog." It was plain the ancient grudge of the courtly parasite had not lost a tooth during all those years.

The Bourgeois was not a man to talk of his private griefs, or seek sympathy, or even ask counsel or help. He knew the world was engrossed with its own cares. The world cares not to look under the surface of things for sake of others, but only for its own sake, its own interests, its own pleasures.

To-day, however, cares, griefs, and resentments were cast aside, and the Bourgeois was all joy at the return of his only son, and proud of Pierre's achievements, and still more of the honors spontaneously paid him. He stood at the door, welcoming arrival after arrival, the happiest man of all the joyous company who honored Belmont that day.

A carriage with outriders brought the Count de la Galissoniere and his friend Herr Kalm and Dr. Gauthier, the last a rich old bachelor, handsome and generous, the physician and savant par excellence of Quebec. After a most cordial reception by the Bourgeois the Governor walked among the guests, who had crowded up to greet him with the respect due to the King's representative, as well as to show their personal regard; for the Count's popularity was unbounded in the Colony except among the partizans of the Grand Company.

Herr Kalm was presently enticed away by a bevy of young ladies, Hortense de Beauharnais leading them, to get the learned professor's opinion on some rare specimens of botany growing in the park. Nothing loath--for he was good-natured as he was clever, and a great enthusiast withal in the study of plants--he allowed the merry, talkative girls to lead him where they would. He delighted them in turn by his agreeable, instructive conversation, which was rendered still more piquant by the odd medley of French, Latin, and Swedish in which it was expressed.

An influx of fresh arrivals next poured into the park--the Chevalier de la Corne, with his pretty daughter, Agathe La Corne St. Luc; the Lady de Tilly and Amelie de Repentigny, with the brothers de Villiers. The brothers had overtaken the Chevalier La Corne upon the road, but the custom of the highway in New France forbade any one passing another without politely asking permission to do so.

"Yes, Coulon," replied the Chevalier; "ride on!" He winked pleasantly at his daughter as he said this. "There is, I suppose, nothing left for an old fellow who dates from the sixteen hundreds but to take the side of the road and let you pass. I should have liked, however, to stir up the fire in my gallant little Norman ponies against your big New England horses. Where did you get them? Can they run?"

"We got them in the sack of Saratoga," replied Coulon, "and they ran well that day, but we overtook them. Would Mademoiselle La Corne care if we try them now?"

Scarcely a girl in Quebec would have declined the excitement of a race on the highroad of St. Foye, and Agathe would fain have driven herself in the race, but being in full dress to-day, she thought of her wardrobe and the company. She checked the ardor of her father, and entered the park demurely, as one of the gravest of the guests.

"Happy youths! Noble lads, Agathe!" exclaimed the Chevalier, admiringly, as the brothers rode rapidly past them. "New France will be proud of them some day!"

The rest of the company now began to arrive in quick succession. The lawn was crowded with guests. "Ten thousand thanks for coming!" exclaimed Pierre Philibert, as he assisted Amelie de Repentigny and the Lady de Tilly to alight from their carriage.

"We could not choose but come to-day, Pierre," replied Amelie, feeling without displeasure the momentary lingering of his hand as it touched hers. "Nothing short of an earthquake would have kept aunt at home," added she, darting a merry glance of sympathy with her aunt's supposed feelings.

"And you, Amelie?" Pierre looked into those dark eyes which shyly turned aside from his gaze.

"I was an obedient niece, and accompanied her. It is so easy to persuade people to go where they wish to go!" She withdrew her hand gently, and took his arm as he conducted the ladies into the house. She felt a flush on her cheek, but it did not prevent her saying in her frank, kindly way,--"I was glad to come to-day, Pierre, to witness this gathering of the best and noblest in the land to honor your fete. Aunt de Tilly has always predicted greatness for you."

"And you, Amelie, doubted, knowing me a shade better than your aunt?"

"No, I believed her; so true a prophet as aunt surely deserved one firm believer!"

Pierre felt the electric thrill run through him which a man feels at the moment he discovers a woman believes in him. "Your presence here to-day, Amelie! you cannot think how sweet it is," said he.

Her hand trembled upon his arm. She thought nothing could be sweeter than such words from Pierre Philibert. With a charming indirectness, however, which did not escape him, she replied, "Le Gardeur is very proud of you to-day, Pierre."

He laid his fingers upon her hand. It was a delicate little hand, but with the strength of an angel's it had moulded his destiny and led him to the honorable position he had attained. He was profoundly conscious at this moment of what he owed to this girl's silent influence. He contented himself, however, with saying, "I will so strive that one day Amelie de Repentigny shall not shame to say she too is proud of me."

She did not reply for a moment. A tremor agitated her low, sweet voice. "I am proud of you now, Pierre,--more proud than words can tell to see you so honored, and proudest to think you deserve it all."

It touched him almost to tears. "Thanks, Amelie; when you are proud of me I shall begin to feel pride of myself. Your opinion is the one thing in life I have most cared for,--your approbation is my best reward."

Her eyes were eloquent with unspoken words, but she thought, "If that were all!" Pierre Philibert had long received the silent reward of her good opinion and approbation.

The Bourgeois at this moment came up to salute Amelie and the Lady de Tilly.

"The Bourgeois Philibert has the most perfect manner of any gentleman in New France," was the remark of the Lady de Tilly to Amelie, as he left them again to receive other guests. "They say he can be rough and imperious sometimes to those he dislikes, but to his friends and strangers, and especially to ladies, no breath of spring can be more gentle and balmy." Amelie assented with a mental reservation in the depths of her dark eyes, and in the dimple that flashed upon her cheek as she suppressed the utterance of a pleasant fancy in reply to her aunt.

Pierre conducted the ladies to the great drawing-room, which was already filled with company, who overwhelmed Amelie and her aunt with the vivacity of their greeting.

In a fine shady grove at a short distance from the house, a row of tables was set for the entertainment of several hundreds of the hardy dependents of the Bourgeois; for while feasting the rich the Bourgeois would not forget his poorer friends, and perhaps his most exquisite satisfaction was in the unrestrained enjoyment of his hospitality by the crowd of happy, hungry fellows and their families, who, under the direction of his chief factor, filled the tables from end to end, and made the park resound with songs and merriment--fellows of infinite gaiety, with appetites of Gargantuas and a capacity for good liquors that reminded one of the tubs of the Danaides. The tables groaned beneath mountains of good things, and in the centre of each, like Mont Blanc rising from the lower Alps, stood a magnificent Easter pie, the confection of which was a masterpiece of the skill of Maitre Guillot Gobet, the head cook of the Bourgeois, who was rather put out, however, when Dame Rochelle decided to bestow all the Easter pies upon the hungry voyageurs, woodmen, and workmen, and banished them from the menu of the more patrician tables set for the guests of the mansion.

"Yet, after all," exclaimed Maitre Guillot, as he thrust his head out of the kitchen door to listen to the song the gay fellows were singing with all their lungs in honor of his Easter pie; "after all, the fine gentlemen and ladies would not have paid my noble pies such honor as that! and what is more the pies would not have been eaten up to the last crumb!" Maitre Guillot's face beamed like a harvest moon, as he chimed in with the well-known ditty in praise of the great pie of Rouen:

"'C'est dans la ville de Rouen,
Ils ont fait un pate si grand,
Ils ont fait un pate si grand,
Qu'ils ont trouve un homme dedans!'"

Maitre Guillot would fain have been nearer, to share in the shouting and clapping of hands which followed the saying of grace by the good Cure of St. Foye, and to see how vigorously knives were handled, and how chins wagged in the delightful task of levelling down mountains of meat, while Gascon wine and Norman cider flowed from ever- replenished flagons.

The Bourgeois and his son, with many of his chief guests, honored for a time the merry feast out-of-doors, and were almost inundated by the flowing cups drunk to the health and happiness of the Bourgeois and of Pierre Philibert.

Maitre Guillot Gobet returned to his kitchen, where he stirred up his cooks and scullions on all sides, to make up for the loss of his Easter pies on the grand tables in the hall. He capered among them like a marionette, directing here, scolding there, laughing, joking, or with uplifted hands and stamping feet despairing of his underlings' cooking a dinner fit for the fete of Pierre Philibert.

Maitre Guilot was a little, fat, red-nosed fellow, with twinkling black eyes, and a mouth irascible as that of a cake-baker of Lerna. His heart was of the right paste, however, and full as a butter-boat of the sweet sauce of good nature, which he was ready to pour over the heads of all his fellows who quietly submitted to his dictation. But woe to man or maid servant who delayed or disputed his royal orders! An Indian typhoon instantly blew. At such a time even Dame Rochelle would gather her petticoats round her and hurry out of the storm, which always subsided quickly in proportion to the violence of its rage.

Maitre Guillot knew what he was about, however. He did not use, he said, to wipe his nose with a herring! and on that day he was going to cook a dinner fit for the Pope after Lent, or even for the Reverend Father De Berey himself, who was the truest gourmet and the best trencherman in New France.

Maitre Guillot honored his master, but in his secret soul he did not think his taste quite worthy of his cook! But he worshipped Father De Berey, and gloried in the infallible judgment and correct taste of cookery possessed by the jolly Recollet. The single approbation of Father De Berey was worth more than the praise of a world full of ordinary eating mortals, who smacked their lips and said things were good, but who knew no more than one of the Cent Suisses why things were good, or could appreciate the talents of an artiste of the cordon bleu.

Maitre Guillot's Easter pie had been a splendid success. "It was worthy," he said, "to be placed as a crown on top of the new Cathedral of St. Marie, and receive the consecration of the Bishop."

Lest the composition of it should be forgotten, Maitre Guillot had, with the solemnity of a deacon intoning the Litany, ravished the ear of Jules Painchaud, his future son-in-law, as he taught him the secrets of its confection.

With his white cap set rakishly on one side of his head and arms akimbo, Maitre Guillot gave Jules the famous recipe:

"Inside of circular walls of pastry an inch thick, and so rich as easily to be pulled down, and roomy enough within for the Court of King Pepin, lay first a thick stratum of mince-meat of two savory hams of Westphalia, and if you cannot get them, of two hams of our habitans."

"Of our habitans!" ejaculated Jules, with an air of consternation.

"Precisely! don't interrupt me!" Maitre Guillot grew red about the gills in an instant. Jules was silenced. "I have said it!" cried he; "two hams of our habitans! what have you to say against it-- stock fish, eh?"

"Oh, nothing, sir," replied Jules, with humility, "only I thought--" Poor Jules would have consented to eat his thought rather than fall out with the father of his Susette.

"You thought!" Maitre Guillot's face was a study for Hogarth, who alone could have painted the alto tone of voice as it proceeded from his round O of a mouth. "Susette shall remain upon my hands an old maid for the term of her natural life if you dispute the confection of Easter pie!"

"Now listen, Jules," continued he, at once mollified by the contrite, submissive air of his future son-in-law: "Upon the foundation of the mince-meat of two hams of Westphalia,--or, if you cannot get them, of two hams of our habitans,--place scientifically the nicely-cut pieces of a fat turkey, leaving his head to stick out of the upper crust, in evidence that Master Dindon lies buried there! Add two fat capons, two plump partridges, two pigeons, and the back and thighs of a brace of juicy hares. Fill up the whole with beaten eggs, and the rich contents will resemble, as a poet might say, 'fossils of the rock in golden yolks embedded and enjellied!' Season as you would a saint. Cover with a slab of pastry. Bake it as you would cook an angel, and not singe a feather. Then let it cool, and eat it! And then, Jules, as the Reverend Father de Berey always says after grace over an Easter pie, 'Dominus vobiscum!'"

## Chapter XXI: Sic Itur ad Astra

The old hall of Belmont had been decorated for many a feast since the times of its founder, the Intendant Talon; but it had never contained a nobler company of fair women and brave men, the pick and choice of their race, than to-day met round the hospitable and splendid table of the Bourgeois Philibert in honor of the fete of his gallant son.

Dinner was duly and decorously despatched. The social fashion of New France was not for the ladies to withdraw when the wine followed the feast, but to remain seated with the gentlemen, purifying the conversation, and by their presence restraining the coarseness which was the almost universal vice of the age.

A troop of nimble servitors carried off the carved dishes and fragments of the splended patisseries of Maitre Guillot, in such a state of demolition as satisfied the critical eye of the chief cook that the efforts of his genius had been very successful. He inspected the dishes through his spectacles. He knew, by what was left, the ability of the guests to discriminate what they had eaten and to do justice to his skill. He considered himself a sort of pervading divinity, whose culinary ideas passing with his cookery into the bodies of the guests enabled them, on retiring from the feast, to carry away as part of themselves some of the fine essence of Maitre Gobet himself.

At the head of his table, peeling oranges and slicing pineapples for the ladies in his vicinity, sat the Bourgeois himself, laughing, jesting, and telling anecdotes with a geniality that was contagious. "'The gods are merry sometimes,' says Homer, 'and their laughter shakes Olympus!'" was the classical remark of Father de Berey, at the other end of the table. Jupiter did not laugh with less loss of dignity than the Bourgeois.

Few of the guests did not remember to the end of their lives the majestic and happy countenance of the Bourgeois on this memorable day.

At his right hand sat Amelie de Repentigny and the Count de la Galissoniere. The Governor, charmed with the beauty and agreeableness of the young chatelaine, had led her in to dinner, and devoted himself to her and the Lady de Tilly with the perfection of gallantry of a gentleman of the politest court in Europe. On his left sat the radiant, dark-eyed Hortense de Beauharnais. With a gay assumption of independence Hortense had taken the arm of La Corne St. Luc, and declared she would eat no dinner unless he would be her cavalier and sit beside her! The gallant old soldier surrendered at discretion. He laughingly consented to be her captive, he said, for he had no power and no desire but to obey. Hortense was proud of her conquest. She seated herself by his side with an air of triumph and mock gravity, tapping him with her fan whenever she detected his eye roving round the table, compassionating, she affirmed, her rivals, who had failed where she had won in securing the youngest, the handsomest, and most gallant of all the gentlemen at Belmont.

"Not so fast, Hortense!" exclaimed the gay Chevalier; "you have captured me by mistake! The tall Swede--he is your man! The other ladies all know that, and are anxious to get me out of your toils, so that you may be free to ensnare the philosopher!"

"But you don't wish to get away from me! I am your garland, Chevalier, and you shall wear me to-day. As for the tall Swede, he has no idea of a fair flower of our sex except to wear it in his button-hole,--this way!" added she, pulling a rose out of a vase and archly adorning the Chevalier's vest with it.

"All pretence and jealousy, mademoiselle. The tall Swede knows how to take down your pride and bring you to a proper sense of your false conceit of the beauty and wit of the ladies of

New France."

Hortense gave two or three tosses of defiance to express her emphatic dissent from his opinions.

"I wish Herr Kalm would lend me his philosophic scales, to weigh your sex like lambs in market," continued La Corne St. Luc; "but I fear I am too old, Hortense, to measure women except by the fathom, which is the measure of a man."

"And the measure of a man is the measure of an angel too scriptum est, Chevalier!" replied she. Hortense had ten merry meanings in her eye, and looked as if bidding him select which he chose. "The learned Swede's philosophy is lost upon me," continued she, "he can neither weigh by sample nor measure by fathom the girls of New France!" She tapped him on the arm. "Listen to me, chevalier," said she, "you are neglecting me already for sake of Cecile Tourangeau!" La Corne was exchanging some gay badinage with a graceful, pretty young lady on the other side of the table, whose snowy forehead, if you examined it closely, was marked with a red scar, in figure of a cross, which, although powdered and partially concealed by a frizz of her thick blonde hair, was sufficiently distinct to those who looked for it; and many did so, as they whispered to each other the story of how she got it.

Le Gardeur de Repentigny sat by Cecile, talking in a very sociable manner, which was also commented on. His conversation seemed to be very attractive to the young lady, who was visibly delighted with the attentions of her handsome gallant.

At this moment a burst of instruments from the musicians, who occupied a gallery at the end of the hall, announced a vocal response to the toast of the King's health, proposed by the Bourgeois. "Prepare yourself for the chorus, Chevalier," exclaimed Hortense. "Father de Berey is going to lead the royal anthem!"

"Vive le Roi!" replied La Corne. "No finer voice ever sang Mass, or chanted 'God Save the King!' I like to hear the royal anthem from the lips of a churchman rolling it out ore rotundo, like one of the Psalms of David. Our first duty is to love God,--our next to honor the King! and New France will never fail in either!" Loyalty was ingrained in every fibre of La Corne St. Luc.

"Never, Chevalier. Law and Gospel rule together, or fall together! But we must rise," replied Hortense, springing up.

The whole company rose simultaneously. The rich, mellow voice of the Rev. Father de Berey, round and full as the organ of Ste. Marie, commenced the royal anthem composed by Lulli in honor of Louis Quatorze, upon an occasion of his visit to the famous Convent of St. Cyr, in company with Madame de Maintenon.

The song composed by Madame Brinon was afterwards translated into English, and words and music became, by a singular transposition, the national hymn of the English nation.

"God Save the King!" is no longer heard in France. It was buried with the people's loyalty, fathoms deep under the ruins of the monarchy. But it flourishes still with pristine vigor in New France, that olive branch grafted on the stately tree of the British Empire. The broad chest and flexile lips of Father de Berey rang out the grand old song in tones that filled the stately old hall:

"'Grand Dieu! Sauvez le Roi!
Grand Dieu! Sauvez le Roi!
Sauvez le Roi!
Que toujours glorieux.
Louis Victorieux,
Voye ses ennemis

Toujours soumis!'"

The company all joined in the chorus, the gentlemen raising their cups, the ladies waving their handkerchiefs, and male and female blending in a storm of applause that made the old walls ring with joy. Songs and speeches followed in quick succession, cutting as with a golden blade the hours of the dessert into quinzaines of varied pleasures.

The custom of the times had reduced speechmaking after dinner to a minimum. The ladies, as Father de Berey wittily remarked, preferred private confession to public preaching; and long speeches, without inlets for reply, were the eighth mortal sin which no lady would forgive.

The Bourgeois, however, felt it incumbent upon himself to express his deep thanks for the honor done his house on this auspicious occasion. And he remarked that the doors of Belmont, so long closed by reason of the absence of Pierre, would hereafter be ever open to welcome all his friends. He had that day made a gift of Belmont, with all its belongings, to Pierre, and he hoped,--the Bourgeois smiled as he said this, but he would not look in a quarter where his words struck home,--he hoped that some one of Quebec's fair daughters would assist Pierre in the menage of his home and enable him to do honor to his housekeeping.

Immense was the applause that followed the short, pithy speech of the Bourgeois. The ladies blushed and praised, the gentlemen cheered and enjoyed in anticipation the renewal of the old hospitalities of Belmont.

"The skies are raining plum cakes!" exclaimed the Chevalier La Corne to his lively companion. "Joy's golden drops are only distilled in the alembic of woman's heart! What think you, Hortense? Which of Quebec's fair daughters will be willing to share Belmont with Pierre?"

"Oh, any of them would!" replied she. "But why did the Bourgeois restrict his choice to the ladies of Quebec, when he knew I came from the Three Rivers?"

"Oh, he was afraid of you, Hortense; you would make Belmont too good for this world! What say you, Father de Berry? Do you ever walk on the cape?"

The friar, in a merry mood, had been edging close to Hortense. "I love, of all things, to air my gray gown on the cape of a breezy afternoon," replied the jovial Recollet, "when the fashionables are all out, and every lady is putting her best foot foremost. It is then I feel sure that Horace is the next best thing to the Homilies:

'"Teretesque suras laudo, et integer ego!'"

The Chevalier La Corne pinched the shrugging shoulder of Hortense as he remarked, "Don't confess to Father de Berey that you promenade on the cape! But I hope Pierre Philibert will soon make his choice! We are impatient to visit him and give old Provencal the butler a run every day through those dark crypts of his, where lie entombed the choicest vintages of sunny France."

The Chevalier said this waggishly, for the benefit of old Provencal, who stood behind his chair looking half alarmed at the threatened raid upon his well-filled cellars.

"But if Pierre should not commit matrimony," replied Hortense, "what will become of him? and especially what will become of us?"

"We will drink his wine all the same, good fellow that he is! But Pierre had as lief commit suicide as not commit matrimony; and who would not? Look here, Pierre Philibert," continued the old soldier, addressing him, with good-humored freedom. "Matrimony is clearly your duty, Pierre; but I need not tell you so: it is written on your face plain as the way betwen Peronne and St. Quintin,--a good, honest way as ever was trod by shoe leather, and as old as Chinon in Touraine! Try it soon, my boy. Quebec is a sack full of pearls!" Hortense pulled him mischievously by the coat, so he caught her hand and held it fast in his, while he proceeded:

"You put your hand in the sack and take out the first that offers. It will be worth a Jew's ransom! If you are lucky to find the fairest, trust me it will be the identical pearl of great price for which the merchant went and sold all that he had and bought it. Is not that Gospel, Father de Berey? I think I have heard something like that preached from the pulpit of the Recollets?"

"Matter of brimborion, Chevalier! not to be questioned by laymen! Words of wisdom for my poor brothers of St. Francis, who, after renouncing the world, like to know that they have renounced something worth having! But not to preach a sermon on your parable, Chevalier, I will promise Colonel Philibert that when he has found the pearl of great price,"--Father de Berey, who knew a world of secrets, glanced archly at Amelie as he said this,--"the bells of our monastery shall ring out such a merry peal as they have not rung since fat Brother Le Gros broke his wind, and short Brother Bref stretched himself out half a yard pulling the bell ropes on the wedding of the Dauphin."

Great merriment followed the speech of Father de Berey. Hortense rallied the Chevalier, a good old widower, upon himself not travelling the plain way between Peronne and St. Quintin, and jestingly offered herself to travel with him, like a couple of gypsies carrying their budget of happiness pick-a-back through the world.

"Better than that!" La Corne exclaimed. Hortense was worthy to ride on the baggage-wagons in his next campaign! Would she go? She gave him her hand. "I expect nothing else!" said she. "I am a soldier's daughter, and expect to live a soldier's wife, and die a soldier's widow. But a truce to jest. It is harder to be witty than wise," continued she. "What is the matter with Cousin Le Gardeur?" Her eyes were fixed upon him as he read a note just handed to him by a servant. He crushed it in his hand with a flash of anger, and made a motion as if about to tear it, but did not. He placed it in his bosom. But the hilarity of his countenance was gone.

There was another person at the table whose quick eye, drawn by sisterly affection, saw Le Gardeur's movement before even Hortense. Amelie was impatient to leave her seat and go beside him, but she could not at the moment leave the lively circle around her. She at once conjectured that the note was from Angelique des Meloises. After drinking deeply two or three times Le Gardeur arose, and with a faint excuse that did not impose on his partner left the table. Amelie rose quickly also, excusing herself to the Bourgeois, and joined her brother in the park, where the cool night air blew fresh and inviting for a walk.

Pretty Cecile Touraugeau had caught a glimpse of the handwriting as she sat by the side of Le Gardeur, and guessed correctly whence it had come and why her partner so suddenly left the table.

She was out of humor; the red mark upon her forehead grew redder as she pouted in visible discontent. But the great world moves on, carrying alternate storms and sunshine upon its surface. The company rose from the table--some to the ball-room, some to the park and conservatories. Cecile's was a happy disposition, easily consoled for her sorrows. Every trace of her displeasure was banished and almost forgotten from the moment the gay, handsome Jumonville de Villiers invited her out to the grand balcony, where, he said, the rarest pastime was going on.

And rare pastime it was! A group of laughing but half-serious girls were gathered round Doctor Gauthier, urging him to tell their fortunes by consulting the stars, which to-night shone out with unusual brilliancy.

At that period, as at the present, and in every age of the world, the female sex, like the Jews of old, asks signs, while the Greeks-- that is, the men--seek wisdom.

The time never was, and never will be, when a woman will cease to be curious,--when her imagination will not forecast the decrees of fate in regard to the culminating event of her life and her whole nature-- marriage. It was in vain Doctor Gauthier protested his inability to read the stars without his celestial eye-glasses.

The ladies would not accept his excuses: he knew the heavens by heart, they said, and could read the stars of destiny as easily as the Bishop his breviary.

In truth the worthy doctor was not only a believer but an adept in astrology. He had favored his friends with not a few horoscopes and nativities, when pressed to do so. His good nature was of the substance of butter: any one that liked could spread it over their bread. Many good men are eaten up in that way by greedy friends.

Hortense de Beauharnais urged the Doctor so merrily and so perseveringly, promising to marry him herself if the stars said so, that he laughingly gave way, but declared he would tell Hortense's fortune first, which deserved to be good enough to make her fulfil her promise just made.

She was resigned, she said, and would accept any fate from the rank of a queen to a cell among the old maids of St. Cyr! The girls of Quebec hung all their hopes on the stars, bright and particular ones especially. They were too loving to live single, and too proud to live poor. But she was one who would not wait for ships to land that never came, and plums to drop into her mouth that never ripened. Hortense would be ruled by the stars, and wise Doctor Gauthier should to-night declare her fate.

They all laughed at this free talk of Hortense. Not a few of the ladies shrugged their shoulders and looked askance at each other, but many present wished they had courage to speak like her to Doctor Gauthier.

"Well, I see there is nothing else for it but to submit to my ruling star, and that is you, Hortense!" cried the Doctor; "so please stand up before me while I take an inventory of your looks as a preliminary to telling your fortune."

Hortense placed herself instantly before him. "It is one of the privileges of our dry study," remarked he, as he looked admiringly on the tall, charming figure and frank countenance of the girl before him.

"The querent," said he gravely, "is tall, straight, slender, arms long, hands and feet of the smallest, hair just short of blackness, piercing, roving eyes, dark as night and full of fire, sight quick, and temperament alive with energy, wit, and sense."

"Oh, tell my fortune, not my character! I shall shame of energy, wit, and sense, if I hear such flattery, Doctor!" exclaimed she, shaking herself like a young eagle preparing to fly.

"We shall see what comes of it, Hortense!" replied he gravely, as with his gold-headed cane he slowly quartered the heavens like an ancient augur, and noted the planets in their houses. The doctor was quite serious, and even Hortense, catching his looks, stood very silent as he studied the celestial aspects,

"Carrying through ether in perpetual round
Decrees and resolutions of the Gods."

"The Lord of the ascendant," said he, "is with the Lord of the seventh in the tenth house. The querent, therefore, shall marry the man made for her, but not the man of her youthful hope and her first love.

"The stars are true," continued he, speaking to himself rather than to her. "Jupiter in the seventh house denotes rank and dignity by marriage, and Mars in sextile foretells successful wars. It is wonderful, Hortense! The blood of Beauharnais shall sit on thrones more than one; it shall rule France, Italy, and Flanders, but not New France, for Saturn in quintile looks darkly upon the twins who rule America!"

"Come, Jumonville," exclaimed Hortense, "congratulate Claude on the greatness awaiting the house of Beauharnais, and condole with me that I am to see none of it myself! I do not care for kings and queens in the third generation, but I do care for happy fortune in the present for those I know and love! Come, Jumonville, have your fortune told now, to keep me in countenance. If the Doctor hits the truth for you I shall believe in him for myself."

"That is a good idea, Hortense," replied Jumonville; "I long ago hung my hat on the stars--let the Doctor try if he can find it."

The Doctor, in great good humor, surveyed the dark, handsome face and lithe, athletic figure of Jumonville de Villiers. He again raised his cane with the gravity of a Roman pontifex, marking off his templum in the heavens. Suddenly he stopped. He repeated more carefully his survey, and then turned his earnest eyes upon the young soldier.

"You see ill-fortune for me, Doctor!" exclaimed Jumonville, with bright, unflinching eyes, as he would look on danger of any kind.

"The Hyleg, or giver of life, is afflicted by Mars in the eighth house, and Saturn is in evil aspect in the ascendant!" said the Doctor slowly.

"That sounds warlike, and means fighting I suppose, Doctor. It is a brave fortune for a soldier. Go on!" Jumonville was in earnest now.

"The pars fortunae," continued the Doctor, gazing upward, "rejoices in a benign aspect with Venus. Fame, true love, and immortality will be yours, Jumonville de Villiers; but you will die young under the flag of your country and for sake of your King! You will not marry, but all the maids and matrons of New France will lament your fate with tears, and from your death shall spring up the salvation of your native land--how, I see not; but decretum est, Jumonville, ask me no more!"

A thrill like a stream of electricity passed through the company. Their mirth was extinguished, for none could wholly free their minds from the superstition of their age. The good Doctor sat down, and wiped his moistened eye-glasses. He would tell no more to-night, he said. He had really gone too far, making jest of earnest and earnest of jest, and begged pardon of Jumonville for complying with his humor.

The young soldier laughed merrily. "If fame, immortality, and true love are to be mine, what care I for death? It will be worth giving up life for, to have the tears of the maids and matrons of New France to lament your fate. What could the most ambitious soldier desire more?"

The words of Jumonville struck a kindred chord in the bosom of Hortense de Beauharnais. They were stamped upon her heart forever. A few years after this prediction, Jumonville de Villiers lay slain under a flag of truce on the bank of the Monongahela, and of all the maids and matrons of New France who wept over his fate, none shed more and bitterer tears than his fair betrothed bride, Hortense de Beauharnais.

The prediction of the Sieur Gauthier was repeated and retold as a strangely true tale; it passed into the traditions of the people, and lingered in their memory generations after the festival of Belmont was utterly forgotten.

When the great revolt took place in the English Colonies, the death of the gallant Jumonville de Villiers was neither forgotten nor forgiven by New France. Congress appealed in vain for union and help from Canadians. Washington's proclamations were trodden under foot, and his troops driven back or captured. If Canada was lost to France partly through the death of Jumonville, it may also be said that his blood helped to save it to England. The ways of

Providence are so mysterious in working out the problems of national existence that the life or death of a single individual may turn the scales of destiny over half a continent.

But all these events lay as yet darkly in the womb of the future. The gallant Jumonville who fell, and his brother Coulon who took his "noble revenge" upon Washington by sparing his life, were to-day the gayest of the gay throng who had assembled to do honor to Pierre Philibert.

While this group of merry guests, half in jest, half in earnest, were trying to discover in the stars the "far-reaching concords" that moulded the life of each, Amelie led her brother away from the busy grounds near the mansion, and took a quiet path that led into the great park which they entered.

A cool salt-water breeze, following the flood tide that was coming up the broad St. Lawrence, swept their faces as Amelie walked by the side of Le Gardeur, talking in her quiet way of things familiar, and of home interests until she saw the fever of his blood abate and his thoughts return into calmer channels. Her gentle craft subdued his impetuous mood--if craft it might be called--for more wisely cunning than all craft is the prompting of true affection, where reason responds like instinct to the wants of the heart.

They sat down upon a garden seat overlooking the great valley. None of the guests had sauntered out so far, but Amelie's heart was full; she had much to say, and wished no interruption.

"I am glad to sit in this pretty spot, Amelie," said he, at last, for he had listened in silence to the sweet, low voice of his sister as she kept up her half sad, half glad monologue, because she saw it pleased him. It brought him into a mood in which she might venture to talk of the matter that pressed sorely upon her heart.

"A little while ago, I feared I might offend you, Le Gardeur," said she, taking his hand tenderly in hers, "if I spoke all I wished. I never did offend you that I remember, brother, did I?"

"Never, my incomparable sister; you never did, and never could. Say what you will, ask me what you like; but I fear I am unworthy of your affection, sister."

"You are not unworthy; God gave you as my only brother, you will never be unworthy in my eyes. But it touches me to the quick to suspect others may think lightly of you, Le Gardeur."

He flinched, for his pride was touched, but he knew Amelie was right. "It was weakness in me," said he, "I confess it, sister. To pour wine upon my vexation in hope to cure it, is to feed a fire with oil. To throw fire into a powder magazine were wisdom compared with my folly, Amelie: I was angry at the message I got at such a time. Angelique des Meloises has no mercy upon her lovers!"

"Oh, my prophetic heart! I thought as much! It was Angelique, then, sent you the letter you read at table?"

"Yes, who else could have moved me so? The time was ill-chosen, but I suspect, hating the Bourgeois as she does, Angelique intended to call me from Pierre's fete. I shall obey her now, but tonight she shall obey me, decide to make or mar me, one way or other! You may read the letter, Amelie, if you will."

"I care not to read it, brother; I know Angelique too well not to fear her influence over you. Her craft and boldness were always a terror to her companions. But you will not leave Pierre's fete tonight?" added she, half imploringly; for she felt keenly the discourtesy to Pierre Philibert.

"I must do even that, sister! Were Angelique as faulty as she is fair, I should only love her the more for her faults, and make them my own. Were she to come to me like Herodias with the Baptist's head in a charger, I should outdo Herod in keeping my pledge to her."

Amelie uttered a low, moaning cry. "O my dear infatuated brother, it is not in nature for a De Repentigny to love irrationally like that! What maddening philtre have you drank, to intoxicate you with a woman who uses you so imperiously? But you will not go, Le Gardeur!" added she, clinging to his arm. "You are safe so long as you are with your sister,--you will be safe no longer if you go to the Maison des Meloises tonight!"

"Go I must and shall, Amelie! I have drank the maddening philtre,-- I know that, Amelie, and would not take an antidote if I had one! The world has no antidote to cure me. I have no wish to be cured of love for Angelique, and in fine I cannot be, so let me go and receive the rod for coming to Belmont and the reward for leaving it at her summons!" He affected a tone of levity, but Amelie's ear easily detected the false ring of it.

"Dearest brother!" said she, "are you sure Angelique returns, or is capable of returning, love like yours? She is like the rest of us, weak and fickle, merely human, and not at all the divinity a man in his fancy worships when in love with a woman." It was in vain, however, for Amelie to try to persuade her brother of that.

"What care I, Amelie, so long as Angelique is not weak and fickle to me?" answered he; "but she will think her tardy lover is both weak and fickle unless I put in a speedy appearance at the Maison des Meloises!" He rose up as if to depart, still holding his sister by the hand.

Amelie's tears flowed silently in the darkness. She was not willing to plant a seed of distrust in the bosom of her brother, yet she remembered bitterly and indignantly what Angelique had said of her intentions towards the Intendant. Was she using Le Gardeur as a foil to set off her attractions in the eyes of Bigot?

"Brother!" said Amelie, "I am a woman, and comprehend my sex better than you. I know Angelique's far-reaching ambition and crafty ways. Are you sure, not in outward persuasion but in inward conviction, that she loves you as a woman should love the man she means to marry?"

Le Gardeur felt her words like a silver probe that searched his heart. With all his unbounded devotion, he knew Angelique too well not to feel a pang of distrust sometimes, as she showered her coquetries upon every side of her. It was the overabundance of her love, he said, but he thought it often fell like the dew round Gideon's fleece, refreshing all the earth about it, but leaving the fleece dry. "Amelie!" said he, "you try me hard, and tempt me too, my sister, but it is useless. Angelique may be false as Cressida to other men, she will not be false to me! She has sworn it, with her hand in mine, before the altar of Notre Dame. I would go down to perdition with her in my arms rather than be a crowned king with all the world of women to choose from and not get her."

Amelie shuddered at his vehemence, but she knew how useless was expostulation. She wisely refrained, deeming it her duty, like a good sister, to make the best of what she could not hinder. Some jasmines overhung the seat; she plucked a handful, and gave them to him as they rose to return to the house.

"Take them with you, Le Gardeur," said she, giving him the flowers, which she tied into a wreath; "they will remind Angelique that she has a powerful rival in your sister's love."

He took them as they walked slowly back. "Would she were like you, Amelie, in all things!" said he. "I will put some of your flowers in her hair to-night for your sake, sister."

"And for her own! May they be for you both an augury of good! Mind and return home, Le Gardeur, after your visit. I shall sit up to await your arrival, to congratulate you;" and, after a pause, she added, "or to console you, brother!"

"Oh, no fear, sister!" replied he, cheeringly. "Angelique is true as steel to me. You shall call her my betrothed tomorrow! Good-by! And now go dance with all delight till morning." He kissed her and departed for the city, leaving her in the ball-room by the side of the Lady de Tilly.

Amelie related to her aunt the result of her conversation with Le Gardeur, and the cause of his leaving the fete so abruptly. The Lady de Tilly listened with surprise and distress. "To think," said she, "of Le Gardeur asking that terrible girl to marry him! My only hope is, she will refuse him. And if it be as I hear, I think she will!"

"It would be the ruin of Le Gardeur if she did, aunt! You cannot think how determined he is on this marriage."

"It would be his ruin if she accepted him!" replied the Lady de Tilly. "With any other woman Le Gardeur might have a fair chance of happiness; but none with her! More than one of her lovers lies in a bloody grave by reason of her coquetries. She has ruined every man whom she has flattered into loving her. She is without affection. Her thoughts are covered with a veil of deceit impenetrable. She would sacrifice the whole world to her vanity. I fear, Amelie, she will sacrifice Le Gardeur as ruthlessly as the most worthless of her admirers."

"We can only hope for the best, aunt; and I do think Angelique loves Le Gardeur as she never loved any other."

They were presently rejoined by Pierre Philibert. The Lady de Tilly and Amelie apologized for Le Gardeur's departure,--he had been compelled to go to the city on an affair of urgency, and had left them to make his excuses. Pierre Philibert was not without a shrewd perception of the state of affairs. He pitied Le Gardeur, and excused him, speaking most kindly of him in a way that touched the heart of Amelie. The ball went on with unflagging spirit and enjoyment. The old walls fairly vibrated with the music and dancing of the gay company.

The music, like the tide in the great river that night, reached its flood only after the small hours had set in. Amelie had given her hand to Pierre for one or two dances, and many a friendly, many a half envious guess was made as to the probable Chatelaine of Belmont.

## Chapter XXII: So Glozed the Tempter

The lamps burned brightly in the boudoir of Angelique des Meloises on the night of the fete of Pierre Philibert. Masses of fresh flowers filled the antique Sevres vases, sending delicious odors through the apartment, which was furnished in a style of almost royal splendor. Upon the white hearth a few billets of wood blazed cheerfully, for, after a hot day, as was not uncommon in New France, a cool salt-water breeze came up the great river, bringing reminders of cold sea-washed rocks and snowy crevices still lingering upon the mountainous shores of the St. Lawrence.

Angelique sat idly watching the wreaths of smoke as they rose in shapes fantastic as her own thoughts.

By that subtle instinct which is a sixth sense in woman, she knew that Le Gardeur de Repentigny would visit her to-night and renew his offer of marriage. She meant to retain his love and evade his proposals, and she never for a moment doubted her ability to accomplish her ends. Men's hearts had hitherto been but potter's clay in her hands, and she had no misgivings now; but she felt that the love of Le Gardeur was a thing she could not tread on without a shock to herself like the counter-stroke of a torpedo to the naked foot of an Indian who rashly steps upon it as it basks in a sunny pool.

She was agitated beyond her wont, for she loved Le Gardeur with a strange, selfish passion, for her own sake, not for his,--a sort of love not uncommon with either sex. She had the frankness to be half ashamed of it, for she knew the wrong she was doing to one of the most noble and faithful hearts in the world. But the arrival of the Intendant had unsettled every good resolution she had once made to marry Le Gardeur de Repentigny and become a reputable matron in society. Her ambitious fantasies dimmed every perception of duty to her own heart as well as his; and she had worked herself into that unenviable frame of mind which possesses a woman who cannot resolve either to consent or deny, to accept her lover or to let him go.

The solitude of her apartment became insupportable to her. She sprang up, opened the window, and sat down in the balcony outside, trying to find composure by looking down into the dark, still street. The voices of two men engaged in eager conversation reached her ear. They sat upon the broad steps of the house, so that every word they spoke reached her ear, although she could scarcely distinguish them in the darkness. These were no other than Max Grimeau and Blind Bartemy, the brace of beggars whose post was at the gate of the Basse Ville. They seemed to be comparing the amount of alms each had received during the day, and were arranging for a supper at some obscure haunt they frequented in the purlieus of the lower town, when another figure came up, short, dapper, and carrying a knapsack, as Angelique could detect by the glimmer of a lantern that hung on a rope stretched across the street. He was greeted warmly by the old mendicants.

"Sure as my old musket it is Master Pothier, and nobody else!" exclaimed Max Grimeau rising, and giving the newcomer a hearty embrace. "Don't you see, Bartemy? He has been foraging among the fat wives of the south shore. What a cheek he blows--red as a peony, and fat as a Dutch Burgomaster!" Max had seen plenty of the world when he marched under Marshal de Belleisle, so he was at no loss for apt comparisons.

"Yes!" replied Blind Bartemy, holding out his hand to be shaken. "I see by your voice, Master Pothier, that you have not said grace over bare bones during your absence. But where have you been this long time?"

"Oh, fleecing the King's subjects to the best of my poor ability in the law! and without half the success of you and Max here, who toll the gate of the Basse Ville more easily than the Intendant gets in the King's taxes!"

"Why not?" replied Bartemy, with a pious twist of his neck, and an upward cast of his blank orbs. "It is pour l'amour de Dieu! We beggars save more souls than the Cure; for we are always exhorting men to charity. I think we ought to be part of Holy Church as well as the Gray Friars."

"And so we are part of Holy Church, Bartemy!" interrupted Max Grimeau. "When the good Bishop washed twelve pair of our dirty feet on Maunday Thursday in the Cathedral, I felt like an Apostle--I did! My feet were just ready for benediction; for see! they had never been washed, that I remember of, since I marched to the relief of Prague! But you should have been out to Belmont to-day, Master Pothier! There was the grandest Easter pie ever made in New France! You might have carried on a lawsuit inside of it, and lived off the estate for a year--I ate a bushel of it. I did!"

"Oh, the cursed luck is every day mine!" replied Master Pothier, clapping his hands upon his stomach. "I would not have missed that Easter pie--no, not to draw the Pope's will! But, as it is laid down in the Coutume d' Orleans (Tit. 17), the absent lose the usufruct of their rights; vide, also, Pothier des Successions-- I lost my share of the pie of Belmont!"

"Well, never mind, Master Pothier," replied Max. "Don't grieve; you shall go with us to-night to the Fleur-de-Lis in the Sault au Matelot. Bartemy and I have bespoken an eel pie and a gallon of humming cider of Normandy. We shall all be jolly as the marguilliers of Ste. Roche, after tithing the parish!"

"Have with you, then! I am free now: I have just delivered a letter to the Intendant from a lady at Beaumanoir, and got a crown for it. I will lay it on top of your eel pie, Max!"

Angelique, from being simply amused at the conversation of the old beggars, became in an instant all eyes and ears at the words of Master Pothier.

"Had you ever the fortune to see that lady at Beaumanoir?" asked Max, with more curiosity than was to be expected of one in his position.

"No; the letter was handed me by Dame Tremblay, with a cup of wine. But the Intendant gave me a crown when he read it. I never saw the Chevalier Bigot in better humor! That letter touched both his purse and his feelings. But how did you ever come to hear of the Lady of Beaumanoir?"

"Oh, Bartemy and I hear everything at the gate of the Basse Ville! My Lord Bishop and Father Glapion of the Jesuits met in the gate one day and spoke of her, each asking the other if he knew who she was-- when up rode the Intendant; and the Bishop made free, as Bishops will, you know, to question him whether he kept a lady at the Chateau.

"'A round dozen of them, my Lord Bishop!' replied Bigot, laughing. La! It takes the Intendant to talk down a Bishop! He bade my Lord not to trouble himself, the lady was under his tutelle! which I comprehended as little, as little--"

"As you do your Nominy Dominy!" replied Pothier. "Don't be angry, Max, if I infer that the Intendant quoted Pigean (Tit. 2, 27): 'Le Tuteur est comptable de sa gestion.'"

"I don't care what the pigeons have to say to it--that is what the Intendant said!" replied Max, hotly, "and THAT, for your law grimoire, Master Pothier!" Max snapped his fingers like the lock of his musket at Prague, to indicate what he meant by THAT!

"Oh, inepte loquens! you don't understand either law or Latin, Max!" exclaimed Pothier, shaking his ragged wig with an air of pity.

"I understand begging; and that is getting without cheating, and much more to the purpose," replied Max, hotly. "Look you, Master Pothier! you are learned as three curates; but I can get more money in the gate of the Basse Ville by simply standing still and crying out Pour l'amour de Dieu! than you with your budget of law lingo- jingo, running up and down the country until the dogs eat off the calves of your legs, as they say in the Nivernois."

"Well, never mind what they say in the Nivernois about the calves of my legs! Bon coq ne fut jamais gras!--a game-cock is never fat--and that is Master Pothier dit Robin. Lean as are my calves, they will carry away as much of your eel pie to-night as those of the stoutest carter in Quebec!"

"And the pie is baked by this time; so let us be jogging!" interrupted Bartemy, rising. "Now give me your arm, Max! and with Master Pothier's on the other side, I shall walk to the Fleur-de-Lis straight as a steeple."

The glorious prospect of supper made all three merry as crickets on a warm hearth, as they jogged over the pavement in their clouted shoes, little suspecting they had left a flame of anger in the breast of Angelique des Meloises, kindled by the few words of Pothier respecting the lady of Beaumanoir.

Angelique recalled with bitterness that the rude bearer of the note had observed something that had touched the heart and opened the purse of the Intendant. What was it? Was Bigot playing a game with Angelique des Meloises? Woe to him and the lady of Beaumanoir if he was! As she sat musing over it a knock was heard on the door of her boudoir. She left the balcony and reentered her room, where a neat, comely girl in a servant's dress was waiting to speak to her.

The girl was not known to Angelique. But courtesying very low, she informed her that she was Fanchon Dodier, a cousin of Lizette's. She had been in service at the Chateau of Beaumanoir, but had just left it. "There is no living under Dame Tremblay," said she, "if she suspect a maid servant of flirting ever so little with M. Froumois, the handsome valet of the Intendant! She imagined that I did; and such a life as she has led me, my Lady! So I came to the city to ask advice of cousin Lizette, and seek a new place. I am sure Dame Tremblay need not be so hard upon the maids. She is always boasting of her own triumphs when she was the Charming Josephine."

"And Lizette referred you to me?" asked Angelique, too occupied just now to mind the gossip about Dame Tremblay, which another time she would have enjoyed immensely. She eyed the girl with intense curiosity; for might she not tell her something of the secret over which she was eating her heart out?

"Yes, my Lady! Lizette referred me to you, and told me to be very circumspect indeed about what I said touching the Intendant, but simply to ask if you would take me into your service. Lizette need not have warned me about the Intendant; for I never reveal secrets of my masters or mistresses, never! never, my Lady!"

"You are more cunning than you look, nevertheless," thought Angelique, "whatever scruple you may have about secrets." "Fanchon," said she, "I will make one condition with you: I will take you into my service if you will tell me whether you ever saw the Lady of Beaumanoir."

Angelique's notions of honor, clear enough in theory, never prevented her sacrificing them without compunction to gain an object or learn a secret that interested her.

"I will willingly tell you all I know, my Lady. I have seen her once; none of the servants are supposed to know she is in the Chateau, but of course all do." Fanchon stood with her two hands in the pockets of her apron, as ready to talk as the pretty grisette who directed Lawrence Sterne to the Opera Comique.

"Of course!" remarked Angelique, "a secret like that could never be kept in the Chateau of Beaumanoir! Now tell me, Fanchon, what is she like?" Angelique sat up eagerly and brushed back the hair from her ear with a rapid stroke of her hand as she questioned the girl. There was a look in her eyes that made Fanchon a little afraid, and brought out more truth than she intended to impart.

"I saw her this morning, my Lady, as she knelt in her oratory: the half-open door tempted me to look, in spite of the orders of Dame Tremblay."

"Ah! you saw her this morning!" repeated Angelique impetuously; "how does she appear? Is she better in looks than when she first came to the Chateau, or worse? She ought to be worse, much worse!"

"I do not know, my Lady, but, as I said, I looked in the door, although forbid to do so. Half-open doors are so tempting, and one cannot shut one's eyes! Even a keyhole is hard to resist when you long to know what is on the other side of it--I always found it so!"

"I dare say you did! But how does she look?" broke in Angelique, impatiently stamping her dainty foot on the floor.

"Oh, so pale, my Lady! but her face is the loveliest I ever saw,-- almost," added she, with an after-thought; "but so sad! she looks like the twin sister of the blessed Madonna in the Seminary chapel, my Lady."

"Was she at her devotions, Fanchon?"

"I think not, my Lady: she was reading a letter which she had just received from the Intendant."

Angelique's eyes were now ablaze. She conjectured at once that Caroline was corresponding with Bigot, and that the letter brought to the Intendant by Master Pothier was in reply to one from him. "But how do you know the letter she was reading was from the Intendant? It could not be!" Angelique's eyebrows contracted angrily, and a dark shadow passed over her face. She said "It could not be," but she felt it could be, and was.

"Oh, but it was from the Intendant, my Lady! I heard her repeat his name and pray God to bless Francois Bigot for his kind words. That is the Intendant's name, is it not, my Lady?"

"To be sure it is! I should not have doubted you, Fanchon! but could you gather the purport of that letter? Speak truly, Fanchon, and I will reward you splendidly. What think you it was about?"

"I did more than gather the purport of it, my Lady: I have got the letter itself!" Angelique sprang up eagerly, as if to embrace Fanchon. "I happened, in my eagerness, to jar the door; the lady, imagining some one was coming, rose suddenly and left the room. In her haste she dropped the letter on the floor. I picked it up; I thought no harm, as I was determined to leave Dame Tremblay to-day. Would my Lady like to read the letter?"

Angelique fairly sprang at the offer. "You have got the letter, Fanchon? Let me see it instantly! How considerate of you to bring it! I will give you this ring for that letter!" She pulled a ring off her finger, and seizing Fanchon's hand, put it on hers. Fanchon was enchanted; she admired the ring, as she turned it round and round her finger.

"I am infinitely obliged, my Lady, for your gift. It is worth a million such letters," said she.

"The letter outweighs a million rings," replied Angelique as she tore it open violently and sat down to read.

The first word struck her like a stone:

"DEAR CAROLINE:"--it was written in the bold hand of the Intendant, which Angelique knew very well--"You have suffered too much for my sake, but I am neither unfeeling nor ungrateful. I have news for you! Your father has gone to France in search of you! No one suspects you to be here. Remain patiently where you are at present, and in the utmost secrecy, or there will be a storm which may upset us both. Try to be happy, and let not the sweetest eyes that were ever seen grow dim with needless regrets. Better and brighter days will surely come. Meanwhile, pray! pray, my Caroline! it will do you good, and perhaps make me more worthy of the love which I know is wholly mine.

"Adieu, FRANCOIS."

Angelique devoured rather than read the letter. She had no sooner perused it than she tore it up in a paroxysm of fury, scattering its pieces like snowflakes over the floor, and stamping on them with her firm foot as if she would tread them into annihilation.

Fanchon was not unaccustomed to exhibitions of feminine wrath; but she was fairly frightened at the terrible rage that shook Angelique from head to foot.

"Fanchon! did you read that letter?" demanded she, turning suddenly upon the trembling maid. The girl saw her mistress's cheeks twitch with passion, and her hands clench as if she would strike her if she answered yes.

Shrinking with fear, Fanchon replied faintly, "No, my Lady; I cannot read."

"And you have allowed no other person to read it?"

"No, my Lady; I was afraid to show the letter to any one; you know I ought not to have taken it!"

"Was no inquiry made about it?" Angelique laid her hand upon the girl's shoulder, who trembled from head to foot.

"Yes, my Lady; Dame Tremblay turned the Chateau upside down, looking for it; but I dared not tell her I had it!"

"I think you speak truth, Fanchon!" replied Angelique, getting somewhat over her passion; but her bosom still heaved, like the ocean after a storm. "And now mind what I say!"-- her hand pressed heavily on the girl's shoulder, while she gave her a look that seemed to freeze the very marrow in her bones. "You know a secret about the Lady of Beaumanoir, Fanchon, and one about me too! If you ever speak of either to man or woman, or even to yourself, I will cut the tongue out of your mouth and nail it to that door-post! Mind my words, Fanchon! I never fail to do what I threaten."

"Oh, only do not look so at me, my Lady!" replied poor Fanchon, perspiring with fear. "I am sure I never shall speak of it. I swear by our Blessed Lady of Ste. Foye! I will never breathe to mortal that I gave you that letter."

"That will do!" replied Angelique, throwing herself down in her great chair. "And now you may go to Lizette; she will attend to you. But REMEMBER!"

The frightened girl did not wait for another command to go. Angelique held up her finger, which to Fanchon looked terrible as a poniard. She hurried down to the servants' hall with a secret held fast between her teeth for once in her life; and she trembled at the very thought of ever letting it escape.

Angelique sat with her hands on her temples, staring upon the fire that flared and flickered in the deep fireplace. She had seen a wild, wicked vision there once before. It came again, as things evil never fail to come again at our bidding. Good may delay, but evil never waits. The red fire turned itself into shapes of lurid dens and caverns, changing from horror to horror until her creative fancy formed them into the secret chamber of Beaumanoir with its one fair, solitary inmate, her rival for the hand of the Intendant,--her fortunate rival, if she might believe the letter brought to her so strangely. Angelique looked fiercely at the fragments of it lying upon the carpet, and wished she had not destroyed it; but every word of it was stamped upon her memory, as if branded with a hot iron.

"I see it all, now!" exclaimed she--"Bigot's falseness, and her shameless effrontery in seeking him in his very house. But it shall not be!" Angelique's voice was like the cry of a wounded panther tearing at the arrow which has pierced his flank. "Is Angelique des Meloises to be humiliated by that woman? Never! But my bright dreams will have no fulfilment so long as she lives at Beaumanoir,-- so long as she lives anywhere!"

She sat still for a while, gazing into the fire; and the secret chamber of Beaumanoir again formed itself before her vision. She sprang up, touched by the hand of her good angel perhaps, and for the last time. "Satan whispered it again in my ear!" cried she. "Ste. Marie! I am not so wicked as that! Last night the thought came to me in the dark--I shook it off at dawn of day. To-night it comes again,--and I let it touch me like a lover, and I neither withdraw my hand nor tremble! To-morrow it will return for the last time and stay with me,--and I shall let it sleep on my pillow! The babe of sin will have been born and waxed to a full demon, and I shall yield myself up to his embraces! O Bigot, Bigot! what have you not done? C'est la faute a vous! C'est la faute a vous!" She repeated this exclamation several times, as if by accusing Bigot she excused her own evil imaginings and cast the blame of them upon him. She seemed drawn down into a vortex from which there was no escape. She gave herself up to its drift in a sort of passionate abandonment. The death or the banishment of Caroline were the only alternatives she could contemplate. "'The sweetest eyes that were ever seen'--Bigot's foolish words!" thought she; "and the influence of those eyes must be killed if Angelique des Meloises is ever to mount the lofty chariot of her ambition."

"Other women," she thought bitterly, "would abandon greatness for love, and in the arms of a faithful lover like Le Gardeur find a compensation for the slights of the Intendant!"

But Angelique was not like other women: she was born to conquer men-- not to yield to them. The steps of a throne glittered in her wild fancy, and she would not lose the game of her life because she had missed the first throw. Bigot was false to her, but he was still worth the winning, for all the reasons which made her first listen to him. She had no love for him--not a spark! But his name, his rank, his wealth, his influence at Court, and a future career of glory there--these things she had regarded as her own by right of her beauty and skill in ruling men. "No rival shall ever boast she has conquered Angelique des Meloises!" cried she, clenching her hands. And thus it was in this crisis of her fate the love of Le Gardeur was blown like a feather before the breath of her passionate selfishness. The weights of gold pulled her down to the nadir. Angelique's final resolution was irrevocably taken before her eager, hopeful lover appeared in answer to her summons recalling him from the festival of Belmont.

# Chapter XXIII: Seals of Love, but Sealed in Vain

She sat waiting Le Gardeur's arrival, and the thought of him began to assert its influence as the antidote of the poisonous stuff she had taken into her imagination. His presence so handsome, his manner so kind, his love so undoubted, carried her into a region of intense satisfaction. Angelique never thought so honestly well of herself as when recounting the marks of affection bestowed upon her by Le Gardeur de Repentigny. "His love is a treasure for any woman to possess, and he has given it all to me!" said she to herself. "There are women who value themselves wholly by the value placed upon them by others; but I value others by the measure of myself. I love Le Gardeur; and what I love I do not mean to lose!" added she, with an inconsequence that fitted ill with her resolution regarding the Intendant. But Angelique was one who reconciled to herself all professions, however opposite or however incongruous.

A hasty knock at the door of the mansion, followed by the quick, well-known step up the broad stair, brought Le Gardeur into her presence. He looked flushed and disordered as he took her eagerly- extended hand and pressed it to his lips.

Her whole aspect underwent a transformation in the presence of her lover. She was unfeignedly glad to see him. Without letting go his hand she led him to the sofa, and sat down by him. Other men had the semblance of her graciousness, and a perfect imitation it was too; but he alone had the reality of her affection.

"O Le Gardeur!" exclaimed she, looking him through and through, and detecting no flaw in his honest admiration, "can you forgive me for asking you to come and see me to-night? and for absolutely no reason--none in the world, Le Gardeur, but that I longed to see you! I was jealous of Belmont for drawing you away from the Maison des Meloises to-night!"

"And what better reason could I have in the world than that you were longing to see me, Angelique? I think I should leave the gate of Heaven itself if you called me back, darling! Your presence for a minute is more to me than hours of festivity at Belmont, or the company of any other woman in the world."

Angelique was not insensible to the devotion of Le Gardeur. Her feelings were touched, and never slow in finding an interpretation for them she raised his hand quickly to her lips and kissed it. "I had no motive in sending for you but to see you, Le Gardeur!" said she; "will that content you? If it won't--"

"This shall," replied he, kissing her cheek--which she was far from averting or resenting.

"That is so like you, Le Gardeur!" replied she,--"to take before it is given!" She stopped-- "What was I going to say?" added she. "It was given, and my contentment is perfect to have you here by my side!" If her thoughts reverted at this moment to the Intendant it was with a feeling of repulsion, and as she looked fondly on the face of Le Gardeur she could not help contrasting his handsome looks with the hard, swarthy features of Bigot.

"I wish my contentment were perfect, Angelique; but it is in your power to make it so-- will you? Why keep me forever on the threshold of my happiness, or of my despair, whichever you shall decree? I have spoken to Amelie tonight of you!"

"O do not press me, Le Gardeur!" exclaimed she, violently agitated, anxious to evade the question she saw burning on his lips, and distrustful of her own power to refuse; "not now! not to-night! Another day you shall know how much I love you, Le Gardeur! Why will not men content themselves with knowing we love them, without stripping our favors of all grace by making them duties, and in the end destroying our love by marrying us?" A flash of her natural archness came over her face as she said this.

"That would not be your case or mine, Angelique," replied he, somewhat puzzled at her strange speech. But she rose up suddenly without replying, and walked to a buffet, where stood a silver salver full of refreshments. "I suppose you have feasted so magnificently at Belmont that you will not care for my humble hospitalities," said she, offering him a cup of rare wine, a recent gift of the Intendant,--which she did not mention, however. "You have not told me a word yet of the grand party at Belmont. Pierre Philibert has been highly honored by the Honnetes Gens I am sure!"

"And merits all the honor he receives! Why were you not there too, Angelique? Pierre would have been delighted," replied he, ever ready to defend Pierre Philibert.

"And I too! but I feared to be disloyal to the Fripponne!" said she, half mockingly. "I am a partner in the Grand Company you know, Le Gardeur! But I confess Pierre Philibert is the handsomest man-- except one--in New France. I own to THAT. I thought to pique Amelie one day by telling her so, but on the contrary I pleased her beyond measure! She agreed without excepting even the one!"

"Amelie told me your good opinions of Pierre, and I thanked you for it!" said he, taking her hand. "And now, darling, since you cannot with wine, words, or winsomeness divert me from my purpose in making you declare what you think of me also, let me tell you I have promised Amelie to bring her your answer to-night!"

The eyes of Le Gardeur shone with a light of loyal affection. Angelique saw there was no escaping a declaration. She sat irresolute and trembling, with one hand resting on his arm and the other held up deprecatingly. It was a piece of acting she had rehearsed to herself for this foreseen occasion. But her tongue, usually so nimble and free, faltered for once in the rush of emotions that well-nigh overpowered her. To become the honored wife of Le Gardeur de Repentigny, the sister of the beauteous Amelie, the niece of the noble Lady de Tilly, was a piece of fortune to have satisfied, until recently, both her heart and her ambition. But now Angelique was the dupe of dreams and fancies. The Royal Intendant was at her feet. France and its courtly splendors and court intrigues opened vistas of grandeur to her aspiring and unscrupulous ambition. She could not forego them, and would not! She knew that, all the time her heart was melting beneath the passionate eyes of Le Gardeur.

"I have spoken to Amelie, and promised to take her your answer to- night," said he, in a tone that thrilled every fibre of her better nature. "She is ready to embrace you as her sister. Will you be my wife, Angelique?"

Angelique sat silent; she dared not look up at him. If she had, she knew her hard resolution would melt. She felt his gaze upon her without seeing it. She grew pale and tried to answer no, but could not; and she would not answer yes.

The vision she had so wickedly revelled in flashed again upon her at this supreme moment. She saw, in a panorama of a few seconds, the gilded halls of Versailles pass before her, and with the vision came the old temptation.

"Angelique!" repeated he, in a tone full of passionate entreaty, "will you be my wife, loved as no woman ever was,--loved as alone Le Gardeur de Repentigny can love you?"

She knew that. As she weakened under his pleading and grasped both his hands tight in hers, she strove to frame a reply which should say yes while it meant no; and say no which he should interpret yes.

"All New France will honor you as the Chatelaine de Repentigny! There will be none higher, as there will be none fairer, than my bride!" Poor Le Gardeur! He had a dim suspicion that Angelique was looking to France as a fitting theatre for her beauty and talents.

She still sat mute, and grew paler every moment. Words formed themselves upon her lips, but she feared to say them, so terrible was the earnestness of this man's love, and no less vivid the consciousness of her own. Her face assumed the hardness of marble, pale as Parian and as rigid; a trembling of her white lips showed the strife going on within her; she covered her eyes with her hand, that he might not see the tears she felt quivering under the full lids, but she remained mute.

"Angelique!" exclaimed he, divining her unexpressed refusal; "why do you turn away from me? You surely do not reject me? But I am mad to think it! Speak, darling! one word, one sign, one look from those dear eyes, in consent to be the wife of Le Gardeur, will bring life's happiness to us both!" He took her hand, and drew it gently from her eyes and kissed it, but she still averted her gaze from him; she could not look at him, but the words dropped slowly and feebly from her lips in response to his appeal:

"I love you, Le Gardeur, but I will not marry you!" said she. She could not utter more, but her hand grasped his with a fierce pressure, as if wanting to hold him fast in the very moment of refusal.

He started back, as if touched by fire. "You love me, but will not marry me! Angelique, what mystery is this? But you are only trying me! A thousand thanks for your love; the other is but a jest,--a good jest, which I will laugh at!" And Le Gardeur tried to laugh, but it was a sad failure, for he saw she did not join in his effort at merriment, but looked pale and trembling, as if ready to faint.

She laid her hands upon his heavily and sadly. He felt her refusal in the very touch. It was like cold lead. "Do not laugh, Le Gardeur, I cannot laugh over it; this is no jest, but mortal earnest! What I say I mean! I love you, Le Gardeur, but I will not marry you!"

She drew her hands away, as if to mark the emphasis she could not speak. He felt it like the drawing of his heartstrings.

She turned her eyes full upon him now, as if to look whether love of her was extinguished in him by her refusal. "I love you, Le Gardeur--you know I do! But I will not--I cannot--marry you now!" repeated she.

"Now!" he caught at the straw like a drowning swimmer in a whirlpool. "Now? I said not now but when you please, Angelique! You are worth a man's waiting his life for!"

"No, Le Gardeur!" she replied, "I am not worth your waiting for; it cannot be, as I once hoped it might be; but love you I do and ever shall!" and the false, fair woman kissed him fatuously. "I love you, Le Gardeur, but I will not marry you!"

"You do not surely mean it, Angelique!" exclaimed he; "you will not give me death instead of life? You cannot be so false to your own heart, so cruel to mine? See, Angelique! My saintly sister Amelie believed in your love, and sent these flowers to place in your hair when you had consented to be my wife,--her sister; you will not refuse them, Angelique?"

He raised his hand to place the garland upon her head, but Angelique turned quickly, and they fell at her feet. "Amelie's gifts are not for me, Le Gardeur--I do not merit them! I confess my fault: I am, I know, false to my own heart, and cruel to yours. Despise me,-- kill me for it if you will, Le Gardeur! better you did kill me, perhaps! but I cannot lie to you as I can to other men! Ask me not to change my resolution, for I neither can nor will." She spoke with impassioned energy, as if fortifying her refusal by the reiteration of it.

"It is past comprehension!" was all he could say, bewildered at her words thus dislocated from all their natural sequence of association. "Love me and not marry me!--that means she will marry another!" thought he, with a jealous pang. "Tell me, Angelique," continued he, after several moments of puzzled silence, "is there some inscrutable reason that makes you keep my love and reject my hand?"

"No reason, Le Gardeur! It is mad unreason,--I feel that,--but it is no less true. I love you, but I will not marry you." She spoke with more resolution now. The first plunge was over, and with it her fear and trembling as she sat on the brink.

The iteration drove him beside himself. He seized her hands, and exclaimed with vehemence,--"There is a man--a rival--a more fortunate lover--behind all this, Angelique des Meloises! It is not yourself that speaks, but one that prompts you. You have given your love to another, and discarded me! Is it not so?"

"I have neither discarded you, nor loved another," Angelique equivocated. She played her soul away at this moment with the mental reservation that she had not yet done what she had resolved to do upon the first opportunity--accept the hand of the Intendant Bigot.

"It is well for that other man, if there be one!" Le Gardeur rose and walked angrily across the room two or three times. Angelique was playing a game of chess with Satan for her soul, and felt that she was losing it.

"There was a Sphinx in olden times," said he, "that propounded a riddle, and he who failed to solve it had to die. Your riddle will be the death of me, for I cannot solve it, Angelique!"

"Do not try to solve it, dear Le Gardeur! Remember that when her riddle was solved the Sphinx threw herself into the sea. I doubt that may be my fate! But you are still my friend, Le Gardeur!" added she, seating herself again by his side, in her old fond, coquettish manner. "See these flowers of Amelie's, which I did not place in my hair; I treasure them in my bosom!" She gathered them up as she spoke, kissed them, and placed them in her bosom.

"You are still my friend, Le Gardeur?" Her eyes turned upon him with the old look she could so well assume.

"I am more than a thousand friends, Angelique!" replied he; "but I shall curse myself that I can remain so and see you the wife of another."

The very thought drove him to frenzy. He dashed her hand away and sprang up towards the door, but turned suddenly round. "That curse was not for you, Angelique!" said he, pale and agitated; "it was for myself, for ever believing in the empty love you professed for me. Good-by! Be happy! As for me, the light goes out of my life, Angelique, from this day forth."

"Oh, stop! stop, Le Gardeur! do not leave me so!" She rose and endeavored to restrain him, but he broke from her, and without adieu or further parley rushed out bareheaded into the street. She ran to the balcony to call him back, and leaning far over it, cried out, "Le Gardeur! Le Gardeur!" That voice would have called him from the dead could he have heard it, but he was already lost in the darkness. A few rapid steps resounded on the distant pavement, and Le Gardeur de Repentigny was lost to her forever!

She waited long on the balcony, looking over it for a chance of hearing his returning steps, but none came. It was the last impulse of her love to save her, but it was useless. "Oh, God!" she exclaimed in a voice of mortal agony, "he is gone forever--my Le Gardeur! my one true lover, rejected by my own madness, and for what?" She thought "For what!" and in a storm of passion, tearing her golden hair over her face, and beating her breast in her rage, she exclaimed,--"I am wicked, unutterably bad, worse and more despicable than the vilest creature that crouches under the bushes on the Batture! How dared I, unwomanly that I am, reject the hand I worship for sake of a hand I should loathe in the very act of accepting it? The slave that is sold in the market is better than I, for she has no choice, while I sell myself to a man whom I already hate, for he is already false to me! The wages of a harlot were more honestly earned than the splendor for which I barter soul and body to this Intendant!"

The passionate girl threw herself upon the floor, nor heeded the blood that oozed from her head, bruised on the hard wood. Her mind was torn by a thousand wild fancies. Sometimes she resolved to go out like the Rose of Sharon and seek her beloved in the city and throw herself at his feet, making him a royal gift of all he claimed of her.

She little knew her own wilful heart. She had seen the world bow to every caprice of hers, but she never had one principle to guide her, except her own pleasure. She was now like a goddess of earth, fallen in an effort to reconcile impossibilities in human hearts, and became the sport of the powers of wickedness.

She lay upon the floor senseless, her hands in a violent clasp. Her glorious hair, torn and disordered, lay over her like the royal robe of a queen stricken from her throne and lying dead upon the floor of her palace.

It was long after midnight, in the cold hours of the morning, when she woke from her swoon. She raised herself feebly upon her elbow, and looked dazedly up at the cold, unfeeling stars that go on shining through the ages, making no sign of sympathy with human griefs. Perseus had risen to his meridian, and Algol, her natal star, alternately darkened and brightened as if it were the scene of some fierce conflict of the powers of light and darkness, like that going on in her own soul.

Her face was stained with hard clots of blood as she rose, cramped and chilled to the bone. The night air had blown coldly upon her through the open lattice; but she would not summon her maid to her assistance. Without undressing she threw herself upon a couch, and utterly worn out by the agitation she had undergone, slept far into the day.

# Chapter XXIV: The Hurried Question of Despair

Le Gardeur plunged headlong down the silent street, neither knowing nor caring whither. Half mad with grief, half with resentment, he vented curses upon himself, upon Angelique, upon the world, and looked upon Providence itself as in league with the evil powers to thwart his happiness,--not seeing that his happiness in the love of a woman like Angelique was a house built on sand, which the first storm of life would sweep away.

"Holla! Le Gardeur de Repentigny! Is that you?" exclaimed a voice in the night. "What lucky wind blows you out at this hour?" Le Gardeur stopped and recognized the Chevalier de Pean. "Where are you going in such a desperate hurry?"

"To the devil!" replied Le Gardeur, withdrawing his hand from De Pean's, who had seized it with an amazing show of friendship. "It is the only road left open to me, and I am going to march down it like a garde du corps of Satan! Do not hold me, De Pean! Let go my arm! I am going to the devil, I tell you!"

"Why, Le Gardeur," was the reply, "that is a broad and well- travelled road--the king's highway, in fact. I am going upon it myself, as fast and merrily as any man in New France."

"Well, go on it then! March either before or after me, only don't go with me, De Pean; I am taking the shortest cuts to get to the end of it, and want no one with me." Le Gardeur walked doggedly on; but De Pean would not be shaken off. He suspected what had happened.

"The shortest cut I know is by the Taverne de Menut, where I am going now," said he, "and I should like your company, Le Gardeur! Our set are having a gala night of it, and must be musical as the frogs of Beauport by this hour! Come along!" De Pean again took his arm. He was not repelled this time.

"I don't care where I go, De Pean!" replied he, forgetting his dislike to this man, and submitting to his guidance,--the Taverne de Menut was just the place for him to rush into and drown his disappointment in wine. The two moved on in silence for a few minutes.

"Why, what ails you, Le Gardeur?" asked his companion, as they walked on arm in arm. "Has fortune frowned upon the cards, or your mistress proved a fickle jade like all her sex?"

His words were irritating enough to Le Gardeur. "Look you, De Pean, said he, stopping, "I shall quarrel with you if you repeat such remarks. But you mean no mischief I dare say, although I would not swear it!" Le Gardeur looked savage.

De Pean saw it would not be safe to rub that sore again. "Forgive me, Le Gardeur!" said he, with an air of sympathy well assumed. "I meant no harm. But you are suspicious of your friends to-night as a Turk of his harem."

I have reason to be! And as for friends, I find only such friends as you, De Pean! And I begin to think the world has no better!" The clock of the Recollets struck the hour as they passed under the shadow of its wall. The brothers of St. Francis slept quietly on their peaceful pillows, like sea birds who find in a rocky nook a refuge from the ocean storms. "Do you think the Recollets are happy, De Pean?" asked he, turning abruptly to his companion.

"Happy as oysters at high water, who are never crossed in love, except of their dinner! But that is neither your luck nor mine, Le Gardeur!" De Pean was itching to draw from his companion something with reference to what had passed with Angelique.

"Well, I would rather be an oyster than a man, and rather be dead than either!" was the reply of Le Gardeur. "How soon, think you, will brandy kill a man, De Pean?" asked he abruptly, after a pause of silence.

"It will never kill you, Le Gardeur, if you take it neat at Master Menut's. It will restore you to life, vigor, and independence of man and woman. I take mine there when I am hipped as you are, Le Gardeur. It is a specific for every kind of ill-fortune,--I warrant it will cure and never kill you."

They crossed the Place d'Armes. Nothing in sight was moving except the sentries who paced slowly like shadows up and down the great gateway of the Castle of St. Louis.

"It is still and solemn as a church-yard here," remarked De Pean; "all the life of the place is down at Menut's! I like the small hours," added he as the chime of the Recollets ceased. "They are easily counted, and pass quickly, asleep or awake. Two o'clock in the morning is the meridian of the day for a man who has wit to wait for it at Menut's!--these small hours are all that are worth reckoning in a man's life!"

Without consenting to accompany De Pean, Le Gardeur suffered himself to be led by him. He knew the company that awaited him there--the wildest and most dissolute gallants of the city and garrison were usually assembled there at this hour.

The famous old hostelry was kept by Master Menut, a burly Breton who prided himself on keeping everything full and plenty about his house--tables full, tankards full, guests full, and himself very full. The house was to-night lit up with unusual brilliance, and was full of company--Cadet, Varin, Mercier, and a crowd of the friends and associates of the Grand Company. Gambling, drinking, and conversing in the loudest strain on such topics as interested their class, were the amusements of the night. The vilest thoughts, uttered in the low argot of Paris, were much affected by them. They felt a pleasure in this sort of protest against the extreme refinement of society, just as the collegians of Oxford, trained beyond their natural capacity in morals, love to fall into slang and, like Prince Hal, talk to every tinker in his own tongue.

De Pean and Le Gardeur were welcomed with open arms at the Taverne de Menut. A dozen brimming glasses were offered them on every side. De Pean drank moderately. "I have to win back my losses of last night," said he, "and must keep my head clear." Le Gardeur, however, refused nothing that was offered him. He drank with all, and drank every description of liquor. He was speedily led up into a large, well-furnished room, where tables were crowded with gentlemen playing cards and dice for piles of paper money, which was tossed from hand to hand with the greatest nonchalance as the game ended and was renewed.

Le Gardeur plunged headlong into the flood of dissipation. He played, drank, talked argot, and cast off every shred of reserve. He doubled his stakes, and threw his dice reckless and careless whether he lost or won. His voice overbore that of the stoutest of the revellers. He embraced De Pean as his friend, who returned his compliments by declaring Le Gardeur de Repentigny to be the king of good fellows, who had the "strongest head to carry wine and the stoutest heart to defy dull care of any man in Quebec."

De Pean watched with malign satisfaction the progress of Le Gardeur's intoxication. If he seemed to flag, he challenged him afresh to drink to better fortune; and when he lost the stakes, to drink again to spite ill luck.

But let a veil be dropped over the wild doings of the Taverne de Menut. Le Gardeur lay insensible at last upon the floor, where he would have remained had not some of the servants of the inn who knew him lifted him up compassionately and placed him upon a couch, where he lay, breathing heavily like one dying. His eyes were fixed; his mouth, where the kisses of his sister still lingered, was partly opened, and his hands were clenched, rigid as a statue's.

"He is ours now!" said De Pean to Cadet. "He will not again put his head under the wing of the Philiberts!"

The two men looked at him, and laughed brutally.

"A fair lady whom you know, Cadet, has given him liberty to drink himself to death, and he will do it."

"Who is that? Angelique?" asked Cadet.

"Of course; who else? and Le Gardeur won't be the first or last man she has put under stone sheets," replied De Pean, with a shrug of his shoulders.

"Gloria patri filioque!" exclaimed Cadet, mockingly; "the Honnetes Gens will lose their trump card. How did you get him away from Belmont, De Pean?"

"Oh, it was not I! Angelique des Meloises set the trap and whistled the call that brought him," replied De Pean.

"Like her, the incomparable witch!" exclaimed Cadet with a hearty laugh. "She would lure the very devil to play her tricks instead of his own. She would beat Satan at his best game to ruin a man."

"It would be all the same, Cadet, I fancy--Satan or she! But where is Bigot? I expected him here."

"Oh, he is in a tantrum to-night, and would not come. That piece of his at Beaumanoir is a thorn in his flesh, and a snow-ball on his spirits. She is taming him. By St. Cocufin! Bigot loves that woman!"

"I told you that before, Cadet. I saw it a month ago, and was sure of it on that night when he would not bring her up to show her to us."

"Such a fool, De Pean, to care for any woman! What will Bigot do with her, think you?"

"How should I know? Send her adrift some fine day I suppose, down the Riviere du Loup. He will, if he is a sensible man. He dare not marry any woman without license from La Pompadour, you know. The jolly fish-woman holds a tight rein over her favorites. Bigot may keep as many women as Solomon--the more the merrier; but woe befall him if he marries without La Pompadour's consent! They say she herself dotes on Bigot,--that is the reason." De Pean really believed that was the reason; and certainly there was reason for suspecting it.

"Cadet! Cadet!" exclaimed several voices. "You are fined a basket of champagne for leaving the table."

"I'll pay it," replied he, "and double it; but it is hot as Tartarus in here. I feel like a grilled salmon." And indeed, Cadet's broad, sensual face was red and glowing as a harvest moon. He walked a little unsteady too, and his naturally coarse voice sounded thick, but his hard brain never gave way beyond a certain point under any quantity of liquor.

"I am going to get some fresh air," said he. "I shall walk as far as the Fleur-de-Lis. They never go to bed at that jolly old inn."

"I will go with you!" "And I!" exclaimed a dozen voices.

"Come on then; we will all go to the old dog-hole, where they keep the best brandy in Quebec. It is smuggled of course, but that makes it all the better."

Mine host of the Taverne de Menut combatted this opinion of the goodness of the liquors at the Fleur-de-Lis. His brandy had paid the King's duties, and bore the stamp of the Grand Company, he said; and he appealed to every gentleman present on the goodness of his liquors.

Cadet and the rest took another round of it to please the landlord, and sallied out with no little noise and confusion. Some of them struck up the famous song which, beyond all others, best expressed the gay, rollicking spirit of the French nation and of the times of the old regime:

"'Vive Henri Quatre!
Vive le Roi vaillant!
Ce diable a quatre

A le triple talent,
De boire et de battre,
Et d'etre un vert galant!'"

When the noisy party arrived at the Fleur-de-Lis, they entered without ceremony into a spacious room--low, with heavy beams and with roughly plastered walls, which were stuck over with proclamations of governors and intendants and dingy ballads brought by sailors from French ports.

A long table in the middle of the room was surrounded by a lot of fellows, plainly of the baser sort,--sailors, boatmen, voyageurs,-- in rough clothes, and tuques--red or blue,--upon their heads. Every one had a pipe in his mouth. Some were talking with loose, loquacious tongues; some were singing; their ugly, jolly visages-- half illumined by the light of tallow candles stuck in iron sconces on the wall--were worthy of the vulgar but faithful Dutch pencils of Schalken and Teniers. They were singing a song as the new company came in.

At the head of the table sat Master Pothier, with a black earthen mug of Norman cider in one hand and a pipe in the other. His budget of law hung on a peg in the corner, as quite superfluous at a free- and-easy at the Fleur-de-Lis.

Max Grimeau and Blind Bartemy had arrived in good time for the eel pie. They sat one on each side of Master Pothier, full as ticks and merry as grigs; a jolly chorus was in progress as Cadet entered.

The company rose and bowed to the gentlemen who had honored them with a call. "Pray sit down, gentlemen; take our chairs!" exclaimed Master Pothier, officiously offering his to Cadet, who accepted it as well as the black mug, of which he drank heartily, declaring old Norman cider suited his taste better than the choicest wine.

"We are your most humble servitors, and highly esteem the honor of your visit," said Master Pothier, as he refilled the black mug.

"Jolly fellows!" replied Cadet, stretching his legs refreshingly, "this does look comfortable. Do you drink cider because you like it, or because you cannot afford better?"

"There is nothing better than Norman cider, except Cognac brandy," replied Master Pothier, grinning from ear to ear. "Norman cider is fit for a king, and with a lining of brandy is drink for a Pope! It will make a man see stars at noonday. Won't it, Bartemy?"

"What! old turn-penny! are you here?" cried Cadet, recognizing the old beggar of the gate of the Basse Ville.

"Oh, yes, your Honor!" replied Bartemy, with his professional whine, "pour l'amour de Dieu!"

"Gad! you are the jolliest beggar I know out of the Friponne," replied Cadet, throwing him a crown.

"He is not a jollier beggar than I am, your Honor," said Max Grimeau, grinning like an Alsatian over a Strasbourg pie. "It was I sang bass in the ballad as you came in--you might have heard me, your Honor?"

"To be sure I did; I will be sworn there is not a jollier beggar in Quebec than you, old Max! Here is a crown for you too, to drink the Intendant's health and another for you, you roving limb of the law, Master Pothier! Come, Master Pothier! I will fill your ragged gown full as a demijohn of brandy if you will go on with the song you were singing."

"We were at the old ballad of the Pont d'Avignon, your Honor," replied Master Pothier.

"And I was playing it," interrupted Jean La Marche; "you might have heard my violin, it is a good one!" Jean would not hide his talent in a napkin on so auspicious an occasion as this.

He ran his bow over the strings and played a few bars,--"that was the tune, your Honor."

"Ay, that was it! I know the jolly old song! Now go on!" Cadet thrust his thumbs into the armholes of his laced waistcoat and listened attentively; rough as he was, he liked the old Canadian music.

Jean tuned his fiddle afresh, and placing it with a knowing jerk under his chin, and with an air of conceit worthy of Lulli, began to sing and play the old ballad:

"'A St. Malo, beau port de mer,
Trois navires sont arrives,
Charges d'avoine, charges de bled;
Trois dames s'en vont les merchander!'"

"Tut!" exclaimed Varin, "who cares for things that have no more point in them than a dumpling! give us a madrigal, or one of the devil's ditties from the Quartier Latin!"

"I do not know a 'devil's ditty,' and would not sing one if I did," replied Jean La Marche, jealous of the ballads of his own New France. "Indians cannot swear because they know no oaths, and habitans cannot sing devil's ditties because they never learned them; but 'St. Malo, beau port de mer,'--I will sing that with any man in the Colony!"

The popular songs of the French Canadians are simple, almost infantine, in their language, and as chaste in expression as the hymns of other countries. Impure songs originate in classes who know better, and revel from choice in musical slang and indecency.

"Sing what you like! and never mind Varin, my good fellow," said Cadet, stretching himself in his chair; "I like the old Canadian ballads better than all the devil's ditties ever made in Paris! You must sing your devil's ditties yourself, Varin; our habitans won't,-- that is sure!"

After an hour's roystering at the Fleur-de-Lis the party of gentlemen returned to the Taverne de Menut a good deal more unsteady and more obstreperous than when they came. They left Master Pothier seated in his chair, drunk as Bacchus, and every one of the rest of his companions blind as Bartemy.

The gentlemen, on their return to the Taverne de Menut, found De Pean in a rage. Pierre Philibert had followed Amelie to the city, and learning the cause of her anxiety and unconcealed tears, started off with the determination to find Le Gardeur.

The officer of the guard at the gate of the Basse Ville was able to direct him to the right quarter. He hastened to the Taverne de Menut, and in haughty defiance of De Pean, with whom he had high words, he got the unfortunate Le Gardeur away, placed him in a carriage, and took him home, receiving from Amelie such sweet and sincere thanks as he thought a life's service could scarcely have deserved.

"Par Dieu! that Philibert is a game-cock, De Pean," exclaimed Cadet, to the savage annoyance of the Secretary. "He has pluck and impudence for ten gardes du corps. It was neater done than at Beaumanoir!" Cadet sat down to enjoy a broad laugh at the expense of his friend over the second carrying off of Le Gardeur.

"Curse him! I could have run him through, and am sorry I did not," exclaimed De Pean.

"No, you could not have run him through, and you would have been sorry had you tried it, De Pean," replied Cadet. "That Philibert is not as safe as the Bank of France to draw upon. I tell you it was well for yourself you did not try, De Pean. But never mind," continued Cadet, "there is never so bad a day but there is a fair to-morrow after it, so make up a hand at cards with me and Colonel Trivio, and put money in your purse; it will salve your bruised feelings." De Pean failed to laugh off his ill humor, but he took Cadet's advice, and sat down to play for the remainder of the night.

"Oh, Pierre Philibert, how can we sufficiently thank you for your kindness to my dear, unhappy brother?" said Amelie to him, her eyes tremulous with tears and her hand convulsively clasping his, as Pierre took leave of her at the door of the mansion of the Lady de Tilly.

"Le Gardeur claims our deepest commiseration, Amelie," replied he; "you know how this has happened?"

"I do know, Pierre, and shame to know it. But you are so generous ever. Do not blame me for this agitation!" She strove to steady herself, as a ship will right up for a moment in veering.

"Blame you! what a thought! As soon blame the angels for being good! But I have a plan, Amelie, for Le Gardeur--we must get him out of the city and back to Tilly for a while. Your noble aunt has given me an invitation to visit the Manor House. What if I manage to accompany Le Gardeur to his dear old home?"

"A visit to Tilly in your company would, of all things, delight Le Gardeur," said she, "and perhaps break those ties that bind him to the city."

These were pleasing words to Philibert, and he thought how delightful would be her own fair presence also at Tilly.

"All the physicians in the world will not help Le Gardeur as will your company at Tilly!" exclaimed she, with a sudden access of hope. "Le Gardeur needs not medicine, only care, and--"

"The love he has set his heart on, Amelie! Men sometimes die when they fail in that." He looked at her as he said this, but instantly withdrew his eyes, fearing he had been overbold.

She blushed, and only replied, with absolute indirection, "Oh, I am so thankful to you, Pierre Philibert!" But she gave him, as he left, a look of gratitude and love which never effaced itself from his memory. In after-years, when Pierre Philibert cared not for the light of the sun, nor for woman's love, nor for life itself, the tender, impassioned glance of those dark eyes wet with tears came back to him like a break in the dark clouds, disclosing the blue heaven beyond; and he longed to be there.

## Chapter XXV: Betwixt the Last Violet and the Earliest Rose

"Do not go out to-day, brother, I want you so particularly to stay with me to-day," said Amelie de Repentigny, with a gentle, pleading voice. "Aunt has resolved to return to Tilly to-morrow; I need your help to arrange these papers, and anyway, I want your company, brother," added she, smiling.

Le Gardeur sat feverish, nervous, and ill after his wild night spent at the Taverne de Menut. He started and reddened as his sister's eyes rested on him. He looked through the open window like a wild animal ready to spring out of it and escape.

A raging thirst was on him, which Amelie sought to assuage by draughts of water, milk, and tea--a sisterly attention which he more than once acknowledged by kissing the loving fingers which waited upon him so tenderly.

"I cannot stay in the house, Amelie," said he; "I shall go mad if I do! You know how it has fared with me, sweet sister! I yesterday built up a tower of glass, high as heaven, my heaven--a woman's love; to-day I am crushed under the ruins of it."

"Say not so, brother! you were not made to be crushed by the nay of any faithless woman. Oh! why will men think more of our sex than we deserve? How few of us do deserve the devotion of a good and true man!"

"How few men would be worthy of you, sweet sister!' replied he, proudly. "Ah! had Angelique had your heart, Amelie!"

"You will be glad one day of your present sorrow, brother," replied she. "It is bitter I know, and I feel its bitterness with you, but life with Angelique would have been infinitely harder to bear."

He shook his head, not incredulously, but defiantly at fate. "I would have accepted it," said he, "had I been sure life with her had been hard as millstones! My love is of the perverse kind, not to be transmuted by any furnace of fiery trial."

"I have no answer, brother, but this:" and Amdlie stooped and kissed his fevered forehead. She was too wise to reason in a case where she knew reason always made default.

"What has happened at the Manor House," asked he after a short silence, "that aunt is going to return home sooner than she expected when she left?"

"There are reports to-day of Iroquois on the upper Chaudiere, and her censitaires are eager to return to guard their homes from the prowling savages; and what is more, you and Colonel Philibert are ordered to go to Tilly to look after the defence of the Seigniory."

Le Gardeur sat bolt upright. His military knowledge could not comprehend an apparently useless order. "Pierre Philibert and I ordered to Tilly to look after the defence of the Seigniory! We had no information yesterday that Iroquois were within fifty leagues of Tilly. It is a false rumor raised by the good wives to get their husbands home again! Don't you think so, Amelie?" asked he, smiling for the first time.

"No, I don't think so, Le Gardeur! but it would be a pretty ruse de guerre, were it true. The good wives naturally feel nervous at being left alone--I should myself," added she, playfully.

"Oh, I don't know! the nervous ones have all come with the men to the city; but I suppose the works are sufficiently advanced, and the men can be spared to return home. But what says Pierre Philibert to the order despatching him to Tilly? You have seen him since?"

Amelie blushed a little as she replied, "Yes, I have seen him; he is well content, I think, to see Tilly once more in your company, brother."

"And in yours, sister!--Why blush, Amelie? Pierre is worthy of you, should he ever say to you what I so vainly said last night to Angelique des Meloises!" Le Gardeur held her tightly by the hand.

Her face was glowing scarlet,--she was in utter confusion. "Oh, stop, brother! Don't say such things! Pierre never uttered such thoughts to me!--never will, in all likelihood!"

"But he will! And, my darling sister, when Pierre Philibert shall say he loves you and asks you to be his wife, if you love him, if you pity me, do not say him nay!" She was trembling with agitation, and without power to reply. But Le Gardeur felt her hand tighten upon his. He comprehended the involuntary sign, drew her to him, kissed her, and left the topic without pressing it further; leaving it in the most formidable shape to take deep root in the silent meditations of Amelie.

The rest of the day passed in such sunshine as Amelie could throw over her brother. Her soft influence retained him at home: she refreshed him with her conversation and sympathy, drew from him the pitiful story of his love and its bitter ending. She knew the relief of disburdening his surcharged heart; and to none but his sister, from whom he had never had a secret until this episode in his life, would he have spoken a word of his heart's trouble.

Numerous were the visitors to-day at the hospitable mansion of the Lady de Tilly; but Le Gardeur would see none of them except Pierre Philibert, who rode over as soon as he was relieved from his military attendance at the Castle of St. Louis.

Le Gardeur received Pierre with an effusion of grateful affection-- touching, because real. His handsome face, so like Amelie's, was peculiarly so when it expressed the emotions habitual to her; and the pleasure both felt in the presence of Pierre brought out resemblances that flashed fresh on the quick, observant eye of Pierre.

The afternoon was spent in conversation of that kind which gives and takes with mutual delight. Le Gardeur seemed more his old self again in the company of Pierre; Amelie was charmed at the visible influence of Pierre over him, and a hope sprang up in her bosom that the little artifice of beguiling Le Gardeur to Tilly in the companionship of Pierre might be the means of thwarting those adverse influences which were dragging him to destruction.

If Pierre Philibert grew more animated in the presence of those bright eyes, which were at once appreciative and sympathizing, Amelie drank in the conversation of Pierre as one drinks the wine of a favorite vintage. If her heart grew a little intoxicated, what the wonder? Furtively as she glanced at the manly countenance of Pierre, she saw in it the reflection of his noble mind and independent spirit; and remembering the injunction of Le Gardeur,-- for, woman-like, she sought a support out of herself to justify a foregone conclusion,--she thought that if Pierre asked her she could be content to share his lot, and her greatest happiness would be to live in the possession of his love.

Pierre Philibert took his departure early from the house of the Lady de Tilly, to make his preparations for leaving the city next day. His father was aware of his project, and approved of it.

The toils of the day were over in the house of the Chien d'Or. The Bourgeois took his hat and sword and went out for a walk upon the cape, where a cool breeze came up fresh from the broad river. It was just the turn of tide. The full, brimming waters, reflecting here and there a star, began to sparkle under the clear moon that rose slowly and majestically over the hills of the south shore.

The Bourgeois sat down on the low wall of the terrace to enjoy the freshness and beauty of the scene which, although he had seen it a hundred times before, never looked lovelier, he thought, than this evening. He was very happy in his silent thoughts over his son's return home; and the general respect paid him on the day of his fete had been more felt, perhaps, by the

Bourgeois than by Pierre himself.

As he indulged in these meditations, a well-known voice suddenly accosted him. He turned and was cordially greeted by the Count de la Galissoniere and Herr Kalm, who had sauntered through the garden of the Castle and directed their steps towards the cape with intention to call upon the Lady de Tilly and pay their respects to her before she left the city.

The Bourgeois, learning their intentions, said he would accompany them, as he too owed a debt of courtesy to the noble lady and her niece Amelie, which he would discharge at the same time.

The three gentlemen walked gravely on, in pleasant conversation. The clearness of the moonlit night threw the beautiful landscape, with its strongly accentuated features, into contrasts of light and shade to which the pencil of Rembrandt alone could have done justice. Herr Kalm was enthusiastic in his admiration,--moonlight over Drachenfels on the Rhine, or the midnight sun peering over the Gulf of Bothnia, reminded him of something similar, but of nothing so grand on the whole as the matchless scene visible from Cape Diamond--worthy of its name.

Lady de Tilly received her visitors with the gracious courtesy habitual to her. She especially appreciated the visit from the Bourgeois, who so rarely honored the houses of his friends by his welcome presence. As for His Excellency, she remarked, smiling, it was his official duty to represent the politeness of France to the ladies of the Colony, while Herr Kalm, representing the science of Europe, ought to be honored in every house he chose to visit,--she certainly esteemed the honor of his presence in her own.

Amelie made her appearance in the drawing-room, and while the visitors stayed exerted herself to the utmost to please and interest them by taking a ready and sympathetic part in their conversation. Her quick and cultivated intellect enabled her to do so to the delight, and even surprise, of the three grave, learned gentlemen. She lacked neither information nor opinions of her own, while her speech, soft and womanly, gave a delicacy to her free yet modest utterances that made her, in their recollections of her in the future, a standard of comparison,--a measure of female perfections.

Le Gardeur, learning who were in the house, came down after a while to thank the Governor, the Bourgeois, and Herr Kalm for the honor of their visit. He exerted himself by a desperate effort to be conversable,--not very successfully, however; for had not Amelie watched him with deepest sympathy and adroitly filled the breaks in his remarks, he would have failed to pass himself creditably before the Governor. As it was, Le Gardeur contented himself with following the flow of conversation which welled up copiously from the lips of the rest of the company.

After a while came in Felix Baudoin in his full livery, reserved for special occasions, and announced to his lady that tea was served. The gentlemen were invited to partake of what was then a novelty in New France. The Bourgeois, in the course of the new traffic with China that had lately sprung up in consequence of the discovery of ginseng in New France, had imported some chests of tea, which the Lady de Tilly, with instinctive perception of its utility, adopted at once as the beverage of polite society. As yet, however, it was only to be seen upon the tables of the refined and the affluent.

A fine service of porcelain of Chinese make adorned her table, pleasing the fancy with its grotesque pictures,--then so new, now so familiar to us all. The Chinese garden and summer-house, the fruit- laden trees, and river with overhanging willows; the rustic bridge with the three long-robed figures passing over it; the boat floating upon the water and the doves flying in the perspectiveless sky--who does not remember them all?

Lady de Tilly, like a true gentlewoman, prized her china, and thought kindly of the mild, industrious race who had furnished her tea-table with such an elegant equipage.

It was no disparagement to the Lady de Tilly that she had not read English poets who sang the praise of tea: English poets were in those days an unknown quantity in French education, and especially in New France until after the conquest. But Wolfe opened the great world of English poetry to Canada as he recited Gray's Elegy with its prophetic line,--

"The paths of glory lead but to the grave,"

as he floated down the St. Lawrence in that still autumnal night to land his forces and scale by stealth the fatal Heights of Abraham, whose possession led to the conquest of the city and his own heroic death, then it was the two glorious streams of modern thought and literature united in New France, where they have run side by side to this day,--in time to be united in one grand flood stream of Canadian literature.

The Bourgeois Philibert had exported largely to China the newly discovered ginseng, for which at first the people of the flowery kingdom paid, in their sycee silver, ounce for ounce. And his Cantonese correspondent esteemed himself doubly fortunate when he was enabled to export his choicest teas to New France in exchange for the precious root.

Amelie listened to an eager conversation between the Governor and Herr Kalm, started by the latter on the nature, culture, and use of the tea-plant,--they would be trite opinions now,-- with many daring speculations on the ultimate conquest of the tea-cup over the wine- cup. "It would inaugurate the third beatitude!" exclaimed the philosopher, pressing together the tips of the fingers of both hands, "and the 'meek would inherit the earth;'" so soon as the use of tea became universal, mankind would grow milder, as their blood was purified from the fiery products of the still and the wine- press! The life of man would be prolonged and made more valuable.

"What has given China four thousand of years of existence?" asked Herr Kaim, abruptly, of the Count.

The Count could not tell, unless it were that the nation was dead already in all that regarded the higher life of national existence,-- had become mummified, in fact,--and did not know it.

"Not at all!" replied Herr Kalm. "It is the constant use of the life-giving infusion of tea that has saved China! Tea soothes the nerves; it clears the blood, expels vapors from the brain, and restores the fountain of life to pristine activity. Ergo, it prolongs the existence of both men and nations, and has made China the most antique nation in the world."

Herr Kalm was a devotee to the tea-cup; he drank it strong to excite his flagging spirits, weak to quiet them down. He took Bohea with his facts, and Hyson with his fancy, and mixed them to secure the necessary afflatus to write his books of science and travel. Upon Hyson he would have attempted the Iliad, upon Bohea he would undertake to square the circle, discover perpetual motion, or reform the German philosophy.

The professor was in a jovial mood, and gambolled away gracefully as a Finland horse under a pack-saddle laden with the learning of a dozen students of Abo, travelling home for the holidays.

"We are fortunate in being able to procure our tea in exchange for our useless ginseng," remarked the Lady de Tilly, as she handed the professor a tiny plate of the leaves, as was the fashion of the day. After drinking the tea, the infused leaves were regarded as quite a fashionable delicacy. Except for the fashion, it had not been perhaps considered a delicacy at all.

The observation of the Lady de Tilly set the professor off on another branch of the subject. "He had observed," he said, "the careless methods of preparing the ginseng in New France, and predicted a speedy end of the traffic, unless it were prepared to suit the fancy of the fastidious Chinese."

"That is true, Herr Kalm," replied the Governor, "but our Indians who gather it are bad managers. Our friend Philibert, who opened this lucrative trade, is alone capable of ensuring its continuance. It is a mine of wealth to New France, if rightly developed. How much made you last year by ginseng, Philibert?"

"I can scarcely answer," replied the Bourgeois, hesitating a moment to mention what might seem like egotism; "but the half million I contributed towards the war in defence of Acadia was wholly the product of my export of ginseng to China."

"I know it was! and God bless you for it, Philibert!" exclaimed the Governor with emotion, as he grasped the hand of the patriotic merchant.

"If we have preserved New France this year, it was through your timely help in Acadia. The King's treasury was exhausted," continued the Governor, looking at Herr Kalm, "and ruin imminent, when the noble merchant of the Chien d'Or fed, clothed, and paid the King's troops for two months before the taking of Grand Pre from the enemy!"

"No great thing in that, your Excellency," replied the Bourgeois, who hated compliments to himself. "If those who have do not give, how can you get from those who have not? You may lay some of it to the account of Pierre too,--he was in Acadia, you know, Governor." A flash of honest pride passed over the usually sedate features of the Bourgeois at the mention of his son.

Le Gardeur looked at his sister. She knew instinctively that his thoughts put into words would say, "He is worthy to be your father, Amelie!" She blushed with a secret pleasure, but spoke not. The music in her heart was without words yet; but one day it would fill the universe with harmony for her.

The Governor noticed the sudden reticence, and half surmising the cause, remarked playfully, "The Iroquois will hardly dare approach Tilly with such a garrison as Pierre Philibert and Le Gardeur, and with you, my Lady de Tilly, as commandant, and you, Mademoiselle Amelie, as aide-de-camp!"

"To be sure! your Excellency," replied the Lady de Tilly. "The women of Tilly have worn swords and kept the old house before now!" she added playfully, alluding to a celebrated defence of the chateau by a former lady of the Manor at the head of a body of her censitaires; "and depend upon it, we shall neither give up Tilly nor Le Gardeur either, to whatever savages claim them, be they red or white!"

The lady's allusion to his late associates did not offend Le Gardeur, whose honest nature despised their conduct, while he liked their company. They all understood her, and laughed. The Governor's loyalty to the King's commission prevented his speaking his thoughts. He only remarked, "Le Gardeur and Pierre Philibert will be under your orders, my Lady, and my orders are that they are not to return to the city until all dangers of the Iroquois are over."

"All right, your Excellency!" exclaimed Le Gardeur. "I shall obey my aunt." He was acute enough to see through their kindly scheming for his welfare; but his good nature and thorough devotion to his aunt and sister, and his affectionate friendship for Pierre, made him yield to the project without a qualm of regret. Le Gardeur was assailable on many sides,--a fault in his character--or a weakness-- which, at any rate, sometimes offered a lever to move him in directions opposite to the malign influences of Bigot and his associates.

The company rose from the tea-table and moved to the drawing-room, where conversation, music, and a few games of cards whiled away a couple of hours very pleasantly.

Amelie sang exquisitely. The Governor was an excellent musician, and accompanied her. His voice, a powerful tenor, had been strengthened by many a conflict with old Boreas on the high seas, and made soft and flexible by his manifold sympathies with all that is kindly and good and true in human nature.

A song of wonderful pathos and beauty had just been brought down from the wilds of the Ottawa, and become universally sung in New France. A voyageur flying from a band of Iroquois had found a hiding-place on a rocky islet in the middle of the Sept Chutes. He concealed himself from his foes, but could not escape, and in the end died of starvation and sleeplessness. The dying man peeled off the white bark of the birch, and with the juice of berries wrote upon it his death song, which was found long after by the side of his remains. His grave is now a marked spot on the Ottawa. La Complainte de Cadieux had seized the imagination of Amelie. She sang it exquisitely, and to-night needed no pressing to do so, for her heart was full of the new song, composed under such circumstances of woe. Intense was the sympathy of the company, as she began:

"'Petit rocher de la haute montagne,
Je viens finir ici cette campagne!
Ah! doux echos, entendez mes soupirs!
En languissant je vais bientot--mourir.'"

There were no dry eyes as she concluded. The last sighs of Cadieux seemed to expire on her lips:

"'Rossignole, va dire a ma maitresse,
A mes enfans, qu'un adieu je leur laisse,
Que j'ai garde mon amour et ma foi,
Et desormais faut renoncer a moi.'"

A few more friends of the family dropped in--Coulon de Villiers, Claude Beauharnais, La Corne St. Luc, and others, who had heard of the lady's departure and came to bid her adieu.

La Corne raised much mirth by his allusions to the Iroquois. The secret was plainly no secret to him. "I hope to get their scalps," said he, "when you have done with them and they with you, Le Gardeur!"

The evening passed on pleasantly, and the clock of the Recollets pealed out a good late hour before they took final leave of their hospitable hostess, with mutual good wishes and adieus, which with some of them were never repeated. Le Gardeur was no little touched and comforted by so much sympathy and kindness. He shook the Bourgeois affectionately by the hand, inviting him to come up to Tilly. It was noticed and remembered that this evening Le Gardeur clung filially, as it were, to the father of Pierre, and the farewell he gave him was tender, almost solemn, in a sort of sadness that left an impress upon all minds. "Tell Pierre--but indeed, he knows we start early," said Le Gardeur, "and the canoes will be waiting on the Batture an hour after sunrise.

The Bourgeois knew in a general way the position of Le Gardeur, and sympathized deeply with him. "Keep your heart up, my boy!" said he on leaving. "Remember the proverb,-- never forget it for a moment, Le Gardeur: Ce que Dieu garde est bien garde!"

"Good-by, Sieur Philibert!" replied he, still holding him by the hand. "I would fain be permitted to regard you as a father, since Pierre is all of a brother to me!"

"I will be a father, and a loving one too, if you will permit me, Le Gardeur," said the Bourgeois, touched by the appeal. "When you return to the city, come home with Pierre. At the Golden Dog, as well as at Belmont, there will be ever welcome for Pierre's friend as for Pierre's self."

The guests then took their departure.

The preparations for the journey home were all made, and the household retired to rest, all glad to return to Tilly. Even Felix Baudoin felt like a boy going back on a holiday. His mind was surcharged with the endless things he had gathered up, ready to pour into the sympathizing ear of Barbara Sanschagrin; and the servants and censitaires were equally eager to return to relate their adventures in the capital when summoned on the King's corvee to build the walls of Quebec.

# Chapter XXVI: The Canadian Boat-Song

"V'la l'bon vent!
V'la l'joli vent!
V'la l'bon vent!
Ma mie m'appelle!
V'la l'bon vent!
V'la l'joli vent!
V'la l'bon vent!
Ma mie m'attend!"

The gay chorus of the voyageurs made the shores ring, as they kept time with their oars, while the silver spray dripped like a shower of diamonds in the bright sunshine at every stroke of their rapid paddles. The graceful bark canoes, things of beauty and almost of life, leaped joyously over the blue waters of the St. Lawrence as they bore the family of the Lady de Tilly and Pierre Philibert with a train of censitaires back to the old Manor House.

The broad river was flooded with sunshine as it rolled majestically between the high banks crowned with green fields and woods in full leaf of summer. Frequent cottages and villages were visible along the shores, and now and then a little church with its bright spire or belfry marked the successive parishes on either hand.

The tide had already forced its way two hundred leagues up from the ocean, and still pressed irresistibly onward, surging and wrestling against the weight of the descending stream.

The wind too was favorable. A number of yachts and bateaux spread their snowy sails to ascend the river with the tide. They were for the most part laden with munitions of war for the Richelieu on their way to the military posts on Lake Champlain, or merchandise for Montreal to be reladen in fleets of canoes for the trading posts up the river of the Ottawas, the Great Lakes, or, mayhap, to supply the new and far-off settlements on the Belle Riviere and the Illinois.

The line of canoes swept past the sailing vessels with a cheer. The light-hearted crews exchanged salutations and bandied jests with each other, laughing immoderately at the well-worn jokes current upon the river among the rough voyageurs. A good voyage! a clear run! short portages and long rests! Some inquired whether their friends had paid for the bear and buffalo skins they were going to buy, or they complimented each other on their nice heads of hair, which it was hoped they would not leave behind as keepsakes with the Iroquois squaws.

The boat-songs of the Canadian voyageurs are unique in character, and very pleasing when sung by a crew of broad-chested fellows dashing their light birch-bark canoes over the waters rough or smooth, taking them, as they take fortune, cheerfully,--sometimes skimming like wild geese over the long, placid reaches, sometimes bounding like stags down the rough rapids and foaming saults.

Master Jean La Marche, clean as a new pin and in his merriest mood, sat erect as the King of Yvetot in the bow of the long canoe which held the Lady de Tilly and her family. His sonorous violin was coquettishly fixed in its place of honor under his wagging chin, as it accompanied his voice while he chanted an old boat-song which had lightened the labor of many a weary oar on lake and river, from the St. Lawrence to the Rocky Mountains.

Amelie sat in the stern of the canoe, laying her white hand in the cool stream which rushed past her. She looked proud and happy to- day, for the whole world of her affections was gathered together in that little bark.

She felt grateful for the bright sun; it seemed to have dispelled every cloud that lately shaded her thoughts on account of her brother, and she silently blessed the light breeze that played with her hair and cooled her cheek, which she felt was tinged with a warm glow of pleasure in the presence of Pierre Philibert.

She spoke little, and almost thanked the rough voyageurs for their incessant melodies, which made conversation difficult for the time, and thus left her to her own sweet silent thoughts, which seemed almost too sacred for the profanation of words.

An occasional look, or a sympathetic smile exchanged with her brother and her aunt, spoke volumes of pure affection. Once or twice the eyes of Pierre Philibert captured a glance of hers which might not have been intended for him, but which Amelie suffered him to intercept and hide away among the secret treasures of his heart. A glance of true affection--brief, it may be, as a flash of lightning--becomes, when caught by the eyes of love, a real thing, fixed and imperishable forever. A tender smile, a fond word of love's creation, contains a universe of light and life and immortality,--small things, and of little value to others, but to him or her whom they concern more precious and more prized than the treasures of Ind.

Master Jean La Marche, after a few minutes' rest, made still more refreshing by a draught from a suspicious-looking flask, which, out of respect for the presence of his mistress, the Lady de Tilly, he said contained "milk," began a popular boat-song which every voyageur in New France knew as well as his prayers, and loved to his very finger-ends.

The canoe-men pricked up their ears, like troopers at the sound of a bugle, as Jean La Marche began the famous old ballad of the king's son who, with his silver gun, aimed at the beautiful black duck, and shot the white one, out of whose eyes came gold and diamonds, and out of whose mouth rained silver, while its pretty feathers, scattered to the four winds, were picked up by three fair dames, who with them made a bed both large and deep--

"For poor wayfaring men to sleep."

Master Jean's voice was clear and resonant as a church bell newly christened; and he sang the old boat-song with an energy that drew the crews of half-a-dozen other canoes into the wake of his music, all uniting in the stirring chorus:

"Fringue! Fringue sur la riviere!

Fringue! Fringue sur l'aviron!"

The performance of Jean La Marche was highly relished by the critical boatmen, and drew from them that flattering mark of approval, so welcome to a vocalist,--an encore of the whole long ballad, from beginning to end.

As the line of canoes swept up the stream, a welcome cheer occasionally greeted them from the shore, or a voice on land joined in the gay refrain. They draw nearer to Tilly, and their voices became more and more musical, their gaiety more irrepressible, for they were going home; and home to the habitans, as well as to their lady, was the world of all delights.

The contagion of high spirits caught even Le Gardeur, and drew him out of himself, making him for the time forget the disappointments, resentments, and allurements of the city.

Sitting there in the golden sunshine, the blue sky above him, the blue waters below,--friends whom he loved around him, mirth in every eye, gaiety on every tongue,--how could Le Gardeur but smile as the music of the boatmen brought back a hundred sweet associations? Nay, he laughed, and to the inexpressible delight of Amelie and Pierre, who watched every change in his demeanor, united in the chorus of the glorious boat-song.

A few hours of this pleasant voyaging brought the little fleet of canoes under the high bank, which from its summit slopes away in a wide domain of forests, park, and cultivated fields, in the midst of which stood the high-pointed and many-gabled Manor House of Tilly.

Upon a promontory--as if placed there for both a land and sea mark, to save souls as well as bodies--rose the belfry of the Chapel of St. Michael, overlooking a cluster of white, old-fashioned cottages, which formed the village of St. Michael de Tilly.

Upon the sandy beach a crowd of women, children, and old men had gathered, who were cheering and clapping their hands at the unexpected return of the lady of the Manor with all their friends and relatives.

The fears of the villagers had been greatly excited for some days past by exaggerated reports of the presence of Iroquois on the upper waters of the Chaudiere. They not unnaturally conjectured, moreover, that the general call for men on the King's corvee, to fortify the city, portended an invasion by the English, who, it was rumored, were to come up in ships from below, as in the days of Sir William Phipps with his army of New Englanders, the story of whose defeat under the walls of Quebec was still freshly remembered in the traditions of the Colony.

"Never fear them!" said old Louis, the one-eyed pilot. "It was in my father's days. Many a time have I heard him tell the story--how, in the autumn of the good year 1690, thirty-four great ships of the Bostonians came up from below, and landed an army of ventres bleus of New England on the flats of Beauport. But our stout Governor, Count de Frontenac, came upon them from the woods with his brave soldiers, habitans, and Indians, and drove them pell-mell back to their boats, and stripped the ship of Admiral Phipps of his red flag, which, if you doubt my word,--which no one does,--still hangs over the high altar of the Church of Notre Dame des Victoires. Blessed be our Lady, who saved our country from our enemies,--and will do so again, if we do not by our wickedness lose her favor! But the arbre sec--the dry tree--still stands upon the Point de Levis, where the Boston fleet took refuge before beating their retreat down the river again,--and you know the old prophecy: that while that tree stands, the English shall never prevail against Quebec!"

Much comforted by this speech of old Louis the pilot, the villagers of Tilly rushed to the beach to receive their friends.

The canoes came dashing into shore. Men, women, and children ran knee-deep into the water to meet them, and a hundred eager hands were ready to seize their prows and drag them high and dry upon the sandy beach.

"Home again! and welcome to Tilly, Pierre Philibert!" exclaimed Lady de Tilly, offering her hand. "Friends like you have the right of welcome here." Pierre expressed his pleasure in fitting terms, and lent his aid to the noble lady to disembark.

Le Gardeur assisted Amelie out of the canoe. As he led her across the beach, he felt her hand tremble as it rested on his arm. He glanced down at her averted face, and saw her eyes directed to a spot well remembered by himself--the scene of his rescue from drowning by Pierre Philibert.

The whole scene came before Amelie at this moment. Her vivid recollection conjured up the sight of the inanimate body of her brother as it was brought ashore by the strong arm of Pierre Philibert and laid upon the beach; her long agony of suspense, and her joy, the greatest she had ever felt before or since, at his resuscitation to life, and lastly, her passionate vow which she made when clasping the neck of his preserver--a vow which she had enshrined as a holy thing in her heart ever since.

At that moment a strange fancy seized her: that Pierre Philibert was again plunging into deep water to rescue her brother, and that she would be called on by some mysterious power to renew her vow or fulfil it to the very letter.

She twitched Le Gardeur gently by the arm and said to him, in a half whisper, "It was there, brother! do you remember?"

"I know it, sister!" replied he; "I was also thinking of it. I am grateful to Pierre; yet, oh, my Amelie, better he had left me at the bottom of the deep river, where I had found my bed! I have no pleasure in seeing Tilly any more!"

"Why not, brother? Are we not all the same? Are we not all here? There is happiness and comfort for you at Tilly."

"There was once, Amelie," replied he, sadly; "but there will be none for me in the future, as I feel too well. I am not worthy of you, Amelie."

"Come, brother!" replied she, cheerily, "you dampen the joy of our arrival. See, the flag is going up on the staff of the turret, and old Martin is getting ready to fire off the culverin in honor of your arrival."

Presently there was a flash, a cloud of smoke, and the report of a cannon came booming down to the shore from the Manor House.

"That was well done of Martin and the women!" remarked Felix Baudoin, who had served in his youth, and therefore knew what was fitting in a military salute. "'The women of Tilly are better than the men of Beauce,' says the proverb."

"Ay, or of Tilly either!" remarked Josephte Le Tardeur, in a sharp, snapping tone. Josephte was a short, stout virago, with a turned-up nose and a pair of black eyes that would bore you through like an auger. She wore a wide-brimmed hat of straw, overtopping curls as crisp as her temper. Her short linsey petticoat was not chary of showing her substantial ankles, while her rolled-up sleeves displayed a pair of arms so red and robust that a Swiss milkmaid might well have envied them.

Her remark was intended for the ear of Jose Le Tardeur, her husband, a lazy, good-natured fellow, whose eyes had been fairly henpecked out of his head all the days of his married life. Josephte's speech hit him without hurting him, as he remarked to a neighbor. Josephte made a target of him every day. He was glad, for his part, that the women of Tilly were better soldiers than the men, and so much fonder of looking after things! It saved the men a deal of worry and a good deal of work.

"What are you saying, Jose?" exclaimed Felix, who only caught a few half words.

"I say, Master Felix, that but for Mere Eve there would have been no curse upon men, to make them labor when they do not want to, and no sin either. As the Cure says, we could have lain on the grass sunning ourselves all day long. Now it is nothing but work and pray, never play, else you will save neither body nor soul. Master Felix, I hope you will remember me if I come up to the Manor house."

"Ay, I will remember you, Jose," replied Felix, tartly; "but if labor was the curse which Eve brought into the world when she ate the apple, I am sure you are free from it. So ride up with the carts, Jose, and get out of the way of my Lady's carriage!"

Jose obeyed, and taking off his cap, bowed respectfully to the Lady de Tilly as she passed, leaning on the arm of Pierre Philibert, who escorted her to her carriage.

A couple of sleek Canadian horses, sure-footed as goats and strong as little elephants, drew the coach with a long, steady trot up the winding road which led to the Manor House.

The road, unfenced and bordered with grass on each side of the track, was smooth and well kept, as became the Grande Chaussee of the Barony of Tilly. It ran sometimes through stretches of cultivated fields--green pastures or corn-lands ripening for the sickle of the censitaire. Sometimes it passed through cool, shady woods, full of primeval grandeur,--part of the great Forest of Tilly, which stretched away far as the eye could reach over the hills of the south shore. Huge oaks that might have stood there from the beginning of the world, wide-branching elms, and dark pines overshadowed the highway, opening now and then into vistas of green fields where stood a cottage or two, with a herd of mottled cows grazing down by the brook. On the higher ridges the trees formed a close phalanx, and with their dark tops cut the horizon into a long, irregular line of forest, as if offering battle to the woodman's axe that was threatening to invade their solitudes.

Half an hour's driving brought the company to the Manor House, a stately mansion, gabled and pointed like an ancient chateau on the Seine.

It was a large, irregular structure of hammered stone, with deeply- recessed windows, mullioned and ornamented with grotesque carvings. A turret, loopholed and battlemented, projected from each of the four corners of the house, enabling its inmates to enfilade every side with a raking fire of musketry, affording an adequate defence against Indian foes. A stone tablet over the main entrance of the Manor House was carved with the armorial bearings of the ancient family of Tilly, with the date of its erection, and a pious invocation placing the house under the special protection of St. Michael de Thury, the patron saint of the House of Tilly.

The Manor House of Tilly had been built by Charles Le Gardeur de Tilly, a gentleman of Normandy, one of whose ancestors, the Sieur de Tilly, figures on the roll of Battle Abbey as a follower of Duke William at Hastings. His descendant, Charles Le Gardeur, came over to Canada with a large body of his vassals in 1636, having obtained from the King a grant of the lands of Tilly, on the bank of the St. Lawrence, "to hold in fief and seigniory,"--so ran the royal patent,--"with the right and jurisdiction of superior, moyenne and basse justice, and of hunting, fishing, and trading with the Indians throughout the whole of this royal concession; subject to the condition of foi et hommage, which he shall be held to perform at the Castle of St. Louis in Quebec, of which he shall hold under the customary duties and dues, agreeably to the coutume de Paris followed in this country."

Such was the style of the royal grants of seignioral rights conceded in New France, by virtue of one of which this gallant Norman gentleman founded his settlement and built this Manor House on the shores of the St. Lawrence.

A broad, smooth carriage road led up to the mansion across a park dotted with clumps of evergreens and deciduous trees. Here and there an ancient patriarch of the forest stood alone,-- some old oak or elm, whose goodly proportions and amplitude of shade had found favor in the eyes of the seigniors of Tilly, and saved it from the axe of the woodman.

A pretty brook, not too wide to be crossed over by a rustic bridge, meandered through the domain, peeping occasionally out of the openings in the woods as it stole away like a bashful girl from the eyes of her admirer.

This brook was the outflow of a romantic little lake that lay hidden away among the wooded hills that bounded the horizon, an irregular sheet of water a league in circumference, dotted with islands and abounding with fish and waterfowl that haunted its quiet pools. That primitive bit of nature had never been disturbed by axe or fire, and was a favorite spot for recreation to the inmates of the Manor House, to whom it was accessible either by boat up the little stream, or by a pleasant drive through the old woods.

As the carriages drew up in front of the Manor House, every door, window, and gable of which looked like an old friend in the eyes of Pierre Philibert, a body of female servants--the men had all been away at the city--stood ranged in their best gowns and gayest ribbons to welcome home their mistress and Mademoiselle Amelie, who was the idol of them all.

Great was their delight to see Monsieur Le Gardeur, as they usually styled their young master, with another gentleman in military costume, whom it did not take two minutes for some of the sharp-eyed lasses to recognize as Pierre Philibert, who had once saved the life of Le Gardeur on a memorable occasion, and who now, they said one to another, was come to the Manor House to--to--they whispered what it was to each other, and smiled in a knowing manner.

Women's wits fly swiftly to conclusions, and right ones too on most occasions. The lively maids of Tilly told one another in whispers that they were sure Pierre Philibert had come back to the Manor House as a suitor for the hand of Mademoiselle Amelie, as was most natural he should do, so handsome and manly looking as he was, and mademoiselle always liked to hear any of them mention his name. The maids ran out the whole chain of logical sequences before either Pierre or Amelie had ventured to draw a conclusion of any kind from the premises of this visit.

Behind the mansion, overlooking poultry-yards and stables which were well hidden from view, rose a high colombiere, or pigeon-house, of stone, the possession of which was one of the rights which feudal law reserved to the lord of the manor. This colombiere was capable of containing a large army of pigeons, but the regard which the Lady de Tilly had for the corn-fields of her censitaires caused her to thin out its population to such a degree that there remained only a few favorite birds of rare breed and plumage to strut and coo upon the roofs, and rival the peacocks on the terrace with their bright colors.

In front of the mansion, contrasting oddly with the living trees around it, stood a high pole, the long, straight stem of a pine- tree, carefully stripped of its bark, bearing on its top the withered remains of a bunch of evergreens, with the fragments of a flag and ends of ribbon which fluttered gaily from it. The pole was marked with black spots from the discharge of guns fired at it by the joyous habitans, who had kept the ancient custom of May-day by planting this May-pole in front of the Manor House of their lady.

The planting of such a pole was in New France a special mark of respect due to the feudal superior, and custom as well as politeness required that it should not be taken down until the recurrence of another anniversary of Flora, which in New France sometimes found the earth white with snow and hardened with frost, instead of covered with flowers as in the Old World whence the custom was derived.

The Lady de Tilly duly appreciated this compliment of her faithful censitaires, and would sooner have stripped her park of half its live trees than have removed that dead pole, with its withered crown, from the place of honor in front of her mansion.

The revels of May in New France, the king and queen of St. Philip, the rejoicings of a frank, loyal peasantry--illiterate in books but not unlearned in the art of life,--have wholly disappeared before the levelling spirit of the nineteenth century.

The celebration of the day of St. Philip has been superseded by the festival of St. John the Baptist, at a season of the year when green leaves and blooming flowers give the possibility of arches and garlands in honor of the Canadian summer.

Felix Beaudoin with a wave of his hand scattered the bevy of maid servants who stood chattering as they gazed upon the new arrivals. The experience of Felix told him that everything had of course gone wrong during his absence from the Manor House, and that nothing could be fit for his mistress's reception until he had set all to rights again himself.

The worthy majordomo was in a state of perspiration lest he should not get into the house before his mistress and don his livery to meet her at the door with his white wand and everything en regle, just as if nothing had interrupted their usual course of housekeeping.

The Lady de Tilly knew the weakness of her faithful old servitor, and although she smiled to herself, she would not hurt his feelings by entering the house before he was ready at his post to receive her. She continued walking about the lawn conversing with Amelie, Pierre, and Le Gardeur, until she saw old Felix with his wand and livery standing at the door, when, taking Pierre's arm, she led the way into the house.

The folding doors were open, and Felix with his wand walked before his lady and her companions into the mansion. They entered without delay, for the day had been warm, and the ladies were weary after sitting several hours in a canoe, a mode of travelling which admits of very little change of position in the voyagers.

The interior of the Manor House of Tilly presented the appearance of an old French chateau. A large hall with antique furniture occupied the center of the house, used occasionally as a court of justice when the Seigneur de Tilly exercised his judicial office for the trial of offenders, which was very rarely, thanks to the good morals of the people, or held a cour pleniere of his vassals, on affairs of the seigniory for apportioning the corvees for road-making and bridge-building, and, not the least important by any means, for the annual feast to his censitaires on the day of St. Michael de Thury.

From this hall, passages led into apartments and suites of rooms arranged for use, comfort, and hospitality. The rooms were of all sizes, panelled, tapestried, and furnished in a style of splendor suited to the wealth and dignity of the Seigneurs of Tilly. A stair of oak, broad enough for a section of grenadiers to march up it abreast, led to the upper chambers, bedrooms, and boudoirs, which looked out of old mullioned windows upon the lawn and gardens that surrounded the house, affording picturesque glimpses of water, hills, and forests far enough off for contemplation, and yet near enough to be accessible by a short ride from the mansion.

Pierre Philibert was startled at the strange familiarity of everything he saw: the passages and all their intricacies, where he, Le Gardeur, and Amelie had hid and found one another with cries of delight,--he knew where they all led to; the rooms with their antique and stately furniture, the paintings on the wall, before which he had stood and gazed, wondering if the world was as fair as those landscapes of sunny France and Italy and why the men and women of the house of Tilly, whose portraits hung upon the walls, looked at him so kindly with those dark eyes of theirs, which seemed to follow him everywhere, and he imagined they even smiled when their lips were illumined by a ray of sunshine. Pierre looked at them again with a strange interest,-- they were like the faces of living friends who welcomed him back to Tilly after years of absence.

Pierre entered a well-remembered apartment which he knew to be the favorite sitting-room of the Lady de Tilly. He walked hastily across it to look at a picture upon the wall which he recognized again with a flush of pleasure.

It was the portrait of Amelie painted by himself during his last visit to Tilly. The young artist, full of enthusiasm, had put his whole soul into the work, until he was himself startled at the vivid likeness which almost unconsciously flowed from his pencil. He had caught the divine upward expression of her eyes, as she turned her head to listen to him, and left upon the canvas the very smile he had seen upon her lips. Those dark eyes of hers had haunted his memory forever after. To his imagination that picture had become almost a living thing. It was as a voice of his own that returned to his ear as the voice of Amelie. In the painting of that portrait Pierre had the first revelation of a consciousness of his deep love which became in the end the master passion of his life.

He stood for some minutes contemplating this portrait, so different from her in age now, yet so like in look and expression. He turned suddenly and saw Amelie; she had silently stepped up behind him, and her features in a glow of pleasure took on the very look of the picture.

Pierre started. He looked again, and saw every feature of the girl of twelve looking through the transparent countenance of the perfect woman of twenty. It was a moment of blissful revelation, for he felt an assurance at that moment that Amelie was the same to him now as in their days of youthful companionship. "How like it is to you yet, Amelie!" said he; "it is more true than I knew how to make it!"

"That sounds like a paradox, Pierre Philibert!" replied she, with a smile. "But it means, I suppose, that you painted a universal portrait of me which will be like through all my seven ages. Such a picture might be true of the soul, Pierre, had you painted that, but I have outgrown the picture of my person."

"I could imagine nothing fairer than that portrait! In soul and body it is all true, Amelie."

"Flatterer that you are!" said she, laughing. "I could almost wish that portrait would walk out of its frame to thank you for the care you bestowed upon its foolish little original."

"My care was more than rewarded! I find in that picture my beau- ideal of the beauty of life, which, belonging to the soul, is true to all ages."

"The girl of twelve would have thanked you more enthusiastically for that remark, Pierre, than I dare do," replied she.

"The thanks are due from me, not from you, Amelie! I became your debtor for a life-long obligation when without genius I could do impossibilities. You taught me that paradox when you let me paint that picture."

Amelie glanced quickly up at him. A slight color came and went on her cheek. "Would that I could do impossibilities," said she, "to thank you sufficiently for your kindness to Le Gardeur and all of us in coming to Tilly at this time.

"It would be a novelty, almost a relief, to put Pierre Philibert under some obligation to us for we all owe him, would it not, Le Gardeur?" continued she, clasping the arm of her brother, who just now came into the room. "We will discharge a portion of our debt to Pierre for this welcome visit by a day on the lake,--we will make up a water-party. What say you, brother? The gentlemen shall light fires, the ladies shall make tea, and we will have guitars and songs, and maybe a dance, brother! and then a glorious return home by moonlight! What say you to my programme, Le Gardeur de Repentigny? What say you, Pierre Philibert?"

"It is a good programme, sister, but leave me out of it. I shall only mar the pleasure of the rest; I will not go to the lake. I have been trying ever since my return home to recognize Tilly; everything looks to me in an eclipse, and nothing bright as it once was, not even you, Amelie. Your smile has a curious touch of sadness in it which does not escape my eyes; accursed as they have been of late, seeing things they ought not to see, yet I can see that, and I know it, too; I have given you cause to be sad, sister."

"Hush, brother! it is a sin against your dear eyes to speak of them thus! Tilly is as bright and joyous as ever. As for my smiles, if you detect in them one trace of that sadness you talk about, I shall grow as melancholy as yourself, and for as little cause. Come! you shall confess before three days, brother, if you will only help me to be gay, that your sister has the lightest heart in New France."

# Chapter XXVII: Cheerful Yesterdays and Confident To-Morrows

The ladies retired to their several rooms, and after a general rearranging of toilets descended to the great parlor, where they were joined by Messire La Lande, the cure of the parish, a benevolent, rosy old priest, and several ladies from the neighborhood, with two or three old gentlemen of a military air and manner, retired officers of the army who enjoyed their pensions and kept up their respectability at a cheaper rate in the country than they could do in the city.

Felix Beaudoin had for the last two hours kept the cooks in hot water. He was now superintending the laying of the table, resolved that, notwithstanding his long absence from home, the dinner should be a marvellous success.

Amelie was very beautiful to-day. Her face was aglow with pure air and exercise, and she felt happy in the apparent contentment of her brother, whom she met with Pierre on the broad terrace of the Manor House.

She was dressed with exquisite neatness, yet plainly. An antique cross of gold formed her only adornment except her own charms. That cross she had put on in honor of Pierre Philibert. He recognized it with delight as a birthday gift to Amelie which he had himself given her during their days of juvenile companionship, on one of his holiday visits to Tilly.

She was conscious of his recognition of it,--it brought a flush to her cheek. "It is in honor of your visit, Pierre," said she, frankly, "that I wear your gift. Old friendship lasts well with me, does it not? But you will find more old friends than me at Tilly who have not forgotten you."

"I am already richer than Croesus, if friendship count as riches, Amelie. The hare had many friends, but none at last; I am more fortunate in possessing one friend worth a million."

"Nay, you have the million too, if good wishes count in your favor, Pierre, you are richer"--the bell in the turret of the chateau began to ring for dinner, drowning her voice somewhat.

"Thanks to the old bell for cutting short the compliment, Pierre," continued she, laughing; "you don't know what you have lost! but in compensation you shall be my cavalier, and escort me to the dining- room."

She took the arm of Pierre, and in a merry mood, which brought back sweet memories of the past, their voices echoed again along the old corridors of the Manor House as they proceeded to the great dining- room, where the rest of the company were assembling.

The dinner was rather a stately affair, owing to the determination of Felix Beaudoin to do especial honor to the return home of the family. How the company ate, talked, and drank at the hospitable table need not be recorded here. The good Cure's face, under the joint influence of good humor and good cheer, was full as a harvest moon. He rose at last, folded his hands, and slowly repeated "agimus gratias." After dinner the company withdrew to the brilliantly lighted drawing-room, where conversation, music, and a few games of cards for such as liked them, filled up a couple of hours longer.

The Lady de Tilly, seated beside Pierre Philibert on the sofa, conversed with him in a pleasant strain, while the Cure, with a couple of old dowagers in turbans, and an old veteran officer of the colonial marine, long stranded on a lee shore, formed a quartette at cards.

These were steady enthusiasts of whist and piquet, such as are only to be found in small country circles where society is scarce and amusements few. They had met as partners or antagonists, and played, laughed, and wrangled over sixpeny stakes and odd tricks and honors, every week for a quarter of a century, and would willingly have gone on playing till the day of judgment without a change of partners if they could have trumped death and won the odd trick of him.

Pierre recollected having seen these same old friends seated at the same card-table during his earliest visits to the Manor House. He recalled the fact to the Lady de Tilly, who laughed and said her old friends had lived so long in the company of the kings and queens that formed the paste-board Court of the Kingdom of Cocagne that they could relish no meaner amusement than one which royalty, although mad, had the credit of introducing.

Amelie devoted herself to the task of cheering her somewhat moody brother. She sat beside him, resting her hand with sisterly affection upon his shoulder, while in a low, sweet voice she talked to him, adroitly touching those topics only which she knew awoke pleasurable associations in his mind. Her words were sweet as manna and full of womanly tenderness and sympathy, skilfully wrapped in a strain of gaiety like a bridal veil which covers the tears of the heart.

Pierre Philibert's eyes involuntarily turned towards her, and his ears caught much of what she said. He was astonished at the grace and perfection of her language; it seemed to him like a strain of music filled with every melody of earth and heaven, surpassing poets in beauty of diction, philosophers in truth,--and in purity of affection, all the saints and sweetest women of whom he had ever read.

Her beauty, her vivacity, her modest reticences, and her delicate tact in addressing the captious spirit of Le Gardeur, filled Pierre with admiration. He could at that moment have knelt at her feet and worshipped in her the realization of every image which his imagination had ever formed of a perfect woman.

Now and then she played on the harp for Le Gardeur the airs which she knew he liked best. His sombre mood yielded to her fond exertions, and she had the reward of drawing at last a smile from his eyes as well as from his lips. The last she knew might be simulated, the former she felt was real, for the smile of the eye is the flash of the joy kindled in the glad heart.

Le Gardeur was not dull nor ungrateful; he read clearly enough the loving purpose of his sister. His brow cleared up under her sunshine. He smiled, he laughed; and Amelie had the exquisite joy of believing she had gained a victory over the dark spirit that had taken possession of his soul, although the hollow laugh struck the ear of Pierre Philibert with a more uncertain sound than that which fluttered the fond hopes of Amelie.

Amelie looked towards Pierre, and saw his eyes fixed upon her with that look which fills every woman with an emotion almost painful in its excess of pleasure when first she meets it-- that unmistakable glance from the eyes of a man who, she is proud to perceive, has singled her out from all other women for his love and homage.

Her face became of a deep glow in spite of her efforts to look calm and cold; she feared Pierre might have misinterpreted her vivacity of speech and manner. Sudden distrust of herself came over her in his presence,--the flow of her conversation was embarrassed, and almost ceased.

To extricate herself from her momentary confusion, which she was very conscious had not escaped the observation of Pierre,--and the thought of that confused her still more,--she rose and went to the harpsichord, to recover her composure by singing a sweet song of her own composition, written in the soft dialect of Provence, the Languedoc, full of the sweet sadness of a tender, impassioned love.

Her voice, tremulous in its power, flowed in a thousand harmonies on the enraptured ears of her listeners. Even the veteran card-players left a game of whist unfinished, to cluster round the angelic singer.

Pierre Philibert sat like one in a trance. He loved music, and understood it passing well. He had heard all the rare voices which Paris prided itself in the possession of, but he thought he had never known what music was till now. His heart throbbed in sympathy with every inflection of the voice of Amelie, which went through him like a sweet spell of enchantment. It was the voice of a disembodied spirit singing in the language of earth, which changed at last into a benediction and good-night for the parting guests, who, at an earlier hour than usual, out of consideration for the fatigue of their hosts, took their leave of the Manor House and its hospitable inmates.

The family, as families will do upon the departure of their guests, drew up in a narrower circle round the fire, that blessed circle of freedom and confidence which belongs only to happy households. The novelty of the situation kept up the interest of the day, and they sat and conversed until a late hour.

The Lady de Tilly reclined comfortably in her fauteuil looking with good-natured complacency upon the little group beside her. Amelie, sitting on a stool, reclined her head against the bosom of her aunt, whose arm embraced her closely and lovingly as she listened with absorbing interest to an animated conversation between her aunt and Pierre Philibert.

The Lady de Tilly drew Pierre out to talk of his travels, his studies, and his military career, of which he spoke frankly and modestly. His high principles won her admiration; the chivalry and loyalty of his character, mingled with the humanity of the true soldier, touched a chord in her own heart, stirring within her the sympathies of a nature akin to his.

The presence of Pierre Philibert, so unforeseen at the old Manor House, seemed to Amelie the work of Providence for a good and great end--the reformation of her brother. If she dared to think of herself in connection with him it was with fear and trembling, as a saint on earth receives a beatific vision that may only be realized in Heaven.

Amelie, with peculiar tact, sought to entangle Le Gardeur's thoughts in an elaborate cobweb of occupations rivalling that of Arachne, which she had woven to catch every leisure hour of his, so as to leave him no time to brood over the pleasures of the Palace of the Intendant or the charms of Angelique des Meloises.

There were golden threads too in the network in which she hoped to entangle him: long rides to the neighboring seigniories, where bright eyes and laughing lips were ready to expel every shadow of care from the most dejected of men, much more from a handsome gallant like Le Gardeur de Repentigny, whose presence at any of these old manors put their fair inmates at once in holiday trim and in holiday humor; there were shorter walks through the park and domain of Tilly, where she intended to botanize and sketch, and even fish and hunt with Le Gardeur and Pierre, although, sooth to say, Amelie's share in hunting would only be to ride her sure-footed pony and look at her companions; there were visits to friends far and near, and visits in return to the Manor House, and a grand excursion of all to the lake of Tilly in boats,--they would colonize its little island for a day, set up tents, make a governor and intendant, perhaps a king and queen, and forget the world till their return home.

This elaborate scheme secured the approbation of the Lady de Tilly, who had, in truth, contributed part of it. Le Gardeur said he was a poor fly whom they were resolved to catch and pin to the wall of a chateau en Espagne, but he would enter the web without a buzz of opposition on condition that Pierre would join him. So it was all settled.

Amelie did not venture again that night to encounter the eyes of Pierre Philibert,--she needed more courage than she felt just now to do that; but in secret she blessed him, and treasured those fond looks of his in her heart, never to be forgotten any more. When she retired to her own chamber and was alone, she threw herself in passionate abandonment before the altar in her little oratory, which she had crowned with flowers to mark her gladness. She poured out her pure soul in invocations of blessings upon Pierre Philibert and upon her brother and all the house. The golden head of her rosary lingered long in her loving fingers that night, as she repeated over and over her accustomed prayers for his safety and welfare.

The sun rose gloriously next morning over the green woods and still greener meadows of Tilly. The atmosphere was soft and pure; it had been washed clean of all its impurities by a few showers in the night. Every object seemed nearer and clearer to the eye, while the delicious odor of fresh flowers filled the whole air with fragrance.

The trees, rocks, waters, and green slopes stood out with marvellous precision of outline, as if cut with a keen knife. No fringe of haze surrounded them, as in a drought or as in the evening when the air is filled with the shimmering of the day dust which follows the sun's chariot in his course round the world.

Every object, great and small, seemed magnified to welcome Pierre Philibert, who was up betimes this morning and out in the pure air viewing the old familiar scenes.

With what delight he recognized each favorite spot! There was the cluster of trees which crowned a promontory overlooking the St. Lawrence where he and Le Gardeur had stormed the eagle's nest. In that sweep of forest the deer used to browse and the fawns crouch in the long ferns. Upon yonder breezy hill they used to sit and count the sails turning alternately bright and dark as the vessels tacked up the broad river. There was a stretch of green lawn, still green as it was in his memory--how everlasting are God's colors! There he had taught Amelie to ride, and, holding fast, ran by her side, keeping pace with her flying Indian pony. How beautiful and fresh the picture of her remained in his memory!--the soft white dress she wore, her black hair streaming over her shoulders, her dark eyes flashing delight, her merry laugh rivalling the trill of the blackbird which flew over their heads chattering for very joy. Before him lay the pretty brook with its rustic bridge reflecting itself in the clear water as in a mirror. That path along the bank led down to the willows where the big mossy stones lay in the stream and the silvery salmon and speckled trout lay fanning the water gently with their fins as they contemplated their shadows on the smooth, sandy bottom.

Pierre Philibert sat down on a stone by the side of the brook and watched the shoals of minnows move about in little battalions, wheeling like soldiers to the right or left at a wave of the hand. But his thoughts were running in a circle of questions and enigmas for which he found neither end nor answer.

For the hundredth time Pierre proposed to himself the tormenting enigma, harder, he thought, to solve than any problem of mathematics,--for it was the riddle of his life: "What thoughts are truly in the heart of Amelie de Repentigny respecting me? Does she recollect me only as her brother's companion, who may possibly have some claim upon her friendship, but none upon her love?" His imagination pictured every look she had given him since his return. Not all! Oh, Pierre Philibert! the looks you would have given worlds to catch, you were unconscious of! Every word she had spoken, the soft inflection of every syllable of her silvery voice lingered in his ear. He had caught meanings where perhaps no meaning was, and missed the key to others which he knew were there-- never, perhaps, to be revealed to him. But although he questioned in the name of love, and found many divine echoes in her words, imperceptible to every ear but his own, he could not wholly solve the riddle of his life. Still he hoped.

"If love creates love, as some say it does," thought he, "Amelie de Repentigny cannot be indifferent to a passion which governs every impulse of my being! But is there any especial merit in loving her whom all the world cannot help admiring equally with myself? I am presumptuous to think so!--and more presumptuous still to expect, after so many years of separation and forgetfulness, that her heart, so loving and so sympathetic, has not already bestowed its affection upon some one more fortunate than me."

While Pierre tormented himself with these sharp thorns of doubt,-- and of hopes painful as doubts,--little did he think what a brave, loving spirit was hid under the silken vesture of Amelie de Repentigny, and how hard was her struggle to conceal from his eyes those tender regards, which, with over-delicacy, she accounted censurable because they were wholly spontaneous.

He little thought how entirely his image had filled her heart during those years when she dreamed of him in the quiet cloister, living in a world of bright imaginings of her own; how she had prayed for his safety and welfare as she would have prayed for the soul of one dead,--never thinking, or even hoping, to see him again.

Pierre had become to her as one of the disembodied saints or angels whose pictures looked down from the wall of the Convent chapel--the bright angel of the Annunciation or the youthful Baptist proclaiming the way of the Lord. Now that Pierre Philibert was alive in the flesh,--a man, beautiful, brave, honorable, and worthy of any woman's love,--Amelie was frightened. She had not looked for that, and yet it had come upon her. And, although trembling, she was glad and proud to find she had been remembered by the brave youth, who recognized in the perfect woman the girl he had so ardently loved as a boy.

Did he love her still? Woman's heart is quicker to apprehend all possibilities than man's. She had caught a look once or twice in the eyes of Pierre Philibert which thrilled the inmost fibres of her being; she had detected his ardent admiration. Was she offended? Far from it! And although her cheek had flushed deeply red, and her pulses throbbed hard at the sudden consciousness that Pierre Philibert admired, nay, more,--she could not conceal it from herself,-- she knew that night that he loved her! She would not have foregone that moment of revelation for all that the world had to offer.

She would gladly at that moment of discovery have fled to her own apartment and cried for joy, but she dared not; she trembled lest his eyes, if she looked up, should discover the secret of her own. She had an overpowering consciousness that she stood upon the brink of her fate; that ere long that look of his would be followed by words--blessed, hoped-for words, from the lips of Pierre Philibert! words which would be the pledge and assurance to her of that love which was hereafter to be the joy--it might be the despair, but in any case the all in all of her life forever.

Amelie had not yet realized the truth that love is the strength, not the weakness of woman; and that the boldness of the man is rank cowardice in comparison with the bravery she is capable of, and the sacrifices she will make for the sake of the man who has won her heart.

God locks up in a golden casket of modesty the yearnings of a woman's heart; but when the hand in which he has placed the key that opens it calls forth her glorified affections, they come out like the strong angels, and hold back the winds that blow from the four corners of the earth that they may not hurt the man whose forehead is sealed with the kiss of her acknowledged love.

# Chapter XXVIII: A Day at the Manor House

Amelie, after a night of wakefulness and wrestling with a tumult of new thoughts and emotions,--no longer dreams, but realities of life,--dressed herself in a light morning costume, which, simple as it was, bore the touch of her graceful hand and perfect taste. With a broad-brimmed straw hat set upon her dark tresses, which were knotted with careless care in a blue ribbon, she descended the steps of the Manor House. There was a deep bloom upon her cheeks, and her eyes looked like fountains of light and gladness, running over to bless all beholders.

She inquired of Felix Beaudoin of her brother. The old majordomo, with a significant look, informed her that Monsieur Le Gardeur had just ordered his horse to ride to the village. He had first called for a decanter of Cognac, and when it was brought to him he suddenly thrust it back and would not taste it. "He would not drink even Jove's nectar in the Manor House, he said; but would go down to the village, where Satan mixed the drink for thirsty souls like his! Poor Le Gardeur!" continued Felix, "you must not let him go to the village this morning, mademoiselle!"

Amelie was startled at this information. She hastened at once to seek her brother, whom she found walking impatiently in the garden, slashing the heads off the poppies and dahlias within reach of his riding-whip. He was equipped for a ride, and waited the coming of the groom with his horse.

Amelie ran up, and clasping his arms with both hands as she looked up in his face with a smile, exclaimed, "Do not go to the village yet, Le Gardeur! Wait for us!"

"Not go to the village yet, Amelie?" replied he; "why not? I shall return for breakfast, although I have no appetite. I thought a ride to the village would give me one."

"Wait until after breakfast, brother, when we will all go with you to meet our friends who come this morning to Tilly,--our cousin Heloise de Lotbiniere is coming to see you and Pierre Philibert; you must be there to welcome her,--gallants are too scarce to allow her to spare the handsomest of all, my own brother!"

Amelie divined truly from Le Gardeur's restless eyes and haggard look that a fierce conflict was going on in his breast between duty and desire,--whether he should remain at home, or go to the village to plunge again into the sea of dissipation out of which he had just been drawn to land half-drowned and utterly desperate.

Amelie resolved not to leave his side, but to cleave to him, and inch by inch to fight the demons which possessed him until she got the victory.

Le Gardeur looked fondly in the face of Amelie. He read her thoughts, and was very conscious why she wished him not to go to the village. His feelings gave way before her love and tenderness. He suddenly embraced her and kissed her cheeks, while the tears stood welling in his eyes. "I am not worthy of you, Amelie," said he; "so much sisterly care is lost on me!"

"Oh, say not that, brother," replied she, kissing him fondly in return. "I would give my life to save you, O my brother!"

Amelie was greatly moved, and for a time unable to speak further; she laid her head on his shoulder, and sobbed audibly. Her love gained the victory where remonstrance and opposition would have lost it.

"You have won the day, Amelie!" said he; "I will not go to the village except with you. You are the best and truest girl in all Christendom! Why is there no other like you? If there were, this curse had not come upon me, nor this trial upon you, Amelie! You are my good angel, and I will try, oh, so faithfully try, to be guided by you! If you fail, you will at least have done all and more than your duty towards your erring brother."

"Le Brun!" cried he to the groom who had brought his horse, and to whom he threw the whip which had made such havoc among the flowers, "lead Black Caesar to the stable again! and hark you! when I bid you bring him out in the early morning another time, lead him to me unbridled and unsaddled, with only a halter on his head, that I may ride as a clown, not as a gentleman!"

Le Brun stared at this speech, and finally regarded it as a capital joke, or else, as he whispered to his fellow-grooms in the stable, he believed his young master had gone mad.

"Pierre Philibert," continued Amelie, "is down at the salmon pool. Let us join him, Le Gardeur, and bid him good morning once more at Tilly."

Amelie, overjoyed at her victory, tripped gaily by the side of her brother, and presently two friendly hands, the hands of Pierre Philibert, were extended to greet her and Le Gardeur.

The hand of Amelie was retained for a moment in that of Pierre Philibert, sending the blood to her cheeks. There is a magnetic touch in loving fingers which is never mistaken, though their contact be but for a second of time: it anticipates the strong grasp of love which will ere long embrace body and soul in adamantine chains of a union not to be broken even by death.

If Pierre Philibert retained the hand of Amelie for one second longer than mere friendship required of him, no one perceived it but God and themselves. Pierre felt it like a revelation--the hand of Amelie yielding timidly, but not unwillingly, to his manly grasp. He looked in her face. Her eyes were averted, and she withdrew her hand quietly but gently, as not upbraiding him.

That moment of time flashed a new influence upon both their lives: it was the silent recognition that each was henceforth conscious of the special regard of the other.

There are moments which contain the whole quintessence of our lives,--our loves, our hopes, our failures, in one concentrated drop of happiness or misery. We look behind us and see that our whole past has led up to that infinitesimal fraction of time which is the consummation of the past in the present, the end of the old and the beginning of the new. We look forward from the vantage ground of the present, and the world of a new revelation lies before us.

Pierre Philibert was conscious from that moment that Amelie de Repentigny was not indifferent to him,--nay, he had a ground of hope that in time she would listen to his pleadings, and at last bestow on him the gift of her priceless love.

His hopes were sure hopes, although he did not dare to give himself the sweet assurance of it, nor did Amelie herself as yet suspect how far her heart was irrevocably wedded to Pierre Philibert.

Deep as was the impression of that moment upon both of them, neither Philibert nor Amelie yielded to its influence more than to lapse into a momentary silence, which was relieved by Le Gardeur, who, suspecting not the cause,--nay, thinking it was on his account that his companions were so unaccountably grave and still, kindly endeavored to force the conversation upon a number of interesting topics, and directed the attention of Philibert to various points of the landscape which suggested reminiscences of his former visits to Tilly.

The equilibrium of conversation was restored, and the three, sitting down on a long, flat stone, a boulder which had dropped millions of years before out of an iceberg as it sailed slowly over the glacial ocean which then covered the place of New France, commenced to talk over Amelie's programme of the previous night, the amusements she had planned for the week, the friends in all quarters they were to visit, and the friends from all quarters they were to receive at the Manor House. These topics formed a source of fruitful comment, as conversation on our friends always does. If the sun shone hot and fierce at noontide in the dog-days, they would enjoy the cool shade of the arbors with books and conversation; they would ride in the forest, or embark in their canoes for a row up the bright little river; there would be dinners and diversions for the day, music and dancing for the night.

The spirits of the inmates of the Manor House could not help but be kept up by these expedients, and Amelie flattered herself that she would quite succeed in dissipating the gloomy thoughts which occupied the mind of Le Gardeur.

They sat on the stone by the brook-side for an hour, conversing pleasantly while they watched the speckled trout dart like silver arrows spotted with blood in the clear pool.

Le Gardeur strove to be gay, and teased Amelie in playfully criticizing her programme, and, half in earnest, half in jest, arguing for the superior attractions of the Palace of the Intendant to those of the Manor House of Tilly. He saw the water standing in her eyes, when a consciousness of what must be her feelings seized him; he drew her to his side, asked her forgiveness, and wished fire were set to the Palace and himself in the midst of it! He deserved it for wounding, even in jest, the heart of the best and noblest sister in the world.

"I am not wounded, dear Le Gardeur," replied she, softly; "I knew you were only in jest. My foolish heart is so sensitive to all mention of the Palace and its occupants in connection with you, that I could not even take in jest what was so like truth."

"Forgive me, I will never mention the Palace to you again, Amelie, except to repeat the malediction I have bestowed upon it a thousand times an hour since I returned to Tilly."

"My own brave brother!" exclaimed she, embracing him, "now I am happy!"

The shrill notes of a bugle were heard sounding a military call to breakfast. It was the special privilege of an old servitor of the family, who had been a trumpeter in the troop of the Seigneur of Tilly, to summon the family of the Manor House in that manner to breakfast only. The old trumpeter had solicited long to be allowed to sound the reveille at break of day, but the good Lady de Tilly had too much regard for the repose of the inmates of her house to consent to any such untimely waking of them from their morning slumbers.

The old, familiar call was recognized by Philibert, who reminded Amelie of a day when Aeolus (the ancient trumpeter bore that windy sobriquet) had accompanied them on a long ramble in the forest,-- how, the day being warm, the old man fell asleep under a comfortable shade, while the three children straggled off into the depths of the woods, where they were speedily lost.

"I remember it like yesterday, Pierre," exclaimed Amelie, sparkling at the reminiscence; "I recollect how I wept and wrung my hands, tired out, hungry, and forlorn, with my dress in tatters, and one shoe left in a miry place! I recollect, moreover, that my protectors were in almost as bad a plight as myself, yet they chivalrously carried the little maiden by turns, or together made a queen's chair for me with their locked hands, until we all broke down together and sat crying at the foot of a tree, reminding one another of the babes in the wood, and recounting stories of bears which had devoured lost naughty children in the forest. I remember how we all knelt down at last and recited our prayers until suddenly we heard the bugle-call of Aeolus sounding close by us. The poor old man, wild with rapture at having found us, kissed and shook us so violently that we almost wished ourselves lost in the forest again."

The recollection of this adventure was very pleasing to Pierre. He recalled every incident of it perfectly, and all three of them seemed for a while transported back into the fairy-land of their happy childhood.

The bugle-call of old Aeolus again sounded, and the three friends rose and proceeded towards the house.

The little brook--it had never looked so bright before to Amelie-- sparkled with joy like her own eyes. The orioles and blackbirds warbled in the bushes, and the insects which love warmth and sunshine chirmed and chirruped among the ferns and branches as Amelie, Pierre, and Le Gardeur walked home along the green footpath under the avenue of elms that led to the chateau.

The Lady de Tilly received them with many pleasant words. Leading them into the breakfast-room, she congratulated Le Gardeur upon the satisfaction it afforded her to see her dear children, so she called them, once more seated round her board in health and happiness. Amelie colored slightly, and looked at her aunt as if questioning whether she included Philibert among her children.

The Lady de Tilly guessed her thought, but pretending not to, bade Felix proceed with the breakfast, and turned the conversation to topics more general. "The Iroquois," she said, "had left the Chaudiere and gone further eastward; the news had just been brought in by messengers to the Seigniory, and it was probable, nay, certain that they would not be heard of again. Therefore Le Gardeur and Pierre Philibert were under no necessity of leaving the Manor to search for the savages, but could arrange with Amelie for as much enjoyment as they could crowd into these summer days."

"It is all arranged, aunt!" replied Amelie. "We have held a cour pleniere this morning, and made a code of laws for our Kingdom of Cocagne during the next eight days. It needs only the consent of our suzeraine lady to be at once acted upon."

"And your suzeraine lady gives her consent without further questioning, Amelie! although I confess you have an admirable way of carrying your point, Amelie," said her aunt, laughing; "you resolve first what you will do, and ask my approbation after."

"Yes, aunt, that is our way in the kingdom of pleasure! And we begin this morning: Le Gardeur and Pierre will ride to the village to meet our cousin Heloise, from Lotbiniere."

"But you will accompany us, Amelie!" exclaimed Le Gardeur. "I will not go else,--it was a bargain!"

"Oh, I did not count myself for anything but an embarrassment! of course I shall go with you, Le Gardeur, but our cousin Heloise de Lotbiniere is coming to see you, not me. She lost her heart," remarked she, turning to Pierre, "when she was last here, at the feast of St. John, and is coming to seek it again."

"Ah! how was that, Amelie?" asked Philibert. "I remember the lovely face, the chestnut curls, and bright black eyes of Heloise de Lotbiniere. And has hers really gone the way of all hearts?"

"Of all good hearts, Pierre,--but you shall hear if you will be good and listen. She saw the portraits of you and Le Gardeur, one day, hung in the boudoir of my aunt. Heloise professed that she admired both until she could not tell which she liked best, and left me to decide."

"Ah! and which of us did you give to the fair Heloise?" demanded Philibert with a sudden interest.

"Not the Abelard she wanted, you may be sure, Pierre," exclaimed Le Gardeur; "she gave me, and kept you! It was a case of clear misappropriation."

"No, brother, not so!" replied Amelie, hastily. "Heloise had tried the charm of the three caskets with the three names without result, and at last watched in the church porch, on the eve of St. John, to see the shade of her destined lover pass by, and lo, Heloise vowed she saw me, and no one else, pass into the church!"

"Ah! I suppose it was you? It is no rare thing for you to visit the shrine of our Lady on the eve of St. John. Pierre Philibert, do you recollect? Oh, not as I do, dear friend," continued Le

Gardeur with a sudden change of voice, which was now filled with emotion: "it was on the day of St. John you saved my poor worthless life. We are not ungrateful! She has kept the eve of St. John in the church ever since, in commemoration of that event."

"Brother, we have much to thank Heaven for!" replied Amelie, blushing deeply at his words, "and I trust we shall never be ungrateful for its favor and protection."

Amelie shied from a compliment like a young colt at its own shadow. She avoided further reference to the subject broached by Le Gardeur by saying,--"It was I whom Heloise saw pass into the church. I never explained the mystery to her, and she is not sure yet whether it was my wraith or myself who gave her that fright on St. John's eve. But I claimed her heart as one authorized to take it, and if I could not marry her myself I claimed the right to give her to whomsoever I pleased, and I gave her to you, Le Gardeur, but you would not accept the sweetest girl in New France!"

"Thanks, Amelie," replied he, laughing, yet wincing. "Heloise is indeed all you say, the sweetest girl in New France! But she was too angelic for Le Gardeur de Repentigny. Pshaw! you make me say foolish things, Amelie. But in penance for my slight, I will be doubly attentive to my fair cousin de Lotbiniere to-day. I will at once order the horses and we will ride down to the village to meet her."

Arrayed in a simple riding-dress of dark blue, which became her as did everything else which she wore,--Amelie's very attire seemed instinct with the living graces and charms of its wearer,--she mounted her horse, accepting the aid of Philibert to do so, although when alone she usually sprang to the saddle herself, saluting the Lady de Tilly, who waved her hand to them from the lawn. The three friends slowly cantered down the broad avenue of the park towards the village of Tilly.

Amelie rode well. The exercise and the pure air brought the fresh color to her face, and her eyes sparkled with animation as she conversed gaily with her brother and Philibert.

They speedily reached the village, where they met Heloise de Lotbiniere, who, rushing to Amelie, kissed her with effusion, and as she greeted Le Gardeur looked up as if she would not have refused a warmer salutation than the kind shake of the hand with which he received her. She welcomed Philibert with glad surprise, recognizing him at once, and giving a glance at Amelie which expressed an ocean of unspoken meaning and sympathy.

Heloise was beautiful, gay, spirited, full of good humor and sensibility. Her heart had long been devoted to Le Gardeur, but never meeting with any response to her shy advances, which were like the wheeling of a dove round and round its wished-for mate, she had long concluded with a sigh that for her the soul of Le Gardeur was insensible to any touch of a warmer regard than sprang from the most sincere friendship.

Amelie saw and understood all this; she loved Heloise, and in her quiet way had tried to awaken a kinder feeling for her in the heart of her brother. As one fights fire with fire in the great conflagrations of the prairies, Amelie hoped also to combat the influence of Angelique des Meloises by raising up a potent rival in the fair Heloise de Lotbiniere but she soon found how futile were her endeavors. The heart of Le Gardeur was wedded to the idol of his fancy, and no woman on earth could win him away from Angelique.

Amelie comforted Heloise by the gift of her whole confidence and sympathy. The poor disappointed girl accepted the decree of fate, known to no other but Amelie, while in revenge upon herself--a thing not rare in proud, sensitive natures--she appeared in society more gay, more radiant and full of mirth than ever before. Heloise hid the asp in her bosom, but so long as its bite was unseen she laughed cruelly at the pain of it, and deceived, as she thought, the eyes of the world as to her suffering.

The arrival of Heloise de Lotbiniere was followed by that of a crowd of other visitors, who came to the Manor House to pay their respects to the family on their return home, and especially to greet Le Gardeur and Colonel Philibert, who was well remembered, and whom the busy tongues of gossip already set down as a suitor for the hand of the young chatelaine.

The report of what was said by so many whispering friends was quickly carried to the ear of Amelie by some of her light-hearted companions. She blushed at the accusation, and gently denied all knowledge of it, laughing as a woman will laugh who carries a hidden joy or a hidden sorrow in her heart, neither of which she cares to reveal to the world's eye. Amelie listened to the pleasant tale with secret complaisance, for, despite her tremor and confusion, it was pleasant to hear that Pierre Philibert loved her, and was considered a suitor for her hand. It was sweet to know that the world believed she was his choice.

She threaded every one of these precious words, like a chaplet of pearls upon the strings of her heart,--contemplating them, counting them over and over in secret, with a joy known only to herself and to God, whom she prayed to guide her right whatever might happen.

That something would happen ere long she felt a premonition, which at times made her grave in the midst of her hopes and anticipations.

The days passed gaily at Tilly. Amelie carried out the elaborate programme which she had arranged for the amusement of Le Gardeur as well as for the pleasures of her guests.

Every day brought a change and a fresh enjoyment. The mornings were devoted by the gentlemen to hunting, fishing, and other sport; by the ladies to reading, music, drawing, needlework, or the arrangements of dress and ornaments. In the afternoons all met together, and the social evening was spent either at the Manor House or some neighboring mansion. The hospitality of all was alike: a profusion of social feeling formed, at that day, a marked characteristic of the people of New France.

The Lady de Tilly spent an hour or two each day with her trusty land steward, or bailli, Master Cote, in attending to the multifarious business of her Seigniory. The feudal law of New France imposed great duties and much labor upon the lords of the manor, by giving them an interest in every man's estate, and making them participators in every transfer of land throughout a wide district of country. A person who acquired, by purchase or otherwise, the lands of a censitaire, or vassal, was held to perform foi et hommage for the lands so acquired, and to acquit all other feudal dues owing by the original holder to his seigneur.

It was during one of these fair summer days at Tilly that Sieur Tranchelot, having acquired the farm of the Bocage, a strip of land a furlong wide and a league in depth, with a pleasant frontage on the broad St. Lawrence, the new censitaire came as in duty bound to render foi et hommage for the same to the lady of the Manor of Tilly, according to the law and custom of the Seigniory.

At the hour of noon, Lady de Tilly, with Le Gardeur, Amelie, and Pierre Philibert, in full dress, stood on a dais in the great hall; Master Cote sat at a table on the floor in front, with his great clasped book of record open before him. A drawn sword lay upon the table, and a cup of wine stood by the side of it.

When all was arranged, three loud knocks were heard on the great door, and the Sieur Tranchelot, dressed in his holiday costume, but bareheaded and without sword or spurs,--not being gentilhomme he was not entitled to wear them,--entered the door, which was ceremoniously opened for him by the majordomo. He was gravely led up to the dais, where stood the lady of the Manor, by the steward bearing his wand of office.

The worthy censitaire knelt down before the lady, and repeating her name three times, pronounced the formula of foi et hommage prescribed by the law, as owing to the lords of the Manor of Tilly.

"My Lady de Tilly! My Lady de Tilly! My Lady de Tilly! I render you fealty and homage due to you on account of my lands of the Bocage, which belong to me by virtue of the deed executed by the Sieur Marcel before the worthy notary Jean Pothier dit Robin, on the day of Palms, 1748, and I avow my willingness to acquit the seigniorial and feudal cens et rentes, and all other lawful dues, whensoever payable by me; beseeching you to be my good liege lady, and to admit me to the said fealty and homage."

The lady accepted the homage of Sieur Tranchelot, graciously remitted the lods et ventes,--the fines payable to the seigneur,-- gave him the cup of wine to drink when he rose to his feet, and ordered him to be generously entertained by her majordomo, and sent back to the Bocage rejoicing.

So the days passed by in alternation of business and pastime, but all made a pleasure for the agreeable inmates of the Manor House. Philibert gave himself up to the delirium of enchantment which the presence of Amelie threw over him. He never tired of watching the fresh developments of her gloriously-endowed nature. Her beauty, rare as it was, grew day by day upon his wonder and admiration, as he saw how fully it corresponded to the innate grace and nobility of her mind.

She was so fresh of thought, so free from all affectation, so gentle and winning in all her ways, and, sooth to say, so happy in the admiration of Philibert, which she was very conscious of now. It darted from his eyes at every look, although no word of it had yet passed his lips. The radiance of her spirits flashed like sunbeams through every part of the old Manor House.

Amelie was carried away in a flood of new emotion; she tried once or twice to be discreetly angry with herself for admitting so unreservedly the pleasure she felt in Pierre's admiration; she placed her soul on a rack of self-questioning torture, and every inquisition she made of her heart returned the self-same answer: she loved Pierre Philibert!

It was in vain she accused herself of possible impropriety: that it was bold, unmaidenly, censurable, nay, perhaps sinful, to give her heart before it had been asked for; but if she had to die for it, she could not conceal the truth, that she loved Pierre Philibert! "I ought to be angry with myself," said she. "I try to be so, but I cannot! Why?"

"Why?" Amelie solved the query as every true woman does, who asks herself why she loves one man rather than another. "Because he has chosen me out in preference to all others, to be the treasure-keeper of his affections! I am proud," continued Amelie, "that he gives his love to me, to me! unworthy as I am of such preference. I am no better than others." Amelie was a true woman: proud as an empress before other men, she was humble and lowly as the Madonna in the presence of him whom she felt was, by right of love, lord and master of her affections.

Amelie could not overcome a feeling of tremor in the presence of Pierre since she made this discovery. Her cheek warmed with an incipient flush when his ardent eyes glanced at her too eloquently. She knew what was in his heart, and once or twice, when casually alone with Philibert, she saw his lips quivering under a hard restraint to keep in the words, the dear words, she thought, which would one day burst forth in a flood of passionate eloquence, overwhelming all denial, and make her his own forever.

Time and tide, which come to all once in our lives, as the poet says, and which must be taken at their flood to lead to fortune, came at length to Amelie de Repentigny.

It came suddenly and in an unlooked-for hour, the great question of questions to her as to every woman.

The hour of birth and the hour of death are in God's hand, but the hour when a woman, yielding to the strong enfolding arm of a man who loves her, falters forth an avowal of her love, and plights her troth, and vows to be one with him till death, God leaves that question to be decided by her own heart. His blessing rests upon her choice, if pure love guides and reason enlightens affection. His curse infallibly follows every faithless pledge where no heart is, every union that is not the marriage of love and truth. These alone can be married, and where these are absent there is no marriage at all in the face of Heaven, and but the simulation of one on earth, an unequal yoking, which, if man will not sunder, God will at last, where there is neither marriage nor giving in marriage, but all are as his angels.

The day appointed for the long-planned excursion to the beautiful Lake of Tilly came round. A numerous and cheerful water-party left the Manor House in the bright, cool morning to spend the day gipsying in the shady woods and quiet recesses of the little lake. They were all there: Amelie's invitation to her young friends far and near had been eagerly accepted. Half a dozen boats and canoes, filled with light-hearted companions and with ample provisions for the day, shot up the narrow river, and after a rapid and merry voyage, disembarked their passengers and were drawn up on the shores and islands of the lake.

That bright morning was followed by a sunny day of blue skies, warm yet breezy. The old oaks wove a carpet of shadows, changing the pattern of its tissue every hour upon the leaf-strewn floor of the forest. The fresh pines shed their resinous perfume on every side in the still shade, but out in the sunshine the birds sang merrily all day.

The groups of merrymakers spent a glorious day of pleasure by the side of the clear, smooth lake, fishing and junketing on shore, or paddling their birch canoes over its waters among the little islands which dotted its surface.

Day was fast fading away into a soft twilight; the shadows which had been drawing out longer and longer as the sun declined, lay now in all their length, like bands stretched over the greensward. The breeze went down with the sun, and the smooth surface of the lake lay like a sheet of molten gold reflecting the parting glories of the day that still lit up the western sky.

A few stars began to twinkle here and there--they were not destined to shine brilliantly to-night, for they would ere long be eclipsed by the splendor of the full moon, which was just at hand, rising in a hemisphere of light, which stood like a royal pavilion on the eastern horizon. From it in a few minutes would emerge the queen of heaven, and mildly replace the vanishing glory of the day.

The company, after a repast under the trees, rose full of life and merriment and rearranged themselves into little groups and couples as chance or inclination led them. They trooped down to the beach to embark in their canoes for a last joyous cruise round the lake and its fairy islands, by moonlight, before returning home.

Amid a shower of lively conversation and laughter, the ladies seated themselves in the light canoes, which danced like corks upon the water. The gentlemen took the paddles, and, expert as Indians in the use of them, swept out over the surface of the lake, which was now all aglow with the bright crimson of sunset.

In the bow of one of the canoes sat the Arion of Tilly, Jean de La Marche; a flute or two accompanied his violin, and a guitar tinkled sweetly under the fingers of Heloise de Lotbiniere. They played an old air, while Jean led the chorus in splendid voice:

"'Nous irons sur l'eau,
Nous y prom-promener,

Nous irons jouer dans l'isle.'"

The voices of all united in the song as the canoes swept away around a little promontory, crowned with three pine-trees, which stood up in the blaze of the setting sun like the three children in the fiery furnace, or the sacred bush that burned and was not consumed.

Faint and fainter, the echoes repeated the receding harmony, until at last they died away. A solemn silence succeeded. A languor like that of the lotus-eaters crept over the face of nature and softened the heart to unwonted tenderness. It was the hour of gentle thoughts, of low spoken confidences, and love between young and sympathizing souls, who alone with themselves and God confess their mutual love and invoke his blessing upon it.

## Chapter XXIX: Felices Ter et Amplius

Amelie, by accident or by contrivance of her fair companions,--girls are so wily and sympathetic with each other,--had been left seated by the side of Philibert, on the twisted roots of a gigantic oak forming a rude but simple chair fit to enthrone the king of the forest and his dryad queen. No sound came to break the quiet of the evening hour save the monotonous plaint of a whippoorwill in a distant brake, and the ceaseless chirm of insects among the leafy boughs and down in the ferns that clustered on the knolls round about.

Philibert let fall upon his knee the book which he had been reading. His voice faltered, he could not continue without emotion the touching tale of Paolo and Francesca da Rimini. Amelie's eyes were suffused with tears of pity, for her heart had beat time to the music of Dante's immortal verse as it dropped in measured cadence from the lips of Philibert.

She had read the pathetic story before, but never comprehended until now the weakness which is the strength of love. Oh, blessed paradox of a woman's heart! And how truly the Commedia, which is justly called Divine, unlocks the secret chambers of the human soul.

"Read no more, Pierre," said she, "that book is too terrible in its beauty and in its sadness! I think it was written by a disembodied spirit who had seen all worlds, knew all hearts, and shared in all sufferings. It sounds to me like the sad voice of a prophet of woe."

"Amelie," replied he, "believe you there are women faithful and true as Francesca da Rimini? She would not forsake Paolo even in the gloomy regions of despair. Believe you that there are such women?"

Amelie looked at him with a quick, confident glance. A deep flush covered her cheek, and her breath went and came rapidly; she knew what to answer, but she thought it might seem overbold to answer such a question. A second thought decided her, however. Pierre Philibert would ask her no question to which she might not answer, she said to herself.

Amelie replied to him slowly, but undoubtingly: "I think there are such women, Pierre," replied she, "women who would never, even in the regions of despair, forsake the man whom they truly love, no, not for all the terrors recorded in that awful book of Dante!"

"It is a blessed truth, Amelie," replied he, eagerly; and he thought, but did not say it, "Such a woman you are; the man who gets your love gets that which neither earth nor heaven nor hell can take away."

He continued aloud, "The love of such a woman is truly given away, Amelie; no one can merit it! It is a woman's grace, not man's deserving."

"I know not," said she; "it is not hard to give away God's gifts: love should be given freely as God gives it to us. It has no value except as the bounty of the heart, and looks for no reward but in its own acceptance."

"Amelie!" exclaimed he, passionately, turning full towards her; but her eyes remained fixed upon the ground. "The gift of such a woman's love has been the dream, the ambition of my life! I may never find it, or having found it may never be worthy of it; and yet I must find it or die! I must find it where alone I seek it--there or nowhere! Can you help me for friendship's sake--for love's sake, Amelie de Repentigny, to find that one treasure that is precious as life, which is life itself to the heart of Pierre Philibert?"

He took hold of her passive hands. They trembled in his, but she offered not to withdraw them. Indeed, she hardly noticed the act in the tide of emotion which was surging in her bosom. Her heart moved with a wild yearning to tell him that he had found the treasure he sought,--that a love as strong and as devoted as that of Francesca da Rimini was her own free gift to him.

She tried to answer him, but could not. Her hand still remained fast locked in his. He held to it as a drowning man holds to the hand that is stretched to save him.

Philibert knew at that moment that the hour of his fate was come. He would never let go that hand again till he called it his own, or received from it a sign to be gone forever from the presence of Amelie de Repentigny.

The soft twilight grew deeper and deeper every moment, changing the rosy hues of the west into a pale ashen gray, over which hung the lamp of love,--the evening star, which shines so brightly and sets so soon,--and ever the sooner as it hastens to become again the morning star of a brighter day.

The shadow of the broad, spreading tree fell darker round the rustic seat where sat these two--as myriads have sat before and since, working out the problems of their lives, and beginning to comprehend each other, as they await with a thrill of anticipation the moment of mutual confidence and fond confession.

Pierre Philibert sat some minutes without speaking. He could have sat so forever, gazing with rapture upon her half-averted countenance, which beamed with such a divine beauty, all aglow with the happy consciousness of his ardent admiration, that it seemed the face of a seraph; and in his heart, if not on his knees, he bent in worship, almost idolatrous, at her feet.

And yet he trembled, this strong man who had faced death in every form but this! He trembled by the side of this gentle girl,--but it was for joy, not for fear. Perfect love casts out fear, and he had no fear now for Amelie's love, although she had not yet dared to look at him. But her little hand lay unreprovingly in his,-- nestling like a timid bird which loved to be there, and sought not to escape. He pressed it gently to his heart; he felt by its magnetic touch, by that dumb alphabet of love, more eloquent than spoken words, that he had won the heart of Amelie de Repentigny.

"Pierre," said she,--she wanted to say it was time to rejoin their companions, but the words would not come. Her face was still half- averted, and suffused with an unseen blush, as she felt his strong arm round her; and his breath, how sweet it seemed, fanning her cheek. She had no power, no will to resist him, as he drew her close, still closer to his heart.

She trembled, but was happy. No eye saw but God's through the blessed twilight; and "God will not reprove Pierre Philibert for loving me," thought she, "and why should I?" She tried, or simulated, an attempt at soft reproof, as a woman will who fears she may be thought too fond and too easily won, at the very moment she is ready to fall down and kiss the feet of the man before her.

"Pierre," said she, "it is time we rejoin our companions; they will remark our absence. We will go."

But she still sat there, and made no effort to go. A gossamer thread could have held her there forever, and how could she put aside the strong arm that was mightier than her own will?

Pierre spoke now; the feelings so long pent up burst forth in a torrent that swept away every bond of restraint but that of love's own laws.

He placed his hand tenderly on her cheek, and turned her glowing face full towards him. Still she dared not look up. She knew well what he was going to say. She might control her words, but not her tell-tale eyes. She felt a wild joy flashing and leaping in her bosom, which no art could conceal, should she look up at this moment in the face of Pierre Philibert.

"Amelie," said he, after a pause, "turn those dear eyes, and see and believe in the truth of mine! No words can express how much I do love you!"

She gave a start of joy,--not of surprise, for she knew he loved her. But the avowal of

Pierre Philibert's love lifted at once the veil from her own feelings. She raised her dark, impassioned eyes to his, and their souls met and embraced in one look both of recognition and bliss. She spake not, but unconsciously nestled closer to his breast, faltering out some inarticulate words of tenderness.

"Amelie," continued he, straining her still harder to his heart, "your love is all I ask of Heaven and of you. Give me that. I must have it, or live henceforth a man forlorn in the wide world. Oh, say, darling, can you, do you care for me?"

"Yes, indeed I do!" replied she, laying her arm over his neck, as if drawing him towards her with a timid movement, while he stooped and kissed her sweet mouth and eyes in an ecstasy of passionate joy. She abandoned herself for a moment to her excess of bliss. "Kiss me, darling!" said he; and she kissed him more than once, to express her own great love and assure him that it was all his own.

They sat in silence for some minutes; her cheek lay upon his, as she breathed his name with many fond, faltering expressions of tenderness.

He felt her tears upon his face. "You weep, Amelie," said he, starting up and looking at her cheeks and eyes suffused with moisture.

"I do," said she, "but it is for joy! Oh, Pierre Philibert, I am so happy! Let me weep now; I will laugh soon. Forgive me if I have confessed too readily how much I love you."

"Forgive you! 'tis I need forgiveness; impetuous that I am to have forced this confession from you to-night. Those blessed words, 'Yes, indeed I do,'--God's finger has written them on my heart forever. Never will I forsake the dear lips which spake them, nor fail in all loving duty and affection to you, my Amelie, to the end of my life."

"Of both our lives, Pierre," replied she; "I can imagine no life, only death, separated from you. In thought you have always been with me from the beginning; my life and yours are henceforth one."

He gave a start of joy, "And you loved me before, Amelie!" exclaimed he.

"Ever and always; but irrevocably since that day of terror and joy when you saved the life of Le Gardeur, and I vowed to pray for you to the end of my life."

"And during these long years in the Convent, Amelie,--when we seemed utterly forgotten to each other?"

"You were not forgotten by me, Pierre! I prayed for you then,-- earnest prayers for your safety and happiness, never hoping for more; least of all anticipating such a moment of bliss as the present. Oh, my Pierre, do not think me bold! You give me the right to love you without shame by the avowal of your love to me."

"Amelie!" exclaimed he, kissing her in an ecstasy of joy and admiration, "what have I done--what can I ever do, to merit or recompense such condescension as your dear words express?"

"Love me, Pierre! Always love me! That is my reward. That is all I ask, all my utmost imagination could desire."

"And this little hand, Amelie, will be forever mine?"

"Forever, Pierre, and the heart along with it."

He raised her hand reverently to his lips and kissed it. "Let it not be long," said he. "Life is too short to curtail one hour of happiness from the years full of trouble which are most men's lot."

"But not our lot, Pierre; not ours. With you I forbode no more trouble in this life, and eternal joy in the next."

She looked at him, and her eyes seemed to dilate with joy. Her hand crept timidly up to his thick locks; she fondly brushed them aside from his broad forehead, which she pressed down to her lips and kissed.

"Tell my aunt and Le Gardeur when we return home," continued she. "They love you, and will be glad--nay, overjoyed, to know that I am to be your--your--"

"My wife!---Amelie, thrice blessed words! Oh, say my wife!"

"Yes, your wife, Pierre! Your true and loving wife forever."

"Forever! Yes. Love like ours is imperishable as the essence of the soul itself, and partakes of the immortality of God, being of him and from him. The Lady de Tilly shall find me a worthy son, and Le Gardeur a true and faithful brother."

"And you, Pierre! Oh, say it; that blessed word has not sounded yet in my ear--what shall I call you?" And she looked in his eyes, drawing his soul from its inmost depths by the magnetism of her look.

"Your husband,--your true and loving husband, as you are my wife, Amelie."

"God be praised!" murmured she in his ear. "Yes, my HUSBAND! The blessed Virgin has heard my prayers." And she pressed him in a fond embrace, while tears of joy flowed from her eyes. "I am indeed happy!"

The words hardly left her lips when a sudden crash of thunder rolled over their heads and went pealing down the lake and among the islands, while a black cloud suddenly eclipsed the moon, shedding darkness over the landscape, which had just begun to brighten in her silvery rays.

Amelie was startled, frightened, clinging hard to the breast of Pierre, as her natural protector. She trembled and shook as the angry reverberations rolled away in the distant forests. "Oh, Pierre!" exclaimed she, "what is that? It is as if a dreadful voice came between us, forbidding our union! But nothing shall ever do that now, shall it? Oh, my love!"

"Nothing, Amelie. Be comforted," replied he. "It is but a thunder- storm coming up. It will send Le Gardeur and all our gay companions quickly back to us, and we shall return home an hour sooner, that is all. Heaven cannot frown on our union, darling."

"I should love you all the same, Pierre," whispered she. Amelie was not hard to persuade; she was neither weak nor superstitious beyond her age and sex. But she had not much time to indulge in alarms.

In a few minutes the sound of voices was heard; the dip and splash of hasty paddles followed, and the fleet of canoes came rushing into shore like a flock of water-fowl seeking shelter in bay or inlet from a storm.

There was a hasty preparation on all sides for departure. The camp- fires were trampled out lest they should kindle a conflagration in the forest. The baskets were tossed into one of the large canoes. Philibert and Amelie embarked in that of Le Gardeur, not without many arch smiles and pretended regrets on the part of some of the young ladies for having left them on their last round of the lake.

The clouds kept gathering in the south, and there was no time for parley. The canoes were headed down the stream, the paddles were plied vigorously: it was a race to keep ahead of the coming storm, and they did not quite win it.

The black clouds came rolling over the horizon in still blacker masses, lower and lower, lashing the very earth with their angry skirts, which were rent and split with vivid flashes of lightning. The rising wind almost overpowered with its roaring the thunder that pealed momentarily nearer and nearer. The rain came down in broad, heavy splashes, followed by a fierce, pitiless hail, as if Heaven's anger was pursuing them.

Amelie clung to Philibert. She thought of Francesca da Rimini clinging to Paolo amidst the tempest of wind and the moving darkness, and uttered tremblingly the words, "Oh, Pierre! what an omen. Shall it be said of us as of them, 'Amor condusse noi ad una morte'?" ("Love has conducted us into one death.")

"God grant we may one day say so," replied he, pressing her to his bosom, "when we have earned it by a long life of mutual love and devotion. But now cheer up, darling; we are home."

The canoes pushed madly to the bank. The startled holiday party sprang out; servants were there to help them. All ran across the lawn under the wildly-tossing trees, and in a few moments, before the storm could overtake them with its greatest fury, they reached the Manor House, and were safe under the protection of its strong and hospitable roof.

## Chapter XXX: "No Speech of Silk Will Serve Your Turn"

Angelique des Meloises was duly informed, through the sharp espionage of Lizette, as to what had become of Le Gardeur after that memorable night of conflict between love and ambition, when she rejected the offer of his hand and gave herself up to the illusions of her imagination.

She was sorry, yet flattered, at Lizette's account of his conduct at the Taverne de Menut; for, although pleased to think that Le Gardeur loved her to the point of self-destruction, she honestly pitied him, and felt, or thought she felt, that she could sacrifice anything except herself for his sake.

Angelique pondered in her own strange, fitful way over Le Gardeur. She had no thought of losing him wholly. She would continue to hold him in her silken string, and keep him under the spell of her fascinations. She still admired him,--nay, loved him, she thought. She could not help doing so; and if she could not help it, where was the blame? She would not, to be sure, sacrifice for him the brilliant hopes which danced before her imagination like fire-flies in a summer night--for no man in the world would she do that! The Royal Intendant was the mark she aimed at. She was ready to go through fire and water to reach that goal of her ambition. But if she gave the Intendant her hand it was enough; it was all she could give him, but not the smallest corner of her heart, which she acknowledged to herself belonged only to Le Gardeur de Repentigny.

While bent on accomplishing this scheme by every means in her power, and which involved necessarily the ruin of Le Gardeur, she took a sort of perverse pride in enumerating the hundred points of personal and moral superiority possessed by him over the Intendant and all others of her admirers. If she sacrificed her love to her ambition, hating herself while she did so, it was a sort of satisfaction to think that Le Gardeur's sacrifice was not less complete than her own; and she rather felt pleased with the reflection that his heart would be broken, and no other woman would ever fill that place in his affections which she had once occupied.

The days that elapsed after their final interview were days of vexation to Angelique. She was angry with herself, almost; angry with Le Gardeur that he had taken her at her word, and still more angry that she did not reap the immediate reward of her treachery against her own heart. She was like a spoiled and wilful child which will neither have a thing nor let it go. She would discard her lover and still retain his love! and felt irritated and even jealous when she heard of his departure to Tilly with his sister, who had thus, apparently, more influence to take him away from the city than Angelique had to keep him there.

But her mind was especially worked upon almost to madness by the ardent professions of love, with the careful avoidance of any proposal of marriage, on the part of the Intendant. She had received his daily visits with a determination to please and fascinate him. She had dressed herself with elaborate care, and no woman in New France equalled Angelique in the perfection of her attire. She studied his tastes in her conversation and demeanor, which were free beyond even her wont, because she saw that a manner bold and unconstrained took best with him. Angelique's free style was the most perfect piece of acting in the world. She laughed loudly at his wit, and heard without blushes his double entendres and coarse jests, not less coarse because spoken in the polished dialect of Paris. She stood it all, but with no more result than is left by a brilliant display of fireworks after it is over. She could read in the eager looks and manner of the Intendant that she had fixed his admiration and stirred his passions, but she knew by a no less sure intuition that she had not, with all her blandishments, suggested to his mind one serious thought of marriage.

In vain she reverted to the subject of matrimony, in apparent jest but secret earnest. The Intendant, quick-witted as herself, would accept the challenge, talk with her and caracole on the topic which she had caparisoned so gaily for him, and amid compliments and pleasantries, ride away from the point, she knew not whither! Then Angelique would be angry after his departure, and swear,--she could swear shockingly for a lady when she was angry!--and vow she would marry Le Gardeur after all; but her pride was stung, not her love. No man had ever defeated her when she chose to subdue him, neither should this proud Intendant! So Angelique collected her scattered forces again, and laid closer siege to Bigot than ever.

The great ball at the Palais had been the object of absorbing interest to the fashionable society of the Capital for many weeks. It came on at last, turning the heads of half the city with its splendor.

Angelique shone the acknowledged queen of the Intendant's ball. Her natural grace and beauty, set off by the exquisite taste and richness of her attire, threw into eclipse the fairest of her rivals. If there was one present who, in admiration of her own charms, claimed for herself the first place, she freely conceded to Angelique the second. But Angelique feared no rival there. Her only fear was at Beaumanoir. She was profoundly conscious of her own superiority to all present, while she relished the envy and jealousy which it created. She cared but little what the women thought of her, and boldly challenging the homage of the men, obtained it as her rightful due.

Still, under the gay smiles and lively badinage which she showered on all around as she moved through the brilliant throng, Angelique felt a bitter spirit of discontent rankling in her bosom. She was angry, and she knew why, and still more angry because upon herself lay the blame! Not that she blamed herself for having rejected Le Gardeur: she had done that deliberately and for a price; but the price was not yet paid, and she had, sometimes, qualms of doubt whether it would ever be paid!

She who had had her own way with all men, now encountered a man who spoke and looked like one who had had his own way with all women, and who meant to have his own way with her!

She gazed often upon the face of Bigot, and the more she looked the more inscrutable it appeared to her. She tried to sound the depths of his thoughts, but her inquiry was like the dropping of a stone into the bottomless pit of that deep cavern of the dark and bloody ground talked of by adventurous voyageurs from the Far West.

That Bigot admired her beyond all other women at the ball, was visible enough from the marked attention which he lavished upon her and the courtly flatteries that flowed like honey from his lips. She also read her preeminence in his favor from the jealous eyes of a host of rivals who watched her every movement. But Angelique felt that the admiration of the Intendant was not of that kind which had driven so many men mad for her sake. She knew Bigot would never go mad for her, much as he was fascinated! and why? why?

Angelique, while listening to his honeyed flatteries as he led her gaily through the ballroom, asked herself again and again, why did he carefully avoid the one topic that filled her thoughts, or spoke of it only in his mocking manner, which tortured her to madness with doubt and perplexity?

As she leaned on the arm of the courtly Intendant, laughing like one possessed with the very spirit of gaiety at his sallies and jests, her mind was torn with bitter comparisons as she remembered Le Gardeur, his handsome face and his transparent admiration, so full of love and ready for any sacrifice for her sake,--and she had cast it all away for this inscrutable voluptuary, a man who had no respect for women, but who admired her person, condescended to be pleased with it, and affected to be caught by the lures she held out to him, but which she felt would be of no more avail to hold him fast than the threads which a spider throws from bush to bush on a summer morn will hold fast a bird which flies athwart them!

The gayest of the gay to all outward appearance, Angelique missed sorely the presence of Le Gardeur, and she resented his absence from the ball as a slight and a wrong to her sovereignty, which never released a lover from his allegiance.

The fair demoiselles at the ball, less resolutely ambitious than Angelique, found by degrees, in the devotion of other cavaliers, ample compensation for only so much of the Intendant's favor as he liberally bestowed on all the sex; but that did not content Angelique: she looked with sharpest eyes of inquisition upon the bright glances which now and then shot across the room where she sat by the side of Bigot, apparently steeped in happiness, but with a serpent biting at her heart, for she felt that Bigot was really unimpressible as a stone under her most subtle manipulation.

Her thoughts ran in a round of ceaseless repetition of the question: "Why can I not subdue Francois Bigot as I have subdued every other man who exposed his weak side to my power?" and Angelique pressed her foot hard upon the floor as the answer returned ever the same: "The heart of the Intendant is away at Beaumanoir! That pale, pensive lady" (Angelique used a more coarse and emphatic word) "stands between him and me like a spectre as she is, and obstructs the path I have sacrificed so much to enter!"

"I cannot endure the heat of the ballroom, Bigot!" said Angelique; "I will dance no more to-night! I would rather sit and catch fireflies on the terrace than chase forever without overtaking it the bird that has escaped from my bosom!"

The Intendant, ever attentive to her wishes, offered his arm to lead her into the pleached walks of the illuminated garden. Angelique rose, gathered up her rich train, and with an air of royal coquetry took his arm and accompanied the Intendant on a promenade down the grand alley of roses.

"What favorite bird has escaped from your bosom, Angelique?" asked the Intendant, who had, however, a shrewd guess of the meaning of her metaphor.

"The pleasure I had in anticipation of this ball! The bird has flown, I know not where or how. I have no pleasure here at all!" exclaimed she, petulantly, although she knew the ball had been really got up mainly for her own pleasure.

"And yet Momus himself might have been your father, and Euphrosyne your mother, Angelique," replied Bigot, "to judge by your gaiety to-night. If you have no pleasure, it is because you have given it all away to others! But I have caught the bird you lost, let me restore it to your bosom pray!" He laid his hand lightly and caressingly upon her arm. Her bosom was beating wildly; she removed his hand, and held it firmly grasped in her own.

"Chevalier!" said she, "the pleasure of a king is in the loyalty of his subjects, the pleasure of a woman in the fidelity of her lover!" She was going to say more, but stopped. But she gave him a glance which insinuated more than all she left unsaid.

Bigot smiled to himself. "Angelique is jealous!" thought he, but he only remarked, "That is an aphorism which I believe with all my heart! If the pleasure of a woman be in the fidelity of her lover, I know no one who should be more happy than Angelique des Meloises! No lady in New France has a right to claim greater devotion from a lover, and no one receives it!"

"But I have no faith in the fidelity of my lover! and I am not happy, Chevalier! far from it!" replied she, with one of those impulsive speeches that seemed frankness itself, but in this woman were artful to a degree.

"Why so?" replied he; "pleasure will never leave you, Angelique, unless you wilfully chase it away from your side! All women envy your beauty, all men struggle to obtain your smiles. For myself, I would gather all the joys and treasures of the world, and lay them at your feet, would you let me!

"I do not hinder you, Chevalier!" she replied, with a laugh of incredulity, "but you do not do it! It is only your politeness to say that. I have told you that the pleasure of a woman is in the fidelity of her lover; tell me now, Chevalier, what is the highest pleasure of a man?"

"The beauty and condescension of his mistress,--at least, I know none greater." Bigot looked at her as if his speech ought to receive acknowledgement on the spot.

"And it is your politeness to say that, also, Chevalier!" replied she very coolly.

"I wish I could say of your condescension, Angelique, what I have said of your beauty: Francois Bigot would then feel the highest pleasure of a man." The Intendant only half knew the woman he was seeking to deceive. She got angry.

Angelique looked up with a scornful flash. "My condescension, Chevalier? to what have I not condescended on the faith of your solemn promise that the lady of Beaumanoir should not remain under your roof? She is still there, Chevalier, in spite of your promise!"

Bigot was on the point of denying the fact, but there was sharpness in Angelique's tone, and clearness of all doubt in her eyes. He saw he would gain nothing by denial.

"She knows the whole secret, I do believe!" muttered he. "Argus with his hundred eyes was a blind man compared to a woman's two eyes sharpened by jealousy."

"The lady of Beaumanoir accuses me of no sin that I repent of!" replied he. "True! I promised to send her away, and so I will; but she is a woman, a lady, who has claims upon me for gentle usage. If it were your case, Angelique--"

Angelique quitted his arm and stood confronting him, flaming with indignation. She did not let him finish his sentence: "If it were my case, Bigot! as if that could ever be my case, and you alive to speak of it!"

Bigot stepped backwards. He was not sure but a poniard glittered in the clenched hand of Angelique. It was but the flash of her diamond rings as she lifted it suddenly. She almost struck him.

"Do not blame me for infidelities committed before I knew you, Angelique!" said he, seizing her hand, which he held forcibly in his, in spite of her efforts to wrench it away.

"It is my nature to worship beauty at every shrine. I have ever done so until I found the concentration of all my divinities in you. I could not, if I would, be unfaithful to you, Angelique des Meloises!" Bigot was a firm believer in the classical faith that Jove laughs at lovers' perjuries.

"You mock me, Bigot!" replied she. "You are the only man who has ever dared to do so twice."

"When did I mock you twice, Angelique?" asked he, with an air of injured innocence.

"Now! and when you pledged yourself to remove the lady of Beaumanoir from your house! I admire your courage, Bigot, in playing false with me and still hoping to win! But never speak to me more of love while that pale spectre haunts the secret chambers of the Chateau!"

"She shall be removed, Angelique, since you insist upon it," replied he, secretly irritated; "but where is the harm? I pledge my faith she shall not stand in the way of my love for you."

"Better she were dead than do so!" whispered Angelique to herself. "It is my due, Bigot!"

replied she aloud, "you know what I have given up for your sake!"

"Yes! I know you have banished Le Gardeur de Repentigny when it had been better to keep him securely in the ranks of the Grand Company. Why did you refuse to marry him, Angelique?"

The question fairly choked her with anger. "Why did I refuse to marry him? Francois Bigot! Do you ask me seriously that question? Did you not tell me of your own love, and all but offer me your hand, giving me to understand--miserable sinner that you are, or as you think me to be--that you pledged your own faith to me, as first in your choice, and I have done that which I had better have been dead and buried with the heaviest pyramid of Egypt on top of me, buried without hope of resurrection, than have done?"

Bigot, accustomed as he was to woman's upbraidings, scarcely knew what to reply to this passionate outburst. He had spoken to her words of love, plenty of them, but the idea of marriage had not flashed across his mind for a moment,--not a word of that had escaped his lips. He had as little guessed the height of Angelique's ambition as she the depths of his craft and wickedness, and yet there was a wonderful similarity between the characters of both,--the same bold, defiant spirit, the same inordinate ambition, the same void of principle in selecting means to ends,--only the one fascinated with the lures of love, the other by the charms of wit, the temptations of money, or effected his purposes by the rough application of force.

"You call me rightly a miserable sinner," said he, half smiling, as one not very miserable although a sinner. "If love of fair women be a sin, I am one of the greatest of sinners; and in your fair presence, Angelique, I am sinning at this moment enough to sink a shipload of saints and angels!"

"You have sunk me in my own and the world's estimation, if you mean what you say, Bigot!" replied she, unconsciously tearing in strips the fan she held in her hand. "You love all women too well ever to be capable of fixing your heart upon one!" A tear, of vexation perhaps, stood in her angry eye as she said this, and her cheek twitched with fierce emotion.

"Come, Angelique!" said he, soothingly, "some of our guests have entered this alley. Let us walk down to the terrace. The moon is shining bright over the broad river, and I will swear to you by St. Picaut, my patron, whom I never deceive, that my love for all womankind has not hindered me from fixing my supreme affection upon you."

Angelique allowed him to press her hand, which he did with fervor. She almost believed his words. She could scarcely imagine another woman seriously preferred to herself, when she chose to flatter a man with a belief of her own preference for him.

They walked down a long alley brilliantly illuminated with lamps of Bohemian glass, which shone like the diamonds, rubies, and emeralds which grew upon the trees in the garden of Aladdin.

At every angle of the geometrically-cut paths of hard-beaten sea- shells, white as snow, stood the statue of a faun, a nymph, or dryad, in Parian marble, holding a torch, which illuminated a great vase running over with fresh, blooming flowers, presenting a vista of royal magnificence which bore testimony to the wealth and splendid tastes of the Intendant.

The garden walks were not deserted: their beauty drew out many a couple who sauntered merrily, or lovingly, down the pleached avenues, which looked like the corridors of a gorgeously-decorated palace.

Bigot and Angelique moved among the guests, receiving, as they passed, obsequious salutations, which to Angelique seemed a foretaste of royalty. She had seen the gardens of the palace many times before, but never illuminated as now. The sight of them so grandly decorated filled her with admiration of their owner, and she resolved that, cost what it would, the homage paid to her to-night, as the partner of the Intendant, should become hers by right on his hearthstone as the first lady in New France.

Angelique threw back her veil that all might see her, that the women might envy and the men admire her, as she leaned confidingly on the arm of Bigot, looking up in his face with that wonderful smile of hers which had brought so many men to ruin at her feet, and talking with such enchantment as no woman could talk but Angelique des Meloises.

Well understanding that her only road to success was to completely fascinate the Intendant, she bent herself to the task with such power of witchery and such simulation of real passion, that Bigot, wary and experienced gladiator as he was in the arena of love, was more than once brought to the brink of a proposal for her hand.

She watched every movement of his features, at these critical moments when he seemed just falling into the snares so artfully set for him. When she caught his eyes glowing with passionate admiration, she shyly affected to withdraw hers from his gaze, turning on him at times flashes of her dark eyes which electrified every nerve of his sensuous nature. She felt the pressure of his hand, the changed and softened inflections of his voice, she knew the words of her fate were trembling on his lips, and yet they did not come! The shadow of that pale hand at Beaumanoir, weak and delicate as it was, seemed to lay itself upon his lips when about to speak to her, and snatch away the words which Angelique, trembling with anticipation, was ready to barter away body and soul to hear spoken.

In a shady passage through a thick greenery where the lights were dimmer and no one was near, she allowed his arm for a moment to encircle her yielding form, and she knew by his quick breath that the words were moulded in his thoughts, and were on the point to rush forth in a torrent of speech. Still they came not, and Bigot again, to her unutterable disgust, shied off like a full-blooded horse which starts suddenly away from some object by the wayside and throws his rider headlong on the ground. So again were dashed the ardent expectations of Angelique.

She listened to the gallant and gay speeches of Bigot, which seemed to flutter like birds round her, but never lit on the ground where she had spread her net like a crafty fowler as she was, until she went almost mad with suppressed anger and passionate excitement. But she kept on replying with badinage light as his own, and with laughter so soft and silvery that it seemed a gentle dew from Heaven, instead of the drift and flying foam of the storm that was raging in her bosom.

She read and re-read glimpses of his hidden thoughts that went and came like faces in a dream, and she saw in her imagination the dark, pleading eyes and pale face of the lady of Beaumanoir. It came now like a revelation, confirming a thousand suspicions that Bigot loved that pale, sad face too well ever to marry Angelique des Meloises while its possessor lived at Beaumanoir,--or while she lived at all!

And it came to that! In this walk with Bigot round the glorious garden, with God's flowers shedding fragrance around them; with God's stars shining overhead above all the glitter and illusion of the thousand lamps, Angelique repeated to herself the terrific words, "Bigot loves that pale, sad face too well ever to marry me while its possessor lives at Beaumanoir--or while she lives at all!"

The thought haunted her! It would not leave her! She leaned heavily upon his arm as she swept like a queen of Cyprus through the flower-bordered walks, brushing the roses and lilies with her proud train, and treading, with as dainty a foot as ever bewitched human eye, the white paths that led back to the grand terrace of the Palace.

Her fevered imagination played tricks in keeping with her fear: more than once she fancied she saw the shadowy form of a beautiful woman walking on the other side of Bigot next his heart! It was the form of Caroline bearing a child in one arm, and claiming, by that supreme appeal to a man's heart, the first place in his affections.

The figure sometimes vanished, sometimes reappeared in the same place, and once and the last time assumed the figure and look of Our Lady of St. Foye, triumphant after a thousand sufferings, and still ever bearing the face and look of the lady of Beaumanoir.

Emerging at last from the dim avenue into the full light, where a fountain sent up showers of sparkling crystals, the figure vanished, and Angelique sat down on a quaintly-carved seat under a mountain- ash, very tired, and profoundly vexed at all things and with everybody.

A servant in gorgeous livery brought a message from the ballroom to the Intendant.

He was summoned for a dance, but he would not leave Angelique, he said. But Angelique begged for a short rest: it was so pleasant in the garden. She would remain by the fountain. She liked its sparkling and splashing, it refreshed her; the Intendant could come for her in half an hour; she wanted to be alone; she felt in a hard, unamiable mood, she said, and he only made her worse by stopping with her when others wanted him, and he wanted others!

The Intendant protested, in terms of the warmest gallantry, that he would not leave her; but seeing Angelique really desired at the present moment to be alone, and reflecting that he was himself sacrificing too much for the sake of one goddess, while a hundred others were adorned and waiting for his offerings, he promised in half an hour to return for her to this spot by the fountain, and proceeded towards the Palace.

Angelique sat watching the play and sparkle of the fountain, which she compared to her own vain exertions to fascinate the Intendant, and thought that her efforts had been just as brilliant, and just as futile!

She was sadly perplexed. There was a depth in Bigot's character which she could not fathom, a bottomless abyss into which she was falling and could not save herself. Whichever way she turned the eidolon of Caroline met her as a bar to all further progress in her design upon the Intendant.

The dim half-vision of Caroline which she had seen in the pleached walk, she knew was only the shadow and projection of her own thoughts, a brooding fancy which she had unconsciously conjured up into the form of her hated rival. The addition of the child was the creation of the deep and jealous imaginings which had often crossed her mind. She thought of that yet unborn pledge of a once mutual affection as the secret spell by which Caroline, pale and feeble as she was, still held the heart of the Intendant in some sort of allegiance.

"It is that vile, weak thing!" said she bitterly and angrily to herself, "which is stronger than I. It is by that she excites his pity, and pity draws after it the renewal of his love. If the hope of what is not yet be so potent with Bigot, what will not the reality prove ere long? The annihilation of all my brilliant anticipations! I have drawn a blank in life's lottery, by the rejection of Le Gardeur for his sake! It is the hand of that shadowy babe which plucks away the words of proposal from the lips of Bigot, which gives his love to its vile mother, and leaves to me the mere ashes of his passion, words which mean nothing, which will never mean anything but insult to Angelique des Meloises, so long as that woman lives to claim the hand which but for her would be mine!"

Dark fancies fluttered across the mind of Angelique during the absence of the Intendant. They came like a flight of birds of evil omen, ravens, choughs, and owls, the embodiments of wicked thoughts. But such thoughts suited her mood, and she neither chid nor banished them, but let them light and brood, and hatch fresh mischief in her soul.

She looked up to see who was laughing so merrily while she was so angry and so sad, and beheld the Intendant jesting and toying with a cluster of laughing girls who had caught him at the turn of the broad stair of the terrace. They kept him there in utter oblivion of Angelique! Not that she cared for his presence at that moment, or felt angry, as she would have done at a neglect of Le Gardeur, but it was one proof among a thousand others that, gallant and gay as he was among the throng of fair guests who were flattering and tempting him on every side, not one of them, herself included, could feel sure she had made an impression lasting longer than the present moment upon the heart of the Intendant.

But Bigot had neither forgotten Angelique nor himself. His wily spirit was contriving how best to give an impetus to his intrigue with her without committing himself to any promise of marriage. He resolved to bring this beautiful but exacting girl wholly under his power. He comprehended fully that Angelique was prepared to accept his hand at any moment, nay, almost demanded it; but the price of marriage was what Bigot would not, dared not pay, and as a true courtier of the period he believed thoroughly in his ability to beguile any woman he chose, and cheat her of the price she set upon her love.

# Chapter XXXI: The Ball at the Intendant's Palace

The bevy of fair girls still surrounded Bigot on the terrace stair. Some of them stood leaning in graceful pose upon the balusters. The wily girls knew his artistic tastes, and their pretty feet patted time to the music, while they responded with ready glee to the gossiping of the gay Intendant.

Amid their idle badinage Bigot inserted an artful inquiry for suggestion, not for information, whether it was true that his friend Le Gardeur de Repentigny, now at the Manor House of Tilly, had become affianced to his cousin, Heloise de Lotbiniere? There was a start of surprise and great curiosity at once manifested among the ladies, some of whom protested that it could not be true, for they knew better in what direction Le Gardeur's inclinations pointed. Others, more compassionate or more spiteful, with a touch of envy, said they hoped it was true, for he had been "jilted by a young lady in the city!" Whom they "all knew!" added one sparkling demoiselle, giving herself a twitch and throwing a side glance which mimicked so perfectly the manner of the lady hinted at, that all knew in a moment she meant no other than Angelique des Meloises. They all laughed merrily at the conceit, and agreed that Le Gardeur de Repentigny would only serve the proud flirt right by marrying Heloise, and showing the world how little he cared for Angelique.

"Or how much!" suggested an experienced and lively widow, Madame La Touche. "I think his marrying Heloise de Lotbiniere will only prove the desperate condition of his feelings. He will marry her, not because he loves her, but to spite Angelique."

The Intendant had reckoned securely on the success of his ruse: the words were scarcely spoken before a couple of close friends of Angelique found her out, and poured into her ears an exaggerated story of the coming marriage of Le Gardeur with Heloise de Lotbiniere.

Angelique believed them because it seemed the natural consequence of her own infidelity.

Her friends, who were watching her with all a woman's curiosity and acuteness, were secretly pleased to see that their news had cut her to the quick. They were not misled by the affected indifference and gay laughter which veiled the resentment which was plainly visible in her agitated bosom.

Her two friends left her to report back to their companions, with many exaggerations and much pursing of pretty lips, how Angelique had received their communication. They flattered themselves they had had the pleasure of first breaking the bad tidings to her, but they were mistaken! Angelique's far-reaching curiosity had touched Tilly with its antennae, and she had already learned of the visit of Heloise de Lotbiniere, an old school companion of her own, to the Manor House of Tilly.

She had scented danger afar off from that visit. She knew that Heloise worshipped Le Gardeur, and now that Angelique had cast him off, what more natural than that he should fall at last into her snares--so Angelique scornfully termed the beauty and amiable character of her rival. She was angry without reason, and she knew it; but that made her still more angry, and with still less reason.

"Bigot!" said she, impetuously, as the Intendant rejoined her when the half-hour had elapsed, "you asked me a question in the Castle of St. Louis, leaning on the high gallery which overlooks the cliffs! Do you remember it?"

"I do: one does not forget easily what one asks of a beautiful woman, and still less the reply she makes to us," replied he, looking at her sharply, for he guessed her drift.

"Yet you seem to have forgotten both the question and the reply, Bigot. Shall I repeat them?" said she, with an air of affected languor.

"Needless, Angelique! and to prove to you the strength of my memory, which is but another name for the strength of my admiration, I will repeat it: I asked you that night--it was a glorious night, the bright moon shone full in our faces as we looked over the shining river, but your eyes eclipsed all the splendor of the heavens--I asked you to give me your love; I asked for it then, Angelique! I ask for it now."

Angelique was pleased with the flattery, even while she knew how hollow and conventional a thing it was.

"You said all that before, Bigot!" replied she, "and you added a foolish speech, which I confess pleased me that night better than now. You said that in me you had found the fair haven of your desires, where your bark, long tossing in cross seas, and beating against adverse winds, would cast anchor and be at rest. The phrase sounded poetical if enigmatical, but it pleased me somehow; what did it mean, Bigot? I have puzzled over it many times since--pray tell me!"

Angelique turned her eyes like two blazing stars full upon him as if to search for every trace of hidden thought that lurked in his countenance.

"I meant what I said, Angelique: that in you I had found the pearl of price which I would rather call mine than wear a king's crown."

"You explain one enigma by another. The pearl of price lay there before you and you picked it up! It had been the pride of its former owner, but you found it ere it was lost. What did you with it, Bigot?"

The Intendant knew as well as she the drift of the angry tide, which was again setting in full upon him, but he doubted not his ability to escape. His real contempt for women was the lifeboat he trusted in, which had carried himself and fortunes out of a hundred storms and tempests of feminine wrath.

"I wore the precious pearl next my heart, as any gallant gentleman should do," replied he blandly; "I would have worn it inside my heart could I have shut it up there."

Bigot smiled in complacent self-approval at his own speech. Not so Angelique! She was irritated by his general reference to the duty of a gallant gentleman to the sex and not to his own special duty as the admirer of herself.

Angelique was like an angry pantheress at this moment. The darts of jealousy just planted by her two friends tore her side, and she felt reckless both as to what she said and what she did. With a burst of passion not rare in women like her, she turned her wrath full upon him as the nearest object. She struck Bigot with her clenched hand upon the breast, exclaiming with wild vehemence,--

"You lie! Francois Bigot, you never wore me next your heart, although you said so! You wear the lady of Beaumanoir next your heart. You have opened your heart to her after pledging it to me! If I was the pearl of price, you have adorned her with it--my abasement is her glory!" Angelique's tall, straight figure stood up, magnified with fury as she uttered this.

The Intendant stepped back in surprise at the sudden attack. Had the blow fallen upon his face, such is human nature, Bigot would have regarded it as an unpardonable insult, but falling upon his breast, he burst out in a loud laugh as he caught hold of her quivering hand, which she plucked passionately away from him.

The eyes of Angelique looked dangerous and full of mischief, but Bigot was not afraid or offended. In truth, her jealousy flattered him, applying it wholly to himself. He was, moreover, a connoisseur in female temper: he liked to see the storm of jealous rage, to watch the rising of its black clouds, to witness the lightning and the thunder, the gusts and whirlwinds of passion, followed by the rain of angry tears, when the tears were on his account. He thought he had never seen so beautiful a fury as Angelique was at that moment.

Her pointed epithet, "You lie!" which would have been death for a man to utter, made no dint on the polished armor of Bigot, although he inly resolved that she should pay a woman's penalty for it.

He had heard that word from other pretty lips before, but it left no mark upon a conscience that was one stain, upon a life that was one fraud. Still his bold spirit rather liked this bold utterance from an angry woman, when it was in his power by a word to change her rage into the tender cooing of a dove.

Bigot was by nature a hunter of women, and preferred the excitement of a hard chase, when the deer turns at bay and its capture gave him a trophy to be proud of, to the dull conquest of a tame and easy virtue, such as were most of those which had fallen in his way.

"Angelique!" said he, "this is perfect madness; what means this burst of anger? Do you doubt the sincerity of my love for you?"

"I do, Bigot! I doubt it, and I deny it. So long as you keep a mistress concealed at Beaumanoir, your pledge to me is false and your love an insult."

"You are too impetuous and too imperious, Angelique! I have promised you she shall be removed from Beaumanoir, and she shall--"

"Whither, and when?"

"To the city, and in a few days: she can live there in quiet seclusion. I cannot be cruel to her, Angelique."

"But you can be cruel to me, Bigot, and will be, unless you exercise the power which I know is placed in your hands by the King himself."

"What is that? to confiscate her lands and goods if she had any?"

"No, to confiscate her person! Issue a lettre de cachet and send her over sea to the Bastile."

Bigot was irritated at this suggestion, and his irritation was narrowly watched by Angelique.

"I would rather go to the Bastile myself!" exclaimed he; "besides, the King alone issues lettres de cachet: it is a royal prerogative, only to be used in matters of State."

"And matters of love, Bigot, which are matters of State in France! Pshaw! as if I did not know that the King delegates his authority, and gives lettres de cachet in blank to his trusted courtiers, and even to the ladies of his Court. Did not the Marquise de Pompadour send Mademoiselle Vaubernier to the Bastile for only smiling upon the King? It is a small thing I ask of you, Bigot, to test your fidelity,--you cannot refuse me, come!" added she, with a wondrous transformation of look and manner from storm and gloom to warmth and sunshine.

"I cannot and will not do it. Hark you, Angelique, I dare not do it! Powerful as I may seem, the family of that lady is too potent to risk the experiment upon. I would fain oblige you in this matter, but it would be the height of madness to do so."

"Well, then, Bigot, do this, if you will not do that! Place her in the Convent of the Ursulines: it will suit her and me both,--no better place in the world to tame an unruly spirit. She is one of the pious souls who will be at home there, with plenty of prayers and penances, and plenty of sins to pray for every day."

"But I cannot force her to enter the Convent, Angelique. She will think herself not good enough to go there; besides, the nuns themselves would have scruples to receive her."

"Not if YOU request her admission of Mere de la Nativite: the Lady Superior will refuse no application of yours, Bigot."

"Won't she! but she will! The Mere de la Nativite considers me a sad reprobate, and has already, when I visited her parlor, read me a couple of sharpest homilies on my evil ways, as she called them. The venerable Mere de la Nativite will not carry coals, I assure you, Angelique."

"As if I did not know her!" she replied impatiently. "Why, she screens with all her authority that wild nephew of hers, the Sieur Varin! Nothing irritates her like hearing a bad report of him, and although she knows all that is said of him to be true as her breviary, she will not admit it. The soeurs converses in the laundry were put on bread and water with prayers for a week, only for repeating some gossip they had heard concerning him."

"Ay! that is because the venerable Mere Superior is touchy on the point of family,--but I am not her nephew, voila la differance!" as the song says.

"Well! but you are her nephew's master and patron," replied Angelique, "and the good Mere will strain many points to oblige the Intendant of New France for sake of the Sieur Varin. You do not know her as I do, Bigot."

"What do you advise, Angelique?" asked he, curious to see what was working in her brain.

"That if you will not issue a lettre de cachet, you shall place the lady of Beaumanoir in the hands of the Mere de la Nativite with instructions to receive her into the community after the shortest probation."

"Very good, Angelique! But if I do not know the Mere Superior, you do not know the lady of Beaumanoir. There are reasons why the nuns would not and could not receive her at all,-- even were she willing to go, as I think she would be. But I will provide her a home suited to her station in the city; only you must promise to speak to me no more respecting her."

"I will promise no such thing, Bigot!" said Angelique, firing up again at the failure of her crafty plan for the disposal of Caroline, "to have her in the city will be worse than to have her at Beaumanoir."

"Are you afraid of the poor girl, Angelique,--you, with your surpassing beauty, grace, and power over all who approach you? She cannot touch you."

"She has touched me, and to the quick too, already," she replied, coloring with passion. "You love that girl, Francois Bigot! I am never deceived in men. You love her too well to give her up, and still you make love to me. What am I to think?"

"Think that you women are able to upset any man's reason, and make fools of us all to your own purposes." Bigot saw the uselessness of argument; but she would not drop the topic.

"So you say, and so I have found it with others," replied she, "but not with you, Bigot. But I shall have been made the fool of, unless I carry my point in regard to this lady."

"Well, trust to me, Angelique. Hark you! there are reasons of State connected with her. Her father has powerful friends at Court, and I must act warily. Give me your hand; we will be friends. I will carry out your wishes to the farthest possible stretch of my power. I can say no more."

Angelique gave him her hand. She saw she could not carry her point with the Intendant, and her fertile brain was now scheming another way to accomplish her ends. She had already undergone a revulsion of feeling, and repented having carried her resentment so far,--not that she felt it less, but she was cunning and artful, although her temper sometimes overturned her craft, and made wreck of her schemes.

"I am sorry I was so angry, Bigot, as to strike you with this feeble hand." Angelique smiled as she extended her dainty fingers, which, delicate as they were, had the strength and elasticity of steel.

"Not so feeble either, Angelique!" replied he, laughing; "few men could plant a better blow: you hit me on the heart fairly, Angelique."

He seized her hand and lifted it to his lips. Had Queen Dido possessed that hand she would have held fast Aeneas himself when he ran away from his engagements.

Angelique pressed the Intendant's hand with a grasp that left every vein bloodless. "As I hold fast to you, Bigot, and hold you to your engagements, thank God that you are not a woman! If you were, I think I should kill you. But as you are a man, I forgive, and take your promise of amendment. It is what foolish women always do!"

The sound of the music and the measured tread of feet in the lively dances were now plainly heard in the pauses of their conversation.

They rose, and entered the ballroom. The music ceased, and recommenced a new strain for the Intendant and his fair partner, and for a time Angelique forgot her wrath in the delirious excitement of the dance.

But in the dance her exuberance of spirits overflowed like a fountain of intoxicating wine. She cared not for things past or future in the ecstatic joy of the present.

Her voluptuous beauty, lissomeness, and grace of movement enthralled all eyes with admiration, as she danced with the Intendant, who was himself no mean votary of Terpsichore. A lock of her long golden hair broke loose and streamed in wanton disorder over her shoulders; but she heeded it not,--carried away by the spirit of the dance, and the triumph of present possession of the courtly Intendant. Her dainty feet flashed under her flying robe and scarcely seemed to touch the floor as they kept time to the swift throbbings of the music.

The Intendant gazed with rapture on his beautiful partner, as she leaned upon his arm in the pauses of the dance, and thought more than once that the world would be well lost for sake of such a woman. It was but a passing fancy, however; the serious mood passed away, and he was weary, long before Angelique, of the excitement and breathless heat of a wild Polish dance, recently first heard of in French society. He led her to a seat, and left her in the centre of a swarm of admirers, and passed into an alcove to cool and rest himself.

# Chapter XXXII: "On with the Dance"

Bigot, a voluptuary in every sense, craved a change of pleasure. He was never satisfied long with one, however pungent. He felt it as a relief when Angelique went off like a laughing sprite upon the arm of De Pean. "I am glad to get rid of the women sometimes, and feel like a man," he said to Cadet, who sat drinking and telling stories with hilarious laughter to two or three boon companions, and indulging in the coarsest jests and broadest scandal about the ladies at the ball, as they passed by the alcove where they were seated.

The eager persistence of Angelique, in her demand for a lettre de cachet to banish the unfortunate Caroline, had wearied and somewhat disgusted Bigot.

"I would cut the throat of any man in the world for the sake of her bright eyes," said he to himself, as she gave him a parting salute with her handkerchief; "but she must not ask me to hurt that poor foolish girl at Beaumanoir. No, by St. Picot! she is hurt enough already, and I will not have Angelique tormenting her! What merciless creatures women are to one another, Cadet!" said he, aloud.

Cadet looked up with red, inflamed eyes at the remark of Bigot. He cared nothing for women himself, and never hesitated to show his contempt for the whole sex.

"Merciless creatures, do you call them, Bigot! the claws of all the cats in Caen could not match the finger-nails of a jealous woman-- still less her biting tongue."

Angelique des Meloises swept past the two in a storm of music, as if in defiance of their sage criticisms. Her hand rested on the shoulder of the Chevalier de Pean. She had an object which made her endure it, and her dissimulation was perfect. Her eyes transfixed his with their dazzling look. Her lips were wreathed in smiles; she talked continually as she danced, and with an inconsistency which did not seem strange in her, was lamenting the absence from the ball of Le Gardeur de Repentigny.

"Chevalier," said she, in reply to some gallantry of her partner, "most women take pride in making sacrifices of themselves; I prefer to sacrifice my admirers. I like a man, not in the measure of what I do for him, but what he will do for me. Is not that a candid avowal, Chevalier? You like frankness, you know."

Frankness and the Chevalier de Pean were unknown quantities together; but he was desperately smitten, and would bear any amount of snubbing from Angelique.

"You have something in your mind you wish me to do," replied he, eagerly. "I would poison my grandmother, if you asked me, for the reward you could give me."

"Yes, I have something in my mind, Chevalier, but not concerning your grandmother. Tell me why you allowed Le Gardeur de Repentigny to leave the city?"

"I did not allow him to leave the city," said he, twitching his ugly features, for he disliked the interest she expressed in Le Gardeur. "I would fain have kept him here if I could. The Intendant, too, had desperate need of him. It was his sister and Colonel Philibert who spirited him away from us."

"Well, a ball in Quebec is not worth twisting a curl for in the absence of Le Gardeur de Repentigny!" replied she. "You shall promise me to bring him back to the city, Chevalier, or I will dance with you no more."

Angelique laughed so gaily as she said this that a stranger would have interpreted her words as all jest.

"She means it, nevertheless," thought the Chevalier. "I will promise my best endeavor, Mademoiselle," said he, setting hard his teeth, with a grimace of dissatisfaction which did not escape the eye of Angelique; "moreover, the Intendant desires his return on affairs of the Grand Company, and has sent more than one message to him already, to urge his return."

"A fig for the Grand Company! Remember, it is I desire his return; and it is my command, not the Intendant's, which you are bound, as a gallant gentleman, to obey." Angelique would have no divided allegiance, and the man who claimed her favors must give himself up, body and soul, without thought of redemption.

She felt very reckless and very wilful at this moment. The laughter on her lips was the ebullition of a hot and angry heart, not the play of a joyous, happy spirit. Bigot's refusal of a lettre de cachet had stung her pride to the quick, and excited a feeling of resentment which found its expression in the wish for the return of Le Gardeur.

"Why do you desire the return of Le Gardeur?" asked De Pean, hesitatingly. Angelique was often too frank by half, and questioners got from her more than they liked to hear.

"Because he was my first admirer, and I never forget a true friend, Chevalier," replied she, with an undertone of fond regret in her voice.

"But he will not be your last admirer," replied De Pean, with what he considered a seductive leer, which made her laugh at him. "In the kingdom of love, as in the kingdom of heaven, the last shall be first and the first last. May I be the last, Mademoiselle?"

"You will certainly be the last, De Pean; I promise that." Angelique laughed provokingly. She saw the eye of the Intendant watching her. She began to think he remained longer in the society of Cadet than was due to herself.

"Thanks, Mademoiselle," said De Pean, hardly knowing whether her laugh was affirmative or negative; "but I envy Le Gardeur his precedence."

Angelique's love for Le Gardeur was the only key which ever unlocked her real feelings. When the fox praised the raven's voice and prevailed on her to sing, he did not more surely make her drop the envied morsel out of her mouth than did Angelique drop the mystification she had worn so coquettishly before De Pean.

"Tell me, De Pean," said she, "is it true or not that Le Gardeur de Repentigny is consoling himself among the woods of Tilly with a fair cousin of his, Heloise de Lotbiniere?"

De Pean had his revenge, and he took it. "It is true; and no wonder," said he. "They say Heloise is, without exception, the sweetest girl in New France, if not one of the handsomest."

"Without exception!" echoed she, scornfully. "The women will not believe that, at any rate, Chevalier. I do not believe it, for one." And she laughed in the consciousness of beauty. "Do you believe it?"

"No, that were impossible," replied he, "while Angelique des Meloises chooses to contest the palm of beauty."

"I contest no palm with her, Chevalier; but I give you this rosebud for your gallant speech. But tell me, what does Le Gardeur think of this wonderful beauty? Is there any talk of marriage?"

"There is, of course, much talk of an alliance." De Pean lied, and the truth had been better for him.

Angelique started as if stung by a wasp. The dance ceased for her, and she hastened to a seat. "De Pean," said she, "you promised to bring Le Gardeur forthwith back to the city; will you do it?"

"I will bring him back, dead or alive, if you desire it; but I must have time. That uncompromising Colonel Philibert is with him. His sister, too, clings to him like a good angel to the skirt of a sinner. Since you desire it,"--De Pean spoke it with bitterness,-- "Le Gardeur shall come back, but I doubt if it will be for his benefit or yours, Mademoiselle."

"What do you mean, De Pean?" asked she, abruptly, her dark eyes alight with eager curiosity, not unmingled with apprehension. "Why do you doubt it will not be for his benefit or mine? Who is to harm him?"

"Nay, he will only harm himself, Angelique. And, by St. Picot! he will have ample scope for doing it in this city. He has no other enemy but himself." De Pean felt that she was making an ox of him to draw the plough of her scheming.

"Are you sure of that, De Pean?" demanded she, sharply.

"Quite sure. Are not all the associates of the Grand Company his fastest friends? Not one of them will hurt him, I am sure."

"Chevalier de Pean!" said she, noticing the slight shrug he gave when he said this, "you say Le Gardeur has no enemy but himself; if so, I hope to save him from himself, nothing more. Therefore I want him back to the city."

De Pean glanced towards Bigot. "Pardon me, Mademoiselle. Did the Intendant never speak to you of Le Gardeur's abrupt departure?" asked he.

"Never! He has spoken to you, though. What did he say?" asked she, with eager curiosity.

"He said that you might have detained him had you wished, and he blamed you for his departure."

De Pean had a suspicion that Angelique had really been instrumental in withdrawing Le Gardeur from the clutches of himself and associates; but in this he erred. Angelique loved Le Gardeur, at least for her own sake if not for his, and would have preferred he should risk all the dangers of the city to avoid what she deemed the still greater dangers of the country,--and the greatest of these, in her opinion, was the fair face of Heloise de Lotbiniere. While, from motives of ambition, Angelique refused to marry him herself, she could not bear the thought of another getting the man whom she had rejected.

De Pean was fairly puzzled by her caprices: he could not fathom, but he dared not oppose them.

At this moment Bigot, who had waited for the conclusion of a game of cards, rejoined the group where she sat.

Angelique drew in her robe and made room for him beside her, and was presently laughing and talking as free from care, apparently, as an oriole warbling on a summer spray. De Pean courteously withdrew, leaving her alone with the Intendant.

Bigot was charmed for the moment into oblivion of the lady who sat in her secluded chamber at Beaumanoir. He forgot his late quarrel with Angelique in admiration of her beauty. The pleasure he took in her presence shed a livelier glow of light across his features. She observed it, and a renewed hope of triumph lifted her into still higher flights of gaiety.

"Angelique," said he, offering his arm to conduct her to the gorgeous buffet, which stood loaded with golden dishes of fruit, vases of flowers, and the choicest confectionery, with wine fit for a feast of Cyprus, "you are happy to-night, are you not? But perfect bliss is only obtained by a judicious mixture of earth and heaven: pledge me gaily now in this golden wine, Angelique, and ask me what favor you will."

"And you will grant it?" asked she, turning her eyes upon him eagerly.

"Like the king in the fairy tale, even to my daughter and half of my kingdom," replied he, gaily.

"Thanks for half the kingdom, Chevalier," laughed she, "but I would prefer the father to the daughter." Angelique gave him a look of ineffable meaning. "I do not desire a king to-night, however. Grant me the lettre de cachet, and then--"

"And then what, Angelique?" He ventured to take her hand, which seemed to tempt the approach of his.

"You shall have your reward. I ask you for a lettre de cachet, that is all." She suffered her hand to remain in his.

"I cannot," he replied sharply to her urgent repetition. "Ask her banishment from Beaumanoir, her life if you like, but a lettre de cachet to send her to the Bastile I cannot and will not give!"

"But I ask it, nevertheless!" replied the wilful, passionate girl. "There is no merit in your love if it fears risk or brooks denial! You ask me to make sacrifices, and will not lift your finger to remove that stumbling-block out of my way! A fig for such love, Chevalier Bigot! If I were a man, there is nothing in earth, heaven, or hell I would not do for the woman I loved!"

Angelique fixed her blazing eyes full upon him, but magnetic as was their fire, they drew no satisfying reply. "Who in heaven's name is this lady of Beaumanoir of whom you are so careful or so afraid?"

"I cannot tell you, Angelique," said he, quite irritated. "She may be a runaway nun, or the wife of the man in the iron mask, or--"

"Or any other fiction you please to tell me in the stead of truth, and which proves your love to be the greatest fiction of all!"

"Do not be so angry, Angelique," said he, soothingly, seeing the need of calming down this impetuous spirit, which he was driving beyond all bounds. But he had carelessly dropped a word which she picked up eagerly and treasured in her bosom. "Her life! He said he would give me her life! Did he mean it?" thought she, absorbed in this new idea.

Angelique had clutched the word with a feeling of terrible import. It was not the first time the thought had flashed its lurid light across her mind. It had seemed of comparatively light import when it was only the suggestion of her own wild resentment. It seemed a word of terrible power heard from the lips of Bigot, yet Angelique knew well he did not in the least seriously mean what he said.

"It is but his deceit and flattery," she said to herself, "an idle phrase to cozen a woman. I will not ask him to explain it, I shall interpret it in my own way! Bigot has said words he understood not himself; it is for me to give them form and meaning."

She grew quiet under these reflections, and bent her head in seeming acquiescence to the Intendant's decision. The calmness was apparent only.

"You are a true woman, Angelique," said he, "but no politician: you have never heard thunder at Versailles. Would that I dared to grant your request. I offer you my homage and all else I have to give you to half my kingdom."

Angelique's eyes flashed fire. "It is a fairy tale after all!" exclaimed she; "you will not grant the lettre de cachet?"

"As I told you before, I dare not grant that, Angelique; anything else--"

"You dare not! You, the boldest Intendant ever sent to New France, and say you dare not! A man who is worth the name dare do anything in the world for a woman if he loves her, and for such a man a true woman will kiss the ground he walks on, and die at his feet if need be!" Angelique's thoughts reverted for a moment to Le Gardeur, not to Bigot, as she said this, and thought how he would do it for her sake if she asked him.

"My God, Angelique, you drive this matter hard, but I like you better so than when you are in your silkiest humor."

"Bigot, it were better you had granted my request." Angelique clenched her fingers hard together, and a cruel expression lit her eyes for a moment. It was like the glance of a lynx seeking a hidden treasure in the ground: it penetrated the thick walls of Beaumanoir! She suppressed her anger, however, lest Bigot should guess the dark imaginings and half-formed resolution which brooded in her mind.

With her inimitable power of transformation she put on her air of gaiety again and exclaimed,--"Pshaw! let it go, Bigot. I am really no politician, as you say; I am only a woman almost stifled with the heat and closeness of this horrid ballroom. Thank God, day is dawning in the great eastern window yonder; the dancers are beginning to depart! My brother is waiting for me, I see, so I must leave you, Chevalier."

"Do not depart just now, Angelique! Wait until breakfast, which will be prepared for the latest guests."

"Thanks, Chevalier," said she, "I cannot wait. It has been a gay and delightful ball--to them who enjoyed it."

"Among whom you were one, I hope," replied Bigot.

"Yes, I only wanted one thing to be perfectly happy, and that I could not get, so I must console myself," said she, with an air of mock resignation.

Bigot looked at her and laughed, but he would not ask what it was she lacked. He did not want a scene, and feared to excite her wrath by mention again of the lettre de cachet.

"Let me accompany you to the carriage, Angelique," said he, handing her cloak and assisting her to put it on.

"Willingly, Chevalier," replied she coquettishly, "but the Chevalier de Pean will accompany me to the door of the dressing-room. I promised him." She had not, but she beckoned with her finger to him. She had a last injunction for De Pean which she cared not that the Intendant should hear.

De Pean was reconciled by this manoevre; he came, and Angelique and he tripped off together. "Mind, De Pean, what I asked you about Le Gardeur!" said she in an emphatic whisper.

"I will not forget," replied he, with a twinge of jealousy. "Le Gardeur shall come back in a few days or De Pean has lost his influence and cunning."

Angelique gave him a sharp glance of approval, but made no further remark. A crowd of voluble ladies were all telling over the incidents of the ball, as exciting as any incidents of flood and field, while they arranged themselves for departure.

The ball was fast thinning out. The fair daughters of Quebec, with disordered hair and drooping wreaths, loose sandals, and dresses looped and pinned to hide chance rents or other accidents of a long night's dancing, were retiring to their rooms, or issuing from them hooded and mantled, attended by obsequious cavaliers to accompany them home.

The musicians, tired out and half asleep, drew their bows slowly across their violins; the very music was steeped in weariness. The lamps grew dim in the rays of morning, which struggled through the high windows, while, mingling with the last strains of good-night and bon repos, came a noise of wheels and the loud shouts of valets and coachmen out in the fresh air, who crowded round the doors of the Palace to convey home the gay revellers who had that night graced the splendid halls of the Intendant.

Bigot stood at the door bowing farewell and thanks to the fair company when the tall, queenly figure of Angelique came down leaning on the arm of the Chevalier de Pean. Bigot tendered her his arm, which she at once accepted, and he accompanied her to her carriage.

She bowed graciously to the Intendant and De Pean, on her departure, but no sooner had she driven off, than, throwing herself back in her carriage, heedless of the presence of her brother, who accompanied her home, she sank into a silent train of thoughts from which she was roused with a start when the carriage drew up sharply at the door of their own home.

## Chapter XXXIII: La Corriveau

Angelique scarcely noticed her brother, except to bid him good-night when she left him in the vestibule of the mansion. Gathering her gay robes in her jewelled hand, she darted up the broad stairs to her own apartment, the same in which she had received Le Gardeur on that memorable night in which she crossed the Rubicon of her fate.

There was a fixedness in her look and a recklessness in her step that showed anger and determination. It struck Lizette with a sort of awe, so that, for once, she did not dare to accost her young mistress with her usual freedom. The maid opened the door and closed it again without offering a word, waiting in the anteroom until a summons should come from her mistress.

Lizette observed that she had thrown herself into a fauteuil, after hastily casting off her mantle, which lay at her feet. Her long hair hung loose over her shoulders as it parted from all its combs and fastenings. She held her hands clasped hard across her forehead, and stared with fixed eyes upon the fire which burned low on the hearth, flickering in the depths of the antique fireplace, and occasionally sending a flash through the room which lit up the pictures on the wall, seeming to give them life and movement, as if they, too, would gladly have tempted Angelique to better thoughts. But she noticed them not, and would not at that moment have endured to look at them.

Angelique had forbidden the lamps to be lighted: it suited her mood to sit in the half-obscure room, and in truth her thoughts were hard and cruel, fit only to be brooded over in darkness and alone. She clenched her hands, and raising them above her head, muttered an oath between her teeth, exclaiming,--

"Par Dieu! It must be done! It must be done!" She stopped suddenly when she had said that. "What must be done?" asked she sharply of herself, and laughed a mocking laugh. "He gave me her life! He did not mean it! No! The Intendant was treating me like a petted child. He offered me her life while he refused me a lettre de cachet! The gift was only upon his false lips, not in his heart! But Bigot shall keep that promise in spite of himself. There is no other way,-- none!"

This was a new world Angelique suddenly found herself in. A world of guilty thoughts and unresisted temptations, a chaotic world where black, unscalable rocks, like a circle of the Inferno, hemmed her in on every side, while devils whispered in her ears the words which gave shape and substance to her secret wishes for the death of her "rival," as she regarded the poor sick girl at Beaumanoir.

How was she to accomplish it? To one unpractised in actual deeds of wickedness, it was a question not easy to be answered, and a thousand frightful forms of evil, stalking shapes of death came and went before her imagination, and she clutched first at one, then at another of the dire suggestions that came in crowds that overwhelmed her power of choice.

In despair to find an answer to the question, "What must be done?" she rose suddenly and rang the bell. The door opened, and the smiling face and clear eye of Lizette looked in. It was Angelique's last chance, but it was lost. It was not Lizette she had rung for. Her resolution was taken.

"My dear mistress!" exclaimed Lizette, "I feared you had fallen asleep. It is almost day! May I now assist you to undress for bed?" Voluble Lizette did not always wait to be first spoken to by her mistress.

"No, Lizette, I was not asleep; I do not want to undress; I have much to do. I have writing to do before I retire; send Fanchon Dodier here." Angelique had a forecast that it was necessary to deceive Lizette, who, without a word, but in no serene humor, went to summon Fanchon to wait on her mistress.

Fanchon presently came in with a sort of triumph glittering in her black eye. She had noticed the ill humor of Lizette, but had not the slightest idea why she had been summoned to wait on Angelique instead of her own maid. She esteemed it quite an honor, however.

"Fanchon Dodier!" said she, "I have lost my jewels at the ball; I cannot rest until I find them; you are quicker-witted than Lizette: tell me what to do to find them, and I will give you a dress fit for a lady."

Angelique with innate craft knew that her question would bring forth the hoped-for reply.

Fanchon's eyes dilated with pleasure at such a mark of confidence. "Yes, my Lady," replied she, "if I had lost my jewels I should know what to do. But ladies who can read and write and who have the wisest gentlemen to give them counsel do not need to seek advice where poor habitan girls go when in trouble and perplexity."

"And where is that, Fanchon? Where would you go if in trouble and perplexity?"

"My Lady, if I had lost all my jewels,"--Fanchon's keen eye noticed that Angelique had lost none of hers, but she made no remark on it,-- "if I had lost all mine, I should go see my aunt Josephte Dodier. She is the wisest woman in all St. Valier; if she cannot tell you all you wish to know, nobody can."

"What! Dame Josephte Dodier, whom they call La Corriveau? Is she your aunt?"

Angelique knew very well she was. But it was her cue to pretend ignorance in order to impose on Fanchon.

"Yes, ill-natured people call her La Corriveau, but she is my aunt, nevertheless. She is married to my uncle Louis Dodier, but is a lady, by right of her mother, who came from France, and was once familiar with all the great dames of the Court. It was a great secret why her mother left France and came to St. Valier; but I never knew what it was. People used to shake their heads and cross themselves when speaking of her, as they do now when speaking of Aunt Josephte, whom they call La Corriveau; but they tremble when she looks at them with her black, evil eye, as they call it. She is a terrible woman, is Aunt Josephte! but oh, Mademoiselle, she can tell you things past, present, and to come! If she rails at the world, it is because she knows every wicked thing that is done in it, and the world rails at her in return; but people are afraid of her all the same."

"But is it not wicked? Is it not forbidden by the Church to consult a woman like her, a sorciere?" Angelique took a sort of perverse merit to herself for arguing against her own resolution.

"Yes, my Lady! but although forbidden by the Church, the girls all consult her, nevertheless, in their losses and crosses; and many of the men, too, for she does know what is to happen, and how to do things, does Aunt Josephte. If the clergy cannot tell a poor girl about her sweetheart, and how to keep him in hand, why should she not go and consult La Corriveau, who can?"

"Fanchon, I would not care to consult your aunt. People would laugh at my consulting La Corriveau, like a simple habitan girl; what would the world say?"

"But the world need not know, my Lady. Aunt Josephte knows secrets, they say, that would ruin, burn, and hang half the ladies of Paris. She learned those terrible secrets from her mother, but she keeps them safe in those close lips of hers. Not the faintest whisper of one of them has ever been heard by her nearest neighbor. Indeed, she has no gossips, and makes no friends, and wants none. Aunt Josephte is a safe confidante, my Lady, if you wish to consult her."

"I have heard she is clever, supernatural, terrible, this aunt of yours! But I could not go to St. Valier for advice and help; I could not conceal my movements like a plain habitan girl."

"No, my Lady," continued Fanchon, "it is not fitting that you should go to Aunt Josephte. I will bring Aunt Josephte here to you. She will be charmed to come to the city and serve a lady like you."

"Well,--no! it is not well, but ill! but I want to recover my jewels, so go for your aunt, and bring her back with you. And mind, Fanchon!" said Angelique, lifting a warning finger, "if you utter one word of your errand to man or beast, or to the very trees of the wayside, I will cut out your tongue, Fanchon Dodier!"

Fanchon trembled and grew pale at the fierce look of her mistress. "I will go, my Lady, and I will keep silent as a fish!" faltered the maid. "Shall I go immediately?"

"Immediately if you will! It is almost day, and you have far to go. I will send old Gujon the butler to order an Indian canoe for you. I will not have Canadian boatmen to row you to St. Valier: they would talk you out of all your errand before you were half-way there. You shall go to St. Valier by water, and return with La Corriveau by land. Do you understand? Bring her in to-night, and not before midnight. I will leave the door ajar for you to enter without noise; you will show her at once to my apartment, Fanchon! Be wary, and do not delay, and say not a word to mortal!"

"I will not, my Lady. Not a mouse shall hear us come in!" replied Fanchon, quite proud now of the secret understanding between herself and her mistress.

"And again mind that loose tongue of yours! Remember, Fanchon, I will cut it out as sure as you live if you betray me."

"Yes, my Lady!" Fanchon's tongue felt somewhat paralyzed under the threat of Angelique, and she bit it painfully as if to remind it of its duty.

"You may go now," said Angelique. "Here is money for you. Give this piece of gold to La Corriveau as an earnest that I want her. The canotiers of the St. Lawrence will also require double fare for bringing La Corriveau over the ferry."

"No, they rarely venture to charge her anything at all, my Lady," replied Fanchon; "to be sure it is not for love, but they are afraid of her. And yet Antoine La Chance, the boatman, says she is equal to a Bishop for stirring up piety; and more Ave Marias are repeated when she is in his boat, than are said by the whole parish on Sunday."

"I ought to say my Ave Marias, too!" replied Angelique, as Fanchon left the apartment, "but my mouth is parched and burns up the words of prayer like a furnace; but that is nothing to the fire in my heart! That girl, Fanchon Dodier, is not to be trusted, but I have no other messenger to send for La Corriveau. I must be wary with her, too, and make her suggest the thing I would have done. My Lady of Beaumanoir!" she apostrophized in a hard monotone, "your fate does not depend on the Intendant, as you fondly imagine. Better had he issued the lettre de cachet than for you to fall into the hands of La Corriveau!"

Daylight now shot into the windows, and the bright rays of the rising sun streamed full in the face of Angelique. She saw herself reflected in the large Venetian mirror. Her countenance looked pale, stern, and fixed as marble. The fire in her eyes startled her with its unearthly glow. She trembled and turned away from her mirror, and crept to her couch like a guilty thing, with a feeling as if she was old, haggard, and doomed to shame for the sake of this Intendant, who cared not for her, or he would not have driven her to such desperate and wicked courses as never fell to the lot of a woman before.

"C'est sa faute! C'est sa faute!" exclaimed she, clasping her hands passionately together. "If she dies, it is his fault, not mine! I prayed him to banish her, and he would not! C'est sa faute! C'est sa faute!" Repeating these words Angelique fell into a feverish slumber, broken by frightful dreams which lasted far on into the day.

The long reign of Louis XIV., full of glories and misfortunes for France, was marked towards its close by a portentous sign indicative of corrupt manners and a falling state. Among these, the crimes of secret poisoning suddenly attained a magnitude which filled the whole nation with terror and alarm.

Antonio Exili, an Italian, like many other alchemists of that period, had spent years in search of the philosopher's stone and the elixir of life. His vain experiments to transmute the baser metals into gold reduced him to poverty and want. His quest after these secrets had led him to study deeply the nature and composition of poisons and their antidotes. He had visited the great universities and other schools of the continent, finishing his scientific studies under a famous German chemist named Glaser. But the terrible secret of the agua tofana and of the poudre de succession, Exili learned from Beatrice Spara, a Sicilian, with whom he had a liaison, one of those inscrutable beings of the gentle sex whose lust for pleasure or power is only equalled by the atrocities they are willing to perpetrate upon all who stand in the way of their desires or their ambition.

To Beatrice Spara, the secret of this subtle preparation had come down like an evil inheritance from the ancient Candidas and Saganas of imperial Rome. In the proud palaces of the Borgias, of the Orsinis, the Scaligers, the Borromeos, the art of poisoning was preserved among the last resorts of Machiavellian statecraft; and not only in palaces, but in streets of Italian cities, in solitary towers and dark recesses of the Apennines, were still to be found the lost children of science, skilful compounders of poisons, at once fatal and subtle in their operation,--poisons which left not the least trace of their presence in the bodies of their victims, but put on the appearance of other and more natural causes of death.

Exili, to escape the vengeance of Beatrice Spara, to whom he had proved a faithless lover, fled from Naples, and brought his deadly knowledge to Paris, where he soon found congenial spirits to work with him in preparing the deadly poudre de succession, and the colorless drops of the aqua tofana.

With all his crafty caution, Exili fell at last under suspicion of the police for tampering in these forbidden arts. He was arrested, and thrown into the Bastile, where he became the occupant of the same cell with Gaudin de St. Croix, a young nobleman of the Court, the lover of the Marchioness de Brinvilliers, for an intrigue with whom the Count had been imprisoned. St. Croix learned from Exili, in the Bastile, the secret of the poudre de succession.

The two men were at last liberated for want of proof of the charges against them. St. Croix set up a laboratory in his own house, and at once proceeded to experiment upon the terrible secrets learned from Exili, and which he revealed to his fair, frail mistress, who, mad to make herself his wife, saw in these a means to remove every obstacle out of the way. She poisoned her husband, her father, her brother, and at last, carried away by a mania for murder, administered on all sides the fatal poudre de succession, which brought death to house, palace, and hospital, and filled the capital, nay, the whole kingdom, with suspicion and terror.

This fatal poison history describes as either a light and almost impalpable powder, tasteless, colorless, and inodorous, or a liquid clear as a dewdrop, when in the form of the aqua tofana. It was capable of causing death either instantaneously or by slow and lingering decline at the end of a definite number of days, weeks, or even months, as was desired. Death was not less sure because deferred, and it could be made to assume the appearance of dumb paralysis, wasting atrophy, or burning fever, at the discretion of the compounder of the fatal poison.

The ordinary effect of the aqua tofana was immediate death. The poudre de succession was more slow in killing. It produced in its pure form a burning heat, like that of a fiery furnace in the chest, the flames of which, as they consumed the patient, darted out of his eyes, the only part of the body which seemed to be alive, while the rest was little more than a dead corpse.

Upon the introduction of this terrible poison into France, Death, like an invisible spirit of evil, glided silently about the kingdom, creeping into the closest family circles, seizing everywhere on its helpless victims. The nearest and dearest relationships of life were no longer the safe guardians of the domestic hearth. The man who to-day appeared in the glow of health dropped to-morrow and died the next day. No skill of the physician was able to save him, or to detect the true cause of his death, attributing it usually to the false appearances of disease which it was made to assume.

The victims of the poudre de succession were counted by thousands. The possession of wealth, a lucrative office, a fair young wife, or a coveted husband, were sufficient reasons for sudden death to cut off the holder of these envied blessings. A terrible mistrust pervaded all classes of society. The husband trembled before his wife, the wife before her husband, father and son, brother and sister,--kindred and friends, of all degrees, looked askance and with suspicious eyes upon one another.

In Paris the terror lasted long. Society was for a while broken up by cruel suspicions. The meat upon the table remained uneaten, the wine undrank, men and women procured their own provisions in the market, and cooked and ate them in their own apartments. Yet was every precaution in vain. The fatal dust scattered upon the pillow, or a bouquet sprinkled with the aqua tofana, looking bright and innocent as God's dew upon the flowers, transmitted death without a warning of danger. Nay, to crown all summit of wickedness, the bread in the hospitals of the sick, the meagre tables of the convent, the consecrated host administered by the priest, and the sacramental wine which he drank himself, all in turn were poisoned, polluted, damned, by the unseen presence of the manna of St. Nicholas, as the populace mockingly called the poudre de succession.

The Court took the alarm when a gilded vial of the aqua tofana was found one day upon the table of the Duchesse de la Valliere, having been placed there by the hand of some secret rival, in order to cast suspicion upon the unhappy Louise, and hasten her fall, already approaching.

The star of Montespan was rising bright in the east, and that of La Valliere was setting in clouds and darkness in the west. But the King never distrusted for a moment the truth of La Valliere, the only woman who ever loved him for his own sake, and he knew it even while he allowed her to be supplanted by another infinitely less worthy--one whose hour of triumph came when she saw the broken- hearted Louise throw aside the velvet and brocade of the Court and put on the sackcloth of the barefooted and repentant Carmelite.

The King burned with indignation at the insult offered to his mistress, and was still more alarmed to find the new mysterious death creeping into the corridors of his palace. He hastily constituted the terrible Chambre Ardente, a court of supreme criminal jurisdiction, and commissioned it to search out, try, and burn, without appeal, all poisoners and secret assassins in the kingdom.

La Regnie, a man of Rhadamanthean justice, as hard of heart as he was subtle and suspicious, was long baffled, and to his unutterable rage, set at naught by the indefatigable poisoners who kept all France awake on its pillows.

History records how Gaudin de St. Croix, the disciple of Exili, while working in his secret laboratory at the sublimation of the deadly poison, accidentally dropped the mask of glass which protected his face. He inhaled the noxious fumes and fell dead by the side of his crucibles. This event gave Desgrais, captain of the police of Paris, a clue to the horrors which had so long baffled his pursuit.

The correspondence of St. Croix was seized. His connection with the Marchioness de Brinvilliers and his relations with Exili were discovered. Exili was thrown a second time into the Bastile. The Marchioness was arrested, and put upon her trial before the Chambre Ardente, where, as recorded in the narrative of her confessor, Pirol, her ravishing beauty of feature, blue eyes, snow-white skin, and gentle demeanor won a strong sympathy from the fickle populace of Paris, in whose eyes her charms of person and manner pleaded hard to extenuate her unparalleled crimes.

But no power of beauty or fascination of look could move the stern La Regnie from his judgment. She was pronounced guilty of the death of her husband, and sentenced first to be tortured and then beheaded and her body burnt on the Place de Greve, a sentence which was carried out to the letter. The ashes of the fairest and most wicked dame of the Court of Lous XIV. were scattered to the four corners of the city which had been the scene of her unparalleled crimes. The arch-poisoner Exili was also tried, and condemned to be burnt. The tumbril that bore him to execution was stopped on its way by the furious rabble, and he was torn in pieces by them.

For a short time the kingdom breathed freely in fancied security; but soon the epidemic of sudden as well as lingering deaths from poison broke out again on all sides. The fatal tree of the knowledge of evil, seemingly cut down with Exili and St. Croix, had sprouted afresh, like a upas that could not be destroyed.

The poisoners became more numerous than ever. Following the track of St. Croix and La Brinvilliers, they carried on the war against humanity without relaxation. Chief of these was a reputed witch and fortune-teller named La Voisin, who had studied the infernal secret under Exili and borne a daughter to the false Italian.

With La Voisin were associated two priests, Le Sage and Le Vigoureux, who lived with her, and assisted her in her necromantic exhibitions, which were visited, believed in, and richly rewarded by some of the foremost people of the Court. These necromantic exhibitions were in reality a cover to darker crimes.

It was long the popular belief in France, that Cardinal Bonzy got from La Voisin the means of ridding himself of sundry persons who stood in the way of his ecclesiastical preferment, or to whom he had to pay pensions in his quality of Archbishop of Narbonne. The Duchesse de Bouillon and the Countess of Soissons, mother of the famous Prince Eugene, were also accused of trafficking with that terrible woman, and were banished from the kingdom in consequence, while a royal duke, Francois de Montmorency, was also suspected of dealings with La Voisin.

The Chambre Ardente struck right and left. Desgrais, chief of the police, by a crafty ruse, penetrated into the secret circle of La Voisin, and she, with a crowd of associates, perished in the fires of the Place de Greve. She left an ill-starred daughter, Marie Exili, to the blank charity of the streets of Paris, and the possession of many of the frightful secrets of her mother and of her terrible father.

Marie Exili clung to Paris. She grew up beautiful and profligate; she coined her rare

Italian charms, first into gold and velvet, then into silver and brocade, and at last into copper and rags. When her charms faded entirely, she began to practise the forbidden arts of her mother and father, but without their boldness or long impunity.

She was soon suspected, but receiving timely warning of her danger, from a high patroness at Court, Marie fled to New France in the disguise of a paysanne, one of a cargo of unmarried women sent out to the colony on matrimonial venture, as the custom then was, to furnish wives for the colonists. Her sole possession was an antique cabinet with its contents, the only remnant saved from the fortune of her father, Exili.

Marie Exili landed in New France, cursing the Old World which she had left behind, and bringing as bitter a hatred of the New, which received her without a shadow of suspicion that under her modest peasant's garb was concealed the daughter and inheritrix of the black arts of Antonio Exili and of the sorceress La Voisin.

Marie Exili kept her secret well. She played the ingenue to perfection. Her straight figure and black eyes having drawn a second glance from the Sieur Corriveau, a rich habitan of St. Valier, who was looking for a servant among the crowd of paysannes who had just arrived from France, he could not escape from the power of their fascination.

He took Marie Exili home with him, and installed her in his household, where his wife soon died of some inexplicable disease which baffled the knowledge of both the doctor and the curate, the two wisest men in the parish. The Sieur Corriveau ended his widowhood by marrying Marie Exili, and soon died himself, leaving his whole fortune and one daughter, the image of her mother, to Marie.

Marie Exili, ever in dread of the perquisitions of Desgrais, kept very quiet in her secluded home on the St. Lawrence, guarding her secret with a life-long apprehension, and but occasionally and in the darkest ways practising her deadly skill. She found some compensation and relief for her suppressed passions in the clinging sympathy of her daughter, Marie Josephte dit La Corriveau, who worshipped all that was evil in her mother, and in spite of an occasional reluctance, springing from some maternal instinct, drew from her every secret of her life. She made herself mistress of the whole formula of poisoning as taught by her grandfather Exili, and of the arts of sorcery practised by her wicked grandmother, La Voisin.

As La Corriveau listened to the tale of the burning of her grandmother on the Place de Greve, her own soul seemed bathed in the flames which rose from the faggots, and which to her perverted reason appeared as the fires of cruel injustice, calling for revenge upon the whole race of the oppressors of her family, as she regarded the punishers of their crimes.

With such a parentage, and such dark secrets brooding in her bosom, Marie Josephte, or, as she was commonly called, La Corriveau, had nothing in common with the simple peasantry among whom she lived.

Years passed over her, youth fled, and La Corriveau still sat in her house, eating her heart out, silent and solitary. After the death of her mother, some whispers of hidden treasures known only to herself, a rumor which she had cunningly set afloat, excited the cupidity of Louis Dodier, a simple habitan of St. Valier, and drew him into a marriage with her.

It was a barren union. No child followed, with God's grace in its little hands, to create a mother's feelings and soften the callous heart of La Corriveau. She cursed her lot that it was so, and her dry bosom became an arid spot of desert, tenanted by satyrs and dragons, by every evil passion of a woman without conscience and void of love.

But La Corriveau had inherited the sharp intellect and Italian dissimulation of Antonio Exili: she was astute enough to throw a veil of hypocrisy over the evil eyes which shot like a glance of death from under the thick black eyebrows.

Her craft was equal to her malice. An occasional deed of alms, done not for charity's sake, but for ostentation; an adroit deal of cards, or a horoscope cast to flatter a foolish girl; a word of sympathy, hollow as a water bubble, but colored with iridescent prettiness, averted suspicion from the darker traits of her character.

If she was hated, she was also feared by her neighbors, and although the sign of the cross was made upon the chair whereon she had sat in a neighbor's house, her visits were not unwelcome, and in the manor- house, as in the cabin of the woodman, La Corriveau was received, consulted, rewarded, and oftener thanked than cursed, by her witless dupes.

There was something sublime in the satanic pride with which she carried with her the terrible secrets of her race, which in her own mind made her the superior of every one around her, and whom she regarded as living only by her permission or forbearance.

For human love other than as a degraded menial, to make men the slaves of her mercenary schemes, La Corriveau cared nothing. She never felt it, never inspired it. She looked down upon all her sex as the filth of creation and, like herself, incapable of a chaste feeling or a pure thought. Every better instinct of her nature had gone out like the flame of a lamp whose oil is exhausted; love of money remained as dregs at the bottom of her heart. A deep grudge against mankind, and a secret pleasure in the misfortunes of others, especially of her own sex, were her ruling passions.

Her mother, Marie Exili, had died in her bed, warning her daughter not to dabble in the forbidden arts which she had taught her, but to cling to her husband and live an honest life as the only means of dying a more hopeful death than her ancestors.

La Corriveau heard much, but heeded little. The blood of Antonio Exili and of La Voisin beat too vigorously in her veins to be tamed down by the feeble whispers of a dying woman who had been weak enough to give way at last. The death of her mother left La Corriveau free to follow her own will. The Italian subtlety of her race made her secret and cautious. She had few personal affronts to avenge, and few temptations in the simple community where she lived to practise more than the ordinary arts of a rural fortune-teller, keeping in impenetrable shadow the darker side of her character as a born sorceress and poisoner.

Fanchon Dodier, in obedience to the order of her mistress, started early in the day to bear the message entrusted to her for La Corriveau. She did not cross the river and take the king's highway, the rough though well-travelled road on the south shore which led to St. Valier. Angelique was crafty enough amid her impulsiveness to see that it were better for Fanchon to go down by water and return by land: it lessened observation, and might be important one day to baffle inquiry. La Corriveau would serve her for money, but for money also she might betray her. Angelique resolved to secure her silence by making her the perpetrator of whatever scheme of wickedness she might devise against the unsuspecting lady of Beaumanoir. As for Fanchon, she need know nothing more than Angelique told her as to the object of her mission to her terrible aunt.

In pursuance of this design, Angelique had already sent for a couple of Indian canoemen to embark Fanchon at the quay of the Friponne and convey her to St. Valier.

Half-civilized and wholly-demoralized red men were always to be found on the beach of Stadacona, as they still called the Batture of the St. Charles, lounging about in blankets, smoking, playing dice, or drinking pints or quarts,--as fortune favored them, or a passenger wanted conveyance in their bark canoes, which they managed with a dexterity unsurpassed by any boatman that ever put oar or paddle in water, salt or fresh.

These rough fellows were safe and trusty in their profession. Fanchon knew them slightly, and felt no fear whatever in seating herself upon the bear skin which carpeted the bottom of their canoe.

They pushed off at once from the shore, with scarcely a word of reply to her voluble directions and gesticulations as they went speeding their canoe down the stream. The turning tide bore them lightly on its bosom, and they chanted a wild, monotonous refrain as their paddles flashed and dipped alternately in stream and sunshine;

"Ah! ah! Tenaouich tenaga!
Tenaouich tenaga, ouich ka!"

"They are singing about me, no doubt," said Fanchon to herself. "I do not care what people say, they cannot be Christians who speak such a heathenish jargon as that: it is enough to sink the canoe; but I will repeat my paternosters and my Ave Marias, seeing they will not converse with me, and I will pray good St. Anne to give me a safe passage to St. Valier." In which pious occupation, as the boatmen continued their savage song without paying her any attention, Fanchon, with many interruptions of worldly thoughts, spent the rest of the time she was in the Indian canoe.

Down past the green hills of the south shore the boatmen steadily plied their paddles, and kept singing their wild Indian chant. The wooded slopes of Orleans basked in sunshine as they overlooked the broad channel through which the canoe sped, and long before meridian the little bark was turned in to shore and pulled up on the beach of St. Valier.

Fanchon leaped out without assistance, wetting a foot in so doing, which somewhat discomposed the good humor she had shown during the voyage. Her Indian boatmen offered her no help, considering that women were made to serve men and help themselves, and not to be waited upon by them.

"Not that I wanted to touch one of their savage hands," muttered Fanchon, "but they might have offered one assistance! Look there," continued she, pulling aside her skirt and showing a very trim foot wet up to the ankle; "they ought to know the difference between their red squaws and the white girls of the city. If they are not worth politeness, WE are. But Indians are only fit to kill Christians or be killed by them; and you might as well courtesy to a bear in the briers as to an Indian anywhere."

The boatmen looked at her foot with supreme indifference, and taking out their pipes, seated themselves on the edge of their canoe, and began to smoke.

"You may return to the city," said she, addressing them sharply; "I pray to the bon Dieu to strike you white;--it is vain to look for manners from an Indian! I shall remain in St. Valier, and not return with you."

"Marry me, be my squaw, Ania?" replied one of the boatmen, with a grim smile; "the bon Dieu will strike out papooses white, and teach them manners like palefaces."

"Ugh! not for all the King's money. What! marry a red Indian, and carry his pack like Fifine Perotte? I would die first! You are bold indeed, Paul La Crosse, to mention such a thing to me. Go back to the city! I would not trust myself again in your canoe. It required courage to do so at all, but Mademoiselle selected you for my boatmen, not I. I wonder she did so, when the brothers Ballou, and the prettiest fellows in town, were idle on the Batture."

"Ania is niece to the old medicine-woman in the stone wigwam at St. Valier; going to see her, eh?" asked the other boatman, with a slight display of curiosity.

"Yes, I am going to visit my aunt Dodier; why should I not? She has crocks of gold buried in the house, I can tell you that, Pierre Ceinture!"

"Going to get some from La Corriveau, eh? crocks of gold, eh?" said Paul La Crosse.

"La Corriveau has medicines, too! get some, eh?" asked Pierre Ceinture.

"I am going neither for gold nor medicines, but to see my aunt, if it concerns you to know, Pierre Ceinture! which it does not!"

"Mademoiselle des Meloises pay her to go, eh? not going back ever, eh?" asked the other Indian.

"Mind your own affairs, Paul La Crosse, and I will mind mine! Mademoiselle des Meloises paid you to bring me to St. Valier, not to ask me impertinences. That is enough for you!" Here is your fare; now you can return to the Sault au Matelot, and drink yourselves blind with the money!"

"Very good, that!" replied the Indian. "I like to drink myself blind, will do it to-night! Like to see me, eh?" Better that than go see La Corriveau! The habitans say she talks with the Devil, and makes the sickness settle like a fog upon the wigwams of the red men. They say she can make palefaces die by looking at them! But Indians are too hard to kill with a look! Fire-water and gun and tomahawk, and fever in the wigwams, only make the Indians die."

"Good that something can make you die, for your ill manners! look at my stocking!" replied Fanchon, with warmth. "If I tell La Corriveau what you say of her there will be trouble in your wigwam, Pierre Ceinture!"

"Do not do that, Ania!" replied the Indian, crossing himself earnestly; "do not tell La Corriveau, or she will make an image of wax and call it Pierre Ceinture, and she will melt it away before a slow fire, and as it melts my flesh and bones will melt away, too! Do not tell her, Fanchon Dodier!" The Indian had picked up this piece of superstition from the white habitans, and, like them, thoroughly believed in the supernatural powers of La Corriveau.

"Well, leave me! get back to the city, and tell Mademoiselle I arrived safe at St. Valier," replied Fanchon, turning to leave them.

The Indians were somewhat taken down by the airs of Fanchon, and they stood in awe of the far-reaching power of her aunt, from the spell of whose witchcraft they firmly believed no hiding-place, even in the deepest woods, could protect them. Merely nodding a farewell to Fanchon, the Indians silently pushed their canoe into the stream, and, embarking, returned to the city by the way they came.

A fine breezy upland lay before Fanchon Dodier. Cultivated fields of corn, and meadows ran down to the shore. A row of white cottages, forming a loosely connected street, clustered into something like a village at the point where the parish church stood, at the intersection of two or three roads, one of which, a narrow green track, but little worn by the carts of the habitans, led to the stone house of La Corriveau, the chimney of which was just visible as you lost sight of the village spire.

In a deep hollow, out of sight of the village church, almost out of hearing of its little bell, stood the house of La Corriveau, a square, heavy structure of stone, inconvenient and gloomy, with narrow windows and an uninviting door. The pine forest touched it on one side, a brawling stream twisted itself like a live snake half round it on the other. A plot of green grass, ill kept and deformed, with noxious weeds, dock, fennel, thistle, and foul stramonium, was surrounded by a rough wall of loose stones, forming the lawn, such as it was, where, under a tree, seated in an armchair, was a solitary woman, whom Fanchon recognized as her aunt, Marie Josephte Dodier, surnamed La Corriveau.

La Corriveau, in feature and person, took after her grand-sire Exili. She was tall and straight, of a swarthy complexion, black- haired, and intensely black-eyed. She was not uncomely of feature, nay, had been handsome, nor was her look at first sight forbidding, especially if she did not turn upon you those small basilisk eyes of hers, full of fire and glare as the eyes of a rattlesnake. But truly those thin, cruel lips of hers never smiled spontaneously, or affected to smile upon you unless she had an object to gain by assuming a disguise as foreign to her as light to an angel of darkness.

La Corriveau was dressed in a robe of soft brown stuff, shaped with a degree of taste and style beyond the garb of her class. Neatness in dress was the one virtue she had inherited from her mother. Her feet were small and well-shod, like a lady's, as the envious neighbors used to say. She never in her life would wear the sabots of the peasant women, nor go barefoot, as many of them did, about the house. La Corriveau was vain of her feet, which would have made her fortune, as she thought with bitterness, anywhere but in St. Valier.

She sat musing in her chair, not noticing the presence of her niece, who stood for a moment looking and hesitating before accosting her. Her countenance bore, when she was alone, an expression of malignity which made Fanchon shudder. A quick, unconscious twitching of the fingers accompanied her thoughts, as if this weird woman was playing a game of mora with the evil genius that waited on her. Her grandsire Exili had the same nervous twitching of his fingers, and the vulgar accused him of playing at mora with the Devil, who ever accompanied him, they believed.

The lips of La Corriveau moved in unison with her thoughts. She was giving expression to her habitual contempt for her sex as she crooned over, in a sufficiently audible voice to reach the ear of Fanchon, a hateful song of Jean Le Meung on women:

"'Toutes vous etes, serez ou futes,
De fait ou de volonte putes!'"

"It is not nice to say that, Aunt Marie!" exclaimed Fanchon, coming forward and embracing La Corriveau, who gave a start on seeing her niece so unexpectedly before her. "It is not nice, and it is not true!"

"But it is true, Fanchon Dodier! if it be not nice. There is nothing nice to be said of our sex, except by foolish men! Women know one another better! But," continued she, scrutinizing her niece with her keen black eyes, which seemed to pierce her through and through, "what ill wind or Satan's errand has brought you to St. Valier to-day, Fanchon?"

"No ill wind, nor ill errand either, I hope, aunt. I come by command of my mistress to ask you to go to the city: she is biting her nails off with impatience to see you on some business."

"And who is your mistress, who dares to ask La Corriveau to go to the city at her bidding?"

"Do not be angry, aunt," replied Fanchon, soothingly. "It was I counselled her to send for you, and I offered to fetch you. My mistress is a high lady, who expects to be still higher,-- Mademoiselle des Meloises!

"Mademoiselle Angelique des Meloises,--one hears enough of her! a high lady indeed! who will be low enough at last! A minx as vain as she is pretty, who would marry all the men in New France, and kill all the women, if she could have her way! What in the name of the Sabbat does she want with La Corriveau?"

"She did not call you names, aunt, and please do not say such things of her, for you will frighten me away before I tell my errand. Mademoiselle Angelique sent this piece of gold as earnest-money to prove that she wants your counsel and advice in an important matter."

Fanchon untied the corner of her handkerchief, and took from it a broad shining louis d'or. She placed it in the hand of La Corriveau, whose long fingers clutched it like the talons of a harpy. Of all the evil passions of this woman, the greed for money was the most ravenous.

"It is long since I got a piece of gold like that to cross my hand with, Fanchon!" said she, looking at it admiringly and spitting on it for good luck.

"There are plenty more where it came from, aunt," replied Fanchon. "Mademoiselle could fill your apron with gold every day of the week if she would: she is to marry the Intendant!"

"Marry the Intendant! ah, indeed! that is why she sends for me so urgently! I see! Marry the Intendant! She will bestow a pot of gold on La Corriveau to accomplish that match!"

"Maybe she would, aunt; I would, myself. But it is not that she wishes to consult you about just now. She lost her jewels at the ball, and wants your help to find them."

"Lost her jewels, eh? Did she say you were to tell me that she had lost her jewels, Fanchon?"

"Yes, aunt, that is what she wants to consult you about," replied Fanchon, with simplicity. But the keen perception of La Corriveau saw that a second purpose lay behind it.

"A likely tale!" muttered she, "that so rich a lady would send for La Corriveau from St. Valier to find a few jewels! But it will do. I will go with you to the city: I cannot refuse an invitation like that. Gold fetches any woman, Fanchon. It fetches me always. It will fetch you, too, some day, if you are lucky enough to give it the chance."

"I wish it would fetch me now, aunt; but poor girls who live by service and wages have small chance to be sent for in that way! We are glad to get the empty hand without the money. Men are so scarce with this cruel war, that they might easily have a wife to each finger, were it allowed by the law. I heard Dame Tremblay say--and I thought her very right--the Church does not half consider our condition and necessities."

"Dame Tremblay! the Charming Josephine of Lake Beauport! She who would have been a witch, and could not: Satan would not have her!" exclaimed La Corriveau, scornfully. "Is she still housekeeper and bedmaker at Beaumanoir?"

Fanchon was honest enough to feel rather indignant at this speech. "Don't speak so of her, aunt; she is not bad. Although I ran away from her, and took service with Mademoiselle des Meloises, I will not speak ill of her."

"Why did you run away from Beaumanoir?" asked La Corriveau.

Fanchon reflected a moment upon the mystery of the lady of Beaumanoir, and something checked her tongue, as if it were not safe to tell all she knew to her aunt, who would, moreover, be sure to find out from Angelique herself as much as her mistress wished her to know.

"I did not like Dame Tremblay, aunt," replied she; I preferred to live with Mademoiselle Angelique. She is a lady, a beauty, who dresses to surpass any picture in the book of modes from Paris, which I often looked at on her dressing-table. She allowed me to imitate them, or wear her cast-off dresses, which were better than any other ladies' new ones. I have one of them on. Look, aunt!" Fanchon spread out very complacently the skirt of a pretty blue robe she wore.

La Corriveau nodded her head in a sort of silent approval, and remarked,--"She is free-handed enough! She gives what costs her nothing, and takes all she can get, and is, after all, a trollop, like the rest of us, Fanchon, who would be very good if there were neither men nor money nor fine clothes in the world, to tempt poor silly women."

"You do say such nasty things, aunt!" exclaimed Fanchon, flashing with indignation. "I will hear no more! I am going into the house to see dear old Uncle Dodier, who has been looking through the window at me for ten minutes past, and dared not come out to speak to me. You are too hard on poor old Uncle Dodier, aunt," said Fanchon, boldly. "If you cannot be kind to him, why did you marry him?"

"Why, I wanted a husband, and he wanted my money, that was all; and I got my bargain, and his too, Fanchon!" and the woman laughed savagely.

"I thought people married to be happy, aunt," replied the girl, persistently.

"Happy! such folly. Satan yokes people together to bring more sinners into the world, and supply fresh fuel for his fires."

"My mistress thinks there is no happiness like a good match," remarked Fanchon; "and I think so, too, aunt. I shall never wait the second time of asking, I assure you, aunt."

"You are a fool, Fanchon," said La Corriveau; "but your mistress deserves to wear the ring of Cleopatra, and to become the mother of witches and harlots for all time. Why did she really send for me?"

The girl crossed herself, and exclaimed, "God forbid, aunt! my mistress is not like that!"

La Corriveau spat at the mention of the sacred name. "But it is in her, Fanchon. It is in all of us! If she is not so already, she will be. But go into the house and see your foolish uncle, while I go prepare for my visit. We will set out at once, Fanchon, for business like that of Angelique des Meloises cannot wait."

# Chapter XXXIV: Weird Sisters

Fanchon walked into the house to see her uncle Dodier. When she was gone, the countenance of La Corriveau put on a dark and terrible expression. Her black eyes looked downwards, seeming to penetrate the very earth, and to reflect in their glittering orbits the fires of the underworld.

She stood for a few moments, buried in deep thought, with her arms tightly folded across her breast. Her fingers moved nervously, as they kept time with the quick motions of her foot, which beat the ground.

"It is for death, and no lost jewels, that girl sends for me!" muttered La Corriveau through her teeth, which flashed white and cruel between her thin lips. "She has a rival in her love for the Intendant, and she will lovingly, by my help, feed her with the manna of St. Nicholas! Angelique des Meloises has boldness, craft, and falseness for twenty women, and can keep secrets like a nun. She is rich and ambitious, and would poison half the world rather than miss the thing she sets her mind on. She is a girl after my own heart, and worth the risk I run with her. Her riches would be endless should she succeed in her designs; and with her in my power, nothing she has would henceforth be her own,--but mine! mine! Besides," added La Corriveau, her thoughts flashing back to the fate which had overtaken her progenitors, Exili and La Voisin, "I may need help myself, some day, to plead with the Intendant on my own account,--who knows?"

A strange thrill ran through the veins of La Corriveau, but she instantly threw it off. "I know what she wants," added she. "I will take it with me. I am safe in trusting her with the secret of Beatrice Spara. That girl is worthy of it as Brinvilliers herself."

La Corriveau entered her own apartment. She locked the door behind her, drew a bunch of keys from her bosom, and turned towards a cabinet of singular shape and Italian workmanship which stood in a corner of the apartment. It was an antique piece of furniture, made of some dark oriental wood, carved over with fantastic figures from Etruscan designs by the cunning hand of an old Italian workman, who knew well how to make secret drawers and invisible concealments for things dangerous and forbidden.

It had once belonged to Antonio Exili, who had caused it to be made, ostensibly for the safe-keeping of his cabalistic formulas and alchemic preparations, when searching for the philosopher's stone and the elixir of life, really for the concealment of the subtle drugs out of which his alembics distilled the aqua tofana and his crucibles prepared the poudre de succession.

In the most secret place of all were deposited, ready for use, a few vials of the crystal liquid, every single drop of which contained the life of a man, and which, administered in due proportion of time and measure, killed and left no sign, numbering its victim's days, hours, and minutes, exactly according to the will and malignity of his destroyer.

La Corriveau took out the vials, and placed them carefully in a casket of ebony not larger than a woman's hand. In it was a number of small flaskets, each filled with pills like grains of mustard- seed, the essence and quintessence of various poisons, that put on the appearance of natural diseases, and which, mixed in due proportion with the aqua tofana, covered the foulest murders with the lawful ensigns of the angel of death.

In that box of ebony was the sublimated dust of deadly nightshade, which kindles the red fires of fever and rots the roots of the tongue. There was the fetid powder of stramonium, that grips the lungs like an asthma; and quinia, that shakes its victims like the cold hand of the miasma of the Pontine marshes. The essence of poppies, ten times sublimated, a few grains of which bring on the stupor of apoplexy; and the sardonic plant, that kills its victim with the frightful laughter of madness on his countenance.

The knowledge of these and many more cursed herbs, once known to Medea in the Colchian land, and transplanted to Greece and Rome with the enchantments of their use, had been handed, by a long succession of sorcerers and poisoners, down to Exili and Beatrice Spara, until they came into the possession of La Corriveau, the legitimate inheritrix of this lore of hell.

Before closing the cabinet, La Corriveau opened one more secret drawer, and took out, with a hesitating hand, as if uncertain whether to do so or no, a glittering stiletto, sharp and cruel to see. She felt the point of it mechanically with her thumb; and, as if fascinated by the touch, placed it under her robe. "I may have need of it," muttered she, "either to save myself OR to make sure of my work on another. Beatrice Spara was the daughter of a Sicilian bravo, and she liked this poignard better than even the poisoned chalice."

La Corriveau rose up now, well satisfied with her foresight and preparation. She placed the ebony casket carefully in her bosom, cherishing it like an only child, as she walked out of the room with her quiet, tiger-like tread. Her look into the future was pleasant to her at this moment. There was the prospect of an ample reward for her trouble and risk, and the anticipated pleasure of practising her skill upon one whose position she regarded as similar to that of the great dames of the Court, whom Exili and La Voisin had poisoned during the high carnival of death, in the days of Louis XIV.

She was now ready, and waited impatiently to depart.

The goodman Dodier brought the caleche to the door. It was a substantial, two-wheeled vehicle, with a curious arrangement of springs, made out of the elastic wood of the hickory. The horse, a stout Norman pony, well harnessed, sleek and glossy, was lightly held by the hand of the goodman, who patted it kindly as an old friend; and the pony, in some sort, after an equine fashion, returned the affection of its master.

La Corriveau, with an agility hardly to be expected from her years, seated herself beside Fanchon in the caleche, and giving her willing horse a sharp cut with the lash for spite, not for need,--goodman Dodier said, only to anger him,--they set off at a rapid pace, and were soon out of sight at the turn of the dark pine-woods, on their way to the city of Quebec.

Angelique des Meloises had remained all day in her house, counting the hours as they flew by, laden with the fate of her unsuspecting rival at Beaumanoir.

Night had now closed in; the lamps were lit, the fire again burned red upon the hearth. Her door was inexorably shut against all visitors. Lizette had been sent away until the morrow; Angelique sat alone and expectant of the arrival of La Corriveau.

The gay dress in which she had outshone all her sex at the ball on the previous night lay still in a heap upon the floor, where last night she had thrown it aside, like the robe of innocence which once invested her. Her face was beautiful, but cruel, and in its expression terrible as Medea's brooding over her vengeance sworn against Creusa for her sin with Jason. She sat in a careless dishabille, with one white arm partly bare. Her long golden locks flowed loosely down her back and touched the floor, as she sat on her chair and watched and waited for the coming footsteps of La Corriveau. Her lips were compressed with a terrible resolution; her eyes glanced red as they alternately reflected the glow of the fire within them and of the fire without. Her hands were clasped nervously together, with a grip like iron, and lay in her lap, while her dainty foot marked the rhythm of the tragical thoughts that swept like a song of doom through her soul.

The few compunctious feelings which struggled up into her mind were instantly overborne by the passionate reflection that the lady of Beaumanoir must die! "I must, or she must--one or other! We cannot both live and marry this man!" exclaimed she, passionately. "Has it come to this: which of us shall be the wife, which the mistress? By God, I would kill him too, if I thought he hesitated in his choice; but he shall soon have no choice but one! Her death be on her own head and on Bigot's--not on mine!"

And the wretched girl strove to throw the guilt of the sin she premeditated upon her victim, upon the Intendant, upon fate, and, with a last subterfuge to hide the enormity of it from her own eyes, upon La Corriveau, whom she would lead on to suggest the crime and commit it!-- a course which Angelique tried to believe would be more venial than if it were suggested by herself! less heinous in her own eyes, and less wicked in the sight of God.

"Why did that mysterious woman go to Beaumanoir and place herself in the path of Angelique des Meloises?" exclaimed she angrily. "Why did Bigot reject my earnest prayer, for it was earnest, for a lettre de cachet to send her unharmed away out of New France?"

Then Angelique sat and listened without moving for a long time. The clock ticked loud and warningly. There was a sighing of the wind about the windows, as if it sought admittance to reason and remonstrate with her. A cricket sang his monotonous song on the hearth. In the wainscot of the room a deathwatch ticked its doleful omen. The dog in the courtyard howled plaintively as the hour of midnight sounded upon the Convent bell, close by. The bell had scarcely ceased ere she was startled by a slight creaking like the opening of a door, followed by a whispering and the rustle of a woman's garments, as of one approaching with cautious steps up the stair. A thrill of expectation, not unmingled with fear, shot through the breast of Angelique. She sprang up, exclaiming to herself, "She is come, and all the demons that wait on murder come with her into my chamber!" A knock followed on the door. Angelique, very agitated in spite of her fierce efforts to appear calm, bade them come in.

Fanchon opened the door, and, with a courtesy to her mistress, ushered in La Corriveau, who walked straight into the room and stood face to face with Angelique.

The eyes of the two women instantly met in a searching glance that took in the whole look, bearing, dress, and almost the very thoughts of each other. In that one glance each knew and understood the other, and could trust each other in evil, if not in good.

And there was trust between them. The evil spirits that possessed each of their hearts shook hands together, and a silent league was sworn to in their souls before a word was spoken.

And yet how unlike to human eye were these two women!--how like in God's eye, that sees the heart and reads the Spirit, of what manner it is! Angelique, radiant in the bloom of youth and beauty, her golden hair floating about her like a cloud of glory round a daughter of the sun, with her womanly perfections which made the world seem brighter for such a revelation of completeness in every external charm; La Corriveau, stern, dark, angular, her fine-cut features crossed with thin lines of cruelty and cunning, no mercy in her eyes, still less on her lips, and none at all in her heart, cold to every humane feeling, and warming only to wickedness and avarice: still these women recognized each other as kindred spirits, crafty and void of conscience in the accomplishment of their ends.

Had fate exchanged the outward circumstances of their lives, each might have been the other easily and naturally. The proud beauty had nothing in her heart better than La Corriveau, and the witch of St. Valier, if born in luxury and endowed with beauty and wealth, would have rivalled Angelique in seductiveness, and hardly fallen below her in ambition and power.

La Corriveau saluted Angelique, who made a sign to Fanchon to retire. The girl obeyed somewhat reluctantly. She had hoped to be present at the interview between her aunt and her mistress, for her curiosity was greatly excited, and she now suspected there was more in this visit than she had been told.

Angelique invited La Corriveau to remove her cloak and broad hat. Seating her in her own luxurious chair, she sat down beside her, and began the conversation with the usual platitudes and commonplaces of the time, dwelling longer upon them than need was, as if she hesitated or feared to bring up the real subject of this midnight conference.

"My Lady is fair to look on. All women will admit that; all men swear to it!" said La Corriveau, in a harsh voice that grated ominously, like the door of hell which she was opening with this commencement of her business.

Angelique replied only with a smile. A compliment from La Corriveau even was not wasted upon her; but just now she was on the brink of an abyss of explanation, looking down into the dark pit, resolved, yet hesitating to make the plunge.

"No witch or witchery but your own charms is needed, Mademoiselle," continued La Corriveau, falling into the tone of flattery she often used towards her dupes, "to make what fortune you will in this world; what pearl ever fished out of the sea could add a grace to this wondrous hair of yours? Permit me to touch it, Mademoiselle!"

La Corriveau took hold of a thick tress, and held it up to the light of the lamp, where it shone like gold. Angelique shrank back as from the touch of fire. She withdrew her hair with a jerk from the hand of La Corriveau. A shudder passed through her from head to foot. It was the last parting effort of her good genius to save her.

"Do not touch it!" said she quickly; "I have set my life and soul on a desperate venture, but my hair--I have devoted it to our Lady of St. Foye; it is hers, not mine! Do not touch it, Dame Dodier."

Angelique was thinking of a vow she had once made before the shrine of the little church of Lorette. "My hair is the one thing belonging to me that I will keep pure," continued she; "so do not be angry with me," she added, apologetically.

"I am not angry," replied La Corriveau, with a sneer. "I am used to strange humors in people who ask my aid; they always fall out with themselves before they fall in with La Corriveau."

"Do you know why I have sent for you at this hour, good Dame Dodier?" asked Angelique, abruptly.

"Call me La Corriveau; I am not good Dame Dodier. Mine is an ill name, and I like it best, and so should you, Mademoiselle, for the business you sent me for is not what people who say their prayers call good. It was to find your lost jewels that Fanchon Dodier summoned me to your abode, was it not?" La Corriveau uttered this with a suppressed smile of incredulity.

"Ah! I bade Fanchon tell you that in order to deceive her, not you! But you know better, La Corriveau! It was not for the sake of paltry jewels I desired you to come to the city to see me at this hour of midnight."

"I conjectured as much!" replied La Corriveau, with a sardonic smile which showed her small teeth, white, even, and cruel as those of a wildcat. "The jewel you have lost is the heart of your lover, and you thought La Corriveau had a charm to win it back; was not that it, Mademoiselle?"

Angelique sat upright, gazing boldly into the eyes of her visitor. "Yes, it was that and more than that I summoned you for. Can you not guess? You are wise, La Corriveau, you know a woman's desire better than she dare avow it to herself!"

"Ah!" replied La Corriveau, returning her scrutiny with the eyes of a basilisk; a green light flashed out of their dark depths. "You have a lover, and you have a rival, too! A woman more potent than yourself, in spite of your beauty and your fascinations, has caught the eye and entangled the affections of the man you love, and you ask my counsel how to win him back and how to triumph over your rival. Is it not for that you have summoned La Corriveau?"

"Yes, it is that, and still more than that!" replied Angelique, clenching her hands hard together, and gazing earnestly at the fire with a look of merciless triumph at what she saw there reflected from her own thoughts distinctly as if she looked at her own face in a mirror.

"It is all that, and still more than that,--cannot you guess yet why I have summoned you here?" continued Angelique, rising and laying her left hand firmly upon the shoulder of La Corriveau, as she bent her head and whispered with terrible distinctness in her ear.

La Corriveau heard her whisper and looked up eagerly. "Yes, I know now, Mademoiselle,--you would kill your rival! There is death in your eye, in your voice, in your heart, but not in your hand! You would kill the woman who robs you of your lover, and you have sent for La Corriveau to help you in the good work! It is a good work in the eyes of a woman to kill her rival! but why should I do that to please you? What do I care for your lover, Angelique des Meloises?"

Angelique was startled to hear from the lips of another, words which gave free expression to her own secret thoughts. A denial was on her lips, but the lie remained unspoken. She trembled before La Corriveau, but her resolution was unchanged.

"It was not only to please me, but to profit yourself that I sent for you!" Angelique replied eagerly, like one trying to outstrip her conscience and prevent it from overtaking her sin. "Hark you! you love gold, La Corriveau! I will give you all you crave in return for your help,--for help me you shall! you will never repent of it if you do; you will never cease to regret it if you do not! I will make you rich, La Corrivean! or else, by God! do you hear? I swear it! I will have you burnt for a witch, and your ashes strewn all over St. Valier!"

La Corriveau spat contemptuously upon the floor at the holy name. "You are a fool, Angelique des Meloises, to speak thus to me! Do you know who and what I am? You are a poor butterfly to flutter your gay wings against La Corriveau; but still I like your spirit! women like you are rare. The blood of Exili could not have spoken bolder than you do; you want the life of a woman who has kindled the hell-fire of jealousy in your heart, and you want me to tell you how to get your revenge!"

"I do want you to do it, La Corriveau, and your reward shall be great!" answered Angelique with a burst of impatience. She could beat about the bush no longer.

"To kill a woman or a man were of itself a pleasure even without the profit," replied La Corriveau, doggedly. "But why should I run myself into danger for you, Mademoiselle des Meloises? Have you gold enough to balance the risk?"

Angelique had now fairly overleaped all barriers of reserve. "I will give you more than your eyes ever beheld, if you will serve me in this matter, Dame Dodier!"

"Perhaps so, but I am getting old and trust neither man nor woman. Give a pledge of your good faith, before you speak one word farther to me on this business, Mademoiselle des Meloises." La Corriveau held out her double hands significantly.

"A pledge? that is gold you want!" replied Angelique. "Yes, La Corriveau; I will bind you to me with chains of gold; you shall have it uncounted, as I get it,--gold enough to make you the richest woman in St. Valier, the richest peasant-woman in New France."

"I am no peasant-woman," replied La Corriveau, with a touch of pride, "I come of a race ancient and terrible as the Roman Caesars! But pshaw! what have you to do with that? Give me the pledge of your good faith and I will help you."

Angelique rose instantly, and, opening the drawer of an escritoire, took out a long silken purse filled with louis d'or, which peeped and glittered through the interstices of the net-work. She gave it with the air of one who cared nothing for money.

La Corriveau extended both hands eagerly, clutching as with the claws of a harpy. She pressed the purse to her thin bloodless lips, and touched with the ends of her bony fingers the edges of the bright coin visible through the silken net.

"This is indeed a rare earnest-penny!" exclaimed La Corriveau. "I will do your whole bidding, Mademoiselle; only I must do it in my own way. I have guessed aright the nature of your trouble and the remedy you seek. But I cannot guess the name of your false lover, nor that of the woman whose doom is sealed from this hour."

"I will not tell you the name of my lover," replied Angelique. She was reluctant to mention the name of Bigot as her lover. The idea was hateful to her. "The name of the woman I cannot tell you, even if I would," added she.

"How, Mademoiselle? you put the death-mark upon one you do not know?"

"I do not know her name. Nevertheless, La Corriveau, that gold, and ten times as much, are yours, if you relieve me of the torment of knowing that the secret chamber of Beaumanoir contains a woman whose life is death to all my hopes, and disappointment to all my plans.

The mention of Beaumanoir startled La Corriveau.

"The lady of Beaumanoir!" she exclaimed, "whom the Abenaquis brought in from Acadia? I saw that lady in the woods of St. Valier, when I was gathering mandrakes one summer day. She asked me for some water in God's name. I cursed her silently, but I gave her milk. I had no water. She thanked me. Oh, how she thanked me! nobody ever before thanked La Corriveau so sweetly as she did! I, even I, bade her a good journey, when she started on afresh with her Indian guides, after asking me the distance and direction of Beaumanoir."

This unexpected touch of sympathy surprised and revolted Angelique a little.

"You know her then! That is rare fortune, La Corriveau," said she; "she will remember you, you will have less difficulty in gaining access to her and winning her confidence."

La Corriveau clapped her hands, laughing a strange laugh, that sounded as if it came from a deep well.

"Know her? That is all I know; she thanked me sweetly. I said so, did I not? but I cursed her in my heart when she was gone. I saw she was both beautiful and good,--two things I hate."

"Do you call her beautiful? I care not whether she be good, that will avail nothing with him; but is she beautiful, La Corriveau? Is she fairer than I, think you?"

La Corriveau looked at Angelique intently and laughed. "Fairer than you? Listen! It was as if I had seen a vision. She was very beautiful, and very sad. I could wish it were another than she, for oh, she spoke to me the sweetest I was ever spoken to since I came into the world."

Angelique ground her teeth with anger. "What did you do, La Corriveau? Did you not wish her dead? Did you think the Intendant or any man could not help loving her to the rejection of any other woman in the world? What did you do?"

"Do? I went on picking my mandrakes in the forest, and waited for you to send for La Corriveau. You desire to punish the Intendant for his treachery in forsaking you for one more beautiful and better!"

It was but a bold guess of La Corriveau, but she had divined the truth. The Intendant Bigot was the man who was playing false with Angelique.

Her words filled up the measure of Angelique's jealous hate, and confirmed her terrible resolution. Jealousy is never so omnipotent as when its rank suspicions are fed and watered by the tales of others.

"There can be but one life between her and me!" replied the vehement girl; "Angelique des Meloises would die a thousand deaths rather than live to feed on the crumbs of any man's love while another woman feasts at his table. I sent for you, La Corriveau, to take my gold and kill that woman!"

"Kill that woman! It is easily said, Mademoiselle; but I will not forsake you, were she the Madonna herself! I hate her for her goodness, as you hate her for her beauty. Lay another purse by the side of this, and in thrice three days there shall be weeping in the Chateau of Beaumanoir, and no one shall know who has killed the cuckquean of the Chevalier Intendant!"

Angelique sprang up with a cry of exultation, like a pantheress seizing her prey. She clasped La Corriveau in her arms and kissed her dark, withered cheek, exclaiming, "Yes, that is her name! His cuckquean she is; his wife she is not and never shall be!--Thanks, a million golden thanks, La Corriveau, if you fulfil your prophecy! In thrice three days from this hour, was it not that you said?"

"Understand me!" said La Corriveau, "I serve you for your money, not for your liking! but I have my own joy in making my hand felt in a world which I hate and which hates me!" La Corriveau held out her hands as if the ends of her fingers were trickling poison. "Death drops on whomsoever I send it," said she, "so secretly and so subtly that the very spirits of air cannot detect the trace of the aqua tofana."

Angelique listened with amaze, yet trembled with eagerness to hear more. "What! La Corriveau, have you the secret of the aqua tofana, which the world believes was burnt with its possessors two generations ago, on the Place de Greve?"

"Such secrets never die," replied the poisoner; "they are too precious! Few men, still fewer women, are there who would not listen at the door of hell to learn them. The king in his palace, the lady in her tapestried chamber, the nun in her cell, the very beggar on the street, would stand on a pavement of fire to read the tablets which record the secret of the aqua tofana. Let me see your hand," added she abruptly, speaking to Angelique.

Angelique held out her hand; La Corriveau seized it. She looked intently upon the slender fingers and oval palm. "There is evil enough in these long, sharp spatulae of yours," said she, "to ruin the world. You are worthy to be the inheritrix of all I know. These fingers would pick fruit off the forbidden tree for men to eat and die! The tempter only is needed, and he is never far off! Angelique des Meloises, I may one day teach you the grand secret; meantime I will show you that I possess it."

## Chapter XXXV: "Flaskets of Drugs, Full to Their Wicked Lips"

La Corriveau took the ebony casket from her bosom and laid it solemnly on the table. "Do not cross yourself," she exclaimed angrily as she saw Angelique mechanically make the sacred sign. "There can come no blessings here. There is death enough in that casket to kill every man and woman in New France."

Angelique fastened her gaze upon the casket as if she would have drawn out the secret of its contents by the very magnetism of her eyes. She laid her hand upon it caressingly, yet tremblingly-- eager, yet fearful, to see its contents.

"Open it!" cried La Corriveau, "press the spring, and you will see such a casket of jewels as queens might envy. It was the wedding- gift of Beatrice Spara, and once belonged to the house of Borgia-- Lucrezia Borgia had it from her terrible father; and he, from the prince of demons!"

Angelique pressed the little spring,--the lid flew open, and there flashed from it a light which for the moment dazzled her eyes with its brilliancy. She thrust the casket from her in alarm, and retreated a few steps, imagining she smelt the odor of some deadly perfume.

"I dare not approach it," said she. "Its glittering terrifies me; its odor sickens me."

"Tush! it is your weak imagination!" replied La Corriveau; "your sickly conscience frightens you! You will need to cast off both to rid Beaumanoir of the presence of your rival! The aqua tofana in the hands of a coward is a gift as fatal to its possessor as to its victim."

Angelique with a strong effort tried to master her fear, but could not. She would not again handle the casket.

La Corriveau looked at her as if suspecting this display of weakness. She then drew the casket to herself and took out a vial, gilt and chased with strange symbols. It was not larger than the little finger of a delicate girl. Its contents glittered like a diamond in the sunshine.

La Corriveau shook it up, and immediately the liquid was filled with a million sparks of fire. It was the aqua tofana undiluted by mercy, instantaneous in its effect, and not medicable by any antidote. Once administered, there was no more hope for its victim than for the souls of the damned who have received the final judgment. One drop of that bright water upon the tongue of a Titan would blast him like Jove's thunderbolt, would shrivel him up to a black, unsightly cinder!

This was the poison of anger and revenge that would not wait for time, and braved the world's justice. With that vial La Borgia killed her guests at the fatal banquet in her palace, and Beatrice Spara in her fury destroyed the fair Milanese who had stolen from her the heart of Antonio Exili.

This terrible water was rarely used alone by the poisoners; but it formed the basis of a hundred slower potions which ambition, fear, avarice, or hypocrisy mingled with the element of time, and colored with the various hues and aspects of natural disease.

Angelique sat down and leaned towards La Corriveau, supporting her chin on the palms of her hands as she bent eagerly over the table, drinking in every word as the hot sand of the desert drinks in the water poured upon it. "What is that?" said she, pointing to a vial as white as milk and seemingly as harmless.

"That," replied La Corriveau, "is the milk of mercy. It brings on painless consumption and decay. It eats the life out of a man while the moon empties and fills once or twice. His friends say he dies of quick decline, and so he does! ha! ha!--when his enemy wills it! The strong man becomes a skeleton, and blooming maidens sink into their graves blighted and bloodless, with white lips and hearts that cease gradually to beat, men know not why. Neither saint nor sacrament can arrest the doom of the milk of mercy."

"This vial," continued she, lifting up another from the casket and replacing the first, licking her thin lips with profound satisfaction as she did so,--"this contains the acrid venom that grips the heart like the claws of a tiger, and the man drops down dead at the time appointed. Fools say he died of the visitation of God. The visitation of God!" repeated she in an accent of scorn, and the foul witch spat as she pronounced the sacred name. "Leo in his sign ripens the deadly nuts of the East, which kill when God will not kill. He who has this vial for a possession is the lord of life." She replaced it tenderly. It was a favorite vial of La Corriveau.

"This one," continued she, taking up another, "strikes with the dead palsy; and this kindles the slow, inextinguishable fires of typhus. Here is one that dissolves all the juices of the body, and the blood of a man's veins runs into a lake of dropsy. "This," taking up a green vial, "contains the quintessence of mandrakes distilled in the alembic when Scorpio rules the hour. Whoever takes this liquid"--La Corriveau shook it up lovingly--"dies of torments incurable as the foul disease of lust which it simulates and provokes."

There was one vial which contained a black liquid like oil. "It is a relic of the past," said she, "an heir-loom from the Untori, the ointers of Milan. With that oil they spread death through the doomed city, anointing its doors and thresholds with the plague until the people died."

The terrible tale of the anointers of Milan has, since the days of La Corriveau, been written in choice Italian by Manzoni, in whose wonderful book he that will may read it.

"This vial," continued the witch, "contains innumerable griefs, that wait upon the pillows of rejected and heartbroken lovers, and the wisest physician is mocked with lying appearances of disease that defy his skill and make a fool of his wisdom."

"Oh, say no more!" exclaimed Angelique, shocked and terrified. However inordinate in her desires, she was dainty in her ways. "It is like a Sabbat of witches to hear you talk, La Corriveau!" cried she, "I will have none of those foul things which you propose. My rival shall die like a lady! I will not feast like a vampire on her dead body, nor shall you. You have other vials in the casket of better hue and flavor. What is this?" continued Angelique, taking out a rose-tinted and curiously-twisted bottle sealed on the top with the mystic pentagon. "This looks prettier, and may be not less sure than the milk of mercy in its effect. What is it?"

"Ha! ha!" laughed the woman with her weirdest laugh. "Your wisdom is but folly, Angelique des Meloises! You would kill, and still spare your enemy! That was the smelling-bottle of La Brinvilliers, who took it with her to the great ball at the Hotel de Ville, where she secretly sprinkled a few drops of it upon the handkerchief of the fair Louise Gauthier, who, the moment she put it to her nostrils, fell dead upon the floor. She died and gave no sign, and no man knew how or why! But she was the rival of Brinvilliers for the love of Gaudin de St. Croix, and in that she resembles the lady of Beaumanoir, as you do La Brinvilliers!"

"And she got her reward! I would have done the same thing for the same reason! What more have you to relate of this most precious vial of your casket?" asked Angelique.

"That its virtue is unimpaired. Three drops sprinkled upon a bouquet of flowers, and its odor breathed by man or woman, causes a sudden swoon from which there is no awakening more in this world. People feel no pain, but die smiling as if angels had kissed away their breath. Is it not a precious toy, Mademoiselle?"

"Oh, blessed vial!" exclaimed Angelique, pressing it to her lips, "thou art my good angel to kiss away the breath of the lady of Beaumanoir! She shall sleep on roses, La Corriveau, and you shall make her bed!"

"It is a sweet death, befitting one who dies for love, or is killed by the jealousy of a dainty rival," replied the witch; "but I like best those draughts which are most bitter and not less sure."

"The lady of Beaumanoir will not be harder to kill than Louise Gauthier," replied Angelique, watching the glitter of the vial in the lamplight. "She is unknown even to the servants of the Chateau; nor will the Intendant himself dare to make public either her life or death in his house."

"Are you sure, Mademoiselle, that the Intendant will not dare to make public the death of that woman in the Chateau?" asked La Corriveau, with intense eagerness; that consideration was an important link of the chain which she was forging.

"Sure? yes, I am sure by a hundred tokens!" said Angelique, with an air of triumph. "He dare not even banish her for my sake, lest the secret of her concealment at Beaumanoir become known. We can safely risk his displeasure, even should he suspect that I have cut the knot he knew not how to untie."

"You are a bold girl!" exclaimed La Corriveau, looking on her admiringly, "you are worthy to wear the crown of Cleopatra, the queen of all the gypsies and enchantresses. I shall have less fear now to do your bidding, for you have a stronger spirit than mine to support you."

"'Tis well, La Corriveau! Let this vial of Brinvilliers bring me the good fortune I crave, and I will fill your lap with gold. If the lady of Beaumanoir shall find death in a bouquet of flowers, let them be roses!"

"But how and where to find roses? they have ceased blooming," said La Corriveau, hating Angelique's sentiment, and glad to find an objection to it.

"Not for her, La Corriveau; fate is kinder than you think!" Angelique threw back a rich curtain and disclosed a recess filled with pots of blooming roses and flowers of various hues. "The roses are blooming here which will form the bouquet of Beaumanoir."

"You are of rare ingenuity, Mademoiselle," replied La Corriveau, admiringly. "If Satan prompts you not, it is because he can teach you nothing either in love or stratagem."

"Love!" replied Angelique quickly, "do not name that! No! I have sacrificed all love, or I should not be taking counsel of La Corriveau!"

Angelique's thoughts flashed back upon Le Gardeur for one regretful moment. "No, it is not love," continued she, "but the duplicity of a man before whom I have lowered my pride. It is the vengeance I have vowed upon a woman for whose sake I am trifled with! It is that prompts me to this deed! But no matter, shut up the casket, La Corriveau; we will talk now of how and when this thing is to be done."

The witch shut up her infernal casket of ebony, leaving the vial of Brinvilliers shining like a ruby in the lamplight upon the polished table.

The two women sat down, their foreheads almost touching together, with their eyes flashing in lurid sympathy as they eagerly discussed the position of things in the Chateau. The apartments of Caroline, the hours of rest and activity, were all well known to Angelique, who had adroitly fished out every fact from the unsuspecting Fanchon Dodier, as had also La Corriveau.

It was known to Angelique that the Intendant would be absent from the city for some days, in consequence of the news from France. The unfortunate Caroline would be deprived of the protection of his vigilant eye.

The two women sat long arranging and planning their diabolical scheme. There was no smile upon the cheek of Angelique now. Her dimples, which drove men mad, had disappeared. Her lips, made to distil words sweeter than honey of Hybla, were now drawn together in hard lines like La Corriveau's,--they were cruel and untouched by a single trace of mercy.

The hours struck unheeded on the clock in the room, as it ticked louder and louder like a conscious monitor beside them. Its slow finger had marked each wicked thought, and recorded for all time each murderous word as it passed their cruel lips.

La Corriveau held the casket in her lap with an air of satisfaction, and sat with eyes fixed on Angelique, who was now silent.

"Water the roses well, Mademoiselle," said she; "in three days I shall be here for a bouquet, and in less than thrice three days I promise you there shall be a dirge sung for the lady of Beaumanoir."

"Only let it be done soon and surely," replied Angelique,--her very tone grew harsh,--"but talk no more of it; your voice sounds like a cry from a dark gallery that leads to hell. Would it were done! I could then shut up the memory of it in a tomb of silence, forever, forever, and wash my hands of a deed done by you, not me!"

"A deed done by you, not me!" She repeated the words, as if repeating them made them true. She would shut up the memory of her crime forever; she reflected not that the guilt is in the evil intent, and the sin the same before God even if the deed be never done.

Angelique was already an eager sophist. She knew better than the wretched creature whom she had bribed with money, how intensely wicked was the thing she was tempting her to do; but her jealousy maddened her, and her ambition could not let her halt in her course.

There was one thought which still tormented her "What would the Intendant think? What would he say should he suspect her of the murder of Caroline?" She feared his scrutinizing investigation; but, trusting in her power, she risked his suspicions, nay, remembering his words, made him in her own mind an accessory in the murder.

If she remembered Le Gardeur de Repentigny at all at this moment, it was only to strangle the thought of him. She shied like a horse on the brink of a precipice when the thought of Le Gardeur intruded itself. Rising suddenly, she bade La Corriveau be gone about her business, lest she should be tempted to change her mind.

La Corriveau laughed at the last struggle of dying conscience, and bade Angelique go to bed. It was two hours past midnight, and she would bid Fanchon let her depart to the house of an old crone in the city who would give her a bed and a blessing in the devil's name.

Angelique, weary and agitated, bade her be gone in the devil's name, if she preferred a curse to a blessing. The witch, with a mocking laugh, rose and took her departure for the night.

Fanchon, weary of waiting, had fallen asleep. She roused herself, offering to accompany her aunt in hopes of learning something of her interview with her mistress. All she got was a whisper that the jewels were found. La Corriveau passed out into the darkness, and plodded her way to the house of her friend, where she resolved to stay until she accomplished the secret and cruel deed she had undertaken to perform.

# Chapter XXXVI: The Broad, Black Gateway of a Lie

The Count de la Galissoniere was seated in his cabinet a week after the arrival of La Corriveau on her fatal errand. It was a plain, comfortable apartment he sat in, hung with arras, and adorned with maps and pictures. It was there he held his daily sittings for the ordinary despatch of business with a few such councillors as the occasion required to be present.

The table was loaded with letters, memorandums, and bundles of papers tied up in official style. Despatches of royal ministers, bearing the broad seal of France. Reports from officers of posts far and near in New France lay mingled together with silvery strips of the inner bark of the birch, painted with hieroglyphics, giving accounts of war parties on the eastern frontier and in the far west, signed by the totems of Indian chiefs in alliance with France. There was a newly-arrived parcel of letters from the bold, enterprising Sieur de Verendrye, who was exploring the distant waters of the Saskatchewan and the land of the Blackfeet, and many a missive from missionaries, giving account of wild regions which remain yet almost a terra incognita to the government which rules over them.

At the Governor's elbow sat his friend Bishop Pontbriand with a secretary immersed in papers. In front of him was the Intendant with Varin, Penisault, and D'Estebe. On one side of the table, La Corne St. Luc was examining some Indian despatches with Rigaud de Vaudreuil; Claude Beauharnais and the venerable Abbe Piquet overlooking with deep interest the rude pictorial despatches in the hands of La Corne. Two gentlemen of the law, in furred gowns and bands, stood waiting at one end of the room, with books under their arms and budgets of papers in their hands ready to argue before the Council some knotty point of controversy arising out of the concession of certain fiefs and jurisdictions granted under the feudal laws of the Colony.

The Intendant, although personally at variance with several of the gentlemen sitting at the council table, did not let that fact be visible on his countenance, nor allow it to interfere with the despatch of public business.

The Intendant was gay and easy to-day, as was his wont, wholly unsuspecting the foul treason that was plotting by the woman he admired against the woman he loved. His opinions were sometimes loftily expressed, but always courteously as well as firmly.

Bigot never drooped a feather in face of his enemies, public or private, but laughed and jested with all at table in the exuberance of a spirit which cared for no one, and only reined itself in when it was politic to flatter his patrons and patronesses at Versailles.

The business of the Council had begun. The mass of papers which lay at the left hand of the Governor were opened and read seriatim by his secretary, and debated, referred, decided upon, or judgment postponed, as the case seemed best to the Council.

The Count was a man of method and despatch, clear-headed and singularly free from prejudice, ambiguity, or hesitation. He was honest and frank in council, as he was gallant on the quarter-deck. The Intendant was not a whit behind him in point of ability and knowledge of the political affairs of the colony, and surpassed him in influence at the court of Louis XV., but less frank, for he had much to conceal, and kept authority in his own hands as far as he was able.

Disliking each other profoundly from the total divergence of their characters, opinions, and habits, the Governor and Intendant still met courteously at the council-table, and not without a certain respect for the rare talents which each recognized in the other.

Many of the papers lying before them were on subjects relating to the internal administration of the Colony,--petitions of the people suffering from the exactions of the commissaries of the army, remonstrances against the late decrees of the Intendant, and arrets of the high court of justice confirming the right of the Grand Company to exercise certain new monopolies of trade.

The discussions were earnest, and sometimes warm, on these important questions. La Corne St. Luc assailed the new regulations of the Intendant in no measured terms of denunciation, in which he was supported by Rigaud de Vaudreuil and the Chevalier de Beauharnais. But Bigot, without condescending to the trouble of defending the ordinances on any sound principle of public policy, which he knew to be useless and impossible with the clever men sitting at the table, contented himself with a cold smile at the honest warmth of La Corne St. Luc, and simply bade his secretary read the orders and despatches from Versailles, in the name of the royal ministers, and approved of by the King himself in a Lit de Justice which had justified every act done by him in favor of the Grand Company.

The Governor, trammelled on all sides by the powers conferred upon the Intendant, felt unable to exercise the authority he needed to vindicate the cause of right and justice in the colony. His own instructions confirmed the pretensions of the Intendant, and of the Grand Company. The utmost he could do in behalf of the true interests of the people and of the King, as opposed to the herd of greedy courtiers and selfish beauties who surrounded him, was to soften the deadening blows they dealt upon the trade and resources of the Colony.

A decree authorizing the issue of an unlimited quantity of paper bills, the predecessors of the assignats of the mother country, was strongly advocated by Bigot, who supported his views with a degree of financial sophistry which showed that he had effectively mastered the science of delusion and fraud of which Law had been the great teacher in France, and the Mississippi scheme, the prototype of the Grand Company, the great exemplar.

La Corne St. Luc opposed the measure forcibly. "He wanted no paper lies," he said, "to cheat the husbandman of his corn and the laborer of his hire. If the gold and silver had all to be sent to France to pamper the luxuries of a swarm of idlers at the Court, they could buy and sell as they had done in the early days of the Colony, with beaver skins for livres, and muskrat skins for sous. These paper bills," continued he, "had been tried on a small scale by the Intendant Hoquart, and on a small scale had robbed and impoverished the Colony. If this new Mississippi scheme propounded by new Laws,"--and here La Corne glanced boldly at the Intendant,--"is to be enforced on the scale proposed, there will not be left in the Colony one piece of silver to rub against another. It will totally beggar New France, and may in the end bankrupt the royal treasury of France itself if called on to redeem them."

The discussion rolled on for an hour. The Count listened in silent approbation to the arguments of the gentlemen opposing the measure, but he had received private imperative instructions from the King to aid the Intendant in the issue of the new paper money. The Count reluctantly sanctioned a decree which filled New France with worthless assignats, the non-redemption of which completed the misery of the Colony and aided materially in its final subjugation by the English.

The pile of papers upon the table gradually diminished as they were opened and disposed of. The Council itself was getting weary of a long sitting, and showed an evident wish for its adjournment. The gentlemen of the law did not get a hearing of their case that day, but were well content to have it postponed, because a postponement meant new fees and increased costs for their clients. The lawyers of Old France, whom LaFontaine depicts in his lively fable as swallowing the oyster and handing to each litigant an empty shell, did not differ in any essential point from their brothers of the long robe in New France, and differed nothing at all in the length of their bills and the sharpness of their practice.

The breaking up of the Council was deferred by the Secretary opening a package sealed with the royal seal, and which contained other sealed papers marked SPECIAL for His Excellency the Governor. The Secretary handed them to the Count, who read over the contents with deep interest and a changing countenance. He laid them down and took them up again, perused them a second time, and passed them over to the Intendant, who read them with a start of surprise and a sudden frown on his dark eyebrows. But he instantly suppressed it, biting his nether lip, however, with anger which he could not wholly conceal.

He pushed the papers back to the Count with a nonchalant air, as of a man who had quite made up his mind about them, saying in a careless manner,--

"The commands of Madame la Marquise de Pompadour shall be complied with," said he. "I will order strict search to be made for the missing demoiselle, who, I suspect, will be found in some camp or fort, sharing the couch of some lively fellow who has won favor in her bright eyes."

Bigot saw danger in these despatches, and in the look of the Governor, who would be sure to exercise the utmost diligence in carrying out the commands of the court in this matter.

Bigot for a few moments seemed lost in reflection. He looked round the table, and, seeing many eyes fixed upon him, spoke boldly, almost with a tone of defiance.

"Pray explain to the councillors the nature of this despatch, your Excellency!" said he to the Count. "What it contains is not surprising to any one who knows the fickle sex, and no gentleman can avoid feeling for the noble Baron de St. Castin!"

"And for his daughter, too, Chevalier!" replied the Governor. "It is only through their virtues that such women are lost. But it is the strangest tale I have heard in New France!"

The gentlemen seated at the table looked at the Governor in some surprise. La Corne St. Luc, hearing the name of the Baron de St. Castin, exclaimed, "What, in God's name, your Excellency,--what is there in that despatch affecting my old friend and companion in arms, the Baron de St. Castin?"

"I had better explain," replied the Count; "it is no secret in France, and will not long be a secret here.

"This letter, gentlemen," continued he, addressing the councillors, and holding it open in his hand, "is a pathetic appeal from the Baron de St. Castin, whom you all know, urging me by every consideration of friendship, honor, and public duty, to aid in finding his daughter, Caroline de St. Castin, who has been abducted from her home in Acadia, and who, after a long and vain search for her by her father in France, where it was thought she might have gone, has been traced to this Colony, where it is said she is living concealed under some strange alias or low disguise.

"The other despatch," continued the Governor, "is from the Marquise de Pompadour, affirming the same thing, and commanding the most rigorous search to be made for Mademoiselle de St. Castin. In language hardly official, the Marquise threatens to make stockfish, that is her phrase, of whosoever has had a hand in either the abduction or the concealment of the missing lady."

The attention of every gentleman at the table was roused by the words of the Count. But La Corne St. Luc could not repress his feelings. He sprang up, striking the table with the palm of his hand until it sounded like the shot of a petronel.

"By St. Christopher the Strong!" exclaimed he, "I would cheerfully have lost a limb rather than heard such a tale told by my dear old friend and comrade, about that angelic child of his, whom I have carried in my arms like a lamb of God many and many a time!

"You know, gentlemen, what befell her!" The old soldier looked as if he could annihilate the Intendant with the lightning of his eyes. "I affirm and will maintain that no saint in heaven was holier in her purity than she was in her fall! Chevalier Bigot, it is for you to answer these despatches! This is your work! If Caroline de St. Castin be lost, you know where to find her!"

Bigot started up in a rage mingled with fear, not of La Corne St. Luc, but lest the secret of Caroline's concealment at Beaumanoir should become known. The furious letter of La Pompadour repressed the prompting of his audacious spirit to acknowledge the deed openly and defy the consequences, as he would have done at any less price than the loss of the favor of his powerful and jealous patroness.

The broad, black gateway of a lie stood open to receive him, and angry as he was at the words of St. Luc, Bigot took refuge in it-- and lied.

"Chevalier La Corne!" said he, with a tremendous effort at self- control, "I do not affect to misunderstand your words, and in time and place will make you account for them! but I will say, for the contentment of His Excellency and of the other gentlemen at the council-table, that whatever in times past have been my relations with the daughter of the Baron de St. Castin, and I do not deny having shown her many courtesies, her abduction was not my work, and if she be lost, I do not know where to find her!"

"Upon your word as a gentleman," interrogated the Governor, "will you declare you know not where she is to be found?"

"Upon my word as a gentleman!" The Intendant's face was suffused with passion. "You have no right to ask that! Neither shall you, Count de La Galissoniere! But I will myself answer the despatch of Madame la Marquise de Pompadour! I know no more, perhaps less, than yourself or the Chevalier La Corne St. Luc, where to look for the daughter of the Baron de St. Castin; and I proclaim here that I am ready to cross swords with the first gentleman who shall dare breathe a syllable of doubt against the word of Francois Bigot!"

Varin and Penisault exchanged a rapid glance, partly of doubt, partly of surprise. They knew well, for Bigot had not concealed from his intimate associates the fact that a strange lady, whose name they had not heard, was living in the secret chambers of the Chateau of Beaumanoir. Bigot never told any who she was or whence she came. Whatever suspicion they might entertain in their own minds, they were too wary to express it. On the contrary, Varin, ever more ready with a lie than Bigot, confirmed with a loud oath the statement of the Intendant.

La Corne St. Luc looked like a baffled lion as Rigaud de Vaudreuil, with the familiarity of an old friend, laid his hand over his mouth, and would not let him speak. Rigaud feared the coming challenge, and whispered audibly in the ear of St. Luc,--

"Count a hundred before you speak, La Corne! The Intendant is to be taken on his word just at present, like any other gentleman! Fight for fact, not for fancy! Be prudent, La Corne! we know nothing to the contrary of what Bigot swears to!"

"But I doubt much to the contrary, Rigaud!" replied La Corne, with accent of scorn and incredulity.

The old soldier chafed hard under the bit, but his suspicions were not facts. He felt that he had no solid grounds upon which to accuse the Intendant in the special matter referred to in the letters. He was, moreover, although hot in temperament, soon master of himself, and used to the hardest discipline of self-control.

"I was, perhaps, over hasty, Rigaud!" replied La Corne St. Luc, recovering his composure; but when I think of Bigot in the past, how can I but mistrust him in the present? However, be the girl above ground or under ground, I will, par Dieu, not leave a stone unturned in New France until I find the lost child of my old friend! La Corne St. Luc pledges himself to that, and he never broke his word!"

He spoke the last words audibly, and looked hard at the Intendant. Bigot cursed him twenty times over between his teeth, for he knew La Corne's indomitable energy and sagacity, that was never at fault in finding or forcing a way to whatever he was in search of. It would not be long before he would discover the presence of a strange lady at Beaumanoir, thought Bigot, and just as certain would he be to find out that she was the lost daughter of the Baron de St. Castin.

The good Bishop rose up when the dispute waxed warmest between the Intendant and La Corne St. Luc. His heart was eager to allay the strife; but his shrewd knowledge of human nature, and manifold experience of human quarrels, taught him that between two such men the intercession of a priest would not, at that moment, be of any avail. Their own notions of honor and self-respect would alone be able to restrain them from rushing into unseemly excesses of language and act; so the good Bishop stood with folded arms looking on, and silently praying for an opportunity to remind them of the seventh holy beatitude, "Beati pacifici!"

Bigot felt acutely the difficulty of the position he had been placed in by the act of La Pompadour, in sending her despatch to the Governor instead of to himself. "Why had she done that?" said he savagely to himself. "Had she suspected him?"

Bigot could not but conclude that La Pompadour suspected him in this matter. He saw clearly that she would not trust the search after this girl to him, because she knew that Caroline de St. Castin had formerly drawn aside his heart, and that he would have married her but for the interference of the royal mistress. Whatever might have been done before in the way of sending Caroline back to Acadia, it could not be done now, after he had boldly lied before the Governor and the honorable Council.

One thing seemed absolutely necessary, however. The presence of Caroline at Beaumanoir must be kept secret at all hazards, until-- until,--and even Bigot, for once, was ashamed of the thoughts which rushed into his mind,--until he could send her far into the wilderness, among savage tribes, to remain there until the search for her was over and the affair forgotten.

This was his first thought. But to send her away into the wilderness was not easy. A matter which in France would excite the gossip and curiosity of a league or two of neighborhood would be carried on the tongues of Indians and voyageurs in the wilds of North America for thousands of miles. To send her away without discovery seemed difficult. To retain her at Beaumanoir in face of the search which he knew would be made by the Governor and the indomitable La Corne St. Luc, was impossible. The quandary oppressed him. He saw no escape from the dilemma; but, to the credit of Bigot be it said, that not for a moment did he entertain a thought of doing injury to the hapless Caroline, or of taking advantage of her lonely condition to add to her distress, merely to save himself.

He fell into a train of sober reflections unusual to him at any time, and scarcely paid any attention to the discussion of affairs at the council-table for the rest of the sitting. He rose hastily at last, despairing to find any outlet of escape from the difficulties which surrounded him in this unlucky affair.

With His Excellency's consent, he said, they would do no more business that day. He was tired, and would rise. Dinner was ready at the Palace, where he had some wine of the golden plant of Ay-Ay, which he would match against the best in the Castle of St. Louis, if His Excellency and the other gentlemen would honor him with their company.

The Council, out of respect to the Intendant, rose at once. The despatches were shoved back to the secretaries, and for the present forgotten in a buzz of lively conversation, in which no man shone to greater advantage than Bigot.

"It is but a fast-day, your Reverence," said he, accosting the Abbe Piquot, "but if you will come and say grace over my graceless table, I will take it kindly of you. You owe me a visit, you know, and I owe you thanks for the way in which you looked reproof, without speaking it, upon my dispute with the Chevalier La Corne. It was better than words, and showed that you know the world we live in as well as the world you teach us to live for hereafter."

The Abbe was charmed with the affability of Bigot, and nourishing some hope of enlisting him heartily in behalf of his favorite scheme of Indian policy, left the Castle in his company. The Intendant also invited the Procureur du Roi and the other gentlemen of the law, who found it both politic, profitable, and pleasant to dine at the bountiful and splendid table of the Palace.

The Governor, with three or four most intimate friends, the Bishop, La Corne St. Luc, Rigaud de Vaudreuil, and the Chevalier de Beauharnais, remained in the room, conversing earnestly together on the affair of Caroline de St. Castin, which awoke in all of them a feeling of deepest pity for the young lady, and of sympathy for the distress of her father. They were lost in conjectures as to the quarter in which a search for her might be successful.

"There is not a fort, camp, house, or wigwam, there is not a hole or hollow tree in New France where that poor broken-hearted girl may have taken refuge, or been hid by her seducer, but I will find her out," exclaimed La Corne St. Luc. "Poor girl! poor hapless girl! How can I blame her? Like Magdalene, if she sinned much, it was because she loved much, and cursed be either man or woman who will cast a stone at her!"

"La Corne," replied the Governor, "the spirit of chivalry will not wholly pass away while you remain to teach by your example the duty of brave men to fair women. Stay and dine with me, and we will consider this matter thoroughly! Nay, I will not have an excuse to- day. My old friend, Peter Kalm, will dine with us too; he is a philosopher as perfectly as you are a soldier! So stay, and we will have something better than tobacco-smoke to our wine to-day!"

"The tobacco-smoke is not bad either, your Excellency!" replied La Corne, who was an inveterate smoker. "I like your Swedish friend. He cracks nuts of wisdom with such a grave air that I feel like a boy sitting at his feet, glad to pick up a kernel now and then. My practical philosophy is sometimes at fault, to be sure, in trying to fit his theories but I feel that I ought to believe many things which I do not understand."

The Count took his arm familiarly, and, followed by the other gentlemen, proceeded to the dining-hall, where his table was spread in a style which, if less luxurious than the Intendant's, left nothing to be desired by guests who were content with plenty of good cheer, admirable cooking, adroit service, and perfect hospitality.

# Chapter XXXVII: Arrival of Pierre Philibert

Dinner at the table of the Count de la Galissoniere was not a dull affair of mere eating and drinking. The conversation and sprightliness of the host fed the minds of his guests as generously as his bread strengthened their hearts, or his wine, in the Psalmist's words, made their faces to shine. Men were they, every one of them possessed of a sound mind in a sound body; and both were well feasted at this hospitable table.

The dishes were despatched in a leisurely and orderly manner, as became men who knew the value of both soul and body, and sacrificed neither to the other. When the cloth was drawn, and the wine-flasks glittered ruby and golden upon the polished board, the old butler came in, bearing upon a tray a large silver box of tobacco, with pipes and stoppers and a wax candle burning, ready to light them, as then the fashion was in companies composed exclusively of gentlemen. He placed the materials for smoking upon the table as reverently as a priest places his biretta upon the altar,--for the old butler did himself dearly love the Indian weed, and delighted to smell the perfume of it as it rose in clouds over his master's table.

"This is a bachelors' banquet, gentlemen," said the Governor, filling a pipe to the brim. "We will take fair advantage of the absence of ladies to-day, and offer incense to the good Manitou who first gave tobacco for the solace of mankind."

The gentlemen were all, as it chanced, honest smokers. Each one took a pipe from the stand and followed the Governor's example, except Peter Kalm, who, more philosophically, carried his pipe with him--a huge meerschaum, clouded like a sunset on the Baltic. He filled it deliberately with tobacco, pressed it down with his finger and thumb, and leaning back in his easy chair after lighting it, began to blow such a cloud as the portly Burgomaster of Stockholm might have envied on a grand council night in the old Raadhus of the city of the Goths.

They were a goodly group of men, whose frank, loyal eyes looked openly at each other across the hospitable table. None of them but had travelled farther than Ulysses, and, like him, had seen strange cities and observed many minds of men, and was as deeply read in the book of human experience as ever the crafty king of Ithaca.

The event of the afternoon--the reading of the royal despatches--had somewhat dashed the spirits of the councillors, for they saw clearly the drift of events which was sweeping New France out of the lap of her mother country, unless her policy were totally changed and the hour of need brought forth a man capable of saving France herself and her faithful and imperilled colonies.

"Hark!" exclaimed the Bishop, lifting his hand, "the Angelus is ringing from tower and belfry, and thousands of knees are bending with the simplicity of little children in prayer, without one thought of theology or philosophy. Every prayer rising from a sincere heart, asking pardon for the past and grace for the future, is heard by our Father in heaven; think you not it is so, Herr Kalm?"

The sad foreboding of colonists like La Corne St. Luc did not prevent the desperate struggle that was made for the preservation of French dominion in the next war. Like brave and loyal men, they did their duty to God and their country, preferring death and ruin in a lost cause to surrendering the flag which was the symbol of their native land. The spirit, if not the words, of the old English loyalist was in them:

"For loyalty is still the same,
  Whether it win or lose the game;
  True as the dial to the sun,

Although it be not shone upon."

New France, after gathering a harvest of glory such as America had never seen reaped before, fell at last, through the neglect of her mother country. But she dragged down the nation in her fall, and France would now give the apple of her eye for the recovery, never to be, of "the acres of snow" which La Pompadour so scornfully abandoned to the English.

These considerations lay in the lap of the future, however; they troubled not the present time and company. The glasses were again replenished with wine or watered, as the case might be, for the Count de la Galissoniere and Herr Kalm kept Horatian time and measure, drinking only three cups to the Graces, while La Corne St. Luc and Rigaud de Vaudreuil drank nine full cups to the Muses, fearing not the enemy that steals away men's brains. Their heads were helmeted with triple brass, and impenetrable to the heaviest blows of the thyrsus of Bacchus. They drank with impunity, as if garlanded with parsley, and while commending the Bishop, who would drink naught save pure water, they rallied gaily Claude Beauharnais, who would not drink at all.

In the midst of a cheerful concert of merriment, the door of the cabinet opened, and the servant in waiting announced the entrance of Colonel Philibert.

All rose to welcome him. Pierre looked anxious and somewhat discomposed, but the warm grasp of the hands of so many true friends made him glad for the moment.

"Why, Pierre!" exclaimed the Count, "I hope no ill wind has blown you to the city so unexpectedly! You are heartily welcome, however, and we will call every wind good that blows our friends back to us again."

"It is a cursed wind that blows me back to-day," replied Philibert, sitting down with an air of disquiet.

"Why, what is the matter, Pierre?" asked the Count. "My honored Lady de Tilly and her lovely niece, are they well?"

"Well, your Excellency, but sorely troubled. The devil has tempted Le Gardeur again, and he has fallen. He is back to the city, wild as a savage and beyond all control."

"Good God! it will break his sister's heart," said the Governor, sympathizingly. "That girl would give her life for her brother. I feel for her; I feel for you, too, Pierre." Philibert felt the tight clasp of the Governor's hand as he said this. He understood well its meaning. "And not less do I pity the unhappy youth who is the cause of such grief to his friends," continued he.

"Yes, your Excellency, Le Gardeur is to be pitied, as well as blamed. He has been tried and tempted beyond human strength."

La Corne St. Luc had risen, and was pacing the floor with impatient strides. "Pierre Philibert!" exclaimed he, "where is the poor lad? He must be sought for and saved yet. What demons have assailed him now? Was it the serpent of strong drink, that bites men mad, or the legion of fiends that rattle the dice-box in their ears? Or was it the last temptation, which never fails when all else has been tried in vain--a woman?"

"It was all three combined. The Chevalier de Pean visited Tilly on business of the Intendant--in reality, I suspect, to open a communication with Le Gardeur, for he brought him a message from a lady you wot of, which drove him wild with excitement. A hundred men could not have restrained Le Gardeur after that. He became infatuated with De Pean, and drank and gambled all night and all day with him at the village inn, threatening annihilation to all who interfered with him. Today he suddenly left Tilly, and has come with De Pean to the city."

"De Pean!" exclaimed La Corne, "the spotted snake! A fit tool for the Intendant's lies and villainy! I am convinced he went not on his own errand to Tilly. Bigot is at the bottom of this foul conspiracy to ruin the noblest lad in the Colony."

"It may be," replied Philibert, "but the Intendant alone would have had no power to lure him back. It was the message of that artful siren which has drawn Le Gardeur de Repentigny again into the whirlpool of destruction."

"Aye, but Bigot set her on him, like a retriever, to bring back the game!" replied La Corne, fully convinced of the truth of his opinion.

"It may be," answered Philibert; "but my impression is that she has influenced the Intendant, rather than he her, in this matter."

The Bishop listened with warm interest to the account of Philibert. He looked a gentle reproof, but did not utter it, at La Corne St. Luc and Philibert, for their outspoken denunciation of the Intendant. He knew--none knew better--how deserved it was; but his ecclesiastical rank placed him at the apex of all parties in the Colony, and taught him prudence in expressing or hearing opinions of the King's representatives in the Colony.

"But what have you done, Pierre Philibert," asked the Bishop, "since your arrival? Have you seen Le Gardeur?"

"No, my Lord; I followed him and the Chevalier to the city. They have gone to the Palace, whither I went and got admittance to the cabinet of the Intendant. He received me in his politest and blandest manner. I asked an interview with Le Gardeur. Bigot told me that my friend unfortunately at that moment was unfit to be seen, and had refused himself to all his city friends. I partly believed him, for I heard the voice of Le Gardeur in a distant room, amid a babble of tongues and the rattle of dice. I sent him a card with a few kind words, and received it back with an insult--deep and damning--scrawled upon it. It was not written, however, in the hand of Le Gardeur, although signed by his name. Read that, your Excellency," said he, throwing a card to the Count. "I will not repeat the foul expressions it contains. Tell Pierre Philibert what he should do to save his honor and save his friend. Poor, wild, infatuated Le Gardeur never wrote that-- never! They have made him sign his name to he knew not what."

"And, by St. Martin!" exclaimed La Corne, who looked at the card, "some of them shall bite dust for that! As for Le Gardeur, poor boy, overlook his fault--pity him, forgive him. He is not so much to blame, Pierre, as those plundering thieves of the Friponne, who shall find that La Corne St. Luc's sword is longer by half an ell than is good for some of their stomachs!"

"Forbear, dear friends," said the Bishop; "it is not the way of Christians to talk thus."

"But it is the way of gentlemen!" replied La Corne, impatiently, "and I always hold that a true gentleman is a true Christian. But you do your duty, my Lord Bishop, in reproving us, and I honor you for it, although I may not promise obedience. David fought a duel with Goliath, and was honored by God and man for it, was he not?"

"But he fought it not in his own quarrel, La Corne," replied the Bishop gently; "Goliath had defied the armies of the living God, and David fought for his king, not for himself."

"Confiteor! my Lord Bishop, but the logic of the heart is often truer than the logic of the head, and the sword has no raison d'etre, except in purging the world of scoundrels."

"I will go home now; I will see your Excellency again on this matter," said Pierre, rising to depart.

"Do, Pierre! my utmost services are at your command," said the Governor, as the guests all rose too. It was very late.

The hour of departure had arrived; the company all rose, and courteously bidding their host good-night, proceeded to their several homes, leaving him alone with his friend Kalm.

They two at once passed into a little museum of minerals, plants, birds, and animals, where they sat down, eager as two boy-students. The world, its battles, and its politics were utterly forgotten, as they conversed far into the night and examined, with the delight of new discoverers, the beauty and variety of nature's forms that exist in the New World.

# Chapter XXXVIII: A Wild Night Indoors and Out

The Chevalier de Pean had been but too successful in his errand of mischief to the Manor House of Tilly.

A few days had sufficed for this accomplished ambassador of Bigot to tempt Le Gardeur to his ruin, and to triumph in his fall.

Upon his arrival at the Seigniory, De Pean had chosen to take up his quarters at the village inn, in preference to accepting the proffered hospitality of the Lady de Tilly, whom, however, he had frequently to see, having been craftily commissioned by Bigot with the settlement of some important matters of business relating to her Seigniory, as a pretext to visit the Manor House and linger in the village long enough to renew his old familiarity with Le Gardeur.

The visits of De Pean to the Manor House were politely but not cordially received. It was only by reason of the business he came upon that he was received at all. Nevertheless he paid his court to the ladies of the Manor, as a gentleman anxious to remove their prejudices and win their good opinion.

He once, and but once, essayed to approach Amelie with gallantry, a hair-breadth only beyond the rigid boundary-line of ordinary politeness, when he received a repulse so quick, so unspoken and invisible, that he could not tell in what it consisted, yet he felt it like a sudden paralysis of his powers of pleasing. He cared not again to encounter the quick glance of contempt and aversion which for an instant flashed in the eyes of Amelie when she caught the drift of his untimely admiration.

A woman is never so Rhadamanthean in her justice, and so quick in her execution of it, as when she is proud and happy in her love for another man: she is then indignant at every suggestion implying any doubt of the strength, purity, and absoluteness of her devotion.

De Pean ground his teeth in silent wrath at this quiet but unequivocal repulse, and vowed a bitter vow that Amelie should ere long repent in sackcloth and ashes for the wound inflicted upon his vanity and still more upon his cupidity.

One of the day-dreams of his fancy was broken, never to return. The immense fortune and high rank of the young Chatelaine de Repentigny had excited the cupidity of De Pean for some time, and although the voluptuous beauty of Angelique fastened his eyes, he would willingly have sacrificed her for the reversion of the lordships of Tilly and Repentigny.

De Pean's soul was too small to bear with equanimity the annihilation of his cherished hopes. As he looked down upon his white hands, his delicate feet, and irreproachable dress and manner, he seemed not to comprehend that a true woman like Amelie cares nothing for these things in comparison with a manly nature that seeks a woman for her own sake by love, and in love, and not by the accessories of wealth and position. For such a one she would go barefoot if need were, while golden slippers would not tempt her to walk with the other.

Amelie's beau-ideal of manhood was embodied in Pierre Philibert, and the greatest king in Christendom would have wooed in vain at her feet, much less an empty pretender like the Chevalier de Pean.

"I would not have treated any gentleman so rudely," said Amelie in confidence to Heloise de Lotbiniere when they had retired to the privacy of their bedchamber. "No woman is justified in showing scorn of any man's love, if it be honest and true; but the Chevalier de Pean is false to the heart's core, and his presumption woke such an aversion in my heart, that I fear my eyes showed less than ordinary politeness to his unexpected advances."

"You were too gentle, not too harsh, Amelie," replied Heloise, with her arm round her friend. "Had I been the object of his hateful addresses, I should have repaid him in his own false coin: I would have led him on to the brink of the precipice of a confession and an offer, and then I would have dropped him as one drops a stone into the deep pool of the Chaudiere."

"You were always more bold than I, Heloise; I could not do that for the world," replied Amelie. "I would not willingly offend even the Chevalier de Pean. Moreover, I fear him, and I need not tell you why, darling. That man possesses a power over my dear brother that makes me tremble, and in my anxiety for Le Gardeur I may have lingered, as I did yesterday, too long in the parlor when in company with the Chevalier de Pean, who, mistaking my motive, may have supposed that I hated not his presence so much as I truly did!"

"Amelie, your fears are my own!" exclaimed Heloise, pressing Amelie to her side. "I must, I will tell you. O loved sister of mine,-- let me call you so!--to you alone I dare acknowledge my hopeless love for Le Gardeur, and my deep and abiding interest in his welfare."

"Nay, do not say hopeless, Heloise!" replied Amelie, kissing her fondly. "Le Gardeur is not insensible to your beauty and goodness. He is too like myself not to love you."

"Alas, Amelie! I know it is all in vain. I have neither beauty nor other attractions in his eyes. He left me yesterday to converse with the Chevalier de Pean on the subject of Angelique des Meloises, and I saw, by the agitation of his manner, the flush upon his cheek, and the eagerness of his questioning, that he cared more for Angelique, notwithstanding her reported engagement with the Intendant, than he did for a thousand Heloises de Lotbiniere!"

The poor girl, overpowered by the recollection, hid her face upon the shoulder of Amelie, and sobbed as if her very heart were breaking,--as in truth it was.

Amelie, so happy and secure in her own affection, comforted Heloise with her tears and caresses, but it was only by picturing in her imagination her own state, should she be so hapless as to lose the love of Pierre Philibert, that she could realize the depth of misery and abandonment which filled the bosom of her fair companion.

She was, moreover, struck to the heart by the words of Heloise regarding the eagerness of her brother to get word of Angelique. "The Chevalier de Pean might have brought a message, perhaps a love- token from Angelique to Le Gardeur to draw him back to the city," thought she. If so, she felt instinctively that all their efforts to redeem him would be in vain, and that neither sister's love nor Pierre's remonstrances would avail to prevent his return. He was the slave of the lamp and Angelique its possessor.

"Heaven forbid, Heloise!" she said faintly; "Le Gardeur is lost if he return to the city now! Twice lost--lost as a gentleman, lost as the lover of a woman who cares for him only as a pastime and as a foil to her ambitious designs upon the Intendant! Poor Le Gardeur! what happiness might not be his in the love of a woman noble-minded as himself! What happiness were he yours, O darling Heloise!" She kissed her pallid cheeks, wet with tears, which lay by hers on the same pillow, and both remained silently brooding over the thoughts which spring from love and sorrow.

"Happiness can never be mine, Amelie," said Heloise, after a lapse of several minutes. "I have long feared it, now I know it. Le Gardeur loves Angelique; he is wholly hers, and not one little corner of his heart is left for poor Heloise to nestle in! I did not ask much, Amelie, but I have not retained the little interest I believed was once mine! He has thrown the whole treasure of his life at her feet. After playing with it, she will spurn it for a more ambitious alliance! Oh, Amelie!" exclaimed she with vivacity, "I could be wicked! Heaven forgive me! I could be cruel and without pity to save Le Gardeur from the wiles of such a woman!"

The night was a stormy one; the east wind, which had lain in a dead lull through the early hours of the evening, rose in all its strength at the turn of the tide. It came bounding like the distant thud of a cannon. It roared and rattled against the windows and casements of the Manor House, sounding a deep bass in the long chimneys and howling like souls in torment amid the distant woods.

The rain swept down in torrents, as if the windows of heaven were opened to wash away the world's defilements. The stout walls of the Manor House were immovable as rocks, but the wind and the rain and the noise of the storm struck an awe into the two girls. They crept closer together in their bed; they dared not separate for the night. The storm seemed too much the reflex of the agitation of their own minds, and they lay clasped in each other's arms, mingling their tears and prayers for Le Gardeur until the gray dawn looked over the eastern hill and they slept.

The Chevalier de Pean was faithful to the mission upon which he had been despatched to Tilly. He disliked intensely the return of Le Gardeur to renew his old ties with Angelique. But it was his fate, his cursed crook, he called it, ever to be overborne by some woman or other, and he resolved that Le Gardeur should pay for it with his money, and be so flooded by wine and debauchery that Angelique herself would repent that she had ever invited his return.

That she would not marry Le Gardeur was plain enough to De Pean, who knew her ambitious views regarding the Intendant; and that the Intendant would not marry her was equally a certainty to him, although it did not prevent De Pean's entertaining an intense jealousy of Bigot.

Despite discouraging prospects, he found a consolation in the reflection that, failing his own vain efforts to please Amelie de Repentigny for sake of her wealth, the woman he most loved for sake of her beauty and spirit would yet drop like a golden fleece into his arms, either through spite at her false lover or through love of himself. De Pean cared little which, for it was the person, not the inclination of Angelique, that carried away captive the admiration of the Chevalier de Pean.

The better to accomplish his crafty design of abducting Le Gardeur, De Pean had taken up his lodging at the village inn. He knew that in the polite hospitalities of the Manor House he could find few opportunities to work upon the susceptible nature of Le Gardeur; that too many loving eyes would there watch over his safety, and that he was himself suspected, and his presence only tolerated on account of the business which had ostensibly brought him there. At the inn he would be free to work out his schemes, sure of success if by any means and on any pretence he could draw Le Gardeur thither and rouse into life and fury the sleeping serpents of his old propensities,--the love of gaming, the love of wine, and the love of Angelique.

Could Le Gardeur be persuaded to drink a full measure to the bright eyes of Angelique des Meloises, and could he, when the fire was kindled, be tempted once more to take in hand the box more fatal than that of Pandora and place fortune on the turn of a die, De Pean knew well that no power on earth could stop the conflagration of every good resolution and every virtuous principle in his mind. Neither aunt nor sister nor friends could withhold him then! He would return to the city, where the Grand Company had a use to make of him which he would never understand until it was too late for aught but repentance.

De Pean pondered long upon a few words he had one day heard drop from the lips of Bigot, which meant more, much more, than they seemed to imply, and they flitted long through his memory like bats in a room seeking an outlet into the night, ominous of some deed of darkness.

De Pean imagined that he had found a way to revenge himself on Le Gardeur and

Amelie--each for thwarting him in a scheme of love or fortune. He brooded long and malignantly how to hatch the plot which he fancied was his own, but which had really been conceived in the deeper brain of Bigot, whose few seemingly harmless words had dropped into the ear of De Pean, casually as it were, but which Bigot knew would take root and grow in the congenial soul of his secretary and one day bring forth terrible fruit.

The next day was wet and autumnal, with a sweeping east wind which blew raw and gustily over the dark grass and drooping trees that edged the muddy lane of the village of Tilly.

At the few houses in the village everything was quiet, except at the old-fashioned inn, with its low, covered gallery and swinging sign of the Tilly Arms.

There, flitting round the door, or occasionally peering through the windows of the tap-room, with pipes in their mouths and perchance a tankard in their hands, were seen the elders of the village, boatmen, and habitans, making use, or good excuse, of a rainy day for a social gathering in the dry, snug chimney-corner of the Tilly Arms.

In the warmest corner of all, his face aglow with firelight and good liquor, sat Master Pothier dit Robin, with his gown tucked up to his waist as he toasted his legs and old gamashes in the genial warmth of a bright fire.

He leaned back his head and twirled his thumbs for a few minutes without speaking or listening to the babble around him, which had now turned upon the war and the latest sweep of the royal commissaries for corn and cattle. "Did you say, Jean La Marche," said he, "that Le Gardeur de Repentigny was playing dice and drinking hot wine with the Chevalier de Pean and two big dogs of the Friponne?"

"I did." Jean spoke with a choking sensation. "Our young Seigneur has broken out again wilder than ever, and is neither to hold nor bind any longer!"

"Ay!" replied Master Pothier reflectively, "the best bond I could draw would not bind him more than a spider's thread! They are stiff-necked as bulls, these De Repentignys, and will bear no yoke but what they put on of themselves! Poor lad! Do they know at the Manor House that he is here drinking and dicing with the Chevalier de Pean?"

"No! Else all the rain in heaven would not have prevented his being looked after by Mademoiselle Amelie and my Lady," answered Jean. "His friend, Pierre Philibert, who is now a great officer of the King, went last night to Batiscan, on some matter of the army, as his groom told me. Had he been here, Le Gardeur would not have spent the day at the Tilly Arms, as we poor habitans do when it is washing-day at home."

"Pierre Philibert!" Master Pothier rubbed his hands at this reminder, "I remember him, Jean! A hero like St. Denis! It was he who walked into the Chateau of the Intendant and brought off young De Repentigny as a cat does her kitten."

"What, in his mouth, Master Pothier?"

"None of your quips, Jean; keep cool!" Master Pothier's own face grew red. "Never ring the coin that is a gift, and do not stretch my comparisons like your own wit to a bare thread. If I had said in his mouth, what then? It was by word of mouth, I warrant you, that he carried him away from Beaumanoir. Pity he is not here to take him away from the Tilly Arms!"

The sound of voices, the rattle and clash of the dice-box in the distant parlor, reached his ear amidst the laughter and gabble of the common room. The night was a hard one in the little inn.

In proportion as the common room of the inn grew quiet by the departure of its guests, the parlor occupied by the gentlemen became more noisy and distinct in its confusion. The song, the laugh, the jest, and jingle of glasses mingled with the perpetual rattle of dice or the thumps which accompanied the play of successful cards.

Paul Gaillard, the host, a timid little fellow not used to such high imperious guests, only ventured to look into the parlor when summoned for more wine. He was a born censitaire of the house of Tilly, and felt shame and pity as he beheld the dishevelled figure of his young Seigneur shaking the dice-box and defying one and all to another cast for love, liquor, or whole handfuls of uncounted coin.

Paul Gaillard had ventured once to whisper something to Le Gardeur about sending his caleche to the Manor House, hoping that his youthful master would consent to be driven home. But his proposal was met by a wild laugh from Le Gardeur and a good-humored expulsion from the room.

He dared not again interfere, but contented himself with waiting until break of day to send a message to the Lady de Tilly informing her of the sad plight of his young master.

De Pean, with a great object in view, had summoned Le Mercier and Emeric de Lantagnac from the city,--potent topers and hard players,-- to assist him in his desperate game for the soul, body, and fortune of Le Gardeur de Repentigny.

They came willingly. The Intendant had laughingly wished them bon voyage and a speedy return with his friend Le Gardeur, giving them no other intimation of his wishes; nor could they surmise that he had any other object in view than the pleasure of again meeting a pleasant companion of his table and a sharer of their pleasures.

De Pean had no difficulty in enticing Le Gardeur down to the village inn, where he had arranged that he should meet, by mere accident, as it were, his old city friends.

The bold, generous nature of Le Gardeur, who neither suspected nor feared any evil, greeted them with warmth. They were jovial fellows, he knew, who would be affronted if he refused to drink a cup of wine with them. They talked of the gossip of the city, its coteries and pleasant scandals, and of the beauty and splendor of the queen of society--Angelique des Meloises.

Le Gardeur, with a painful sense of his last interview with Angelique, and never for a moment forgetting her reiterated words, "I love you, Le Gardeur, but I will not marry you," kept silent whenever she was named, but talked with an air of cheerfulness on every other topic.

His one glass of wine was soon followed by another. He was pressed with such cordiality that he could not refuse. The fire was rekindled, at first with a faint glow upon his cheek and a sparkle in his eye; but the table soon overflowed with wine, mirth, and laughter. He drank without reflection, and soon spoke with warmth and looseness from all restraint.

De Pean, resolved to excite Le Gardeur to the utmost, would not cease alluding to Angelique. He recurred again and again to the splendor of her charms and the fascination of her ways. He watched the effect of his speech upon the countenance of Le Gardeur, keenly observant of every expression of interest excited by the mention of her.

"We will drink to her bright eyes," exclaimed De Pean, filling his glass until it ran over, "first in beauty and worthy to be first in place in New France--yea, or Old France either! and he is a heathen who will not drink this toast!"

"Le Gardeur will not drink it! Neither would I, in his place," replied Emeric de Lantagnac, too drunk now to mind what he said. "I would drink to the bright eyes of no woman who had played me the trick Angelique has played upon Le Gardeur!"

"What trick has she played upon me?" repeated Le Gardeur, with a touch of anger.

"Why, she has jilted you, and now flies at higher game, and nothing but a prince of the blood will satisfy her!"

"Does she say that, or do you invent it?" Le Gardeur was almost choking with angry feelings. Emeric cared little what he said, drunk or sober. He replied gravely,--

"Oh, all the women in the city say she said it! But you know, Le Gardeur, women will lie of one another faster than a man can count a hundred by tens."

De Pean, while enjoying the vexation of Le Gardeur, feared that the banter of Emeric might have an ill effect on his scheme. "I do not believe it, Le Gardeur;" said he, "Angelique is too true a woman to say what she means to every jealous rival. The women hope she has jilted you. That counts one more chance for them, you know! Is not that feminine arithmetic, Le Mercier?" asked he.

"It is at the Friponne," replied Le Mercier, laughing. "But the man who becomes debtor to Angelique des Meloises will never, if I know her, be discharged out of her books, even if he pay his debt."

"Ay, they say she never lets a lover go, or a friend either," replied De Pean. "I have proof to convince Le Gardeur that Angelique has not jilted him. Emeric reports women's tattle, nothing more."

Le Gardeur was thoroughly roused. "Par Dieu!" exclaimed he, "my affairs are well talked over in the city, I think! Who gave man or woman the right to talk of me thus?"

"No one gave them the right. But the women claim it indefeasibly from Eve, who commenced talking of Adam's affairs with Satan the first time her man's back was turned."

"Pshaw! Angelique des Meloises is as sensible as she is beautiful: she never said that! No, par Dieu! she never said to a man or woman that she had jilted me, or gave reason for others to say so!"

Le Gardeur in his vexation poured out with nervous hand a large glass of pure brandy and drank it down. It had an instant effect. His forehead flushed, and his eyes dilated with fresh fire. "She never said that!" repeated he fiercely. "I would swear it on my mother's head, she never did! and would kill any man who would dare affirm it of her!"

"Right! the way to win a woman is never to give her up," answered De Pean. "Hark you, Le Gardeur, all the city knows that she favored you more than any of the rest of her legion of admirers. Why are you moping away your time here at Tilly when you ought to be running down your game in the city?"

"My Atalanta is too fleet of foot for me, De Pean," replied Le Gardeur. "I have given up the chase. I have not the luck of Hippomanes."

"That is, she is too fast!" said De Pean mockingly. "But have you thrown a golden apple at her feet to stop your runaway nymph?"

"I have thrown myself at her feet, De Pean! and in vain," said Le Gardeur, gulping down another cup of brandy.

De Pean watched the effect of the deep potations which Le Gardeur now poured down to quench the rising fires kindled in his breast. "Come here, Le Gardeur," said he; "I have a message for you which I would not deliver before, lest you might be angry."

De Pean led him into a recess of the room. "You are wanted in the city," whispered he. "Angelique sent this little note by me. She put it in my hand as I was embarking for Tilly, and blushed redder than a rose as she did so. I promised to deliver it safely to you."

It was a note quaintly folded in a style Le Gardeur recognized well, inviting him to return to the city. Its language was a mixture of light persiflage and tantalizing coquetry,--she was dying of the dullness of the city! The late ball at the Palace had been a failure, lacking the presence of Le Gardeur! Her house was forlorn without the visits of her dear friend, and she wanted his trusty counsel in an affair of the last importance to her welfare and happiness!

"That girl loves you, and you may have her for the asking!" continued De Pean, as Le Gardeur sat crumpling the letter up in his hand. De Pean watched his countenance with the eye of a basilisk.

"Do you think so?" asked Le Gardeur eagerly. "But no, I have no more faith in woman; she does not mean it!"

"But if she does mean it, would you go, Le Gardeur?"

"Would I go?" replied he, excitedly. "Yes, I would go to the lowest pit in hell for her! But why are you taunting me, De Pean!"

"I taunt you? Read her note again! She wants your trusty counsel in an affair of the last importance to her welfare and happiness. You know what is the affair of last importance to a woman! Will you refuse her now, Le Gardeur?"

"No, par Dieu! I can refuse her nothing; no, not if she asked me for my head, although I know it is but mockery."

"Never mind! Then you will return with us to the city? We start at daybreak."

"Yes, I will go with you, De Pean; you have made me drunk, and I am willing to stay drunk till I leave Amelie and my aunt and Heloise, up at the Manor House. Pierre Philibert, he will be angry that I leave him, but he can follow, and they can all follow! I hate myself for it, De Pean! But Angelique des Meloises is to me more than creature or Creator. It is a sin to love a woman as I love her, De Pean!"

De Pean fairly writhed before the spirit he evoked. He was not so sure of his game but that it might yet be lost. He knew Angelique's passionate impulses, and he thought that no woman could resist such devotion as that of Le Gardeur.

He kept down his feelings, however. He saw that Le Gardeur was ripe for ruin. They returned to the table and drank still more freely. Dice and cards were resumed; fresh challenges were thrown out; Emeric and Le Mercier were already deep in a game; money was pushed to and fro. The contagion fastened like a plague upon Le Gardeur, who sat down at the table, drew forth a full purse, and pulling up every anchor of restraint, set sail on the flood-tide of drinking and gaming which lasted without ceasing until break of day.

De Pean never for a moment lost sight of his scheme for the abduction of Le Gardeur. He got ready for departure, and with a drunken rush and a broken song the four gallants, with unwashed faces and disordered clothes, staggered into their canoe and with a shout bade the boatmen start.

The hardy canotiers were ready for departure. They headed their long canoes down the flowing river, dashed their paddles into the water just silvered with the rays of the rising sun, and shot down stream towards the city of Quebec.

De Pean, elate with his success, did not let the gaiety of the party flag for a moment during their return. They drank, sang, and talked balderdash and indecencies in a way to bring a look of disgust upon the cheeks of the rough boatmen.

Much less sober than when they left Tilly, the riotous party reached the capital. The canotiers with rapid strokes of the paddle passed the high cliffs and guarded walls, and made for the quay of the Friponne, De Pean forcing silence upon his companions as they passed the Sault au Matelot, where a crowd of idle boatmen hailed them with volleys of raillery, which only ceased when the canoe was near enough for them to see whom it contained. They were instantly silent. The rigorous search made by order of the Intendant after the late rioters, and the summary punishment inflicted upon all who had been convicted, had inspired a careful avoidance of offence toward Bigot and the high officers of his staff.

De Pean landed quietly, few caring to turn their heads too often towards him. Le Gardeur, wholly under his control, staggered out of the canoe, and, taking his arm, was dragged rather than led up to the Palace, where Bigot greeted the party with loud welcome. Apartments were assigned to Le Gardeur, as to a most honored guest in the Palace. Le Gardeur de Repentigny was finally and wholly in the power of the Intendant.

Bigot looked triumphant, and congratulated De Pean on the success of his mission. "We will keep him now!" said he. "Le Gardeur must never draw a sober breath again until we have done with him!"

De Pean looked knowingly at Bigot; "I understand," said he; "Emeric and Le Mercier will drink him blind, and Cadet, Varin, and the rest of us will rattle the dice like hail. We must pluck the pigeon to his last feather before he will feel desperate enough to play your game, Chevalier."

"As you like, De Pean, about that," replied Bigot; "only mind that he does not leave the Palace. His friends will run after him. That accursed Philibert will be here; on your life, do not let him see him! Hark you! When he comes, make Le Gardeur affront him by some offensive reply to his inquiry. You can do it."

De Pean took the hint, and acted upon it by forging that infamous card in the name of Le Gardeur, and sending it as his reply to Pierre Philibert.

# Chapter XXXIX: Mere Malheur

La Corriveau, eager to commence her work of wickedness, took up her abode at the house of her ancient friend, Mere Malheur, whither she went on the night of her first interview with Angelique.

It was a small house, built of uncut stones, with rough stone steps and lintels, a peaked roof, and low overhanging eaves, hiding itself under the shadow of the cliff, so closely that it seemed to form a part of the rock itself.

Its sole inmate, an old crone who had reached the last degree of woman's ugliness and woman's heartlessness,--Mere Malheur--sold fair winds to superstitious sailors and good luck to hunters and voyageurs. She was not a little suspected of dabbling in other forbidden things. Half believing in her own impostures, she regarded La Corriveau with a feeling akin to worship, who in return for this devotion imparted to her a few secrets of minor importance in her diabolic arts.

La Corriveau was ever a welcome guest at the house of Mere Malheur, who feasted her lavishly, and served her obsequiously, but did not press with undue curiosity to learn her business in the city. The two women understood one another well enough not to pry too closely into each other's secrets.

On this occasion La Corriveau was more than usually reserved, and while Mere Malheur eagerly detailed to her all the doings and undoings that had happened in her circle of acquaintance, she got little information in return. She shrewdly concluded that La Corriveau had business on hand which would not bear to be spoken of.

"When you need my help, ask for it without scruple, Dame Dodier," said the old crone. "I see you have something on hand that may need my aid. I would go into the fire to serve you, although I would not burn my finger for any other woman in the world, and you know it."

"Yes, I know it, Mere Malheur," La Corriveau spoke with an air of superiority, "and you say rightly: I have something on hand which I cannot accomplish alone, and I need your help, although I cannot tell you yet how or against whom."

"Is it a woman or a man? I will only ask that question, Dame Dodier," said the crone, turning upon her a pair of green, inquisitive eyes.

"It is a woman, and so of course you will help me. Our sex for the bottom of all mischief, Mere Malheur! I do not know what women are made for except to plague one another for the sake of worthless men!"

The old crone laughed a hideous laugh, and playfully pushed her long fingers into the ribs of La Corriveau. "Made for! quotha! men's temptation, to be sure, and the beginning of all mischief!"

"Pretty temptations you and I are, Mere Malheur!" replied La Corriveau, with a scornful laugh.

"Well, we were pretty temptations once! I will never give up that! You must own, Dame Dodier, we were both pretty temptations once!"

"Pshaw! I wish I had been a man, for my part," replied La Corriveau, impetuously. "It was a spiteful cross of fate to make me a woman!"

"But, Dame Dodier, I like to be a woman, I do. A man cannot be half as wicked as a woman, especially if she be young and pretty," said the old woman, laughing till the tears ran out of her bleared eyes.

"Nay, that is true, Mere Malheur; the fairest women in the world are ever the worst! fair and false! fair and false! they are always so. Not one better than another. Satan's mark is upon all of us!" La Corriveau looked an incarnation of Hecate as she uttered this calumny upon her sex.

"Ay, I have his mark on my knee, Dame Dodier," replied the crone. "See here! It was pricked once in the high court of Arras, but the fool judge decided that it was a mole, and not a witch-mark! I escaped a red gown that time, however. I laughed at his stupidity, and bewitched him for it in earnest. I was young and pretty then! He died in a year, and Satan sat on his grave in the shape of a black cat until his friends set a cross over it. I like to be a woman, I do, it is so easy to be wicked, and so nice! I always tell the girls that, and they give me twice as much as if I had told them to be good and nice, as they call it! Pshaw! Nice! If only men knew us as we really are!"

"Well, I do not like women, Mere Malheur," replied La Corriveau; "they sneer at you and me and call us witch and sorceress, and they will lie, steal, kill, and do worse themselves for the sake of one man to-day, and cast him off for sake of another to-morrow! Wise Solomon found only one good woman in a thousand; the wisest man now finds not one in a worldful! It were better all of us were dead, Mere Malheur; but pour me out a glass of wine, for I am tired of tramping in the dark to the house of that gay lady I told you of."

Mere Malheur poured out a glass of choice Beaume from a dame-jeanne which she had received from a roguish sailor, who had stolen it from his ship.

"But you have not told me who she is, Dame Dodier," replied Mere Malheur, refilling the glass of La Corriveau.

"Nor will I yet. She is fit to be your mistress and mine, whoever she is; but I shall not go again to see her."

And La Corriveau did not again visit the house of Angelique. She had received from her precise information respecting the movements of the Intendant. He had gone to the Trois Rivieres on urgent affairs, and might be absent for a week.

Angelique had received from Varin, in reply to her eager question for news, a short, falsified account of the proceedings in the Council relative to Caroline and of Bigot's indignant denial of all knowledge of her.

Varin, as a member of the Council, dared not reveal the truth, but would give his familiars half-hints, or tell to others elaborate lies, when pressed for information. He did not, in this case, even hint at the fact that a search was to be made for Caroline. Had he done so, Angelique would herself have given secret information to the Governor to order the search of Beaumanoir, and thus got her rival out of the way without trouble, risk, or crime.

But it was not to be. The little word that would have set her active spirit on fire to aid in the search for Caroline was not spoken, and her thoughts remained immovably fixed upon her death.

But if Angelique had been misled by Varin as to what had passed at the Council, Mere Malheur, through her intercourse with a servant of Varin, had learned the truth. An eavesdropping groom had overheard his master and the Intendant conversing on the letters of the Baron and La Pompadour. The man told his sweetheart, who, coming with some stolen sweetmeats to Mere Malheur, told her, who in turn was not long in imparting what she had heard to La Corriveau.

La Corriveau did not fail to see that, should Angelique discover that her rival was to be searched for, and taken to France if found, she would at once change her mind, and Caroline would be got rid of without need of her interference. But La Corriveau had got her hand in the dish. She was not one to lose her promised reward or miss the chance of so cursed a deed by any untimely avowal of what she knew.

So Angelique was doomed to remain in ignorance until too late. She became the dupe of her own passions and the dupe of La Corriveau, who carefully concealed from her a secret so important.

Bigot's denial in the Council weighed nothing with her. She felt certain that the lady was no other than Caroline de St. Castin. Angelique was acute enough to perceive that Bigot's bold assertion that he knew nothing of her bound him in a chain of obligation never to confess afterwards aught to the contrary. She eagerly persuaded herself that he would not regret to hear that Caroline had died by some sudden and, to appearance, natural death, and thus relieved him of a danger, and her of an obstacle to her marriage.

Without making a full confidant of Mere Malheur, La Corriveau resolved to make use of her in carrying out her diabolical scheme. Mere Malheur had once been a servant at Beaumanoir. She knew the house, and in her heyday of youth and levity had often smuggled herself in and out by the subterranean passage which connected the solitary watchtower with the vaults of the Chateau. Mere Malheur knew Dame Tremblay, who, as the Charming Josephine, had often consulted her upon the perplexities of a heart divided among too many lovers.

The memory of that fragrant period of her life was the freshest and pleasantest of all Dame Tremblay's experience. It was like the odor of new-mown hay, telling of early summer and frolics in the green fields. She liked nothing better than to talk it all over in her snug room with Mere Malheur, as they sat opposite one another at her little table, each with a cup of tea in her hand, well laced with brandy, which was a favorite weakness of them both.

Dame Tremblay was, in private, neither nice nor squeamish as to the nature of her gossip. She and the old fortune-teller, when out of sight of the rest of the servants, had always a dish of the choicest scandal fresh from the city.

La Corriveau resolved to send Mere Malheur to Beaumanoir, under the pretence of paying a visit to Dame Tremblay, in order to open a way of communication between herself and Caroline. She had learned enough during her brief interview with Caroline in the forest of St. Valier, and from what she now heard respecting the Baron de St. Castin, to convince her that this was no other than his missing daughter.

"If Caroline could only be induced to admit La Corriveau into her secret chamber and take her into her confidence, the rest--all the rest," muttered the hag to herself, with terrible emphasis, "would be easy, and my reward sure. But that reward shall be measured in my own bushel, not in yours, Mademoiselle des Meloises, when the deed is done!"

La Corriveau knew the power such a secret would enable her to exercise over Angelique. She already regarded the half of her reputed riches as her own. "Neither she nor the Intendant will ever dare neglect me after that!" said she. "When once Angelique shall be linked in with me by a secret compact of blood, the fortune of La Corriveau is made. If the death of this girl be the elixir of life to you, it shall be the touchstone of fortune forever to La Corriveau!"

Mere Malheur was next day despatched on a visit to her old gossip, Dame Tremblay. She had been well tutored on every point, what to say and how to demean herself. She bore a letter to Caroline, written in the Italian hand of La Corriveau, who had learned to write well from her mother, Marie Exili.

The mere possession of the art of writing was a rarity in those days in the class among whom she lived. La Corriveau's ability to write at all was a circumstance as remarkable to her illiterate neighbors as the possession of the black art which they ascribed to her, and not without a strong suspicion that it had the same origin.

Mere Malheur, in anticipation of a cup of tea and brandy with Dame Tremblay, had dressed herself with some appearance of smartness in a clean striped gown of linsey. A peaked Artois hat surmounted a broad-frilled cap, which left visible some tresses of coarse gray hair and a pair of silver ear-rings, which dangled with every motion of her head. Her shoes displayed broad buckles of brass, and her short petticoat showed a pair of stout ankles enclosed in red clocked stockings. She carried a crutched stick in her hand, by help of which she proceeded vigorously on her journey.

Starting in the morning, she trudged out of the city towards the ferry of Jean Le Nocher, who carefully crossed himself and his boat too as he took Mere Malheur on board. He wafted her over in a hurry, as something to be got rid of as quickly as possible.

Mere Malheur tramped on, like a heavy gnome, through the fallen and flying leaves of the woods of Beaumanoir, caring nothing for the golden, hazy sky, the soft, balmy air, or the varicolored leaves-- scarlet, yellow, and brown, of every shade and tinge--that hung upon the autumnal trees.

A frosty night or two had ushered in the summer of St. Martin, as it was called by the habitans,--the Indian summer,--that brief time of glory and enchantment which visits us like a gaudy herald to announce the approach of the Winter King. It is Nature's last rejoicing in the sunshine and the open air, like the splendor and gaiety of a maiden devoted to the cloister, who for a few weeks is allowed to flutter like a bird of paradise amid the pleasures and gaieties of the world, and then comes the end. Her locks of pride are shorn off; she veils her beauty, and kneels a nun on the cold stones of her passionless cell, out of which, even with repentance, there comes no deliverance.

Mere Malheur's arrival at Beaumanoir was speedily known to all the servants of the Chateau. She did not often visit them, but when she did there was a hurried recital of an Ave or two to avert any harm, followed by a patronizing welcome and a rummage for small coins to cross her hand withal in return for her solutions of the grave questions of love, jealousy, money, and marriage, which fermented secretly or openly in the bosoms of all of them. They were but human beings, food for imposture, and preyed on by deceivers. The visit of Mere Malheur was an event of interest in both kitchen and laundry of the Chateau.

Dame Tremblay had the first claim, however, upon this singular visitor. She met her at the back door of the Chateau, and with a face beaming with smiles, and dropping all dignity, exclaimed,--

"Mere Malheur, upon my life! Welcome, you wicked old soul! you surely knew I wanted to see you! come in and rest! you must be tired, unless you came on a broom! ha! ha! come to my room and never mind anybody!"

This last remark was made for the benefit of the servants who stood peeping at every door and corner, not daring to speak to the old woman in the presence of the housekeeper, but knowing that their time would come, they had patience.

The housekeeper, giving them a severe look, proceeded to her own snug apartment, followed by the crone, whom she seated in her easiest chair and proceeded to refresh with a glass of cognac, which was swallowed with much relish and wiping of lips, accompanied by a little artificial cough. Dame Tremblay kept a carafe of it in her room to raise the temperature of her low spirits and vapors to summer heat, not that she drank, far from it, but she liked to sip a little for her stomach's sake.

"It is only a thimbleful I take now and then," she said. "When I was the Charming Josephine I used to kiss the cups I presented to the young gallants, and I took no more than a fly! but they always drank bumpers from the cup I kissed!" The old dame looked grave as she shook her head and remarked, "But we cannot be always young and handsome, can we, Mere Malheur?"

"No, dame, but we can be jolly and fat, and that is what we are! You don't quaff life by thimblefuls, and you only want a stout offer to show the world that you can trip as briskly to church yet as any girl in New France!"

The humor of the old crone convulsed Dame Tremblay with laughter, as if some invisible fingers were tickling her wildly under the armpits.

She composed herself at last, and drawing her chair close to that of Mere Malheur, looked her inquiringly in the face and asked, "What is the news?"

Dame Tremblay was endowed with more than the ordinary curiosity of her sex. She knew more news of city and country than any one else, and she dispensed it as freely as she gathered. She never let her stock of gossip run low, and never allowed man or woman to come to speak with her without pumping them dry of all they knew. A secret in anybody's possession set her wild to possess it, and she gave no rest to her inordinate curiosity until she had fished it out of even the muddiest waters.

The mystery that hung around Caroline was a source of perpetual irritation to the nerves of Dame Tremblay. She had tried as far as she dared by hint and suggestion to draw from the lady some reference to her name and family, but in vain. Caroline would avow nothing, and Dame Tremblay, completely baffled by a failure of ordinary means to find out the secret, bethought herself of her old resource in case of perplexity, Mere Malheur.

For several days she had been brooding over this mode of satisfying her curiosity, when the unexpected visit of Mere Malheur set aside all further hesitation about disobeying the Intendant's orders not to inquire or allow any other person to make inquisition respecting Caroline.

"Mere Malheur, you feel comfortable now!" said she. "That glass of cognac has given you a color like a peony!"

"Yes, I am very comfortable now, dame! your cognac is heavenly: it warms without burning. That glass is the best news I have to tell of to-day!"

"Nay, but there is always something stirring in the city; somebody born, married, or dead; somebody courted, won, lost, or undone; somebody's name up, somebody's reputation down! Tell me all you know, Mere Malheur! and then I will tell you something that will make you glad you came to Beaumanoir to-day. Take another sip of cognac and begin!"

"Ay, dame, that is indeed a temptation!" She took two deep sips, and holding her glass in her hand, began with loose tongue to relate the current gossip of the city, which was already known to Dame Tremblay; but an ill-natured version of it from the lips of her visitor seemed to give it a fresh seasoning and a relish which it had not previously possessed.

"Now, Mere Malheur! I have a secret to tell you," said Dame Tremblay, in a low, confidential tone, "a dead secret, mind you, which you had better be burnt than reveal. There is a lady, a real lady if I ever saw one, living in the Chateau here in the greatest privacy. I and the Intendant only see her. She is beautiful and full of sorrow as the picture of the blessed Madonna. What she is, I may guess; but who she is, I cannot conjecture, and would give my little finger to know!"

"Tut, dame!" replied Mere Malheur, with a touch of confidence, "I will not believe any woman could keep a secret from you! But this is news, indeed, you tell me! A lady in concealment here, and you say you cannot find her out, Dame Tremblay!"

"In truth, I cannot; I have tried every artifice, but she passes all my wit and skill. If she were a man, I would have drawn her very teeth out with less difficulty than I have tried to extract the name of this lady. When I was the Charming Josephine of Lake Beauport, I could wind men like a thread around which finger I liked; but this is a tangled knot which drives me to despair to unravel it."

"What do you know about her, dame? Tell me all you suspect!" said Mere Malheur.

"Truly," replied the dame, without the least asperity, "I suspect the poor thing, like the rest of us, is no better than she should be; and the Intendant knows it, and Mademoiselle des Meloises knows it too; and, to judge by her constant prayers and penitence, she knows it herself but too well, and will not say it to me!"

"Ay, dame! but this is great news you tell me!" replied Mere Malheur, eagerly clutching at the opportunity thus offered for the desired interview. "But what help do you expect from me in the matter?"

Mere Malheur looked very expectant at her friend, who continued, "I want you to see that lady under promise of secrecy, mark you!--and look at her hands, and tell me who and what she is."

Dame Tremblay had an unlimited faith in the superstitions of her age.

"I will do all you wish, dame, but you must allow me to see her alone," replied the crone, who felt she was thus opening the door to La Corriveau.

"To be sure I will,--that is, if she will consent to be seen, for she has in some things a spirit of her own! I am afraid to push her too closely! The mystery of her is taking the flesh off my bones, and I can only get sleep by taking strong possets, Mere Malheur! Feel my elbow! Feel my knee! I have not had so sharp an elbow or knee since Goodman Tremblay died! And he said I had the sharpest elbow and knee in the city! But I had to punch him sometimes to keep him in order! But set that horrid cap straight, Mere Malheur, while I go ask her if she would like to have her fortune told. She is not a woman if she would not like to know her fortune, for she is in despair, I think, with all the world; and when a woman is in despair, as I know by my own experience, she will jump at any chance for spite, if not for love, as I did when I took the Sieur Tremblay by your advice, Mere Malheur!"

Dame Tremblay left the old crone making hideous faces in a mirror. She rubbed her cheeks and mouth with the corner of her apron as she proceeded to the door of Caroline's apartment. She knocked gently, and a low, soft voice bade her enter.

Caroline was seated on a chair by the window, knitting her sad thoughts into a piece of work which she occasionally lifted from her lap with a sudden start, as something broke the train of her reflections.

She was weighing over and over in her thoughts, like gold in a scale, by grains and pennyweights, a few kind words lately spoken to her by Bigot when he ran in to bid her adieu before departing on his journey to Trois Rivieres. They seemed a treasure inexhaustible as she kept on repeating them to herself. The pressure of his hand had been warmer, the tone of his voice softer, the glance of his eye more kind, and he looked pityingly, she thought, upon her wan face when he left her in the gallery, and with a cheery voice and a kiss bade her take care of her health and win back the lost roses of Acadia.

These words passed through her mind with unceasing repetition, and a white border of light was visible on the edge of the dark cloud which hung over her. "The roses of Acadia will never bloom again," thought she sadly. "I have watered them with salt tears too long, and all in vain. O Bigot, I fear it is too late, too late!" Still, his last look and last words reflected a faint ray of hope and joy upon her pallid countenance.

Dame Tremblay entered the apartment, and while busying herself on pretence of setting it in order, talked in her garrulous way of the little incidents of daily life in the Chateau, and finished by a mention, as if it were casual, of the arrival of the wise woman of the city, who knew everything, who could interpret dreams, and tell, by looking in a glass or in your hand, things past, present, and to come.

"A wonderful woman," Dame Tremblay said, "a perilous woman too, not safe to deal with; but for all that, every one runs after her, and she has a good or bad word for every person who consults her. For my part," continued the dame, "she foretold my marriage with the Goodman Tremblay long before it happened, and she also foretold his death to the very month it happened. So I have reason to believe in her as well as to be thankful!"

Caroline listened attentively to the dame's remarks. She was not superstitious, but yet not above the beliefs of her age, while the Indian strain in her lineage and her familiarity with the traditions of the Abenaquis inclined her to yield more than ordinary respect to dreams.

Caroline had dreamed of riding on a coal-black horse, seated behind the veiled figure of a man whose face she could not see, who carried her like the wind away to the ends of the earth, and there shut her up in a mountain for ages and ages, until a bright angel cleft the rock, and, clasping her in his arms, bore her up to light and liberty in the presence of the Redeemer and of all the host of heaven.

This dream lay heavy on her mind. For the veiled figure she knew was one she loved, but who had no honest love for her. Her mind had been brooding over the dream all day, and the announcement by Dame Tremblay of the presence in the Chateau of one who was able to interpret dreams seemed a stroke of fortune, if not an act of Providence.

She roused herself up, and with more animation than Dame Tremblay had yet seen in her countenance, requested her to send up the visitor, that she might ask her a question.

Mere Malheur was quickly summoned to the apartment of Caroline, where Dame Tremblay left them alone.

The repulsive look of the old crone sent a shock through the fine, nervous organization of the young girl. She requested Mere Malheur to be seated, however, and in her gentle manner questioned her about the dream.

Mere Malheur was an adept in such things, and knew well how to humor human nature, and lead it to put its own interpretations upon its own visions and desires while giving all the credit of it to herself.

Mere Malheur therefore interpreted the dream according to Caroline's secret wishes. This inspired a sort of confidence, and Mere Malheur seized the opportunity to deliver the letter from La Corriveau.

"My Lady," said she, looking carefully round the room to note if the door was shut and no one was present, "I can tell you more than the interpretation of your dream. I can tell who you are and why you are here!"

Caroline started with a frightened look, and stared in the face of Mere Malheur. She faltered out at length,--"You know who I am and why I am here? Impossible! I never saw you before."

"No, my Lady, you never saw me before, but I will convince you that I know you. You are the daughter of the Baron de St. Castin! Is it not so?" The old crone looked frightfully knowing as she uttered these words.

"Mother of mercies! what shall I do?" ejaculated the alarmed girl. "Who are you to say that?"

"I am but a messenger, my Lady. Listen! I am sent here to give you secretly this letter from a friend who knows you better than I, and who above all things desires an interview with you, as she has things of the deepest import to communicate."

"A letter! Oh, what mystery is all this? A letter for me! Is it from the Intendant?"

"No, my Lady, it is from a woman." Caroline blushed and trembled as she took it from the old crone.

A woman! It flashed upon the mind of Caroline that the letter was important. She opened it with trembling fingers, anticipating she knew not what direful tidings when her eyes ran over the clear handwriting.

La Corriveau had written to the effect that she was an unknown friend, desirous of serving her in a moment of peril. The Baron de St. Castin had traced her to New France, and had procured from the King instructions to the Governor to search for her everywhere and to send her to France. Other things of great import, the writer said, she had also to communicate, if Caroline would grant her a private interview in the Chateau.

There was a passage leading from the old deserted watch-tower to the vaulted chamber, continued the letter, and the writer would without further notice come on the following night to Beaumanoir, and knock at the arched door of her chamber about the hour of midnight, when, if Caroline pleased to admit her, she would gladly inform her of very important matters relating to herself, to the Intendant, and to the Baron de St. Castin, who was on his way out to the Colony to conduct in person the search after his lost daughter.

The letter concluded with the information that the Intendant had gone to Trois Rivieres, whence he might not return for a week, and that during his absence the Governor would probably order a search for her to be made at Beaumanoir.

Caroline held the letter convulsively in her hand as she gathered its purport rather than read it. Her face changed color, from a deep flush of shame to the palest hue of fear, when she comprehended its meaning and understood that her father was on his way to New France to find out her hiding-place.

"What shall I do! Oh, what shall I do!" exclaimed she, wringing her hands for very anguish, regardless of the presence of Mere Malheur, who stood observing her with eyes glittering with curiosity, but void of every mark of womanly sympathy or feeling.

"My father, my loving father!" continued Caroline, "my deeply- injured father coming here with anger in his face to drag me from my concealment! I shall drop dead at his feet for very shame. Oh, that I were buried alive with mountains piled over me to hide me from my father! What shall I do? Whither shall I go? Bigot, Bigot, why have you forsaken me?"

Mere Malheur continued eyeing her with cold curiosity, but was ready at the first moment to second the promptings of the evil spirit contained in the letter.

"Mademoiselle," said she, "there is but one way to escape from the search to be made by your father and the Governor,--take counsel of her who sends you that friendly letter. She can offer you a safe hiding-place until the storm blows over. Will you see her, my Lady?"

"See her! I, who dare see no one! Who is she that sends me such strange news? Is it truth? Do you know her?" continued she, looking fixedly at Mere Malheur, as if in hope of reading on her countenance some contradiction of the matter contained in the letter.

"I think it is all true, my Lady," replied she, with mock humility; "I am but a poor messenger, however, and speak not myself of things I do not know, but she who sends me will tell you all."

"Does the Intendant know her?"

"I think he told her to watch over your safety during his absence. She is old and your friend; will you see her?" replied Mere Malheur, who saw the point was gained.

"Oh, yes, yes! tell her to come. Beseech her not to fail to come, or I shall go mad. O woman, you too are old and experienced and ought to know,--can she help me in this strait, think you?" exclaimed Caroline, clasping her hands in a gesture of entreaty.

"No one is more able to help you," said the crone; "she can counsel you what to do, and if need be find means to conceal you from the search that will be made for you."

"Haste, then, and bid her come to-morrow night! Why not tonight?" Caroline was all nervous impatience. "I will wait her coming in the vaulted chamber; I will watch for her as one in the valley of death watches for the angel of deliverance. Bid her come, and at midnight to-morrow she shall find the door of the secret chamber open to admit her."

The eagerness of the ill-fated girl to see La Corriveau outran every calculation of Mere Malheur. It was in vain and useless for her to speak further on the subject; Caroline would say no more. Her thoughts ran violently in the direction suggested by the artful letter. She would see La Corriveau to-morrow night, and would make no more avowals to Mere Malheur, she said to herself.

Seeing no more was to be got out of her, the crone bade her a formal farewell, looking at her curiously as she did so, and wondering in her mind if she should ever see her again. For the old creature had a shrewd suspicion that La Corriveau had not told her all her intentions with respect to this singular girl.

Caroline returned her salute, still holding the letter in her hand. She sat down to peruse it again, and observed not Mere Malheur's equivocal glance as she turned her eyes for the last time upon the innocent girl, doomed to receive the midnight visit from La Corriveau.

"There is death in the pot!" the crone muttered as she went out,-- "La Corriveau comes not here on her own errand either! That girl is too beautiful to live, and to some one her death is worth gold! It will go hard, but La Corriveau shall share with me the reward of the work of tomorrow night!"

In the long gallery she encountered Dame Tremblay "ready to eat her up," as she told La Corriveau afterwards, in the eagerness of her curiosity to learn the result of her interview with Caroline.

Mere Malheur was wary, and accustomed to fence with words. It was necessary to tell a long tale of circumstances to Dame Tremblay, but not necessary nor desirable to tell the truth. The old crone therefore, as soon as she had seated herself in the easy chair of the housekeeper and refreshed herself by twice accepting the dame's pressing invitation to tea and cognac, related with uplifted hands and shaking head a narrative of bold lies regarding what had really passed during her interview with Caroline.

"But who is she, Mere Malheur? Did she tell you her name? Did she show you her palm?"

"Both, dame, both! She is a girl of Ville Marie who has run away from her parents for love of the gallant Intendant, and is in hiding from them. They wanted to put her into the Convent to cure her of love. The Convent always cures love, dame, beyond the power of philtres to revive it!" and the old crone laughed inwardly to herself, as if she doubted her own saying.

Eager to return to La Corriveau with the account of her successful interview with Caroline, she bade Dame Tremblay a hasty but formal farewell, and with her crutched stick in her hand trudged stoutly back to the city.

Mere Malheur, while the sun was yet high, reached her cottage under the rock, where La

Corriveau was eagerly expecting her at the window. The moment she entered, the masculine voice of La Corriveau was heard asking loudly,--

"Have you seen her, Mere Malheur? Did you give her the letter? Never mind your hat! tell me before you take it off!" The old crone was tugging at the strings, and La Corriveau came to help her.

"Yes! she took your letter," replied she, impatiently. "She took my story like spring water. Go at the stroke of twelve to-morrow night and she will let you in, Dame Dodier; but will she let you out again, eh?" The crone stood with her hat in her hand, and looked with a wicked glance at La Corriveau.

"If she will let me in, I shall let myself out, Mere Malheur," replied Corriveau in a low tone. "But why do you ask that?"

"Because I read mischief in your eye and see it twitching in your thumb, and you do not ask me to share your secret! Is it so bad as that, Dame Dodier?"

"Pshaw! you are sharing it! wait and you will see your share of it! But tell me, Mere Malheur, how does she look, this mysterious lady of the Chateau?" La Corriveau sat down, and placed her long, thin hand on the arm of the old crone.

"Like one doomed to die, because she is too good to live. Sorrow is a bad pasture for a young creature like her to feed on, Dame Dodier!" was the answer, but it did not change a muscle on the face of La Corriveau.

"Ay! but there are worse pastures than sorrow for young creatures like her, and she has found one of them," she replied, coldly.

"Well! as we make our bed so must we lie on it, Dame Dodier,--that is what I always tell the silly young things who come to me asking their fortunes; and the proverb pleases them. They always think the bridal bed must be soft and well made, at any rate."

"They are fools! better make their death-bed than their bridal bed! But I must see this piece of perfection of yours to-morrow night, dame! The Intendant returns in two days, and he might remove her. Did she tell you about him?"

"No! Bigot is a devil more powerful than the one we serve, dame. I fear him!"

"Tut! I fear neither devil nor man. It was to be at the hour of twelve! Did you not say at the hour of twelve, Mere Malheur?"

"Yes! go in by the vaulted passage and knock at the secret door. She will admit you. But what will you do with her, Dame Dodier? Is she doomed? Could you not be gentle with her, dame?"

There was a fall in the voice of Mere Malheur,--an intonation partly due to fear of consequences, partly to a fibre of pity which--dry and disused--something in the look of Caroline had stirred like a dead leaf quivering in the wind.

"Tut! has she melted your old dry heart to pity, Mere Malheur! Ha, ha! who would have thought that! and yet I remember she made a soft fool of me for a minute in the wood of St. Valier!" La Corriveau spoke in a hard tone, as if in reproving Mere Malheur she was also reproving herself.

"She is unlike any other woman I ever saw," replied the crone, ashamed of her unwonted sympathy. "The devil is clean out of her as he is out of a church."

"You are a fool, Mere Malheur! Out of a church, quotha!" and La Corriveau laughed a loud laugh; "why I go to church myself, and whisper my prayers backwards to keep on terms with the devil, who stands nodding behind the altar to every one of my petitions,--that is more than some people get in return for their prayers," added she.

"I pray backwards in church too, dame, but I could never get sight of him there, as you do: something always blinds me!" and the two old sinners laughed together at the thought of the devil's litanies they recited in the church.

"But how to get to Beaumanoir? I shall have to walk, as you did, Mere Malheur. It is a vile road, and I must take the byway through the forest. It were worth my life to be seen on this visit," said La Corriveau, conning on her fingers the difficulties of the by- path, which she was well acquainted with, however.

"There is a moon after nine, by which hour you can reach the wood of Beaumanoir," observed the crone. "Are you sure you know the way, Dame Dodier?"

"As well as the way into my gown! I know an Indian canotier who will ferry me across to Beauport, and say nothing. I dare not allow that prying knave, Jean Le Nocher, or his sharp wife, to mark my movements."

"Well thought of, Dame Dodier; you are of a craft and subtlety to cheat Satan himself at a game of hide and seek!" The crone looked with genuine admiration, almost worship, at La Corriveau as she said this; "but I doubt he will find both of us at last, dame, when we have got into our last corner."

"Well, vogue la galere!" exclaimed La Corriveau, starting up. "Let it go as it will! I shall walk to Beaumanoir, and I shall fancy I wear golden garters and silver slippers to make the way easy and pleasant. But you must be hungry, Mere, with your long tramp. I have a supper prepared for you, so come and eat in the devil's name, or I shall be tempted to say grace in nomine Domini, and choke you."

The two women went to a small table and sat down to a plentiful meal of such things as formed the dainties of persons of their rank of life. Upon the table stood the dish of sweetmeats which the thievish maidservant had brought to Mere Malheur with the groom's story of the conversation between Bigot and Varin, a story which, could Angelique have got hold of it, would have stopped at once her frightful plot to kill the unhappy Caroline.

"I were a fool to tell her that story of the groom's," muttered La Corriveau to herself, "and spoil the fairest experiment of the aqua tofana ever made, and ruin my own fortune too! I know a trick worth two of that," and she laughed inwardly to herself a laugh which was repeated in hell and made merry the ghosts of Beatrice Spara, Exili, and La Voisin.

All next day La Corriveau kept closely to the house, but she found means to communicate to Angelique her intention to visit Beaumanoir that night.

The news was grateful, yet strangely moving to Angelique; she trembled and turned pale, not for truth, but for doubt and dread of possible failure or discovery.

She sent by an unknown hand to the house of Mere Malheur a little basket containing a bouquet of roses so beautiful and fragrant that they might have been plucked in the garden of Eden.

La Corriveau carried the basket into an inner chamber, a small room, the window of which never saw the sun, but opened against the close, overhanging rock, which was so near that it might be touched by the hand. The dark, damp wall of the cliff shed a gloomy obscurity in the room even at midday.

The small black eyes of La Corriveau glittered like poniards as she opened the basket, and taking out the bouquet, found attached to it by a ribbon a silken purse containing a number of glittering pieces of gold. She pressed the coins to her cheek, and even put them between her lips to taste their sweetness, for money she loved beyond all things. The passion of her soul was avarice; her wickedness took its direction from the love of money, and scrupled at no iniquity for the sake of it.

She placed the purse carefully in her bosom, and took up the roses, regarding them with a strange look of admiration as she muttered, "They are beautiful and they are sweet! men would call them innocent! they are like her who sent them, fair without as yet; like her who is to receive them, fair within." She stood reflecting for a few moments, and exclaimed as she laid the bouquet upon the table,--

"Angelique des Meloises, you send your gold and your roses to me because you believe me to be a worse demon than yourself, but you are worthy to be crowned tonight with these roses as queen of hell and mistress of all the witches that ever met in Grand Sabbat at the palace of Galienne, where Satan sits on a throne of gold!"

La Corriveau looked out of the window and saw a corner of the rock lit up with the last ray of the setting sun. She knew it was time to prepare for her journey. She loosened her long black and gray elfin locks, and let them fall dishevelled over her shoulders. Her thin, cruel lips were drawn to a rigid line, and her eyes were filled with red fire as she drew the casket of ebony out of her bosom and opened it with a reverential touch, as a devotee would touch a shrine of relics. She took out a small, gilded vial of antique shape, containing a clear, bright liquid, which, as she shook it up, seemed filled with a million sparks of fire.

Before drawing the glass stopper of the vial, La Corriveau folded a handkerchief carefully over her mouth and nostrils, to avoid inhaling the volatile essence of its poisonous contents. Then, holding the bouquet with one hand at arm's length, she sprinkled the glowing roses with the transparent liquid from the vial which she held in the other hand, repeating, in a low, harsh tone, the formula of an ancient incantation, which was one of the secrets imparted to Antonio Exili by the terrible Beatrice Spara.

La Corriveau repeated by rote, as she had learned from her mother, the ill-omened words, hardly knowing their meaning, beyond that they were something very potent, and very wicked, which had been handed down through generations of poisoners and witches from the times of heathen Rome:

"'Hecaten voco!
Voco Tisiphonem!
Spargens avernales aquas,
Te morti devoveo, te diris ago!'"

The terrible drops of the aqua tofana glittered like dew on the glowing flowers, taking away in a moment all their fragrance, while leaving all their beauty unimpaired. The poison sank into the very hearts of the roses, whence it breathed death from every petal and every leaf, leaving them fair as she who had sent them, but fatal to the approach of lip or nostril, fit emblems of her unpitying hate and remorseless jealousy.

La Corriveau wrapped the bouquet in a medicated paper of silver tissue, which prevented the escape of the volatile death, and replacing the roses carefully in the basket, prepared for her departure to Beaumanoir.

## Chapter XL: Quoth the Raven, "Nevermore!"

It was the eve of St. Michael. A quiet autumnal night brooded over the forest of Beaumanoir. The moon, in her wane, had risen late, and struggled feebly among the broken clouds that were gathering slowly in the east, indicative of a storm. She shed a dim light through the glades and thickets, just enough to discover a path where the dark figure of a woman made her way swiftly and cautiously towards the Chateau of the Intendant.

She was dressed in the ordinary costume of a peasant-woman, and carried a small basket on her arm, which, had she opened it, would have been found to contain a candle and a bouquet of fresh roses carefully covered with a paper of silver tissue,--nothing more. An honest peasant-woman would have had a rosary in her basket, but this was no honest-peasant woman, and she had none.

The forest was very still,--it was steeped in quietness. The rustling of the dry leaves under the feet of the woman was all she heard, except when the low sighing of the wind, the sharp bark of a fox, or the shriek of an owl, broke the silence for a moment, and all was again still.

The woman looked watchfully around as she glided onwards. The path was known to her, but not so familiarly as to prevent the necessity of stopping every few minutes to look about her and make sure she was right.

It was long since she had travelled that way, and she was looking for a landmark--a gray stone that stood somewhere not far from where she was, and near which she knew that there was a footpath that led, not directly to the Chateau, but to the old deserted watch-tower of Beaumanoir.

That stone marked a spot not to be forgotten by her, for it was the memorial of a deed of wickedness now only remembered by herself and by God. La Corriveau cared nothing for the recollection. It was not terrible to her, and God made no sign; but in his great book of account, of which the life of every man and woman forms a page, it was written down and remembered.

On the secret tablets of our memory, which is the book of our life, every thought, word, and deed, good or evil, is written down indelibly and forever; and the invisible pen goes on writing day after day, hour after hour, minute after minute, every thought, even the idlest, every fancy the most evanescent: nothing is left out of our book of life which will be our record in judgment! When that book is opened and no secrets are hid, what son or daughter of Adam is there who will not need to say, "God be merciful?"

La Corriveau came suddenly upon the gray stone. It startled her, for its rude contour, standing up in the pale moonlight, put on the appearance of a woman. She thought she was discovered, and she heard a noise; but another glance reassured her. She recognized the stone, and the noise she had heard was only the scurrying of a hare among the dry leaves.

The habitans held this spot to be haunted by the wailing spirit of a woman in a gray robe, who had been poisoned by a jealous lover. La Corriveau gave him sweatmeats of the manna of St. Nicholas, which the woman ate from his hand, and fell dead at his feet in this trysting-place, where they met for the last time. The man fled to the forest, haunted by a remorseful conscience, and died a retributive death: he fell sick, and was devoured by wolves. La Corriveau alone of mortals held the terrible secret.

La Corriveau gave a low laugh as she saw the pale outline of the woman resolve itself into the gray stone. "The dead come not again!" muttered she, "and if they do she will soon have a companion to share her midnight walks round the Chateau!" La Corriveau had no conscience; she knew not remorse, and would probably have felt no great fear had that pale spirit really appeared at that moment, to tax her with wicked complicity in her murder.

The clock of the Chateau struck twelve. Its reverberations sounded far into the night as La Corriveau emerged stealthily out of the forest, crouching on the shady side of the high garden hedges, until she reached the old watch-tower, which stood like a dead sentinel at his post on the flank of the Chateau.

There was an open doorway, on each side of which lay a heap of fallen stones. This was the entrance into a square room, dark and yawning as a cavern. It was traversed by one streak of moonshine, which struggled through a grated window set in the thick wall.

La Corriveau stood for a few moments looking intently into the gloomy ruin; then, casting a sharp glance behind her, she entered. Tired with her long walk through the forest, she flung herself upon a stone seat to rest, and to collect her thoughts for the execution of her terrible mission.

The dogs of the Chateau barked vehemently, as if the very air bore some ominous taint; but La Corriveau knew she was safe: they were shut up in the courtyard, and could not trace her to the tower. A harsh voice or two and the sound of whips presently silenced the barking dogs, and all was still again.

She had got into the tower unseen and unheard. "They say there is an eye that sees everything," muttered she, "and an ear that hears our very thoughts. If God sees and hears, he does nothing to prevent me from accomplishing my end; and he will not interfere to- night! No, not for all the prayers she may utter, which will not be many more! God if there be one--lets La Corriveau live, and will let the lady of Beaumanoir die!"

There was a winding stair of stone, narrow and tortuous, in one corner of the tower. It led upwards to the roof and downwards to a deep vault which was arched and groined. Its heavy, rough columns supported the tower above, and divided the vaults beneath. These vaults had formerly served as magazines for provisions and stores for the use of the occupants of the Chateau upon occasions when they had to retire for safety from a sudden irruption of Iroquois.

La Corriveau, after a short rest, got up with a quick, impatient movement. She went over to an arched doorway upon which her eyes had been fixed for several minutes. "The way is down there," she muttered; "now for a light!"

She found the entrance to the stair open; she passed in, closing the door behind her so that the glimmer might not be seen by any chance stroller, and struck a light. The reputation which the tower had of being haunted made the servants very shy of entering it, even in the day-time; and the man was considered bold indeed who came near it after dark.

With her candle in her hand, La Corriveau descended slowly into the gloomy vault. It was a large cavern of stone, a very habitation of darkness, which seemed to swallow up the feeble light she carried. It was divided into three portions, separated by rough columns.

A spring of water trickled in and trickled out of a great stone trough, ever full and overflowing with a soft, tinkling sound, like a clepsydra measuring the movements of eternity. The cool, fresh, living water diffused throughout the vaults an even, mild temperature the year round. The gardeners of the Chateau took advantage of this, and used the vault as a favorite storeroom for their crops of fruit and vegetables for winter use in the Chateau.

La Corriveau went resolutely forward, as one who knew what she sought and where to find it, and presently stood in front of a recess containing a wooden panel similar to that in the Chateau, and movable in the same manner. She considered it for some moments, muttering to herself as she held aloft the candle to inspect it closely and find the spring by which it was moved.

La Corriveau had been carefully instructed by Mere Malheur in every point regarding the mechanism of this door. She had no difficulty in finding the secret of its working. A slight touch sufficed when the right place was known. She pressed it hard with her hand; the panel swung open, and behind it gaped a dark, narrow passage leading to the secret chamber of Caroline.

She entered without hesitation, knowing whither it led. It was damp and stifling. Her candle burned dimmer and dimmer in the impure air of the long shut-up passage. There were, however, no other obstacles in her way. The passage was unincumbered; but the low arch, scarcely over her own height, seemed to press down upon her as she passed along, as if to prevent her progress. The fearless, wicked heart bore her up,--nothing worse than herself could meet her; and she felt neither fear at what lay before her nor remorse at what was behind.

The distance to be traversed was not far, although it seemed to her impatience to be interminable. Mere Malheur, with her light heels, could once run through it in a minute, to a tryst in the old tower. La Corriveau was thrice that time in groping her way along it before she came to a heavy, iron-ribbed door set in a deep arch, which marked the end of the passage.

That black, forbidding door was the dividing of light from darkness, of good from evil, of innocence from guilt. On one side of it, in a chamber of light, sat a fair girl, confiding, generous, and deceived only through her excess of every virtue; on the other, wickedness, fell and artful, was approaching with stealthy footsteps through an unseen way, and stood with hand upraised to knock, but incapable of entering in unless that unsuspecting girl removed the bar.

As the hour of midnight approached, one sound after another died away in the Chateau. Caroline, who had sat counting the hours and watching the spectral moon as it flickered among the drifting clouds, withdrew from the window with a trembling step, like one going to her doom.

She descended to the secret chamber, where she had appointed to meet her strange visitor and hear from strange lips the story that would be told her.

She attired herself with care, as a woman will in every extremity of life. Her dark raven hair was simply arranged, and fell in thick masses over her neck and shoulders. She put on a robe of soft, snow-white texture, and by an impulse she yielded to, but could not explain, bound her waist with a black sash, like a strain of mourning in a song of innocence. She wore no ornaments save a ring, the love-gift of Bigot, which she never parted with, but wore with a morbid anticipation that its promises would one day be fulfilled. She clung to it as a talisman that would yet conjure away her sorrows; and it did! but alas! in a way little anticipated by the constant girl! A blast from hell was at hand to sweep away her young life, and with it all her earthly troubles.

She took up a guitar mechanically, as it were, and as her fingers wandered over the strings, a bar or two of the strain, sad as the sigh of a broken heart, suggested an old ditty she had loved formerly, when her heart was full of sunshine and happiness, when her fancy used to indulge in the luxury of melancholic musings, as every happy, sensitive, and imaginative girl will do as a counterpoise to her high-wrought feelings.

In a low voice, sweet and plaintive as the breathings of an Aeolian harp, Caroline sang her Minne-song:--

"'A linnet sat upon a thorn
At evening chime.
Its sweet refrain fell like the rain
Of summer-time.
Of summer-time when roses bloomed,
And bright above

A rainbow spanned my fairy-land
   Of hope and love!
Of hope and love! O linnet, cease
   Thy mocking theme!
I ne'er picked up the golden cup
   In all my dream!
In all my dream I missed the prize
   Should have been mine;
And dreams won't die! though fain would I,
   And make no sign!'"

The lamps burned brightly, shedding a cheerful light upon the landscapes and figures woven into the tapestry behind which was concealed the black door that was to admit La Corriveau.

It was oppressively still. Caroline listened with mouth and ears for some sound of approaching footsteps until her heart beat like the swift stroke of a hammer, as it sent the blood throbbing through her temples with a rush that almost overpowered her.

She was alone, and lonely beyond expression. Down in these thick foundations no sound penetrated to break the terrible monotony of the silence around her, except the dull, solemn voice of the bell striking the hour of midnight.

Caroline had passed a sleepless night after the visit of Mere Malheur, sometimes tossing on her solitary couch, Sometimes starting up in terror. She rose and threw herself despairingly upon her knees, calling on Christ to pardon her, and on the Mother of Mercies to plead for her, sinner that she was, whose hour of shame and punishment had come!

The mysterious letter brought by Mere Malheur, announcing that her place of concealment was to be searched by the Governor, excited her liveliest apprehensions. But that faded into nothingness in comparison with the absolute terror that seized her at the thoughts of the speedy arrival of her father in the Colony.

Caroline, overwhelmed with a sense of shame and contrition, pictured to herself in darkest colors the anger of her father at the dishonor she had brought upon his unsullied name.

She sat down, she rose up, she walked her solitary chamber, and knelt passionately on the floor, covering her face with her hands, crying to the Madonna for pity and protection.

Poor self-accuser! The hardest and most merciless wretch who ever threw stones at a woman was pitiful in comparison with Caroline's inexorable condemnation of herself.

Yet her fear was not on her own account. She could have kissed her father's hand and submitted humbly to death itself, if he chose to inflict it; but she trembled most at the thought of a meeting between the fiery Baron and the haughty Intendant. One or the other, or both of them, she felt instinctively, must die, should the Baron discover that Bigot had been the cause of the ruin of his idolized child. She trembled for both, and prayed God that she might die in their stead and the secret of her shame never be known to her fond father.

A dull sound, like footsteps shuffling in the dark passage behind the arras, struck her ear; she knew her strange visitant was come. She started up, clasping her hands hard together as she listened, wondering who and what like she might be. She suspected no harm,-- for who could desire to harm her who had never injured a living being? Yet there she stood on the one side of that black door of doom, while the calamity of her life stood on the other side like a tigress ready to spring through.

A low knock, twice repeated on the thick door behind the arras, drew her at once to her feet. She trembled violently as she lifted up the tapestry; something rushed through her mind telling her not to do it. Happy had it been for her never to have opened that fatal door!

She hesitated for a moment, but the thought of her father and the impending search of the Chateau flashed suddenly upon her mind. The visitant, whoever she might be, professed to be a friend, and could, she thought, have no motive to harm her.

Caroline, with a sudden impulse, pushed aside the fastening of the door, and uttering the words, "Dieu! protege moi!" stood face to face with La Corriveau.

The bright lamp shone full on the tall figure of the strange visitor, and Caroline, whose fears had anticipated some uncouth sight of terror, was surprised to see only a woman dressed in the simple garb of a peasant, with a little basket on her arm, enter quietly through the secret door.

The eyes of La Corriveau glared for a moment with fiendish curiosity upon the young girl who stood before her like one of God's angels. She measured her from head to foot, noted every fold of her white robe, every flexure of her graceful form, and drank in the whole beauty and innocence of her aspect with a feeling of innate spite at aught so fair and good. On her thin, cruel lips there played a smile as the secret thought hovered over them in an unspoken whisper,--"She will make a pretty corpse! Brinvilliers and La Voisin never mingled drink for a fairer victim than I will crown with roses to-night!"

Caroline retreated a few steps, frightened and trembling, as she encountered the glittering eyes and sinister smile of La Corriveau. The woman observed it, and instantly changed her mien to one more natural and sympathetic; for she comprehended fully the need of disarming suspicion and of winning the confidence of her victim to enable her more surely to destroy her.

Caroline, reassured by a second glance at her visitor, thought she had been mistaken in her first impression. The peasant's dress, the harmless basket, the quiet manner assumed by La Corriveau as she stood in a respectful attitude as if waiting to be spoken to, banished all fears from the mind of Caroline, and left her only curious to know the issue of this mysterious visit.

## Chapter XLI: A Deed Without a Name

Caroline, profoundly agitated, rested her hands on the back of a chair for support, and regarded La Corriveau for some moments without speaking. She tried to frame a question of some introductory kind, but could not. But the pent-up feelings came out at last in a gush straight from the heart.

"Did you write this?" said she, falteringly, to La Corriveau, and holding out the letter so mysteriously placed in her hand by Mere Malheur. "Oh, tell me, is it true?"

La Corriveau did not reply except by a sign of assent, and standing upright waited for further question.

Caroline looked at her again wonderingly. That a simple peasant-woman could have indited such a letter, or could have known aught respecting her father, seemed incredible.

"In heaven's name, tell me who and what you are!" exclaimed she. "I never saw you before!"

"You have seen me before!" replied La Corriveau quietly.

Caroline looked at her amazedly, but did not recognize her. La Corriveau continued, "Your father is the Baron de St. Castin, and you, lady, would rather die than endure that he should find you in the Chateau of Beaumanoir. Ask me not how I know these things; you will not deny their truth; as for myself, I pretend not to be other than I seem."

"Your dress is that of a peasant-woman, but your language is not the language of one. You are a lady in disguise visiting me in this strange fashion!" said Caroline, puzzled more than ever. Her thoughts at this instant reverted to the Intendant. "Why do you come here in this secret manner?" asked she.

"I do not appear other than I am," replied La Corriveau evasively, "and I come in this secret manner because I could get access to you in no other way."

"You said that I had seen you before; I have no knowledge or recollection of it," remarked Caroline, looking fixedly at her.

"Yes, you saw me once in the wood of St. Valier. Do you remember the peasant-woman who was gathering mandrakes when you passed with your Indian guides, and who gave you milk to refresh you on the way?"

This seemed like a revelation to Caroline; she remembered the incident and the woman. La Corriveau had carefully put on the same dress she had worn that day.

"I do recollect!" replied Caroline, as a feeling of confidence welled up like a living spring within her. She offered La Corriveau her hand. "I thank you gratefully," said she; "you were indeed kind to me that day in the forest, and I am sure you must mean kindly by me now."

La Corriveau took the offered hand, but did not press it. She could not for the life of her, for she had not heart to return the pressure of a human hand. She saw her advantage, however, and kept it through the rest of the brief interview.

"I mean you kindly, lady," replied she, softening her harsh voice as much as she could to a tone of sympathy, "and I come to help you out of your trouble."

For a moment that cruel smile played on her thin lips again, but she instantly repressed it. "I am only a peasant-woman," repeated she again, "but I bring you a little gift in my basket to show my good-will." She put her hand in her basket, but did not withdraw it at the moment, as Caroline, thinking little of gifts but only of her father, exclaimed,--

"I am sure you mean well, but you have more important things to tell me of than a gift. Your letter spoke of my father. What, in God's name, have you to tell me of my father?"

La Corriveau withdrew her hand from the basket and replied, "He is on his way to New France in search of you. He knows you are here, lady."

"In Beaumanoir? Oh, it cannot be! No one knows I am here!" exclaimed Caroline, clasping her hands in an impulse of alarm.

"Yes, more than you suppose, lady, else how did I know? Your father comes with the King's letters to take you hence and return with you to Acadia or to France." La Corriveau placed her hand in her basket, but withdrew it again. It was not yet time.

"God help me, then!" exclaimed Caroline, shrinking with terror. "But the Intendant; what said you of the Intendant?"

"He is ordered de par le Roi to give you up to your father, and he will do so if you be not taken away sooner by the Governor."

Caroline was nigh fainting at these words. "Sooner! how sooner?" asked she, faintly.

"The Governor has received orders from the King to search Beaumanoir from roof to foundation-stone, and he may come to-morrow, lady, and find you here."

The words of La Corriveau struck like sharp arrows into the soul of the hapless girl.

"God help me, then!" exclaimed she, clasping her hands in agony. "Oh, that I were dead and buried where only my Judge could find me at the last day, for I have no hope, no claim upon man's mercy! The world will stone me, dead or living, and alas! I deserve my fate. It is not hard to die, but it is hard to bear the shame which will not die with me!"

She cast her eyes despairingly upward as she uttered this, and did not see the bitter smile return to the lips of La Corriveau, who stood upright, cold and immovable before her, with fingers twitching nervously, like the claws of a fury, in her little basket, while she whispered to herself, "Is it time, is it time?" but she took not out the bouquet yet.

Caroline came still nearer, with a sudden change of thought, and clutching the dress of La Corriveau, cried out, "O woman, is this all true? How can you know all this to be true of me, and you a stranger?"

"I know it of a certainty, and I am come to help you. I may not tell you by whom I know it; perhaps the Intendant himself has sent me," replied La Corriveau, with a sudden prompting of the spirit of evil who stood beside her. "The Intendant will hide you from this search, if there be a sure place of concealment in New France."

The reply sent a ray of hope across the mind of the agonized girl. She bounded with a sense of deliverance. It seemed so natural that Bigot, so deeply concerned in her concealment, should have sent this peasant woman to take her away, that she could not reflect at the moment how unlikely it was, nor could she, in her excitement, read the lie upon the cold face of La Corriveau.

She seized the explanation with the grasp of despair, as a sailor seizes the one plank which the waves have washed within his reach, when all else has sunk in the seas around him.

"Bigot sent you?" exclaimed Caroline, raising her hands, while her pale face was suddenly suffused with a flush of joy. "Bigot sent you to conduct me hence to a sure place of concealment? Oh, blessed messenger! I believe you now." Her excited imagination outflew even the inventions of La Corriveau. "Bigot has heard of my peril, and sent you here at midnight to take me away to your forest home until this search be over. Is it not so? Francois Bigot did not forget me in my danger, even while he was away!"

"Yes, lady, the Intendant sent me to conduct you to St. Valier, to hide you there in a sure retreat until the search be over," replied La Corriveau, calmly eyeing her from head to foot.

"It is like him! He is not unkind when left to himself. It is so like the Francois Bigot I once knew! But tell me, woman, what said he further? Did you see him, did you hear him? Tell me all he said to you."

"I saw him, lady, and heard him," replied La Corriveau, taking the bouquet in her fingers," but he said little more than I have told you. The Intendant is a stern man, and gives few words save commands to those of my condition. But he bade me convey to you a token of his love; you would know its meaning, he said. I have it safe, lady, in this basket,--shall I give it to you?"

"A token of his love, of Francois Bigot's love to me! Are you a woman and could delay giving it so long? Why gave you it not at first? I should not have doubted you then. Oh, give it to me, and be blessed as the welcomest messenger that ever came to Beaumanoir!"

La Corriveau held her hand a moment more in the basket. Her dark features turned a shade paler, although not a nerve quivered as she plucked out a parcel carefully wrapped in silver tissue. She slipped off the cover, and held at arm's length towards the eager, expectant girl, the fatal bouquet of roses, beautiful to see as the fairest that ever filled the lap of Flora.

Caroline clasped it with both hands, exclaiming in a voice of exultation, while every feature radiated with joy, "It is the gift of God, and the return of Francois's love! All will yet be well!"

She pressed the glowing flowers to her lips with passionate kisses, breathed once or twice their mortal poison, and suddenly throwing back her head with her dark eyes fixed on vacancy, but holding the fatal bouquet fast in her hands, fell dead at the feet of La Corriveau.

A weird laugh, terrible and unsuppressed, rang around the walls of the secret chamber, where the lamps burned bright as ever; but the glowing pictures of the tapestry never changed a feature. Was it not strange that even those painted men should not have cried out at the sight of so pitiless a murder?

Caroline lay amid them all, the flush of joy still on her cheek, the smile not yet vanished from her lips. A pity for all the world, could it have seen her; but in that lonely chamber no eye pitied her.

But now a more cruel thing supervened. The sight of Caroline's lifeless form, instead of pity or remorse, roused all the innate furies that belonged to the execrable race of La Corriveau. The blood of generations of poisoners and assassins boiled and rioted in her veins. The spirits of Beatrice Spara and of La Voisin inspired her with new fury. She was at this moment like a pantheress that has brought down her prey and stands over it to rend it in pieces.

Caroline lay dead, dead beyond all doubt, never to be resuscitated, except in the resurrection of the just. La Corriveau bent over her and felt her heart; it was still. No sign of breath flickered on lip or nostril.

The poisoner knew she was dead, but something still woke her suspicions, as with a new thought she drew back and looked again at the beauteous form before her. Suddenly, as if to make assurance doubly sure, she plucked the sharp Italian stiletto from her bosom, and with a firm, heavy hand plunged it twice into the body of the lifeless girl. "If there be life there," she said, "it too shall die! La Corriveau leaves no work of hers half done!"

A faint trickle of blood in red threads ran down the snow-white vestment, and that was all! The heart had forever ceased to beat, and the blood to circulate. The golden bowl was broken and the silver cord of life loosed forever, and yet this last indignity would have recalled the soul of Caroline, could she have been conscious of it. But all was well with her now; not in the sense of the last joyous syllables she spoke in life, but in a higher, holier sense, as when God interprets our words, and not men, all was well with her now.

The gaunt, iron-visaged woman knelt down upon her knees, gazing with unshrinking eyes upon the face of her victim, as if curiously marking the effect of a successful experiment of the aqua tofana.

It was the first time she had ever dared to administer that subtle poison in the fashion of La Borgia.

"The aqua tofana does its work like a charm!" muttered she. "That vial was compounded by Beatrice Spara, and is worthy of her skill and more sure than her stiletto! I was frantic to use that weapon, for no purpose than to redden my hands with the work of a low bravo!"

A few drops of blood were on the hand of La Corriveau. She wiped them impatiently upon the garment of Caroline, where it left the impress of her fingers upon the snowy muslin. No pity for her pallid victim, who lay with open eyes looking dumbly upon her, no remorse for her act touched the stony heart of La Corriveau.

The clock of the Chateau struck one. The solitary stroke of the bell reverberated like an accusing voice through the house, but failed to awaken one sleeper to a discovery of the black tragedy that had just taken place under its roof.

That sound had often struck sadly upon the ear of Caroline, as she prolonged her vigil of prayer through the still watches of the night. Her ear was dull enough now to all earthly sound! But the toll of the bell reached the ear of La Corriveau, rousing her to the need of immediately effecting her escape, now that her task was done.

She sprang up and looked narrowly around the chamber. She marked with envious malignity the luxury and magnificence of its adornments. Upon a chair lay her own letter sent to Caroline by the hands of Mere Malheur. La Corriveau snatched it up. It was what she sought. She tore it in pieces and threw the fragments from her; but with a sudden thought, as if not daring to leave even the fragments upon the floor, she gathered them up hastily and put them in her basket with the bouquet of roses, which she wrested from the dead fingers of Caroline in order to carry it away and scatter the fatal flowers in the forest.

She pulled open the drawers of the escritoire to search for money, but finding none, was too wary to carry off aught else. The temptation lay sore upon her to carry away the ring from the finger of Caroline. She drew it off the pale wasted finger, but a cautious consideration restrained her. She put it on again, and would not take it.

"It would only lead to discovery!" muttered she. "I must take nothing but myself and what belongs to me away from Beaumanoir, and the sooner the better!"

La Corriveau, with her basket again upon her arm, turned to give one last look of fiendish satisfaction at the corpse, which lay like a dead angel slain in God's battle. The bright lamps were glaring full upon her still beautiful but sightless eyes, which, wide open, looked, even in death, reproachfully yet forgivingly upon their murderess.

Something startled La Corriveau in that look. She turned hastily away, and, relighting her candle, passed through the dark archway of the secret door, forgetting to close it after her, and retraced her steps along the stone passage until she came to the watch-tower, where she dashed out her light.

Creeping around the tower in the dim moonlight, she listened long and anxiously at door and window to discover if all was still about the Chateau. Not a sound was heard but the water of the little brook gurgling in its pebbly bed, which seemed to be all that was awake on this night of death.

La Corriveau emerged cautiously from the tower. She crept like a guilty thing under the shadow of the hedge, and got away unperceived by the same road she had come. She glided like a dark spectre through the forest of Beaumanoir, and returned to the city to tell Angelique des Meloises that the arms of the Intendant were now empty and ready to clasp her as his bride; that her rival was dead, and she had put herself under bonds forever to La Corriveau as the price of innocent blood.

La Corriveau reached the city in the gray of the morning; a thick fog lay like a winding-sheet upon the face of nature. The broad river, the lofty rocks, every object, great and small, was hidden from view.

To the intense satisfaction of La Corriveau, the fog concealed her return to the house of Mere Malheur, whence, after a brief repose, and with a command to the old crone to ask no questions yet, she sallied forth again to carry to Angelique the welcome news that her rival was dead.

No one observed La Corriveau as she passed, in her peasant dress, through the misty streets, which did not admit of an object being discerned ten paces off.

Angelique was up. She had not gone to bed that night, and sat feverishly on the watch, expecting the arrival of La Corriveau.

She had counted the minutes of the silent hours of the night as they passed by her in a terrible panorama. She pictured to her imagination the successive scenes of the tragedy which was being accomplished at Beaumanoir.

The hour of midnight culminated over her head, and looking out of her window at the black, distant hills, in the recesses of which she knew lay the Chateau, her agitation grew intense. She knew at that hour La Corriveau must be in the presence of her victim. Would she kill her? Was she about it now? The thought fastened on Angelique like a wild beast, and would not let go. She thought of the Intendant, and was filled with hope; she thought of the crime of murder and shrunk now that it was being done.

It was in this mood she waited and watched for the return of her bloody messenger. She heard the cautious foot on the stone steps. She knew by a sure instinct whose it was, and rushed down to admit her.

They met at the door, and without a word spoken, one eager glance of Angelique at the dark face of La Corriveau drank in the whole fatal story. Caroline de St. Castin was dead! Her rival in the love of the Intendant was beyond all power of rivalry now! The lofty doors of ambitious hope stood open--what! to admit the queen of beauty and of society? No! but a murderess, who would be forever haunted with the fear of justice! It seemed at this moment as if the lights had all gone out in the palaces and royal halls where her imagination had so long run riot, and she saw only dark shadows, and heard inarticulate sounds of strange voices babbling in her ear. It was the unspoken words of her own troubled thoughts and the terrors newly awakened in her soul!

Angelique seized the hand of La Corriveau, not without a shudder. She drew her hastily up to her chamber and thrust her into a chair. Placing both hands upon the shoulders of La Corriveau, she looked wildly in her face, exclaiming in a half exultant, half piteous tone, "Is it done? Is it really done? I read it in your eyes! I know you have done the deed! Oh, La Corriveau!"

The grim countenance of the woman relaxed into a half smile of scorn and surprise at the unexpected weakness which she instantly noted in Angelique's manner.

"Yes, it is done!" replied she, coldly, "and it is well done! But, by the manna of St. Nicholas!" exclaimed she, starting from the chair and drawing her gaunt figure up to its full height, while her black eyes shot daggers, "you look, Mademoiselle, as if you repented its being done. Do you?"

"Yes! No! No, not now!" replied Angelique, touched as with a hot iron. "I will not repent now it is done! that were folly, needless, dangerous, now it is done! But is she dead? Did you wait to see if she were really dead? People look dead sometimes and are not! Tell me truly, and conceal nothing!"

"La Corriveau does not her work by halves, Mademoiselle, neither do you; only you talk of repentance after it is done, I do not! That is all the difference! Be satisfied; the lady of Beaumanoir is dead! I made doubly sure of that, and deserve a double reward from you!"

"Reward! You shall have all you crave! But what a secret between you and me!" Angelique looked at La Corriveau as if this thought now struck her for the first time. She was in this woman's power. She shivered from head to foot. "Your reward for this night's work is here," faltered she, placing her hand over a small box. She did not touch it, it seemed as if it would burn her. It was heavy with pieces of gold. "They are uncounted," continued she. "Take it, it is all yours!"

La Corriveau snatched the box off the table and held it to her bosom. Angelique continued, in a monotonous tone, as one conning a lesson by rote,--"Use it prudently. Do not seem to the world to be suddenly rich: it might be inquired into. I have thought of everything during the past night, and I remember I had to tell you that when I gave you the gold. Use it prudently! Something else, too, I was to tell you, but I think not of it at this moment."

"Thanks, and no thanks, Mademoiselle!" replied La Corriveau, in a hard tone. "Thanks for the reward so fully earned. No thanks for your faint heart that robs me of my well-earned meed of applause for a work done so artistically and perfectly that La Brinvilliers, or La Borgia herself, might envy me, a humble paysanne of St. Valier!"

La Corriveau looked proudly up as she said this, for she felt herself to be anything but a humble paysanne. She nourished a secret pride in her heart over the perfect success of her devilish skill in poisoning.

"I give you whatever praise you desire," replied Angelique, mechanically. "But you have not told me how it was done. Sit down again," continued she, with a touch of her imperative manner, "and tell me all and every incident of what you have done."

"You will not like to hear it. Better be content with the knowledge that your rival was a dangerous and a beautiful one." Angelique looked up at this. "Better be content to know that she is dead, without asking any more."

"No, you shall tell me everything. I cannot rest unless I know all!"

"Nor after you do know all will you rest!" replied La Corriveau slightingly, for she despised the evident trepidation of Angelique.

"No matter! you shall tell me. I am calm now." Angelique made a great effort to appear calm while she listened to the tale of tragedy in which she had played so deep a part.

La Corriveau, observing that the gust of passion was blown over, sat down in the chair opposite Angelique, and placing one hand on the knee of her listener, as if to hold her fast, began the terrible recital.

She gave Angelique a graphic, minute, and not untrue account of all she had done at Beaumanoir, dwelling with fierce unction on the marvellous and sudden effects of the aqua tofana, not sparing one detail of the beauty and innocent looks of her victim; and repeating, with a mocking laugh, the deceit she had practised upon her with regard to the bouquet as a gift from the Intendant.

Angelique listened to the terrible tale, drinking it in with eyes, mouth, and ears. Her countenance changed to a mask of ugliness, wonderful in one by nature so fair to see. Cloud followed cloud over her face and eyes as the dread recital went on, and her imagination accompanied it with vivid pictures of every phase of the diabolical crime.

When La Corriveau described the presentation of the bouquet as a gift of Bigot, and the deadly sudden effect which followed its joyous acceptance, the thoughts of Caroline in her white robe, stricken as by a thunderbolt, shook Angelique with terrible emotion. But when La Corriveau, coldly and with a bitter spite at her softness, described with a sudden gesticulation and eyes piercing her through and through, the strokes of the poniard upon the lifeless body of her victim, Angelique sprang up, clasped her hands together, and, with a cry of woe, fell senseless upon the floor.

"She is useless now," said La Corriveau, rising and spurning Angelique with her foot. "I deemed she had courage to equal her wickedness. She is but a woman after all,--doomed to be the slave of some man through life, while aspiring to command all men! It is not of such flesh that La Corriveau is made!"

La Corriveau stood a few moments, reflecting what was best to be done.

All things considered, she decided to leave Angelique to come to of herself, while she made the best of her way back to the house of Mere Malheur, with the intention, which she carried out, of returning to St. Valier with her infamous reward that very day.

# Chapter XLII: "Let's Talk of Graves and Worms and Epitaphs"

About the hour that La Corriveau emerged from the gloomy woods of Beauport, on her return to the city, the night of the murder of Caroline, two horsemen were battering at full speed on the highway that led to Charlebourg. Their dark figures were irrecognizable in the dim moonlight. They rode fast and silent, like men having important business before them, which demanded haste; business which both fully understood and cared not now to talk about.

And so it was. Bigot and Cadet, after the exchange of a few words about the hour of midnight, suddenly left the wine, the dice, and the gay company at the Palace, and mounting their horses, rode, unattended by groom or valet, in the direction of Beaumanoir.

Bigot, under the mask of gaiety and indifference, had felt no little alarm at the tenor of the royal despatch, and at the letter of the Marquise de Pompadour concerning Caroline de St. Castin.

The proximate arrival of Caroline's father in the Colony was a circumstance ominous of trouble. The Baron was no trifler, and would as soon choke a prince as a beggar, to revenge an insult to his personal honor or the honor of his house.

Bigot cared little for that, however. The Intendant was no coward, and could brazen a thing out with any man alive. But there was one thing which he knew he could not brazen out or fight out, or do anything but miserably fail in, should it come to the question. He had boldly and wilfully lied at the Governor's council-table-- sitting as the King's councillor among gentlemen of honor--when he declared that he knew not the hiding-place of Caroline de St. Castin. It would cover him with eternal disgrace, as a gentleman, to be detected in such a flagrant falsehood. It would ruin him as a courtier in the favor of the great Marquise should she discover that, in spite of his denials of the fact, he had harbored and concealed the missing lady in his own chateau.

Bigot was sorely perplexed over this turn of affairs. He uttered a thousand curses upon all concerned in it, excepting upon Caroline herself, for although vexed at her coming to him at all, he could not find it in his heart to curse her. But cursing or blessing availed nothing now. Time was pressing, and he must act.

That Caroline would be sought after in every nook and corner of the land, he knew full well, from the character of La Corne St. Luc and of her father. His own chateau would not be spared in the general search, and he doubted if the secret chamber would remain a secret from the keen eyes of these men. He surmised that others knew of its existence besides himself: old servitors, and women who had passed in and out of it in times gone by. Dame Tremblay, who did know of it, was not to be trusted in a great temptation. She was in heart the Charming Josephine still, and could be bribed or seduced by any one who bid high enough for her.

Bigot had no trust whatever in human nature. He felt he had no guarantee against a discovery, farther than interest or fear barred the door against inquiry. He could not rely for a moment upon the inviolability of his own house. La Corne St. Luc would demand to search, and he, bound by his declarations of non-complicity in the abduction of Caroline, could offer no reason for refusal without arousing instant suspicion; and La Corne was too sagacious not to fasten upon the remotest trace of Caroline and follow it up to a complete discovery.

She could not, therefore, remain longer in the Chateau--this was absolute; and he must, at whatever cost and whatever risk, remove her to a fresh place of concealment, until the storm blew over, or some other means of escape from the present difficulty offered themselves in the chapter of accidents.

In accordance with this design, Bigot, under pretence of business, had gone off the very next day after the meeting of the Governor's Council, in the direction of the Three Rivers, to arrange with a band of Montagnais, whom he could rely upon, for the reception of Caroline, in the disguise of an Indian girl, with instructions to remove their wigwams immediately and take her off with them to the wild, remote valley of the St. Maurice.

The old Indian chief, eager to oblige the Intendant, had assented willingly to his proposal, promising the gentlest treatment of the lady, and a silent tongue concerning her.

Bigot was impressive in his commands upon these points, and the chief pledged his faith upon them, delighted beyond measure by the promise of an ample supply of powder, blankets, and provisions for his tribe, while the Intendant added an abundance of all such delicacies as could be forwarded, for the use and comfort of the lady.

To carry out this scheme without observation, Bigot needed the help of a trusty friend, one whom he could thoroughly rely upon, to convey Caroline secretly away from Beaumanoir, and place her in the keeping of the Montagnais, as well as to see to the further execution of his wishes for her concealment and good treatment.

Bigot had many friends,--men living on his bounty, who ought only to have been too happy to obey his slightest wishes,--friends bound to him by disgraceful secrets, and common interests, and pleasures. But he could trust none of them with the secret of Caroline de St. Castin.

He felt a new and unwonted delicacy in regard to her. Her name was dear to him, her fame even was becoming dearer. To his own surprise it troubled him now as it had never troubled him before. He would not have her name defiled in the mouths of such men as drank his wine daily and nightly, and disputed the existence of any virtue in woman.

Bigot ground his teeth as he muttered to himself that they might make a mock of whatever other women they pleased. He himself could out-do them all in coarse ribaldry of the sex, but they should not make a mock and flash obscene jests at the mention of Caroline de St. Castin! They should never learn her name. He could not trust one of them with the secret of her removal. And yet some one of them must perforce be entrusted with it!

He conned over the names of his associates one by one, and one by one condemned them all as unworthy of confidence in a matter where treachery might possibly be made more profitable than fidelity. Bigot was false himself to the heart's core, and believed in no man's truth.

He was an acute judge of men. He read their motives, their bad ones especially, with the accuracy of a Mephistopheles, and with the same cold contempt for every trace of virtue.

Varin was a cunning knave, he said, ambitious of the support of the Church; communing with his aunt, the Superior of the Ursulines, whom he deceived, and who was not without hope of himself one day rising to be Intendant. He would place no such secret in the keeping of Varin!

Penisault was a sordid dog. He would cheat the Montagnais of his gifts, and so discontent them with their charge. He had neither courage nor spirit for an adventure. He was in his right place superintending the counters of the Friponne. He despised Penisault, while glad to use him in the basest offices of the Grand Company.

Le Mercier was a pickthank, angling after the favor of La Pompadour,--a pretentious knave, as hollow as one of his own mortars. He suspected him of being a spy of hers upon himself. Le Mercier would be only too glad to send La Pompadour red-hot information of such an important secret as that of Caroline, and she would reward it as good service to the King and to herself.

Deschenaux was incapable of keeping a secret of any kind when he got drunk, or in a passion, which was every day. His rapacity reached to the very altar. He would rob a church, and was one who would rather take by force than favor. He would strike a Montagnais who would ask for a blanket more than he had cheated him with. He would not trust Deschenaux.

De Pean, the quiet fox, was wanted to look after that desperate gallant, Le Gardeur de Repentigny, who was still in the Palace, and must be kept there by all the seductions of wine, dice, and women, until we have done with him. De Pean was the meanest spirit of them all. "He would kiss my foot in the morning and sell me at night for a handful of silver," said Bigot. Villains, every one of them, who would not scruple to advance their own interests with La Pompadour by his betrayal in telling her such a secret as that of Caroline's.

De Repentigny had honor and truth in him, and could be entirely trusted if he promised to serve a friend. But Bigot dared not name to him a matter of this kind. He would spurn it, drunk as he was. He was still in all his instincts a gentleman and a soldier. He could only be used by Bigot through an abuse of his noblest qualities. He dared not broach such a scheme to Le Gardeur de Repentigny!

Among his associates there was but one who, in spite of his brutal manners and coarse speech, perhaps because of these, Bigot would trust as a friend, to help him in a serious emergency like the present.

Cadet, the Commissary General of New France, was faithful to Bigot as a fierce bull-dog to his master. Cadet was no hypocrite, nay, he may have appeared to be worse than in reality he was. He was bold and outspoken, rapacious of other men's goods, and as prodigal of his own. Clever withal, fearless, and fit for any bold enterprise. He ever allowed himself to be guided by the superior intellect of Bigot, whom he regarded as the prince of good fellows, and swore by him, profanely enough, on all occasions, as the shrewdest head and the quickest hand to turn over money in New France.

Bigot could trust Cadet. He had only to whisper a few words in his ear to see him jump up from the table where he was playing cards, dash his stakes with a sweep of his hand into the lap of his antagonist, a gift or a forfeit, he cared not which, for not finishing the game. In three minutes Cadet was booted, with his heavy riding-whip in his hand ready to mount his horse and accompany Bigot "to Beaumanoir or to hell," he said, "if he wanted to go there."

In the short space of time, while the grooms saddled their horses, Bigot drew Cadet aside and explained to him the situation of his affairs, informing him, in a few words, who the lady was who lived in such retirement in the Chateau, and of his denial of the fact before the Council and Governor. He told him of the letters of the King and of La Pompadour respecting Caroline, and of the necessity of removing her at once far out of reach before the actual search for her was begun.

Cadet's cynical eyes flashed in genuine sympathy with Bigot, and he laid his heavy hand upon his shoulder and uttered a frank exclamation of admiration at his ruse to cheat La Pompadour and La Galissoniere both.

"By St. Picot!" said he, "I would rather go without dinner for a month than you should not have asked me, Bigot, to help you out of this scrape. What if you did lie to that fly-catching beggar at the Castle of St. Louis, who has not conscience to take a dishonest stiver from a cheating Albany Dutchman! Where was the harm in it? Better lie to him than tell the truth to La Pompadour about that girl! Egad! Madame Fish would serve you as the Iroquois served my fat clerk at Chouagen--make roast meat of you--if she knew it! Such a pother about a girl! Damn the women, always, I say, Bigot! A man is never out of hot water when he has to do with them!"

Striking Bigot's hand hard with his own, he promised; wet or dry, through flood or fire, to ride with him to Beaumanoir, and take the girl, or lady,--he begged the Intendant's pardon,--and by such ways as he alone knew he would, in two days, place her safely among the Montagnais, and order them at once, without an hour's delay, to pull up stakes and remove their wigwams to the tuque of the St. Maurice, where Satan himself could not find her. And the girl might remain there for seven years without ever being heard tell of by any white person in the Colony.

Bigot and Cadet rode rapidly forward until they came to the dark forest, where the faint outline of road, barely visible, would have perplexed Bigot to have kept it alone in the night. But Cadet was born in Charlebourg; he knew every path, glade, and dingle in the forest of Beaumanoir, and rode on without drawing bridle.

Bigot, in his fiery eagerness, had hitherto ridden foremost. Cadet now led the way, dashing under the boughs of the great trees that overhung the road. The tramp of their horses woke the echoes of the woods. But they were not long in reaching the park of Beaumanoir.

They saw before them the tall chimney-stacks and the high roofs and the white walls of the Chateau, looking spectral enough in the wan moonlight,--ghostly, silent, and ominous. One light only was visible in the porter's lodge; all else was dark, cold, and sepulchral.

The watchful old porter at the gate was instantly on foot to see who came at that hour, and was surprised enough at sight of his master and the Sieur Cadet, without retinue or even a groom to accompany them.

They dismounted and tied their horses outside the gate. "Run to the Chateau, Marcele, without making the least noise," said Bigot. "Call none of the servants, but rap gently at the door of Dame Tremblay. Bid her rise instantly, without waking any one. Say the Intendant desires to see her. I expect guests from the city."

The porter returned with the information that Dame Tremblay had got up and was ready to receive his Excellency.

Bidding old Marcele take care of the horses, they walked across the lawn to the Chateau, at the door of which stood Dame Tremblay, hastily dressed, courtesying and trembling at this sudden summons to receive the Intendant and Sieur Cadet.

"Good night, dame!" said Bigot, in a low tone, "conduct us instantly to the grand gallery."

"Oh, your Excellency!" replied the dame, courtesying, "I am your humble servant at all times, day and night, as it is my duty and my pleasure to serve my master!"

"Well, then!" returned Bigot, impatiently, "let us go in and make no noise."

The three, Dame Tremblay leading the way with a candle in each hand, passed up the broad stair and into the gallery communicating with the apartments of Caroline. The dame set her candles on the table and stood with her hands across her apron in a submissive attitude, waiting the orders of her master.

"Dame!" said he, "I think you are a faithful servant. I have trusted you with much. Can I trust you with a greater matter still?"

"Oh, your Excellency! I would die to serve so noble and generous a master! It is a servant's duty!"

"Few servants think so, nor do I! But you have been faithful to your charge respecting this poor lady within, have you not, dame?" Bigot looked as if his eyes searched her very vitals.

"O Lord! O Lord!" thought the dame, turning pale. "He has heard about the visit of that cursed Mere Malheur, and he has come to hang me up for it in the gallery!" She stammered out in reply, "Oh, yes! I have been faithful to my charge about the lady, your Excellency! I have not failed wilfully or negligently in any one point, I assure you! I have been at once careful and kind to her, as you bade me to be, your Excellency! Indeed, I could not be otherwise to a live angel in the house like her!"

"So I believe, dame!" said Bigot, in a tone of approval that quite lifted her heart. This spontaneous praise of Caroline touched him somewhat. "You have done well! Now can you keep another secret, dame?"

"A secret! and entrusted to me by your Excellency!" replied she, in a voice of wonder at such a question. "The marble statue in the grotto is not closer than I am, your Excellency. I was always too fond of a secret ever to part with it! When I was the Charming Josephine of Lake Beauport I never told, even in confession, who they were who--"

"Tut! I will trust you, dame, better than I would have trusted the Charming Josephine! If all tales be true, you were a gay girl, dame, and a handsome one in those days, I have heard!" added the Intendant, with well-planned flattery.

A smile and a look of intelligence between the dame and Bigot followed this sally, while Cadet had much to do to keep in one of the hearty horse-laughs he used to indulge in, and which would have roused the whole Chateau.

The flattery of the Intendant quite captivated the dame. "I will go through fire and water to serve your Excellency, if you want me," said she. "What shall I do to oblige your Excellency?"

"Well, dame, you must know then that the Sieur Cadet and I have come to remove that dear lady from the Chateau to another place, where it is needful for her to go for the present time; and if you are questioned about her, mind you are to say she never was here, and you know nothing of her!"

"I will not only say it," replied the dame with promptness, "I will swear it until I am black in the face if you command me, your Excellency! Poor, dear lady! may I not ask where she is going?"

"No, she will be all right! I will tell you in due time. It is needful for people to change sometimes, you know, dame! You comprehend that! You had to manage matters discreetly when you were the Charming Josephine. I dare say you had to change, too, sometimes! Every woman has an intrigue once, at least, in her lifetime, and wants a change. But this lady is not clever like the Charming Josephine, therefore we have to be clever for her!"

The dame laughed prudently yet knowingly at this, while Bigot continued, "Now you understand all! Go to her chamber, dame. Present our compliments with our regrets for disturbing her at this hour. Tell her that the Intendant and the Sieur Cadet desire to see her on important business."

Dame Tremblay, with a broad smile all over her countenance at her master's jocular allusions to the Charming Josephine, left at once to carry her message to the chamber of Caroline.

She passed out, while the two gentlemen waited in the gallery, Bigot anxious but not doubtful of his influence to persuade the gentle girl to leave the Chateau, Cadet coolly resolved that she must go, whether she liked it or no. He would banish every woman in New France to the tuque of the St. Maurice had he the power, in order to rid himself and Bigot of the eternal mischief and trouble of them!

Neither Bigot nor Cadet spoke for some minutes after the departure of the dame. They listened to her footsteps as the sound of them died away in the distant rooms, where one door opened after another as she passed on to the secret chamber.

"She is now at the door of Caroline!" thought Bigot, as his imagination followed Dame Tremblay on her errand. "She is now speaking to her. I know Caroline will make no delay to admit us." Cadet on his side was very quiet and careless of aught save to take the girl and get her safely away before daybreak.

A few moments of heavy silence and expectation passed over them. The howl of a distant watch-dog was heard, and all was again still. The low, monotonous ticking of the great clock at the head of the gallery made the silence still more oppressive. It seemed to be measuring off eternity, not time.

The hour, the circumstance, the brooding stillness, waited for a cry of murder to ring through the Chateau, waking its sleepers and bidding them come and see the fearful tragedy that lay in the secret chamber.

But no cry came. Fortunately for Bigot it did not! The discovery of Caroline de St. Castin under such circumstances would have closed his career in New France, and ruined him forever in the favor of the Court.

Dame Tremblay returned to her master and Cadet with the information "that the lady was not in her bedchamber, but had gone down, as was her wont, in the still hours of the night, to pray in her oratory in the secret chamber, where she wished never to be disturbed.

"Well, dame," replied Bigot, "you may retire to your own room. I will go down to the secret chamber myself. These vigils are killing her, poor girl! If your lady should be missing in the morning, remember, dame, that you make no remark of it; she is going away to- night with me and the Sieur Cadet and will return soon again; so be discreet and keep your tongue well between your teeth, which, I am glad to observe," remarked he with a smile, "are still sound and white as ivory."

Bigot wished by such flattery to secure her fidelity, and he fully succeeded. The compliment to her teeth was more agreeable than would have been a purse of money. It caught the dame with a hook there was no escape from.

Dame Tremblay courtesied very low, and smiled very broadly to show her really good teeth, of which she was extravagantly vain. She assured the Intendant of her perfect discretion and obedience to all his commands.

"Trust to me, your Excellency," said she with a profound courtesy. "I never deceived a gentleman yet, except the Sieur Tremblay, and he, good man, was none! When I was the Charming Josephine, and all the gay gallants of the city used to flatter and spoil me, I never deceived one of them, never! I knew that all is vanity in this world, but my eyes and teeth were considered very fine in those days, your Excellency."

"And are yet, dame. Zounds! Lake Beauport has had nothing to equal them since you retired from business as a beauty. But mind my orders, dame! keep quiet and you will please me. Good-night, dame!"

"Good-night, your Excellency! Good-night, your Honor!" replied she, flushed with gratified vanity. She left Bigot vowing to herself that he was the finest gentleman and the best judge of a woman in New France! The Sieur Cadet she could not like. He never looked pleasant on a woman, as a gentleman ought to do!

The dame left them to themselves, and went off trippingly in high spirits to her own chamber, where she instantly ran to the mirror to look at her teeth, and made faces in the glass like a foolish girl in her teens.

Bigot, out of a feeling of delicacy not usual with him, bid Cadet wait in the anteroom while he went forward to the secret chamber of Caroline. "The sudden presence of a stranger might alarm her," he said.

He descended the stair and knocked softly at the door, calling in a low tone, "Caroline! Caroline!" No answer came. He wondered at that, for her quick ear used always to catch the first sound of his footsteps while yet afar off.

He knocked louder, and called again her name. Alas! he might have called forever! That voice would never make her heart flutter again or her eyes brighten at his footstep, that sounded sweeter than any music as she waited and watched for him, always ready to meet him at the door.

Bigot anticipated something wrong, and with a hasty hand pushed open the door of the secret chamber and went in. A blaze of light filled his eyes. A white form lay upon the floor. He saw it and he saw nothing else! She lay there with her unclosed eyes looking as the dead only look at the living. One hand was pressed to her bosom, the other was stretched out, holding the broken stem and a few green leaves of the fatal bouquet which La Corriveau had not wholly plucked from her grasp.

Bigot stood for a moment stricken dumb and transfixed with horror, then sprang forward and knelt over her with a cry of agony. He thought she might have fallen in a swoon. He touched her pale forehead, her lips, her hands. He felt her heart, it did not beat; he lifted her head to his bosom, it fell like the flower of a lily broken on its stem, and he knew she was dead. He saw the red streaks of blood on her snowy robe, and he knew she was murdered.

A long cry like the wail of a man in torture burst from him. It woke more than one sleeper in the distant chambers of the Chateau, making them start upon their pillows to listen for another cry, but none came. Bigot was a man of iron; he retained self-possession enough to recollect the danger of rousing the house.

He smothered his cries in suffocating sobs, but they reached the ear of Cadet, who, foreboding some terrible catastrophe, rushed into the room where the secret door stood open. The light glared up the stair. He ran down and saw the Intendant on his knees, holding in his arms the half raised form of a woman which he kissed and called by name like a man distraught with grief and despair.

Cadet's coarse and immovable nature stood him in good stead at this moment. He saw at a glance what had happened. The girl they had come to bear away was dead! How? He knew not; but the Intendant must not be suffered to make an alarm. There was danger of discovery on all sides now, and the necessity of concealment was a thousand times greater than ever. There was no time to question, but instant help was needed. In amaze at the spectacle before him, Cadet instantly flew to the assistance of the Intendant.

He approached Bigot without speaking a word, although his great eyes expressed a look of sympathy never seen there before. He disengaged the dead form of Caroline tenderly from the embrace of Bigot, and laid it gently upon the floor, and lifting Bigot up in his stout arms, whispered hoarsely in his ear, "Keep still, Bigot! keep still! not one word! make no alarm! This is a dreadful business, but we must go to another room to consider calmly, calmly, mind, what it means and what is to be done."

"Oh, Cadet! Cadet!" moaned the Intendant, still resting on his shoulder, "she is dead! dead! when I just wanted her to live! I have been hard with women, but if there was one I loved it was she who lies dead before me! Who, who has done this bloody deed to me?"

"Who has done it to her, you mean! You are not killed yet, old friend, but will live to revenge this horrid business!" answered Cadet with rough sympathy.

"I would give my life to restore hers!" replied Bigot despairingly. "Oh, Cadet, you never knew what was in my heart about this girl, and how I had resolved to make her reparation for the evil I had done her!"

"Well, I can guess what was in your heart, Bigot. Come, old friend, you are getting more calm, you can walk now. Let us go upstairs to consider what is to be done about it. Damn the women! They are man's torment whether alive or dead!"

Bigot was too much absorbed in his own tumultuous feelings to notice Cadet's remark.

He allowed himself to be led without resistance to another room, out of sight of the murdered girl, in whose presence Cadet knew calm council was impossible.

Cadet seated Bigot on a couch and, sitting beside him, bade him be a man and not a fool. He tried to rouse Bigot by irritating him, thinking, in his coarse way, that that was better than to be maudlin over him, as he considered it, with vain expressions of sympathy.

"I would not give way so," said he, "for all the women in and out of Paradise! and you are a man, Bigot! Remember you have brought me here, and you have to take me safely back again, out of this den of murder."

"Yes, Cadet," replied Bigot, rousing himself up at the sharp tone of his friend. "I must think of your safety; I care little for my own at this moment. Think for me."

"Well, then, I will think for you, and I think this, Bigot, that if the Governor finds out this assassination, done in your house, and that you and I have been here at this hour of night with the murdered girl, by God! he will say we have alone done it, and the world will believe it! So rouse up, I for one do not want to be taxed with the murder of a woman, and still less to be hung innocently for the death of one. I would not risk my little finger for all the women alive, let alone my neck for a dead one!"

The suggestion was like a sharp probe in his flesh. It touched Bigot to the quick. He started up on his feet. "You are right, Cadet, it only wants that accusation to make me go mad! But my head is not my own yet! I can think of nothing but her lying there, dead in her loveliness and in her love! Tell me what to do, and I will do it."

"Ay, now you talk reasonably. Now you are coming to yourself, Bigot. We came to remove her alive from here, did we not? We must now remove her dead. She cannot remain where she is at the risk of certain discovery to-morrow."

"No, the secret chamber would not hide such a secret as that," replied Bigot, recovering his self-possession. "But how to remove her? We cannot carry her forth without discovery." Bigot's practical intellect was waking up to the danger of leaving the murdered girl in the Chateau.

Cadet rose and paced the room with rapid strides, rubbing his forehead, and twitching his mustache violently. "I will tell you what we have got to do, Bigot! Par Dieu! we must bury her where she is, down there in the vaulted chamber."

"What, bury her?" Bigot looked at him with intense surprise.

"Yes, we must bury her in that very chamber, Bigot. We must cover up somebody's damnable work to avert suspicion from ourselves! A pretty task for you and me, Bigot! Par Dieu! I could laugh like a horse, if I were not afraid of being overheard."

"But who is to dig a grave for her? surely not you or I," replied Bigot with a look of dismay.

"Yes, gentlemen as we are, you and I must do it, Bigot. Zounds! I learned to dig and delve when I was a stripling at Charlebourg, and in the trenches at Louisbourg, and I have not yet forgotten the knack of it! But where to get spades, Bigot; you are master here and ought to know."

"I, how should I know? It is terrible, Cadet, to bury her as if we had murdered her! Is there no other way?"

"None. We are in a cahot and must get our cariole out of it as best we can! I see plainly we two shall be taxed with this murder, Bigot, if we let it be discovered! Besides, utter ruin awaits you from La Pompadour if she finds out you ever had this girl at Beaumanoir in keeping. Come! time for parley is past; where shall we find spades? We must to work, Bigot!"

A sudden thought lighted up the eyes of the Intendant, who saw the force of Cadet's suggestion, strange and repulsive as it was. "I think I know," said he; "the gardeners keep their tools in the old tower, and we can get there by the secret passage and return."

"Bravo!" exclaimed Cadet, encouragingly, "come, show the way, and we will get the tools in a trice! I always heard there was a private way underground to the old tower. It never stood its master in better stead than now; perhaps never worse if it has let in the murderer of this poor girl of yours."

Bigot rose up, very faint and weak; Cadet took his arm to support him, and bidding him be firm and not give way again at sight of her dead body, led him back to the chamber of death. "Let us first look around a moment," said he, "to find, if possible, some trace of the hellish assassins."

The lamps burned brightly, shedding a glare of light over every object in the secret chamber.

Cadet looked narrowly round, but found little trace of the murderers. The drawers of the escritoire stood open, with their contents in great disorder, a circumstance which at once suggested robbers. Cadet pointed it out to Bigot with the question:

"Kept she much money, Bigot?"

"None that I know of. She asked for none, poor girl! I gave her none, though I would have given her the King's treasury had she wished for it."

"But she might have had money when she came, Bigot," continued Cadet, not doubting but robbery had been the motive for the murder.

"It may be, I never questioned her," replied Bigot; "she never spoke of money; alas! all the money in the world was as dross in her estimation. Other things than money occupied her pure thoughts."

"Well, it looks like robbers: they have ransacked the drawers and carried off all she had, were it much or little," remarked Cadet, still continuing his search.

"But why kill her? Oh, Cadet, why kill the gentle girl, who would have given every jewel in her possession for the bare asking?"

"Nay, I cannot guess," said Cadet. "It looks like robbers, but the mystery is beyond my wit to explain. What are you doing, Bigot?"

Bigot had knelt down by the side of Caroline; he lifted her hand first to his lips, then towards Cadet, to show him the stalk of a rose from which the flower had been broken, and which she held with a grip so hard that it could not be loosened from her dead fingers.

The two men looked long and earnestly at it, but failed to make a conjecture even why the flower had been plucked from that broken stalk and carried away, for it was not to be seen in the room.

The fragment of a letter lay under a chair. It was a part of that which La Corriveau had torn up and missed to gather up again with the rest. Cadet picked it up and thrust it into his pocket.

The blood streaks upon her white robe and the visible stabs of a fine poniard riveted their attention. That that was the cause of her death they doubted not, but the mute eloquence of her wounds spoke only to the heat. It gave no explanation to the intellect. The whole tragedy seemed wrapped in inexplicable mystery.

"They have covered their track up well!" remarked Cadet. "Hey! but what have we here?" Bigot started up at the exclamation. The door of the secret passage stood open. La Corriveau had not closed it after her when making her escape. "Here is where the assassins have found entrance and exit! Egad! More people know the secret of your Chateau than you think, Bigot!"

They sprang forward, and each seizing a lamp, the two men rushed into the narrow passage. It was dark and still as the catacombs. No trace of anything to the purpose could they perceive in the vaulted subterranean way to the turret.

They speedily came to the other end; the secret door there stood open also. They ascended the stairs in the tower, but could see no trace of the murderers. "It is useless to search further for them at this time," remarked Cadet, "perhaps not safe at any time, but I would give my best horse to lay hands on the assassins at this moment."

Gardeners' tools lay around the room. "Here," exclaimed Cadet, "is what is equally germane to the matter, and we have no time to lose."

He seized a couple of spades and a bar of iron, and bidding Bigot go before him with the lights, they returned to the chamber of death.

"Now for work! This sad business must be done well, and done quickly!" exclaimed Cadet. "You shall see that I have not forgotten how to dig, Bigot!"

Cadet threw off his coat, and setting to work, pulled up the thick carpet from one side of the chamber. The floor was covered with broad, smooth flags, one of which he attacked with the iron bar, raised the flagstone and turned it over; another easily followed, and very soon a space in the dry brown earth was exposed, large enough to make a grave.

Bigot looked at him in a sort of dream. "I cannot do it, Cadet! I cannot dig her grave!" and he threw down the spade which he had taken feebly in his hand.

"No matter, Bigot! I will do it! Indeed, you would only be in my way. Sit down while I dig, old friend. Par Dieu! this is nice work for the Commissary General of New France, with the Royal Intendant overseeing him!"

Bigot sat down and looked forlornly on while Cadet with the arms of a Hercules dug and dug, throwing out the earth without stopping for the space of a quarter of an hour, until he had made a grave large and deep enough to contain the body of the hapless girl.

"That will do!" cried he, leaping out of the pit. "Our funeral arrangements must be of the briefest, Bigot! So come help me to shroud this poor girl."

Cadet found a sheet of linen and some fine blankets upon a couch in the secret chamber. He spread them out upon the floor, and motioned to Bigot without speaking. The two men lifted Caroline tenderly and reverently upon the sheet. They gazed at her for a minute in solemn silence, before shrouding her fair face and slender form in their last winding-sheet. Bigot was overpowered with his feelings, yet strove to master them, as he gulped down the rising in his throat which at times almost strangled him.

Cadet, eager to get his painful task over, took from the slender finger of Caroline a ring, a love-gift of Bigot, and from her neck a golden locket containing his portrait and a lock of his hair. A rosary hung at her waist; this Cadet also detached, as a precious relic to be given to the Intendant by and by. There was one thread of silk woven into the coarse hempen nature of Cadet.

Bigot stooped down and gave her pale lips and eyes, which he had tenderly closed, a last despairing kiss, before veiling her face with the winding-sheet as she lay, white as a snow-drift, and as cold. They wrapped her softly in the blankets, and without a word spoken, lowered the still, lissom body into its rude grave.

The awful silence was only broken by the spasmodic sobs of Bigot as he leaned over the grave to look his last upon the form of the fair girl whom he had betrayed and brought to this untimely end. "Mea culpa! Mea maxima culpa!" said he, beating his breast. "Oh, Cadet, we are burying her like a dog! I cannot, I cannot do it!"

The Intendant's feelings overcame him again, and he rushed from the chamber, while Cadet, glad of his absence for a few moments, hastily filled up the grave and, replacing with much care the stone slabs over it, swept the debris into the passage and spread the carpet again smoothly over the floor. Every trace of the dreadful deed was obliterated in the chamber of murder.

Cadet, acutely thinking of everything at this supreme moment, would leave no ground of suspicion for Dame Tremblay when she came in the morning to visit the chamber. She should think that her lady had gone away with her master as mysteriously as she had come, and no further inquiry would be made after her. In this Cadet was right.

It was necessary for Cadet and Bigot now to depart by the secret passage to the tower. The deep-toned bell of the chateau struck three.

"We must now be gone, Bigot, and instantly," exclaimed Cadet. "Our night work is done! Let us see what day will bring forth! You must see to it to-morrow, Bigot, that no man or woman alive ever again enter this accursed chamber of death!"

Cadet fastened the secret door of the stair, and gathering up his spades and bar of iron, left the chamber with Bigot, who was passive as a child in his hands. The Intendant turned round and gave one last sorrowful look at the now darkened room as they left it. Cadet and he made their way back to the tower. They sallied out into the open air, which blew fresh and reviving upon their fevered faces after escaping from the stifling atmosphere below.

They proceeded at once towards their horses and mounted them, but Bigot felt deadly faint and halted under a tree while Cadet rode back to the porter's lodge and roused up old Marcele to give him some brandy, if he had any, "as of course he had," said Cadet. "Brandy was a gate-porter's inside livery, the lining of his laced coat which he always wore. Cadet assumed a levity which he did not really feel.

Marcele fortunately could oblige the Sieur Cadet. "He did line his livery a little, but lightly, as his Honor would see!" said he, bringing out a bottle of cognac and a drinking-cup.

"It is to keep us from catching cold!" continued Cadet in his peculiar way. "Is it good?" He placed the bottle to his lips and tasted it.

Marcele assured him it was good as gold.

"Right!" said Cadet, throwing Marcele a louis d'or. "I will take the bottle to the Intendant to keep him from catching cold too! Mind, Marcele, you keep your tongue still, or else--!" Cadet held up his whip, and bidding the porter "good-night!" rejoined Bigot.

Cadet had a crafty design in this proceeding. He wanted not to tell Marcele that a lady was accompanying them; also not to let him perceive that they left Beaumanoir without one. He feared that the old porter and Dame Tremblay might possibly compare notes together, and the housekeeper discover that Caroline had not left Beaumanoir with the Intendant.

Bigot sat faint and listless in his saddle when Cadet poured out a large cupful of brandy and offered it to him. He drank it eagerly. Cadet then filled and gulped down a large cupful himself, then gave another to the Intendant, and poured another and another for himself until, he said, he "began to feel warm and comfortable, and got the damnable taste of grave-digging out of his mouth!"

The heavy draught which Cadet forced the Intendant to take relieved him somewhat, but he groaned inwardly and would not speak. Cadet respected his mood, only bidding him ride fast. They spurred their horses, and rode swiftly, unobserved by any one, until they entered the gates of the Palace of the Intendant.

The arrival of the Intendant or the Sieur Cadet at the Palace at any untimely hour of the night excited no remark whatever, for it was the rule, rather than the exception with them both.

Dame Tremblay was not surprised next morning to find the chamber empty and the lady gone.

She shook her head sadly. "He is a wild gallant, is my master! No wilder ever came to Lake Beauport when I was the Charming Josephine and all the world ran after me. But I can keep a secret, and I will! This secret I must keep at any rate, by the Intendant's order, and I would rather die than be railed at by that fierce Sieur Cadet! I will keep the Intendant's secret safe as my teeth, which he praised so handsomely and so justly!"

The fact that Caroline never returned to the Chateau, and that the search for her was so long and so vainly carried on by La Corne St. Luc and the Baron de St. Castin, caused the dame to suspect at last that some foul play had been perpetrated, but she dared not speak openly.

The old woman's suspicions grew with age into certainties, when at last she chanced to talk with her old fellow servant, Marcele, the gatekeeper, and learned from him that Bigot and Cadet had left the Chateau alone on that fatal night. Dame Tremblay was more perplexed than ever. She talked, she knew not what, but her talk passed into the traditions of the habitans.

It became the popular belief that a beautiful woman, the mistress of the powerful Intendant Bigot, had been murdered and buried in the Chateau of Beaumanoir.

## Chapter XLIII: Silk Gloves over Bloody Hands

It was long before Angelique came to herself from the swoon in which she had been left lying on the floor by La Corriveau. Fortunately for her it was without discovery. None of the servants happened to come to her room during its continuance, else a weakness so strange to her usual hardihood would have become the city's talk before night, and set all its idle tongues conjecturing or inventing a reason for it. It would have reached the ears of Bigot, as every spray of gossip did, and set him thinking, too, more savagely than he was yet doing, as to the causes and occasions of the murder of Caroline.

All the way back to the Palace, Bigot had scarcely spoken a word to Cadet. His mind was in a tumult of the wildest conjectures, and his thoughts ran to and fro like hounds in a thick brake darting in every direction to find the scent of the game they were in search of. When they reached the Palace, Bigot, without speaking to any one, passed through the anterooms to his own apartment, and threw himself, dressed and booted as he was, upon a couch, where he lay like a man stricken down by a mace from some unseen hand.

Cadet had coarser ways of relieving himself from the late unusual strain upon his rough feelings. He went down to the billiard-room, and joining recklessly in the game that was still kept up by De Pean, Le Gardeur, and a number of wild associates, strove to drown all recollections of the past night at Beaumanoir by drinking and gambling with more than usual violence until far on in the day.

Bigot neither slept nor wished to sleep. The image of the murdered girl lying in her rude grave was ever before him, with a vividness so terrible that it seemed he could never sleep again. His thoughts ran round and round like a mill-wheel, without advancing a step towards a solution of the mystery of her death.

He summoned up his recollections of every man and woman he knew in the Colony, and asked himself regarding each one, the question, "Is it he who has done this? Is it she who has prompted it? And who could have had a motive, and who not, to perpetrate such a bloody deed?"

One image came again and again before his mind's eye as he reviewed the list of his friends and enemies. The figure of Angelique appeared and reappeared, intruding itself between every third or fourth personage which his memory called up, until his thoughts fixed upon her with the maddening inquiry, "Could Angelique des Meloises have been guilty of this terrible deed?"

He remembered her passionate denunciation of the lady of Beaumanoir, her fierce demand for her banishment by a lettre de cachet. He knew her ambition and recklessness, but still, versed as he was in all the ways of wickedness, and knowing the inexorable bitterness of envy, and the cruelty of jealousy in the female breast,--at least in such women as he had for the most part had experience of,--Bigot could hardly admit the thought that one so fair as Angelique, one who held him in a golden net of fascination, and to whom he had been more than once on the point of yielding, could have committed so great a crime.

He struggled with his thoughts like a man amid tossing waves, groping about in the dark for a plank to float upon, but could find none. Still, in spite of himself, in spite of his violent asseverations that "it was IMPOSSIBLE;" in spite of Cadet's plausible theory of robbers,--which Bigot at first seized upon as the likeliest explanation of the mystery,--the thought of Angelique ever returned back upon him like a fresh accusation.

He could not accuse her yet, though something told him he might have to do so at last. He grew angry at the ever-recurring thought of her, and turning his face to the wall, like a man trying to shut out the light, resolved to force disbelief in her guilt until clearer testimony than his own suspicions should convict her of the death of Caroline. And yet in his secret soul he dreaded a discovery that might turn out as he feared. But he pushed the black thoughts aside; he would wait and watch for what he feared to find.

The fact of Caroline's concealment at Beaumanoir, and her murder at the very moment when the search was about to be made for her, placed Bigot in the cruelest dilemma. Whatever his suspicions might be, he dared not, by word or sign, avow any knowledge of Caroline's presence, still less of her mysterious murder, in his Chateau. Her grave had been dug; she had been secretly buried out of human sight, and he was under bonds as for his very life never to let the dreadful mystery be discovered.

So Bigot lay on his couch, for once a weak and frightened man, registering vain vows of vengeance against persons unknown, vows which he knew at the moment were empty as bubbles, because he dared not move hand or foot in the matter to carry them out, or make open accusation against any one of the foul crime. What thoughts came to Bigot's subtle mind were best known to himself, but something was suggested by the mocking devil who was never far from him, and he caught and held fast the wicked suggestion with a bitter laugh. He then grew suddenly still and said to himself, "I will sleep on it!" and pillowing his head quietly, not in sleep, but in thoughts deeper than sleep, he lay till day.

Angelique, who had never in her life swooned before, felt, when she awoke, like one returning to life from death. She opened her eyes wondering where she was, and half remembering the things she had heard as things she had seen, looked anxiously around the room for La Corriveau. She rose up with a start when she saw she was gone, for Angelique recollected suddenly that La Corriveau now held the terrible secret which concerned her life and peace for evermore.

The thing she had so long wished for, and prayed for, was at last done! Her rival was out of the way! But she also felt that if the murder was discovered her own life was forfeit to the law, and the secret was in the keeping of the vilest of women.

A mountain, not of remorse, but of apprehension, overwhelmed her for a time. But Angelique's mind was too intensely selfish, hard, and superficial, to give way to the remorse of a deeper nature.

She was angry at her own cowardice, but she feared the suspicions of Bigot. There was ever something in his dark nature which she could not fathom, and deep and crafty as she knew herself to be, she feared that he was more deep and more crafty than herself.

What if he should discover her hand in this bloody business? The thought drove her frantic, until she fancied she repented of the deed.

Had it brought a certainty, this crime, then--why, then--she had found a compensation for the risk she was running, for the pain she was enduring, which she tried to believe was regret and pity for her victim. Her anxiety redoubled when it occurred to her that Bigot, remembering her passionate appeals to him for the removal of Caroline, might suspect her of the murder as the one alone having a palpable interest in it.

"But Bigot shall never believe it even if he suspect it!" exclaimed she at last, shaking off her fears. "I have made fools of many men for my pleasure, I can surely blind one for my safety; and, after all, whose fault is it but Bigot's? He would not grant me the lettre de cachet nor keep his promise for her removal. He even gave me her life! But he lied; he did not mean it. He loved her too well, and meant to deceive me and marry her, and I have deceived him and shall marry him, that is all!" and Angelique laughed a hysterical laugh, such as Dives in his torments may sometimes give way to.

"La Corriveau has betrayed her trust in one terrible point," continued she, "she promised a death so easy that all men would say the lady of Beaumanoir died of heartbreak only, or by God's visitation! A natural death! The foul witch has used her stiletto and made a murder of that which, without it, had been none! Bigot will know it, must know it even if he dare not reveal it! for how in the name of all the saints is it to be concealed?

"But, my God! this will never do!" continued she, starting up, "I look like very guilt!" She stared fiercely in the mirror at her hollow eyes, pale cheeks, and white lips. She scarcely recognized herself. Her bloom and brightness had vanished for the time.

"What if I have inhaled some of the poisoned odor of those cursed roses?" thought she, shuddering at the supposition; but she reassured herself that it could not be. "Still, my looks condemn me! The pale face of that dead girl is looking at me out of mine! Bigot, if he sees me, will not fail to read the secret in my looks."

She glanced at the clock: the morning was far advanced towards noon; visitors might soon arrive, Bigot himself might come, she dare not deny herself to him. She would deny herself to no one to-day! She would go everywhere and see everybody, and show the world, if talk of it should arise, that she was wholly innocent of that girl's blood.

She would wear her brightest looks, her gayest robe, her hat and feathers, the newest from Paris. She would ride out into the city,-- go to the Cathedral,--show herself to all her friends, and make every one say or think that Angelique des Meloises had not a care or trouble in the world.

She rang for Fanchon, impatient to commence her toilet, for when dressed she knew that she would feel like herself once more, cool and defiant. The touch of her armor of fashionable attire would restore her confidence in herself, and enable her to brave down any suspicion in the mind of the Intendant,--at any rate it was her only resource, and Angelique was not one to give up even a lost battle, let alone one half gained through the death of her rival.

Fanchon came in haste at the summons of her mistress. She had long waited to hear the bell, and began to fear she was sick or in one of those wild moods which had come over her occasionally since the night of her last interview with Le Gardeur.

The girl started at sight of the pale face and paler lips of her mistress. She uttered an exclamation of surprise, but Angelique, anticipating all questions, told her she was unwell, but would dress and take a ride out in the fresh air and sunshine to recruit.

"But had you not better see the physician, my Lady?--you do look so pale to-day, you are really not well!"

"No, but I will ride out;" and she added in her old way, "perhaps, Fanchon, I may meet some one who will be better company than the physician. Qui sait?" And she laughed with an appearance of gaiety which she was far from feeling, and which only half imposed on the quick-witted maid who waited upon her.

"Where is your aunt, Fanchon? When did you see Dame Dodier?" asked she, really anxious to learn what had become of La Corriveau.

"She returned home this morning, my Lady! I had not seen her for days before, but supposed she had already gone back to St. Valier,-- but Aunt Dodier is a strange woman, and tells no one her business."

"She has, perhaps, other lost jewels to look after besides mine," replied Angelique mechanically, yet feeling easier upon learning the departure of La Corriveau.

"Perhaps so, my Lady. I am glad she is gone home. I shall never wish to see her again."

"Why?" asked Angelique, sharply, wondering if Fanchon had conjectured anything of her aunt's business.

"They say she has dealings with that horrid Mere Malheur, and I believe it," replied Fanchon, with a shrug of disgust.

"Ah! do you think Mere Malheur knows her business or any of your aunt's secrets, Fanchon?" asked Angelique, thoroughly roused.

"I think she does, my Lady,--you cannot live in a chimney with another without both getting black alike, and Mere Malheur is a black witch as sure as my aunt is a white one," was Fanchon's reply.

"What said your aunt on leaving?" asked her mistress.

"I did not see her leave, my Lady; I only learned from Ambroise Gariepy that she had crossed the river this morning to return to St. Valier."

"And who is Ambroise Gariepy, Fanchon? You have a wide circle of acquaintance for a young girl, I think!" Angelique knew the dangers of gossiping too well not to fear Fanchon's imprudences.

"Yes, my Lady," replied Fanchon with affected simplicity, "Ambroise Gariepy keeps the Lion Vert and the ferry upon the south shore; he brings me news and sometimes a little present from the pack of the Basque pedlers,--he brought me this comb, my Lady!" Fanchon turned her head to show her mistress a superb comb in her thick black hair, and in her delight of talking of Ambroise Gariepy, the little inn of the ferry, and the cross that leaned like a failing memory over the grave of his former wife, Fanchon quite forgot to ease her mind further on the subject of La Corriveau, nor did Angelique resume the dangerous topic.

Fanchon's easy, shallow way of talking of her lover touched a sympathetic chord in the breast of her mistress. Grand passions were grand follies in Angelique's estimation, which she was less capable of appreciating than even her maid; but flirtation and coquetry, skin-deep only, she could understand, and relished beyond all other enjoyments. It was just now like medicine to her racking thoughts to listen to Fanchon's shallow gossip.

She had done what she had done, she reflected, and it could not be undone! why should she give way to regret, and lose the prize for which she had staked so heavily? She would not do it! No, par Dieu! She had thrown Le Gardeur to the fishes for the sake of the Intendant, and had done that other deed! She shied off from the thought of it as from an uncouth thing in the dark, and began to feel shame of her weakness at having fainted at the tale of La Corriveau.

The light talk of Fanchon while dressing the long golden hair of her mistress and assisting her to put on a new riding-dress and the plumed hat fresh from Paris, which she had not yet displayed in public, did much to restore her equanimity.

Her face had, however, not recovered from its strange pallor. Her eager maid, anxious for the looks of her mistress, insisted on a little rouge, which Angelique's natural bloom had never before needed. She submitted, for she intended to look her best to-day, she said. "Who knows whom I shall fall in with?"

"That is right, my Lady," exclaimed Fanchon admiringly, "no one could be dressed perfectly as you are and be sick! I pity the gentleman you meet to-day, that is all! There is murder in your eye, my Lady!"

Poor Fanchon believed she was only complimenting her mistress, and at other times her remark would only have called forth a joyous laugh; now the word seemed like a sharp knife: it cut, and Angelique did not laugh. She pushed her maid forcibly away from her, and was on the point of breaking out into some violent exclamation when, recalled by the amazed look of

Fanchon, she turned the subject adroitly, and asked, "Where is my brother?"

"Gone with the Chevalier de Pean to the Palace, my Lady!" replied Fanchon, trembling all over, and wondering how she had angered her mistress.

"How know you that, Fanchon?" asked Angelique, recovering her usual careless tone.

"I overheard them speaking together, my Lady. The Chevalier de Pean said that the Intendant was sick, and would see no one this morning."

"Yes, what then?" Angelique was struck with a sudden consciousness of danger in the wind. "Are you sure they said the Intendant was sick?" asked she.

"Yes, my Lady! and the Chevalier de Pean said that he was less sick than mad, and out of humor to a degree he had never seen him before!"

"Did they give a reason for it? that is, for the Intendant's sickness or madness?" Angelique's eyes were fixed keenly upon her maid, to draw out a full confession.

"None, my Lady, only the Chevalier des Meloises said he supposed it was the news from France which sat so ill on his stomach."

"And what then, Fanchon? you are so long of answering!" Angelique stamped her foot with impatience.

Fanchon looked up at the reproof so little merited, and replied quickly, "The Chevalier de Pean said it must be that, for he knew of nothing else. The gentlemen then went out and I heard no more."

Angelique was relieved by this turn of conversation. She felt certain that if Bigot discovered the murder he would not fail to reveal it to the Chevalier de Pean, who was understood to be the depository of all his secrets. She began to cheer up under the belief that Bigot would never dare accuse any one of a deed which would be the means of proclaiming his own falseness and duplicity towards the King and the Marquise de Pompadour.

"I have only to deny all knowledge of it," said she to herself, "swear to it if need be, and Bigot will not dare to go farther in the matter. Then will come my time to turn the tables upon him in a way he little expects! Pshaw!" continued she, glancing at her gay hat in the mirror, and with her own dainty fingers setting the feather more airily to her liking. "Bigot is bound fast enough to me now that she is gone! and when he discovers that I hold his secret he will not dare meddle with mine."

Angelique, measurably reassured and hopeful of success in her desperate venture, descended the steps of her mansion, and, gathering up her robes daintily, mounted her horse, which had long been chafing in the hands of her groom waiting for his mistress.

She bade the man remain at home until her return, and dashed off down the Rue St. Louis, drawing after her a hundred eyes of admiration and envy.

She would ride down to the Place d'Armes, she thought, where she knew that before she had skirted the length of the Castle wall half a dozen gallants would greet her with offers of escort, and drop any business they had in hand for the sake of a gallop by her side.

She had scarcely passed the Monastery of the Recollets when she was espied by the Sieur La Force, who, too, was as quickly discovered by her, as he loitered at the corner of the Rue St. Ann, to catch sight of any fair piece of mischief that might be abroad that day from her classes in the Convent of the Ursulines.

"Angelique is as fair a prize as any of them," thought La Force, as he saluted her with Parisian politeness, and with a request to be her escort in her ride through the city.

"My horse is at hand, and I shall esteem it such an honor," said La Force, smiling, "and such a profit too," added he; "my credit is low in a certain quarter, you know where!" and he laughingly pointed towards the Convent. "I desire to make HER jealous, for she has made me madly so, and no one can aid in an enterprise of that kind better than yourself, Mademoiselle des Meloises!"

"Or more willingly, Sieur La Force!" replied she, laughing. "But you overrate my powers, I fear."

"Oh, by no means," replied La Force; "there is not a lady in Quebec but feels in her heart that Angelique des Meloises can steal away her lover when and where she will. She has only to look at him across the street, and presto, change! he is gone from her as if by magic. But will you really help me, Mademoiselle?"

"Most willingly, Sieur La Force,--for your profit if not for your honor! I am just in the humor for tormenting somebody this morning; so get your horse and let us be off!"

Before La Force had mounted his horse, a number of gaily-dressed young ladies came in sight, in full sail down the Rue St. Ann, like a fleet of rakish little yachts, bearing down upon Angelique and her companion.

"Shall we wait for them, La Force?" asked she. "They are from the Convent!"

"Yes, and SHE is there too! The news will be all over the city in an hour that I am riding with you!" exclaimed La Force in a tone of intense satisfaction.

Five girls just verging on womanhood, perfect in manner and appearance--as the Ursulines knew well how to train the young olive- plants of the Colony,--walked on demurely enough, looking apparently straight forward, but casting side glances from under their veils which raked the Sieur La Force and Angelique with a searching fire that nothing could withstand, La Force said; but which Angelique remarked was simply "impudence, such as could only be found in Convent girls!"

They came nearer. Angelique might have supposed they were going to pass by them had she not known too well their sly ways. The foremost of the five, Louise Roy, whose glorious hair was the boast of the city, suddenly threw back her veil, and disclosing a charming face, dimpled with smiles and with a thousand mischiefs lurking in her bright gray eyes, sprang towards Angelique, while her companions--all Louises of the famous class of that name--also threw up their veils, and stood saluting Angelique and La Force with infinite merriment.

Louise Roy, quizzing La Force through a coquettish eyeglass which she wore on a ribbon round her pretty neck, as if she had never seen him before, motioned to him in a queenly way as she raised her dainty foot, giving him a severe look, or what tried to be such but was in truth an absurd failure.

He instantly comprehended her command, for such it was, and held out his hand, upon which she stepped lightly, and sprang up to Angelique, embracing and kissing her with such cordiality that, if it were not real, the acting was perfect. At the same time Louise Roy made her understand that she was not the only one who could avail herself of the gallant attentions of the Sieur La Force.

In truth Louise Roy was somewhat piqued at the Sieur La Force, and to punish him made herself as heavy as her slight figure would admit of. She stood perched up as long as she could, and actually enjoyed the tremor which she felt plainly enough in his hand as he continued to support her, and was quite disposed to test how long he could or would hold her up, while she conversed in whispers with Angelique.

"Angelique!" said she. "They say in the Convent that you are to marry the Intendant. Your old mistress, Mere St. Louis, is crazy with delight. She says she always predicted you would make a great match."

"Or none at all, as Mere St. Helene used to say of me; but they know everything in the Convent, do they not?" Angelique pinched the arm of Louise, as much as to say, "Of course it is true." "But who told you that, Louise?" asked she.

"Oh, every bird that flies! But tell me one thing more. They say the Intendant is a Bluebeard, who has had wives without number,-- nobody knows how many or what became of them, so of course he kills them. Is that true?"

Angelique shrank a little, and little as it was the movement was noticed by Louise. "If nobody knows what became of them, how should I know, Louise?" replied she. "He does not look like a Bluebeard, does he?"

"So says Mere St. Joseph, who came from the Convent at Bordeaux, you know, for she never tires telling us. She declares that the Chevalier Bigot was never married at all, and she ought to know that surely, as well as she knows her beads, for coming from the same city as the Intendant, and knowing his family as she does--"

"Well, Louise," interrupted Angelique impatiently, "but do you not see the Sieur La Force is getting tired of holding you up so long with his hand? For heaven's sake, get down!"

"I want to punish him for going with you, and not waiting for me," was the cool whisper of Louise. "But you will ask me, Angelique, to the wedding, will you not? If you do not," continued she, "I shall die!" and delaying her descent as long as possible, she commenced a new topic concerning the hat worn by Angelique.

"Mischief that you are, get down! The Sieur La Force is my cavalier for the day, and you shall not impose on his gallantry that way! He is ready to drop," whispered Angelique.

"One word more, Angelique." Louise was delighted to feel the hand of La Force tremble more and more under her foot.

"No, not a word! Get down!"

"Kiss me then, and good-by, cross thing that you are! Do not keep him all day, or all the class besides myself will be jealous," replied Louise, not offering to get down.

Angelique had no mind to allow her cavalier to be made a horse-block of for anybody but herself. She jerked the bridle, and making her horse suddenly pirouette, compelled Louise to jump down. The mischievous little fairy turned her bright laughing eyes full upon La Force and thanked him for his great courtesy, and with a significant gesture--as much as to say he was at liberty now to escort Angelique, having done penance for the same--rejoined her expectant companions, who had laughed heartily at her manoeuvre.

"She paints!" was Louise's emphatic whisper to her companions, loud enough to be heard by La Force, for whom the remark was partly intended. "She paints! and I saw in her eyes that she has not slept all night! She is in love! and I do believe it is true she is to marry the Intendant!"

This was delicious news to the class of Louises, who laughed out like a chime of silver bells as they mischievously bade La Force and Angelique bon voyage, and passed down the Place d'Armes in search of fresh adventures to fill their budgets of fun--budgets which, on their return to the Convent, they would open under the very noses of the good nuns (who were not so blind as they seemed, however), and regale all their companions with a spicy treat, in response to the universal question ever put to all who had been out in the city, "What is the news?"

La Force, compliant as wax to every caprice of Angelique, was secretly fuming at the trick played upon him by the Mischief of the Convent,--as he called Louise Roy,--for which he resolved to be revenged, even if he had to marry her. He and Angelique rode down the busy streets, receiving salutations on every hand. In the great square of the market-place Angelique pulled up in front of the Cathedral.

Why she stopped there would have puzzled herself to explain. It was not to worship, not to repent of her heinous sin: she neither repented nor desired to repent. But it seemed pleasant to play at repentance and put on imaginary sackcloth.

Angelique's brief contact with the fresh, sunny nature of Louise Roy had sensibly raised her spirits. It lifted the cloud from her brow, and made her feel more like her former self. The story, told half in jest by Louise, that she was to marry the Intendant, flattered her vanity and raised her hopes to the utmost. She liked the city to talk of her in connection with the Intendant.

The image of Beaumanoir grew fainter and fainter as she knelt down upon the floor, not to ask pardon for her sin, but to pray for immunity for herself and the speedy realization of the great object of her ambition and her crime!

The pealing of the organ, rising and falling in waves of harmony, the chanting of choristers, and the voice of the celebrant during the service in honor of St. Michael and all the angels, touched her sensuous nature, but failed to touch her conscience.

A crowd of worshippers were kneeling upon the floor of the Cathedral, unobstructed in those days by seats and pews, except on one side, where rose the stately bancs of the Governor and the Intendant, on either side of which stood a sentry with ported arms, and overhead upon the wall blazed the royal escutcheons of France.

Angelique, whose eyes roved incessantly about the church, turned them often towards the gorgeous banc of the Intendant, and the thought intruded itself to the exclusion of her prayers, "When shall I sit there, with all these proud ladies forgetting their devotions through envy of my good fortune?"

Bigot did not appear in his place at church to-day. He was too profoundly agitated and sick, and lay on his bed till evening, revolving in his astute mind schemes of vengeance possible and impossible, to be carried out should his suspicions of Angelique become certainties of knowledge and fact. His own safety was at stake. The thought that he had been outwitted by the beautiful, designing, heartless girl, the reflection that he dare not turn to the right hand nor to the left to inquire into this horrid assassination, which, if discovered, would be laid wholly to his own charge, drove him to the verge of distraction.

The Governor and his friend Peter Kalm occupied the royal banc. Lutheran as he was, Peter Kalm was too philosophical and perhaps too faithful a follower of Christ to consider religion as a matter of mere opinion or of form rather than of humble dependence upon God, the Father of all, with faith in Christ and the conscientious striving to love God and his neighbor.

A short distance from Angelique, two ladies in long black robes, and evidently of rank, were kneeling with downcast faces, and hands clasped over their bosoms, in a devout attitude of prayer and supplication.

Angelique's keen eye, which nothing escaped, needed not a second glance to recognize the unmistakable grace of Amelie de Repentigny and the nobility of the Lady de Tilly.

She started at sight of these relatives of Le Gardeur's, but did not wonder at their presence, for she already knew that they had returned to the city immediately after the abduction of Le Gardeur by the Chevalier de Pean.

Startled, frightened, and despairing, with aching hearts but unimpaired love, Amelie and the Lady de Tilly had followed Le Gardeur and reoccupied their stately house in the city, resolved to leave no means untried, no friends unsolicited, no prayers unuttered to rescue him from the gulf of perdition into which he had again so madly plunged.

Within an hour after her return, Amelie, accompanied by Pierre Philibert, had gone to the

Palace to seek an interview with her brother. They were rudely denied. "He was playing a game of piquet for the championship of the Palace with the Chevalier de Pean, and could not come if St. Peter, let alone Pierre Philibert, stood at the gate knocking!"

This reply had passed through the impure lips of the Sieur de Lantagnac before it reached Amelie and Pierre. They did not believe it came from their brother. They left the Palace with heavy hearts, after long and vainly seeking an interview, Philibert resolving to appeal to the Intendant himself and call him to account at the sword's point, if need be, for the evident plot in the Palace to detain Le Gardeur from his friends.

Amelie, dreading some such resolution on the part of Pierre, went back next day alone to the Palace to try once more to see Le Gardeur.

She was agitated and in tears at the fate of her brother. She was anxious over the evident danger which Pierre seemed to court, for his sake and--she would not hide the truth from herself--for her own sake too; and yet she would not forbid him. She felt her own noble blood stirred within her to the point that she wished herself a man to be able to walk sword in hand into the Palace and confront the herd of revellers who she believed had plotted the ruin of her brother.

She was proud of Pierre, while she trembled at the resolution which she read in his countenance of demanding as a soldier, and not as a suppliant, the restoration of Le Gardeur to his family.

Amelie's second visit to the Palace had been as fruitless as her first. She was denied admittance, with the profoundest regrets on the part of De Pean, who met her at the door and strove to exculpate himself from the accusation of having persuaded Le Gardeur to depart from Tilly, and of keeping him in the Palace against the prayers of his friends.

De Pean remembered his presumption as well as his rejection by Amelie at Tilly, and while his tongue ran smooth as oil in polite regrets that Le Gardeur had resolved not to see his sister to-day, her evident distress filled him with joy, which he rolled under his tongue as the most delicate morsel of revenge he had ever tasted.

Bowing with well-affected politeness, De Pean attended her to her carriage, and having seen her depart in tears, returned laughing into the Palace, remarking, as he mimicked the weeping countenance of Amelie, that "the Honnetes Gens had learned it was a serious matter to come to the burial of the virtues of a young gentleman like Le Gardeur de Repentigny."

On her return home Amelie threw herself on the neck of her aunt, repeating in broken accents, "My poor Le Gardeur! my brother! He refuses to see me, aunt! He is lost and ruined in that den of all iniquity and falsehood!"

"Be composed, Amelie," replied the Lady de Tilly; "I know it is hard to bear, but perhaps Le Gardeur did not send that message to you. The men about him are capable of deceiving you to an extent you have no conception of,--you who know so little of the world's baseness."

"O aunt, it is true! He sent me this dreadful thing; I took it, for it bears the handwriting of my brother."

She held in her hand a card, one of a pack. It was the death-card of superstitious lookers into futurity. Had he selected it because it bore that reputation, or was it by chance?

On the back of it he had written, or scrawled in a trembling hand, yet plainly, the words: "Return home, Amelie. I will not see you. I have lost the game of life and won the card you see. Return home, dear sister, and forget your unworthy and ruined brother, Le Gardeur."

Lady de Tilly took the card, and read and re-read it, trying to find a meaning it did not contain, and trying not to find the sad meaning it did contain.

She comforted Amelie as best she could, while needing strength herself to bear the bitter cross laid upon them both, in the sudden blighting of that noble life of which they had been so proud.

She took Amelie in her arms, mingling her own tears with hers, and bidding her not despair. "A sister's love," said she, "never forgets, never wearies, never despairs." They had friends too powerful to be withstood, even by Bigot, and the Intendant would be compelled to loosen his hold upon Le Gardeur. She would rely upon the inherent nobleness of the nature of Le Gardeur himself to wash itself pure of all stain, could they only withdraw him from the seductions of the Palace. "We will win him from them by counter charms, Amelie, and it will be seen that virtue is stronger than vice to conquer at last the heart of Le Gardeur."

"Alas, aunt!" replied the poor girl, her eyes suffused with tears, "neither friend nor foe will avail to turn him from the way he has resolved to go. He is desperate, and rushes with open eyes upon his ruin. We know the reason of it all. There is but one who could have saved Le Gardeur if she would. She is utterly unworthy of my brother, but I feel now it were better Le Gardeur had married even her than that he should be utterly lost to himself and us all. I will see Angelique des Meloises myself. It was her summons brought him back to the city. She alone can withdraw him from the vile companionship of Bigot and his associates at the Palace."

Angelique had been duly informed of the return of Amelie to the city, and of her fruitless visits to the Palace to see her brother.

It was no pleasure, but a source of angry disappointment to Angelique that Le Gardeur, in despair of making her his wife, refused to devote himself to her as her lover. He was running wild to destruction, instead of letting her win the husband she aspired to, and retain at the same time the gallant she loved and was not willing to forego.

She had seen him at the first sober moment after his return from Tilly, in obedience to her summons. She had permitted him to pour out again his passion at her feet. She had yielded to his kisses when he claimed her heart and hand, and had not refused to own the mutual flame that covered her cheek with a blush at her own falseness. But driven to the wall by his impetuosity, she had at last killed his reviving hopes by her repetition of the fatal words, "I love you, Le Gardeur, but I will not marry you!"

Angelique was seized with a sudden impulse to withdraw from the presence of Amelie in the Cathedral before being discovered by her. She was half afraid that her former school companion would speak to her on the subject of Le Gardeur. She could not brazen it out with Amelie, who knew her too well, and if she could, she would gladly avoid the angry flash of those dark, pure eyes.

The organ was pealing the last notes of the Doxology, and the voices of the choristers seemed to reecho from the depths of eternity the words, "in saecula saeculorum," when Angelique rose up suddenly to leave the church.

Her irreverent haste caused those about her to turn their heads at the slight confusion she made, Amelie among the rest, who recognized at once the countenance of Angelique, somewhat flushed and irritated, as she strove vainly, with the help of La Force, to get out of the throng of kneeling people who covered the broad floor of the Cathedral.

Amelie deemed it a fortunate chance to meet Angelique so opportunely--just when her desire to do so was strongest. She caught her eye, and made her a quick sign to stay, and approaching her, seized her hands in her old, affectionate way.

"Wait a few moments, Angelique," said she, "until the people depart. I want to speak to you alone. I am so fortunate to find you here."

"I will see you outside, Amelie. The Sieur La Force is with me, and cannot stay."

Angelique dreaded an interview with Amelie.

"No, I will speak to you here. It will be better here in God's temple than elsewhere. The Sieur La Force will wait for you if you ask him; or shall I ask him?" A faint smile accompanied these words of Amelie, which she partly addressed to La Force.

La Force, to Angelique's chagrin, understanding that Amelie desired him to wait for Angelique outside, at once offered to do so.

"Or perhaps," continued Amelie, offering her hand, "the Sieur La Force, whom I am glad to see, will have the politeness to accompany the Lady de Tilly, while I speak to Mademoiselle des Meloises?"

La Force was all compliance. "He was quite at the service of the ladies," he said politely, "and would esteem it an honor to accompany the noble Lady de Tilly."

The Lady de Tilly at once saw through the design of her niece. She acceded to the arrangement, and left the Cathedral in company with the Sieur La Force, whom she knew as the son of an old and valued friend.

He accompanied her home, while Amelie, holding fast to the arm of Angelique until the church was empty of all but a few scattered devotees and penitents, led her into a side chapel, separated from the body of the church by a screen of carved work of oak, wherein stood a small altar and a reliquary with a picture of St. Paul.

The seclusion of this place commended itself to the feelings of Amelie. She made Angelique kneel down by her side before the altar. After breathing a short, silent prayer for help and guidance, she seized her companion by both hands and besought her "in God's name to tell her what she had done to Le Gardeur, who was ruining himself, both soul and body."

Angelique, hardy as she was, could ill bear the searching gaze of those pure eyes. She quailed under them for a moment, afraid that the question might have some reference to Beaumanoir, but reassured by the words of Amelie, that her interview had relation to Le Gardeur only, she replied: "I have done nothing to make Le Gardeur ruin himself, soul or body, Amelie. Nor do I believe he is doing so. Our old convent notions are too narrow to take out with us into the world. You judge Le Gardeur too rigidly, Amelie."

"Would that were my fault, Angelique!" replied she earnestly, "but my heart tells me he is lost unless those who led him astray remit him again into the path of virtue whence they seduced him."

Angelique winced, for she took the allusion to herself, although in the mind of Amelie it referred more to the Intendant. "Le Gardeur is no weakling to be led astray," replied she. "He is a strong man, to lead others, not to be led, as I know better than even his sister."

Amelie looked up inquiringly, but Angelique did not pursue the thought nor explain the meaning of her words.

"Le Gardeur," continued Angelique, "is not worse, nay, with all his faults, is far better than most young gallants, who have the laudable ambition to make a figure in the world, such as women admire. One cannot hope to find men saints, and we women to be such sinners. Saints would be dull companions. I prefer mere men, Amelie!"

"For shame, Angelique! to say such things before the sacred shrine," exclaimed Amelie, indignantly stopping her. "What wonder that men are wicked, when women tempt them to be so! Le Gardeur was like none of the gallants you compare him with! He loved virtue and hated vice, and above all things he despised the companionship of such men as now detain him at the Palace. You first took him from me, Angelique! I ask you now to give him back to me. Give me back my brother, Angelique des Meloises!" Amelie grasped her by the arm in the earnestness of her appeal.

"I took him from you?" exclaimed Angelique hotly. "It is untrue! Forgive my saying so, Amelie! I took him no more than did Heloise de Lotbiniere or Cecile Tourangeau! Will you hear the truth? He fell in love with me, and I had not the heart to repulse him,--nay, I could not, for I will confess to you, Amelie, as I often avowed to you in the Convent, I loved Le Gardeur the best of all my admirers! And by this blessed shrine," continued she, laying her hand upon it, "I do still! If he be, as some say he is, going too fast for his own good or yours or mine, I regret it with my whole heart; I regret it as you do! Can I say more?"

Angelique was sincere in this. Her words sounded honest, and she spoke with a real warmth in her bosom, such as she had not felt in a long time.

Her words impressed Amelie favorably.

"I think you speak truly, Angelique," replied she, "when you say you regret Le Gardeur's relapse into the evil ways of the Palace. No one that ever knew my noble brother could do other than regret it. But oh, Angelique, why, with all your influence over him did you not prevent it? Why do you not rescue him now? A word from you would have been of more avail than the pleading of all the world beside!"

"Amelie, you try me hard," said Angelique, uneasily, conscious of the truth of Amelie's words, "but I can bear much for the sake of Le Gardeur! Be assured that I have no power to influence his conduct in the way of amendment, except upon impossible conditions! I have tried, and my efforts have been vain as your own!"

"Conditions!" replied Amelie, "what conditions?--but I need not ask you! He told me in his hour of agony of your inexplicable dealing with him, and yet not so inexplicable now! Why did you profess to love my brother, leading him on and on to an offer of his hand, and then cruelly reject him, adding one more to the list of your heartless triumphs? Le Gardeur de Repentigny was too good for such a fate from any woman, Angelique!" Amelie's eyes swam in tears of indignation as she said this.

"He was too good for me!" said Angelique, dropping her eyes. "I will acknowledge that, if it will do you any good, Amelie! But can you not believe that there was a sacrifice on my part, as well as on his or yours?"

"I judge not between you, Angelique! or between the many chances wasted on you; but I say this Angelique des Meloises, you wickedly stole the heart of the noblest brother in New France, to trample it under your feet!"

"'Fore God, I did not, Amelie!" she replied indignantly. "I loved and do love Le Gardeur de Repentigny, but I never plighted my troth to him, I never deceived him! I told him I loved him, but I could not marry him! And by this sacred cross," said she, placing her hands upon it, "it is true! I never trampled upon the heart of Le Gardeur; I could kiss his hands, his feet, with true affection as ever loving woman gave to man; but my duty, my troth, my fate, were in the hands of another!"

Angelique felt a degree of pleasure in the confession to Amelie of her love for her brother. It was the next thing to confessing it to himself, which had been once the joy of her life, but it changed not one jot her determination to wed only the Intendant, unless--yes, her busy mind had to-day called up a thousand possible and impossible contingencies that might spring up out of the unexpected use of the stiletto by Corriveau. What if the Intendant, suspecting her complicity in the murder of Caroline, should refuse to marry her? Were it not well in that desperate case to have Le Gardeur to fall back upon?

Amelie watched nervously the changing countenance of Angelique. She knew it was a beautiful mask covering impenetrable deceit, and that no principle of right kept her from wrong when wrong was either pleasant or profitable.

The conviction came upon Amelie like a flash of inspiration that she was wrong in seeking to save Le Gardeur by seconding his wild offer of marriage to Angelique. A union with this false and capricious woman would only make his ruin more complete and his latter end worse than the first. She would not urge it, she thought.

"Angelique," said she, "if you love Le Gardeur, you will not refuse your help to rescue him from the Palace. You cannot wish to see him degraded as a gentleman because he has been rejected by you as a lover."

"Who says I wish to see him degraded as a gentleman? and I did not reject him as a lover! not finally--that is, I did not wholly mean it. When I sent to invite his return from Tilly it was out of friendship,--love, if you will, Amelie, but from no desire that he should plunge into fresh dissipation."

"I believe you, Angelique! You could not, if you had the heart of a woman loving him ever so little, desire to see him fall into the clutches of men who, with the wine-cup in one hand and the dice-box in the other, will never rest until they ruin him, body, soul, and estate."

"Before God, I never desired it, and to prove it, I have cursed De Pean to his face, and erased Lantagnac from my list of friends, for coming to show me the money he had won from Le Gardeur while intoxicated. Lantagnac brought me a set of pearls which he had purchased out of his winnings. I threw them into the fire and would have thrown him after them, had I been a man! 'fore God, I would, Amelie! I may have wounded Le Gardeur, but no other man or woman shall injure him with my consent."

Angelique spoke this in a tone of sincerity that touched somewhat the heart of Amelie, although the aberrations and inconsistencies of this strange girl perplexed her to the utmost to understand what she really felt.

"I think I may trust you, Angelique, to help me to rescue him from association with the Palace?" said Amelie, gently, almost submissively, as if she half feared a refusal.

"I desire nothing more," replied Angelique. "You have little faith in me, I see that,"--Angelique wiped her eyes, in which a shade of moisture could be seen,--"but I am sincere in my friendship for Le Gardeur. The Virgin be my witness, I never wished his injury, even when I injured him most. He sought me in marriage, and I was bound to another."

"You are to marry the Intendant, they say. I do not wonder, and yet I do wonder, at your refusing my brother, even for him."

"Marry the Intendant! Yes, it is what fools and some wise people say. I never said it myself, Amelie."

"But you mean it, nevertheless; and for no other would you have thrown over Le Gardeur de Repentigny."

"I did not throw him over," she answered, indignantly. "But why dispute? I cannot, Amelie, say more, even to you! I am distraught with cares and anxieties, and know not which way to turn."

"Turn here, where I turn in my troubles, Angelique!" replied Amelie, moving closer to the altar. "Let us pray for Le Gardeur." Angelique obeyed mechanically, and the two girls prayed silently for a few moments, but how differently in spirit and feeling! The one prayed for her brother,--the other tried to pray, but it was more for herself, for safety in her crime and success in her deep-laid scheming. A prayer for Le Gardeur mingled with Angelique's devotions, giving them a color of virtue. Her desire for his welfare was sincere enough, and she thought it disinterested of herself to pray for him.

Suddenly Angelique started up as if stung by a wasp. "I must take leave of you, my Amelie," said she; "I am glad I met you here. I trust you understand me now, and will rely on my being as a sister to Le Gardeur, to do what I can to restore him perfect to you and the good Lady de Tilly."

Amelie was touched. She embraced Angelique and kissed her; yet so cold and impassive she felt her to be, a shiver ran through her as she did so. It was as if she had touched the dead, and she long afterwards thought of it. There was a mystery in this strange girl that Amelie could not fathom nor guess the meaning of. They left the Cathedral together. It was now quite empty, save of a lingering penitent or two kneeling at the shrines. Angelique and Amelie parted at the door, the one eastward, the other westward, and, carried away by the divergent currents of their lives, they never met again.

## Chapter XLIV: The Intendant's Dilemma

"Did I not know for a certainty that she was present till midnight at the party given by Madame de Grandmaison, I should suspect her, by God!" exclaimed the Intendant, as he paced up and down his private room in the Palace, angry and perplexed to the uttermost over the mysterious assassination at Beaumanoir. "What think you, Cadet?"

"I think that proves an alibi," replied Cadet, stretching himself lazily in an armchair and smoking with half-shut eyes. There was a cynical, mocking tone in his voice which seemed to imply that although it proved an alibi, it did not prove innocence to the satisfaction of the Sieur Cadet.

"You think more than you say, Cadet. Out with it! Let me hear the worst of your suspicions. I fancy they chime with mine," said the Intendant, in quick reply.

"As the bells of the Cathedral with the bells of the Recollets," drawled out Cadet. "I think she did it, Bigot, and you think the same; but I should not like to be called upon to prove it, nor you either,--not for the sake of the pretty witch, but for your own."

"I could prove nothing, Cadet. She was the gayest and most light- hearted of all the company last night at Madame de Grandmaison's. I have made the most particular inquiries of Varin and Deschenaux. They needed no asking, but burst out at once into praise and admiration of her gaiety and wit. It is certain she was not at Beaumanoir."

"You often boasted you knew women better than I, and I yielded the point in regard to Angelique," replied Cadet, refilling his pipe. "I did not profess to fathom the depths of that girl, but I thought you knew her. Egad! she has been too clever for you, Bigot! She has aimed to be the Lady Intendant, and is in a fair way to succeed! That girl has the spirit of a war-horse; she would carry any man round the world. I wish she would carry me. I would rule Versailles in six weeks, with that woman, Bigot!"

"The same thought has occurred to me, Cadet, and I might have been entrapped by it had not this cursed affair happened. La Pompadour is a simpleton beside Angelique des Meloises! My difficulty is to believe her so mad as to have ventured on this bold deed."

"'Tis not the boldness, only the uselessness of it, would stop Angelique!" answered Cadet, shutting one eye with an air of lazy comfort.

"But the deceitfulness of it, Cadet! A girl like her could not be so gay last night with such a bloody purpose on her soul. Could she, think you?"

"Couldn't she? Tut! Deceit is every woman's nature! Her wardrobe is not complete unless it contains as many lies for her occasions as ribbons for her adornment!"

"You believe she did it then? What makes you think so, Cadet?" asked Bigot eagerly, drawing near his companion.

"Why, she and you are the only persons on earth who had an interest in that girl's death. She to get a dangerous rival out of the way,-- you to hide her from the search-warrants sent out by La Pompadour. You did not do it, I know: ergo, she did! Can any logic be plainer? That is the reason I think so, Bigot."

"But how has it been accomplished, Cadet? Have you any theory? SHE can not have done it with her own hand."

"Why, there is only one way that I can see. We know she did not do the murder herself, therefore she has done it by the hand of another. Here is proof of a confederate, Bigot,--I picked this up in the secret chamber." Cadet drew out of his pocket the fragment of the letter torn in pieces by La Corriveau. "Is this the handwriting of Angelique?" asked he.

Bigot seized the scrap of paper, read it, turned it over and scrutinized it, striving to find resemblances between the writing and that of every one known to him. His scrutiny was in vain.

"This writing is not Angelique's," said he. "It is utterly unknown to me. It is a woman's hand, but certainly not the hand of any woman of my acquaintance, and I have letters and billets from almost every lady in Quebec. It is proof of a confederate, however, for listen, Cadet! It arranges for an interview with Caroline, poor girl! It was thus she was betrayed to her death. It is torn, but enough remains to make the sense clear,--listen: 'At the arched door about midnight--if she pleased to admit her she would learn important matters concerning herself--the Intendant and the Baron de St. Castin--speedily arrive in the Colony.' That throws light upon the mystery, Cadet! A woman was to have an interview with Caroline at midnight! Good God, Cadet! not two hours before we arrived! And we deferred starting in order that we might rook the Signeur de Port Neuf! Too late! too late! Oh cursed word that ever seals our fate when we propose a good deed!" and Bigot felt himself a man injured and neglected by Providence.

"'Important matters relating to herself,'" repeated Bigot, reading again the scrap of writing. "'The Intendant and the Baron de St. Castin--speedily to arrive in the Colony.' No one knew but the sworn Councillors of the Governor that the Baron de St. Castin was coming out to the Colony. A woman has done the deed, and she has been informed of secrets spoken in Council by some Councillor present on that day at the Castle. Who was he? and who was she?" questioned Bigot, excitedly.

"The argument runs like water down hill, Bigot! but, par Dieu! I would not have believed that New France contained two women of such mettle as the one to contrive, the other to execute, a masterpiece of devilment like that!"

"Since we find another hand in the dish, it may not have been Angelique after all," remarked Bigot. "It is hard to believe one so fair and free-spoken guilty of so dark and damnable a crime." Bigot would evidently be glad to find himself in error touching his suspicions.

"Fairest without is often foulest within, Bigot," answered Cadet, doggedly. "Open speech in a woman is often an open trap to catch fools! Angelique des Meloises is free-spoken and open-handed enough to deceive a conclave of cardinals; but she has the lightest heels in the city. Would you not like to see her dance a ballet de triomphe on the broad flagstone I laid over the grave of that poor girl? If you would, you have only to marry her, and she will give a ball in the secret chamber!"

"Be still, Cadet! I could take you by the throat for suggesting it! But I will make her prove herself innocent!" exclaimed Bigot, angry at the cool persistence of Cadet.

"I hope you will not try it to-day, Bigot." Cadet spoke gravely now. "Let the dead sleep, and let all sleeping dogs and bitches lie still. Zounds! we are in greater danger than she is! you cannot stir in this matter without putting yourself in her power. Angelique has got hold of the secret of Caroline and of the Baron de St. Castin; what if she clear herself by accusing you? The King would put you in the Bastile for the magnificent lie you told the Governor, and La Pompadour would send you to the Place de Greve when the Baron de St. Castin returned with the bones of his daughter, dug up in your Chateau!"

"It is a cursed dilemma!" Bigot fairly writhed with perplexity. "Dark as the bottomless pit, turn which way we will. Angelique knows too much, that is clear; it were a charity, if it were a safe thing, to kill her too, Cadet!"

"Not to be thought of, Bigot; she is too much in every man's eye, and cannot be stowed away in a secret corner like her poor victim. A dead silence on every point of this cursed business is our only policy, our only safety." Cadet had plenty of common sense in the rough, and Bigot was able to appreciate it.

The Intendant strode up and down the room, clenching his hands in a fury. "If I were sure! sure! she did it, I would kill her, by God! such a damnable cruel deed as this would justify any measure of vengeance!" exclaimed he, savagely.

"Pshaw! not when it would all rebound upon yourself. Besides, if you want vengeance, take a man's revenge upon a woman; you can do that! It will be better than killing her, much more pleasant, and quite as effectual."

Bigot looked as Cadet said this and laughed: "You would send her to the Parc aux cerfs, eh, Cadet? Par Dieu! she would sit on the throne in six months!"

"No, I do not mean the Parc aux cerfs, but the Chateau of Beaumanoir. But you are in too ill humor to joke to-day, Bigot." Cadet resumed his pipe with an air of nonchalance.

"I never was in a worse humor in my life, Cadet! I feel that I have a padlock upon every one of my five senses; and I cannot move hand or foot in this business."

"Right, Bigot, do not move hand or foot, eye or tongue, in it. I tell you the slightest whisper of Caroline's life or death in your house, reaching the ears of Philibert or La Corne St. Luc, will bring them to Beaumanoir with warrants to search for her. They will pick the Chateau to pieces stone by stone. They will drag Caroline out of her grave, and the whole country will swear you murdered her, and that I helped you, and with appearances so strong against us that the mothers who bore us would not believe in our innocence! Damn the women! The burying of that girl was the best deed I did for one of the sex in my life, but it will be the worst if you breath one word of it to Angelique des Meloises, or to any other person living. I am not ready to lose my head yet, Bigot, for the sake of any woman, or even for you!"

The Intendant was staggered by the vehemence of Cadet, and impressed by the force of his remarks. It was hard to sit down quietly and condone such a crime, but he saw clearly the danger of pushing inquiry in any direction without turning suspicion upon himself. He boiled with indignation. He fumed and swore worse than his wont when angry, but Cadet looked on quietly, smoking his pipe, waiting for the storm to calm down.

"You were never in a woman's clutches so tight before, Bigot," continued Cadet. "If you let La Pompadour suspect one hair of your head in this matter, she will spin a cart-rope out of it that will drag you to the Place de Greve."

"Reason tells me that what you say is true, Cadet," replied Bigot, gloomily.

"To be sure; but is not Angelique a clever witch to bind Francois Bigot neck and heels in that way, after fairly outwitting and running him down?"

Cadet's cool comments drove Bigot beside himself. "I will not stand it; by St. Maur! she shall pay for all this! I, who have caught women all my life, to be caught by one thus! she shall pay for it!"

"Well, make her pay for it by marrying her!" replied Cadet. "Par Dieu! I am mistaken if you have not got to marry her in the end! I would marry her myself, if you do not, only I should be afraid to sleep nights! I might be put under the floor before morning if she liked another man better!"

Cadet gave way to a feeling of hilarity at this idea, shaking his sides so long and heartily that Bigot caught the infection, and joined in with a burst of sardonic laughter.

Bigot's laughter was soon over. He sat down at the table again, and, being now calm, considered the whole matter over, point by point, with Cadet, who, though coarse and unprincipled, was a shrewd counsellor in difficulties.

It was determined between the two men that nothing whatever should be said of the assassination. Bigot should continue his gallantries to Angelique, and avoid all show of suspicion in that quarter. He should tell her of the disappearance of Caroline, who had gone away mysteriously as she came, but profess absolute ignorance as to her fate.

Angelique would be equally cautious in alluding to the murder; she would pretend to accept all his statements as absolute fact. Her tongue, if not her thoughts, would be sealed up in perpetual silence on that bloody topic. Bigot must feed her with hopes of marriage, and if necessary set a day for it, far enough off to cover all the time to be taken up in the search after Caroline.

"I will never marry her, Cadet!" exclaimed Bigot, "but will make her regret all her life she did not marry me!"

"Take care, Bigot! It is dangerous playing with fire. You don't half know Angelique."

"I mean she shall pull the chestnuts out of the fire for me with her pretty fingers, until she burn them," remarked Bigot, gruffly.

"I would not trust her too far! In all seriousness, you have but the choice of two things, Bigot: marry her or send her to the Convent."

"I would not do the one, and I could not do the other, Cadet," was Bigot's prompt reply to this suggestion.

"Tut! Mere Migeon de la Nativite will respect your lettre de cachet, and provide a close, comfortable cell for this pretty penitent in the Ursulines," said Cadet.

"Not she! Mere Migeon gave me one of her parlor-lectures once, and I care not for another. Egad, Cadet! she made me the nearest of being ashamed of Francois Bigot of any one I ever listened to! Could you have seen her, with her veil thrown back, her pale face still paler with indignation, her black eyes looking still blacker beneath the white fillet upon her forehead, and then her tongue, Cadet! Well, I withdrew my proposal and felt myself rather cheapened in the presence of Mere Migeon."

"Ay, I hear she is a clipper when she gets a sinner by the hair! What was the proposal you made to her, Bigot?" asked Cadet, smiling as if he knew.

"Oh, it was not worth a livre to make such a row about! I only proposed to send a truant damsel to the Convent to repent of MY faults, that was all! But I could never dispose of Angelique in that way," continued the Intendant, with a shrug.

"Egad! she will fool any man faster than he can make a fool of her! But I would try Mere Migeon, notwithstanding," replied Cadet. "She is the only one to break in this wild filly and nail her tongue fast to her prayers!"

"It is useless trying. They know Angelique too well. She would turn the Convent out of the windows in the time of a neuvaine. They are all really afraid of her," replied Bigot.

"Then you must marry her, or do worse, Bigot. I see nothing else for it," was Cadet's reply.

"Well, I will do worse, if worse can be; for marry her I will not!" said Bigot, stamping his foot upon the floor.

"It is understood, then, Bigot, not a word, a hint, a look is to be given to Angelique regarding your suspicions of her complicity in this murder?"

"Yes, it is understood. The secret is like the devil's tontine,--he catches the last possessor of it."

"I expect to be the last, then, if I keep in your company, Bigot," remarked Cadet.

Cadet having settled this point to his mind, reclined back in his easy chair and smoked on in silence, while the Intendant kept walking the floor anxiously, because he saw farther than his companion the shadows of coming events.

Sometimes he stopped impatiently at the window, beating a tattoo with his nails on the polished casement as he gazed out upon the beautiful parterres of autumnal flowers, beginning to shed their petals around the gardens of the Palace. He looked at them without seeing them. All that caught his eye was a bare rose-bush, from which he remembered he had plucked some white roses which he had sent to Caroline to adorn her oratory; and he thought of her face, more pale and delicate than any rose of Provence that ever bloomed. His thoughts ran violently in two parallel streams side by side, neither of them disappearing for a moment amid the crowd of other affairs that pressed upon his attention,--the murder of Caroline and the perquisition that was to be made for her in all quarters of the Colony. His own safety was too deeply involved in any discovery that might be made respecting her to allow him to drop the subject out of his thought for a moment.

By imposing absolute silence upon himself in the presence of Angelique, touching the death of Caroline, he might impose a like silence upon her whom he could not acquit of the suspicion of having prompted the murder. But the certainty that there was a confederate in the deed--a woman, too, judging by the fragment of writing picked up by Cadet--tormented him with endless conjectures.

Still, he felt, for the present, secure from any discovery on that side; but how to escape from the sharp inquisition of two men like La Corne St. Luc and Pierre Philibert? And who knew how far the secret of Beaumanoir was a secret any longer? It was known to two women, at any rate; and no woman, in Bigot's estimation of the sex, would long keep a secret which concerned another and not herself.

"Our greatest danger, Cadet, lies there!" continued the Intendant, stopping in his walk and turning suddenly to his friend. "La Corne St. Luc and Pierre Philibert are commissioned by the Governor to search for that girl. They will not leave a stone unturned, a corner unransacked in New France. They will find out through the Hurons and my own servants that a woman has been concealed in Beaumanoir. They will suspect, if they do not discover who she was. They will not find her on earth,--they will look for her under the earth. And, by St. Maur! it makes me quake to think of it, Cadet, for the discovery will be utter ruin! They may at last dig up her murdered remains in my own Chateau! As you said, the Bastile and the Place de Greve would be my portion, and ruin yours and that of all our associates."

Cadet held up his pipe as if appealing to Heaven. "It is a cursed reward for our charitable night's work, Bigot," said he. "Better you had never lied about the girl. We could have brazened it out or fought it out with the Baron de St. Castin or any man in France! That lie will convict us if found out!"

"Pshaw! the lie was a necessity," answered Bigot, impatiently." But who could have dreamed of its leading us such a dance as it has done! Par Dieu! I have not often lied except to women, and such lies do not count! But I had better have stuck to truth in this matter, Cadet. I acknowledge that now."

"Especially with La Pompadour! She is a woman. It is dangerous to lie to her,--at least about other women."

"Well, Cadet, it is useless blessing the Pope or banning the Devil! We are in for it, and we must meet La Corne St. Luc and Pierre Philibert as warily as we can. I have been thinking of making safe ground for us to stand upon, as the trappers do on the great prairies, by kindling a fire in front to escape from the fire in the rear!"

"What is that, Bigot? I could fire the Chateau rather than be tracked out by La Corne and

Philibert," said Cadet, sitting upright in his chair.

"What, burn the Chateau!" answered Bigot. "You are mad, Cadet! No; but it were well to kindle such a smoke about the eyes of La Corne and Philibert that they will need to rub them to ease their own pain instead of looking for poor Caroline."

"How, Bigot? Will you challenge and fight them? That will not avert suspicion, but increase it," remarked Cadet.

"Well, you will see! A man will need as many eyes as Argus to discover our hands in this business."

Cadet started, without conjecturing what the Intendant contemplated. "You will kill the bird that tells tales on us, Bigot,--is that it?" added he.

"I mean to kill two birds with one stone, Cadet! Hark you; I will tell you a scheme that will put a stop to these perquisitions by La Corne and Philibert--the only two men I fear in the Colony--and at the same time deliver me from the everlasting bark and bite of the Golden Dog!"

Bigot led Cadet to the window, and poured in his ear the burning passions which were fermenting in his own breast. He propounded a scheme of deliverance for himself and of crafty vengeance upon the Philiberts which would turn the thoughts of every one away from the Chateau of Beaumanoir and the missing Caroline into a new stream of public and private troubles, amid the confusion of which he would escape, and his present dangers be overlooked and forgotten in a great catastrophe that might upset the Colony, but at any rate it would free Bigot from his embarrassments and perhaps inaugurate a new reign of public plunder and the suppression of the whole party of the Honnetes Gens.

## Chapter XLV: "I Will Feed Fat the Ancient Grudge I Bear Him"

The Treaty of Aix La Chapelle, so long tossed about on the waves of war, was finally signed in the beginning of October. A swift- sailing goelette of Dieppe brought the tidings to New France, and in the early nights of November, from Quebec to Montreal. Bonfires on every headland blazed over the broad river; churches were decorated with evergreens, and Te Deums sung in gratitude for the return of peace and security to the Colony.

New France came out of the struggle scathed and scorched as by fire, but unshorn of territory or territorial rights; and the glad colonists forgot and forgave the terrible sacrifices they had made in the universal joy that their country, their religion, language, and laws were still safe under the Crown of France, with the white banner still floating over the Castle of St. Louis.

On the day after the arrival of the Dieppe goelette bringing the news of peace, Bigot sat before his desk reading his despatches and letters from France, when the Chevalier de Pean entered the room with a bundle of papers in his hand, brought to the Palace by the chief clerk of the Bourgeois Philibert, for the Intendant's signature.

The Bourgeois, in the course of his great commercial dealings, got possession of innumerable orders upon the royal treasury, which in due course had to be presented to the Intendant for his official signature. The signing of these treasury orders in favor of the Bourgeois never failed to throw Bigot into a fit of ill humor.

On the present occasion he sat down muttering ten thousand curses upon the Bourgeois, as he glanced over the papers with knitted eyebrows and teeth set hard together. He signed the mass of orders and drafts made payable to Nicolas Philibert, and when done, threw into the fire the pen which had performed so unwelcome an office. Bigot sent for the chief clerk who had brought the bills and orders, and who waited for them in the antechamber. "Tell your master, the Bourgeois," said he, "that for this time, and only to prevent loss to the foolish officers, the Intendant has signed these army bills; but that if he purchase more, in defiance of the sole right of the Grand Company, I shall not sign them. This shall be the last time, tell him!"

The chief clerk, a sturdy, gray-haired Malouin, was nothing daunted by the angry look of the Intendant. "I shall inform the Bourgeois of your Excellency's wishes," said he, "and--"

"Inform him of my commands!" exclaimed Bigot, sharply. "What! have you more to say? But you would not be the chief clerk of the Bourgeois without possessing a good stock of his insolence!"

"Pardon me, your Excellency!" replied the chief clerk, "I was only going to observe that His Excellency the Governor and the Commander of the Forces both have decided that the officers may transfer their warrants to whomsoever they will."

"You are a bold fellow, with your Breton speech; but by all the saints in Saintonge, I will see whether the Royal Intendant or the Bourgeois Philibert shall control this matter! And as for you--"

"Tut! cave canem! let this cur go back to his master," interrupted Cadet, amused at the coolness of the chief clerk. "Hark you, fellow!" said he, "present my compliments--the Sieur Cadet's compliments--to your master, and tell him I hope he will bring his next batch of army bills himself, and remind him that it is soft falling at low tide out of the windows of the Friponne."

"I shall certainly advise my master not to come himself, Sieur Cadet," replied the chief clerk; "and I am very certain of returning in three days with more army bills for the signature of his Excellency the Intendant."

"Get out, you fool!" shouted Cadet, laughing at what he regarded the insolence of the clerk. "You are worthy of your master!" And Cadet pushed him forcibly out of the door, and shut it after him with a bang that resounded through the Palace.

"Don't be angry at him, Bigot, he is not worth it," said Cadet. "'Like master like man,' as the proverb says. And, after all, I doubt whether the furred law-cats of the Parliament of Paris would not uphold the Bourgeois in an appeal to them from the Golden Dog."

Bigot was excessively irritated, for he was lawyer enough to know that Cadet's fear was well founded. He walked up and down his cabinet, venting curses upon the heads of the whole party of the Honnetes Gens, the Governor and Commander of the Forces included. The Marquise de Pompadour, too, came in for a full share of his maledictions, for Bigot knew that she had forced the signing of the treaty of Aix la Chapelle,--influenced less by the exhaustion of France than by a feminine dislike to camp life, which she had shared with the King, and a resolution to withdraw him back to the gaieties of the capital, where he would be wholly under her own eye and influence.

"She prefers love to honor, as all women do!" remarked Bigot; "and likes money better than either." The Grand Company pays the fiddler for the royal fetes at Versailles, while the Bourgeois Philibert skims the cream off the trade of the Colony. This peace will increase his power and make his influence double what it is already!"

"Egad, Bigot!" replied Cadet, who sat near him smoking a large pipe of tobacco, "you speak like a preacher in Lent. We have hitherto buttered our bread on both sides, but the Company will soon, I fear, have no bread to butter! I doubt we shall have to eat your decrees, which will be the only things left in the possession of the Friponne."

"My decrees have been hard to digest for some people who think they will now eat us. Look at that pile of orders, Cadet, in favor of the Golden Dog!"

The Intendant had long regarded with indignation the ever increasing trade and influence of the Bourgeois Philibert, who had become the great banker as well as the great merchant of the Colony, able to meet the Grand Company itself upon its own ground, and fairly divide with it the interior as well as the exterior commerce of the Colony.

"Where is this thing going to end?" exclaimed Bigot, sweeping from him the pile of bills of exchange that lay upon the table. "That Philibert is gaining ground upon us every day! He is now buying up army bills, and even the King's officers are flocking to him with their certificates of pay and drafts on France, which he cashes at half the discount charged by the Company!"

"Give the cursed papers to the clerk and send him off, De Pean!" said Bigot.

De Pean obeyed with a grimace, and returned.

"This thing must be stopped, and shall!" continued the Intendant, savagely.

"That is true, your Excellency," said De Pean. "And we have tried vigorously to stop the evil, but so far in vain. The Governor and the Honnetes Gens, and too many of the officers themselves, countenance his opposition to the Company. The Bourgeois draws a good bill upon Paris and Bordeaux, and they are fast finding it out."

"The Golden Dog is drawing half the money of the Colony into his coffers, and he will blow up the credit of the Friponne some fine day when we least expect it, unless he be chained up," replied Bigot.

"'A mechant chien court lien,' says the proverb, and so say I," replied Cadet. "The Golden Dog has barked at us for a long time; par Dieu! he bites now!--ere long he will gnaw our bones in reality, as he does in effigy upon that cursed tablet in the Rue Buade."

"Every dog has his day, and the Golden Dog has nearly had his, Cadet. But what do you advise?" asked Bigot.

"Hang him up with a short rope and a shorter shrift, Bigot! You have warrant enough if your Court friends are worth half a handful of chaff."

"But they are not worth half a handful of chaff, Cadet. If I hung the Bourgeois there would be such a cry raised among the Honnetes Gens in the Colony, and the whole tribe of Jansenists in France, that I doubt whether even the power of the Marquise could sustain me."

Cadet looked quietly truculent. He drew Bigot aside. "There are more ways than one to choke a dog, Bigot," said he. "You may put a tight collar outside his throat, or a sweetened roll inside of it. Some course must be found, and that promptly. We shall, before many days, have La Corne St. Luc and young Philibert like a couple of staghounds in full cry at our heels about that business at the Chateau. They must be thrown off that scent, come what will, Bigot!"

The pressure of time and circumstance was drawing a narrower circle around the Intendant. The advent of peace would, he believed, inaugurate a personal war against himself. The murder of Caroline was a hard blow, and the necessity of concealing it irritated him with a sense of fear foreign to his character.

His suspicion of Angelique tormented him day and night. He had loved Angelique in a sensual, admiring way, without one grain of real respect. He worshipped her one moment as the Aphrodite of his fancy; he was ready to strip and scourge her the next as the possible murderess of Caroline. But Bigot had fettered himself with a lie, and had to hide his thoughts under degrading concealments. He knew the Marquise de Pompadour was jealously watching him from afar. The sharpest intellects and most untiring men in the Colony were commissioned to find out the truth regarding the fate of Caroline. Bigot was like a stag brought to bay. An ordinary man would have succumbed in despair, but the very desperation of his position stirred up the Intendant to a greater effort to free himself.

He walked gloomily up and down the room, absorbed in deep thought. Cadet, who guessed what was brooding in his mind, made a sign to De Pean to wait and see what would be the result of his cogitations.

Bigot, gesticulating with his right hand and his left, went on balancing, as in a pair of scales, the chances of success or failure in the blow he meditated against the Golden Dog. A blow which would scatter to the winds the inquisition set on foot to discover the hiding-place of Caroline.

He stopped suddenly in his walk, striking both hands together, as if in sign of some resolution arrived at in his thoughts.

"De Pean!" said he, "has Le Gardeur de Repentigny shown any desire yet to break out of the Palace?"

"None, your Excellency. He is fixed as a bridge to fortune. You can no more break him down than the Pont Neuf at Paris. He lost, last night, a thousand at cards and five hundred at dice; then drank himself dead drunk until three o'clock this afternoon. He has just risen; his valet was washing his head and feet in brandy when I came here."

"You are a friend that sticks closer than a brother, De Pean. Le Gardeur believes in you as his guardian angel, does he not?" asked Bigot with a sneer.

"When he is drunk he does," replied De Pean; "when he is sober I care not to approach him too nearly! He is a wild colt that will kick his groom when rubbed the wrong way; and every way is wrong when the wine is out of him."

"Keep him full then!" exclaimed Bigot; "you have groomed him well, De Pean! but he must now be saddled and ridden to hunt down the biggest stag in New France!"

De Pean looked hard at the Intendant, only half comprehending his allusion.

"You once tried your hand with Mademoiselle de Repentigny, did you not?" continued Bigot.

"I did, your Excellency; but that bunch of grapes was too high for me. They are very sour now."

"Sly fox that you were! Well, do not call them sour yet, De Pean. Another jump at the vine and you may reach that bunch of perfection!" said Bigot, looking hard at him.

"Your Excellency overrates my ability in that quarter, and if I were permitted to choose--"

"Another and a fairer maid would be your choice. I see, De Pean, you are a connoisseur in women. Be it as you wish! Manage this business of Philibert discreetly, and I will coin the Golden Dog into doubloons for a marriage portion for Angelique des Meloises. You understand me now?"

De Pean started. He hardly guessed yet what was required of him, but he cared not in the dazzling prospect of such a wife and fortune as were thus held out to him.

"Your Excellency will really support my suit with Angelique?" De Pean seemed to mistrust the possibility of such a piece of disinterestedness on the part of the Intendant.

"I will not only commend your suit, but I will give away the bride, and Madame de Pean shall not miss any favor from me which she has deserved as Angelique des Meloises," was Bigot's reply, without changing a muscle of his face.

"And your Excellency will give her to me?" De Pean could hardly believe his ears.

"Assuredly you shall have her if you like," cried Bigot, "and with a dowry such as has not been seen in New France!"

"But who would like to have her at any price?" muttered Cadet to himself, with a quiet smile of contempt,--Cadet thought De Pean a fool for jumping at a hook baited with a woman; but he knew what the Intendant was driving at, and admired the skill with which he angled for De Pean.

"But Angelique may not consent to this disposal of her hand," replied De Pean with an uneasy look; "I should be afraid of your gift unless she believed that she took me, and not I her."

"Hark you, De Pean! you do not know what women like her are made of, or you would be at no loss how to bait your hook! You have made four millions, they say, out of this war, if not more."

"I never counted it, your Excellency; but, much or little, I owe it all to your friendship," replied De Pean with a touch of mock humility.

"My friendship! Well, so be it. It is enough to make Angelique des Meloises Madame de Pean when she finds she cannot be Madame Intendant. Do you see your way now, De Pean?"

"Yes, your Excellency, and I cannot be sufficiently grateful for such a proof of your goodness."

Bigot laughed a dry, meaning laugh. "I truly hope you will always think so of my friendship, De Pean. If you do not, you are not the man I take you to be. Now for our scheme of deliverance!

"Hearken, De Pean," continued the Intendant, fixing his dark, fiery eyes upon his secretary; "you have craft and cunning to work out this design and good will to hasten it on. Cadet and I, considering the necessities of the Grand Company, have resolved to put an end to the rivalry and arrogance of the Golden Dog. We will treat the Bourgeois," Bigot smiled meaningly, "not as a trader with a baton, but as a gentleman with a sword; for, although a merchant, the Bourgeois is noble and wears a sword, which under proper provocation he will draw, and remember he can use it too! He can be tolerated no longer by the gentlemen of the Company. They have often pressed me in vain to take this step, but now I yield. Hark, De Pean! The Bourgeois must be INSULTED, CHALLENGED, and KILLED by some gentleman of the Company with courage and skill enough to champion its rights. But mind you! it must be done fairly and in open day, and without my knowledge or approval! Do you understand?"

Bigot winked at De Pean and smiled furtively, as much as to say, "You know how to interpret my words."

"I understand your Excellency, and it shall be no fault of mine if your wishes, which chime with my own, be not carried out before many days. A dozen partners of the Company will be proud to fight with the Bourgeois if he will only fight with them."

"No fear of that, De Pean! give the devil his due. Insult the Bourgeois and he will fight with the seven champions of Christendom! so mind you get a man able for him, for I tell you, De Pean, I doubt if there be over three gentlemen in the Colony who could cross swords fairly and successfully with the Bourgeois."

"It will be easier to insult and kill him in a chance medley than to risk a duel!" interrupted Cadet, who listened with intense eagerness. "I tell you, Bigot, young Philibert will pink any man of our party. If there be a duel he will insist on fighting it for his father. The old Bourgeois will not be caught, but we shall catch a Tartar instead, in the young one."

"Well, duel or chance medley be it! I dare not have him assassinated," replied the Intendant. "He must be fought with in open day, and not killed in a corner. Eh, Cadet, am I not right?"

Bigot looked for approval from Cadet, who saw that he was thinking of the secret chamber at Beaumanoir.

"You are right, Bigot! He must be killed in open day and not in a corner. But who have we among us capable of making sure work of the Bourgeois?"

"Leave it to me," replied De Pean. "I know one partner of the Company who, if I can get him in harness, will run our chariot wheels in triumph over the Golden Dog."

"And who is that'?" asked Bigot eagerly.

"Le Gardeur de Repentigny!" exclaimed De Pean, with a look of exultation.

"Pshaw! he would draw upon us more readily! Why, he is bewitched with the Philiberts!" replied Bigot.

"I shall find means to break the spell long enough to answer our purpose, your Excellency!" replied De Pean. "Permit me only to take my own way with him."

"Assuredly, take your own way, De Pean! A bloody scuffle between De Repentigny and the Bourgeois would not only be a victory for the Company, but would breakup the whole party of the Honnetes Gens!"

The Intendant slapped De Pean on the shoulder and shook him by the hand. "You are more clever than I believed you to be, De Pean. You have hit on a mode of riddance which will entitle you to the best reward in the power of the Company to bestow."

"My best reward will be the fulfilment of your promise, your Excellency," answered De Pean.

"I will keep my word, De Pean. By God you shall have Angelique, with such a dowry as the Company can alone give! Or, if you do not want the girl, you shall have the dowry without the wife!"

"I shall claim both, your Excellency! But--"

"But what? Confess all your doubts, De Pean."

"Le Gardeur may claim her as his own reward!" De Pean guessed correctly enough the true bent of Angelique's fancy.

"No fear! Le Gardeur de Repentigny, drunk or sober, is a gentleman. He would reject the Princess d'Elide were she offered on such conditions as you take her on. He is a romantic fool; he believes in woman's virtue and all that stuff!"

"Besides, if he kill the Bourgeois, he will have to fight Pierre Philibert before his sword is dry!" interjected Cadet. "I would not give a Dutch stiver for Le Gardeur's bones five hours after he has pinked the Bourgeois!"

An open duel in form was not to be thought of, because in that they would have to fight the son and not the father, and the great object would be frustrated. But the Bourgeois might be killed in a sudden fray, when blood was up and swords drawn, when no one, as De Pean remarked, would be able to find an i undotted or a t uncrossed in a fair record of the transaction, which would impose upon the most critical judge as an honorable and justifiable act of self-defence.

This was Cadet's real intent, and perhaps Bigot's, but the Intendant's thoughts lay at unfathomable depths, and were not to be discovered by any traces upon the surface. No divining-rod could tell where the secret spring lay hid which ran under Bigot's motives.

Not so De Pean. He meditated treachery, and it were hard to say whether it was unnoted by the penetrating eye of Bigot. The Intendant, however, did not interfere farther, either by word or sign, but left De Pean to accomplish in his own way the bloody object they all had in view, namely, the death of the Bourgeois and the break-up of the Honnetes Gens. De Pean, while resolving to make Le Gardeur the tool of his wickedness, did not dare to take him into his confidence. He had to be kept in absolute ignorance of the part he was to play in the bloody tragedy until the moment of its denouement arrived. Meantime he must be plied with drink, maddened with jealousy, made desperate with losses, and at war with himself and all the world, and then the whole fury of his rage should, by the artful contrivance of De Pean, be turned, without a minute's time for reflection, upon the head of the unsuspecting Bourgeois.

To accomplish this successfully, a woman's aid was required, at once to blind Le Gardeur and to sharpen his sword.

In the interests of the Company Angelique des Meloises was at all times a violent partisan. The Golden Dog and all its belongings were objects of her open aversion. But De Pean feared to impart to her his intention to push Le Gardeur blindly into the affair. She might fear for the life of one she loved. De Pean reflected angrily on this, but he determined she should be on the spot. The sight of her and a word from her, which De Pean would prompt at the critical moment, should decide Le Gardeur to attack the Bourgeois and kill him; and then, what would follow? De Pean rubbed his hands with ecstasy at the thought that Le Gardeur would inevitably bite the dust under the avenging hand of Pierre Philibert, and Angelique would be his beyond all fear of rivals.

## Chapter XLVI: The Bourgeois Philibert

The Bourgeois Philibert, after an arduous day's work, was enjoying in his armchair a quiet siesta in the old comfortable parlor of his city home.

The sudden advent of peace had opened the seas to commerce, and a fleet of long-shut-up merchantmen were rapidly loading at the quays of the Friponne as well as at those of the Bourgeois, with the products of the Colony for shipment to France before the closing in of the St. Lawrence by ice. The summer of St. Martin was lingering soft and warm on the edge of winter, and every available man, including the soldiers of the garrison, were busy loading the ships to get them off in time to escape the hard nip of winter.

Dame Rochelle sat near the window, which to-day was open to the balmy air. She was occupied in knitting, and occasionally glancing at a volume of Jurieu's hard Calvinistic divinity, which lay upon the table beside her. Her spectacles reposed upon the open page, where she had laid them down while she meditated, as was her custom, upon knotty points of doctrine, touching free will, necessity, and election by grace; regarding works as a garment of filthy rags, in which publicans and sinners who trusted in them were damned, while in practice the good soul was as earnest in performing them as if she believed her salvation depended exclusively thereupon.

Dame Rochelle had received a new lease of life by the return home of Pierre Philibert. She grew radiant, almost gay, at the news of his betrothal to Amelie de Repentigny, and although she could not lay aside the black puritanical garb she had worn so many years, her kind face brightened from its habitual seriousness. The return of Pierre broke in upon her quiet routine of living like a prolonged festival. The preparation of the great house of Belmont for his young bride completed her happiness.

In her anxiety to discover the tastes and preferences of her young mistress, as she already called her, Dame Rochelle consulted Amelie on every point of her arrangements, finding her own innate sense of the beautiful quickened by contact with that fresh young nature. She was already drawn by that infallible attraction which every one felt in the presence of Amelie.

"Amelie was too good and too fair," the dame said, "to become any man's portion but Pierre Philibert's!"

The dame's Huguenot prejudices melted like wax in her presence, until Amelie almost divided with Grande Marie, the saint of the Cevennes, the homage and blessing of Dame Rochelle.

Those were days of unalloyed delight which she spent in superintending the arrangements for the marriage which had been fixed for the festivities of Christmas.

It was to be celebrated on a scale worthy of the rank of the heiress of Repentigny and of the wealth of the Philiberts. The rich Bourgeois, in the gladness of his heart, threw open all his coffers, and blessed with tears of happiness the money he flung out with both hands to honor the nuptials of Pierre and Amelie.

The Bourgeois was profoundly happy during those few brief days of Indian summer. As a Christian, he rejoiced that the long desolating war was over. As a colonist, he felt a pride that, unequal as had been the struggle, New France remained unshorn of territory, and by its resolute defence had forced respect from even its enemies. In his eager hope he saw commerce revive, and the arts and comforts of peace take the place of war and destruction. The husbandman would now reap for himself the harvest he had sown, and no longer be crushed by the exactions of the Friponne!

There was hope for the country. The iniquitous regime of the Intendant, which had pleaded the war as its justification, must close, the Bourgeois thought, under the new conditions of peace. The hateful monopoly of the Grand Company must be overthrown by the constitutional action of the Honnetes Gens, and its condemnation by the Parliament of Paris, to which an appeal would presently be carried, it was hoped, would be secured.

The King was quarreling with the Jesuits. The Molinists were hated by La Pompadour, and he was certain His Majesty would never hold a lit de justice to command the registration of the decrees issued in his name by the Intendant of New France after they had been in form condemned by the Parliament of Paris.

The Bourgeois still reclined very still on his easy chair. He was not asleep. In the daytime he never slept. His thoughts, like the dame's, reverted to Pierre. He meditated the repurchase of his ancestral home in Normandy and the restoration of its ancient honors for his son.

Personal and political enmity might prevent the reversal of his own unjust condemnation, but Pierre had won renown in the recent campaigns. He was favored with the friendship of many of the noblest personages in France, who would support his suit for the restoration of his family honors, while the all-potent influence of money, the open sesame of every door in the palace of Versailles, would not be spared to advance his just claims.

The crown of the Bourgeois's ambition would be to see Pierre restored to his ancestral chateau as the Count de Philibert, and Amelie as its noble chatelaine, dispensing happiness among the faithful old servitors and vassals of his family, who in all these long years of his exile never forgot their brave old seigneur who had been banished to New France.

His reflections took a practical turn, and he enumerated in his mind the friends he could count upon in France to support, and the enemies who were sure to oppose the attainment of this great object of his ambition. But the purchase of the chateau and lands of Philibert was in his power. Its present possessor, a needy courtier, was deeply in debt, and would be glad, the Bourgeois had ascertained, to sell the estates for such a price as he could easily offer him.

To sue for simple justice in the restoration of his inheritance would be useless. It would involve a life-long litigation. The Bourgeois preferred buying it back at whatever price, so that he could make a gift of it at once to his son, and he had already instructed his bankers in Paris to pay the price asked by its owner and forward to him the deeds, which he was ambitious to present to Pierre and Amelie on the day of their marriage.

The Bourgeois at last looked up from his reverie. Dame Rochelle closed her book, waiting for her master's commands.

"Has Pierre returned, dame?" asked he.

"No, master; he bade me say he was going to accompany Mademoiselle Amelie to Lorette."

"Ah! Amelie had a vow to Our Lady of St. Foye, and Pierre, I warrant, desired to pay half the debt! What think you, dame, of your godson? Is he not promising?" The Bourgeois laughed quietly, as was his wont sometimes.

Dame Rochelle sat a shade more upright in her chair. "Pierre is worthy of Amelie and Amelie of him," replied she, gravely; "never were two out of heaven more fitly matched. If they make vows to the Lady of St. Foye they will pay them as religiously as if they had made them to the Most High, to whom we are commanded to pay our vows!"

"Well, Dame, some turn to the east and some to the west to pay their vows, but the holiest shrine is where true love is, and there alone the oracle speaks in response to young hearts. Amelie, sweet, modest flower that she is, pays her vows to Our Lady of St. Foye, Pierre his to Amelie! I will be bound, dame, there is no saint in the calendar so holy in his eyes as herself!"

"Nor deserves to be, master! Theirs is no ordinary affection. If love be the fulfilling of the law, all law is fulfilled in these two, for never did the elements of happiness mingle more sweetly in the soul of a man and a woman than in Pierre and Amelie!"

"It will restore your youth, dame, to live with Pierre and Amelie," replied the Bourgeois. "Amelie insists on it, not because of Pierre, she says, but for your own sake. She was moved to tears one day, dame, when she made me relate your story."

Dame Rochelle put on her spectacles to cover her eyes, which were fast filling, as she glanced down on the black robe she wore, remembering for whom she wore it.

"Thanks, master. It would be a blessed thing to end the remaining days of my mourning in the house of Pierre and Amelie, but my quiet mood suits better the house of my master, who has also had his heart saddened by a long, long day of darkness and regret."

"Yes, dame, but a bright sunset, I trust, awaits it now. The descending shadow of the dial goes back a pace on the fortunes of my house! I hope to welcome my few remaining years with a gayer aspect and a lighter heart than I have felt since we were driven from France. What would you say to see us all reunited once more in our old Norman home?"

The dame gave a great start, and clasped her thin hands.

"What would I say, master? Oh, to return to France, and be buried in the green valley of the Cote d'Or by the side of him, were next to rising in the resurrection of the just at the last day."

The Bourgeois knew well whom she meant by "him." He reverenced her feeling, but continued the topic of a return to France.

"Well, dame, I will do for Pierre what I would not do for myself. I shall repurchase the old chateau, and use every influence at my command to prevail on the King to restore to Pierre the honors of his ancestors. Will not that be a glorious end to the career of the Bourgeois Philibert?"

"Yes, master, but it may not end there for you. I hear from my quiet window many things spoken in the street below. Men love you so, and need you so, that they will not spare any supplication to bid you stay in the Colony; and you will stay and die where you have lived so many years, under the shadow of the Golden Dog. Some men hate you, too, because you love justice and stand up for the right. I have a request to make, dear master."

"What is that, dame?" asked he kindly, prepared to grant any request of hers.

"Do not go to the market to-morrow," replied she earnestly.

The Bourgeois glanced sharply at the dame, who continued to ply her needles. Her eyes were half closed in a semi-trance, their lids trembling with nervous excitement. One of her moods, rare of late, was upon her, and she continued:

"Oh, my dear master! you will never go to France; but Pierre shall inherit the honors of the house of Philibert!"

The Bourgeois looked up contentedly. He respected, without putting entire faith in Dame Rochelle's inspirations. "I shall be resigned," he said, "not to see France again, if the King's Majesty makes it a condition that he restore to Pierre the dignity, while I give him back the domain of his fathers."

Dame Rochelle clasped her hands hard together and sighed. She spake not, but her lips moved in prayer as if deprecating some danger, or combating some presentiment of evil.

The Bourgeois watched her narrowly. Her moods of devout contemplation sometimes perplexed his clear worldly wisdom. He could scarcely believe that her intuitions were other than the natural result of a wonderfully sensitive and apprehensive nature; still, in his experience he had found that her fancies, if not supernatural, were not unworthy of regard as the sublimation of rcason by intellectual processes of which the possessor was unconscious.

"You again see trouble in store for me, dame," said he smiling; "but a merchant of New France setting at defiance the decrees of the Royal Intendant, an exile seeking from the King the restoration of the lordship of Philibert, may well have trouble on his hands."

"Yes, master, but as yet I only see trouble like a misty cloud which as yet has neither form nor color of its own, but only reflects red rays as of a setting sun. No voice from its midst tells me its meaning; I thank God for that. I like not to anticipate evil that may not be averted!"

"Whom does it touch, Pierre or Amelie, me, or all of us?" asked the Bourgeois.

"All of us, master? How could any misfortune do other than concern us all? What it means, I know not. It is now like the wheel seen by the Prophet, full of eyes within and without, like God's providence looking for his elect."

"And finding them?"

"Not yet, master, but ere long,--finding all ere long," replied she in a dreamy manner. "But go not to the market to-morrow."

"These are strange fancies of yours, Dame Rochelle. Why caution me against the market to-morrow? It is the day of St. Martin; the poor will expect me; if I go not, many will return empty away."

"They are not wholly fancies, master. Two gentlemen of the Palace passed to-day, and looking up at the tablet, one wagered the other on the battle to-morrow between Cerberus and the Golden Dog. I have not forgotten wholly my early lessons in classical lore," added the dame.

"Nor I, dame. I comprehend the allusion, but it will not keep me from the market! I will be watchful, however, for I know that the malice of my enemies is at this time greater than ever before."

"Let Pierre go with you, and you will be safe," said the dame half imploringly.

The Bourgeois laughed at the suggestion and began good-humoredly to rally her on her curious gift and on the inconvenience of having a prophetess in his house to anticipate the evil day.

Dame Rochelle would not say more. She knew that to express her fears more distinctly would only harden the resolution of the Bourgeois. His natural courage would make him court the special danger he ought to avoid.

"Master," said she, suddenly casting her eyes in the street, "there rides past one of the gentlemen who wagered on the battle between Cerberus and the Golden Dog."

The Bourgeois had sufficient curiosity to look out. He recognized the Chevalier de Pean, and tranquilly resumed his seat with the remark that "that was truly one of the heads of Cerberus which guards the Friponne, a fellow who wore the collar of the Intendant and was worthy of it. The Golden Dog had nothing to fear from him."

Dame Rochelle, full of her own thoughts, followed with her eyes the retreating figure of the Chevalier de Pean, whom she lost sight of at the first turn, as he rode rapidly to the house of Angelique des Meloises. Since the fatal eve of St. Michael, Angelique had been tossing in a sea of conflicting emotions, sometimes brightened by a wild hope of the Intendant, sometimes darkened with fear of the discovery of her dealings with La Corriveau.

It was in vain she tried every artifice of female blandishment and cunning to discover what was really in the heart and mind of Bigot. She had sounded his soul to try if he entertained a suspicion of herself, but its depth was beyond her power to reach its bottomless darkness, and to the last she could not resolve whether he suspected her or not of complicity with the death of the unfortunate Caroline.

She never ceased to curse La Corriveau for that felon stroke of her mad stiletto which changed what might have passed for a simple death by heartbreak into a foul assassination.

The Intendant she knew must be well aware that Caroline had been murdered; but he had never named it or given the least token of consciousness that such a crime had been committed in his house.

It was in vain that she repeated, with a steadiness of face which sometimes imposed even on Bigot, her request for a lettre de cachet, or urged the banishment of her rival, until the Intendant one day, with a look which for a moment annihilated her, told her that her rival had gone from Beaumanoir and would never trouble her any more.

What did he mean? Angelique had noted every change of muscle, every curve of lip and eyelash as he spake, and she felt more puzzled than before.

She replied, however, with the assurance she could so well assume, "Thanks, Bigot; I did not speak from jealousy. I only asked for justice and the fulfilment of your promise to send her away."

"But I did not send her away. She has gone away, I know not whither,--gone, do you mind me, Angelique? I would give half my possessions to know who helped her to ESCAPE--yes, that is the word--from Beaumanoir."

Angelique had expected a burst of passion from Bigot; she had prepared herself for it by diligent rehearsal of how she would demean herself under every possible form of charge, from bare innuendo to direct impeachment of herself.

Keenly as Bigot watched Angelique, he could detect no sign of confusion in her. She trembled in her heart, but her lips wore their old practised smile. Her eyes opened widely, looking surprise, not guilt, as she shook him by the sleeve or coquettishly pulled his hair, asking if he thought that "she had stolen away his lady-love!"

Bigot though only half deceived, tried to persuade himself of her innocence, and left her after an hour's dalliance with the half belief that she did not really merit the grave suspicions he had entertained of her.

Angelique feared, however, that he was only acting a part. What part? It was still a mystery to her, and likely to be; she had but one criterion to discover his real thoughts. The offer of his hand in marriage was the only test she relied upon to prove her acquittal in the mind of Bigot of all complicity with the death of Caroline.

But Bigot was far from making the desired offer of his hand. That terrible night in the secret chamber of Beaumanoir was not absent from his mind an hour. It could never be forgotten, least of all in the company of Angelique, whom he was judging incessantly, either convicting or acquitting her in his mind as he was alternately impressed by her well-acted innocent gaiety or stung by a sudden perception of her power of deceit and unrivalled assurance.

So they went on from day to day, fencing like two adepts in the art of dissimulation, Bigot never glancing at the murder, and speaking of Caroline as gone away to parts unknown, but, as Angelique observed with bitterness, never making that a reason for pressing his suit; while she, assuming the role of innocence and ignorance of all that had happened at Beaumanoir, put on an appearance of satisfaction, or pretending still to fits of jealousy, grew fonder in her demeanor and acted as though she assumed as a matter of course that Bigot would now fulfill her hopes of speedily making her his bride.

The Intendant had come and gone every day, unchanged in his manner, full of spirits and gallantry, and as warm in his admiration as before; but her womanly instinct told her there was something hidden under that gay exterior.

Bigot accepted every challenge of flirtation, and ought to have declared himself twenty times over, but he did not. He seemed to bring himself to the brink of an avowal only to break into her confidence and surprise the secret she kept so desperately concealed.

Angelique met craft by craft, duplicity by duplicity, but it began to be clear to herself that she had met with her match, and although the Intendant grew more pressing as a lover, she had daily less hope of winning him as a husband.

The thought was maddening. Such a result admitted of a twofold meaning: either he suspected her of the death of Caroline, or her charms, which had never failed before with any man, failed now to entangle the one man she had resolved to marry.

She cursed him in her heart while she flattered him with her tongue, but by no art she was mistress of, neither by fondness nor by coyness, could she extract the declaration she regarded as her due and was indignant at not receiving. She had fairly earned it by her great crime. She had still more fully earned it, she thought, by her condescensions. She regarded Providence as unjust in withholding her reward, and for punishing as a sin that which for her sake ought to be considered a virtue.

She often reflected with regretful looking back upon the joy which Le Gardeur de Repentigny would have manifested over the least of the favors which she had lavished in vain upon the inscrutable Intendant. At such moments she cursed her evil star, which had led her astray to listen to the promptings of ambition and to ask fatal counsel of La Corriveau.

Le Gardeur was now in the swift downward road of destruction. This was the one thing that caused Angelique a human pang. She might yet fail in all her ambitious prospects, and have to fall back upon her first love,--when even that would be too late to save Le Gardeur or to save her.

De Pean rode fast up the Rue St. Louis, not unobservant of the dark looks of the Honnetes Gens or the familiar nods and knowing smiles of the partisans of the Friponne whom he met on the way.

Before the door of the mansion of the Chevalier des Meloises he saw a valet of the Intendant holding his master's horse, and at the broad window, half hid behind the thick curtains, sat Bigot and Angelique engaged in badinage and mutual deceiving, as De Pean well knew.

Her silvery laugh struck his ear as he drew up. He cursed them both; but fear of the Intendant, and a due regard to his own interests, two feelings never absent from the Chevalier De Pean, caused him to ride on, not stopping as he had intended.

He would ride to the end of the Grande Allee and return. By that time the Intendant would be gone, and she would be at liberty to receive his invitation for a ride to-morrow, when they would visit the Cathedral and the market.

De Pean knew enough of the ways of Angelique to see that she aimed at the hand of the Intendant. She had slighted and vilipended himself even, while accepting his gifts and gallantries. But with a true appreciation of her character, he had faith in the ultimate power of money, which represented to her, as to most women, position, dress, jewels, stately houses, carriages, and above all, the envy and jealousy of her own sex.

These things De Pean had wagered on the head of Angelique against the wild love of Le Gardeur, the empty admiration of Bigot, and the flatteries of the troop of idle gentlemen who dawdled around her.

He felt confident that in the end victory would be his, and the fair Angelique would one day lay her hand in his as the wife of Hugues de Pean.

De Pean knew that in her heart she had no love for the Intendant, and the Intendant no respect for her. Moreover, Bigot would not venture to marry the Queen of Sheba without the sanction of his jealous patroness at Court. He might possess a hundred mistresses if he liked, and be congratulated on his bonnes fortunes, but not one wife, under the penalty of losing the favor of La Pompadour, who had chosen a future wife for him out of the crowd of intriguantes who fluttered round her, basking like butterflies in the sunshine of her semi-regal splendor.

Bigot had passed a wild night at the Palace among the partners of the Grand Company, who had met to curse the peace and drink a speedy renewal of the war. Before sitting down to their debauch, however, they had discussed, with more regard to their peculiar interests than to the principles of the Decalogue, the condition and prospects of the Company.

The prospect was so little encouraging to the associates that they were glad when the Intendant bade them cheer up and remember that all was not lost that was in danger. "Philibert would yet undergo the fate of Actaeon, and be torn in pieces by his own dog." Bigot, as he said this, glanced from Le Gardeur to De Pean, with a look and a smile which caused Cadet, who knew its meaning, to shrug his shoulders and inquire of De Pean privately, "Is the trap set?"

"It is set!" replied De Pean in a whisper. "It will spring to- morrow and catch our game, I hope."

"You must have a crowd and a row, mind! this thing, to be safe, must be done openly," whispered Cadet in reply.

"We will have both a crowd and a row, never fear! The new preacher of the Jesuits, who is fresh from Italy and knows nothing about our plot, is to inveigh in the market against the Jansenists and the Honnetes Gens. If that does not make both a crowd and a row, I do not know what will."

"You are a deep devil, De Pean! So deep that I doubt you will cheat yourself yet," answered Cadet gruffly.

"Never fear, Cadet! To-morrow night shall see the Palace gay with illumination, and the Golden Dog in darkness and despair."

## Chapter XLVII: A Drawn Game

Le Gardeur was too drunk to catch the full drift of the Intendant's reference to the Bourgeois under the metaphor of Actaeon torn in pieces by his own dog. He only comprehended enough to know that something was intended to the disparagement of the Philiberts, and firing up at the idea, swore loudly that "neither the Intendant nor all the Grand Company in mass should harm a hair of the Bourgeois's head!"

"It is the dog!" exclaimed De Pean, "which the Company will hang, not his master, nor your friend his son, nor your friend's friend the old Huguenot witch! We will let them hang themselves when their time comes; but it is the Golden Dog we mean to hang at present, Le Gardeur!"

"Yes! I see!" replied Le Gardeur, looking very hazy. "Hang the Golden Dog as much as you will, but as to the man that touches his master, I say he will have to fight ME, that is all." Le Gardeur, after one or two vain attempts, succeeded in drawing his sword, and laid it upon the table.

"Do you see that, De Pean? That is the sword of a gentleman, and I will run it through the heart of any man who says he will hurt a hair of the head of Pierre Philibert, or the Bourgeois, or even the old Huguenot witch, as you call Dame Rochelle, who is a lady, and too good to be either your mother, aunt, or cater cousin, in any way, De Pean!"

"By St. Picot! You have mistaken your man, De Pean!" whispered Cadet. "Why the deuce did you pitch upon Le Gardeur to carry out your bright idea?"

"I pitched upon him because he is the best man for our turn. But I am right. You will see I am right. Le Gardeur is the pink of morality when he is sober. He would kill the devil when he is half drunk, but when wholly drunk he would storm paradise, and sack and slay like a German ritter. He would kill his own grandfather. I have not erred in choosing him."

Bigot watched this by-play with intense interest. He saw that Le Gardeur was a two-edged weapon just as likely to cut his friends as his enemies, unless skilfully held in hand, and blinded as to when and whom he should strike.

"Come, Le Gardeur, put up your sword!" exclaimed Bigot, coaxingly; "we have better game to bring down to-night than the Golden Dog. Hark! They are coming! Open wide the doors, and let the blessed peacemakers enter!"

"The peacemakers!" ejaculated Cadet; "the cause of every quarrel among men since the creation of the world! What made you send for the women, Bigot?"

"Oh, not to say their prayers, you may be sure, old misogynist, but this being a gala-night at the Palace, the girls and fiddlers were ordered up by De Pean, and we will see you dance fandangoes with them until morning, Cadet."

"No you won't! Damn the women! I wish you had kept them away, that is all. It spoils my fun, Bigot!"

"But it helps the Company's! Here they come!"

Their appearance at the door caused a hubbub of excitement among the gentlemen, who hurried forward to salute a dozen or more women dressed in the extreme of fashion, who came forward with plentiful lack of modesty, and a superabundance of gaiety and laughter.

Le Gardeur and Cadet did not rise like the rest, but kept their seats. Cadet swore that De Pean had spoiled a jolly evening by inviting the women to the Palace.

These women had been invited by De Pean to give zest to the wild orgie that was intended to prepare Le Gardeur for their plot of to- morrow, which was to compass the fall of the

Bourgeois. They sat down with the gentlemen, listening with peals of laughter to their coarse jests, and tempting them to wilder follies. They drank, they sang, they danced and conducted, or misconducted, themselves in such a thoroughly shameless fashion that Bigot, Varin, and other experts of the Court swore that the petits appartements of Versailles, or even the royal fetes of the Parc aux cerfs, could not surpass the high life and jollity of the Palace of the Intendant.

In that wild fashion Bigot had passed the night previous to his present visit to Angelique. The Chevalier de Pean rode the length of the Grande Allee and returned. The valet and horse of the Intendant were still waiting at the door, and De Pean saw Bigot and Angelique still seated at the window engaged in a lively conversation, and not apparently noticing his presence in the street as he sat pulling hairs out of the mane of his horse, "with the air of a man in love," as Angelique laughingly remarked to Bigot.

Her quick eye, which nothing could escape, had seen De Pean the first time he passed the house. She knew that he had come to visit her, and seeing the horse of the Intendant at the door, had forborne to enter,--that would not have been the way with Le Gardeur, she thought. He would have entered all the readier had even the Dauphin held her in conversation.

Angelique was woman enough to like best the bold gallant who carries the female heart by storm and puts the parleying garrison of denial to the sword, as the Sabine women admired the spirit of their Roman captors and became the most faithful of wives.

De Pean, clever and unprincipled, was a menial in his soul, as cringing to his superiors as he was arrogant to those below him.

"Fellow!" said he to Bigot's groom, "how long has the Intendant been here?"

"All the afternoon, Chevalier," replied the man, respectfully uncovering his head.

"Hum! and have they sat at the window all the time?"

"I have no eyes to watch my master," replied the groom; "I do not know."

"Oh!" was the reply of De Pean, as he suddenly reflected that it were best for himself also not to be seen watching his master too closely. He uttered a spurt of ill humor, and continued pulling the mane of his horse through his fingers.

"The Chevalier de Pean is practising patience to-day, Bigot," said she; "and you give him enough time to exercise it."

"You wish me gone, Angelique!" said he, rising; "the Chevalier de Pean is naturally waxing impatient, and you too!"

"Pshaw!" exclaimed she; "he shall wait as long as I please to keep him there."

"Or as long as I stay. He is an accommodating lover, and will make an equally accommodating husband for his wife's friend some day!" remarked Bigot laughingly.

Angelique's eyes flashed out fire, but she little knew how true a word Bigot had spoken in jest. She could have choked him for mentioning her in connection with De Pean, but remembering she was now at his mercy, it was necessary to cheat and cozen this man by trying to please him.

"Well, if you must go, you must, Chevalier! Let me tie that string," continued she, approaching him in her easy manner. The knot of his cravat was loose. Bigot glanced admiringly at her slightly flushed cheek and dainty fingers as she tied the loose ends of his rich steinkirk together.

"'Tis like love," said she, laughingly; "a slip-knot that looks tied until it is tried."

She glanced at Bigot, expecting him to thank her, which he did with a simple word. The thought of Caroline flashed over his mind like lightning at that moment. She, too, as they walked on the shore of the Bay of Minas had once tied the string of his cravat, when for the first time he read in her flushed cheek and trembling fingers that she loved him. Bigot, hardy as he was and reckless, refrained from touching the hand or even looking at Angelique at this moment.

With the quick perception of her sex she felt it, and drew back a step, not knowing but the next moment might overwhelm her with an accusation. But Bigot was not sure, and he dared not hint to Angelique more than he had done.

"Thanks for tying the knot, Angelique," said he at length. "It is a hard knot, mine, is it not, both to tie and to untie?"

She looked at him, not pretending to understand any meaning he might attach to his words. "Yes, it is a hard knot to tie, yours, Bigot, and you do not seem particularly to thank me for my service. Have you discovered the hidden place of your fair fugitive yet?" She said this just as he turned to depart. It was the feminine postscript to their interview.

Bigot's avoidance of any allusion to the death of Caroline was a terrible mark of suspicion; less in reality, however, than it seemed.

Bigot, although suspicious, could find no clue to the real perpetrators of the murder. He knew it had not been Angelique herself in person. He had never heard her speak of La Corriveau. Not the smallest ray of light penetrated the dark mystery.

"I do not believe she has left Beaumanoir, Bigot," continued Angelique; "or if she has, you know her hiding-place. Will you swear on my book of hours that you know not where she is to be found?"

He looked fixedly at Angelique for a moment, trying to read her thoughts, but she had rehearsed her part too often and too well to look pale or confused. She felt her eyebrow twitch, but she pressed it with her fingers, believing Bigot did not observe it, but he did.

"I will swear and curse both, if you wish it, Angelique," replied he. "Which shall it be?"

"Well, do both,--swear at me and curse the day that I banished Le Gardeur de Repentigny for your sake, Francois Bigot! If the lady be gone, where is your promise?"

Bigot burst into a wild laugh, as was his wont when hard-pressed. He had not, to be sure, made any definite promise to Angelique, but he had flattered her with hopes of marriage never intended to be realized.

"I keep my promises to ladies as if I had sworn by St. Dorothy," replied he.

"But your promise to me, Bigot! Will you keep it, or do worse?" asked she, impatiently.

"Keep it or do worse! What mean you, Angelique?" He looked up in genuine surprise. This was not the usual tone of women towards him.

"I mean that nothing will be better for Francois Bigot than to keep his promise, nor worse than to break it, to Angelique des Meloises!" replied she, with a stamp of her foot, as was her manner when excited.

She thought it safe to use an implied threat, which at any rate might reach the thought that lay under his heart like a centipede under a stone which some chance foot turns over.

But Bigot minded not the implied threat. He was immovable in the direction she wished him to move. He understood her allusion, but would not appear to understand it, lest worse than she meant should come of it.

"Forgive me, Angelique!" said he, with a sudden change from frigidity to fondness. "I am not unmindful of my promises; there is nothing better to myself than to keep them, nothing worse than to break them. Beaumanoir is now without reproach, and you can visit it without fear of aught but the ghosts in the gallery."

Angelique feared no ghosts, but she did fear that the Intendant's words implied a suggestion of one which might haunt it for the future, if there were any truth in tales.

"How can you warrant that, Bigot?" asked she dubiously.

"Because Pierre Philibert and La Corne St. Luc have been with the King's warrant and searched the chateau from crypt to attic, without finding a trace of your rival."

"What, Chevalier, searched the Chateau of the Intendant?"

"Par bleu! yes, I insisted upon their doing so; not, however, till they had gone through the Castle of St. Louis. They apologized to me for finding nothing. What did they expect to find, think you?"

"The lady, to be sure! Oh, Bigot," continued she, tapping him with her fan, "if they would send a commission of women to search for her, the secret could not remain hid."

"No, truly, Angelique! If you were on such a commission to search for the secret of her."

"Well, Bigot, I would never betray it, if I knew it," answered she, promptly.

"You swear to that, Angelique?" asked he, looking full in her eyes, which did not flinch under his gaze.

"Yes; on my book of hours, as you did!" said she.

"Well, there is my hand upon it, Angelique. I have no secret to tell respecting her. She has gone, I cannot tell WHITHER."

Angelique gave him her hand on the lie. She knew he was playing with her, as she with him, a game of mutual deception, which both knew to be such. And yet they must, circumstanced as they were, play it out to the end, which end, she hoped, would be her marriage with this arch-deceiver. A breach of their alliance was as dangerous as it would be unprofitable to both.

Bigot rose to depart with an air of gay regret at leaving the company of Angelique to make room for De Pean, "who," he said, "would pull every hair out of his horse's mane if he waited much longer."

"Your visit is no pleasure to you, Bigot," said she, looking hard at him. "You are discontented with me, and would rather go than stay!"

"Well, Angelique, I am a dissatisfied man to-day. The mysterious disappearance of that girl from Beaumanoir is the cause of my discontent. The defiant boldness of the Bourgeois Philibert is another. I have heard to-day that the Bourgeois has chartered every ship that is to sail to France during the remainder of the autumn. These things are provoking enough, but they drive me for consolation to you. But for you I should shut myself up in Beaumanoir, and let every thing go helter-skelter to the devil."

"You only flatter me and do not mean it!" said she, as he took her hand with an over-empressement as perceptible to her as was his occasional coldness.

"By all the saints! I mean it," said he. But he did not deceive her. His professions were not all true, but how far they were true was a question that again and again tormented her, and set her bosom palpitating as he left her room with his usual courteous salute.

"He suspects me! He more than suspects me!" said she to herself as Bigot passed out of the mansion and mounted his horse to ride off. "He would speak out plainer if he dared avow that that woman was in truth the missing Caroline de St. Castin!" thought she with savage bitterness.

"I have a bit in your mouth there, Francois Bigot, that will forever hold you in check. That missing demoiselle, no one knows as you do where she is. I would give away every jewel I own to know what you did with the pretty piece of mortality left on your hands by La Corriveau."

Thus soliloquized Angelique for a few moments, looking gloomy and beautiful as Medea, when the step of De Pean sounded up the broad stair.

With a sudden transformation, as if touched by a magic wand, Angelique sprang forward, all smiles and fascinations to greet his entrance.

The Chevalier de Pean had long made distant and timid pretensions to her favor, but he had been overborne by a dozen rivals. He was incapable of love in any honest sense; but he had immense vanity. He had been barely noticed among the crowd of Angelique's admirers. "He was only food for powder," she had laughingly remarked upon one occasion, when a duel on her account seemed to be impending between De Pean and the young Captain de Tours; and beyond doubt Angelique would have been far prouder of him shot for her sake in a duel than she was of his living attentions.

She was not sorry, however, that he came in to-day after the departure of the Intendant. It kept her from her own thoughts, which were bitter enough when alone. Moreover, she never tired of any amount of homage and admiration, come from what quarter it would.

De Pean stayed long with Angelique. How far he opened the details of the plot to create a riot in the market-place that afternoon can only be conjectured by the fact of her agreeing to ride out at the hour designated, which she warmly consented to do as soon as De Pean informed her that Le Gardeur would be there and might be expected to have a hand in the tumult raised against the Golden Dog. The conference over, Angelique speedily dismissed De Pean. She was in no mood for flirtation with him. Her mind was taken up with the possibility of danger to Le Gardeur in this plot, which she saw clearly was the work of others, and not of himself, although he was expected to be a chief actor in it.

## Chapter XLVIII: "In Gold Clasps Locks in the Golden Story"

Love is like a bright river when it springs from the fresh fountains of the heart. It flows on between fair and ever-widening banks until it reaches the ocean of eternity and happiness.

The days illuminated with the brightest sunshine are those which smile over the heads of a loving pair who have found each other, and with tender confessions and mutual avowals plighted their troth and prepared their little bark for sailing together down the changeful stream of time.

So it had been through the long Indian summer days with Pierre Philibert and Amelie de Repentigny. Since the blessed hour they plighted their troth in the evening twilight upon the shore of the little lake of Tilly, they had showed to each other, in the heart's confessional, the treasures of true human affection, holy in the eyes of God and man.

When Amelie gave her love to Pierre, she gave it utterly and without a scruple of reservation. It was so easy to love Pierre, so impossible not to love him; nay, she remembered not the time it was otherwise, or when he had not been first and last in her secret thoughts as he was now in her chaste confessions, although whispered so low that her approving angel hardly caught the sound as it passed into the ear of Pierre Philibert.

A warm, soft wind blew gently down the little valley of the Lairet, which wound and rippled over its glossy brown pebbles, murmuring a quiet song down in its hollow bed. Tufts of spiry grass clung to its steep banks, and a few wild flowers peeped out of nooks among the sere fallen leaves that lay upon the still greensward on each shore of the little rivulet.

Pierre and Amelie had been tempted by the beauty of the Indian summer to dismount and send their horses forward to the city in charge of a servant while they walked home by way of the fields to gather the last flowers of autumn, which Amelie said lingered longest in the deep swales of the Lairet.

A walk in the golden sunshine with Amelie alone amid the quiet fields, free to speak his love, and she to hear him and be glad, was a pleasure Pierre had dreamt of but never enjoyed since the blessed night when they plighted their troth to each other by the lake of Tilly.

The betrothal of Pierre and Amelie had been accepted by their friends on both sides as a most fitting and desirable match, but the manners of the age with respect to the unmarried did not admit of that freedom in society which prevails at the present day.

They had seldom met save in the presence of others, and except for a few chance but blissful moments, Pierre had not been favored with the company all to himself of his betrothed.

Amelie was not unmindful of that when she gave a willing consent to- day to walk with him along the banks of the Lairet, under the shady elms, birches, and old thorns that overhung the path by the little stream.

"Pierre," said she smiling, "our horses are gone and I must now walk home with you, right or wrong. My old mistress in the Convent would shake her head if she heard of it, but I care not who blames me to- day, if you do not, Pierre!"

"Who can blame you, darling? What you do is ever wisest and best in my eyes, except one thing, which I will confess now that you are my own, I cannot account for--"

"I had hoped, Pierre, there was no exception to your admiration; you are taking off my angel's wings already, and leaving me a mere woman!" replied she merrily.

"It is a woman I want you to be, darling, a woman not faultless, but human as myself, a wife to hold to me and love me despite my faults, not an angel too bright and too perfect to be my other self."

"Dear Pierre," said she, pressing his arm, "I will be that woman to you, full enough of faults to satisfy you. An angel I am not and cannot be, nor wish to be until we go together to the spirit-land. I am so glad I have a fault for which you can blame me, if it makes you love me better. Indeed I own to many, but what is that one fault, Pierre, which you cannot account for?"

"That you should have taken a rough soldier like me, Amelie! That one so fair and perfect in all the graces of womanhood, with the world to choose from, should have permitted Pierre Philibert to win her loving heart of hearts."

Amelie looked at him with a fond expression of reproach. "Does that surprise you, Pierre? You rough soldier, you little know, and I will not tell you, the way to a woman's heart; but for one blindfolded by so much diffidence to his own merits, you have found the way very easily! Was it for loving you that you blamed me? What if I should recall the fault?" added she, laughing.

Pierre raised her hand to his lips, kissing devotedly the ring he had placed upon her finger. "I have no fear of that, Amelie! The wonder to me is that you could think me worthy of the priceless trust of your happiness."

"And the wonder to me," replied she, "is that your dear heart ever burdened itself with my happiness. I am weak in myself, and only strong in my resolution to be all a loving wife should be to you, my Pierre! You wonder how you gained my love? Shall I tell you? You never gained it; it was always yours, before you formed a thought to win it! You are now my betrothed, Pierre Philibert, soon to be my husband; I would not exchange my fortune to become the proudest queen that ever sat on the throne of France."

Amelie was very happy to-day. The half-stolen delight of walking by the side of Pierre Philibert was enhanced by the hope that the fatal spell that bound Le Gardeur to the Palace had been broken, and he would yet return home, a new man.

Le Gardeur had only yesterday, in a moment of recollection of himself and of his sister, addressed a note to Amelie, asking pardon for his recent neglect of home, and promising to come and see them on St. Martin's day.

He had heard of her betrothal to Pierre. It was the gladdest news, he said, that had ever come to him in his life. He sent a brother's blessing upon them both, and claimed the privilege of giving away her hand to the noblest man in New France, Pierre Philibert.

Amelie showed the precious note to Pierre. It only needed that to complete their happiness for the day. The one cloud that had overshadowed their joy in their approaching nuptials was passing away, and Amelie was prouder in the anticipation that Le Gardeur, restored to himself, sober, and in his right mind, was to be present at her wedding and give her away, than if the whole Court of France, with thousands of admiring spectators, were to pay her royal honors.

They sauntered on towards a turn of the stream where a little pool lay embayed like a smooth mirror reflecting the grassy bank. Amelie sat down under a tree while Pierre crossed over the brook to gather on the opposite side some flowers which had caught her eye.

"Tell me which, Amelie!" exclaimed he, "for they are all yours; you are Flora's heiress, with right to enter into possession of her whole kingdom!"

"The water-lilies, Pierre, those, and those, and those; they are to deck the shrine of Notre Dame des Victoires. Aunt has a vow there, and to-morrow it must be paid; I too."

He looked up at her with eyes of admiration. "A vow! Let me share in its payment, Amelie," said he.

"You may, but you shall not ask me what it is. There now, do not wet yourself further!

You have gathered more lilies than we can carry home."

"But I have my own thank-offering to make to Notre Dame des Victoires, for I think I love God even better for your sake, Amelie."

"Fie, Pierre, say not that! and yet I know what you mean. I ought to reprove you, but for your penance you shall gather more lilies, for I fear you need many prayers and offerings to expiate,--"she hesitated to finish the sentence.

"My idolatry, Amelie," said he, completing her meaning.

"I doubt it is little better, Pierre, if you love me as you say. But you shall join in my offering, and that will do for both. Please pull that one bunch of lilies and no more, or Our Lady of Victory will judge you harder than I do."

Pierre stepped from stone to stone over the gentle brook, gathering the golden lilies, while Amelie clasped her hands and silently thanked God for this happy hour of her life.

She hardly dared trust herself to look at Pierre except by furtive glances of pride and affection; but as his form and features were reflected in a shadow of manly beauty in the still pool, she withdrew not her loving gaze from his shadow, and leaning forward towards his image,

"A thousand times she kissed him in the brook,
Across the flowers with bashful eyelids down!"

Amelie had royally given her love to Pierre Philibert. She had given it without stint or measure, and with a depth and strength of devotion of which more facile natures know nothing.

Pierre, with his burden of golden lilies, came back over the brook and seated himself beside her; his arm encircled her, and she held his hand firmly clasped in both of hers.

"Amelie," said he, "I believe now in the power of fate to remove mountains of difficulty and cast them into the sea. How often, while watching the stars wheel silently over my head as I lay pillowed on a stone, while my comrades slumbered round the campfires, have I repeated my prayer for Amelie de Repentigny! I had no right to indulge a hope of winning your love; I was but a rough soldier, very practical, and not at all imaginative. 'She would see nothing in me,' I said; and still I would not have given up my hope for a kingdom."

"It was not so hard, after all, to win what was already yours, Pierre, was it?" said she with a smile and a look of unutterable sweetness; "but it was well you asked, for without asking you would be like one possessing a treasure of gold in his field without knowing it, although it was all the while there and all his own. But not a grain of it would you have found without asking me, Pierre!"

"But having found it I shall never lose it again, darling!" replied he, pressing her to his bosom.

"Never, Pierre, it is yours forever!" replied she, her voice trembling with emotion. "Love is, I think, the treasure in heaven which rusts not, and which no thief can steal."

"Amelie," said he after a few minutes' silence, "some say men's lives are counted not by hours but by the succession of ideas and emotions. If it be so, I have lived a century of happiness with you this afternoon. I am old in love, Amelie!"

"Nay, I would not have you old in love, Pierre! Love is the perennial youth of the soul. Grand'mere St. Pierre, who has been fifty years an Ursuline, and has now the visions which are promised to the old in the latter days, tells me that in heaven those who love God and one another grow ever more youthful; the older the more beautiful! Is not that better than the philosophers teach, Pierre?"

He drew her closer, and Amelie permitted him to impress a kiss on each eyelid as she closed it; suddenly she started up.

"Pierre," said she, "you said you were a soldier and so practical. I feel shame to myself for being so imaginative and so silly. I too would be practical if I knew how. This was to be a day of business with us, was it not, Pierre?"

"And is it not a day of business, Amelie? or are we spending it like holiday children, wholly on pleasure? But after all, love is the business of life, and life is the business of eternity,-- we are transacting it to-day, Amelie! I never was so seriously engaged as at this moment, nor you either, darling; tell the truth!"

Amelie pressed her hands in his. "Never, Pierre, and yet I cannot see the old brown woods of Belmont rising yonder upon the slopes of St. Foye without remembering my promise, not two hours old, to talk with you to-day about the dear old mansion."

"That is to be the nest of as happy a pair of lovers as ever went to housekeeping; and I promised to keep soberly by your side as I am doing," said he, mischievously twitching a stray lock of her dark hair, "and talk with you on the pretty banks of the Lairet about the old mansion."

"Yes, Pierre, that was your promise, if I would walk this way with you. Where shall we begin?"

"Here, Amelie," replied he, kissing her fondly; "now the congress is opened! I am your slave of the wonderful lamp, ready to set up and pull down the world at your bidding. The old mansion is your own. It shall have no rest until it becomes, within and without, a mirror of the perfect taste and fancy of its lawful mistress."

"Not yet, Pierre. I will not let you divert me from my purpose by your flatteries. The dear old home is perfect, but I must have the best suite of rooms in it for your noble father, and the next best for good Dame Rochelle. I will fit them up on a plan of my own, and none shall say me nay; that is all the change I shall make."

"Is that all? and you tried to frighten the slave of the lamp with the weight of your commands. A suite of rooms for my father, and one for good Dame Rochelle! Really, and what do you devote to me, Amelie?"

"Oh, all the rest, with its mistress included, for the reason that what is good enough for me is good enough for you, Pierre," said she gaily.

"You little economist! Why, one would say you had studied housekeeping under Madame Painchaud."

"And so I have. You do not know what a treasure I am, Pierre," said she, laughing merrily. "I graduated under mes tantes in the kitchen of the Ursulines, and received an accessit as bonne menagere which in secret I prize more than the crown of honor they gave me."

"My fortune is made, and I am a rich man for life," exclaimed Pierre, clapping his hands; "why, I shall have to marry you like the girls of Acadia, with a silver thimble on your finger and a pair of scissors at your girdle, emblems of industrious habits and proofs of a good housewife!"

"Yes, Pierre, and I will comb your hair to my own liking. Your valet is a rough groom," said she, taking off his hat and passing her finger through his thick, fair locks.

Pierre, although always dressed and trimmed like a gentleman, really cared little for the petit maitre fashions of the day. Never had he felt a thrill of such exquisite pleasure as when Amelie's hands arranged his rough hair to her fancy.

"My blessed Amelie!" said he with emotion, pressing her finger to his lips, "never since my mother combed my boyish locks has a woman's hand touched my hair until now."

Leaning her head fondly against the shoulder of Pierre, she bade him repeat to her again, to her who had not forgotten one word or syllable of the tale he had told her before, the story of his love.

She listened with moistened eyelids and heaving bosom as he told her again of his faithfulness in the past, his joys in the present, and his hopes in the future. She feared to look up lest she should break the charm, but when he had ended she turned to him passionately and kissed his lips and his hands, murmuring, "Thanks, my Pierre, I will be a true and loving wife to you!"

He strained her to his bosom, and held her fast, as if fearful to let her go.

"Her image at that last embrace,
Ah! little thought he 'twas the last!"

Dim twilight crept into the valley. It was time to return home. Pierre and Amelie, full of joy in each other, grateful for the happiest day in their lives, hopeful of to-morrow and many to-morrows after it, and mercifully blinded to what was really before them, rose from their seat under the great spreading elm. They slowly retraced the path through the meadow leading to the bridge, and reentered the highway which ran to the city, where Pierre conducted Amelie home.

# Chapter XLIX: The Market-Place on St. Martin's Day

The market-place then as now occupied the open square lying between the great Cathedral of Ste. Marie and the College of the Jesuits. The latter, a vast edifice, occupied one side of the square. Through its wide portal a glimpse was had of the gardens and broad avenues of ancient trees, sacred to the meditation and quiet exercises of the reverend fathers, who walked about in pairs, according to the rule of their order, which rarely permitted them to go singly.

The market-place itself was lively this morning with the number of carts and stalls ranged on either side of the bright little rivulet which ran under the old elms that intersected the square, the trees affording shade and the rivulet drink for man and beast.

A bustling, loquacious crowd of habitans and citizens, wives and maid-servants, were buying, selling, exchanging compliments, or complaining of hard times. The marketplace was full, and all were glad at the termination of the terrible war, and hopeful of the happy effect of peace in bringing plenty back again to the old market.

The people bustled up and down, testing their weak purses against their strong desires to fill their baskets with the ripe autumnal fruits and the products of field and garden, river and basse cour, which lay temptingly exposed in the little carts of the marketmen and women who on every side extolled the quality and cheapness of their wares.

There were apples from the Cote de Beaupre, small in size but impregnated with the flavor of honey; pears grown in the old orchards about Ange Gardien, and grapes worthy of Bacchus, from the Isle of Orleans, with baskets of the delicious bilberries that cover the wild hills of the north shore from the first wane of summer until late in the autumn.

The drain of the war had starved out the butchers' stalls, but Indians and hunters took their places for the nonce with an abundance of game of all kinds, which had multiplied exceedingly during the years that men had taken to killing Bostonnais and English instead of deer and wild turkeys.

Fish was in especial abundance; the blessing of the old Jesuits still rested on the waters of New France, and the fish swarmed metaphorically with money in their mouths.

There were piles of speckled trout fit to be eaten by popes and kings, taken in the little pure lakes and streams tributary to the Montmorency; lordly salmon that swarmed in the tidal weirs along the shores of the St. Lawrence, and huge eels, thick as the arm of the fisher who drew them up from their rich river-beds.

There were sacks of meal ground in the banal mills of the seigniories for the people's bread, but the old tinettes of yellow butter, the pride of the good wives of Beauport and Lauzon, were rarely to be seen, and commanded unheard-of prices. The hungry children who used to eat tartines of bread buttered on both sides were now accustomed to the cry of their frugal mother as she spread it thin as if it were gold-leaf: "Mes enfants, take care of the butter!"

The Commissaries of the Army, in other words the agents of the Grand Company, had swept the settlements far and near of their herds, and the habitans soon discovered that the exposure for sale in the market of the products of the dairy was speedily followed by a visit from the purveyors of the army, and the seizure of their remaining cattle.

Roots and other esculents of field and garden were more plentiful in the market, among which might have been seen the newly introduced potato,--a vegetable long despised in New France, then endured, and now beginning to be liked and widely cultivated as a prime article of sustenance.

At the upper angle of the square stood a lofty cross or Holy Rood, overtopping the low roofs of the shops and booths in its neighborhood. About the foot of the cross was a platform of timber raised a few feet from the ground, giving a commanding view of the whole market-place.

A crowd of habitans were gathered round this platform listening, some with exclamations of approval, not unmingled on the part of others with sounds of dissent, to the fervent address of one of the Jesuit Fathers from the College, who with crucifix in hand was preaching to the people upon the vices and backslidings of the times.

Father Glapion, the Superior of the order in New France, a grave, saturnine man, and several other fathers in close black cassocks and square caps, stood behind the preacher, watching with keen eyes the faces of the auditory as if to discover who were for and who were against the sentiments and opinions promulgated by the preacher.

The storm of the great Jansenist controversy, which rent the Church of France from top to bottom, had not spared the Colony, where it had early caused trouble; for that controversy grew out of the Gallican liberties of the national Church and the right of national participation in its administrations and appointments. The Jesuits ever fiercely contested these liberties; they boldly set the tiara above the crown, and strove to subordinate all opinions of faith, morals, education, and ecclesiastical government to the infallible judgment of the Pope alone.

The Bishop and clergy of New France had labored hard to prevent the introduction of that mischievous controversy into the Colony, and had for the most part succeeded in reserving their flocks, if not themselves, from its malign influence. The growing agitation in France, however, made it more difficult to keep down troublesome spirits in the Colony, and the idea got abroad, not without some foundation, that the Society of Jesus had secret commercial relations with the Friponne. This report fanned the smouldering fires of Jansenism into a flame visible enough and threatening enough to the peace of the Church.

The failure and bankruptcy of Father Vallette's enormous speculations in the West Indies had filled France with bad debts and protested obligations which the Society of Jesus repudiated, but which the Parliament of Paris ordered them to pay. The excitement was intense all over the Kingdom and the Colonies. On the part of the order it became a fight for existence.

They were envied for their wealth, and feared for their ability and their power. The secular clergy were for the most part against them. The Parliament of Paris, in a violent decree, had declared the Jesuits to have no legal standing in France. Voltaire and his followers, a growing host, thundered at them from the one side. The Vatican, in a moment of inconsistency and ingratitude, thundered at them from the other. They were in the midst of fire, and still their ability and influence over individual consciences, and especially over the female sex, prolonged their power for fifteen years longer, when Louis XV., driven to the wall by the Jansenists, issued his memorable decree declaring the Jesuits to be rebels, traitors, and stirrers up of mischief. The King confiscated their possessions, proscribed their persons, and banished them from the kingdom as enemies of the State.

Padre Monti, an Italian newly arrived in the Colony, was a man very different from the venerable Vimont and the Jogues and the Lallements, who had preached the Evangel to the wild tribes of the forest, and rejoiced when they won the crown of martyrdom for themselves.

Monti was a bold man in his way, and ready to dare any bold deed in the interests of religion, which he could not dissociate from the interests of his order. He stood up, erect and commanding, upon the platform under the Holy Rood, while he addressed with fiery eloquence and Italian gesticulation the crowd of people gathered round him.

The subject he chose was an exciting one. He enlarged upon the coming of Antichrist and upon the new philosophy of the age, the growth of Gallicanism in the Colony, with its schismatic progeny of Jansenists and Honnetes Gens, to the discouragement of true religion and the endangering of immortal souls.

His covert allusions and sharp innuendoes were perfectly understood by his hearers, and signs of dissentient feeling were rife among the crowd. Still, the people continued to listen, on the whole respectfully; for, whatever might be the sentiment of Old France with respect to the Jesuits, they had in New France inherited the profound respect of the colonists, and deserved it.

A few gentlemen, some in military, some in fashionable civil attire, strolled up towards the crowd, but stood somewhat aloof and outside of it. The market people pressed closer and closer round the platform, listening with mouths open and eager eyes to the sermon, storing it away in their retentive memories, which would reproduce every word of it when they sat round the fireside in the coming winter evenings.

One or two Recollets stood at a modest distance from the crowd, still as statues, with their hands hid in the sleeves of their gray gowns, shaking their heads at the arguments, and still more at the invectives of the preacher; for the Recollets were accused, wrongfully perhaps, of studying the five propositions of Port Royal more than beseemed the humble followers of St. Francis to do, and they either could not or would not repel the accusation.

"Padre Monti deserves the best thanks of the Intendant for this sermon," remarked the Sieur d'Estebe to Le Mercier, who accompanied him.

"And the worst thanks of His Excellency the Count! It was bold of the Italian to beard the Governor in that manner! But La Galissoniere is too great a philosopher to mind a priest!" was the half-scoffing reply of Le Mercier.

"Is he? I do not think so, Le Mercier. I hate them myself, but egad! I am not philosophic enough to let them know it. One may do so in Paris, but not in New France. Besides, the Jesuits are just now our fast friends, and it does not do to quarrel with your supporters."

"True, D'Estebe! We get no help from the Recollets. Look yonder at Brothers Ambrose and Daniel! They would like to tie Padre Monti neck and heels with the cords of St. Francis, and bind him over to keep the peace towards Port Royal; but the gray gowns are afraid of the black robes. Padre Monti knew they would not catch the ball when he threw it. The Recollets are all afraid to hurl it back."

"Not all," was the reply; "the Reverend Father de Berey would have thrown it back with a vengeance. But I confess, Le Mercier, the Padre is a bold fellow to pitch into the Honnetes Gens the way he does. I did not think he would have ventured upon it here in the market, in face of so many habitans, who swear by the Bourgeois Philibert."

The bold denunciations by the preacher against the Honnetes Gens and against the people's friend and protector, the Bourgeois Philibert, caused a commotion in the crowd of habitans, who began to utter louder and louder exclamations of dissent and remonstrance. A close observer would have noticed angry looks and clenched fists in many parts of the crowd, pressing closer and closer round the platform.

The signs of increasing tumult in the crowd did not escape the sharp eyes of Father Glapion, who, seeing that the hot-blooded Italian was overstepping the bounds of prudence in his harangue, called him by name, and with a half angry sign brought his sermon suddenly to a close. Padre Monti obeyed with the unquestioning promptness of an automaton. He stopped instantly, without rounding the period or finishing the sentence that was in his mouth.

His flushed and ardent manner changed to the calmness of marble as, lifting up his hands with a devout oremus, he uttered a brief prayer and left the puzzled people to finish his speech and digest at leisure his singular sermon.

# Chapter L: "Blessed They Who Die Doing Thy Will"

It was the practice of the Bourgeois Philibert to leave his counting-room to walk through the market-place, not for the sake of the greetings he met, although he received them from every side, nor to buy or sell on his own account, but to note with quick, sympathizing eye the poor and needy and to relieve their wants.

Especially did he love to meet the old, the feeble, the widow, and the orphan, so numerous from the devastation of the long and bloody war.

The Bourgeois had another daily custom which he observed with unfailing regularity. His table in the House of the Golden Dog was set every day with twelve covers and dishes for twelve guests, "the twelve apostles," as he gayly used to say, "whom I love to have dine with me, and who come to my door in the guise of poor, hungry, and thirsty men, needing meat and drink. Strangers to be taken in, and sick wanting a friend." If no other guests came he was always sure of the "apostles" to empty his table, and, while some simple dish sufficed for himself, he ordered the whole banquet to be given away to the poor. His choice wines, which he scarcely permitted himself to taste, were removed from his table and sent to the Hotel Dieu, the great convent of the Nuns Hospitalieres, for the use of the sick in their charge, while the Bourgeois returned thanks with a heart more content than if kings had dined at his table.

To-day was the day of St. Martin, the anniversary of the death of his wife, who still lived in his memory fresh as upon the day he took her away as his bride from her Norman home. Upon every recurrence of that day, and upon some other special times and holidays, his bounty was doubled, and the Bourgeois made preparations, as he jocularly used to say, "not only for the twelve apostles, but for the seventy disciples as well!"

He had just dressed himself with scrupulous neatness in the fashion of a plain gentleman, as was his wont, without a trace of foppery. With his stout gold-headed cane in his hand, he was descending the stairs to go out as usual to the market, when Dame Rochelle accosted him in the hall.

Her eyes and whole demeanor wore an expression of deep anxiety as the good dame looked up in the face of the Bourgeois.

"Do not go to the market to-day, dear master!" said she, beseechingly; "I have been there myself and have ordered all we need for the due honor of the day."

"Thanks, good dame, for remembering the blessed anniversary, but you know I am expected in the market. It is one of my special days. Who is to fill the baskets of the poor people who feel a delicacy about coming for alms to the door, unless I go? Charity fulfills its mission best when it respects the misfortune of being poor in the persons of its recipients. I must make my round of the market, good dame."

"And still, dear master, go not to-day; I never asked you before; I do this time. I fear some evil this morning!"

The Bourgeois looked at her inquiringly. He knew the good dame too well not to be sure she had some weighty reason for her request.

"What particularly moves you to this singular request, Dame Rochelle?" asked he.

"A potent reason, master, but it would not weigh a grain with you as with me. There is this morning a wild spirit afloat,--people's minds have been excited by a sermon from one of the college fathers. The friends of the Intendant are gathered in force, they say, to clear the market of the Honnetes Gens. A disturbance is impending. That, master, is one reason. My other is a presentiment that some harm will befall you if you go to the market in the midst of such excitement."

"Thanks, good dame," replied the Bourgeois calmly, "both for your information and your presentiment; but they only furnish an additional reason why I should go to try to prevent any disturbance among my fellow-citizens."

"Still, master, you see not what I see, and hear not what I hear, and would not believe it did I tell you! I beseech you, go not to- day!" exclaimed she imploringly, clasping her hands in the eagerness of her appeal.

"Good dame," replied he, "I deeply respect your solicitude, but I could not, without losing all respect for myself as a gentleman, stay away out of any consideration of impending danger. I should esteem it my duty all the more to go, if there be danger, which I cannot believe."

"Oh, that Pierre were here to accompany you! But at least take some servants with you, master," implored the dame, persisting in her request.

"Good dame, I cannot consult fear when I have duty to perform; besides, I am in no danger. I have enemies enough, I know; but he would be a bold man who would assail the Bourgeois Philibert in the open market-place of Quebec."

"Yet there may be such a bold man, master," replied she. "There are many such men who would consider they did the Intendant and themselves good service by compassing your destruction!"

"May be so, dame; but I should be a mark of scorn for all men if I evaded a duty, small or great, through fear of the Intendant or any of his friends."

"I knew my appeal would be in vain, master, but forgive my anxiety. God help you! God defend you!"

She looked at him fixedly for a moment. He saw her features were quivering with emotion and her eyes filled with tears.

"Good dame," said he kindly, taking her hand, "I respect your motives, and will so far show my regard for your forecast of danger as to take my sword, which, after a good conscience, is the best friend a gentleman can have to stand by him in peril. Please bring it to me."

"Willingly, master, and may it be like the sword of the cherubim, to guard and protect you to-day!"

She went into the great hall for the rapier of the Bourgeois, which he only wore on occasions of full dress and ceremony. He took it smilingly from her hand, and, throwing the belt over his shoulder, bade Dame Rochelle good-by, and proceeded to the market.

The dame looked earnestly after him until he turned the corner of the great Cathedral, when, wiping her eyes, she went into the house and sat down pensively for some minutes.

"Would that Pierre had not gone to St. Ann's to-day!" cried she. "My master! my noble, good master! I feel there is evil abroad for him in the market to-day." She turned, as was her wont in time of trouble, to the open Bible that ever lay upon her table, and sought strength in meditation upon its sacred pages.

There was much stir in the market when the Bourgeois began his accustomed walk among the stalls, stopping to converse with such friends as he met, and especially with the poor and infirm, who did not follow him--he hated to be followed,--but who stood waiting his arrival at certain points which he never failed to pass. The Bourgeois knew that his poor almsmen would be standing there, and he would no more avoid them than he would avoid the Governor.

A group of girls very gaily dressed loitered through the market, purchasing bouquets of the last of autumnal flowers, and coquetting with the young men of fashion who chose the market-place for their morning promenade, and who spent their smiles and wit freely, and sometimes their money, upon the young ladies they expected to find there.

This morning the Demoiselles Grandmaison and Hebert were cheapening immortelles and dry flowers to decorate their winter vases,--a pleasant fashion, not out of date in the city at the present day.

The attention of these young ladies was quite as much taken up with the talk of their cavaliers as with their bargaining when a quick exclamation greeted them from a lady on horseback, accompanied by the Chevalier de Pean. She drew bridle sharply in front of the group, and leaning down from her saddle gave her hand to the ladies, bidding them good morning in a cheery voice which there was no mistaking, although her face was invisible behind her veil. It was Angelique des Meloises, more gay and more fascinating than ever.

She noticed two gentlemen in the group. "Oh, pardon me, Messieurs Le Mercier and d'Estebe!" said she. "I did not perceive you. My veil is so in the way!" She pushed it aside coquettishly, and gave a finger to each of the gentlemen, who returned her greeting with extreme politeness.

"Good morning! say you, Angelique?" exclaimed Mademoiselle Hebert; "it is a good noon. You have slept rarely! How bright and fresh you look, darling!"

"Do I not!" laughed Angelique in reply. "It is the morning air and a good conscience make it! Are you buying flowers? I have been to Sillery for mine!" said she, patting her blooming cheeks with the end of her riding-whip. She had no time for further parley, for her attention was suddenly directed by De Pean to some stir upon the other side of the market, with an invitation to her to ride over and see what was the matter. Angelique at once wheeled her horse to accompany De Pean.

The group of girls felt themselves eclipsed and overborne by the queenly airs of Angelique, and were glad when she moved off, fearing that by some adroit manoeuvre she would carry off their cavaliers. It needed but a word, as they knew, to draw them all after her.

Angelique, under the lead of De Pean, rode quickly towards the scene of confusion, where men were gesticulating fiercely and uttering loud, angry words such as usually precede the drawing of swords and the rush of combatants.

To her surprise, she recognized Le Gardeur de Repentigny, very drunk and wild with anger, in the act of leaping off his horse with oaths of vengeance against some one whom she could not distinguish in the throng.

Le Gardeur had just risen from the gaming-table, where he had been playing all night. He was maddened with drink and excited by great losses, which in his rage he called unfair.

Colonel St. Remy had rooked him at piquet, he said, and refused him the chance of an honorable gamester to win back some part of his losses. His antagonist had left the Palace like a sneak, and he was riding round the city to find him, and horsewhip him if he would not fight like a gentleman.

Le Gardeur was accompanied by the Sieur de Lantagnac, who, by splendid dissipation, had won his whole confidence. Le Gardeur, when drunk, thought the world did not contain a finer fellow than Lantagnac, whom he thoroughly despised when sober.

At a hint from De Pean, the Sieur de Lantagnac had clung to Le Gardeur that morning like his shadow, had drunk with him again and again, exciting his wrath against St. Remy; but apparently keeping his own head clear enough for whatever mischief De Pean had put into it.

They rode together to the market-place, hearing that St. Remy was at the sermon. Their object, as Le Gardeur believed, was to put an unpardonable insult upon St. Remy, by striking him with his whip and forcing him to fight a duel with Le Gardeur or his friend. The reckless De Lantagnac asserted loudly, he "did not care a straw which!"

Le Gardeur and De Lantagnac rode furiously through the market, heedless of what they encountered or whom they ran over, and were followed by a yell of indignation from the people, who recognized them as gentlemen of the Grand Company.

It chanced that at that moment a poor almsman of the Bourgeois Philibert was humbly and quietly leaning on his crutches, listening with bowing head and smiling lips to the kind inquiries of his benefactor as he received his accustomed alms.

De Lantagnac rode up furiously, followed by Le Gardeur. De Lantagnac recognized the Bourgeois, who stood in his way talking to the crippled soldier. He cursed him between his teeth, and lashed his horse with intent to ride him down as if by accident.

The Bourgeois saw them approach and motioned them to stop, but in vain. The horse of De Lantagnac just swerved in its course, and without checking his speed ran over the crippled man, who instantly rolled in the dust, his face streaming with blood from a sharp stroke of the horse's shoe upon his forehead.

Immediately following De Lantagnac came Le Gardeur, lashing his horse and yelling like a demon to all to clear the way.

The Bourgeois was startled at this new danger, not to himself,--he thought not of himself,--but to the bleeding man lying prostrate upon the ground. He sprang forward to prevent Le Gardeur's horse going over him.

He did not, in the haste and confusion of the moment, recognize Le Gardeur, who, inflamed with wine and frantic with passion, was almost past recognition by any who knew him in his normal state. Nor did Le Gardeur, in his frenzy, recognize the presence of the Bourgeois, whose voice calling him by name, with an appeal to his better nature, would undoubtedly have checked his headlong career.

The moment was critical. It was one of those points of time where the threads of many lives and many destinies cross and intersect each other, and thence part different ways, leading to life or death, happiness or despair, forever!

Le Gardeur spurred his horse madly over the wounded man who lay upon the ground; but he did not hear him, he did not see him. Let it be said for Le Gardeur, if aught can be said in his defence, he did not see him. His horse was just about to trample upon the prostrate cripple lying in the dust, when his bridle was suddenly and firmly seized by the hand of the Bourgeois, and his horse wheeled round with such violence that, rearing back upon his haunches, he almost threw his rider headlong.

Le Gardeur, not knowing the reason of this sudden interference, and flaming with wrath, leaped to the ground just at the moment when Angelique and De Pean rode up. Le Gardeur neither knew nor cared at that moment who his antagonist was; he saw but a bold, presumptuous man who had seized his bridle, and whom it was his desire to punish on the spot.

De Pean recognized the stately figure and fearless look of the Bourgeois confronting Le Gardeur. The triumph of the Friponne was at hand. De Pean rubbed his hands with ecstasy as he called out to Le Gardeur, his voice ringing above the din of the crowd, "Achevez- le! Finish him, Le Gardeur!"

Angelique sat upon her horse fixed as a statue and as pale as marble, not at the danger of the Bourgeois, whom she at once recognized, but out of fear for her lover, exposed to the menaces of the crowd, who were all on the side of the Bourgeois.

Le Gardeur leaped down from his horse and advanced with a terrible imprecation upon the Bourgeois, and struck him with his whip. The brave old merchant had the soul of a marshal of France. His blood boiled at the insult; he raised his staff to ward off a second blow and struck Le Gardeur sharply upon the wrist, making his whip fly out of his hand. Le Gardeur instantly advanced again upon him, but was pressed back by the habitans, who rushed to the defence of the Bourgeois. Then came the tempter to his ear,--a word or two, and the fate of many innocent lives was decided in a moment!

Le Gardeur suddenly felt a hand laid upon his shoulder, and heard a voice, a woman's voice, speaking to him in passionate tones.

Angelique had forced her horse into the thick of the crowd. She was no longer calm, nor pale with apprehension, but her face was flushed redder than fire, and her eyes, those magnetic orbs which drove men mad, blazed upon Le Gardeur with all their terrible influence. She had seen him struck by the Bourgeois, and her anger was equal to his own.

De Pean saw the opportunity.

"Angelique," exclaimed he, "the Bourgeois strikes Le Gardeur! What an outrage! Can you bear it?"

"Never!" replied she; "neither shall Le Gardeur!"

With a plunge of her horse she forced her way close to Le Gardeur, and, leaning over him, laid her hand upon his shoulder and exclaimed in a voice choking with passion,--

"Comment, Le Gardeur! vous souffrez qu'un Malva comme ca vous abime de coups, et vous portez l'epee!" "What, Le Gardeur! you allow a ruffian like that to load you with blows, and you wear a sword!"

It was enough! That look, that word, would have made Le Gardeur slaughter his father at that moment.

Astonished at the sight of Angelique, and maddened by her words as much as by the blow he had received, Le Gardeur swore he would have revenge upon the spot. With a wild cry and the strength and agility of a panther he twisted himself out of the grasp of the habitans, and drawing his sword, before any man could stop him, thrust it to the hilt through the body of the Bourgeois, who, not expecting this sudden assault, had not put himself in an attitude of defense to meet it.

The Bourgeois fell dying by the side of the bleeding man who had just received his alms, and in whose protection he had thus risked and lost his own life.

"Bravo, Le Gardeur!" exclaimed De Pean; "that was the best stroke ever given in New France. The Golden Dog is done for, and the Bourgeois has paid his debt to the Grand Company."

Le Gardeur looked up wildly. "Who is he, De Pean?" exclaimed he. "What man have I killed?"

"The Bourgeois Philibert, who else?" shouted De Pean with a tone of exultation.

Le Gardeur uttered a wailing cry, "The Bourgeois Philibert! have I slain the Bourgeois Philibert? De Pean lies, Angelique," said he, suddenly turning to her. "I would not kill a sparrow belonging to the Bourgeois Philibert! Oh, tell me De Pean lies."

"De Pean does not lie, Le Gardeur," answered she, frightened at his look. "The Bourgeois struck you first. I saw him strike you first with his staff. You are a gentleman and would kill the King if he struck you like a dog with his staff. Look where they are lifting him up. You see it is the Bourgeois and no other."

Le Gardeur gave one wild look and recognized the well-known form and features of the Bourgeois. He threw his sword on the ground, exclaiming, "Oh! oh! unhappy man that I am! It is parricide! parricide! to have slain the father of my brother Pierre! Oh, Angelique des Meloises! you made me draw my sword, and I knew not who it was or what I did!"

"I told you, Le Gardeur, and you are angry with me. But see! hark! what a tumult is gathering; we must get out of this throng or we shall all be killed as well as the Bourgeois. Fly, Le Gardeur, fly! Go to the Palace!"

"To hell sooner! Never shall the Palace see me again!" exclaimed he madly. "The people shall kill me if they will, but save yourself, Angelique. De Pean, lead her instantly away from this cursed spot, or all the blood is not spilt that will be spilt to-day. This is of your contriving, De Pean," cried he, looking savagely, as if about to spring upon him.

"You would not harm me or her, Le Gardeur?" interrupted De Pean, turning pale at his fierce look.

"Harm her, you fool, no! but I will harm you if you do not instantly take her away out of this tumult. I must see the Bourgeois. Oh God, if he be dead!"

A great cry now ran through the market-place: "The Bourgeois is killed. The Grand Company have assassinated the Bourgeois." Men ran up from every side shouting and gesticulating. The news spread like wild-fire through the city, and simultaneously a yell for vengeance rose from the excited multitude.

The Recollet Brother Daniel had been the first to fly to the help of the Bourgeois. His gray robe presently was dyed red with the blood of the best friend and protector of their monastery. But death was too quick for even one prayer to be heard or uttered by the dying man.

The gray Brother made the sign of the cross upon the forehead of the Bourgeois, who opened his eyes once for a moment, and looked in the face of the good friar while his lips quivered with two inarticulate words, "Pierre! Amelie!" That was all. His brave eyes closed again forever from the light of the sun. The good Bourgeois Philibert was dead.

"'Blessed are the dead who die in the Lord,'" repeated the Recollet. "'Even so, saith the Spirit, for they rest from their labors.'"

De Pean had foreseen the likelihood of a popular commotion. He was ready to fly on the instant, but could not prevail on Angelique to leave Le Gardeur, who was kneeling down by the side of the Bourgeois, lifting him in his arms and uttering the wildest accents of grief as he gazed upon the pallid, immovable face of the friend of his youth.

"That is the assassin, and the woman, too," cried a sturdy habitan. "I heard her bid him draw his sword upon the Bourgeois."

The crowd for the moment believed that De Pean had been the murderer of Philibert.

"No, not he; it was the other. It was the officer who dismounted,-- the drunken officer. Who was he? Where is he?" cried the habitan, forcing his way into the presence of Le Gardeur, who was still kneeling by the side of the Bourgeois and was not seen for a few moments; but quickly he was identified.

"That is he!" cried a dozen voices. "He is looking if he has killed him, by God!"

A number of men rushed upon Le Gardeur, who made no defence, but continued kneeling beside the Recollet Brother Daniel over the body of the Bourgeois. He was instantly seized by some of the crowd. He held out his hands and bade them take him prisoner or kill him on the spot, if they would, for it was he who had killed the Bourgeois.

Half a dozen swords were instantly drawn as if to take him at his word, when the terrible shrieks of Angelique pierced every ear. The crowd turned in astonishment to see who it was on horseback that cried so terribly, "Do not kill him! Do not kill Le Gardeur de Repentigny!" She called several citizens by name and entreated them to help to save him.

By her sudden interference Angelique caused a diversion in the crowd. Le Gardeur rose up to his feet, and many persons recognized him with astonishment and incredulity, for no one could believe that he had killed the good Bourgeois, who was known to have been the warm friend of the whole family of De Repentigny.

De Pean, taking advantage of the sudden shift of feeling in the crowd and anxious for the safety of Angelique, seized the bridle of her horse to drag her forcibly out of the press, telling her that her words had been heard and in another instant the whole mob would turn its fury upon her, and in order to save her life she must fly.

"I will not fly, De Pean. You may fly yourself, for you are a coward. They are going to kill Le Gardeur, and I will not forsake him. They shall kill me first."

"But you must! You shall fly! Hark! Le Gardeur is safe for the present. Wheel your horse around, and you will see him standing up yonder quite safe! The crowd rather believe it was I who killed the Bourgeois, and not Le Gardeur! I have a soul and body to be saved as well as he!"

"Curse you, soul and body, De Pean! You made me do it! You put those hellish words in my mouth! I will not go until I see Le Gardeur safe!"

Angelique endeavored frantically to approach Le Gardeur, and could not, but as she looked over the surging heads of the people she could see Le Gardeur standing up, surrounded by a ring of agitated men who did not appear, however, to threaten him with any injury,-- nay, looked at him more with wonder and pity than with menace of injury.

He was a prisoner, but Angelique did not know it or she would not have left him. As it was, urged by the most vehement objurgations of De Pean, and seeing a portion of the crowd turning their furious looks towards herself as she sat upon her horse, unable either to go or stay, De Pean suddenly seized her rein, and spurring his own horse, dragged her furiously in spite of herself out of the tumult. They rode headlong to the casernes of the Regiment of Bearn, where they took refuge for the moment from the execrations of the populace.

The hapless Le Gardeur became suddenly sobered and conscious of the enormity of his act. He called madly for death from the raging crowd. He held out his hands for chains to bind a murderer, as he called himself! But no one would strike him or offer to bind him. The wrath of the people was so mingled with blank astonishment at his demeanor, his grief and his despair were so evidently genuine and so deep, that many said he was mad, and more an object of pity than of punishment.

At his own reiterated command, he was given over to the hands of some soldiers and led off, followed by a great crowd of people, to the main guard of the Castle of St. Louis, where he was left a prisoner, while another portion of the multitude gathered about the scene of the tragedy, surrounded the body of the Bourgeois, which was lifted off the ground and borne aloft on men's shoulders, followed by wild cries and lamentations to the House of the Golden Dog,-- the house which he had left but half an hour before, full of life, vigor and humanity, looking before and after as a strong man looks who has done his duty, and who feels still able to take the world upon his shoulders and carry it, if need were.

The sad procession moved slowly on amid the pressing, agitated crowd, which asked and answered a hundred eager questions in a breath. The two poor Recollet brothers, Daniel and Ambrose, walked side by side before the bleeding corpse of their friend, and stifled their emotions by singing, in a broken voice that few heard but themselves, the words of the solitary hymn of St. Francis d'Assisi, the founder of their order:

"Praised be the Lord, by our sweet sister Death,
From whom no man escapes, howe'er he try!

Woe to all those who yield their parting breath
In mortal sin! But blessed those who die
Doing thy will in that decisive hour!
The second death o'er such shall have no power.
    Praise, blessing, and thanksgiving to my Lord!
    For all He gives and takes be He adored!"

Dame Rochelle heard the approaching noise and tumult. She looked out of the window and could see the edge of the crowd in the market- place tossing to and fro like breakers upon a rocky shore. The people in the streets were hurrying towards the market. Swarms of men employed in the magazines of the Bourgeois were running out of the edifice towards the same spot.

The dame divined at once that something had happened to her master. She uttered a fervent prayer for his safety. The noise grew greater, and as she reached out of the window to demand of passers- by what was the matter, a voice shouted up that the Bourgeois was dead; that he had been killed by the Grand Company, and they were bringing him home.

The voice passed on, and no one but God heeded the long wail of grief that rose from the good dame as she fell upon her knees in the doorway, unable to proceed further. She preserved her consciousness, however.

The crowd now swarmed in the streets about the doors of the house. Presently were heard the shuffling steps of a number of men in the great hall, bearing the body of the Bourgeois into the large room where the sunshine was playing so gloriously.

The crowd, impelled by a feeling of reverence, stood back; only a few ventured to come into the house.

The rough habitans who brought him in laid him upon a couch and gazed for some moments in silent awe upon the noble features, so pale and placid, which now lay motionless before them.

Here was a man fit to rule an empire, and who did rule the half of New France, who was no more now, save in the love and gratitude of the people, than the poorest piece of human clay in the potter's field. The great leveller had passed his rule over him as he passes it over every one of us. The dead lion was less now than the living dog, and the Golden Dog itself was henceforth only a memory, and an epitaph forever of the tragedy of this eventful day.

"Oh, my master! my good, noble master!" exclaimed Dame Rochelle as she roused herself up and rushed to the chamber of the dead. "Your implacable enemies have killed you at last! I knew it! Oh, I knew that your precious life would one day pay the penalty of your truth and justice! And Pierre! Oh, where is he on this day of all days of grief and sorrow?"

She wrung her hands at the thought of Pierre's absence to-day, and what a welcome home awaited him.

The noise and tumult in the street continued to increase. The friends of the Bourgeois poured into the house, among them the Governor and La Corne St. Luc, who came with anxious looks and hasty steps to inquire into the details of the murder.

The Governor, after a short consultation with La Corne St. Luc, who happened to be at the Castle, fearing a riot and an attack upon the magazines of the Grand Company, ordered the troops immediately under arms and despatched strong detachments under the command of careful and trusty officers to the Palace of the Intendant, and the great warehouse of the Friponne, and also into the market-place, and to the residence of the Lady de Tilly, not knowing in what direction the fury of the populace might direct itself.

The orders were carried out in a few minutes without noise or confusion. The Count, with La Corne St. Luc, whose countenance bore a concentration of sorrow and anger wonderful to see, hastened down to the house of mourning. Claude Beauharnais and Rigaud de Vaudreuil followed hastily after them. They pushed through the crowd that filled the Rue Buade, and the people took off their hats, while the air resounded with denunciations of the Friponne and appeals for vengeance upon the assassin of the Bourgeois.

The Governor and his companions were moved to tears at the sight of their murdered friend lying in his bloody vesture, which was open to enable the worthy Dr. Gauthier, who had run in all haste, to examine the still oozing wound. The Recollet Brother Daniel still knelt in silent prayer at his feet, while Dame Rochelle with trembling hands arranged the drapery decently over her dead master, repeating to herself:

"It is the end of trouble, and God has mercifully taken him away before he empties the vials of his wrath upon this New France, and gives it up for a possession to our enemies! What says the prophet? 'The righteous perisheth and no man layeth it to heart, and merciful men are taken away, none considering that the righteous are taken away from the evil to come!'"

The very heart of La Corne St. Luc seemed bursting in his bosom, and he choked with agony as he placed his hand upon the forehead of his friend, and reflected that the good Bourgeois had fallen by the sword of his godson, the old man's pride,--Le Gardeur de Repentigny!

"Had death come to him on the broad, common road of mortality,--had he died like a soldier on the battlefield," exclaimed La Corne, "I would have had no spite at fate. But to be stabbed in the midst of his good deeds of alms, and by the hand of one whom he loved! Yes, by God! I will say it! and by one who loved him! Oh, it is terrible, Count! Terrible and shameful to me as if it had been the deed of my own son!"

"La Corne, I feel with you the grief and shame of such a tragedy. But there is a fearful mystery in this thing which we cannot yet unravel. They say the Chevalier de Pean dropped an expression that sounded like a plot. I cannot think Le Gardeur de Repentigny would deliberately and with forethought have killed the Bourgeois."

"On my life he never would! He respected the Bourgeois, nay, loved him, for the sake of Pierre Philibert as well as for his own sake. Terrible as is his crime, he never committed it out of malice aforethought. He has been himself the victim of some hellish plot,-- for a plot there has been. This has been no chance melee, Count," exclaimed La Corne St. Luc impetuously.

"It looks like a chance melee, but I suspect more than appears on the surface," replied the Governor. "The removal of the Bourgeois decapitates the party of the Honnetes Gens, does it not?"

"Gospel is not more true! The Bourgeois was the only merchant in New France capable of meeting their monopoly and fighting them with their own weapons. Bigot and the Grand Company will have everything their own way now."

"Besides, there was the old feud of the Golden Dog," continued the Governor. "Bigot took its allusion to the Cardinal as a personal insult to himself, did he not, La Corne?"

"Yes; and Bigot knew he deserved it equally with his Eminence, whose arch-tool he had been," replied La Corne. "By God! I believe Bigot has been at the bottom of this plot. It would be worthy of his craft."

"These are points to be considered, La Corne. But such is the secrecy of these men's councils, that I doubt we may suspect more than we shall ever be able to prove." The Governor looked much agitated.

"What amazes me, Count, is not that the thing should be done, but that Le Gardeur should have done it!" exclaimed La Corne, with a puzzled expression.

"That is the strangest circumstance of all, La Corne," observed the Governor. "The same thought has struck me. But he was mad with wine, they say; and men who upset their reason do not seldom reverse their conduct towards their friends; they are often cruelest to those whom they love best."

"I will not believe but that he was made drunk purposely to commit this crime!" exclaimed La Corne, striking his hand upon his thigh. "Le Gardeur in his senses would have lost his right hand sooner than have raised it against the Bourgeois."

"I feel sure of it; his friendship for Pierre Philibert, to whom he owed his life, was something rarely seen now-a-days," remarked the Count.

La Corne felt a relief in bearing testimony in favor of Le Gardeur. "They loved one another like brothers," said he, "and more than brothers. Bigot had corrupted the habits, but could never soil the heart or lessen the love of Le Gardeur for Pierre Philibert, or his respect for the Bourgeois, his father."

"It is a mystery, La Corne; I cannot fathom it. But there is one more danger to guard against," said the Governor meditatively, "and we have sorrow enough already among our friends."

"What is that, Count?" La Corne stood up erect as if in mental defiance of a new danger.

"Pierre Philibert will return home to-night," replied the Governor; "he carries the sharpest sword in New France. A duel between him and Le Gardeur would crown the machinations of the secret plotters in this murder. He will certainly avenge his father's death, even upon Le Gardeur."

La Corne St. Luc started at this suggestion, but presently shook his head. "My life upon it," said he, "Le Gardeur would stand up to receive the sword of Pierre through his heart, but he would never fight him! Besides, the unhappy boy is a prisoner."

"We will care well for him and keep him safe. He shall have absolute justice, La Corne, but no favor."

An officer entered the room to report to the Governor that the troops had reached their assigned posts, and that there was no symptom of rioting among the people in any quarter of the city.

The Governor was greatly relieved by these tidings. "Now, La Corne," said he, "we have done what is needful for the public. I can spare you, for I know where your heart yearns most to go, to offer the consolations of a true friend."

"Alas, yes," replied La Corne sadly. "Men weep tears of water, but women tears of blood! What is our hardest grief compared with the overwhelming sorrow and desolation that will pass over my poor goddaughter, Amelie de Repentigny, and the noble Lady de Tilly at this doleful news?"

"Go comfort them, La Corne, and the angel of consolation go with you!" The Governor shook him by the hand and wished him Godspeed.

La Corne St. Luc instantly left the house. The crowd uncovered and made way for him as they would have done for the Governor himself, as with hasty strides he passed up the Rue du Fort and on towards the Cape, where stood the mansion of the Lady de Tilly.

"Oh, Rigaud, what a day of sorrow this is!" exclaimed the Governor to De Vaudreuil, on their return to the Castle of St. Louis. "What a bloody and disgraceful event to record in the annals of New France!"

"I would give half I have in the world could it be forever blotted out," replied De

Vaudreuil. "Your friend, Herr Kalm, has left us, fortunately, before he could record in his book, for all Europe to read, that men are murdered in New France to sate the vengeance of a Royal Intendant and fill the purses of the greatest company of thieves that ever plundered a nation."

"Hark, Rigaud! do not say such things," interrupted the Governor; "I trust it is not so bad as that; but it shall be seen into, if I remain Governor of New France. The blood of the noble Bourgeois shall be requited at the hands of all concerned in his assassination. The blame of it shall not rest wholly upon that unhappy Le Gardeur. We will trace it up to its very origin and fountain-head."

"Right, Count; you are true as steel. But mark me! if you begin to trace this assassination up to its origin and fountain-head, your letters of recall will be despatched by the first ship that leaves France after the news reaches Versailles." Rigaud looked fixedly at the Count as he said this.

"It may be so, Rigaud," replied the Count, sadly; "strange things take place under the regime of the strange women who now rule the Court. Nevertheless, while I am here my whole duty shall be done. In this matter justice shall be meted out with a firm and impartial hand, no matter who shall be incriminated!"

The Count de la Galissoniere at once summoned a number of his most trusted and most sagacious councillors together--the Intendant was not one of those summoned--to consider what steps it behooved them to take to provide for the public safety and to ensure the ends of justice in this lamentable tragedy.

## Chapter LI: Evil News Rides Post

The sunbeams never shone more golden through the casement of a lady's bower than on that same morning of St. Martin's through the window of the chamber of Amelie de Repentigny, as she sat in the midst of a group of young ladies holding earnest council over the dresses and adornments of herself and companions, who were to be her bridesmaids on her marriage with Pierre Philibert.

Amelie had risen from pleasant dreams. The tender flush of yesterday's walk on the banks of the Lairet lingered on her cheek all night long, like the rosy tint of a midsummer's sunset. The loving words of Pierre floated through her memory like a strain of divine music, with the sweet accompaniment of her own modest confessions of love, which she had so frankly expressed.

Amelie's chamber was vocal with gaiety and laughter; for with her to-day were the chosen friends and lifelong companions who had ever shared her love and confidence.

These were, Hortense Beauharnais, happy also in her recent betrothal to Jumonville de Villiers; Heloise de Lotbiniere, so tenderly attached to Amelie, and whom of all her friends Amelie wanted most to call by the name of sister; Agathe, the fair daughter of La Corne St. Luc, so like her father in looks and spirit; and Amelie's cousin, Marguerite de Repentigny, the reflection of herself in feature and manners.

There was rich material in that chamber for the conversation of such a group of happy girls. The bridal trousseau was spread out before them, and upon chairs and couches lay dresses of marvellous fabric and beauty,--muslins and shawls of India and Cashmere, and the finest products of the looms of France and Holland. It was a trousseau fit for a queen, and an evidence at once of the wealth of the Lady de Tilly and of her unbounded love for her niece, Amelie. The gifts of Pierre were not mingled with the rest, nor as yet had they been shown to her bridesmaids,--Amelie kept them for a pretty surprise upon another day.

Upon the table stood a golden casket of Venetian workmanship, the carvings of which represented the marriage at Cana in Galilee. It was stored with priceless jewels which dazzled the sight and presented a constellation of starry gems, the like of which had never been seen in the New World. It was the gift of the Bourgeois Philibert, who gave this splendid token of his affection and utter contentment with Amelie as the bride of his son and heir.

The girls were startled in the midst of their preparations by the sudden dashing past of a horseman, who rode in a cloud of dust, followed by a wild, strange cry, as of many people shouting together in lamentation and anger.

Amelie and Heloise looked at each other with a strange feeling, but sat still while the rest rushed to the balcony, where they leaned eagerly over to catch sight of the passing horseman and discover the meaning of the loud and still repeated cry.

The rider had disappeared round the angle of the Cape, but the cry from the city waxed still louder, as if more and more voices joined in it.

Presently men on horseback and on foot were seen hurrying towards the Castle of St. Louis, and one or two shot up the long slope of the Place d'Armes, galloping towards the mansion of the Lady de Tilly, talking and gesticulating in the wildest manner.

"In God's name, what is the matter, Monsieur La Force?" exclaimed Hortense as that gentleman rode furiously up and checked his horse violently at the sight of the ladies upon the balcony.

Hortense repeated her question. La Force took off his hat and looked up, puzzled and distressed. "Is the Lady de Tilly at home?" inquired he eagerly.

"Not just now, she has gone out; but what is the matter, in heaven's name?" repeated she, as another wild cry came up from the city.

"Is Mademoiselle Amelie home?" again asked La Force with agitated voice.

"She is home. Heavens! have you some bad news to tell her or the Lady de Tilly?" breathlessly inquired Hortense.

"Bad news for both of them; for all of us, Hortense. But I will not be the bearer of such terrible tidings,--others are following me; ask them. Oh, Hortense, prepare poor Amelie for the worst news that ever came to her."

The Sieur La Force would not wait to be further questioned,--he rode off furiously.

The bridesmaids all turned pale with affright at these ominous words, and stood looking at each other and asking what they could mean.

Amelie and Heloise caught some of the conversation between Hortense and La Force. They sprang up and ran to the balcony just as two of the servants of the house came rushing up with open mouths, staring eyes, and trembling with excitement. They did not wait to be asked what was the matter, but as soon as they saw the ladies they shouted out the terrible news, as the manner of their kind is, without a thought of the consequences: that Le Gardeur had just killed the Bourgeois Philibert in the market-place, and was himself either killed or a prisoner, and the people were going to burn the Friponne and hang the Intendant under the tablet of the Golden Dog, and all the city was going to be destroyed.

The servants, having communicated this piece of wild intelligence, instantly rushed into the house and repeated it to the household, filling the mansion in a few moments with shrieks and confusion.

It was in vain Hortense and Agathe La Corne St. Luc strove to withhold the terrible truth from Amelie. Her friends endeavored with kindly force and eager exhortations to prevent her coming to the balcony, but she would not be stayed; in her excitement she had the strength of one of God's angels. She had caught enough of the speech of the servants to gather up its sense into a connected whole, and in a moment of terrible enlightenment, that came like a thunderbolt driven through her soul, she understood the whole significance of their tidings.

Her hapless brother, maddened with disappointment, drink, and desperation, had killed the father of Pierre, the father of her betrothed husband, his own friend and hers; why or how, was a mystery of amazement.

She saw at a glance all the ruin of it. Her brother a murderer, the Bourgeois a bleeding corpse. Pierre, her lover and her pride, lost,--lost to her forever! The blood of his father rising up between them calling for vengeance upon Le Gardeur and invoking a curse upon the whole house of Repentigny.

The heart of Amelie, but a few moments ago expanding with joy and overflowing with the tenderest emotions of a loving bride, suddenly collapsed and shrivelled like a leaf in the fire of this unlooked- for catastrophe.

She stared wildly and imploringly in the countenances of her trembling companions as if for help, but no human help could avail her. She spake not, but uttering one long, agonizing scream, fell senseless upon the bosom of Heloise de Lotbiniere, who, herself nigh fainting, bore Amelie with the assistance of her friends to a couch, where she lay unconscious of the tears and wailing that surrounded her.

Marguerite de Repentigny with her weeping companions remained in the chamber of Amelie, watching eagerly for some sign of returning consciousness, and assiduously administering such restoratives as were at hand.

Their patience and tenderness were at last rewarded,--Amelie gave a flutter of reviving life. Her dark eyes opened and stared wildly for a moment at her companions with a blank look, until they rested upon the veil and orange blossoms on the head of Agathe, who had put them on in such a merry mood and forgotten in the sudden catastrophe to take them off again.

The sight of the bridal veil and wreath seemed to rouse Amelie to consciousness. The terrible news of the murder of the Bourgeois by Le Gardeur flashed upon her mind, and she pressed her burning eyelids hard shut with her hands, as if not to see the hideous thought.

Her companions wept, but Amelie found no relief in tears as she murmured the name of the Bourgeois, Le Gardeur, and Pierre.

They spoke softly to her in tones of tenderest sympathy, but she scarcely heeded them, absorbed as she was in deepest despair, and still pressing her eyes shut as if she had done with day and cared no more to see the bright sunshine that streamed through the lattice. The past, present, and future of her whole life started up before her in terrible distinctness, and seemed concentrated in one present spot of mental anguish.

Amelie came of a heroic race, stern to endure pain as to inflict it, capable of unshrinking fortitude and of desperate resolves. A few moments of terrible contemplation decided her forever, changed the whole current of her life, and overthrew as with an earthquake the gorgeous palace of her maiden hopes and long-cherished anticipations of love and happiness as the wife of Pierre Philibert.

She saw it all; there was no room for hope, no chance of averting the fatal doom that had fallen upon her. Her life, as she had long pictured it to her imagination, was done and ended. Her projected marriage with Pierre Philibert? It was like sudden death! In one moment the hand of God had transported her from the living to the dead world of woman's love. A terrible crime had been perpetrated, and she, innocent as she was, must bear the burden of punishment. She had but one object now to live for: to put on sackcloth and ashes, and wear her knees out in prayer before God, imploring forgiveness and mercy upon her unhappy brother, and expiate the righteous blood of the just man who had been slain by him.

She rose hastily and stood up. Her face was beautiful as the face of a marble Niobe, but as pale and as full of anguish.

"My loving bridesmaids," said she, "it is now all over with poor Amelie de Repentigny; tell Pierre," and here she sobbed, almost choking in her grief, "tell Pierre not to hate me for this blood that lies on the threshold of our house! Tell him how truly and faithfully I was preparing to devote myself to his happiness as his bride and wife; tell him how I loved him, and I only forsake him because it is the inexorable decree of my sad fate; not my will, but my cruel misfortune. But I know his noble nature; he will pity, not hate me. Tell him it will even rejoice me where I am going to know that Pierre Philibert still loves me. I cannot, dare not ask him to pardon Le Gardeur! I dare not pardon him myself! But I know Pierre will be just and merciful to my poor brother, even in this hour of doom."

"And now," continued she, speaking with a terrible energy, "put away these bridal deceits; they will never be worn by me! I have a garb more becoming the bridal of death; more fitting to wear by the sister of--O God! I was going to say, of a murderer!"

Amelie, with a wild desperation, gathered up the gay robes and garlands and threw them in a heap in the corner of the chamber. "My glory is departed!" said she. "Oh, Hortense, I am punished for the pride I took in them! Yet it was not for myself, but for the sake of him, I took pride in them! Bestow them, I pray you, upon some more happy girl, who is poor in fortune, but rich in love, who will wear them at her bridal, instead of the unhappy Amelie."

The group of girls beheld her, while their eyes were swimming with tears. "I have long, long kept a bridal veil in my closet," she went on, "and knew not it was to be mine!" Opening a wardrobe, she took out a long black veil. It had belonged to her grandaunt, the nun, Madelaine de Repentigny, and was kept as an heirloom in her family.

"This," said she, "shall be mine till death! Embrace me, O my sisters, my bridesmaids and companions. I go now to the Ursulines to kneel at the door and crave admittance to pass a life of penitence for Le Gardeur, and of prayer for my beloved Pierre."

"O Amelie, think what you do!" exclaimed Hortense Beauharnais; "be not hasty, take not a step that cannot be recalled. It will kill Pierre!"

"Alas! I have killed him already!" said she; "but my mind is made up! Dear Hortense, I love Pierre, but oh, I could never look at his face again without shame that would burn like guilt. I give myself henceforth to Christ, not for my own sake, but for his, and for my unhappy brother's! Do not hinder me, dear friends, and do not follow me! May you all be happy in your happiness, and pray for poor Amelie, whom fate has stricken so hard and so cruelly in the very moment of her brightest hopes! And now let me go--alone--and God bless you all! Bid my aunt to come and see me," added she; "I cannot even wait her return."

The girls stood weeping around her, and kissed and embraced her over and over. They would not disobey her request to be allowed to go alone to the Convent, but as she turned to depart, she was clasped around the neck by Heloise de Lotbiniere, exclaiming that she should not go alone, that the light of the world had gone out for her as well as for Amelie, and she would go with her.

"But why, Heloise, would you go with me to the Convent?" asked Amelie, sadly. She knew but too well why.

"Oh, my cousin! I too would pray for Le Gardeur! I too--but no matter! I will go with you, Amelie! If the door of the Ursulines open for you, it shall open for Heloise de Lotbiniere also."

"I have no right to say nay, Heloise, nor will I," replied Amelie, embracing her; "you are of my blood and lineage, and the lamp of Repentigny is always burning in the holy chapel to receive broken- hearted penitents like you and me!"

"Oh, Heloise, do not you also leave us! Stay till to-morrow!" exclaimed the agitated girls, amazed at this new announcement.

"My mind is made up; it has long been made up!" replied Heloise. "I only waited the marriage of Amelie before consummating my resolution to enter the convent. I go now to comfort Amelie, as no other friend in the world can comfort her. We shall be more content in the midst of our sorrows to be together."

It was in vain to plead with or to dissuade them. Amelie and Heloise were inexorable and eager to be gone. They again kissed their companions, with many tears bidding them a last farewell, and the two weeping girls, hiding their heads under their veils, left the bright mansion that was their home, and proceeded with hasty steps towards the Convent of the Ursulines.

# Chapter LII: The Lamp of Repentigny

Closely veiled, acknowledging no one, looking at no one, and·not themselves recognized by any, but clinging to each other for mutual support, Amelie and Heloise traversed swiftly the streets that led to the Convent of the Ursulines.

At the doors, and in the porches and galleries of the old-fashioned houses, women stood in groups, discussing eagerly the wild reports that were flying to and fro through the city, and looking up and down the streets for further news of the tragedy in the market- place. The male part of the population had run off and gathered in excited masses around the mansion of the Golden Dog, which was suddenly shut up, and long streamers of black crape were hanging at the door.

Many were the inquisitive glances and eager whisperings of the good wives and girls as the two ladies, deeply veiled in black, passed by with drooping heads and handkerchiefs pressed against their faces, while more than one quick ear caught the deep, suppressed sobs that broke from their bosoms. No one ventured to address them, however, although their appearance caused no little speculation as to who they were and whither they were going.

Amelie and Heloise, almost fainting under their sorrow, stood upon the broad stone step which formed the threshold that separated the world they were entering into from the world they were leaving.

The high gables and old belfry of the Monastrey stood bathed in sunlight. The figure of St. Joseph that dominated over the ancient portal held out his arms and seemed to welcome the trembling fugitives into the house with a gesture of benediction.

The two ladies paused upon the stone steps. Amelie clasped her arm round Heloise, whom she pressed to her bosom and said, "Think before you knock at this door and cross the threshold for the last time, Heloise! You must not do it for my sake, darling."

"No, Amelie," replied she sadly. "It is not wholly for your sake. Would I could say it were! Alas! If I remained in the world, I could even now pity Le Gardeur, and follow him to the world's end; but it must not--cannot be. Do not seek to dissuade me, Amelie, for it is useless."

"Your mind is made up, then, to go in with me, my Heloise?" said Amelie, with a fond, questioning look.

"Fully, finally, and forever!" replied she, with energy that left no room for doubt. "I long ago resolved to ask the community to let me die with them. My object, dear sister, is like yours: to spend my life in prayers and supplications for Le Gardeur, and be laid, when God calls me to his rest, by the side of our noble aunt, Mere Madelaine de Repentigny, whose lamp still burns in the Chapel of the Saints, as if to light you and me to follow in her footsteps."

"It is for Le Gardeur's sake I too go," replied Amelie; "to veil my face from the eyes of a world I am ashamed to see, and to expiate, if I can, the innocent blood that has been shed. But the sun shines very bright for those to whom its beams are still pleasant!" said she, looking around sadly, as if it were for the last time she bade adieu to the sun, which she should never again behold under the free vault of heaven.

Heloise turned slowly to the door of the Convent. "Those golden rays that shine through the wicket," said she, "and form a cross upon the pavement within, as we often observed with schoolgirl admiration, are the only rays to gladden me now. I care no more for the light of the sun. I will live henceforth in the blessed light of the lamp of Repentigny. My mind is fixed, and I will not leave you, Amelie. 'Where thou goest I will go, where thou lodgest I will lodge; thy people shall be my people, and thy God my God.'"

Amelie kissed her cousin tenderly. "So be it, then, Heloise. Your heart is broken as well as mine. We will pray together for Le Gardeur, beseeching God to pity and forgive."

Amelie knocked at the door twice before a sound of light footsteps was heard within. A veiled nun appeared at the little wicket and looked gravely for a moment upon the two postulantes for admission, repeating the formula usual on such occasions.

"What seek you, my sisters?"

"To come in and find rest, good Mere des Seraphins," replied Amelie, to whom the portiere was well known. "We desire to leave the world and live henceforth with the community in the service and adoration of our blessed Lord, and to pray for the sins of others as well as our own."

"It is a pious desire, and no one stands at the door and knocks but it is opened. Wait, my sisters, I will summon the Lady Superior to admit you."

The nun disappeared for a few minutes. Her voice was heard again as she returned to the wicket: "The Lady Superior deputes to Mere Esther the privilege, on this occasion, of receiving the welcome postulantes of the house of Repentigny."

The portiere retired from the wicket. The heavy door swung noiselessly back, opening the way into a small antechamber, floored with smooth flags, and containing a table and a seat or two. On either side of the interior door of the antechamber was a turnstile or tourelle, which enabled the inmates within to receive anything from the outside world without being themselves seen. Amelie and Heloise passed through the inner door, which opened as of its own accord, as they approached it with trembling steps and troubled mien.

A tall nun, of commanding figure but benign aspect, received the two ladies with the utmost affection, as well-known friends.

Mere Esther wore a black robe sweeping the ground. It was bound at the waist by a leathern girdle. A black veil fell on each side of the snowy fillet that covered her forehead, and half covered the white wimple upon her neck and bosom.

At the first sight of the veil thrown over the heads of Amelie and Heloise, and the agitation of both, she knew at once that the time of these two girls, like that of many others, had come. Their arrival was a repetition of the old, old story, of which her long experience had witnessed many instances.

"Good mother," exclaimed Amelie, throwing her arms around the nun, who folded her tenderly to her bosom, although her face remained calm and passionless, "we are come at last! Heloise and I wish to live and die in the monastery. Good Mother Esther, will you take us in?"

"Welcome both!" replied Mere Esther, kissing each of them on the forehead. "The virgins who enter in with the bridegroom to the marriage are those whose lamps are burning! The lamp of Repentigny is never extinguished in the Chapel of Saints, nor is the door of the monastery ever shut against one of your house."

"Thanks, good mother! But we bring a heavy burden with us. No one but God can tell the weight and the pain of it!" said Amelie sadly.

"I know, Amelie, I know; but what says our blessed Lord? 'Come unto me all ye that are weary and heavy-laden, and I will give you rest.'"

"I seek not rest, good mother," replied she sadly, "but a place for penance, to melt Heaven with prayers for the innocent blood that has been shed to-day, that it be not recorded forever against my brother. Oh, Mere Esther, you know my brother, Le Gardeur; how generous and kind he was! You have heard of the terrible occurrence in the market-place?"

"Yes, I have heard," said the nun. "Bad news reaches us ever soonest. It fills me with amazement that one so noble as your brother should have done so terrible a deed."

"Oh, Mere Esther!" exclaimed Amelie eagerly, "it was not Le Gardeur in his senses who did it. No, he never knowingly struck the blow that has killed me as well as the good Bourgeois! Alas! he knew not what he did. But still he has done it, and my remaining time left on earth must be spent in sackcloth and ashes, beseeching God for pardon and mercy for him."

"The community will join you in your prayers, Amelie," replied the Mere.

Esther stood wrapt in thought for a few moments. "Heloise!" said she, addressing the fair cousin of Amelie, "I have long expected you in the monastery. You struggled hard for the world and its delights, but God's hand was stronger than your purposes. When He calls, be it in the darkest night, happy is she who rises instantly to follow her Lord!"

"He has indeed called me, O mother! and I desire only to become a faithful servant of His tabernacle forever. I pray, good Mere Esther, for your intercession with the Mere de la Nativite. The venerable Lady Superior used to say we were dowerless brides, we of the house of Lotbiniere."

"But you shall not be dowerless, Heloise!" burst out Amelie. "You shall enter the convent with as rich a dowry as ever accompanied an Ursuline."

"No, Amelie; if they will not accept me for myself, I will imitate my aunt, the admirable queteuse, who, being, like me, a dowerless postulante, begged from house to house throughout the city for the means to open to her the door of the monastery.

"Heloise," replied Mere Esther, "this is idle fear. We have waited for you, knowing that one day you would come, and you will be most welcome, dowered or not!"

"You are ever kind, Mere Esther, but how could you know I should come to you?" asked Heloise with a look of inquiry.

"Alas, Heloise, we know more of the world and its doings than is well for us. Our monastery is like the ear of Dionysius: not a whisper in the city escapes it. Oh, darling, we knew you had failed in your one great desire upon earth, and that you would seek consolation where it is only to be found, in the arms of your Lord."

"It is true, mother; I had but one desire upon earth, and it is crushed; one little bird that nestled a while in my bosom, and it has flown away. The event of to-day has stricken me and Amelie alike, and we come together to wear out the stones of your pavement praying for the hapless brother of Amelie."

"And the object of Heloise's faithful love!" replied the nun with tender sympathy. "Oh! how could Le Gardeur de Repentigny refuse a heart like yours, Heloise, for the sake of that wild daughter of levity, Angelique des Meloises?

"But come, I will conduct you to the venerable Lady Superior, who is in the garden conversing with Grand'mere St. Pierre, and your old friend and mistress, Mere Ste. Helene."

The news of the tragedy in the market-place had been early carried to the Convent by the ubiquitous Bonhomme Michael, who was out that day on one of his multifarious errands in the service of the community.

The news had passed quickly through the Convent, agitating the usually quiet nuns, and causing the wildest commotion among the classes of girls, who were assembled at their morning lessons in the great schoolroom. The windows were clustered with young, comely heads, looking out in every direction, while nuns in alarm streamed from the long passages to the lawn, where sat the venerable Superior, Mere Migeon de la Nativite, under a broad ash-tree, sacred to the Convent by the memories that clustered around it. The Ste. Therese of Canada, Mere Marie de l'Incarnation, for lack of a better roof, in the first days of her mission, used to gather around her under that tree the wild Hurons as well as the young children of the colonists, to give them their first lessons in religion and letters.

Mere Esther held up her finger warningly to the nuns not to speak, as she passed onward through the long corridors, dim with narrow lights and guarded by images of saints, until she came into an open square flagged with stones. In the walls of this court a door opened upon the garden into which a few steps downwards conducted them.

The garden of the monastery was spacious and kept with great care. The walks meandered around beds of flowers, and under the boughs of apple-trees, and by espaliers of ancient pears and plums.

The fruit had long been gathered in, and only a few yellow leaves hung upon the autumnal trees, but the grass was still green on the lawn where stood the great ash-tree of Mere Marie de l'Incarnation. The last hardy flowers of autumn lingered in this sheltered spot.

In these secluded alleys the quiet recluses usually walked and meditated in peace, for here man's disturbing voice was never heard.

But to-day a cluster of agitated nuns gathered around the great ash- tree, and here and there stood groups of black and white veils; some were talking, while others knelt silently before the guardian of the house, the image of St. Joseph, which overlooked this spot, considered particularly sacred to prayer and meditation.

The sight of Mere Esther, followed by the well-known figures of Amelie and Heloise, caused every head to turn with a look of recognition; but the nuns were too well disciplined to express either surprise or curiosity in the presence of Mere Migeon, however much they felt of both. They stood apart at a sign from the Lady Superior, leaving her with a nun attendant on each side to receive Mere Esther and her two companions.

Mere Migeon de la Nativite was old in years, but fresh in looks and alert in spirit. Her features were set in that peculiar expression of drooping eyelids and placid lips which belongs to the Convent, but she could look up and flash out on occasion with an air of command derived from high birth and a long exercise of authority as Superior of the Ursulines, to which office the community had elected her as many trienniums as their rules permitted.

Mere Migeon had been nearly half a century a nun, and felt as much pride as humility in the reflection. She liked power, which, however, she exercised wholly for the benefit of her subjects in the Convent, and wore her veil with as much dignity as the Queen her crown. But, if not exempt from some traces of human infirmity, she made amends by devoting herself night and day to the spiritual and temporal welfare of the community, who submitted to her government with extreme deference and unquestioning obedience.

Mere Migeon had directed the two sorrowing ladies to be brought into the garden, where she would receive them under the old tree of Mere Marie de l'Incarnation.

She rose with affectionate eagerness as they entered, and embraced them one after the other, kissing them on the cheek; "her little prodigals returning to the house of their father and mother, after feeding on the husks of vanity in the gay world which was never made for them."

"We will kill the fatted calf in honor of your return, Amelie. Will we not, Mere Esther?" said the Lady Superior, addressing Amelie rather than Heloise.

"Not for me, reverend Mere; you shall kill no fatted calf, real or symbolical, for me!" exclaimed Amelie. "I come only to hide myself in your cloister, to submit myself to your most austere discipline. I have given up all. Oh, my Mere, I have given up all! None but God can know what I have given up forever!"

"You were to have married the son of the Bourgeois, were you not, Amelie?" asked the

Superior, who, as the aunt of Varin, and by family ties connected with certain leading spirits of the Grand Company, had no liking for the Bourgeois Philibert; her feelings, too, had been wrought upon by a recital of the sermon preached in the marketplace that morning.

"Oh, speak not of it, good Mere! I was betrothed to Pierre Philibert, and how am I requiting his love? I should have been his wife, but for this dreadful deed of my brother. The Convent is all that is left to me now."

"Your aunt called herself the humble handmaid of Mary, and the lamp of Repentigny will burn all the brighter trimmed by a daughter of her noble house," answered Mere Migeon.

"By two daughters, good Mere! Heloise is equally a daughter of our house," replied Amelie, with a touch of feeling.

Mere Esther whispered a few words in the ear of the Superior, advising her to concede every request of Amelie and Heloise, and returned to the wicket to answer some other hasty call from the troubled city.

Messengers despatched by Bonhomme Michael followed one another at short intervals, bringing to the Convent exact details of all that occurred in the streets, with the welcome tidings at last that the threatened outbreak had been averted by the prompt interposition of the Governor and troops. Comparative quietness again reigned in every quarter of the city.

Le Gardeur de Repentigny had voluntarily surrendered himself to the guard and given up his sword, being overwhelmed with remorse for his act. He had been placed, not in irons as he had demanded, but as a prisoner in the strong ward of the Castle of St. Louis.

"I pray you, reverend Mere Superior," said Amelie, "permit us now to go into the Chapel of Saints to lay our hearts, as did our kinswoman, Madelaine de Repentigny, at the feet of our Lady of Grand Pouvoir."

"Go, my children, and our prayers shall go with you," replied the Superior; "the lamp of Repentigny will burn brighter than ever to- night to welcome you."

The Chapel of Saints was held in reverence as the most sacred place in the monastery. It contained the shrines and relics of many saints and martyrs. The devout nuns lavished upon it their choicest works of embroidery, painting, and gilding, in the arts of which they were eminent. The old Sacristaine was kneeling before the altar as Amelie and Heloise entered the Chapel.

An image of the Virgin occupied a niche in the Chapel wall, and before it burned the silver lamp of Repentigny which had been hung there two generations before, in memory of the miraculous call of Madelaine de Repentigny and her victory over the world.

The high-bred and beautiful Madelaine had been the delight and pride of Ville Marie. Stricken with grief by the death of a young officer to whom she was affianced, she retired to Quebec, and knelt daily at the feet of our Lady of Pouvoir, beseeching her for a sign if it was her will that she should become an Ursuline.

The sign was given, and Madelaine de Repentigny at once exchanged her gay robes for the coarse black gown and veil, and hung up this votive lamp before the Madonna as a perpetual memorial of her miraculous call.

Seven generations of men have passed away since then. The house of Repentigny has disappeared from their native land. Their name and fame lie buried in oblivion, except in that little Chapel of the Saints where their lamp still burns brightly as ever. The pious nuns of St. Ursule, as the last custodians of the traditions of New France, preserve that sole memorial of the glories and misfortunes of the noble house,--the lamp of Repentigny.

Amelie and Heloise remained long in the Chapel of Saints, kneeling upon the hard floor as they prayed with tears and sobs for the soul of the Bourgeois and for God's pity and forgiveness upon Le Gardeur.

To Amelie's woes was added the terrible consciousness that, by this deed of her brother, Pierre Philibert was torn from her forever. She pictured to herself his grief, his love, his despair, perhaps his vengeance; and to add to all, she, his betrothed bride, had forsaken him and fled like a guilty thing, without waiting to see whether he condemned her.

An hour ago Amelie had been the envy and delight of her gay bridesmaids. Her heart had overflowed like a fountain of wine, intoxicating all about her with joy at the hope of the speedy coming of her bridegroom. Suddenly the idols of her life had been shattered as by a thunderbolt, and lay in fragments around her feet.

The thought came upon her like the rush of angry wings. She knew that all was over between her and Pierre. The cloister and the veil were all that were left to Amelie de Repentigny.

"Heloise, dearest sister!" exclaimed she, "my conscience tells me I have done right, but my heart accuses me of wrong to Pierre, of falseness to my plighted vows in forsaking him; and yet, not for heaven itself would I have forsaken Pierre. Would that I were dead! Oh, what have I done, Heloise, to deserve such a chastisement as this from God?"

Amelie threw her arms around the neck of Heloise, and leaning her head on her bosom, wept long and without restraint, for none saw them save God.

"Listen!" said Heloise, as the swelling strain of the organ floated up from the convent chapel. The soft voices of the nuns mingled in plaintive harmony as they sang the hymn of the Virgin:

"Pia Mater! Fons amoris!
Me sentire vim doloris
Fac, ut tecum lugeam!"

Again came the soft pleading notes of the sacred hymn:

"Quando corpus morietur,
Fac ut animae donetur
Paradisi gloria! Amen!"

The harmony filled the ears of Amelie and Heloise, like the lap of the waves of eternity upon the world's shore. It died away, and they continued praying before Our Lady of Grand Pouvoir.

The silence was suddenly broken. Hasty steps traversed the little chapel. A rush of garments caused Amelie and Heloise to turn around, and in an instant they were both clasped in the passionate embrace of the Lady de Tilly, who had arrived at the Convent.

"My dear children, my poor, stricken daughters," exclaimed she, kissing them passionately and mingling her tears with theirs, "what have you done to be dashed to the earth by such a stroke of divine wrath?"

"Oh, aunt, pardon us for what we have done!" exclaimed Amelie, "and for not asking your consent, but alas! it is God's will and doing! I have given up the world; do not blame me, aunt!"

"Nor me, aunt!" added Heloise; "I have long known that the cloister was my sole heritage, and I now claim it."

"Blame you, darling! Oh, Amelie, in the shame and agony of this day I could share the cloister with you myself forever, but my work is out in the wide world, and I must not withdraw my hand!"

"Have you seen Le Gardeur? Oh, aunt! have you seen my brother?" asked Amelie, seizing her hand passionately.

"I have seen him, and wept over him," was the reply. "Oh, Amelie! great as is his offence, his crime, yes, I will be honest calling it such,--no deeper contrition could rend his heart had he committed all the sins forbidden in the Decalogue. He demands a court martial to condemn him at once to death, upon his own self-accusation and confession of the murder of the good Bourgeois."

"Oh, aunt, and he loved the Bourgeois so! It seems like a hideous dream of fright and nightmare that Le Gardeur should assail the father of Pierre Philibert, and mine that was to be!"

At this thought the poor girl flung herself upon the bosom of the Lady de Tilly, convulsed and torn by as bitter sobs as ever drew human pity.

"Le Gardeur! Le Gardeur! Good God! what will they do with him, aunt? Is he to die?" cried she imploringly, as with streaming eyes she looked up at her aunt.

"Listen, Amelie! Compose yourself and you shall hear. I was in the Church of Notre Dame des Victoires when I received the tidings. It was long before the messenger found me. I rose instantly and hastened to the house of the Bourgeois, where its good master lay dead in his bloody vesture. I cannot describe the sad sight, Amelie! I there learned that the Governor and La Corne St. Luc had been to the house of the Bourgeois and had returned to the Castle."

"Oh, aunt, did you see him? Did you see the good old Bourgeois? And you know he is dead?"

"Yes, Amelie, I saw him, and could have wished my eyesight blasted forever after. Do not ask me more."

"But I must, aunt! Did you see--oh, why may I not yet utter his dear name?--did you see Pierre?"

"Yes, Amelie. Pierre came home unexpectedly while I was weeping over the dead corpse of his father. Poor Pierre! my own sorrows were naught to his silent grief! It was more terrible than the wildest outburst of passion I ever saw!"

"And what did he say? Oh, aunt, tell me all! Do not spare me one word, however bitter! Did he not curse you? Did he not curse me? And above all, Le Gardeur? Oh, he cursed us all; he heaped a blasting malediction upon the whole house of Repentigny, did he not?"

"Amelie, be composed! Do not look at me so wildly with these dear eyes, and I will tell you." Her aunt tried to soothe her with fond caresses.

"I will be composed! I am calm! Look now, aunt, I am calm!" exclaimed the grief-stricken girl, whose every nerve was quivering with wild excitement.

The Lady de Tilly and Heloise made her sit down, while each held forcibly a hand to prevent an access of hysteria. Mere Ste. Vierge rose and hastily left the chapel to fetch water.

"Amelie, the nobleness of Pierre Philibert is almost beyond the range of fallible mortals," said the Lady de Tilly. "In the sudden crash of all his hopes he would not utter a word of invective against your brother. His heart tells him that Le Gardeur has been made the senseless instrument of others in this crime."

"A thousand thanks, dearest aunt, for your true appreciation of Pierre! I know he deserves it all; and when the veil covers my head forever from the eyes of men, it will be my sole joy to reflect that Pierre Philibert was worthy, more than worthy, of my love! But what said he further, aunt? Oh, tell me all!"

"He rose from his knees beside the corpse of his father," continued the lady, "and seeing me kneeling, raised me and seated me in a chair beside him. He asked me where you were, and who was with you to support and comfort you in this storm of affliction. I told him, and he kissed me, exclaiming, 'Oh, aunt,--mother, what shall I do?'"

"Oh, aunt! did Pierre say that? Did he call you aunt and mother? And he did not curse me at all? Poor Pierre!" And she burst out into a flood of tears which nothing could control.

"Yes Amelie! His heart is bleeding to death with this dreadful sword-stroke of Le Gardeur's," said the Lady de Tilly, after waiting till she recovered somewhat.

"And will he not slay Le Gardeur? Will he not deem it his duty to kill my brother and his?" cried she. "He is a soldier and must!"

"Listen, Amelie. There is a divinity in Pierre that we see only in the noblest of men; he will not slay Le Gardeur. He is his brother and yours, and will regard him as such. Whatever he might have done in the first impulse of anger, Pierre will not now seek the life of Le Gardeur. He knows too well whence this blow has really come. He has been deeply touched by the remorse and self-accusation of Le Gardeur."

"I could kiss his feet! my noble Pierre! Oh, aunt, aunt! what have I not lost! But I was betrothed to him, was I not?" She started up with a shriek of mortal agony. "They never can recall that!" she cried wildly. "He was to have been mine! He is still mine, and forever will be mine! Death will reunite what in life is sundered! Will it not, aunt?"

"Yes; be composed, darling, and I will tell you more. Nay, do not look at me so, Amelie!" The Lady de Tilly stroked her cheek and kissed the dark eyes that seemed flaring out of their sockets with maddening excitement.

"When I had recovered strength enough to go to the Castle to see the Count, Pierre supported me thither. He dared not trust himself to see Le Gardeur, who from his prison sent message after message to him to beg death at his hand.

"I held a brief conference with the Governor, La Corne St. Luc, and a few gentlemen, who were hastily gathered together in the council- chamber. I pleaded long, not for pardon, not even for Le Gardeur could I ask for pardon, Amelie!" exclaimed the just and noble woman,--"but for a calm consideration of the terrible circumstances which had surrounded him in the Palace of the Intendant, and which had led directly to the catastrophe."

"And what said they? Oh, be quick, aunt! Is not Le Gardeur to be tried by martial law and condemned at once to death?"

"No, Amelie! The Count de la Galissoniere, with the advice of his wisest counsellors, among whom is your godfather and others, the dearest friends of both families, have resolved to send Le Gardeur to France by the Fleur de Lys, which sails to-morrow. They do this in order that the King may judge of his offence, as also to prevent the conflict that may arise between the contending factions in the Colony, should they try him here. This resolution may be wise, or not, I do not judge; but such is the determination of the Governor and Council, to which all must submit."

Amelie held her head between her palms for some moments. She was violently agitated, but she tried to consider, as best she might, the decision with regard to her brother.

"It is merciful in them," she said, "and it is just. The King will judge what is right in the sight of God and man. Le Gardeur was but a blind instrument of others in this murder, as blind almost as the sword he held in his hand. But shall I not see him, aunt, before he is sent away?"

"Alas, no! The Governor, while kind, is inexorable on one point. He will permit no one, after this, to see Le Gardeur, to express either blame or approval of his deed, or to report his words. He will forbid you and me and his nearest friends from holding any communication with him before he leaves the Colony. The Count has remitted his case to the King, and resolved that it shall be accompanied by no self-accusation which Le Gardeur may utter in his frantic grief. The Count does this in justice as well as mercy, Amelie."

"Then I shall never see my brother more in this world,--never!" exclaimed Amelie, supporting herself on the arm of Heloise. "His fate is decided as well as mine, and yours too, O Heloise."

"It may not be so hard with him as with us, Amelie," replied Heloise, whose bosom was agitated with fresh emotions at every allusion to Le Gardeur. "The King may pardon him, Amelie." Heloise in her soul hoped so, and in her heart prayed so.

"Alas! If we could say God pardoned him!" replied Amelie, her thoughts running suddenly in a counter-current. "But my life must be spent in imploring God's grace and forgiveness all the same, whether man forgive him or no."

"Say not my life, but our lives, Amelie. We have crossed the threshold of this house together for the last time. We go no more out to look upon a world fair and beautiful to see, but so full of disappointment and wretchedness to have experience of!"

"My daughters," exclaimed the Lady de Tilly, "another time we will speak of this. Harken, Amelie! I did not tell you that Pierre Philibert came with me to the gate of the Convent to see you. He would have entered, but the Lady Superior refused inexorably to admit him even to the parlor."

"Pierre came to the Convent,--to the Convent?" repeated Amelie with fond iteration, "and they would not admit him. Why would they not admit him? But I should have died of shame to see him. They were kind in their cruelty. Poor Pierre! he thinks me still worthy of some regard." She commenced weeping afresh.

"He would fain have seen you, darling," said her aunt. "Your flight to the Convent--he knows what it means--overwhelms him with a new calamity."

"And yet it cannot be otherwise. I dare not place my hand in his now, for it would redden it! But it is sweet amid my affliction to know that Pierre has not forgotten me, that he does not hate me, nay, that he still loves me, although I abandon the world and him who to me was the light of it. Why would they not admit him?"

"Mere Migeon is as hard as she is just, Amelie. I think too she has no love for the Philiberts. Her nephew Varin has all the influence of a spoilt son over the Lady Superior."

Amelie scarcely regarded the last remark of her aunt, but repeated the words, "Hard and just! Yes, it is true, and hardness and justice are what I crave in my misery. The flintiest couch shall be to me a bed of down, the scantiest fare a royal feast, the hardest penance a life of pleasure. Mere Migeon cannot be more hard nor more just to me than I would be to myself."

"My poor Amelie! My poor Heloise!" repeated the lady, stroking their hair and kissing them both alternately; "be it as God wills. When it is dark every prospect lies hid in the darkness, but it is there all the same, though we see it not; but when the day returns everything is revealed. We see naught before us now but the image of our Lady of Grand Pouvoir illumined by the lamp of Repentigny, but the sun of righteousness will yet arise with healing on his wings for us all! But oh, my children, let nothing be done hastily, rashly, or unbecoming the daughters of our honorable house."

# Chapter LIII: "Lovely in Death the Beauteous Ruin Lay"

The chant of vespers had long ceased. The Angelus had rung its last summons to invoke a blessing upon life and death at the close of the day. The quiet nuns filed off from their frugal meal in the long refectory and betook themselves to the community or to their peaceful cells. The troop of children in their charge had been sent with prayer to their little couches in the dormitory, sacred to sleep and happy dreams.

Candles flickered through the long passages as veiled figures slowly and noiselessly passed towards the chapel to their private devotions. Scarcely a footfall reached the ear, nor sound of any kind, except the sweet voice of Mere Madelaine de St. Borgia. Like the flow of a full stream in the still moonlight, she sang her canticle of praise to the guardian of the house, before she retired to rest:

"Ave, Joseph! Fili David juste!
Vir Mariae de qua natus est Jesus!"

Lady de Tilly sat listening as she held the hands of her two nieces, thinking how merciless was Fate, and half rebelling in her mind against the working of Providence. The sweet song of Mere St. Borgia fell like soft rain upon her hard thoughts, and instilled a spirit of resignation amid the darkness, as she repeated the words, "Ave, Joseph!" She fought bitterly in her soul against giving up her two lambs, as she called them, to the cold, scant life of the cloister, while her judgment saw but too plainly that naught else seemed left to their crushed and broken spirits. But she neither suggested their withdrawal from the Convent, nor encouraged them to remain.

In her secret thought, the Lady de Tilly regarded the cloister as a blessed refuge for the broken-hearted, a rest for the weary and overladen with earthly troubles, a living grave, which such may covet and not sin; but the young, the joyous, the beautiful, and all capable of making the world fairer and better, she would inexorably shut out. Christ calls not these from the earthly paradise; but the afflicted, the disappointed, the despairing, they who have fallen helplessly down in the journey of life, and are of no further use in this world, these he calls by their names and comforts them. But for those rare souls who are too cold for aught but spiritual joys, he reserves a peculiar though not his choicest benediction.

The Lady de Tilly pondered these thoughts over and over, in the fulness of pity for her children. She would not leave the Convent at the closing of the gates for the night, but remained the honored guest of Mere Migeon, who ordered a chamber to be prepared for her in a style that was luxurious compared with the scantily furnished rooms allotted to the nuns.

Amelie prevailed, after much entreaty, upon Mere Esther, to intercede with the Superior for permission to pass the night with Heloise in the cell that had once been occupied by her pious kinswoman, Mere Madelaine.

"It is a great thing to ask," replied Mere Esther as she returned with her desired boon, "and a greater still to be obtained! But Mere Migeon is in a benevolent mood tonight; for the sake of no one else would she have granted a dispensation of the rules of the house."

That night Lady de Tilly held a long and serious conference with Mere Migeon and Mere Esther, upon the event which had driven her nieces to the cloister, promising that if, at the end of a month, they persisted in their resolutions, she would consent to their assumption of the white veil; and upon the completion of their novitiate, when they took the final vows, she would give them up with such a dower as would make all former gifts of the house of Repentigny and Tilly poor in the comparison.

Mere Migeon was especially overjoyed at this prospect of relieving the means of her house, which had been so terribly straitened of late years. The losses occasioned by the war had been a never- ending source of anxiety to her and Mere Esther, who, however, kept their troubles as far as possible to themselves, in order that the cares of the world might not encroach too far upon the minds of the community. Hence they were more than ordinarily glad at this double vocation in the house of Repentigny. The prospect of its great wealth falling to pious uses they regarded as a special mark of divine providence and care for the house of Ste. Ursule.

"Oh, Mere Esther! Mere Esther!" exclaimed the Lady Superior. "I feel too great a satisfaction in view of the rich dower of these two girls. I need much self-examination to weed out worldly thoughts. Alas! Alas! I would rather be the humblest aunt in our kitchen than the Lady Superior of the Ursulines. Blessed old Mere Marie used to say 'a good turn in the kitchen was as good as a prayer in the chapel.'"

Mere Esther reflected a moment, and said, "We have long found it easier to pray for souls than to relieve bodies. I thank good St. Joseph for this prospective blessing upon our monastery."

During the long and wasting war, Mere Migeon had seen her poor nuns reduced to grievous straits, which they bore cheerfully, however, as their share of the common suffering of their country. The cassette of St. Joseph, wherein were deposited the oboli for the poor, had long been emptied. The image of St. Joseph au Ble, that stood at the great stair, and kept watch over the storeroom of corn and bread, had often guarded an empty chamber. St. Joseph au Labeur, overlooking the great kitchen of the Convent, had often been deaf to the prayers of "my aunts," who prepared the food of the community. The meagre tables of the refectory had not seldom been the despair of the old depositaire, Mere St. Louis, who devoutly said her longest graces over her scantiest meals.

"I thank St. Joseph for what he gives, and for what he withholds; yea, for what he takes away!" observed Mere St. Louis to her special friend and gossip, Mere St. Antoine, as they retired from the chapel. "Our years of famine are nearly over. The day of the consecration of Amelie de Repentigny will be to us the marriage at Cana. Our water will be turned into wine. I shall no longer need to save the crumbs, except for the poor at our gate."

The advent of Amelie de Repentigny was a circumstance of absorbing interest to the nuns, who regarded it as a reward for their long devotions and prayers for the restoration of their house to its old prosperity. We usually count Providence upon our side when we have consciously done aught to merit the good fortune that befalls us.

And now days came and went, went and came, as Time, the inexorable, ever does, regardless of human joys or sorrows. Amelie, weary of the world, was only desirous of passing away from it to that sphere where time is not, and where our affections and thoughts alone measure the periods of eternity. For time, there, is but the shadow that accompanies the joys of angels, or the woes of sinners,--not the reality. It is time here, eternity there!

The two postulantes seemed impressed with the spirit that, to their fancies, lingered in the cell of their kinswoman, Mere Madelaine. They bent their gentle necks to the heaviest yoke of spiritual service which their Superior would consent to lay upon them.

Amelie's inflexible will made her merciless towards herself. She took pleasure in the hardest of self-imposed penances, as if the racking of her soul by incessant prayers, and wasting of her body by vigils and cruel fastings, were a vicarious punishment, borne for the sake of her hapless brother.

She could not forget Pierre, nor did she ever try to forget him. It was observed by the younger nuns that when, by chance or design, they mentioned his name, she looked up and her lips moved in silent prayer; but she spoke not of him, save to her aunt and to Heloise. These two faithful friends alone knew the inexpressible anguish with which she had heard of Pierre's intended departure for France.

The shock caused by the homicide of the Bourgeois, and the consequent annihilation of all the hopes of her life in a happy union with Pierre Philibert, was too much for even her naturally sound and elastic constitution. Her health gave way irrecoverably. Her face grew thin and wan without losing any of its spiritual beauty, as her soul looked through its ever more transparent covering, which daily grew more and more aetherialized as she faded away. A hectic flush, like a spot of fire, came and went for a time, and at last settled permanently upon her cheek. Her eyes, those glorious orbs, filled with unquenchable love, grew supernaturally large and brilliant with the flames that fed upon her vital forces. Amelie sickened and sank rapidly. The vulture of quick consumption had fastened upon her young life.

Mere Esther and Mere Migeon shook their heads, for they were used to broken hearts, and knew the infallible signs which denote an early death in the young and beautiful. Prayers and masses were offered for the recovery of Amelie, but all in vain. God wanted her. He alone knew how to heal that broken heart. It was seen that she had not long to live. It was known she wished to die.

Pierre heard the tidings with overwhelming grief. He had been permitted but once to see her for a few brief moments, which dwelt upon his mind forever. He deferred his departure to Europe in consequence of her illness, and knocked daily at the door of the Convent to ask after her and leave some kind message or flower, which was faithfully carried to her by the friendly nuns who received him at the wicket. A feeling of pity and sympathy for these two affianced and unfortunate lovers stole into the hearts of the coldest nuns, while the novices and the romantic convent girls were absolutely wild over the melancholy fate of Pierre and Amelie.

He long solicited in vain for another interview with Amelie, but until it was seen that she was approaching the end, it was not granted him. Mere Esther interceded strongly with the Lady Superior, who was jealous of the influence of Pierre with her young novice. At length Amelie's prayers overcame her scruples. He was told one day that Amelie was dying, and wished to see him for the last time in this world.

Amelie was carried in a chair to the bars to receive her sorrowing lover. Her pale face retained its statuesque beauty of outline, but so thin and wasted!

"Pierre will not know me;" whispered she to Heloise, "but I shall smile at the joy of meeting him, and then he will recognize me."

Her flowing veil was thrown back from her face. She spoke little, but her dark eyes were fixed with devouring eagerness upon the door by which she knew Pierre would come in. Her aunt supported her head upon her shoulder, while Heloise knelt at her knee and fanned her with sisterly tenderness, whispering words of sisterly sympathy in her ear.

Pierre flew to the Convent at the hour appointed. He was at once admitted, with a caution from Mere Esther to be calm and not agitate the dying girl. The moment he entered the great parlor, Amelie sprang from her seat with a sudden cry of recognition, extending her poor thin hands through the bars towards him. Pierre seized them, kissing them passionately, but broke down utterly at the sight of her wasted face and the seal of death set thereon.

"Amelie, my darling Amelie!" exclaimed he; "I have prayed so long to see you, and they would not let me in."

"It was partly my fault, Pierre," said she fondly. "I feared to let you see me. I feared to learn that you hate, as you have cause to do, the whole house of Repentigny! And yet you do not curse me, dear Pierre?"

"My poor angel, you break my heart! I curse the house of Repentigny? I hate you? Amelie, you know me better."

"But your good father, the noble and just Bourgeois! Oh, Pierre, what have we not done to you and yours!"

She fell back upon her pillow, covering her eyes with her semi- transparent hands, bursting, as she did so, into a flood of passionate tears and passing into a dead faint.

Pierre was wild with anguish. He pressed against the bars. "For God's sake, let me in!" exclaimed he; "she is dying!"

The two quiet nuns who were in attendance shook their heads at Pierre's appeal to open the door. They were too well disciplined in the iron rule of the house to open it without an express order from the Lady Superior, or from Mere Esther. Their bosoms, abounding in spiritual warmth, responded coldly to the contagion of mere human passion. Their ears, unused to the voice of man's love, tingled at the words of Pierre. Fortunately, Mere Esther, ever on the watch, came into the parlor, and, seeing at a glance the need of the hour, opened the iron door and bade Pierre come in. He rushed forward and threw himself at the feet of Amelie, calling her by the most tender appellatives, and seeking to recall her to a consciousness of his presence.

That loved, familiar voice overtook her spirit, already winging its flight from earth, and brought it back for a few minutes longer. Mere Esther, a skilful nurse, administered a few drops of cordial, and, seeing her dying condition, sent instantly for the physician and the chaplain.

Amelie opened her eyes and turned them inquiringly around the group until they fastened upon Pierre. A flash of fondness suddenly suffused her face, as she remembered how and why he was there. She threw her arms around his neck and kissed him many times, murmuring, "I have often prayed to die thus, Pierre! close to you, my love, close to you; in your arms and God's, where you could receive my last breath, and feel in the last throb of my heart that it is wholly yours!"

"My poor Amelie," cried he, pressing her to his bosom, "you shall not die! Courage, darling! It is but weakness and the air of the convent; you shall not die."

"I am dying now, Pierre," said she, falling back upon her pillow. "I feel I have but a short time to live. I welcome death, since I cannot be yours. But, oh, the unutterable pang of leaving you, my dear love!"

Pierre could only reply by sobs and kisses. Amelie was silent for a few moments, as if revolving some deep thought in her mind.

"There is one thing, Pierre, I have to beg of you," said she, faltering as if doubting his consent to her prayer. "Can you, will you, accept my life for Le Gardeur's? If I die for HIM, will you forgive my poor blood-stained and deluded brother, and your own? Yes, Pierre," repeated she, as she raised his hand to her lips and kissed it, "your brother, as well as mine! Will you forgive him, Pierre?"

"Amelie! Amelie!" replied he with a voice broken with emotion, "can you fancy other than that I would forgive him? I forgave Le Gardeur from the first. In my heart I never accused him of my father's death. Alas, he knew not what he did! He was but a sword in the hands of my father's enemies. I forgave him then, darling, and I forgive him wholly now, for your sake and his own."

"My noble Pierre!" replied she, putting out her arms towards him. "Why might not God have suffered me to reward such divine goodness? Thanks, my love! I now die content with all things but parting with you." She held him fast by his hands, one of which she kept pressed to her lips. They all looked at her expectantly, waiting for her to speak again, for her eyes were wide open and fixed with a look of ineffable love upon the face of Pierre, looking like life, after life was fled. She still held him in her rigid clasp, but she moved not. Upon her pale lips a smile seemed to hover. It was but the shadow left behind of her retreating soul. Amelie de Repentigny was dead! The angel of death had kissed her lovingly, and unnoticed of any she had passed with him away.

The watchful eye of the Lady de Tilly was the first to see that Amelie's breath had gone so quietly that no one caught her latest sigh. The physician and chaplain rushed hurriedly into the chamber, but too late. The great physician of souls had already put his beloved to sleep,--the blessed sleep, whose dream is of love on earth, and whose waking is in heaven. The great high priest of the sons and daughters of men had anointed her with the oil of his mercy, and sent his blessed angels to lead her to the mansions of everlasting rest.

The stroke fell like the stunning blow of a hammer upon the heart of Pierre. He had, indeed, foreseen her death, but tried in vain to realize it. He made no outcry, but sat still, wrapped in a terrible silence as in the midst of a desert. He held fast her dead hands, and gazed upon her dead face until the heart-breaking sobs of Heloise, and the appeals of Mere Esther, roused him from his stupor.

He rose up, and, lifting Amelie in his arms, laid her upon a couch tenderly and reverently, as a man touches the holiest object of his religion. Amelie was to him a sacrament, and in his manly love he worshipped her more as a saint than as a woman, a creation of heavenly more than of earthly perfections.

Pierre bent over her and closed for the last time those dear eyes which had looked upon him so pure and so lovingly. He embraced her dead form, and kissed those pallid lips which had once confessed her unalterable love and truth for Pierre Philibert.

The agitated nuns gathered round them at the news of death in the Convent. They looked wonderingly and earnestly at an exhibition of such absorbing affection, and were for the most part in tears. With some of these gentle women this picture of true love, broken in the midst of its brightest hopes, woke sympathies and recollections which the watchful eye of Mere Migeon promptly checked as soon as she came into the parlor.

The Lady Superior saw that all was over, and that Pierre's presence was an uneasiness to the nuns, who glanced at him with eyes of pity and womanly sympathy. She took him kindly by the hand, with a few words of condolence, and intimated that, as he had been permitted to see the end, he must now withdraw from those forbidden precincts and leave his lost treasure to the care of the nuns who take charge of the dead.

# Chapter LIV: "The Mills of God Grind Slowly"

Pierre was permitted to see the remains of his affianced bride interred in the Convent chapel. Her modest funeral was impressive from the number of sad, sympathizing faces which gathered around her grave.

The quiet figure of a nun was seen morn and eve, for years and years after, kneeling upon the stone slab that covered her grave, laying upon it her daily offering of flowers, and if the name of Le Gardeur mingled with her prayers, it was but a proof of the unalterable affection of Heloise de Lotbiniere, known in religion as Mere St. Croix.

The lamp of Repentigny shed its beams henceforth over the grave of the last representative of that noble house, where it still shines to commemorate their virtues, and perpetuate the memory of their misfortunes; but God has long since compensated them for all.

Lady de Tilly was inconsolable over the ruin of her fondest hopes. She had regarded Pierre as her son, and intended to make him and Amelie joint inheritors with Le Gardeur of her immense wealth. She desired still to bequeath it to Pierre, not only because of her great kindness for him, but as a sort of self-imposed amercement upon her house for the death of his father.

Pierre refused. "I have more of the world's riches already than I can use," said he; "and I value not what I have, since she is gone for whose sake alone I prized them. I shall go abroad to resume my profession of arms, not seeking, yet not avoiding an honorable death, which may reunite me to Amelie, and the sooner the more welcome."

Lady de Tilly sought, by assiduous devotion to the duties of her life and station, distraction from the gnawing cares that ever preyed upon her. She but partially succeeded. She lived through the short peace of Aix-la-Chapelle, and shared in the terrible sufferings of the seven years' war that followed in its wake. When the final conquest of New France overwhelmed the Colony, to all appearances in utter ruin, she endowed the Ursulines with a large portion of her remaining wealth, and retired with her nearest kinsmen to France. The name of Tilly became extinct among the noblesse of the Colony, but it still flourishes in a vigorous branch upon its native soil of Normandy.

Pierre Philibert passed a sad winter in arranging and settling the vast affairs of his father before leaving New France. In the spring following the death of Amelie, he passed over to the old world, bidding a long and last adieu to his native land.

Pierre endeavored manfully to bear up under the load of recollections and sorrows which crushed his heart, and made him a grave and melancholy man before his time. He rejoined the army of his sovereign, and sought danger--his comrades said for danger's sake--with a desperate valor that was the boast of the army; but few suspected that he sought death and tempted fate in every form.

His wish was at last accomplished,--as all earnest, absorbing wishes ever are. He fell valorously, dying a soldier's death upon the field of Minden, his last moments sweetened by the thought that his beloved Amelie was waiting for him on the other side of the dark river, to welcome him with the bridal kiss promised upon the banks of the Lake of Tilly. He met her joyfully in that land where love is real, and where its promises are never broken.

The death of the Bourgeois Philibert, affecting so many fortunes, was of immense consequence to the Colony. It led to the ruin of the party of the Honnetes Gens, to the supremacy of the Grand company, and the final overthrow of New France.

The power and extravagance of Bigot after that event grew without check or challenge, and the departure of the virtuous La Galissoniere left the Colony to the weak and corrupt administrations of La Jonquiere, and De Vaudreuil. The latter made the Castle of St. Louis as noted for its venality as was the Palace of the Intendant. Bigot kept his high place through every change. The Marquis de Vaudreuil gave him free course, and it was more than suspected shared with the corrupt Intendant in the plunder of the Colony.

These public vices bore their natural fruit, and all the efforts of the Honnetes Gens to stay the tide of corruption were futile. Montcalm, after reaping successive harvests of victories, brilliant beyond all precedent in North America, died a sacrifice to the insatiable greed and extravagance of Bigot and his associates, who, while enriching themselves, starved the army and plundered the Colony of all its resources. The fall of Quebec, and the capitulation of Montreal were less owing to the power of the English than to the corrupt misgovernment of Bigot and Vaudreuil, and the neglect by the court of France of her ancient and devoted Colony.

Le Gardeur, after a long confinement in the Bastille, where he incessantly demanded trial and punishment for his rank offence of the murder of the Bourgeois, as he ever called it, was at last liberated by express command of the King, without trial and against his own wishes. His sword was restored to him, accompanied by a royal order bidding him, upon his allegiance, return to his regiment, as an officer of the King, free from all blame for the offence laid to his charge. Whether the killing of the Bourgeois was privately regarded at Court as good service was never known. But Le Gardeur, true to his loyal instincts, obeyed the King, rejoined the army, and once more took the field.

Upon the outbreak of the last French war in America, he returned to New France, a changed and reformed man; an ascetic in his living, and, although a soldier, a monk in the rigor of his penitential observances. His professional skill and daring were conspicuous among the number of gallant officers upon whom Montcalm chiefly relied to assist him in his long and desperate struggle against the ever-increasing forces of the English. From the capture of Chouaguen and the defence of the Fords of Montmorency, to the last brave blow struck upon the plains of St. Foye, Le Gardeur de Repentigny fulfilled every duty of a gallant and desperate soldier. He carried his life in his hand, and valued it as cheaply as he did the lives of his enemies.

He never spoke to Angelique again. Once he met her full in the face, upon the perron of the Cathedral of St. Marie. She started as if touched by fire,--trembled, blushed, hesitated, and extended her hand to him in the old familiar way,--with that look of witchery in her eyes, and that seductive smile upon her lips, which once sent the hot blood coursing madly in his veins. But Le Gardeur's heart was petrified now. He cared for no woman more,--or if he did, his thought dwelt with silent regret upon that pale nun in the Convent of the Ursulines--once Heloise de Lotbiniere--who he knew was wasting her young life in solitary prayers for pardon for his great offence.

His anger rose fiercely at the sight of Angelique, and Le Gardeur forgot for a moment that he was a gentleman, a man who had once loved this woman. He struck her a blow, and passed on. It shattered her last illusion. The proud, guilty woman still loved Le Gardeur, if she loved any man. But she felt she had merited his scorn. She staggered, and sat down on the steps of the Cathedral, weeping the bitterest tears her eyes had ever wept in her life. She never saw Le Gardeur again.

After the conquest of New France, Le Gardeur retired with the shattered remnant of the army of France, back to their native land. His sovereign loaded him with honors which he cared not for. He had none to share them with now! Lover, sister, friends, all were lost and gone! But he went on performing his military duties with an iron rigor and punctuality that made men admire, while they feared him. His life was more mechanical than human. Le Gardeur spared neither himself nor others. He never married, and never again looked with kindly eye upon a woman. His heart was proof against every female blandishment. He ended his life in solitary state and greatness, as Governor of Mahe in India, many years after he had left his native Canada.

One day, in the year of grace 1777, another council of war was sitting in the great chamber of the Castle of St. Louis, under a wonderful change of circumstances. An English governor, Sir Guy Carleton, presided over a mixed assemblage of English and Canadian officers. The royal arms and colors of England had replaced the emblems and ensigns of France upon the walls of the council-chamber, and the red uniform of her army was loyally worn by the old, but still indomitable, La Corne St. Luc, who, with the De Salaberrys, the De Beaujeus, Duchesnays, De Gaspes, and others of noblest name and lineage in New France, had come forward as loyal subjects of England's Crown to defend Canada against the armies of the English Colonies, now in rebellion against the King.

"Read that, La Corne," said Sir Guy Carleton, handing him a newspaper just received from England. "An old friend of yours, if I mistake not, is dead. I met him once in India. A stern, saturnine man he was, but a brave and able commander; I am sorry to hear of his death, but I do not wonder at it. He was the most melancholy man I ever saw."

La Corne took the paper and gave a start of intense emotion as he read an obituary notice as follows:

"East Indies. Death of the Marquis de Repentigny. The Marquis Le Gardeur de Repentigny, general of the army and Governor of Mahe, died last year in that part of India, which he had, by his valor and skill, preserved to France. This officer had served in Canada with the reputation of an able and gallant soldier."

La Corne was deeply agitated; his lips quivered, and tears gathered in the thick gray eyelashes that formed so prominent a feature of his rugged but kindly face. He concluded his reading in silence, and handed the paper to De Beaujeu, with the single remark, "Le Gardeur is dead! Poor fellow! He was more sinned against than sinning! God pardon him for all the evil he meant not to do! Is it not strange that she who was the cursed cause of his ruin still flourishes like the Queen of the Kingdom of Brass? It is hard to justify the ways of Providence, when wickedness like hers prospers, and virtues like those of the brave old Bourgeois find a bloody grave! My poor Amelie, too! poor girl, poor girl!" La Corne St. Luc sat silent a long time, immersed in melancholy reflections.

The Canadian officers read the paragraph, which revived in their minds also sad recollections of the past. They knew that, by her who had been the cursed cause of the ruin of Le Gardeur and of the death of the Bourgeois, La Corne referred to the still blooming widow of the Chevalier de Pean,--the leader of fashion and gaiety in the capital now, as she had been thirty years before, when she was the celebrated Angelique des Meloises.

Angelique had played desperately her game of life with the juggling fiend of ambition, and had not wholly lost. Although the murder of Caroline de St. Castin pressed hard upon her conscience, and still harder upon her fears, no man read in her face the minutest asterisk that pointed to the terrible secret buried in her bosom, nor ever discovered it. So long as La Corriveau lived, Angelique never felt safe. But fear was too weak a counsellor for her to pretermit either her composure or her pleasures. She redoubled her gaiety and her devotions; and that was the extent of her repentance! The dread secret of Beaumanoir was never revealed. It awaited, and awaits still, the judgment of the final day of account.

Angelique had intrigued and sinned in vain. She feared Bigot knew more than he really did, in reference to the death of Caroline, and oft, while laughing in his face, she trembled in her heart, when he played and equivocated with her earnest appeals to marry her. Wearied out at length with waiting for his decisive yes or no, Angelique, mortified by wounded pride and stung by the scorn of Le Gardeur on his return to the Colony, suddenly accepted the hand of the Chevalier de Pean, and as a result became the recognized mistress of the Intendant,--imitating as far as she was able the splendor and the guilt of La Pompadour, and making the Palace of Bigot as corrupt, if not as brilliant, as that of Versailles.

Angelique lived thenceforth a life of splendid sin. She clothed herself in purple and fine linen, while the noblest ladies of the land were reduced by the war to rags and beggary. She fared sumptuously, while men and women died of hunger in the streets of Quebec. She bought houses and lands, and filled her coffers with gold out of the public treasury, while the brave soldiers of Montcalm starved for the want of their pay. She gave fetes and banquets while the English were thundering at the gates of the capital. She foresaw the eventual fall of Bigot and the ruin of the country, and resolved that, since she had failed in getting himself, she would make herself possessor of all that he had.

The fate of Bigot was a warning to public peculators and oppressors. He returned to France soon after the surrender of the Colony, with Cadet, Varin, Penisault, and others of the Grand Company, who were now useless tools, and were cast aside by their court friends. The Bastille opened its iron doors to receive the godless and wicked crew, who had lost the fairest Colony of France, the richest jewel in her crown. Bigot and the others were tried by a special commission, were found guilty of the most heinous malversations of office, and sentenced to make full restitution of the plunder of the King's treasures, to be imprisoned until their fines and restitutions were paid, and then banished from the kingdom forever.

It is believed that, by favor of La Pompadour, Bigot's heavy sentence was commuted, and he retained a sufficiency of his ill- gotten wealth to enable him, under a change of name, to live in ease and opulence at Bordeaux, where he died.

Angelique had no sympathy for Bigot in his misfortunes, no regrets save that she had failed to mould him more completely to her own purposes, flattering herself that had she done so, the fortunes of the war and the fate of the Colony might have been different. What might have been, had she not ruined herself and her projects by the murder of Caroline, it were vain to conjecture. But she who had boldly dreamed of ruling king and kingdom by the witchery of her charms and the craft of her subtle intellect, had to content herself with the name of De Pean and the shame of a lawless connection with the Intendant.

She would fain have gone to France to try her fortunes when the Colony was lost, but La Pompadour forbade her presence there, under pain of her severest displeasure. Angelique raved at the inhibition, but was too wise to tempt the wrath of the royal mistress by disobeying her mandate. She had to content herself with railing at La Pompadour with the energy of three furies, but she never ceased, to the end of her life, to boast of the terror which her charms had exercised over the great favorite of the King.

Rolling in wealth and scarcely faded in beauty, Angelique kept herself in the public eye. She hated retirement, and boldly claimed her right to a foremost place in the society of Quebec. Her great wealth and unrivalled power of intrigue enabled her to keep that place, down to the last.

The fate of La Corriveau, her confederate in her great wickedness, was peculiar and terrible. Secured at once by her own fears, as well as by a rich yearly allowance paid her by Angelique, La Corriveau discreetly bridled her tongue over the death of Caroline, but she could not bridle her own evil passions in her own household.

One summer day, of the year following the conquest of the Colony, the Goodman Dodier was found dead in his house at St. Valier. Fanchon, who knew something and suspected more, spoke out; an investigation into the cause of death of the husband resulted in the discovery that he had been murdered by pouring melted lead into his ear while he slept. La Corriveau was arrested as the perpetrator of the atrocious deed.

A special court of justice was convened in the great hall of the Convent of the Ursulines, which, in the ruinous state of the city after the siege and bombardment, had been taken for the headquarters of General Murray. Mere Migeon and Mere Esther, who both survived the conquest, had effected a prudent arrangement with the English general, and saved the Convent from all further encroachment by placing it under his special protection.

La Corriveau was tried with all the fairness, if not with all the forms, of English law. She made a subtle and embarrassing defence, but was at last fairly convicted of the cruel murder of her husband. She was sentenced to be hung, and gibbetted in an iron cage, upon the hill of Levis, in sight of the whole city of Quebec.

La Corriveau made frantic efforts during her imprisonment to engage Angelique to intercede in her behalf; but Angelique's appeals were fruitless before the stern administrators of English law. Moreover, Angelique, to be true to herself, was false to her wicked confederate. She cared not to intercede too much, or enough to ensure success. In her heart she wished La Corriveau well out of the way, that all memory of the tragedy of Beaumanoir might be swept from the earth, except what of it remained hid in her own bosom. She juggled with the appeals of La Corriveau, keeping her in hopes of pardon until the fatal hour came, when it was too late for La Corriveau to harm her by a confession of the murder of Caroline.

The hill of Levis, where La Corriveau was gibbetted, was long remembered in the traditions of the Colony. It was regarded with superstitious awe by the habitans. The ghost of La Corriveau long haunted, and, in the belief of many, still haunts, the scene of her execution. Startling tales, raising the hair with terror, were told of her around the firesides in winter, when the snow-drifts covered the fences, and the north wind howled down the chimney and rattled the casement of the cottages of the habitans; how, all night long, in the darkness, she ran after belated travellers, dragging her cage at her heels, and defying all the exorcisms of the Church to lay her evil spirit!

Our tale is now done. There is in it neither poetic nor human justice. But the tablet of the Chien d'Or still overlooks the Rue Buade; the lamp of Repentigny burns in the ancient chapel of the Ursulines; the ruins of Beaumanoir cover the dust of Caroline de St. Castin; and Amelie sleeps her long sleep by the side of Heloise de Lotbiniere.

THE END

Printed in the USA
CPSIA information can be obtained
at www.ICGtesting.com
LVHW070854241223
767331LV00005B/550